MICHAEL MOORCOCK

The Dancers at the End of Time

An Alien Heat
The Hollow Lands
The End of All Songs

GRAFTON BOOKS
A Division of the Collins Publishing Group
───────────
LONDON GLASGOW
TORONTO SYDNEY AUCKLAND

Grafton Books
A Division of the Collins Publishing Group
8 Grafton Street, London W1X 3LA

Published by Grafton Books 1983
Reprinted 1984, 1986, 1988

This one-volume edition of *The Dancers at the End of
Time* Trilogy first published in Great Britain by
Granada Publishing in 1981

An Alien Heat	Copyright © Michael Moorcock 1972
The Hollow Lands	Copyright © Michael Moorcock 1974
The End of All Songs	Copyright © Michael Moorcock 1976

ISBN 0-583-13639-7

Printed and bound in Great Britain by
Collins, Glasgow

Set in Baskerville

VOLUME ONE

An Alien Heat

For Nik Turner, Dave Brock, Bob Calvert,
DikMik, Del Dettmar, Terry Ollis, Simon King and
Lemmy of Hawkwind.

The silver lips of lilies virginal,
The full deep bosom of the enchanted rose
Please less than flowers glass-hid from frosts and snows
For whom an alien heat makes festival.

THEODORE WRATISLAW
Hothouse Flowers
1896

Contents

PROLOGUE

The cycle of the Earth (indeed, the universe, if the truth had been known) was nearing its end and the human race had at last ceased to take itself seriously. Having inherited millennia of scientific and technological knowledge it used this knowledge to indulge its richest fantasies to play immense imaginative games, to relax and create beautiful monstrosities. After all, there was little else left to do. An earlier age might have been horrified at what it would have judged a waste of resources, an appalling extravagance in the uses to which materials and energies were put. An earlier age would have seen the inhabitants of this world as 'decadent' or 'amoral', to say the least. But even if these inhabitants were not conscious of the fact that they lived at the end of time some unconscious knowledge informed their attitudes and made them lose interest in ideals, creeds, philosophies and the conflicts to which such things give rise. They found pleasure in paradox, aesthetics and baroque wit; if they had a philosophy, then it was a philosophy of taste, of sensuality. Most of the old emotions had atrophied, meant little to them. They had rivalry without jealousy, affection without lust, malice without rage, kindness without pity. Their schemes – often grandiose and perverse – were pursued without obsession and left uncompleted without regret, for death was rare and life might cease only when Earth herself died.

Yet this particular story is about an obsession which overtook one of these people, much to his own astonishment. And because he was overtaken by an obsession that is why we have a story to tell. It is probably the last story in the annals of the human race and, as it happens, it is not dissimilar to that which many believe is the first.

What follows, then, is the story of Jherek Carnelian, who did not know the meaning of morality, and Mrs Amelia Underwood, who knew everything about it.

CHAPTER ONE

A CONVERSATION WITH THE IRON ORCHID

Dressed in various shades of light brown, the Iron Orchid and her son sat upon a cream-coloured beach of crushed bone. Some distance off a white sea sparkled and whispered. It was the afternoon.

Between the Iron Orchid and her son, Jherek Carnelian, lay the remains of a lunch. Spread on a cloth of plain damask were ivory plates containing pale fish, potatoes, meringue, vanilla ice-cream and, glaring rather dramatically, from the centre of it all, a lemon.

The Iron Orchid smiled with her amber lips and, reaching for an oyster, asked: 'How do you mean, my love, "virtuous"?' Her perfect hand, powdered the very lightest shade of gold, hovered for a second over the oyster and then withdrew. She used the hand, instead, to cover a small yawn.

Her son stretched on his soft pillows. He, too, felt tired after the exertions of eating, but dutifully he continued with the subject. 'I'm not thoroughly sure what it means. As you know, most devastating of minerals, most enchanting of flowers, I have studied the language of the time quite extensively. I must possess every tape that still exists. It provides considerable amusement. But I cannot understand every nuance. I found the word in a dictionary and the dictionary told me it meant acting with "moral rectitude" or in conformity with "moral laws" – "good, just, righteous". Bewildering!'

He did take an oyster. He slid it into his mouth. He rolled it down his throat. It had been the Iron Orchid who had discovered oysters and he had been delighted when she suggested they meet on this beach and eat them. She had made some champagne to go with them, but they had both agreed that they did not care for it and had cheerfully returned it to its component atoms.

'However,' he continued, 'I should like to try it for a bit. It is supposed to involve "self-denial"' – he forestalled her question – 'which means doing nothing pleasurable.'

'But *everything*, body of velvet, bones of steel, is pleasurable!'

'True – and there lies our paradox! You see the ancients, mother, divided their sensations into different groupings – categories of sensations, some of which they did not find pleasurable, it seems. Or they did find them pleasurable and therefore were displeased! Oh, dearest Iron Orchid, I can see you are ready to dismiss the whole thing. And I despair, often, of puzzling out the answer. Why was one thing considered worth pursuing and another not? But,' his handsome lips curved in a smile, 'I shall settle the problem in one way or another, sooner or later.' And he closed his heavy lids.

'Oh, Carnelian!'

She laughed softly and affectionately and stretched across the cloth to slip her slender hands into his loose robe and stroke his warmth and his blood.

'Oh, my dear! How swift you are! How ripe and rich you are today!'

And he drew himself to his feet and he stepped over the cloth and he laid his tall body down upon her and he kissed her slowly.

And the sea sighed.

When they awoke, still in each other's arms, it was morning, though no night had passed. For their own pleasure someone had doubtless been engaged in rearranging time. It was not important.

Jherek noticed that the sea had turned a deep pink, almost a cerise, and was clashing dreadfully with the beach, while on the horizon behind him he saw that two palms and a cliff had disappeared altogether. In their place stood a silver pagoda, about twelve storeys high and glittering in the morning sun.

Jherek looked to his left and was pleased to see that his aircar (resembling a steam locomotive of the early 20th century, but of about half the size, in gold, ebony and rubies) was still where they had left it.

He looked again at the pagoda, craning his neck, for his mother still relaxed with her head against his shoulder. His mother, too, turned to look as a winged figure left the roof of the pagoda and flew crazily away towards the east, swerving and dipping, circling back, narrowly missing the sharp edge of the pagoda's crest, and at last disappearing.

'Oh,' said the Iron Orchid getting to her feet. 'It is the Duke of Queens and his wings. Why will he insist that they are successful?' She waved a vague hand at the departed duke. 'Goodbye. Playing one of his solitary games, again, I suppose.' She looked down at the remains of the lunch and made a face. 'I must clear this away.' With a wave of the ring on her left hand she disseminated the lunch and watched the dust drift away on the air. 'Will you be going there, this evening? To his party?' She moved her slender arm, heavy with brown brocade, and touched her forehead with her fingertips.

'I think so.' He disseminated his own pillows. 'I have a great liking for the Duke of Queens.'

His lips pursed a trifle, Jherek Carnelian pondered the pink sea. 'Even if I do not always appreciate his colour sense.'

He turned and walked over the crushed bone beach to his aircar. He clambered into the cabin.

3

'All aboard, my strong, my sweet, Iron Orchid!'

She chuckled and reached up to him.

From the footplate he reached down, seized her waist and swung her aboard.

'Off to Pasadena!'

He sounded his whistle.

'Shuffle off to Buffalo!'

Responding to the sonic signal, the little locomotive took magnificently to the air, shunting up the sky, with lovely, lime-coloured steam puffing from its smokestack and from beneath its wheels.

'Oh, they gave him his augurs at Racine-Virginia,' sang Jherek Carnelian, donning a scarlet and cloth-of-gold engineer's cap, 'saying steam-up, you're way behind time! It ain't '98, it's old '97. You got to get on down that old Nantucket line!'

The Iron Orchid settled back in her seat of plush and ermine (an exact reproduction, she understood, of the original) and watched her son with amusement as he opened the firedoor and shovelled in the huge black diamonds which he had made specially to go with the train and which, though of no particular use in fuelling the aircar, added aesthetic texture to the recreation.

'Where do you *find* all these old songs, Carnelian, my own?'

'I came across a cache of "platters",' he told her, wiping honest sweat from his face with a silk rag. The train swept rapidly over a sea and a range of mountains. 'A form of sound-storage of the same period as the original of this aircar. A. million years old, at least, though there's some evidence that they, themselves, are reproductions of other originals. Kept in perfect condition by a succession of owners.'

He slammed the firedoor shut and discarded the platinum shovel, joining her upon the couch and staring down at the quaintly moulded countryside which Mistress Christia, the Everlasting Concubine, had begun to build a while ago and then abandoned.

It was not elegant. In fact it was something of a mess. Two-thirds of a hill, in the fashion of the 91st century post-Aryan landscapers, supported a snake-tree done after the Saturnian

4

manner but left uncoloured; part of an 11th century Gothic ruin stood beside a strip of river of the Bengali Empire period. You could see why she had decided not to finish it, but it seemed to Jherek that it was a pity she had not bothered to disseminate it. Someone else would, of course, sooner or later.

'Carrie Joan,' he sang, 'she kept her boiler going. Carrie Joan, she filled it full of wine. Carrie Joan didn't stop her rowing. She had to get to Brooklyn by a quarter-past nine!'

He turned to the Iron Orchid.

'Do you like it? The quality of the platters isn't all it could be, but I think I've worked out all the words now.'

'Is that what you were doing last year?'

She raised her fine eyebrows. 'I heard the noises coming from your Hi-Rise.' She laughed. 'And I thought it was to do with sex.' She frowned. 'Or animals.' She smiled. 'Or both.'

The locomotive began to spiral down, hooting, towards Jherek's ranch. The ranch had taken the place of the Hi-Rise. A typical building of the 19th century, done in fiba-fome and thatch, each corner of its veranda roof was supported by a wooden Indian, some forty feet high. Each Indian had a magnificent pearl, twelve inches in diameter, in his turban, and a beard of real hair. The Indians were the only extravagant detail in the otherwise simple building.

The locomotive landed in the corral and Jherek, whose interest in the ancient world had, off and on, sustained itself for nearly two years, held out his hand to help the Iron Orchid disembark. For a moment she hesitated as she attempted to remember what she must do. Then she grasped his hand and jumped to the ground crying:

'Geronimo!'

Together they made for the house.

The surrounding landscape had been designed to fit in with the ranch. The sky contained a sunset, which silhouetted the purple hills, and the black pines, which topped them. On the other side was a range containing a herd of bison. Every few days there would emerge from a cunningly hidden opening in the ground a group of mechanical 7th cavalrymen who would whoop and shout and ride round and round the bison shooting their arrows into the air before roping and branding the beasts.

5

The bison had been specially grown from Jherek's own extensive gene-bank and didn't seem to care for the operation although it should have been instinctive to them. The 7th cavalry, on the other hand, had been manufactured in his machine shop because he had a distaste for growing people (who were inclined to be bad-mannered when the time came for their dissemination).

'What a beautiful sunset,' said his mother, who had not visited him since the Hi-Rise days. 'Was the sun really as huge as that in those days?'

'Bigger,' he said, 'by all accounts. I toned it down rather, for this.'

She touched his arm. 'You were always inclined to be restrained. I like it.'

'Thank you.'

They went up the white winding staircase to the veranda, breathing in the delicious scent of magnolia which grew on the ground beside the basement section of the house. They crossed the veranda and Jherek manipulated a lever which, depressed, allowed the door to open so that they could enter the parlour – a single room occupying the whole of this floor. The remaining eight floors were given over to kitchens, bedrooms, cupboards and the like.

The parlour was a treasure house of 19th century reproductions, including a magnificent pot-bellied stove carved from a single oak and a flowering aspidistra which grew from the centre of the grass carpet and spread its rubbery branches over the best part of the room.

The Iron Orchid hovered beside the intricate lattice-work shape which Jherek had seen in an old holograph and reproduced in steel and chrome. It was like a huge egg standing on its end and it rose as high as the ceiling.

'And what is this, my life force?' she asked him.

'A spaceship,' he explained. 'They were constantly attempting to fly to the moon or striving to repel invasions from Mars. I'm not sure if they were successful, though of course there are no Martians these days. Some of their writers were inclined to tell rather tall tales, you know, doubtless with a view to entertaining their companions.'

6

'Whatever possessed them to *try*! Into *space*!'

She shuddered. People had lost the inclination to leave the Earth centuries ago.

Naturally, space-travellers called on the planet from time to time, but they were, as often as not, boring fellows with not much to offer. They were usually encouraged to leave as soon as possible or, if one should catch somebody's fancy, he would be retained in a collection.

Even Jherek had no impulse to time-travel, though time-travellers would arrive occasionally in his era. He could have travelled through time himself, if he had wished, and very briefly visited his beloved 19th century. But, like most people, he found that the real places were rather disappointing. It was much better to indulge in imaginative recreation of the periods or places. Nothing, therefore, would spoil the full indulgence of one's fancies, or the thrill of discovery as one unearthed some new piece of information and added it to the texture of one's reproduction.

A servo entered and bowed. The Iron Orchid handed it her clothes (as she had been instructed to do by Jherek – another custom of the time) and went to stretch her wonderful body under the aspidistra tree.

Jherek was pleased to note she was wearing breasts again and thus did not clash with her surroundings. Everything was in period. Even the servo wore a derby, an ulster, chaps and stout brogues and carried several meerschaum pipes in its steel teeth. At a sign from its master it rolled away.

Jherek went to sit with his back against the bole of the aspidistra. 'And now, lovely Iron Orchid, tell me what you have been doing.'

She looked up at him, her eyes shining. 'I've been making babies, dearest. Hundreds of them!' She giggled. 'I couldn't stop. Cherubs, mainly. I built a little aviary for them, too. And I made them trumpets to blow and harps to pluck and I composed the sweetest music you ever heard. And they played it!'

'I should like to hear it.'

'What a shame.' She was genuinely upset that she had not thought of him, her favourite, her only real son. 'I'm making

7

microscopes now. And gardens, of course, to go with them. And tiny beasts. But perhaps I'll do the cherubs again some day. And you shall hear them, then.'

'If I am not being "virtuous",' he said archly.

'Ah, now I begin to understand the meaning. If you have an impulse to do something – you do the opposite. You want to be a man, so you become a woman. You wish to fly somewhere, so you go underground. You wish to drink, but instead you emit fluid. And so on. Yes, that's splendid. You'll set a fashion, mark my words. In a month, blood of my blood, *everyone* will be virtuous. And what shall we do then? Is there anything else? Tell me!'

'Yes. We could be "evil" – or "modest" – or "lazy" – or "poor" – or, oh, I don't know – "worthy". There's hundreds.'

'And you would tell us how to be it?'

'Well . . .' He frowned. 'I still have to work out exactly what's involved. But by that time I should know a little more.'

'We'll all be grateful to you. I remember when you taught us Lunar Cannibals. And Swimming. And – what was it – Flags?'

'I enjoyed Flags,' he said. 'Particularly when My Lady Charlotina made that delicious one which covered the whole of the western hemisphere. In metal cloth the thickness of an ant's web. Do you remember how we laughed when it fell on us?'

'Oh, yes!' She clapped her hands. 'Then Lord Jagged built a Flag Pole on which to fly it and the pole melted so we each made a Niagara to see who could do the biggest and used up every drop of water and had to make a whole new batch and you went round and round in a cloud raining on everyone, even on Mongrove. And Mongrove dug himself an underground Hell, with devils and everything, out of that book the time-traveller brought us, and he set fire to Bulio Himmler's "Bunkerworld 2" which he didn't know was right next door to him and Bulio was so upset he kept dropping atom bombs on Mongrove's Hell, not knowing that he was supplying Mongrove with all the heat he needed!'

They laughed heartily.

'Was it really three hundred years ago?' said Jherek nostalgically.

He plucked a leaf from the aspidistra and reflectively began to chew it. A little blue juice ran down his beige chin.

'I sometimes think,' he continued, 'that I haven't known a better sequence of events. It seemed to go on and on, one thing leading neatly to another. Mongrove's Hell, you know, also ruined my menagerie, except for one creature that escaped and broke most of his devils. Everything went up, in my menagerie, otherwise. Because of Himmler, really. Or because of Lady Charlotina. Who's to say?'

He discarded the leaf.

'It's strange,' he said. 'I haven't kept a menagerie since. I mean, almost everyone has some sort of menagerie, even you, Iron Orchid.'

'Mine is so *small*. Compare it with the Everlasting Concubine's, even.'

'You've three Napoleons. She has none.'

'True. But I'm honestly not sure whether any one of them is genuine.'

'It is hard to tell,' he agreed.

'And she does have an absolutely genuine Attila the Hun. The trouble she went to, too, to make that particular trade. But he's such a bore.'

'I think that's why I stopped collecting,' he said. 'The genuine items are often less interesting than the fakes.'

'It's usually the case, fruit of my loins.' She sank into the grass again. This last reference was not to the literal truth. In fact, as Jherek remembered, his mother had been some sort of male anthropoid at the actual moment of his birth and had forgotten all about him until, by accident, six months later she came upon the incubator in the jungle she had built. He had still been nursed as a new-born baby by the incubator. But she had kept him. He was glad of that. So few human beings, as such, were born these days.

Perhaps that was why, being a natural born baby, as it were, he felt such an affinity with the past, thought Jherek. Many of the time-travellers – even some of the space-travellers – had been children, too.

He did get on well with some of the people who had chosen to live outside the menageries and adopt the ways of this society.

Pereg Tralo, for instance, who had ruled the world in the

9

30th century simply because he had been the last person to be born out of an actual womb! A splendid, witty companion. And Clare Cyrato, the singer from the 500th – a peculiar freak, due to some experiment of her mother's, she too had entered life as a baby. Babies, children, adolescents – everything!

It was an experience he had not regretted. What experience could be regretted? And he had been the darling of all his mother's friends. His novelty lasted well into his teens. With delight they had watched him *grow*! Everyone envied him. Everyone envied the Iron Orchid, though for a while she had distinctly tired of him and gone away to live in the middle of a mountain. Everyone envied him, that is, except Mongrove (who would certainly not have admitted it, anyway) and Werther de Goethe, who had also been born a baby. Werther, of course, had been a trial and had not enjoyed himself nearly so much. Even though he no longer had six arms, he still felt a certain amount of resentment about the way he had been altered, never having the same limbs or the same head, even, from one day to the next.

Jherek noticed that his mother had fallen asleep again. She only had to lie down for a moment and she was dreaming. It was a habit she had always encouraged in herself, for she thought up many of her best new ideas in dreams.

Jherek hardly dreamed at all.

If he had, he supposed he would not have to seek out old tapes and platters to read, watch or hear.

Still, he was acknowledged as being one of the very best recreators, even if his originality would not equal either his mother's or that of the Duke of Queens. Privately Jherek felt that the Duke of Queens lost on aesthetic sensibility what he made up for in invention.

Jherek remembered that both he and the Iron Orchid were invited to the Duke's that evening. He had not been to a party for some time and was determined to wear something stunning.

He considered what to put on. He would stick to the 19th century, of course, for he believed very much in consistency of style. And it must be nothing fanciful. It must be spare. It must be a clean, quiet image, striking and absolutely without a

10

personal touch. A personal touch would, again, mar the effect. The choice became obvious.

He would wear full evening dress, an opera hat and an opera cloak.

And, he thought with a self-satisfied smile, he would have the whole thing in a low-keyed combination of russet orange and midnight blue. With a carnation, naturally, at the throat.

CHAPTER TWO

A SOIRÉE AT THE DUKE OF QUEENS

A few million years ago, perhaps less (for time was terribly difficult to keep track of), there had flourished as a province of legendary New York City a magnificent district known as the Queen's. It was here that some New York king's escort had established her summer residence, building a vast palace and gardens and inviting from all over the world the most talented and the most amusing people to share the summer months with her. To the Queen's court flocked great painters, writers, composers, sculptors, craftsmen and wits, to display their new creations, to perform plays, dances and operas, to gossip, to entertain their queen (who had probably been the mythical Queen Eleanor of the Red Veldt), their patron.

Although in the meantime a few continents had drowned and others emerged, while various land masses had joined

12

together and some had divided, there had been little doubt in the mind of Liam Ty Pam Caesar Lloyd George Zatopek Finsbury Ronnie Michelangelo Yurio Iopu 4578 Rew United that he had found the site of the original court and established his own residence there and was thus able to style himself, reasonably enough, the Duke of Queens. One of the few permanent landmarks of the world was his statue of the Queen of the Red Veldt herself, stretching half a mile into the sky and covering an area of some six miles, showing the heroic queen in her cadillac (or chariot) drawn by six dragons, with her oddly curved spear in one hand, her square shield on her other arm and with her bizarre helmet upon her head, looking splendidly heroic as she must have done when she led her victorious armies against the might of the United Nations, that grandiose and ambitious alliance which had, in the legends, once sought to dominate the entire planet. So long had the statue stood in the grounds of the Duke's residence that few really ever noticed it, for the residence itself changed frequently and the Duke of Queens often managed to astonish everyone with the originality and scope of his invention.

As Jherek Carnelian and his mother, the Iron Orchid, approached, the first thing they saw was the statue, but almost immediately they took note of the house which the Duke must have erected especially for this evening's party.

'Oh!' breathed the Iron Orchid, peering out from the cabin of the locomotive and shielding her eyes against the light, 'How clever he is! How delightful!'

Jherek pretended to be unimpressed as he joined her on the footplate, his opera cloak swirling.

'It's pretty,' he said, 'and striking, of course. The Duke of Queens is always striking.'

Clad in poppies, marigolds and cornflowers from throat to ankle, the Iron Orchid turned with a smile and wagged a finger at him. 'Come now, my dear. Admit that it is magnificent.'

'I have admitted that it is striking. It is striking.'

'It is magnificent!'

His disdain melted before her enthusiasm. He laughed. 'Very well, lushest of blooms, it is *magnificent*! Without parallel! Gorgeous! Breathtaking! A work of genius!'

'And you will tell him so, my ghost?' Her eyes were sardonic. 'Will you tell him?'

He bowed. 'I will.'

'Splendid. And then, you see, we shall enjoy the party so much more.'

Of course, there was no doubting the Duke's ingenuity but as usual, thought Jherek, he had overdone everything. The sky had been coloured a lurid purple as a background and in it swirled the remaining planets of the Solar System – Mars as a great ruby, Venus as an emerald, Herod as a diamond, and so on – thirty in all.

The residence itself was a reproduction of the Great Fire of Africa. There were a number of separate buildings, each in the shape of some famous city of the time, blazing merrily away. Durban, Kilwa-Kivinje, Yola, Timbuctoo and others all burned, yet each detailed building, which was certain to be in perfect scale, was sculpted from water and the water was brightly (garishly, in Jherek's opinion) coloured, as were the flames. There were flames of every conceivable, flickering shade. And among the flames and the water wandered the guests who had already arrived. Naturally there was no heat to the fire – or barely any – for the Duke of Queens had no intention of burning his guests to death. In a way, Jherek thought, that was why the residence seemed to him to lack any real creative force. But then he was inclined to take such matters too seriously – everyone told him of that.

The locomotive landed just outside Smithsmith, whose towers and terraces would crumble as if in a blaze and then swiftly reform themselves before the water fell on anybody. People shouted with delight and giggled in surprise. Smithsmith seemed at present the most popular attraction in the residence. Food and beverages, mainly 28th century African, were laid about everywhere and people wandered from table to table sampling them.

Dismounting from the footplate and absently offering his hand to his mother (whose 'Geronimo' was *sotto voce* because she was becoming bored with the ritual) Jherek noticed many people he knew and a few whom he did not. Some of those he did not know were plainly from menageries, probably all time-

14

travellers. He could tell by the awkward way in which they stood, either conversing or keeping to themselves, either amused or unhappy. Jherek saw a time-traveller he did recognise. Li Pao, clad in his usual blue overalls, was casting a disapproving eye over Smithsmith.

Jherek and the Iron Orchid approached him.

'Good evening, Li Pao,' said the Iron Orchid. She kissed him on his lovely, round yellow face. 'You're evidently critical of Smithsmith. Is it the usual? Lack of authenticity? You're from the 28th century, aren't you?'

'27th,' said Li Pao, 'but I don't imagine things would have changed that much. Ah, you bourgeois individualists – you're so bad at it. That's always been my main contention.'

'You could be a better "bourgeois individualist" if you wanted to be, eh?' Another menagerie member approached. He was dressed in the long, silver skirts of the 32nd century whipperman. 'You're always quibbling over details, Li Pao.'

Li Pao sighed. 'I know. I'm boring. But there it is.'

'It's why we love you,' said the Iron Orchid, kissing him again and then waving her hand to her dear friend Gaf the Horse in Tears who had looked up from her conversation with Sweet Orb Mace (whom some thought might be Jherek's father) and smiled at the Iron Orchid, motioning her to join them. The Iron Orchid drifted away.

'And it's why we won't listen to you time-travellers,' said Jherek. 'You can be so dreadfully pedantic. This detail isn't right – that one's out of period – and so on. It spoils everyone's pleasure. You must admit, Li Pao, that you are a trifle literal minded.'

'That was the strength of our Republic,' said Li Pao, sipping his wine. 'That was why it lasted fifty thousand years.'

'Off and on,' said the 32nd century whipperman.

'More on than off,' said Li Pao.

'Well, it depends what you call a republic,' said the whipperman.

They were at it again. Jherek Carnelian smoothed himself off and saw Mongrove, the bitter giant, all overblown and unloved, who stood moping in the very centre of blazing Smithsmith as if he wished the buildings would really fall down on him and consume him. Jherek knew that Mongrove's whole persona was an affectation, but he had kept it so long that it was almost possible Mongrove had become the thing itself. But Mongrove was not really unloved. He was a favourite at parties – when he deigned to attend them. This must be his first in twenty years.

'How are you, Lord Mongrove?' Jherek asked, staring up at the giant's lugubrious face.

'The worse for seeing you, Jherek Carnelian. I have not forgotten all the slights, you know.'

'You would not be Mongrove if you had.'

'The turning of my feet into rats. You were only a boy, then.'

'Correct. The first slight.' Jherek bowed.

'The theft of my private poems.'

'True – and my publishing them.'

'Just so.' Mongrove nodded, continuing: 'The shifting of my lair and its environs from the North to the South pole.'

'You were confused.'

'Confused and angry with you, Jherek Carnelian. The list is endless. I know that I am your butt, your fool, your plaything. I know what you think of me.'

'I think well of you, Lord Mongrove.'

'You know me for what I am. A monster. A horror. A thing which does not deserve to live. And I hate you for that, Jherek Carnelian.'

'You love me for it, Mongrove. Admit it.'

A deep sigh, almost a windy bellow, escaped the giant's lips and tears fell from his eyes as he turned away. 'Do your worst, Jherek Carnelian. Do your worst to me.'

'If you insist, my darling Mongrove.'

Jherek smiled as he watched Mongrove plod deeper into the holocaust, his great shoulders slumped, his huge hands hanging heavily at his hips. Dressed all in black, was Mongrove, with his skin, hair and eyes stained black, too. Jherek wondered if he and Mongrove would ever consummate their love for each other. Perhaps Mongrove had learned the secret of 'virtue'? Perhaps the giant deliberately sought the opposite of everything he really desired to think and do? Jherek felt he was beginning to understand. However, he didn't much like the idea of turning into another Mongrove. That would be an awful thing to do. It was the only thing which Mongrove would truly resent.

However, thought Jherek as he strolled on through the flames and the liquids, if *he* became Mongrove would not Mongrove then have an incentive to become something else? But would that new Mongrove be as delightful as the old? It was unlikely.

'Jherek, my delicious fancy! Here!'

Jherek turned with a crack of his russet cloak and saw Lord Jagged of Canaria, a mass of quilted yellow, his head barely visible in his puffy collar, signalling to be joined at a table of fruits.

'Lord Jagged.' Jherek embraced his friend. 'Well, cosy one, are your battles ended?'

'They are ended at last. It has been five years. But they are ended. And every little man dead, I fear.' Lord Jagged had invented a perfect facsimile of the Solar System and had played out every war on it he had ever heard of. Each soldier had been complete in every detail, though of sub-microscopic proportions. A tiny personality. The entire set had been built in a cube measuring just over two feet square. Lord Jagged yawned and for a moment his face disappeared altogether into his collar. 'Yes, I quite lost affection for them in the end. Silly things. And you, handsome Jherek, what do you do?'

'Nothing very ambitious. Reproductions of the ancient world. Have you seen my locomotive?'

'I don't even know the word!' Lord Jagged roared. 'Shall I see it now?'

'It's over there, somewhere,' said Jherek, pointing through a tumbling skyscraper. 'It can wait until you are nearer.'

'Your costume is admirable,' said Lord Jagged, fingering the cloak. 'I have always envied your taste, Jherek. Is this, too, something the ancients wore?'

'Exactly.'

'Exactly! Oh, your patience! Your care! Your *eye*!'

Jherek stretched his arms and looked about him, pleased by the compliment. 'It is fine,' he said, 'my eye.'

'But where is our host, the magnificent Duke of Queens, the

inventor of all this excitement?'

Jherek knew that Lord Jagged shared his view of the Duke's taste. He shook his head. 'I haven't seen him. Perhaps in one of the other cities. Is there a main one?'

'I think not. It is possible, of course, that he has not yet arrived – or left already. You know how he loves to absent himself. Such a strong, *dramatic* sense.'

'And droll,' said Jherek, meeting his friend's eyes and smiling.

'Now, now,' said Lord Jagged. 'Let us, Jherek, *circulate*. Then, perhaps, we'll find our host and be able to compliment him to his face.'

Arm in arm they moved through the blazing city, crossed the lawns and entered Timbuctoo, whose slender oblongs, crowned by minarets, fell in upon each other, criss-crossed, nearly struck the ground and then sprang upright again, to be consumed by the flames afresh.

'Chrome,' Jherek heard Li Pao saying. 'They were chrome. Not silver and quartz and gold at all. To me, I'm afraid, that spoils the whole idea.'

Jherek chuckled. 'Do you know Li Pao? I suspect that he did not travel willingly through time. I suspect, my padded Jagged, that his comrades *sent* him off! I am learning "virtue", by the way.'

'And what is "virtue"?'

'I think it involves being like Mongrove.'

'Oh!' Lord Jagged rounded his lips in an ironic expression of dismay.

'I know. But you're familiar with my perfectionism.'

'Of its kind it is the sweetest.'

'I think you taught me that – when I was a boy.'

'I remember! I remember!' Lord Jagged sighed reminiscently.

'And I am grateful.'

'Nonsense. A boy needs a father. I was there.' The puffed sleeve stretched out and a pale hand emerged to touch Jherek lightly upon his carnation, to pluck a tiny petal from it and touch it so elegantly to the pale lips. 'I was there, my heart.'

'One day,' said Jherek, 'we must make love, Lord Jagged.'

'One day. When the mood comes upon us at the same time. Yes.' Lord Jagged's lips smiled. 'I look forward to it. And how is your mother?'

'She is sleeping a great deal again.'

'Then we may expect something extraordinary from her soon.'

'I think so. She is here.'

Lord Jagged drew away from Jherek. 'Then I shall look for her. Farewell.'

'Goodbye, golden Lord Jagged.'

Jherek watched his friend disappear through an archway of fire which was there for a moment before the towers reformed.

It was true that Lord Jagged of Canaria had helped form his taste and was, perhaps, the kindest, most affectionate person in all the world. Yet there was a certain sadness about him which Jherek could never understand. Lord Jagged, it was sometimes said, had not been created in this age at all, but had been a time-traveller. Jherek had once put this to Lord Jagged but had met with an amused denial. Yet still Jherek was not sure. He wondered why, if Jagged were a time-traveller, he would wish to make a secret of it.

Jherek realised that he was frowning. He rearranged his expression and sauntered on through Timbuctoo. How dull the 28th century must have been. Odd that things could change so swiftly in the course of a few hundred years so that a century like the 19th could be full of richness and a century like the 28th could only offer the Great Fire of Africa. Still, it was all a matter of what happened to amuse the individual. He really must try to be less critical of the Duke of Queens.

A pride of lions appeared and prowled menacingly around Jherek, growling and sniffing. They were real. He wondered if the Duke of Queens had gone so far as to allow them all their instincts. But they lost interest in him and swaggered on. Their colours, predominantly blue and green, clashed as usual. Elsewhere Jherek heard people giggling in fear as the lions found them. Most people found such sensations gratifying. He wondered if his pursuit of virtue was making him bad-tempered. If so, he would swiftly become a bore and had best abandon the whole idea. He saw Mistress Christia, the

Everlasting Concubine, lying on her back near the edge of the burning city and humping up and down with glad cries as O'Kala Incarnadine, who had turned himself into a gorilla for the occasion, enjoyed her. She saw Jherek and waved. 'Jherek!' she panted. 'I – would – *love* – to – see – – Oh, Kala, my love, that's enough. Do you mind? But I want to talk to Jherek now.' The gorilla turned its head and saw Jherek and grinned at him.

'Hello, Jherek. I didn't realise,' said O'Kala Incarnadine. He got up, smoothing down his fur. 'Thank you, Mistress Christia.'

'Thank you, O'Kala. That was lovely.' She spoke vaguely as she concentrated on rearranging her skirts. 'How are you, Jherek. Can I serve?'

'Always, as you know. But I would rather chat.'

'So would I, to be frank. O'Kala has been a gorilla now for several weeks and I'm *constantly* bumping into him and I'm beginning to suspect that these meetings aren't accidental. Not that I mind, of course. But I'll admit that I'm thinking of going back to being a man again. And maybe a gorilla. Your mother was a gorilla for a while, wasn't she? How did she enjoy it?'

'I was too young to remember, Mistress Christia.'

'Of course you were!' She looked him over. 'A baby! I remember.'

'You would, my delicacy.'

'There is nothing to stop anyone *becoming* a child for a while. I wonder why more people don't do it?'

'The fashion never did catch on,' Jherek agreed, seizing her about the waist and kissing her neck and shoulders. She kissed him back. She really was one of the most perfect identity-creations in the world. No man could resist her. Whatever he felt like he had to kiss her and often had to make love to her. Even Mongrove. Even Werther de Goethe who, as a boy, had never enjoyed her.

'Have you seen Werther de Goethe?' Jherek asked.

'He *was* here, earlier,' said Mistress Christia looking about her. 'I saw him with Mongrove. They do like one another's company, don't they?'

'Mongrove learns from Werther, I think,' said Jherek. 'And

20

Werther says that Mongrove is the only sane person in the whole world.'

'Perhaps it's true. What does "sane" mean?'

'I shan't tell you. I've had enough of defining difficult words and ideas today.'

'Oh, Jherek! What are you up to?'

'Very little. My interests have always tended towards the abstract. It makes me poor company and I am determined to improve.'

'You're lovely company, Jherek. Everyone loves you.'

'I know. And I intend to continue being loved. You know how tiresome I'd become – like Li Pao – if I did nothing but talk and invented little.'

'Everyone loves Li Pao!'

'Of course. But I do not wish to be loved in the way Li Pao is loved.'

She offered him a glance of secret amusement.

'Is *that* how I'm loved!' he asked in horror.

'Not quite. But you *were* a child, Jherek. The questions you asked!'

'I'm mortified.' He was not. He realised that he did not really care. He laughed.

'You're right,' she said. 'Li Pao is a bore and even I find him tiresome occasionally. Have you heard that the Duke of Queens has a surprise for us?'

'Another.'

'Jherek – you are not generous to the Duke of Queens. And that isn't fair, for the Duke is a very generous host.'

'Yes, I know. What is the nature of this new surprise?'

'That, too, is a surprise.' High above little African flying machines began to bomb the city. Bright lights burst everywhere and screamed as they burst. 'Oh, that's how it started!' exclaimed Mistress Christia. 'He's put it on again for the people who missed it.' Mistress Christia could have been the only witness to the original display. She was always the first to arrive anywhere.

'Come on, Jherek. Everyone's to go to Wolverhampton. That's where we'll be shown the surprise.'

'Very well.' Jherek let her take his hand and lead him

towards Wolverhampton, on the far side of the collection of cities.

And then suddenly all the flames went out and they were in complete darkness.

Silence fell.

'Delicious,' whispered Mistress Christia, squeezing his hand.

Jherek closed his eyes.

CHAPTER THREE

A VISITOR WHO IS LESS THAN ENTERTAINING

At last, after a longer pause than Jherek would have thought absolutely necessary, the voice of the Duke of Queens came to them through the darkness.

'Dear friends, you have doubtless already guessed that this party has a theme. That theme, needless to say, is "Disaster".'

A cool, soft voice said to Jherek: 'It's interesting to compare this expression of the theme with that of the Earl of Carbolic who gave it to us two years ago.'

Jherek smiled as he recognised Lord Jagged's voice. 'Wait for the lights to go up,' he said.

And then the lights did come on. They focused upon an odd, asymmetrical sort of mound which had been set on a dais of transparent steel. The mound seemed covered with a greenish-yellow mould. The mould pulsed. It made small squeaking sounds. It was less than charming.

'Well,' whispered Lord Jagged, still in darkness, for only the mound itself was lit, 'it certainly appears to fit the theme: what disaster could have caused that, I wonder!'

Mistress Christia squeezed Jherek's hand tighter and giggled. 'One of the Duke's experiments gone wrong, I'd have thought. Or perhaps the Duke himself?'

'Ah,' said Lord Jagged. 'How intelligent you are, Mistress Christia. As well as desirable, of course.'

The Duke of Queens, still unseen, continued with his introduction:

'This, my friends, is a spaceship. It landed near here a day or two ago.'

Jherek was disappointed and he could tell from their silence that the rest of the guests were just as disappointed. It was not unusual for spaceships to come to the planet, although none had called here in the last few years, as he remembered.

'It has come the furthest of any spaceship ever to visit our old Earth,' said the voice of the Duke of Queens. 'It's travelled simply millions of light years to get here! Sensational in itself!'

This was still not good enough, thought Jherek, to make such a fuss about.

'Travelling at much the fastest speed of any spaceship to visit us before! Stupendous speed!' continued the Duke.

Jherek shrugged.

'Astounding,' came Lord Jagged's dry voice from beside him. 'A scientific lecture. The Duke of Queens is taking a leaf out of Li Pao's book. I suppose it makes a change. But somewhat out of character for our Duke, I'd have thought.'

'Perhaps even he has tired of sensationalism for its own sake,' said Jherek. 'But a rather dramatic reaction, surely?'

'Ah, these problems of taste. They'll remain a subject of debate until every one of us decides to end his existence, I fear.' Lord Jagged sighed.

'But you are thinking that this is not of sufficient moment to make a great fuss about,' said the Duke of Queens, as if in answer to Jherek and Lord Jagged. 'And, of course, you are right. The occupant of this particular spacecraft by coincidence happened to bring a certain amplification to the theme

24

of my party tonight. I felt he would amuse you all. So here he is. His name, as far as I can pronounce it at all, is Yusharisp. He will address you through his own translation system (which is not quite of the quality to which we are used) and I'm sure you will find him as delightful as did I when I first spoke with him a little while ago. My dear friends, I give you the space-traveller Yusharisp.'

The light dimmed and then refocused on a creature standing on the other side of the transparent steel dais. The creature was about four feet tall, stood upon four bandy legs, had a round body, no head and no arms. Near the top of the body was a row of circular eyes, dotted at regular intervals about the entire circumference. There was a small triangular opening below these, which Jherek took to be the mouth. The creature was predominantly dark, muddy brown, with little flecks of green here and there. The eyes were bright, china blue. All in all, the space-traveller had a rather sour look to him.

'Greetings, people of this planet,' began Yusharisp. 'I come from the civilisation of Pweeli' – here the translator he was using screeched for a few seconds and Yusharisp had to cough to readjust it – 'many galaxies distant. It is my self-appointed mission to travel the universe bringing with me my message. I believe it to be my duty to tell all intelligent life-forms what I know. I srrti oowo...' again a pause and a cough while Yusharisp adjusted his translator, which seemed to be a mechanical rather than an organic device of some kind, probably implanted in his equivalent of a throat by crude surgery. Jherek was interested in the device for its own sake, for he had heard of such things existing in the 19th century, or possibly a little later. 'I apologise,' Yusharisp continued, 'for the inefficiency of my equipment. It has been put to much use over the past two or three thousand years as I have travelled the universe bearing my tidings. After I leave here, I will continue my work until, at last, I perish. It will be several thousand years more before everyone I can possibly warn has been warned.' There was a sudden roaring and Jherek thought at first that it must be the lions, for he could not imagine a sound like it issuing from the tiny mouth cavity. But it was plain, from the alien's embarrassed gestures and coughs, that the translator was again malfunctioning. Jherek began to feel impatient.

'Well, I suppose it *is* an experience,' said Lord Jagged. 'Though I'm not sure that it was entirely tactful of the Duke of Queens to make it impossible for us to leave should we so desire. After all, not everyone enjoys being bored.'

'Oh, you are not kind, Lord Jagged,' said the equally invisible Mistress Christia. 'I feel a certain sympathy for the little creature.'

'Dry sgog,' said the alien. 'I am sorry. Dry sgog.' He cleared his throat again. 'I had best be as brief as possible.'

The guests were beginning to talk quite loudly among themselves now.

'In short,' said the alien, trying to make himself heard above a rising babble, 'my people have reached the inescapable conclusion that we are living at what you might call the End of Time. The universe is about to undergo a reformation of such massive proportions that not an atom of it will remain the same. All life will, effectively, die. All suns and planets will be destroyed as the universe ends one cycle and begins another. We are doomed, fellow intelligences. We are doomed.'

Jherek yawned. He wished the alien would get to the point. He began to stroke Mistress Christia's breasts.

The babble died. It was obvious that everyone was now waiting for the alien to finish.

'I see you are shocked, skree, skree, skree,' said the alien. 'Perhaps I could have (roar) put the news more tactfully, but I, skree, skree, have so little time. There is nothing we can do, of course, to avert our fate. We can only prepare ourselves, philosophically, skree, skree, for (roar) death.'

Mistress Christia giggled. She and Jherek sank to the ground and Jherek tried to remember how the lower garment of his set was removed. Mistress Christia's had already drifted open to receive him.

'Buttons,' said Jherek, who had not forgotten even this small detail.

'Isn't that amazing!' said the voice of the Duke of Queens. The voice was strained; it was disappointed; it was eager to infect them with the interest which he himself felt but which, it appeared, had failed to communicate itself to his guests. 'The end of the universe! Delightful!'

'I suppose so,' said Lord Jagged, feeling for Jherek's heaving back and patting it good-bye. 'But it is not a very *new* idea, is it?'

'We are all going to *die*!' The Duke of Queens laughed rather mechanically. 'Oh, it's delicious!'

'Good-bye, Jherek. Farewell, beautiful Mistress Christia.' Lord Jagged went away. It was plain that he was disappointed in the Duke of Queens; offended, even.

'Good-bye, Lord Jagged,' said Mistress Christia and Jherek together. Really, there hadn't been such a dull party in a thousand years. They separated and sat side by side on the lawn. By the sound of it, many others were drifting away, stumbling against people in the dark and apologising. It was, indeed, a disaster.

Jherek, now trying to be generous to the Duke of Queens, wondered if the thing had been deliberately engineered. Well, it was a relatively *fresh* experience – a party which failed.

The cities of Africa burst into flame once again and Jherek could see the dais and the Duke of Queens standing talking to the alien on the dais.

Lady Charlotina went past, not noticing Jherek and Mistress Christia, who were still sitting on the ground.

'Duke,' called Lady Charlotina, 'is your friend part of your menagerie?'

The Duke of Queens turned, his fine, bearded face full of dejection. It was obvious that he had not planned the failure at all.

'He must be tired, poor thing,' said Mistress Christia.

'It was almost bound to happen. Sensation piled on sensation but rooted in nothing, no proper artistic conception,' said Jherek maliciously. 'It is what I've always said.'

'Oh, Jherek. Don't be unkind.'

'Well . . .' Jherek did feel ashamed of himself. He had been on the point of revelling in the Duke's appalling mistake. 'Very well, Mistress Christia. You and I shall go and comfort him. Congratulate him, if you like, though I fear he won't believe in my sincerity.' They got up.

The Duke of Queens was taken aback by Lady Charlotina's question. He said vaguely: 'Menagerie? Why, no . . .'

'Then might I have him?'

'Yes, yes, of course.'

'Thank you.' Lady Charlotina gestured to the alien. 'Will you come with me, please.'

The alien turned several of his eyes upon her. 'But I must leave. My message. You are kind to, skree, skree, invite, skree, me. Howev (roar) er, I shall have to, skree, decline.' He began to move towards his ship.

Regretfully Lady Charlotina gestured with one hand and froze the alien while with the other hand she disseminated his spaceship.

'*Disgusting!*'

Jherek heard the voice behind him and turned, delightedly, to identify it. The person had spoken in the language of the 19th century. A woman stood there. She wore a tight-fitting grey jacket and a voluminous grey skirt which covered all but the toes of her black boots. Beneath the jacket could just be seen a white blouse with a small amount of lacework on the bodice. She had a straw, wide-brimmed hat upon her heavily coiled chestnut hair and an expression of outrage on her pretty, heart-shaped face. A time-traveller, without doubt. Jherek grinned with pleasure.

'Oh!' he exclaimed. 'An ancient!'

She ignored him, calling out to Lady Charlotina (who, of course, did not understand 19th century speech at all): '*Let the poor creature go! Though he is neither human nor Christian, he is still one of God's creatures and has a right to his liberty!*'

Jherek was speechless with delight as he watched the time-traveller stride forward, the heavy skirts swinging. Mistress Christia raised her eyebrows. 'What is she saying, Jherek?'

'She must be new,' he said. 'She has yet to take a translation pill. She seems to want the little alien for herself. I don't understand every word, of course.' He shook his head in admiration as the time-traveller laid a small hand upon Lady Charlotina's shoulder. Lady Charlotina turned in surprise.

Jherek and Mistress Christia approached the pair. The Duke of Queens peered down from the dais looking first at them and then at the frozen space creature without any understanding at all.

'*What you have done you can undo, degenerate soul,*' said the time-traveller to the bewildered Lady Charlotina.

'She's speaking 19th century – one of many dialects,' explained Jherek, proud of his knowledge.

Lady Charlotina inspected the grey-clad woman. 'Does she want to make love to me? I suppose I will, if . . .'

Jherek shook his head. 'No. I think she wants your alien. Or, perhaps, she doesn't want you to have it. I'll speak to her. Just a moment.' He turned and smiled at the ancient.

'*Good evening, Fräulein. I parle the yazhak. Nây m̂-sdi pâ,*' said Jherek.

She did not appear to be reassured. But now she stared at him in equal astonishment.

'*The Fräulein this,*' said Jherek indicating Lady Charlotina, who listened with mild interest, '*is pense que t'a make love to elle.*' He was about to continue and point out that he knew that this was not the case when the time-traveller transferred her attention to him altogether and delivered a heavy smack on his cheek. This baffled him. He had no knowledge of the custom or, indeed, how to respond to it.

'I think,' he said to Lady Charlotina regretfully, 'that we ought to give her a pill before we go any further.'

'*Disgusting!*' said the time-traveller again. '*I shall seek someone in authority. This must be stopped. I'm beginning to believe I've had the misfortune to find myself in a colony of lunatics!*'

They all watched her stalk away.

'Isn't she fine,' said Jherek. 'I wonder if anyone's claimed her. It almost makes me want to start my own menagerie.'

The Duke of Queens lowered himself from the dais and settled beside them. He was dressed in a force-form chastity belt, feather cloak and had a conical hat of shrunken human heads. 'I must apologise,' he began.

'The whole thing was superb,' said Jherek, all malice forgotten in his delight at meeting the time-traveller. 'How did you think of it?'

'Well,' said the Duke of Queens fingering his beard. 'Ah . . .'

'A wonderful joke, juiciest of Dukes,' said Mistress Christia. 'We shall be talking about it for days!'

'Oh?' The Duke of Queens brightened.

29

'And you have shown your enormous kindness once again,' said Lady Charlotina, pressing her sky blue lips and nose to his cheek, 'in giving me the morbid space-traveller for my menagerie. I haven't got a round one.'

'Of course, of course,' said the Duke of Queens, his normal ebullience returning, though Jherek thought that the Duke rather regretted making the gift.

The Lady Charlotina made an adjustment to one of her rings and the stiff body of the little alien floated from the dais and hovered over her head, bobbing slightly, in the manner of a captive balloon.

Jherek said: 'The time-traveller. Is she yours, My Lord Duke?'

'The grey one who slapped you? No. I've never seen her before. Perhaps a maverick?'

'Perhaps so.' Jherek took off his opera hat and made a sweeping bow to the company. 'If you will forgive me, then, I'll see if I can find her. She will add a touch to my present collection which will bring it close to perfection. Farewell.'

'Good-bye, Jherek,' said the Duke, almost gratefully. Sympathetically Lady Charlotina and Mistress Christia took each of his arms and led him away while Jherek bowed once more and then struck off in pursuit of his quarry.

CHAPTER FOUR

CARNELIAN CONCEIVES A NEW AFFECTATION

After an hour of searching, Jherek realised that the grey time-traveller was no longer at the party. Because most of the guests had left, it had not been a difficult search. Disconsolate, he returned to his locomotive and swung aboard, throwing himself upon the long seat of plush and ermine, but hesitating before he pulled the whistle and set the aircar in motion, for he wanted something to happen to him – a compensation for his disappointment.

Either, he thought, the time-traveller had been returned to the menagerie of whomever it was that owned her, or else she had gone somewhere of her own volition. He hoped that she did not have a time-travelling machine capable of carrying her back to her own age. If she had, then it was likely she was gone forever. He seemed to remember that there was some evidence to suggest that the people of the late 19th century had possessed a crude form of time-travel.

'Ah, well,' he sighed to himself, 'if she has gone, she has gone.'

His mother, the Iron Orchid, had left with the Lady Voiceless and Ulianov of the Palms, doubtless to revive memories of times before he had been born. Being naturally gregarious, he felt deserted. There was hardly anyone left whom he knew well or would care to take back with him to his ranch. He wanted the time-traveller. His heart was set on her. She was charming. He fingered his cheek and smiled.

Peering through one of the observation windows, he saw Mongrove and Werther de Goethe approaching and he stood up to hail them. But both pointedly ignored him and so increased his sense of desolation where normally he would have been amused by the perfection with which they played their roles. He slumped, once more, into his cushions, now thoroughly reluctant to return home but with no idea of any alternative. Mistress Christia, always a willing companion, had gone off with the Duke of Queens and My Lady Charlotina. Even Li Pao was nowhere to be seen. He yawned and closed his eyes.

'Sleeping, my dear?'

It was Lord Jagged. He stood peering up over the footplate. 'Is this the machine you were telling me about. The —?'

'The locomotive. Oh, Lord Jagged, I am so pleased to see you. I thought you left hours ago.'

'I was diverted.' The pale head emerged a fraction further from the yellow collar. 'And then deserted.' Lord Jagged smiled his familiar, wistful smile. 'May I join you?'

'Of course.'

Lord Jagged floated up, a cloud of lemon-coloured down, and sat beside Jherek.

'So the Duke's display was not a deliberate disaster?' said Lord Jagged. 'But we all pretended that it was.'

Jherek Carnelian drew off his opera hat and flung it from the locomotive. It became a puff of orange smoke which dissipated in the air. He loosened the cord of his cloak. 'Yes,' he said, 'even I managed to compliment him. He was so miserable. But what could have possessed him to think that anyone would be interested in an ordinary little alien? And a mad, prophesying one, at that.'

'You don't think he told the truth, then? The alien?'

'Oh, yes. I'm sure he spoke the truth. Why shouldn't he? But what is particularly interesting about the *truth*? Very little, when it comes down to it, as we all know. Look at Li Pao. He is forever telling the truth, too. And what is a truth, anyway? There are so many different kinds.'

'And his message did not disturb you?'

'His message? No. The lifetime of the universe is finite. That was his message.'

'And we are near the end of that lifetime. He said that.' Lord Jagged made a motion with his hand and disrobed himself, stretching his thin, pale body upon the couch.

'Why are you making so much of this, white Lord Jagged?'

Lord Jagged laughed. 'I am not. I am not. Just conversation. And a touch or two of curiosity. Your mind is so much fresher than mine – than almost anyone's in the world. That is why I ask questions. If it bores you I'll stop.'

'No. The poor little space-traveller was a bore, wasn't he? Wasn't he, Lord Jagged? Or did you find something interesting about him?'

'Not really. People used to fear death once, you know, and I suppose whatever-his-name-was still fears it. I believe that people used to wish to communicate their fear. To spread it somehow comforted them. I suppose that is his impulse. Well, he shall find plenty to comfort him in My Lady Charlotina's menagerie.'

'Speaking of menageries, did you see a girl time-traveller dressed in rather heavy grey garments, wearing a straw-coloured hat with a wide brim, at the party?'

'I believe I did.'

'Did you notice where she went? Did you see her leave?'

'I think Mongrove took a fancy to her and sent her in his aircar to his menagerie before he left with Werther de Goethe.'

'Mongrove! How unfortunate.'

'You wanted her yourself?'

'Yes.'

'But you've no menagerie.'

'I have a 19th century collection. She would have suited it perfectly.'

'She's 19th century, then?'

'Yes.'

'Perhaps Mongrove will give her to you.'

'Mongrove had best not know I want her at all. He would disseminate her or send her back to her own time or give her away rather than think he was contributing to my pleasure. You must know that, Lord Jagged.'

'You couldn't trade something for her? What about the item Mongrove wanted from you so much? The elderly writer – from the same period, wasn't he?'

'Yes, before I became interested in it. I remember, Ambrose Bierce.'

'The same!'

'He went up with the others. In the fire. I couldn't be bothered to reconstitute him and now, of course, it's too late.'

'You were never prudent, tender Jherek.'

Jherek's brows knitted. 'I *must* have her, Lord Jagged, I think, in fact, that I shall fall in love with her. Yes! in *love*.'

'Oho!' Lord Jagged threw back his head, arching his exquisite neck. 'Love! Love! How splendid, Jherek.'

'I will plunge into it. I will encourage the passion until I am as involved in it as Mongrove is involved in his misery.'

'An excellent affectation. It will power your mind. It will make you so ingenious. You will succeed. You will get her away from Mongrove, though it will turn the world upside down! You will entertain us all. You will thrill us. You will hold our attention for months! For years! We shall speculate upon your success or your failure. We shall wonder how far you have really involved yourself in this game. We shall watch to see how your grey time-traveller responds. Will she return your love? Will she spurn it? Will she decide to love Mongrove, the more to complicate your schemes?' Lord Jagged reached over and kissed Jherek heartily upon the lips. 'Yes! It must be played out in every small detail. Your friends will help. They will give you tips. They'll consult the literatures of the ages to glean the best of the love stories and you will act them out. Gorgon and Queen

Elizabeth. Romeo and Julius Caesar. Windermere and Lady Oscar. Hitler and Mussolini. Fred and Louella. Ojiba and Obija. Sero and Fidsekalak. The list goes on – and on! And on, dear Jherek!'

Fired by his friend's enthusiasm Jherek stood up and yelled with laughter.

'I shall be a *lover*!'

'A lover!'

'Nothing shall thwart me!'

'Nothing!'

'I shall win my love and live with her in ardent happiness until the very universe grows old and cold.'

'Or whatever our space-travelling friend said would happen. Now that factor should give it an edge.' Lord Jagged fingered his linen-coloured nose. 'Oh, you'll be doomed, desired, deceived, debunked and delivered!' (Lord Jagged seemed to be fond, tonight, of his d's.) 'Demonic, demonstrative, determined, destructive.' He was dangerously close to overdoing it. 'You'll be destiny's fool, my dear! Your story shall ring down the ages (whatever's left, at any rate). Jherek Carnelian – the most laudable, the most laborious, the most literal, the very *last* of lovers!' And with a yell he flung his arms around his friend while Jherek Carnelian seized the whistle string and tugged wildly making the locomotive shriek and moan and thrust itself throbbing into the warm, black night.

'Love!' shouted Jherek.

'Love,' whispered Lord Jagged, kissing him once more.

'Oh, Jagged!' Jherek gave himself up to his lascivious lord's embrace.

'She must have a name,' said Jagged, rolling over in the eight-poster bed and taking a sip of beer from the bronze barrel he held between the forefinger and thumb of his left hand. 'We must find it out.' He got up and crossed the corrugated iron floor to brush aside the sheets from the window and peer through. 'Is that a sunset or a sunrise? It looks like a sunset.'

'I'm sorry.' Jherek opened his eyes and turned one of his rings a fraction of a degree to the right.

'Much better,' said Lord Jagged of Canaria, admiring the golden dawn. 'And what are the birds?' He pointed through the window at the black silhouettes circling high above in the sky.

'Parrots,' said Jherek. 'They're supposed to eat the branded buffalo.'

'Supposed to?'

'They won't. And they should be perfect reproductions. I made a mistake somewhere. I really ought to put them back in my gene-bank and start again.'

'What if we paid Mongrove a visit this morning?' Lord Jagged suggested, returning to his original subject.

'He wouldn't receive me.'

'He would receive *me*, however. And you will be my companion. I will feign an interest in his menagerie and that way you shall be able to meet again the object of your desire.'

'I'm not sure it's such a good idea now, darling Jagged,' said Jherek. 'I was carried away last night.'

'Indeed, my love, you were. And why not? How often does it happen? No, Jherek Carnelian, you shall not falter. It will delight so many.'

Jherek laughed. 'Lord Jagged, I think there is some other motive involved here – a motive of your own. Would you not rather take my place?'

'I? I have no interest at all in the period.'

'Aren't you interested in falling in love?'

'I am interested in *your* falling in love. You should. It will complete you, Jherek. You were *born*, do you see? The rest of us came into the world as adults (apart from poor Werther, but that was a somewhat different story) or created ourselves or were created by our friends. But you, Jherek, were born – a baby. And so you must also fall in love. Oh, yes. There is no question of it. In any other one of us it would be silly.'

'I think you have already pointed out that it would be ludicrous in me, too,' said Jherek mildly.

'Love was always *ludicrous*, Jherek. That's another thing again.'

'Very well,' smiled Jherek. 'To please you, my lean lord, I will do my best.'

'To please us all. Including yourself, Jherek. Especially yourself, Jherek.'

'I must admit that I might consider...'

Lord Jagged began, suddenly, to sing.

The notes trilled and warbled from his throat. A most delightful rush of song and such a complicated melody that Jherek could hardly follow it.

Jherek glanced thoughtfully and with some irony at his friend.

It had seemed for a moment that Lord Jagged had deliberately cut Jherek short.

But why?

He had only been about to point out that the Lord of Canaria had all the qualities of affection, wit and imagination that might be desired in a lover and that Jherek would willingly fall in love with him rather than some time-traveller whom he did not know at all.

And, Jherek suspected, Lord Jagged had known that he was about to say this. Would the declaration have been in doubtful taste, perhaps? The point about falling in love with the grey time-traveller was that she would find nothing strange in it. In her age *everyone* had fallen in love (or, at very least, had been able to deceive themselves that they had, which was much the same thing). Yes, Lord Jagged had acted with great generosity and stopped him from embarrassing himself. It would have been vulgar to have declared his love for Lord Jagged but it was witty to fall in love with the grey timetraveller.

Not that there was anything wrong with intentional vulgarity. Or even unintentional vulgarity, thought Jherek, in the case, for instance, of the Duke of Queens.

He recalled the party with horror. 'The poor Duke of Queens!'

'His party was absolutely perfect. Not a thing went right.' Lord Jagged left the window and wandered over the bumpy floor. 'May I use this for a suit?' He gestured towards a stuffed mammoth which filled one corner of the room.

'Of course,' said Jherek. 'I was never quite sure if it was in period, anyway. How clever of you to pick that.' He watched with interest as Lord Jagged broke the mammoth down into its component atoms and then, from the hovering cloud of particles, concocted for himself a loose, lilac-coloured robe with the kind of high, stiff collar he often favoured, and huge puffed sleeves from which peeped the tips of his fingers, and silver slippers with long, pointed toes, and a circlet to contain his long platinum hair; a circlet in the form of a rippling, living 54th century Uranian lizard.

'How haughty you look!' said Jherek. 'A prince of fifty planets!'

Lord Jagged bowed in acknowledgement of the compliment. 'We are the sum of all previous ages, are we not? And as a result there is nothing that marks this age of ours, save that one thing. We are the sum.'

'I had never thought of it.' Jherek swung his long legs from the bed and stood up.

'Nor I, until this moment. But it is true. I can think of nothing else typical. Our technologies, our tricks, our conceits – they all imitate the past. We benefit from everything our ancestors worked to achieve. But we invent nothing of our own – we merely ring a few changes on what already exists.'

'There is nothing left to invent, my lilac lord. The long history of mankind, if it has a purpose at all, has found complete fulfilment in us. We can indulge any fancy. We can choose to be whatever we wish and do whatever we wish. What else is there? We are happy. Even Mongrove is happy in his misery – it is his choice. No one would try to alter it. I am rather at a loss, therefore, to follow where your argument is leading.' Jherek sipped from his own beer barrel.

'There was no argument, my jaunty Jherek. It was an observation I made. That was all.'

'And accurate.' Jherek was at a loss to add anything more.

'Accurate.'

Lord Jagged stood back to admire Jherek, still unclothed for the day.

'And what will you wear?'

'I have been considering that very question,' Jherek put a finger to his chin. 'It must be in keeping with all this – especially since I am to pay court to a lady of the 19th century. But it cannot be the same as yesterday.'

'No,' agreed Lord Jagged.

38

And then Jherek had it. He was delighted at his own brilliance. 'I know! I shall wear exactly the same costume as she wore last night! It will be a compliment she cannot fail to notice.'

'Jherek,' crooned Lord Jagged, hugging him, 'you are the best of us!'

CHAPTER FIVE

A MENAGERIE OF TIME AND SPACE

'The very best of us,' yawned Lord Jagged of Canaria, lying back upon the couch of plush and ermine as Jherek, clad in his new costume, pulled the whistle of the locomotive which took off from the corral and left the West behind, heading for gloomy Mongrove's domain.

The locomotive steered a course for the tropics, passing through a dozen different skies. Some of the skies were still being completed, while others were being dismantled as their creators wearied of them.

They puffed over the old cities which nobody used any more, but which were not destroyed because the sources of many forms of energy were still stored there – the energy in particular, which powered the rings everyone wore. Once whole star systems had been converted to store the energy banks of Earth, during the manic Engineering Millennium, when everyone, it appeared, had devoted themselves to that single purpose.

They travelled through several daytimes and a few night-times on their way to Mongrove's. The giant, save for his brief Hell-making fad, had always lived in the same place, where a sub-continent called Indi had once been. It was well over an hour before they sighted the grey clouds which perpetually hung over Mongrove's domain, pouring down either snow or sleet or hail or rain, depending on the giant's mood. The sun never shone through those clouds. Mongrove hated sunshine.

Lord Jagged pretended to shiver, though his garments had naturally adjusted to the change in temperature. 'There are Mongrove's miserable cliffs. I can see them now.' He pointed through the observation window.

Jherek looked and saw them. Mile high crags met the grey clouds. They were black, gleaming and melancholy crags, without symmetry, without a single patch of relieving colour, for even the rain which fell on them seemed to turn black as it struck them and ran in weeping black rivers down their rocky flanks. And Jherek shivered, too. It had been many years since he had visited Mongrove and he had forgotten with what uncompromising misery the giant had designed his home.

At a murmured command from Jherek, the locomotive rolled up the sky to get above the clouds. The rain and the cold would not affect the aircar, but Jherek found the mere sight too glum for his taste. But soon they had passed over the cliffs and Jherek could tell from the way in which the cloud bank seemed to dip in the middle that they were over Mongrove's valley. Now they would have to pass through the clouds. There was no choice.

The locomotive began to descend, passing through layer after grey layer of the thick, swirling mist until it emerged, finally, over Mongrove's valley. Jherek and Lord Jagged looked down upon a blighted landscape of festering marsh and leafless, stunted trees, of bleak boulders, of withered shrubs and dank moss. In the very centre of all this desolation squatted the vast, cheerless complex of buildings and enclosures which was surrounded by a great, glabrous wall and dominated by

Mongrove's dark, obsidian castle. From the castle's ragged towers shone a few dim, yellowish lights.

Almost immediately a force dome appeared over the castle and its environs. It turned the falling rain to steam. Then Mongrove's voice, amplified fiftyfold, boomed from the now partially hidden castle:

'What enemy approaches to plague and threaten despondent Mongrove?'

Although Mongrove's detectors would already have identified them, Jagged answered with good humour.

'It is I, dear Mongrove. Your good friend Lord Jagged of Canaria.'

'And another.'

'Yes, another. Jherek Carnelian is well known to you surely?'

'Well known and well hated. He is not welcome here, Lord Jagged.'

'And I? Am I not welcome?'

'None are welcome at Castle Mongrove, but you may enter, if you wish.'

'And my friend Jherek?'

'If you insist upon bringing him with you – and if I have his word, Lord Jagged, that he is not here to play one of his cruel jests upon me.'

'You have my word, Mongrove,' said Jherek.

'Then,' said Mongrove reluctantly, 'enter.'

The force dome vanished; the rain fell unhindered upon the basalt and the obsidian. For the sake of politeness, Jherek did not take his locomotive over the wall. Instead he brought the aircar to the swampy ground and waited until the massive iron gates groaned open just wide enough to admit the locomotive, which shuffled merrily through, giving out multicoloured smoke from its funnel and its bogies – a most incongruous sight and one which was bound to displease Mongrove. Yet Jherek could not resist it. Mongrove desired so much to be baited, he felt, and he desired so much to bait him that he let few opportunities go. Lord Jagged placed a hand on Jherek's shoulder.

'It would improve matters and make our task the easier if we were to forgo the smoke, jolly Jherek.'

'Very well!' Jherek laughed and ordered the smoke to stop.

'Perhaps I should have designed a more funereal carriage altogether. For the occasion. One of those black ships of the Four Year Empire would do. Oh, death meant so much to them in those days. Are we missing something, I wonder?'

'I have wondered that. Still, we have all of us died so many times and been recreated so many times that the thrill is gone. For them – especially the heavy folk of the Four Year Empire – it was an experience they could have only three or four times at most before their systems gave out. Strange.'

They were nearing the main entrance of the castle itself, passing through narrow streets full of lowering, dark walls and iron fences behind which dim shapes could be seen moving occasionally. The large part of all this was Mongrove's menagerie.

'He has added a great deal to it since I was last here,' said Jherek. 'I hadn't realised.'

'You had best follow my lead,' said Lord Jagged. 'I will gauge Mongrove's mood and ask, casually, if we can see the menagerie. Perhaps after lunch, if he offers us lunch.'

'I remember the last lunch I had here,' Jherek said with a shudder. 'Raw Turyian dungwhale prepared in the style of the Zhadash primitives who hunted it, I gather, on Ganesha in the 89th century.'

'You do remember it well.'

'I could never forget it. I have never questioned Mongrove's *artistry*, Lord Jagged. Like me, he is a stickler for detail.'

'And that is why this rivalry exists between you, I shouldn't wonder. You are of similar temperaments, really.'

Jherek laughed. 'Perhaps. Though I think I prefer the way in which I *express* mine!'

They went under a portcullis and entered a cobbled courtyard. The locomotive stopped.

Rain fell on the cobbles. Somewhere a sad bell tolled and tolled and tolled.

And there was Mongrove. He was dressed in dark green robes, his great chin sunk upon his huge chest, his brooding eyes regarding them from a head which seemed itself carved from rock. His monstrous, ten foot frame did not move as they dismounted from the aircar and, from politeness, allowed

43

themselves to be soaked by the chill rain.

'Good morning, Mongrove.' Lord Jagged of Canaria made one of his famous sweeping bows and then tip-toed forward to reach up and grasp the giant's bulky hands which were folded on his stomach.

'Jagged,' said Mongrove. 'I am feeling suspicious. Why are you and that wretch Jherek Carnelian here? What plot's hatching? What devious brew are you boiling? What new ruse are you rascals ripening to make a rift in my peace of mind?'

'Oh, come, Mongrove – peace of mind! Isn't that the last thing you desire?' Jherek could not resist the jibe. He stood before his old rival in his new grey gown with his straw boater upon his chestnut curls and his hands on his hips and he grinned up at the giant. 'It is despair you seek – exquisite despair. It is agony of soul such as the ancients knew. You wish to discover the secret of what they called "the human condition" and recreate it in all its terror and its pain. And yet you have never quite discovered that secret, have you, Mongrove? Is that why you keep this vast menagerie with creatures culled from all the ages, all the places of the universe? Do you hope that, in their misery, they will show you the way from despair to utter despair, from melancholy to the deepest melancholy, from gloom to unspeakable gloom?'

'Be silent!' groaned Mongrove. 'You *did* come here to plague me. You cannot stay! You cannot stay!' He covered his monstrous ears with his monstrous hands and closed his great, sad eyes.

'I apologise for Jherek, Mongrove,' said Lord Jagged softly. 'He only hopes to please you.'

Mongrove's reply was in the form of a vast, shuddering moan. He began to turn to go back into his castle.

'Please, Mongrove,' said Jherek. 'I do apologise. I really do. I wish there was some release for you from this terror, this gloom, this unbearable depression.'

Mongrove turned back again, brightening just a trifle. 'You understand?'

'Of course. Though I have felt only a fraction of what you must feel – I understand.' Jherek placed his hand on his bosom. 'The aching sorrow of it all.'

44

'Yes,' whispered Mongrove. A tear fell from his huge right eye. 'That is very true, Jherek.' A tear fell from his left eye. 'Nobody understands, as a rule. I am a joke. A laughing-stock. They know that in this great frame is a tiny, frightened, pathetic creature incapable of any generosity, without creative talent, with a capacity only to weep, to mourn, to sigh and to watch the tragedy that is human life play itself to its awful conclusion.'

'Yes,' said Jherek. 'Yes, Mongrove.'

Lord Jagged, who now stood behind Mongrove, sheltering in the doorway of the castle and leaning against the obsidian wall, gave Jherek a look of pure admiration and added to this look one of absolute approval. He nodded his pale head. He smiled. He winked his encouragement, the white lid falling over his almost colourless eye.

Jherek did admire Mongrove for the pains he took to make his role complete. When he, Jherek, became a lover, he would pursue his role with the same dedication.

'You see,' said Lord Jagged. 'You see, Mongrove. Jherek understands and sympathises better than anyone. In the past he has played the odd practical joke upon you, it is true, but that was because he was trying to cheer you up. Before he realised that nothing can hope to ease the misery in your bleak soul and so on.'

'Yes,' said Mongrove. 'I do see, Lord Jagged.' He threw a huge arm around Jherek's shoulders and almost flung Jherek to the cobbled ground, muddying his skirts. Jherek feared for his set. It was already getting wet and yet politeness forbade him to use any form of force protection. He felt his straw hat begin to sag a little. He looked down at his blouse and saw that the lace was looking a bit straggly.

'Come,' Mongrove went on. 'You shall lunch with me. My honoured guests. I never realised before, Jherek, how sensitive you were. And you tried to hide your sensitivity with rough humour, with coarse badinage and crude japes.'

Jherek thought many of his jokes had been rather subtle, but it was not politic to say so at the moment. He nodded, instead, and smiled.

Mongrove led them at last into the castle. For all the winds

45

whistling through the passages and howling along stairwells; for all that the only light was from guttering brands and that the walls ran with damp or were festooned with mildew; for all the rats glimpsed from time to time; for all the bloodless faces of Mongrove's living-dead retainers, the thick cobwebs, the chilly odours, the peculiar little sounds, Jherek was pleased to be inside and walked quite merrily with Mongrove as they made their way up several flights of unclad stone stairs, through a profusion of twisting corridors until at last they arrived in Mongrove's banqueting hall.

'And where is Werther,' asked Lord Jagged, 'de Goethe, I mean? I was sure he left with you last night. At the Duke of Queens?'

'The Duke of Queens.' Mongrove's massive brow frowned. 'Aye. Aye. The Duke of Queens. Yes, Werther was here for a while. But he left. Some new nightmare or other he promised to show me when he'd completed it.'

'Nightmare?'

'A play. Something. I'm not sure. He said I would like it.'

'Excellent.'

'Ah,' sighed Mongrove. 'That space-traveller. How I would love to converse longer with him. Did you hear him? Doom, he said. We are *doomed*!'

'Doom, doom,' echoed Lord Jagged, signing for Jherek to join in.

'Doom,' said Jherek a little uncertainly. 'Doom, doom.'

'Yes, dark damnation. Dejection. Doom. Doom. Doom.' Mongrove stared into the middle distance.

Jherek thought that Mongrove seemed to have picked up Lord Jagged's predilection for words beginning with 'd'.

'You covet, then, the alien?' he said.

'Covet him?'

'You want him in your menagerie?' explained Lord Jagged. 'That's the question.'

'Of course I would like him here. He is very *morbid*, isn't he? He would make an excellent companion.'

'Oh, he would!' said Lord Jagged, staring significantly at Jherek as the three men seated themselves at Mongrove's chipped and stained dining table. But Jherek couldn't quite work out why Jagged stared at him significantly. 'He would! What a shame he is in My Lady's Charlotina's collection.'

'Is that where he is? I wondered.'

'Lady Charlotina wouldn't *give* you the little alien, I suppose,' said Lord Jagged. 'Since his companionship would mean so much to you.'

'Lady Charlotina hates me,' said Mongrove simply.

'Surely not!'

'Oh, yes she does. She would give me nothing. She is jealous of my collection, I suppose.' Mongrove went on, with gloomy pride: 'My collection is large. Possibly the largest there is.'

'I have heard that it is magnificent,' Jherek told him.

'Thank you, Jherek,' said the giant gratefully.

Mongrove's attitude had changed completely. Evidently all he asked for was that his misery should be taken seriously. Then he could forget every past slight, every joke at his expense, that Jherek had ever made. In a few minutes they had changed, in Mongrove's eyes, from being bitter enemies to the closest of friends.

It was plain to Jherek that Lord Jagged understood Mongrove very well – as well as he knew Jherek, if not better. He was constantly astonished at the insight of the Lord of Canaria. Sometimes Lord Jagged could appear almost sinister!

'I would very much like to see your menagerie,' said Lord Jagged. 'Would that be possible, my miserable Mongrove?'

'Of course, of course,' said Mongrove. 'There is little to see, really. I expect it lacks the glamour of My Lady Charlotina's, the colour of the Duke of Queens', even the variety of your mother's, Jherek, the Iron Orchid's.'

'I am sure that is not the case,' said Jherek diplomatically.

'And would you like to see my menagerie also?' asked Mongrove.

'Very much,' said Jherek. 'Very much. I hear you have —'

'Those cracks,' said Lord Jagged suddenly and deliberately interrupting his friend, 'they are new, are they not, dear Mongrove?'

He gestured towards several large fissures in the far wall of the hall.

'Yes, they're comparatively recent,' Mongrove agreed. 'Do you like them?'

'They are *prime*!'

'Not excessive? You don't think they are excessive?' Mongrove asked anxiously.

'Not a bit. They are just right. The touch of a true artist.'

'I'm so glad, Lord Jagged, that two men of such understanding taste have visited me. You must forgive me if earlier I seemed surly.'

'Surly? No, no. Naturally cautious, yes. But not surly.'

'We must eat,' said Mongrove and Jherek's heart sank. 'Lunch – and then I'll show you round my menagerie.'

Mongrove clapped his hands and food appeared on the table.

'Splendid!' said Lord Jagged, surveying the discoloured meats and the watery vegetables, the withered salads and lumpy dressings. 'And what are these delicacies?'

'It is a banquet of the time of the Kalean Plague Century,' said Mongrove proudly. 'You've heard of the plague? It swept the Solar System in I think, the 1000th century. It infected everyone and everything.'

'Wonderful,' said Lord Jagged with what seemed to be genuine enthusiasm. Jherek, struggling to restrain an expression of nausea, was amazed at his friend's self-control.

'And what,' said Lord Jagged, picking up a dish on which sat a piece of quivering, bloody flesh, 'would this be?'

'Well, it's my own reproduction, of course, but I think it's authentic.' Mongrove half-rose to peer at the dish, looming over the pair. 'Ah, yes – that's Snort – or is it Snout? It's confusing. I've studied all I could of the period. One of my favourites. If it's Snort, they had to change their entire religious attitude in order to justify eating it. If it's Snout, I'm not sure it would be wise for you to eat it. Although, if you've never died from food-poisoning, it's an interesting experience.'

'I never have,' said Lord Jagged. 'But on the other hand, it would take a while, I suppose, and I was rather keen to see your menagerie this afternoon.'

'Perhaps another time, then,' said Mongrove politely, though it seemed he was a trifle disappointed. 'Snout is one of my favourites. Or is it Snort? But I had better resist the temptation, too. Jherek?'

Jherek reached for the nearest dish. 'This looks tasty.'

'Well, *tasty* is not the word I'd choose.' Mongrove uttered a strange, humourless laugh. 'Very little Plague Century food was that. Indeed, taste is not the criterion I apply in planning my meals...'

'No, no,' nodded Jherek. 'I meant it looked – um...'

'Diseased?' suggested Lord Jagged, munching his new choice (very little different in appearance from the Snout or Snort he had rejected) with every apparent relish.

Jherek looked at Mongrove, who nodded his approval of Lord Jagged's description.

'Yes,' said Jherek in a small, strangled voice. 'Diseased.'

'It was. But it will do you no great harm. They had slightly different metabolisms, as you can imagine.' Mongrove pushed the dish towards Jherek. In it was some kind of greenish vegetable in a brown, murky sauce. 'Help yourself.'

Jherek ladled the smallest possible amount on to his plate.

'More,' said Mongrove, munching. 'Have more. There's plenty.'

'More,' whispered Jherek, and heaped another spoonful or two from the dish to his plate.

He had never had much of an appetite for crude food at the best of times, preferring more direct (and invisible) means of sustaining himself. And this was the most ghastly crude food he had ever seen in his entire life.

He began to wish that he had suggested they have the Turyian dungwhale, after all.

At last the ordeal ended and Mongrove got up, wiping his lips.

Jherek, who had been concentrating on controlling his spasms as he forced the food down his throat, noticed that while Lord Jagged had eaten with every sign of heartiness he had actually consumed very little. He must get Jagged to teach him that trick.

'And now,' said Mongrove, 'my menagerie awaits us.' He looked with despondent kindness upon Jherek, who had not yet risen. 'Are you unwell? Perhaps the food was more diseased than it should have been?'

'Perhaps,' said Jherek, pressing his palms on the wood of the table and pushing his body upright.

'Do you feel dizzy?' asked Mongrove, grasping Jherek's elbow to support him.

'A little.'

'Are there pains in the stomach? Have you a stomach?'

'I think I have. There *are* a few small pains.'

'Hmm.' Mongrove frowned. 'Maybe we should make the tour another day.'

'No, no,' said Jagged. 'Jherek will appreciate things all the more if he is feeling a little low. He enjoys feeling low. It brings him closer to a true understanding of the essential pain of human existence. Doesn't it, Jherek?'

Jherek moved his head up and down in assent. He could not quite bring himself to speak to Lord Jagged at that moment.

'Very good,' said Mongrove, propelling Jherek forward. 'Very good. I wish that we had settled our differences much earlier, gentle Jherek. I can see now how much I have misunderstood you.'

And Jherek, while Mongrove's attention was diverted, darted a look of pure hatred at his friend Lord Jagged.

He had recovered a little by the time they left the courtyard and plodded through the rain to the first menagerie building. Here Mongrove kept his collection of bacteria; his viruses, his cancers – all magnified by screens, some of which measured nearly an eighth of a mile across. Mongrove seemed to have an affinity with plagues.

'Some of these illnesses are more than a million years old,' he said proudly. 'Brought by time-travellers, mostly. Others come from all over the universe. We have missed a lot, you know, my friends, by not having diseases of our own.'

He paused before one of the larger screens. Here were examples of how the bacteria infected the creatures from which they had originally been taken.

A bearlike alien writhed in agony as his flesh bubbled and burst.

A reptilian space-traveller sat and watched with bleary eyes as his webbed hands and feet grew small tentacles which gradually wrapped themselves around the rest of his body and strangled him.

'I sometimes wonder if we, the most imaginative of creatures, lack a certain kind of imagination,' murmured Lord Jagged to Jherek as they paused to look at the poor reptile.

Elsewhere a floral intelligence was attacked by a fungus which gradually ate at its beautiful blossoms and turned its stems to dry twigs.

There were hundreds of them. They were all so interesting that Jherek began to forget his own qualms and left Jagged behind as he strode beside Mongrove, asking questions and, often, giving close attention to the answers.

Lord Jagged was inclined to linger, examining this specimen, exclaiming about that one, and was late in following them when they left the Bacteria House and entered the Fluctuant House.

Here was a wide variety of creatures which could change shape or colour at will. Each creature was allowed a large space of its own in which its environment had been recreated in absolute detail. The environments were not separated by walls but by unseen force fields, each environment phasing tastefully into another. Most of the fluctuants were not indigenous to Earth at any period in her history (save for a few primitive chameleons, offapeckers and the like) but were drawn from many distant planets beyond the Solar System. Virtually all were intelligent, especially the mimics.

As the three people walked through the various environments, protected from attack by their own force shields, creature after creature encountered them and changed shape, mimicking crudely or perfectly either Jherek, or Jagged, or Mongrove. Some changed shape so swiftly (from Jagged, say, to Mongrove, to Jherek) that Jherek himself began to feel quite strange.

The Human House was next and it was in this that Jherek hoped to find the woman he intended to love.

The Human House was the largest in the menagerie and whereas many of the other houses were stocked from different areas of space, this was stocked from different ages in Earth's history. The house stretched for several square miles and, like the Fluctuant House, its environments were phased into each other (in chronological order), recreating different habitats from many periods. In the broader categories were represented Neanderthal Man, Piltdown Man, Religious Man and Scientific Man and there were, of course, many sub-divisions.

'I have here,' said Mongrove, almost animatedly, 'men and women from virtually every major period in our history.'

He paused. 'Have you, my friends, any particular interest? The Phradracean Tyrannies, possibly?' He indicated the environment in which they now stood. The houses were square, sandy blocks, standing on a sand-coloured concrete. The representative of this age was wearing a garment (if it was a garment) of similar material and colour, also square. His head and limbs projected rather incongruously from it and he looked a comical sight as he walked about shouting at the three men in his own language and waving his fists. He nonetheless kept a safe distance.

'He seems angry,' said Lord Jagged, watching him with quizzical amusement.

'It was an angry age,' said Mongrove. 'Like so many.'

They passed through that environment and through several more before Mongrove stopped again.

'Or the glorious Irish Empire,' he said. 'Five hundred years of the most marvellous Celtic Twilight, covering forty planets. This is the guinness, or ruler, himself.'

They were in an environment of lush green grass and soft light in which stood a two-storey building in wood and stone with a sign hanging from it. Outside the building, on a wooden bench, sat a handsome, red-faced individual dressed in a rather strange dun-coloured garment which was belted tightly at the waist and had a collar turned up to shade the face. On the head was a soft brown hat with a brim turned down over the eyes. In one hand was a pot of dark liquid on which floated a thick, white scum. The man raised this pot frequently to his lips and drained it, whereupon it instantly filled again, to the man's constant, smiling delight. He sang all the time, too, a lugubrious dirge-like melody, which seemed to please him, though sometimes he would lower his head and weep.

'He can be so sad,' said Mongrove admiringly. 'He laughs, he sings, but the sadness fills him. He is one of my favourites.'

They moved on, through examples of the prehistoric Greek Golden Age, the British Renaissance, the Corinian Republican era, the Imperial American Confederation, the Mexican Overlordship, the Yulinish Emperors, the Twelve Planet Union, the Thirty Planet Union, the Anarchic States, the Cool Theocracy, the Dark Green Council, the Farajite Warlord period, the Herodian Empire, the Gienic Empire, the Sugar Dictatorship, the Sonic Assassination period, the time of the Invisible Mark (most peculiar of many similar periods), the Rope Girl age, the First, Second and Third Paternalisms, the Ship Cultures, the Engineering Millennium, the age of the Planet Builders and hundreds more.

And all the time Jherek looked about him for a sign of the grey time-traveller while, mechanically, he praised Mongrove's collection, leaving most of the expressions of awe and delight to Lord Jagged, who deliberately drew attention away from Jherek.

And yet it was Mongrove who pointed her out first as they entered an environment somewhat barer than the rest.

'And here is the latest addition to my collection. I'm very proud to have acquired her, but as yet she will not tell me what to build so that she may be happy in a habitat which suits her best.'

Jherek turned and looked full into the face of the grey time-traveller.

She was glaring. She was red with rage. At first Jherek did not realise that he was the object of that rage. He thought that when she recognised him, when she saw what he was wearing, her expression would soften.

But it grew harder.

'Has she had a translation pill yet?' he asked of Mongrove. But Mongrove was staring at him with a tinge of suspicion.

'Your costumes are very similar, Jherek.'

'Yes,' said Jherek. 'I have already met the time-traveller. Last night. At the Duke of Queens'. I was so impressed by the costume that I made one for myself.'

'I see.' Mongrove's brow cleared a little.

'But what a coincidence,' said Lord Jagged briskly. 'We had

no idea she was in *your* collection, Lord Mongrove. How extraordinary.'

'Yes,' said Mongrove quietly.

Jherek cleared his throat.

'I wonder . . .' began Mongrove.

Jherek turned to address the lady, making a low bow and saying courteously: 'I trust you are well, madam, and that you can now understand me better.'

'Understand! Understand!' The lady's voice was hysterical. She did not seem at all flattered. 'I understand you to be a depraved, disgusting, corrupt and abominable *thing*, sir!'

Some of the words still meant nothing to Jherek. He smiled politely. 'Perhaps another translation pill would . . .'

'You are the foulest creature I have ever encountered in my entire life,' said the lady. 'And now I am convinced that I have died and am in a more horrible Hell than any that Man could imagine. Oh, my sins must have been terrible when I lived.'

'Hell?' said Mongrove, his interest awakened. 'Are you from Hell?'

'Is that another name for the 19th century?' asked Lord Jagged. He seemed amused.

'There is much I can learn from you,' said Mongrove, eagerly. 'How glad I am that it was I who claimed you.'

'What is your name?' said Jherek wildly, completely taken aback by her reaction.

She drew herself up, her lip curling in disdain as she eyed him from head to toe.

'My name, sir, is Mrs Amelia Underwood and, if this is not Hell, but some dreadful foreign land, I demand that I be allowed to speak to the British Consul at once!'

Jherek looked up at Mongrove and Mongrove looked down in astonishment at Jherek.

'She is one of the strangest I have ever acquired,' said Mongrove.

'I will take her off your hands,' said Jherek.

'No, no,' said Mongrove, 'though the thought is kind. No, I think I will enjoy studying her.' He turned his attention back to Mrs Underwood, speaking politely. 'How hot would you like the flames?'

CHAPTER SIX

A PLEASING MEETING: THE IRON ORCHID
DEVISES A SCHEME

Having successfully convinced melancholy Mongrove that
flames would not be the best environment for the grey time-
traveller and having made one or two alternative suggestions
based on his own detailed knowledge of the period, Jherek
decided that it was time to offer his adieux. Mongrove was still
inclined to dart at him the odd suspicious glance; Mrs Amelia
Underwood was plainly in no mood at the moment to receive
his declarations of love and, it seemed to him, Lord Jagged was
becoming bored and wanting to leave.

Mongrove escorted them from the Human House and back
to where the gold and ebony locomotive awaited them, its
colours clashing horribly with the blacks, dark greens and
muddy browns of Mongrove's lair.

'Well,' said Mongrove, 'thank you for your advice, Jherek, I think my new specimen should settle down soon. Of course, some creatures are inclined to pine, no matter how much care you take of them. Some die and have to be resurrected and sent back to where they came from.'

'If there's any further help I can give . . .' murmured Jherek anxiously, horrified at the idea.

'I shall ask for it of course.' There was perhaps a trace of coolness in Mongrove's tone.

'Or if I can spend some time with . . .'

'You have been,' said Lord Jagged of Canaria, posing above them on the footplate, 'a gracious host, and gigantic, Mongrove, in your generosity. I'll remember how much you would like to add that gloomy space-traveller to your collection. I'll try to acquire him for you in some way. Would you, incidentally, be interested in making a trade?'

'A trade?' Mongrove shrugged. 'Yes, why not? But what for? What have I worth offering?'

'Oh, I thought I'd take the 19th century specimen off your hands,' Jagged said airily. 'I honestly don't think you'll have much joy from it. Also, there is someone to whom it would make a suitable gift.'

'Jherek?' Mongrove was alert. 'Is that whom you mean?' He turned his huge head to look soulfully at Jherek, who was pretending that he hadn't been listening to the conversation.

'Ah, now,' said Lord Jagged, 'that would not be tactful, would it, Mongrove, to reveal?'

'I suppose it wouldn't.' Mongrove gave a great sniff. The rain ran down his face and soaked his dull, shapeless garments. 'But you would never get My Lady Charlotina to give up her alien. So there is no point to this discussion.'

'It might be possible,' said Lord Jagged. The lizard circlet on his head hissed its complaint at the soaking it was receiving. He ducked back into the cabin of the locomotive. 'Are you coming, Jherek?'

Jherek bowed to Mongrove. 'You have been very kind, Mongrove. I am glad we understand each other better now.'

Mongrove's eyes narrowed as he watched Jherek drift up to the footplate. 'Yes,' said the giant, 'I am glad of that, too, Jherek.'

'And you will be pleased to make the trade?' said Jagged. 'If I can bring you the alien?'

Mongrove pursed his enormous lips. 'If you *can* bring me the alien, you may have the time-traveller.'

'It's a bargain!' said Lord Jagged gaily. 'I shall bring him to you shortly.'

And at last Mongrove found it in himself to voice his suspicions. 'Lord Jagged. Did you come here with the specific desire to acquire my new specimen?'

Lord Jagged laughed. 'So that is why your manner has seemed reserved! It was bothering me, Mongrove, for I felt I had offended you in some way.'

'But is that the reason?' Mongrove continued insistently. He turned to Jherek. 'Have you been deceiving me, pretending to be my friends, while all the time it was your intention to take my specimen away from me?'

'I am shocked!'

Lord Jagged drew himself up in a swirl of draperies.

'Shocked, Mongrove.'

Jherek could not restrain a grin as he marvelled at Lord Jagged's histrionic powers. But then Lord Jagged turned his grim frown upon Jherek, too.

'And why do you smile, Jherek Carnelian? Do you believe Mongrove? Do you think that I brought you with me on a mere pretence – that my intention was *not* to heal the rift between you?'

'No,' said Jherek, casting down his eyes and trying to rid himself of the unwelcome grin. 'I am sorry, Lord Jagged.'

'And I am sorry, too.' Mongrove's lips trembled. 'I have wronged you both. Forgive me.'

'Of course, most miserable of Mongroves,' said Lord Jagged kindly. 'Of course! Of course! Of course! You were right to be suspicious. Your collection is the envy of the planet. Each one of your specimens is a gem. *Remain* cautious! There are others, less scrupulous than myself or Jherek Carnelian, who *would* deceive you.'

'How unkind I have been. How ungenerous. How ill-mannered. How mean-spirited!' Mongrove groaned. 'What a wretch I am, Lord Jagged. Now I hate myself. And now you see me for what I am, you will despise me forever!'

'Despise? Never! Your prudence is admirable. I admire it. I admire you. And now, dearest Mongrove, we must leave. Perhaps I will return with the specimen you desire. In a day or so.'

'You are more than gracious. Farewell, Lord Jagged. Farewell, Jherek. Please feel free to visit me whenever you wish. Though I realise I am poor company and that therefore you will have little inclination to ...'

'Farewell, weeping Mongrove!' Jherek pulled the whistle and the train made a mournful noise – a kind of despairing honk – before it began to ascend slowly into the drooping day.

Lord Jagged had resumed his position on the couch. His eyes were closed, his face expressionless. Jherek turned from where he stood looking through the observation window. 'Lord Jagged, you are a model of deviousness.'

'Come now, my cunning Carnelian,' murmured Lord Jagged, his eyes still shut, 'you, too, show a fine talent in that direction.'

'Poor Mongrove. How neatly his suspicion was turned.' Jherek sat down beside his friend. 'But how are we to acquire Mrs Amelia Underwood? The Lady Charlotina might not hate Mongrove, but she is jealous of her treasures. She will not give the little alien to us.'

'Then we must *steal* him, eh?' Jagged opened his pale eyes and there was a mischievous ecstacy shining from them. 'We shall be *thieves*, Jherek, you and I.'

The idea was so astonishing that it took Jherek a while to understand its implications. And then he laughed in delight. 'You are so inventive, Lord Jagged! And it fits so well!'

'It does. Mad with love, you will go to any lengths to have possession of the object of that love. All other considerations – friendship, prestige, dignity – are swept aside. I see you like it.' Lord Jagged put a slender finger to his lips, which now bore just a trace of a smile. 'What a succulent drama we are beginning to build. Ah, Jherek, my dear, you were *born* – for *love*!'

'Hm,' said Jherek, without rancour, 'I am beginning to suspect that I was born so that you might be supplied with raw

58

materials with which to exercise your own considerable literary gifts, my lord.'

'You flatter, flatter, *flatter* me!'

Later a voice spoke gently in Jherek's ear. 'My son, my ruby! Is that your aircar?'

Jherek recognised the voice of the Iron Orchid. 'Yes, mother, it is..And where are you?'

'Below you, dear.'

He got up and looked down. On a chequered landscape of blue, purple and yellow, flat, save for a few crystal trees dotted here and there, he could make out two figures. He looked at Jagged. 'Do you mind if we pause a while?'

'Not at all.'

Jherek ordered the locomotive to descend and was standing on the footplate by the time it landed in one of the orange squares, measuring about twelve feet across and made of tightly packed tiny shamrocks. In the neighbouring square, a green one, sat the Iron Orchid with Li Pao upon her knee. Even as Jherek lowered himself from his car the colours of the squares changed again.

'I just can't make up my mind, today,' she explained. 'Can you help me, Jherek?'

She had always had a predilection for fur and now a fine, golden down covered her body, save for her face which she had coloured to match Li Pao's. Li Pao wore the same blue overalls as usual and seemed embarrassed. He tried to get off the Iron Orchid's furry knee, but she held him firmly. She was seated in a beautiful, shimmering force chair. Bluebirds wheeled and dipped just above her head.

The chequered plain stretched away for a mile on all sides. Jherek contemplated it. His mind was occupied with other matters and he found it difficult to offer advice. At last he said: 'I think any arrangement that you make is perfect, most ornamental of Orchids. Good afternoon, Li Pao.'

'Good afternoon,' said Li Pao rather distantly. Although a member of the Duke of Queens' menagerie, he chose to wander abroad most of the time. Jherek thought that Li Pao didn't really like the austere environment which the Duke of

Queens had created for him, though Li Pao claimed that it was all he really needed. Li Pao looked beyond Jherek. 'I see you have your decadent friend, Lord Jagged, with you.'

Lord Jagged acknowledged Li Pao with a bow that set all his lilac robes a-flutter and made the living lizard rear upon his brow and snap its teeth. Then Lord Jagged took one of the Iron Orchid's fur-covered hands and pressed it to his lips. 'Softest of beasts,' he murmured. He stroked her shoulder. 'Prettiest of pelts.'

Li Pao got up. He was sulking. He stood some distance off and pretended an interest in a crystal tree. The Iron Orchid laughed, her hand encircling the back of Lord Jagged's neck and pulling his head down to kiss his lizard upon its serrated snout.

Leaving them to their ritual, Jherek joined Li Pao beside the tree. 'We have just returned from Mongrove's. Aren't you a friend of his?'

Li Pao nodded. 'Something of a friend. We have one or two ideas in common. But I suspect that Mongrove's views are not always his own. Not always sincere.'

'Mongrove? There is nobody less insincere.'

'In this world? Perhaps not. But the fact remains . . .' Li Pao flicked a silver crystal fruit and it emitted a single pure, sweet note for two seconds before falling silent again. 'I mean, it is not a great deal to say of someone native to your society.'

'Aha!' said Jherek portentously. He had not actually been listening. 'I have tumbled, Li Pao, in love,' he announced. 'I am desperately in love – mindlessly in love – with a girl.'

'You don't know the meaning of love,' Li Pao replied dismissively. 'Love involves dedication, self-denial, nobility of temperament. All of them qualities which you people no longer possess. Is this another of your frightful travesties? Why are you dressed like that? What ghosts you are. What pathetic fantasies you pursue. You play mindless games, without purpose or meaning, while the universe dies around you.'

'I am sure that's true,' said Jherek politely. 'But if it is, Li Pao, why do you not return to your own time? It is difficult, but not impossible.'

'It is virtually impossible. You must surely have heard of the

60

Morphail Effect. One can go back in time, certainly – perhaps for a few minutes at most. No scientist in the Earth's long history has ever been able to solve that problem. But – even if there was a good chance of my remaining there once I *had* returned – what could I tell my people? That all their work, their self-sacrifice, their idealism, their establishment of justice, finally led to the creation of your putrid world? I would be a monster if I tried. Would I describe your over-ripe and rotting technologies, your foul sexual practices, your degenerate bourgeois pastimes at which you idle away the centuries? No!'

Li Pao's eyes shone as he warmed to his theme and felt the full power of his own heroism surging through him.

'No! It is my lot to remain a prisoner here. My self-appointed lot. My sacrifice. It is my duty to warn you of the consequences of your decadent behaviour. My duty to try to steer you on to straighter paths, to consider more serious matters, before it is too late!' He paused, panting and proud.

'And meanwhile,' came the languid tones of the Iron Orchid as she approached, hanging on to the arm of Lord Jagged, who raised a complimentary eyebrow at Li Pao, 'it is also your lot, Li Pao, to entertain your Orchid, to pleasure her, to adore her (as I know you do) and most caustic of critics, to sweeten her days with your fine displays of emotion.'

'Oh, you are wicked! You are imperialistic! You are vile!' Li Pao stalked away.

'But mark my words,' he said over his shoulder, 'the apocalypse is not that far away. You will wish, Iron Orchid, that you had not made sport of me.'

'What dark, dark hints! Does Li Pao love you?' asked Lord Jagged. There was a speculative expression on his white features. He glanced sardonically at Jherek. 'Perhaps he can teach you a few responses, my novice?'

'Perhaps.' Jherek yawned. The strain of his visit to Mongrove had tried him a bit.

'Why?' The Iron Orchid stared with interest at her son. 'Are you learning "jealousy" now, blood of my blood? Instead of virtue? Isn't jealousy what Li Pao is doing now?'

Jherek had forgotten his craze of the day before.

'I believe so,' he replied. 'Perhaps I should cultivate Li Pao. Isn't jealousy one of the components of true love, Lord Jagged?'

'You know more of the details of the period than I, joyful Jherek. All I have helped you do is to put them into a *context*.'

'And a splendid context, too,' Jherek added. He looked after the departing Li Pao.

'Come now, Jherek,' said his mother, laying down her sleekness upon a padded couch and dismissing the chequered field (it *had* been awful, thought Jherek). The field became a desert. The bluebirds became eagles. Not far off a clump of palms sprang up beside a waterhole. The Iron Orchid pretended not to notice that the oasis had appeared directly beneath where Li Pao had been standing. The Chinese was now glowering at her. All that could be seen above the surface of the water was his head. 'What,' she continued, 'is this game you and Lord Jagged have invented?'

'Mother, I'm in love with such a wonderful girl,' began Jherek.

'Ah!' She sighed with delight.

'My heart sings when I see her, mother. My pulse throbs when I think of her. My life means nothing when she's not there.'

'Charming!'

'And, dear mother, she is everything that a girl should be. She's beautiful, intelligent, understanding, imaginative, cruel. And, mother, I mean to *marry* her!'

Exhausted by his performance, Jherek fell back upon the sand.

The Iron Orchid clapped her hands enthusiastically. It was a somewhat muffled clap, because of the fur.

'Admirable!' She blew him a kiss. 'Jherek, my doll, you are a *genius*! No other description will do!' She leaned forward. 'Now. The background?'

And Jherek explained all that had happened since he had last seen his mother, and all that he and Jagged had planned – including the Theft.

'Luscious,' she said. 'So we must somehow steal the dreary alien from My Lady Charlotina. She'd never give it away. I know her. You're right. A difficult task.' She looked at the oasis, crying petulantly: 'Oh, Li Pao, *do* come out of there.'

Li Pao scowled across the water. He refused to speak. His body remained submerged.

'That's why I'm so attached to him, really,' the Iron Orchid explained. 'He sulks so prettily.' She rested her chin upon her furry fist and considered the problem at hand.

Jherek looked about him, contemplating the enterprise afresh and wondering if it were not becoming too complicated. Too boring even. Perhaps he should invent a simpler affectation. Being in love took up so much *time*.

At last the Iron Orchid looked up. 'The first thing we must do is visit My Lady Charlotina. A large group of us. As many as possible. We shall make merry. The party will be exciting, confused. While it is at its height, we steal the alien. We shall have to decide the actual method of theft when we are there. I don't remember how her menagerie is arranged, and anyway it has probably changed since I visited her last. What do you think, Jagged?'

'I think that you are the genius, my blossom, from which this genius sprang.' Grinning, Lord Jagged put his arm around Jherek's grey-clad shoulders. 'Most fragrant of flowers it is an excellent notion. But none should be aware of our true intent. We three alone shall plan the robbery. The others will, unknowingly, cover our attempt. Do you agree, Jherek?'

'I agree. What a complimentary pair you are. You praise me for your own cleverness. You credit me with your inventiveness. I – I am merely your tool.'

'Nonsense.' Lord Jagged closed his eyes as if in modesty. 'You sketch out the grand design. We are merely your pupils – we block out the less interesting details of the canvas.'

The Iron Orchid stretched out her paw to stroke Lord Jagged's lizard, which had become dormant and was almost asleep. 'Our friends must be fired with the idea of visiting My Lady Charlotina. We can only *trust* that she is at home. *And* that she welcomes us. Then,' she laughed her delicate laugh, 'we must hope we are not detected in our deceit. Before the theft's accomplished, at least. And the *consequences*! Can you imagine the complications which are bound to arise? You remember, Jherek, we were hoping for another series of events to rival that which followed Flags?'

'This should easily rival Flags,' said Lord Jagged. 'It makes me feel young again.'

'Were you ever *young*, Jagged?' asked the Iron Orchid in surprise.

'Well, you know what I mean,' he said.

CHAPTER SEVEN

TO STEAL A SPACE-TRAVELLER

My Lady Charlotina had always preferred the subterranean existence.

Her territory of Below-the-Lake was not merely subterranean, it was subaqueous, too, in the truest sense. It was made up of mile upon mile of high, muggy caverns linked by tunnels and smaller caves, into which one might put whole cities and towns without difficulty. My Lady Charlotina had hollowed the whole place out herself, many years before, under the bed and following the contours of one of the few permanent lakes left on the planet.

This lake was, of course, Lake Billy the Kid.

Lake Billy the Kid was named after the legendary American explorer, astronaut and bon-vivant, who had been crucified around the year 2000 because it was discovered that he possessed the hindquarters of a goat. In Billy the Kid's time such permutations were apparently not fashionable.

Lake Billy the Kid was perhaps the most ancient landmark in the world. It had been moved only twice in the past fifty thousand years.

At Below-the-Lake, the revels were in full swing.

A hundred or so of My Lady Charlotina's closest friends had arrived to entertain their delighted (if surprised) hostess and themselves. The party was noisy. It was chaotic.

Jherek Carnelian had had no difficulty, in this atmosphere, in slipping away to the menagerie and at last discovering My Lady Charlotina's latest acquisition in one of the two or three thousand smaller caverns she used to house her specimens.

The cavern containing Yusharisp's environment was between one containing a flickering, hissing flame-creature (which had been discovered on the Sun, but had probably originally come from another star altogether) and another containing a microscopic dog-like alien from nearby Betelgeux.

Yusharisp's environment was rather dark and chilly. Its main feature was a pulsing, squeaking black and purple tower which was covered in a most unappealing kind of mould. The tower was doubtless what Yusharisp lived in on his home planet. Apart from the tower there was a profusion of drooping grey plants and jagged dark yellow rocks. The tower resembled the spaceship which My Lady Charlotina had had to disseminate (if it *had* disseminated, as such, being of unearthly origin).

Yusharisp sat on a rock outside his tower, his four little legs folded under his spherical body. Most of his eyes were closed, save one at the front and one at the back. He seemed lost in sullen thoughts and did not notice Jherek at first. Jherek adjusted one of his rings, broke the force-barrier for a second, and walked through.

'You're Yusharisp, aren't you?' said Jherek. 'I came to say how interested I was in your speech of the other day.'

All Yusharisp's eyes opened round his head. His body swayed a little so that for a moment Jherek thought it would roll off and bounce over the ground like a ball. Yusharisp's many eyes were filled with gloom. 'You, skree, responded to it?' he said in a small, despairing voice.

'It was very pleasant,' said Jherek vaguely, thinking that perhaps he had begun on the wrong tack. 'Very pleasant indeed.'

'Pleasant? Now I am completely confused.' Yusharisp began to rise on the rock upon his four little legs. 'You found what I had to say *pleasant*?'

Jherek realised he had not said the right thing. 'I meant,' he went on, 'that it was pleasant to hear such sentiments expressed.' He racked his brains to remember exactly what the alien had said. He knew the general drift of it. He had heard it many times before. It had been about the end of the universe or the end of the galaxy, or something like that. Very similar in tone to a lot of what Li Pao had to say. Was it because the people on Earth were not living according to the principles and customs currently fashionable on the alien's home planet? That was the usual message: 'You do not live like us. Therefore you are going to die. It is inevitable. And it will be your own fault.'

'Refreshing, I meant,' said Jherek lamely.

'I see, skree, what you mean, skree.' Mollified, the alien hopped from the rock and stood quite close to Jherek, his front row of eyes staring roundly up into Jherek's face.

'I am pleased that there are *some* serious-minded people on this planet,' Yusharisp continued. 'In all my travels I have never had such a reception. Most beings have been moved and (roar) saddened by my news. Some have accepted it with dignity, skree, and calm. Some have been angry or disbelieving, even attacked me. Some have not been moved at all, for death holds no fear for, skree, them. But, skree, on Earth (roar) I have been *imprisoned* and my spaceship has quite casually been *destroyed*! And no one has expressed regret, anger – anything but – what? – amusement. As if what I had to say was a joke. They do not take me seriously, yet they lock me in this cell as if I had, skree, committed some kind of crime (roar)! Can you explain?'

'Oh, yes,' said Jherek. 'My Lady Charlotina wanted you for

67

her collection. You see, she hasn't got a space-traveller of your shape and size.'

'Collection? This is a (roar) *zoo*, skree, then?'

'Of sorts. She hasn't explained? She can be a bit vague, My Lady Charlotina, I agree. But she *has* made you comfortable. Your own environment in all its details.'

Jherek looked without enthusiasm at the drooping plants and dark yellow rocks, the mouldy tower sticking up into the chill air. It was easy to see why the alien had chosen to leave. 'Nice.'

Yusharisp turned away and began to waddle towards his tower. 'It is useless. My translator is malfunctioning more than I realised. I cannot transmit my message properly. It is my fault, not yours. I deserve this.'

'What exactly was the message,' said Jherek. He saw a chance to find out without appearing to have forgotten. 'Perhaps if you could repeat it I could tell you if I understood.'

The alien appeared to brighten and walk backwards. The only difference between his back and his front, as far as Jherek could see, was that his mouth was in the front. The eyes looked exactly the same. He swivelled round so that his mouth aperture faced Jherek.

'Well,' Yusharisp began, 'basically what has happened is that the universe, having ceased to expand, is contracting. Our researches have shown that this is what always happens – expansion/contraction, expansion/contraction, expansion/ contraction – the universe forming and re-forming all the time. Perhaps that formation is always the same – each cycle being more or less a repeat of the previous one – I don't know. Anyway that takes us into the realm of Time, not Space, and I know nothing at all of Time.'

'An interesting theory,' said Jherek, who found it somewhat boring.

'It is not a theory.'

'Aha.'

'The universe has begun to contract. As a result, skree, all matter not in a completely gaseous (roar) state already, will be destroyed as it is pulled into what you might call the central vortex of the universe. My own, skree, planet has already gone

68

by now, I should think.' The alien sighed a deep sigh. 'It's a matter of millennia, perhaps even less time than that, before your galaxy goes the same way.'

'There, there.' Jherek patted the alien on the top part of its body. Yusharisp looked up, offended.

'This is (roar) no time for sexual advances, skree, my friend!' Jherek took his hand away. 'My apologies.'

'At another time, perhaps...' Yusharisp's translator growled and moaned and he kept clearing his throat until it had stopped. 'I am, I must admit, rather dispirited,' he said. 'A trifle on (roar) edge, as you might expect.'

Jherek's plan (or at least an important part of it) now crystallised. He said:

'That is why I intend to help you escape from My Lady Charlotina's menagerie.'

'You do? But the force-field and so on? The security must be, skree, very tight.'

Jherek did not tell the alien that he could, if he wished, wander at large across the whole planet. The only intelligent creatures who remained in menageries remained there because they desired it. Jherek reasoned that it was best, for his purposes, if Yusharisp really did think he was a prisoner.

'I can deal with all that,' he said airily.

'I am deeply grateful to you.' One of the alien's brown, bandy legs rose and touched Jherek on the thigh. 'I could not believe that *every* creature on this planet could be so, skree, skree, inhumane. But my spaceship? How will I escape from your world to continue my journey, to carry my message?'

'We'll cope with that problem later,' Jherek assured him.

'Very, skree, well. I understand. You are risking so much already.' The alien hopped eagerly about on his four legs. 'Can we leave now? Or must secret preparations be made, skree?'

'The important thing is that you shouldn't be detected leaving by My Lady Charlotina,' Jherek answered. 'Therefore, I must ask you if you will object to a little restructuring. Temporary, of course. And not very sophisticated – there isn't time. I'll put you back to your original form before we go to Mongrove's...'

'Mon(roar)grove's?'

'Our, um, hideout. A friend. A sympathiser.'

'And what, skree, is "restructuring"?' Yusharisp's manner had become suspicious.

'A disguise,' said Jherek. 'I must alter your body.'

'A skree – a skree – a skree – a *trick*. Another cruel trick! (roar)' The alien became agitated and made as if to run into his tower. Jherek could see why Mongrove had seen a fellow spirit in Yusharisp. They would get on splendidly.

'Not a trick upon you. Upon the woman who has imprisoned you here.'

Yusharisp calmed down, but a score of his eyes were darting from side to side, crossing in an alarming manner.

'And what (roar) then? Where will you take, skree, me?'

'To Mongrove's. He sympathises with your plight. He wishes to listen to all you have to say. He is perhaps the one person on the planet (apart, of course, from myself) who really understands what you are trying to do.'

Perhaps, thought Jherek, he was not deceiving the alien, after all. It was quite likely that Mongrove would want to help Yusharisp when he heard the whole of the little fellow's story. 'Now —' Jherek fiddled with one of his rings. 'If you will allow me...'

'Very well,' said the alien, seeming to slump in resignation. 'After all, there is, skree, nothing more (roar) to lose, is there?'

'Jherek! Sweet child. Child of nature. Son of the Earth! Over here!'

My Lady Charlotina, surrounded by many of her guests, including the Iron Orchid and Lord Jagged of Canaria (who were both working hard to keep her attention) waved to Jherek.

Jherek and Yusharisp (his body restructured to resemble that of an apeman) moved through a throng of laughing guests in one of the main caverns, close to the Gateway in the Water through which Jherek hoped to make his escape.

This cavern had glowing golden walls and a roof and floor of mirrored silver so that it seemed that everything took place simultaneously a hundred times upon the floor and the ceiling

70

of the cavern. My Lady Charlotina floated in a force-hammock while the dwarfish scientist, Brannart Morphail, lay gasping between her knees. Morphail was perhaps the last true scientist on Earth, experimenting in the only possible field left for such a person – the field of time-manipulation. Morphail raised his head as My Lady Charlotina signalled Jherek. Morphail peered through ragged tufts of white, yellow and blue hair. He licked red lips surrounded by a tattered beard of orange and black. His dark eyes glowered, as if he blamed Jherek for the interrupted intercourse.

Jherek had to acknowledge her. He bowed, smiled and tried to think of some polite phrase on which to leave.

My Lady Charlotina was naked. All four of her latest breasts were tinted gold with silver nipples to match her cavern's décor. Her body was rose-pink and radiated softness and comfort. Her long, thin face, with its sharp nose and pointed chin, was embroidered in threads of scintillating light-thread which shifted colour constantly and sometimes appeared to alter the whole outline of her features.

Jherek, with the alien clinging nervously to him with one of its feet, tried to move on but then had to pause to instruct the alien, in a whisper, to use one of the upper appendages if it wished to hold to him at all. He was afraid My Lady Charlotina had already detected his theft.

Yusharisp looked as if he were about to bolt now. Jherek laid a restraining hand on the alien's new body.

'Who is that with you?'

My Lady Charlotina's embroidered face was, for a moment, scarlet all over.

'Is that a time-traveller?' Her force-hammock began to drift towards Jherek and Yusharisp. The sudden motion threw Brannart Morphail to the floor of the cavern. Moodily, he lay where he had fallen, looking at himself in the mirrored surface and refusing the proffered hands of both Lord Jagged of Canaria and the Iron Orchid. They stood near him, trying not to look at Jherek who, in turn, tried to ignore them. An exchange of glances at this stage might easily make My Lady Charlotina that much more suspicious.

'Yes,' said Jherek quickly. 'A time-traveller.'

At this, Brannart Morphail looked up.

'He recently arrived. I found him. He'll be the basis of what will be my new collection.'

'Oh, so you are to vie with me? I must watch you, Jherek. You're so *clever*.'

'Yes, you must watch. My collection, though, will never match yours, my charming Charlotina.'

'Have you seen my new space-traveller?' She cast her eyes over the alien as she spoke.

'Yes. Yesterday, I think. Or the day before. Very fine.'

'Thank you. This *is* an odd specimen. Are you sure it's genuine, dear?'

'Oh, yes. Absolutely.'

Jherek had given him the form of a pre-10th century, or Piltdown, Man. He was apelike, somewhat shaggy and inclined (because of Yusharisp's normal method of perambulation) to drop to all fours. He was dressed in animal skins and (an authentic touch) carried a pistol (a club with a metal handle and a blunt, wooden end).

'He didn't, surely, come in his own machine?' said My Lady Charlotina.

Jherek looked about for his mother and Lord Jagged, but both had slipped away. Only Brannart Morphail was left, slowly rising from the floor.

'No,' said Jherek. 'A machine from some other age must have brought him. A temporal accident no doubt. Some poor time-traveller plunged into the past, dragged back to his present without his machine. The primitive gets in, pushes a button or two and – heigh-ho – here he is!'

'He told you this, juicy Jherek?'

'Speculation. He is, of course, not intelligent, as we understand it. An interesting mixture of human and animal though.'

'Can he speak?'

'In grunts,' said Jherek, nodding furiously for no real reason. 'He can communicate in grunts.' He looked hard at the alien, warning him not to speak. The alien was a fool. He could easily ruin the whole thing. But Yusharisp remained silent.

'What a shame. Well, it's a *start* to a collection, I suppose,

72

dear,' she added kindly.

Brannart Morphail was now on his feet. He hobbled over to join them. He did not need to have a hump-back and a club-foot, but he was a traditionalist in almost everything and he knew that once all true scientists had looked as he did now. He was touchily proud of his appearance and had not changed it for centuries.

'What machine did he come in?' queried Brannart Morphail. 'I ask because it could not be one of the four or five basic kinds which have been invented and re-invented through the course of our history.'

'And why could it not be?' Jherek was beginning to feel disturbed. Morphail knew everything there was to know about time. Perhaps he should have concocted a slightly better story. Still, it was too late now to change it.

'Because I should have detected it in my laboratories. My scanners are constantly checking the chronowaves. Any object such as a time machine is immediately registered on its arrival in our time.'

'Ah.' Jherek was at a loss for an explanation.

'So I should like to see the time machine in which your specimen arrived,' said Brannart Morphail. 'It must be a new type. To us, that is.'

'Tomorrow,' said Jherek Carnelian wildly, guiding his charge forward and away from My Lady Charlotina and Brannart Morphail. 'You must visit me tomorrow.'

'I will.'

'Jherek. Are you *leaving* my party?' My Lady Charlotina seemed offended. 'After all, weren't you one of the people who thought of it? Really, my tulip, you should stay a little longer.'

'I am sorry.' Jherek felt trapped. He adjusted the animal skin to cover as much of Yusharisp's body as possible. He had not had time to adjust the skin colour, which was still pretty much the same, a muddy brown with green fleck in it. 'You see, my specimen must be, um, fed.'

'Fed? We can feed him here.'

'Special food,' said Jherek. 'Only I know the recipe.'

'But we *pride* ourselves on our cuisine at my menagerie,' said My Lady Charlotina. 'Let me know what he eats and it shall be prepared instantly.'

'Oh,' said Jherek.

My Lady Charlotina laughed and her embroidery went through a sudden and startling series of colours. 'Jherek. You are looking positively *shifty*. What on earth are you planning?'

'Planning? Nothing.' He felt miserable and wished deeply that he had not embarked upon this scheme.

'Your time-traveller. Did you really acquire him as you said, or is there some secret? Have you been back in time yourself?'

'No. No.' His lips were dry. He adjusted his body moisture. It didn't seem to make much difference.

'Or did you make the time-traveller yourself, as I suspected? Could he be a fake?'

She was getting altogether too close. Jherek fixed his eye on the exit and murmured to Yusharisp. 'That is the way to freedom. We must ...'

My Lady Charlotina drifted closer, bent forward to peer at the disguised alien. Her perfume was so strong that Jherek felt faint. She addressed Yusharisp, her eyes narrowing:

'What's your name?' she said.

'He doesn't speak —' Jherek's voice cracked.

'Skree,' said Yusharisp.

'His name is Skree,' said Jherek, pushing the space-traveller forward with the flat of his hand. The space-traveller fell forward and, upon all fours, began to skitter in the direction of one of several tunnels leading from the cavern. His club lay gleaming on the floor behind him.

Lady Charlotina's brows drew closer together as an expression of dawning suspicion gradually spread over her embroidered face.

'I'll see you tomorrow, then,' said Brannart Morphail briskly, unaware of any other level of conversation taking place. 'About the time machine.' He turned to My Lady Charlotina, who had risen on one elbow in her force-hammock and was staring, open-mouthed, as Jherek sped away after the alien.

'Exciting,' said Brannart Morphail. 'A new form of time-travel, evidently.'

74

'Or a new form of affectation,' said My Lady Charlotina grimly. However, her voice was more melodramatic than sincere as she called, on a fading note: 'Jherek! Jherek!'

Jherek kept running. But he turned, shouting: 'My alien – I mean my time-traveller – he's escaping. Must catch him. Wonderful party. Farewell, coruscating Charlotina, for now!'

'Oh, oh, Jherek!'

And he fled after Yusharisp, through the tunnels to the Gateway in the Water – a tube of energy pushed up from the bottom of the lake to the surface – and thence to where his little locomotive hovered, awaiting him.

Jherek shot into the sky, dragging the alien (who had no anti-gravity ring) with him.

'Into the aircar!' Jherek panted, floating towards the locomotive.

Together they tumbled in and collapsed on the plush and ermine couch.

Jherek pulled the whistle cord.

'Mongrove's,' he said, watching the lake for signs of pursuit, 'and speedily.'

With a wild hoot, the locomotive chugged rapidly towards the East, letting out great clouds of scarlet steam.

Looking back and down Jherek saw My Lady Charlotina emerge with a gush from the shimmering lake and, still in her force-hammock, still raised on one elbow, shout after him as he disappeared into the evening sky.

Jherek strained to catch the words, for she was using no form of projection. He hoped, too, she would be sporting enough not to use any kind of tracer on his aircar, or a traction beam to haul him back to Below-the-Lake. Possibly she still didn't realise what he had done.

But he heard the words clearly enough. 'Stop,' she called theatrically, languidly. 'Stop thief!'

And Jherek felt his legs grow weak. He experienced one of the most exquisite thrills of his entire life. Even certain experiences of his adolescence hadn't done this for him. He sighed with pleasure.

'Stop,' he murmured to himself as the locomotive moved

rapidly towards Mongrove's. 'Stop thief! Oh! Ah! Thief, thief, *thief*!' His breathing became heavier. He felt dizzy. 'Stop thief!'

Yusharisp, who had been practising how to sit on the couch, gave up and sat on the floor. 'Will there be trouble?' he said.

'I expect so,' said Jherek, hugging himself. 'Yes. *Trouble*.' His eyes were glassy. He stared through the alien.

Yusharisp was touched by what he interpreted as Jherek's nobility. 'Why are you risking so much, then, for a stranger like myself?'

'For love!' whispered Jherek, and another shudder of pleasure ran through him. 'For *love*!'

'You are a great-hearted, skree, creature,' said Yusharisp tenderly. He rose on his hands and knees and looked up at Jherek, his eyes shining. 'Greater, skree, skree, skree, love, as we (roar) say on my planet, hath skree, skree, no man skree, ryof chio lar, oof.' He stopped in embarrassment. 'It must skree, be untranslatable.'

'I'd better change you back into your proper shape before we get to Mongrove's,' said Jherek, his tone becoming business-like.

CHAPTER EIGHT

A PROMISE FROM MRS AMELIA UNDERWOOD:
A MYSTERY

Mongrove had been delighted to receive Yusharisp. He had embraced, and almost smothered, the little round space-traveller, beginning immediately to question him on all aspects of his message of doom.

The space-traveller had been pleased by the reception, though he was still under the impression that he was soon to be helped to leave the planet. That was why Jherek Carnelian had made the transaction as quickly as possible and left with his new treasure while Mongrove and Yusharisp were still deep in conversation.

Mrs Amelia Underwood had been stiffened for easy transportation (without her realising that she was to belong to Jherek now) and shipped aboard the locomotive.

Jherek had lost no time in returning to his ranch and there

depositing Mrs Underwood in what in ancient times had always been the most important section of the house, the cellar. The cellar was immediately above his bedroom and contained towering transparent tanks of carnelian- and pearl-coloured wine. It was also the prettiest room in the house and he felt Mrs Underwood would be pleased to wake up in such lovely surroundings.

Laying her upon an ottoman bed in the exact centre of the room, Jherek adjusted Mrs Underwood so that she would sleep and awake slowly and naturally the following morning.

He then went to his own bedroom, impatient to prepare himself for when he next encountered her, determined that he should this time make a good impression. Though it was still many hours until morning, he began to make his plans. He intended to wear something ordinary and give up trying to please her by imitation, since she had made no comment on his earlier costume. He made a solid holograph of himself and dressed it in several different styles, making the holograph move about the room wearing the styles until he was satisfied and had selected the one he wanted.

He would wear everything – robes, shoes, hair, eyebrows and lips – in white. He would blend in well with the main décor of the cellar, particularly if he wore only one ring, the rich, red garnet, which clung to the third finger of his right hand like a drop of fresh blood.

Jherek wondered if Mrs Underwood would like to change into something different. The grey suit, the white blouse and the straw hat were beginning to look rather crumpled and faded. He decided to construct some clothes for her and take them with him as one of his courting gifts. He had seen enough of the literature of the period to know that the offering of such a gift was a necessary part of the courting ritual and would surely be welcome.

He must think of another gift, too. Something traditional. And music. There must be music playing in the background . . .

When he had made his plans, there were still several hours left and they gave him time to review recent events. He felt a little nervous. My Lady Charlotina was bound to want to repay him for his trick, his theft of her alien. At present he did not want to be interrupted in his courtship and if My Lady Charlotina decided to act at once it could prove inconvenient. He had hoped, of course, to have more time before she discovered his deception. However, it could not be helped. He could only hope now that her vengeance would not take too complicated or prolonged a form.

He lounged in his eight-poster, his body sunk in white cushions, and waited impatiently for morning, refusing to speed up the period of time by a second, for he knew that time-travellers were often thrown out by such things.

He contemplated his situation. He did find Mrs Underwood most attractive. She had a beautiful skin. Her face was lovely. And she seemed quite intelligent, which was pleasant. If she fell in love with him tomorrow (which was pretty inevitable, really) there were all sorts of games they could play – separations, suicides, melancholy walks, bitter-sweet partings and so on. It really depended on her and how her imagination worked with his. The important thing at present was to get the groundwork done.

He slept for a little while, a relaxed, seraphic smile upon his handsome lips.

Then, in the morning, Jherek Carnelian went a-courting.

In his translucent white robes, with his milk-white hair all coiffed and curled, with his white lips smiling, a bunch of little chocolates on long leafy stalks in one hand, a silver 'suitcase' full of clothing in the other, he paused outside the cellar door (of genuine silk stretched on a frame of plaited gold) and stamped twice on the floor in lieu of a knock (how had they managed to knock on the doors? One of many such mysteries). The stamping also had the effect of making the music begin to play. It was a piece by a composer who was a close contemporary of Mrs Underwood's. His name was Charles St Ives, the Cornish Caruso, and his pleasant counter-melodies, though un-sophisticated, were probably just the sort of thing that Mrs Underwood would enjoy.

Jherek made the music soft, virtually unhearable at first.

'Mrs Amelia Underwood,' he said. 'Did you hear me knock?

Or stamp?'

'I would be grateful if you went away,' said her voice from the other side of the door. 'I know who you are and I can guess why I have been abducted – and to where. If you intend to soften my resolve by inducing madness in me, you shall not have that satisfaction. I will destroy myself first! Monster.'

'My servo brought you breakfast, did it not? I trust it was to your taste.'

Her tone was mocking, a little strained. 'I have never been overfond of raw beef, sir. Neither is neat whisky my idea of a suitable breakfast drink. At least in my other prison I received the food I requested.'

'Request, then. I'm sorry, Mrs Amelia Underwood. I was sure I had it right. Perhaps in your region of the world at that time the customs were dissimilar . . . Still, you must tell me —'

'If I am to be a prisoner here, sir,' she said firmly, 'I shall require for breakfast two slices of lightly toasted bread, unsalted butter, Chetwynd's Cheshire Marmalade, café au lait and, occasionally, two medium boiled eggs.'

He made a gesture with his red ring. 'It is done. Programmed.'

Her voice continued:

'For luncheon – well, that will vary. But, since the climate is constantly far too warm, salads of various varieties shall form the basis of the meals. No tomatoes. They are bad for the complexion. I will specify the varieties later. On Sundays – roast beef, mutton, pork or veal. Venison from time to time, in season (though it's inclined to heat the blood, I know) and game when suitable. Mutton cutlets. Stewed ox-cheek and so forth. I'll make you a list. And Yorkshire pudding with the beef, and horseradish sauce, of course, et cetera. Mint sauce with the mutton. Apple sauce with the pork. Peppercorns or sage and onion with the veal, perhaps, though I have certain preferences regarding veal which I will also list. For dinner . . .'

'Mrs Amelia Underwood!' cried Jherek Carnelian in confusion. 'You shall have every food you wish, any dish which delights you. You shall eat turkeys and turtles, heads, hearts and haunches, gravies and gateaux, fish, fowl and beast shall be created and shall die for the pleasure of your palate! I swear to you that you shall never breakfast off beef and whisky again. And now, Mrs Underwood, may I please come in?'

There was a note of surprise in her voice. 'You are the gaoler, sir. You may do as you please, I am sure!'

The music of Charles St Ives (*Three New Places in England*) grew louder and Jherek stepped backward and then plunged through the silk, catching his foot in a trailing fragment of the stuff and hopping forward without much style, noticing that she was covering her ears and crying:

'Awful! Awful!'

'You are not pleased with the music? It is of your time.'

'It is cacophony.'

'Ah, well.' He snapped his fingers and the music died. He turned and reformed the silk in its frame. Then, with a sweeping bow which rivalled one of Lord Jagged's, he presented himself in all his whiteness to her.

She was dressed in her usual costume, although her hat lay on the neatly made twelve foot long ottoman. She stood framed against a tank of sparkling champagne, her hands folded together under her breasts, her lips pursed. She really was the most beautiful human being apart from himself that Jherek had ever seen. He could have imagined and created nothing better. Little strands of chestnut hair fell over her face. Her grey-green eyes were bright and steady. Her shoulders were straight, her back stiff, her little booted feet together.

'Well, sir?' she said. Her voice was sharp, even cold. 'I see you have abducted me. If you have my body, I guarantee that you shall not have my soul!'

He hardly heard her as he drank in her beauty. He offered her the bunch of chocolates. She did not accept them. 'Drugs,' she said, 'shall not willingly pass my lips.'

'Chocolates,' he explained. He indicated the blue ribbon bound around their stalks. 'See? Blue ribbon.'

'Chocolates.' She peered at them more closely. For a moment she seemed almost amused, but then her face resumed its set, stern expression. She would not take them. At last he was forced to make the chocolates drift over to the ottoman and settle beside her hat. They went well together. He disseminated the suitcase so that the contents tumbled to the floral floor.

'And what is this?'

'Clothes,' he said, 'for you to wear. Aren't they pretty?'

She looked down at the profusion of colours, the variety of materials. They scintillated. Their beauty was undeniable and all the colours suited her. Her lips parted, her cheeks flushed. And then she spurned the clothes with her buttoned boot. 'These are not suitable clothes for a well-bred lady,' she said. 'You may take them away.'

He was disappointed. He was almost *hurt*. 'But —? Away?'

'My own clothes are perfectly satisfactory. I would like the opportunity to wash them, that is all. I have found nowhere in this – this cell – that offers – washing facilities.'

'You are not bored, Mrs Amelia Underwood, with what you are wearing?'

'I am not. As I was saying. Regarding the facilities . . .'

'Well.' He made a gesture with his ring. The clothes at her feet rose into the air, altering shape and colour until they, too, drifted to the ottoman. Beside the chocolates and the straw hat there now lay neatly side by side six identical outfits (complete with straw boaters) each exactly the same as the one she presently wore.

'Thank you.' She seemed just a fraction less cool in manner. 'That is much better.' She frowned. 'I wonder if, after all, you are not . . .'

Grateful that at last he had done something to meet with her approval, he decided to make his announcement. Gathering his robes around him, he went carefully down on one knee upon the curtains of fresh flowers which covered the floor. He placed his two hands upon his heart. He raised his eyes to heaven in a gaze of adoration.

'Mrs Amelia Underwood!'

She took a startled step backward and bumped against a wine tank. It made a faint sloshing.

'I am Jherek Carnelian,' he continued. 'I was born. I love you!'

'Good heavens!'

'I love you more than I love life, dignity, or deities,' he went on. 'I shall love you until the cows come home, until the pigs cease to fly. I, Jherek Carnelian . . .'

'Mr Carnelian!' She was stunned, it seemed, by his devotion. But why should she be stunned? After all, everyone was always declaring their love to everyone else in her time! 'Get up, sir, please. I am a respectable woman. I believe that perhaps you are under some misunderstanding considering the position I hold in society. That is, Mr Carnelian – I am a housewife. A housewife from, in fact, Bromley, in Kent, near London. I have no – no *other* occupation, sir.'

'Housewife?'

He looked imploringly at her for an explanation. 'Misunderstanding?'

'I have, I emphasise – no – other – calling.'

He was puzzled. 'You must explain.'

'Mr Carnelian. Earlier I was trying to hint – to touch upon a rather *delicate* matter concerning the, ah, appointments. I cannot find them.'

'Appointments?' Still on one knee he glanced around the cellar, at the great tanks of wine, the jacaranda trees, the sarcophagi, the stuffed alligators and bears, the mangles, the wurlitzer. 'I'm afraid I do not follow...'

'Mr Carnelian.' She coughed and lowered her eyes to the floor, murmuring: 'The *bathroom*.'

'But Mrs Amelia Underwood, if you wish to bathe, there are the tanks of wine. Or I can bring aphid's milk, if you prefer.'

Evidently in some embarrassment, but with her manner becoming increasingly insistent, she said: 'I do not wish to bathe, Mr Carnelian. I am referring' – she took a deep breath – 'to the water closet.'

Realisation dawned. How obtuse he was. He smiled helpfully. 'I suppose it could be arranged. I can easily fill a closet with water. And we can make love. Oh, in water. Liquid!'

Her lip trembled. She was plainly in distress. Had he again misinterpreted her? Helplessly he stared up at her. 'I love you,' he said.

Her hands leapt to her face. Her shoulders began to heave. 'You must hate me dreadfully.' Her voice was muffled. 'I cannot believe that you do not understand me. As another human being... Oh, how you must hate me!'

'No!' He rose with a cry. 'No! I love you. Your every desire will be met by me. Whatever is in my power to do I shall do. It is simply, Mrs Amelia Underwood, that you have not made your request explicit. I do not understand you.' He spread his arms to indicate everything in the room. 'I have carefully reconstructed a whole house in the fashion of your own time. I have done everything, I hope, to suit you. If you will only explain further, I will be happy to make what you ask.' He paused. She was lowering her hands from her face and offering him a peculiar, searching look. 'Perhaps a sketch?' he suggested.

She covered her face again. Again her shoulders began to heave.

It took some time before he could discover from her what she wanted. She told him in halting, nervous tones. She blushed deep scarlet.

He laughed delightedly when he understood.

'Such functions have long since been dispensed with by our people. I could restructure your body slightly and you would not need . . .'

'I will not be interfered with!'

'If that is your desire.'

At last he had manufactured her 'bathroom', according to her instructions and put it in one corner of the cellar. Then, at her further request, he boxed it in, adding a touch or two of his own, the vermilion marble, the green baize.

The moment it was finished, she ran inside and closed the door with a slam. He was reminded of a small, nervous animal. He wondered if the box offered her a sense of security which the cellar could not. How long would she remain in the appointment? Forever, like a menagerie specimen which refused to leave its environment? How long *could* she stay there, hidden behind the marble door, refusing to see him? After all, she must fall in love with him soon.

He waited for what seemed to him to be a very long time indeed. Then he weakened and called:

'Mrs Amelia Underwood?'

Her voice came sharply from the other side of the door. 'Mr

Carnelian, you have no tact! I may have mistaken your intentions, but I cannot ignore the fact that your manners are abominable!'

'Oh!' He was offended. 'Mrs Amelia Underwood! I am known for my tact. I am famous for it. I was born!'

'So was I, Mr Carnelian. I cannot understand why you keep harping on the fact. I am reminded of some tribesmen we had the misfortune to meet when my father, my mother and myself were in South America. They had some similar phrase . . .'

'They were impolite?'

'It does not matter. Let us say that yours is not the kind of tact an English gentlewoman recognises. One moment.'

There came a gurgling noise and at last she emerged. She looked a little fresher, but she gave him a glance of puzzled displeasure.

Jherek Carnelian had never experienced anything particularly close to misery before, but he was beginning to understand the meaning of the word as he sighed with frustration at his inability to communicate with Mrs Underwood. She was forever misunderstanding his intentions. According to his original calculations they should at this moment be together in the ottoman exchanging kisses and so forth and pledging eternal love to each other. It was all extremely upsetting. He determined to try again.

'I want to make love to you,' he said reasonably. 'Does that mean nothing? I am sure that people constantly made love to each other in your age. I *know* they did. Everything I have studied shows that it was one of the chief obsessions of the time!'

'It is not something we speak about, Mr Carnelian.'

'I want to – to — What do you say instead?'

'There is, Mr Carnelian, such a thing as the institution of Christian marriage.' Her tone, while softening, also became rather patronising. 'Such love as you speak of is sanctioned by society only if the two people involved are married. I believe you might not be the monster I thought you. You have, in your fashion, behaved in an almost gentlemanly way. I must conclude, therefore, that you are merely misguided. If you wish to learn proper behaviour, then I shall not stand in the way of your learning it. I will do my best to teach you all I can of civilised comportment.'

'Yes?' He brightened. 'This marriage. Shall we do that, then?'

'You wish to marry me?' She gave a tiny, icy laugh.

'Yes.' He began to lower himself to his knees again.

'I am already married,' she explained. 'To Mr Underwood.'

'I have married, too,' he said, unable to interpret the significance of her last statement.

'Then we *cannot* marry, Mr Carnelian.' She laughed again. 'People who are already married must remain married to those people to whom they are – ah – already married. To whom are you married?'

'Oh,' he smiled and shrugged, 'I have been married to many people. To my mother, of course, the Iron Orchid. She was the first, I think, being the closest to hand at the time. And then (second, if not first) Mistress Christia, the Everlasting Concubine. And My Lady Charlotina. And to Werther de Goethe, but that came to very little as I recall. And most recently to Lord Jagged of Canaria, my old friend. And perhaps a hundred others in between.'

'A – a *hundred* others?' She sat down suddenly upon the ottoman. 'A hundred?' She gave him a queer look. 'Do you understand me correctly, Mr Carnelian, when I speak of marriage. Your mother? A male friend? Oh dear!'

'I do not understand you, I am sure. Marriage means making love, does it not.' He paused, trying to think of a more direct phrase. 'Sexual love,' he said.

She leaned back on the ottoman, one delicate hand against her perfect brow. She spoke in a whisper. 'Please, Mr Carnelian! Stop at once. I wish to hear no more. Leave me, I beg you.'

'You do not wish to marry me now?'

'Leave . . .' She pointed a trembling finger at the door. 'Leave . . .'

But he continued patiently: 'I love you, Mrs Amelia Underwood. I brought chocolates – clothes. I made the – the appointments – for you. I declared my everlasting affection. I have stolen for you, cheated and lied for you.' He paused, apologetically. 'I admit I have not yet lost the respect of my friends, but I am trying to think of a way to accomplish that. What else must I do, Mrs Amelia Underwood?'

She rallied a little. She sat upright on the couch and took a very deep breath. 'It is not your fault,' she said, staring fixedly into the middle distance. 'And it is my duty to help. You have asked for my help. I must give it. It would be wicked and un-Christian of me to do otherwise. But, frankly, it will be a herculean task. I have lived in India. I have visited Africa. There are few areas of the Empire I have not, in my time, seen. My father was a missionary. He devoted his life to teaching savages the Christian virtues. Therefore . . .'

'Virtue.' Eagerly he shuffled forward on his knees. 'Virtue? That is it. Will you teach me Virtue, Mrs Amelia Underwood?'

She sighed. She had a dazed look on her face now as she looked down at him. It seemed as if she were about to faint. 'How can a Christian refuse? But now you must leave, Mr Carnelian, while I consider the full implications of this situation.'

Again he got to his feet.

'If you say so. I think we're making progress, aren't we? When I have learned virtue – may I then become your lover?'

She made a weary gesture. 'If only you had a bottle of sal volatile, I think it could make all the difference at this moment.'

'Yes? You shall have it. Describe it.'

'No, no. Leave me now. I *must* proceed, I suppose, as if you were not trying to make a joke of my situation, though I have my suspicions. So, until I have complete evidence to the contrary . . . Oh, dear.' She fell back on the ottoman again, having just enough strength to adjust her grey skirt so that its hem did not reveal her ankle.

'I will return later,' he promised. 'To begin my lessons.'

'Later,' she gasped. 'Yes . . .'

He stepped, with a rippling of silk, through the door. He turned and bowed a low, gallant bow.

She stared at him glassily, shaking her head from side to side and running her hand through her chestnut curls.

'My own dear heart,' he murmured.

She felt for the pendant watch lying on her shirt front. She opened the case and looked at the time.

'I shall expect lunch,' she said, 'at exactly one o'clock.'

Almost cheerfully Jherek returned to his bedroom and flung himself upon his cushions.

The courtship was, he had to admit, proving more difficult, more complicated, than he had at first imagined. At least, though, he was soon to learn the secret of that mysterious Virtue. So he had gained something by his acquisition of Mrs Underwood.

His reverie was interrupted by Lord Jagged of Canaria's voice murmuring in his ear:

'May I speak to you, my tasty Jherek, if you are not otherwise engaged? I am below. In your main compartment.'

'Of course.' Jherek got up. 'I'll join you directly.'

Jherek was pleased that Jagged had come. He needed to tell his friend all that had so far taken place between himself and his lady love. Also he wished to seek Lord Jagged's advice on his next moves. Because really, when he thought about it, this was all Lord Jagged's idea . . .

He slipped down into the main room and found Lord Jagged leaning against the bole of the aspidistra, a fruit in his hand. He was nibbling the fruit with a certain clinical interest but no great pleasure. He was dressed in ice blue fog which followed the contours of his body and rose around his pale face in a kind of hood. His limbs were entirely hidden. 'Good morning, Jherek,' he said. He disseminated the fruit. 'And how is your new guest?'

'At first she was unresponsive,' Jherek told him. 'She seemed to think I was unsympathetic. But I think I have broken down her reserve at last. It will not be long before the curtain rises on the main act.'

'She loves you as you love her?'

'She is beginning to love me, I think. She is taking an interest in me, at any rate.'

'So you have not made love?'

'Not yet. There are more rituals involved than you and I guessed. All kinds of things. But it is extremely interesting.'

'You remain in love with her, of course?'

'Oh, of course. Desperately. I'm not one to back out of an

affectation just like that, Lord Jagged. You know me better, I hope.'

'I do. I apologise,' murmured the Lord of Canaria, displaying his sharp, golden teeth.

'But, if the story is to assume true *dramatic*, even *tragic*, dimensions, she must, of course, learn to love me. Otherwise the thing becomes a farce, a low comedy, and barely worth pursuing at all!'

'Agreed – oh, *agreed*!' said Jagged. And his smile was strange.

'She is to teach me the customs of her people. She is to prepare me for the main ritual which is called "marriage". Then, doubtless, she will pledge her own love and the thing can begin in earnest.'

'And how long will all this take?'

'Oh, at least a day or two,' said Jherek seriously. 'Perhaps a week.' He remembered another matter. 'And how did My Lady Charlotina take my, um, *crime*?'

'Extremely well.' Lord Jagged strode about the room, leaving little clouds of blue fog behind him. 'She has vowed – let me see – everlasting vengeance upon you. She is even now contemplating the most exquisite form of revenge. The possibilities! You should have been there last night. You would *never* guess some of them. Retribution, my darling Jherek, will strike at the best possible dramatic moment for you, rest assured. And it will be *cruel*! It will be apt. It will be witty!'

Jherek was hardly listening. 'She is very imaginative,' he said.

'Highly.'

'But she plans nothing immediate?'

'I think not.'

'Good. I would rather have time to establish the ritual between Mrs Amelia Underwood and myself before I have to think of My Lady Charlotina's vengeance.'

'I understand.' Lord Jagged lifted his fine head and looked through the wall. 'You're neglecting the scenery a bit, aren't you? Your herds of buffalo haven't moved for quite a while. And your parrots seem to have disappeared altogether. Still, I suppose that is in keeping with someone who is nurturing an obsession.'

'I must, however, extinguish that sunset.' Jherek removed the sunset and the scenery was suddenly flooded with ordinary sunlight, from the sun. It clashed a little, but he didn't mind. 'I'm becoming bored with all the peripheral stuff, I think.'

'And why shouldn't you be? And who is this come to see you?'

An ornithopter, awkward and heavy, came lumbering through the sky, its huge metal wings clashing as they flapped unevenly earthward. It slumped into the corral near Jherek's locomotive. A small figure emerged from the machine.

'Why!' exclaimed Lord Jagged of Canaria. 'It's Brannart Morphail himself. On an errand from My Lady Charlotina perhaps? The opening sally?'

'I hope not.'

Jherek watched the hunchbacked scientist limp slowly up the steps to the veranda. When he did not use a vehicle, Brannart Morphail insisted on limping everywhere. It was another of his idiosyncracies. He came through the door and greeted the two friends.

'Good morning, Brannart,' said Lord Jagged, moving forward and clapping the scientist upon his hump. 'What brings you from your laboratories?'

'You remember, I hope, Jherek,' said the chronologist, 'that you agreed to let me see that time-machine today. The new one?'

Jherek had forgotten entirely his hasty – and lying – conversation with Morphail the previous evening.

'The time machine?' he echoed. He tried to remember what he had said. 'Oh, yes.' He decided to make a clean breast of it. 'I'm sorry to say that that was a joke, my dear Morphail. A joke with My Lady Charlotina. Did you not hear about it?'

'No. She seemed pensive when she returned, but I left soon afterward on account of her losing interest in me. What a pity.' Brannart ran his fingers through his streaky, multi-hued beard and hair, but he had accepted the news philosophically enough. 'I had hoped . . .'

'Of course you had, my crusty,' said Lord Jagged, tactfully stepping in. 'Of course, of course, my twisted, tattered love. But Jherek *does* have a time-traveller here.'

'The Piltdown Man?'

'Not exactly. A slightly later specimen. 19th century isn't it, Jherek?' said Lord Jagged. 'A lady.'

'19th century England,' said Jherek, a trifle pedantically, for he was proud of his thorough knowledge of the period.

But Brannart was disappointed. 'Came in a conventional machine, eh? Did she? 19th – 20th – 21st century or thereabouts. The kind with the big wheels, was it?'

'I suppose so.' Jherek had not thought to ask her. 'I didn't see the machine. Have you seen it, Lord Jagged?'

Lord Jagged shrugged and shook his head.

'When did she arrive?' old Morphail asked.

'Two or three days ago.'

'No time-machine has been recorded arriving then,' Morphail said decisively. 'None. We haven't had one through for more than a score of days. And even the last few barely stayed long enough to register on my chronographs. You must find out from your time-traveller, Jherek, what sort of machine she used. It could be important. You could help me, after all! A new kind of machine. Possibly not a machine at all. A mystery, eh?' His eyes were bright.

'If I can help, I'll be pleased to. I feel I have already brought you here on a fool's errand, Brannart,' Jherek assured the scientist. 'I will find out as soon as possible.'

'You are very kind, Jherek.' Brannart Morphail paused. 'Well, I suppose . . .'

'You'll stay to lunch?'

'Ah. I don't lunch, really. And my experiments await. Await. Await.' He waved a thin hand. 'Good-bye for now, my dears.'

They saw him to his ornithopter. It began to clank skyward after a few false starts. Jherek waved to it, but Lord Jagged was looking back at the house and frowning. 'A mystery, eh?' said Jagged.

'A mystery?' Jherek turned.

'A mystery, *too*,' said Lord Jagged. He winked at Jherek.

Wearily, Jherek returned the wink.

CHAPTER NINE

SOMETHING OF AN IDYLL: SOMETHING OF A TRAGEDY

The days passed.

My Lady Charlotina took no vengeance.

Lord Jagged of Canaria disappeared upon an errand of his own and no longer visited Jherek.

Mongrove and Yusharisp became enormously good friends and Mongrove was determined to help Yusharisp (who was no engineer) build a new spaceship.

The Iron Orchid became involved with Werther de Goethe and took to wearing nothing but black. She even turned her blood a deep black. They slept together in a big black coffin in a huge tomb of black marble and ebony.

It was, it seemed, to be a season of gloom, of tragedy, of despair. For everyone had by now heard of Jherek's having fallen in love, of his hopeless passion for Mrs Amelia

Underwood, of his misery. He had set another fashion into which the world was plunging with even more enthusiasm than it had plunged into Flags.

Ironically, only Jherek Carnelian and Mrs Amelia Underwood were largely untouched by the fashion. They were having a reasonably pleasant time together, as soon as Jherek realised that he was not to consummate his love for a while, and Mrs Underwood understood that he was, in her expression, 'more like a misguided nabob than a consciously evil Caesar'. He did not really know what she was talking about, but he was content to let the subject go since it meant she agreed to share his company during most of her waking hours.

They explored the world in his locomotive. They went for drives in a horse-drawn carriage. They punted on a river which Jherek made for her. She taught him the art of riding the bicycle and they cycled through lovely broadleaf woods which he built according to her instructions, taking packed lunches, a thermos of tea, the occasional bottle of hock. She relaxed (to a large extent) and consented to change her costume from time to time (though remaining faithful to the fashions of her own age). He made her a piano, after some false starts and peculiar mutations, and she sang hymns to him, or sometimes patriotic songs like *Drake's Drum* or *There'll Always Be An England*. At very rare moments she would sing a sentimental song, such as *Come Into the Garden, Maud* or *If Those Lips Could Only Speak*. For a short time he took up the banjo in order to accompany her, but she disapproved of the instrument, it seemed, so he abandoned it.

With a sunshade on her shoulder, with a wide-brimmed Gainsborough hat on her chestnut curls, wearing a frothy summer frock of white cotton trimmed with green lace, she would allow him to take a punt into the air and soar over the world, looking at Mongrove's mountains or the hotsprings of the Duke of Queens, Werther de Goethe's brooding black tomb, Mistress Christia's scented ocean. On the whole they tended to avoid Lake Billy the Kid and the territory of My Lady Charlotina. There was no point, said Mrs Amelia Underwood, in tempting providence.

She described the English Lake District to him and he built

her fells and lakes to her specifications, but she was never really happy with the environment.

'You are always inclined to overdo things, Mr Carnelian,' she explained, studying a copy of Lake Thirlmere which stretched for fifty miles in all directions. 'Though you have got the peculiar shifting light right,' she said consolingly. She sighed. 'No. It won't do. I'm sorry.'

And he destroyed it.

This was one of her few disappointments, however, although she had still to get him to understand the meaning of Virtue. She had given up the direct approach and hoped that he would learn by example and through conversations they had concerning various aspects of her own world.

Once, remembering Brannart Morphail's request, he asked her how she had been brought to his world.

'I was abducted,' she told him simply.

'Abducted? By some passing time-traveller who fell in love with you?'

'I never discovered his feelings towards me. I was asleep in my own bed one night when this hooded figure appeared in my room. I tried to scream, but my vocal cords were frozen. He told me to dress. I refused. He told me again, insisting that I wear clothes "typical of my period". I refused and suddenly my clothes were on and I was standing up. He seized me. I fainted. The world spun and then I was in your world, wandering about and trying to find someone in authority, preferably the British Consul. I realise now, of course, that you don't have a British Consul here. That, naturally, is why I am inclined to despair of ever returning to 23 Collins Avenue, Bromley.'

'It sounds very romantic,' said Jherek. 'I can see why you regret leaving.'

'Romantic? Bromley? Well . . .' She let the subject go. She sat with her back straight and her knees together on the plush and ermine seat of his locomotive, peering out at the scenery floating past below. 'However, I should very much like to go back, Mr Carnelian.'

'I fear that's not possible,' he said.

'For technical reasons?' She had never pursued this subject very far before. He had always managed to give her the impression that it was totally impossible rather than simply very difficult to move backward in Time.

'Yes,' he said. 'Technical reasons.'

'Couldn't we visit this scientist you mention? Brannart Morphail? And ask him?'

He didn't want to lose her. His love for her had grown profound (or, at least, he thought it had, not being absolutely sure what 'profound' meant). He shook his head emphatically. Also there were indications that she was begining to warm towards him. It might be quite soon that she would agree to become his lover. He didn't want her sidetracked.

'Not possible,' he said. 'Particularly since, it seems, you didn't come in a time machine. I've never heard of that before. I thought a machine was always required. Who do you think it was abducted you? Nobody from my age, surely?'

'He wore a hood.'

'Yes.'

'His whole body was hidden by his garments. It might not even have been a man. It could have been a woman. Or a beast from some other planet, such as those kept in your menageries.'

'It really is very strange. Perhaps,' said Jherek fancifully, 'it was a Messenger of Fate – Spanning the Centuries to bring Two Immortal Lovers Together Again.' He leaned towards her, taking her hand. 'And here at last —'

She snatched her hand away.

'Mr Carnelian! I thought we had agreed to stop such nonsense!'

He sighed. 'I can hide my feelings from you, Mrs Amelia Underwood, but I cannot banish them altogether. They remain with me night and day.'

She offered him a kind smile. 'It is just infatuation, I am sure, Mr Carnelian. I must admit I would find you quite attractive – in a Bohemian sort of way, of course – if I were not already married to Mr Underwood.'

'But Mr Underwood is a million years away!'

'That makes no difference.'

'It must. He is dead. You are a widow!' He had not wasted his time. He had questioned her closely on such matters. 'And a widow may marry again!' he added cunningly.

'I am only technically a widow, Mr Carnelian, as well you know.' She looked primly up at him as he stalked moodily about the footplate. Once he almost fell from the locomotive so great was his agitation. 'It is my duty to bear in mind always the possibility that I might find a means of returning to my own age.'

'The Morphail Effect,' he said. 'You can't *stay* in the past once you have visited the future. Well, not often. And not for long. I don't know why. Neither does Morphail. Reconcile yourself, Mrs Amelia Underwood, to the knowledge that you must spend eternity here (such as it is). Spend it with me!'

'Mr Carnelian. No more!'

He slouched to the far side of the footplate.

'I agree to accompany you, to spend my time with you, because I felt it was my duty to try to imbue in you some vestige of a moral education. I shall continue in that attempt. However, if, after a while, it seems to me that there is no hope for you, I shall give up. Then I shall refuse to see you for any reason, whether you keep me prisoner or not!'

He sighed. 'Very well, Mrs Amelia Underwood. But months ago you promised to explain what Virtue was and how I might pursue it. You have still not managed a satisfactory explanation.'

'Nil desperandum,' she said. Her back grew imperceptibly straighter. 'Now...'

And she told him the story of Sir Parsifal as the gold, ebony and ruby locomotive puffed across the sky, trailing glorious clouds of blue and silver smoke behind it.

And so the time went by, until both Mrs Amelia Underwood and Jherek Carnelian had become thoroughly used to each other's company. It was almost as if they *were* married (save for one thing – and that did not seem as important as it had, for Jherek was, like all his people, extremely adaptable) and on terms of friendly equality, at that. Even Mrs Amelia Underwood had to admit there were some advantages to her situation.

She had few responsibilities (save her self-appointed responsibility concerning Jherek's moral improvement) and no household duties. She did not need to hold her tongue when she felt like making an astute observation. Jherek certainly did not demand the attention and respect which Mr Underwood had demanded when they had lived together in Bromley. And there had been moments in Mrs Underwood's life in this disgusting and decadent age when she had, for the first time ever, sensed what freedom might mean. Freedom from fear, from care, from the harsher emotions. And Jherek *was* kind. There was no doubting his enormous willingness to please her, his genuine liking for her character as well as her beauty. She wished that things had been different, sometimes, and that she really was a widow. Or, at least, single. Or single and in her own time where she and Jherek might be married in a proper church by a proper priest. When these thoughts came she drove them away firmly.

It was her duty to remember that one day she might have the opportunity of returning to 23 Collins Avenue, Bromley, preferably in the spring of 1896. Preferably on the night of April 4 at three o'clock in the morning (more or less the time she had been abducted) so that then no one might have to wonder what had happened. She was sensible enough to know that no one would believe the truth and that the speculation would be at once more mundane and more lurid than the actuality. That aspect of her return was not, in fact, very attractive.

None the less, duty was duty.

It was often hard for her to remember what duty actually was in this - this rotting paradise. It was hard, indeed, to cling to all one's proper moral ideals when there was so little evidence of Satan here - no war, no disease, no sadness (unless it was desired), no death, even. Yet Satan *must* be present. And was, of course, she recalled, in the sexual behaviour of these people. But somehow that did not shock her as much as it had, though it *was* evidence of the most dreadful decadence. Still, no worse, really than those innocent children, natives of Pawtow Island in the South Seas, where she had spent two years as her father's assistant after Mother had died. They had had no conception of sin, either.

An intelligent, if conventional, woman, Mrs Amelia Underwood sometimes wondered momentarily if she were doing the right thing in teaching Mr Jherek Carnelian the meaning of virtue.

Not, of course, that he showed any particular alacrity in absorbing her lessons. She did, on occasions, feel tempted to give the whole thing up and merely enjoy herself (within reason) as she might upon a holiday. Perhaps that was what this age represented – a holiday for the human race after millennia of struggle? It *was* a pleasant thought. And Mr Carnelian had been right in one thing – all her friends, her relatives and, naturally, Mr Underwood, her whole society, the British Empire itself (unbelievable though *that* was!) were not only dead a million years, crumbled to dust, they were *forgotten*. Even Mr Carnelian had to piece together what he knew of her world from a few surviving records, references by other, later, ages to the 19th century. And Mr Carnelian was regarded as the planet's greatest specialist in the 19th century. This depressed her. It made her desperate. The desperation made her defiant. The defiance led her to reject certain values which had once seemed to her to be immutable and built solidly into her character. These feelings, luckily, came mainly at night when she was in her own bed and Mr Carnelian was elsewhere.

And sometimes, when she was tempted to leave the sanctuary of her bed, she would sing a hymn until she fell asleep.

Jherek Carnelian would often hear Mrs Amelia Underwood singing at night (he had taken to keeping the same hours as the object of his love) and would wake up in some alarm. The alarm would turn to speculation. He would have liked to have believed that Mrs Underwood was calling to him; some ancient love song like that of the Factory Siren who had once lured men to slavery in the plastic mines. Unfortunately the tunes and the words were more than familiar to him and he associated them with the very antithesis of sexual joy. He would sigh and try, without much success, to go back to sleep as her high, sweet voice sang 'Jesus bids us shine with a pure, clear light . . .' over and over again.

Little by little Jherek's ranch began to change its appearance as Mrs Underwood made a suggestion here, offered an alternative there, and slowly altered the house until, she assured him, it was almost all that a good Victorian family house should be. Jherek found the rooms rather small and cluttered. He felt uncomfortable in them. He found the food, which she insisted they both eat, heavy and somewhat dull. The little Gothic towers, the wooden balconies, the carved gables, the red bricks offended his aesthetic sensibilities even more than the grandiose creations of the Duke of Queens. One day, while they ate a lunch of cold roast beef, lettuce, cucumber, watercress and boiled potatoes, he put down the cumbersome knife and fork with which, at her request, he had been eating the food and said:

'Mrs Amelia Underwood. I love you. You know that I would do anything for you.'

'Mr Carnelian, we agreed . . .'

He raised his hand. 'But I put it to you, dear lady, that this environment you have had me create has become just a little boring, to say the least. Do you not feel like a change?'

'A – change? But, sir, this is a proper house. You told me yourself that you wished me to live as I had always lived. This is very similar, now, to my own house in Bromley. A little larger, perhaps, and a little better furnished – but I could not resist that. I saw no point in not taking the opportunity to have one or two of the things I might not have had in my – my past life.'

With a deep sigh he contemplated the fireplace with its mantelpiece crammed with little china articles, the absolutely tiny aspidistras and potted palms, the occasional tables, the sideboard, the thick carpets, the dark wallpaper, the gas-mantles, the dull curtains (at the windows), the pictures and the motifs which read, in Mrs Underwood's people's own script VIRTUE IS ITS OWN REWARD or WHAT MEAN THESE STONES?

'A little colour,' he said. 'A little light. A little space.'

'The house is very comfortable,' she insisted.

'Aha.' He returned his attention to the animal flesh and unseasoned vegetables before him (reminiscent, he feared, of Mongrove's table).

'You told me how delighted you were in it all,' she said reasonably. She was puzzled by his despondent manner. Her voice was sympathetic.

'And I was,' he murmured.

'Then?'

'It has gone on,' he said, 'for a long time now, you see. I thought this was merely *one* of the environments you would choose.'

'Oh.' She frowned. 'Hm,' she said. 'Well, we believe in stability, you see, Mr Carnelian. In constancy. In solid, permanent things.' She added apologetically: 'It was our impression that our way of life would endure pretty much unchanged for ever. Improving, of course, but not actually altering very much. We visualised a time when all people would live like us. We believed that everyone wanted to live like us, you see.' She put down her knife and fork. She reached over and touched his shoulder. 'Perhaps we were misguided. We were *evidently* wrong. That is indisputable to me, of course. But I thought you wanted a nice house, that it would help you . . .' She removed her hand from his shoulder and sat back in her mahogany chair. 'I do feel just a little guilty, I must say. I did not consider that your feelings might be less than gratified by all this . . .' She waved her hands about to indicate the room and its furnishings. 'Oh, dear.'

He rallied. He smiled. He got up. 'No, no. If this is what you want, then it is what *I* want, of course. It will take a bit of getting used to, but . . .' He was at a loss for words.

'You are unhappy, Mr Carnelian,' she said softly. 'I do not believe I have ever seen you unhappy before.'

'I have never *been* unhappy before,' he said. 'It is an experience. I must learn to relish it, as Mongrove relishes his misery. Though Mongrove's misery seems to have rather more flair than mine. Well, this is what I desired. This is what is doubtless involved in love – and Virtue, too, perhaps.'

'If you wish to send me back to Mr Mongrove . . .' she began nobly.

'No! Oh, no! I love you too much.'

This time she made no verbal objection to his declaration.

'Well,' she said determinedly, 'we must make an effort to cheer you up. Come —' She stretched out her hand. Jherek took her hand. He thrilled. He wondered.

She led him into the parlour where the piano was. 'Perhaps some jolly hymn?' she suggested. 'What about "All Things Bright and Beautiful"?' She smoothed her skirt under her as she sat down on the stool. 'Do you know the words now?'

He could not get the words out of his mind. He had heard them too often, by night as well as by day. Dumbly he nodded.

She struck a few introductory chords on the piano and began to sing. He tried to join in, but the words would not come out. His throat felt both dry and tight. Amazed, he put his hand to his neck. Her own voice petered out and she stopped playing, swinging round on the stool to look up at him. 'What about a walk?' she said.

He cleared his throat. He tried to smile. 'A walk?'

'A good brisk walk, Mr Carnelian, often has a palliative effect.'

'All right.'

'I'll get my hat.'

A few moments later she joined him outside the house. The grounds of the house were not very large either, now. The prairie, the buffalo, the cavalrymen and the parrots had been replaced by neat privet hedges (some clipped into ornamental shapes), shrubs and rock gardens. The most colour was supplied by the rose garden which had several different varieties, including one which she had allowed him to invent for her, the Mrs Amelia Underwood, which was a bluish green.

She closed the front door and put her arm in his. 'Where shall we go?' she said.

Again the touch of her hand produced the thrill and the thrill was, astonishingly, translated into a feeling of utter misery.

'Wherever you think,' he said.

They went up the crazy-paving path to the garden gate, out of the gate and along the little white road in which stood several gas lamps. The road led up between two low, green hills. 'We'll go this way,' she said.

He could smell her. She was warm. He looked bleakly at her lovely face, her glowing hair, her pretty summer frock, her neat, well-proportioned figure. He turned his head away with a stifled sob.

'Oh, come along now, Mr Carnelian. You'll soon feel better

once you've some of this good, fresh air in your lungs.' Passively he allowed her to lead him up the hill until they walked between lines of tall cypresses which fringed fields in which cows and sheep grazed, tended by mechanical cowherds and shepherds who could not, even close to, be told from real people.

'I must say,' she told him, 'this landscape is as much a work of art as any of Reynolds' pictures. I could almost believe I was in my own, dear Kent countryside.'

The compliment did not relieve his gloom.

They crossed a little crooked bridge over a tinkling stream. They entered a cool, green wood of oaks and elms. There were even rooks nesting in the elms and red squirrels running along the boughs of oaks.

But Jherek's feet dragged. His step became slower and slower and at last she stopped and looked closely up into his face, her own face full of tenderness.

And, in silence, he took her awkwardly in his arms. She did not resist him. Slowly the depression began to lift as their faces drew closer together. Gradually his spirits rose until, at the very moment their lips touched, he knew an ecstasy such as he had never known before.

'My dear,' said Mrs Amelia Underwood. She was trembling as she pressed her precious form against him and put her arms around him. 'My own, dear, Jherek . . .'

And then she vanished.

She was gone. He was alone.

He gave a great scream of pain. He whirled, looking everywhere for some sign of her. 'Mrs Amelia Underwood! Mrs Amelia Underwood!'

But all there was of her was the wood, with its oaks and its elms, its rocks and its squirrels.

He rose into the air and sped back to the little house, his coat-tails flapping, his hat flying from his head.

He ran through the overfurnished rooms. He called to her but she did not reply. He knew that she would not. Everything she had had him create for her – the tables, the sofas, the chairs, the beds, the cabinets, the knick-knacks, seemed to mock him in his grief and thus increase the pain.

And at last he collapsed upon the grass of the rose garden and, holding a rose of a peculiar bluish-green, he wept, for he knew very well what had happened.

Lord Jagged? Where was he? Lord Jagged had told Jherek that it *would* happen like this.

But Jherek had changed. He could no longer appreciate the splendid irony of the joke. For everyone but Jherek would see it as a joke and a clever one.

My Lady Charlotina had claimed her vengeance.

CHAPTER TEN

THE GRANTING OF HER HEART'S DESIRE

My Lady Charlotina would have hidden Mrs Amelia Underwood very well. As he recovered a little of his composure Jherek began to wonder how he might rescue his love. There would be no point in going to My Lady Charlotina's (his first impulse) and simply demanding the return of Mrs Underwood. My Lady Charlotina would only laugh at him the more. No, he must visit Lord Jagged of Canaria and seek his advice. He wondered now, why Lord Jagged had not come to visit him since he had taken up with Mrs Amelia Underwood. Perhaps Jagged had stayed away out of a rather overdeveloped sense of tact?

With a heavy heart Jherek Carnelian went to the outbuilding where, at Mrs Underwood's suggestion he had stored his locomotive.

The door of the outbuilding was opened with a key, but he could not find the key. Mrs Underwood had always kept it.

He was reluctant to disseminate the outbuilding now (she had been a stickler about observing certain proprieties of her own day and the business of keys and locks was one of the chief ones, it seemed), for all that it was frightfully ugly. But, with her disappearance, everything of Mrs Underwood's had become sacred to him. If he never found her again this little Gothic house would stand in the same spot forever.

At length, however, he was forced to disseminate the door, order the locomotive out, and remake the door behind him. Then he set off.

As he flew towards Lord Jagged's the thought kept recurring to him that My Lady Charlotina would have seen nothing particularly wrong in disseminating Mrs Amelia Underwood completely and irrevocably. It was unlikely that My Lady Charlotina would have gone that far – but it *was* possible. In that case Mrs Underwood might be gone forever. She could not be resurrected if every single atom of her being had been broken down and spread across the face of the Earth. Jherek kept this sort of thought back as best he could. If he brooded on it there was every chance, he feared, of his falling into a depressive trance from which he would never wake.

The locomotive at last reached Lord Jagged's castle – all bright yellow, in the shape of an ornamental bird cage and a modest seventy-five feet tall – and began to circle while Jherek sent a message to his friend.

'Lord Jagged? Can you receive a visitor? It is I, Jherek Carnelian, and my business is of the gravest importance.'

There was no reply. The locomotive circled lower. There were various 'boxes' suspended on antigravity beams in the birdcage. Each box was a room used by Lord Jagged. He might be in any one of them. But, no matter which room he occupied, he would be bound to hear Jherek's request.

'Lord Jagged?'

It was plain that Lord Jagged was not at home. There was a sense of desertion about his castle as if it had not been used for several months. Had something happened to the Lord of Canaria?

Had My Lady Charlotina taken vengeance on him, too, for his part in the theft of the alien?

Oh, this was savage!

Jherek turned his locomotive towards the North and Werther de Goethe's tomb, expecting to find that his mother, the Iron Orchid, had also vanished.

But Werther's tomb – a vast statue of himself lying serenely dead with a gigantic Angel of Death hovering over his body and several sorrowing women kneeling beside him – was still occupied by the black pair. They were, in fact, on the roof near the feet of the reclining statue but Jherek did not see them at first, for both they and the statue were completely black.

'Jherek, my sorrow!' His mother sounded almost animated. Werther merely glowered and gnawed his fingernails in the background as the locomotive landed on the flat parapet, bringing a startling dash of colour to the scene. 'Jherek, what ill tidings bring you here?' His mother produced a black handkerchief and wiped black tears from her black cheeks.

'Ill tidings, indeed,' he said. He felt offended by what at the present moment seemed to him to be a mockery of his real anguish. 'Mrs Amelia Underwood has been abducted – perhaps destroyed – and My Lady Charlotina is almost certainly the cause of it.'

'Her *vengeance,* of course!' breathed the Iron Orchid, her black eyes widening and a certain kind of amusement glinting in them. 'Oh! Oh! Woe! Thus is great Jherek brought low! Thus is the House of Carnelian ruined! Oi moi! Oi moi!' And she added, conversationally, 'What do you think of that last touch?'

'This is serious, mother, who brought me precious life . . .'

'Only so that you might suffer its torments! I know! I know! Oh, woe!'

'Mother!' Jherek was screaming. 'What shall I do?'

'What *can* you do?' Werther de Goethe broke in. 'You are doomed, Jherek. You are damned! Fate has singled you out, as it has singled me out, for an eternity of anguish.' He uttered his bitter laugh. 'Accept this dreadful knowledge. There is no solution. No escape. You were granted a few short moments of bliss so that you might suffer all the more exquisitely when the

106

object of your bliss was snatched from you.'

'You know what happened?' Jherek asked suspiciously.

Werther looked embarrassed. 'Well, My Lady Charlotina did take me into her confidence a week or two ago...'

'Devil!' cried Jherek. 'You did not try to warn me?'

'Of the inevitable? What good would it have done? And,' said Werther sardonically, 'we all know how prophets are treated these days! People do not like to hear the truth!'

'Wretch!' Jherek turned to confront the Iron Orchid. 'And you, mother, did you know what Charlotina planned?'

'Not exactly, my misery. She merely said something about granting Mrs Underwood her heart's desire.'

'And what is that? What can it be but a life with me?'

'She did not explain.' The Iron Orchid dabbed at her eyes. 'She feared, no doubt, that I would betray her plan to you. After all, we are of the same fickle flesh, my egg.'

Jherek said grimly: 'I see there is nothing for me to do but confront My Lady Charlotina herself.'

'Is this not what you wanted?' said Werther, sitting on a ledge above their heads, leaning his black back against his statue's marble knee and moodily swinging his legs. 'Did you not court disaster when you courted Mrs Underwood? I seem to recall some plan...'

'Be silent! I love Mrs Underwood more than I love myself!'

'Jherek,' said his mother reasonably, 'you can take these things too far, you know.'

'There it is! I am thoroughly in love. I am totally in love. My passion rules me. It is no longer a game!'

'No longer a game!' Even Werther de Goethe sounded shocked.

'Farewell, black, black betrayers. Traitors in jet – farewell!'

And Jherek swept back to his locomotive, pulled the whistle and hurled his aircar high into the dark and cheerless sky.

'Do not struggle against your destiny, Jherek!' he heard Werther cry. 'Shake not your fist against uncompromising Fate! Plead not for mercy from the Norns, for they are deaf and blind!'

Jherek did not reply. Instead he let a great sob escape his lips and he murmured her name and the sound of her name brought all the aching anguish back to his soul so that at last he was silent.

And he came to Lake Billy the Kid, all serene and dancing in the sunlight, and he had a mind to destroy the Lake and Under-the-Lake and My Lady Charlotina and her menagerie and her caverns – to destroy the whole globe if need be. But he contained his rage, for Mrs Amelia Underwood might even now be a prisoner in one of those caverns.

He left his locomotive drifting a few inches above the surface of the lake and he went through the Gateway in the Water and came to the cave with the walls of gold and the roof and floor of mirrored silver and My Lady Charlotina was waiting for him, knowing that he would come.

'I knew that you would come, my victim,' she purred.

She was dressed in a gown of lily-coloured stuff through which her soft, pink body might be observed. And her pale hair was piled upon her head and secured by a coronet of platinum and pearls. And her face was serene and stern and proud and her eyes were narrowed and pleased and she smiled at him. She smiled at him. And she lay upon a couch covered in white samite over which white roses had been strewn. All the roses were white save one and that one she fingered. It was a rose of a peculiar bluish-green colour. Even as he approached her she opened her mouth and, with sharp ivory teeth, plucked a petal from the rose and tore that petal into tiny pieces which flecked her red lips and her chin and fell upon her bodice.

'I knew you would come.'

He stretched out his arms and his hands became claws and he walked on stiff legs with his eyes on her long throat and would have seized her had not a force barrier stopped him, a force barrier of her own recipe which he could not neutralise.

He paused then.

'You are without wit, or charm, or beauty, or grace,' he said sharply.

She was taken aback. 'Jherek! Isn't that a little strong?'

'I mean it!'

'Jherek! Your humour! Where is it? Where? I thought you'd be amused at this turn of events. I planned it so carefully.' She had the air of a disappointed hostess, of someone who had given

108

a party like that of the Duke of Queens (which nobody, of course, had forgotten or would forget until the Duke of Queens, who was still upset by it, managed to conceive some really out of the ordinary entertainment).

'Yes! And all knew of the plan, save myself and Mrs Amelia Underwood.'

'But that, naturally, was an important part of the jest!'

'My Lady Charlotina, you have gone too far! Where is Mrs Amelia Underwood? Return her to me at once!'

'I shall not!'

'And, for that matter, what have you done with Lord Jagged of Canaria? He is not in his castle.'

'I know nothing of Lord Jagged. I haven't seen him for months. Jherek! What is the matter with you? I was expecting some counter-jest. Is this it? If so, it is a poor return for mine . . .'

'The Iron Orchid said that you granted Mrs Underwood her heart's desire. What did you mean by that?'

'Jherek! You're becoming dull. This is extraordinary. Come and make love to me, Jherek, if nothing else!'

'I loathe you.'

'Loathe? How interesting! Come and make —'

'What did you mean?'

'What I said. I gave her the thing she desired most.'

'How could you know what she desired most?'

'Well, I took the liberty of sending a little eavesdropper, a mechanical flea, to listen to some of your conversations. It soon became evident what she wanted most. And so I waited for the right moment, today – and then I did it!'

'Did what? Did what?'

'Jherek you have lost all your wit. Can't you guess?'

He frowned. 'Death? She did at one point say that she would prefer death to . . .'

'No, no!'

'Then what?'

'Oh, what a bore you have become! Let me make love to you and then . . .'

'Jealousy! Now I understand. You love me yourself. You have destroyed Mrs Underwood because you think that then I will love you. Well, madam, let me tell you —'

'Jealousy? Destroyed? Love? Jherek you have thrown yourself thoroughly into your part, I can see. You are most convincing. But I fear, something is missing – some hint of irony which would give the role a little more substance.'

'You must tell me, My Lady Charlotina, what you have done with Mrs Amelia Underwood.'

She yawned.

'Tell me!'

'Mad, darling Jherek, I granted her...'

'What did you do?'

'Oh, very well! Brannart!'

'Brannart?'

The hunchbacked scientist limped from one of the tunnel mouths and began to cross the mirrored floor, looking down appreciatively at his appearance.

'What has Brannart Morphail to do with this?' Jherek demanded.

'I had to employ his help. And he was eager to experiment.'

'Experiment?' said Jherek in a horrible whisper.

'Hello, Jherek. Well, she'll be there now. I only hope it's successful. If so, then it will open up new roads of inquiry for me. I am still interested in the fact that she did not come here in a time-machine...'

'What have you done, Brannart?'

'What? Well, I sent her back to her own time, of course. In one of the machines in my collection. If all went well she should be there by now. April 4, 1896, 3 a.m. Bromley, Kent, England. Temporal co-ordinates should offer no real trouble, but there might be a slight variance on the spatial. So unless something happened on the way back – you know, a chronostorm or something – she will ?..'

'You mean – you sent her back to... Oh!' Jherek sank to his knees in despair.

'Her heart's desire,' said My Lady Charlotina. 'Now do you appreciate the succulent irony of it, my tragic Jherek? See how I have produced your reversal? Isn't it a charming revenge? Surely you are amused?'

Jherek did his best to rally himself. Shaking, he raised himself to his feet and he looked past the smiling Lady

Charlotina at Brannart Morphail, who, as usual, had missed all the nuances.

'Brannart. You must send me there, too. I must follow her. She loves me. She was on the point of declaring that love . . .'

'I know! I know!' My Lady Charlotina clapped her hands.

'Of declaring that love, when she was snatched from me. I must pursue her – across a million years if need be – and bring her back. You must help me, Brannart.'

'Ah!' My Lady Charlotina giggled with delight. 'Now I understand you, Jherek. How daring! How clever! Of course – it has to be! Brannart, you must help him.'

'But the Morphail Effect . . .' Brannart Morphail stretched his hands imploringly out to her. 'It is highly unlikely that the past will accept Mrs Underwood back. It might propel her into her own near future – in fact that's the most likely thing – but it will send Jherek anywhere, back here, further forward, to oblivion possibly. Visitors from the future cannot exist in the past. The traffic is, effectively, one-way. That is the Morphail Effect.'

'You will do as I ask, Brannart,' said Jherek. 'You will send me back to 1896.'

'You may have only a few seconds in that time – I cannot guarantee how long – before it – it spits you out.' Brannart Morphail spoke slowly, as if to an idiot. 'To make the attempt is dangerous enough. You could be destroyed in any one of a dozen different ways, Jherek. Take my advice . . .'

'You will do as he asks, Brannart,' said My Lady Charlotina, tossing aside the rose of a peculiar bluish-green. 'Can you not appreciate a properly realised drama when it is presented to you? What else can Jherek do? It is inevitable.'

Again Brannart objected, growling to himself. But My Lady Charlotina drifted over to him and whispered something in his ear and the growling ceased and he nodded. 'I will do what you want, Jherek, though it is, in all senses, a waste of time.'

CHAPTER ELEVEN

THE QUEST FOR BROMLEY

The time machine was a sphere full of milky fluid in which the traveller floated enclosed in a rubber suit, breathing through a mask attached to a hose leading into the wall of the machine.

Jherek Carnelian looked at it in some distaste. It was rather small, rather battered. There were what looked like scorch marks on its metallic sides.

'Where did it come from, Brannart?' He stretched his rubber-swathed limbs.

'Oh, it could be from almost anywhere. In deciphering the internal dating system I came to the conclusion that it's from a period about two thousand years before the period you want to visit. That's why I chose it for you. It seemed that it might slightly improve your chances.' Brannart Morphail pottered about his laboratory, which was crammed with instruments and machinery, most of them in various stages of disrepair, from many different ages. Most of the least sophisticated looking instruments were the inventions of Brannart Morphail himself.

'Is it safe?' Gingerly Jherek touched the pitted metal of the sphere. Some cracks appeared to have been welded over. It had done a lot of service, that time machine.

'Safe? What time machine is safe? It's as safe as any other.' Brannart waved a dismissive hand. 'It is you, Jherek, who want to travel in it. I have tried to dissuade you from pursuing this folly further.'

'Brannart, you have no imagination. No sense of drama, Brannart,' chided My Lady Charlotina, her eyes twinkling as she lounged on her couch in a corner of the laboratory.

Taking a deep breath, Jherek clambered into the machine and adjusted his breathing apparatus before lowering himself into the fluid.

'You are a *martyr*, Jherek Carnelian!' sighed My Lady Charlotina. 'You may *perish* in the service of temporal exploration. You will be remembered as a Hero, should you die – crucified, tempestuous time-traveller, Casanova of Chrononauts, upon the Cross of Time!' Her couch sped forward and she reached out to press in his right hand a translation pill and, into his left, a crushed rose of a peculiar bluish-green.

'I intend to save her, My Lady Charlotina, to bring her back.' His voice came out as a somewhat muffled squeak.

'Of course you do! And you are a splendid saviour Jherek!'

'Thank you.' He still maintained a cool attitude towards her. She seemed to have forgotten that it was because of her that he was forced into this dangerous action.

Her couch fell back. She waved a green handkerchief. 'Speed through the hours, my Horos! Through the days and the months! The centuries and the millennia, most dedicated of lovers – as Hitler sped to Eva. As Oscar sped to Bosie! On! On! Oh, I am *moved*. I am entranced. I am *faint* with rapture!'

Jherek scowled at her, but he took her gifts with him as he slipped deeper into the sphere and felt the airlock close over his head. He floated, uncomfortably weightless, and readied himself for his plunge into the timestream.

Through the fluid he could see the instruments, crypto-graphic, unconventional, seeming to swim, as he swam, in the fluid. They made no sound, there was no movement on their faces.

Then one of the dials flickered. A series of green and red figures came and went. Jherek's stomach grew tight.

He felt his body shift. Then it was still again. It seemed that the machine had rolled over.

He could hear his breath hissing in the tube. The machine was so uncomfortable, the rubber suit so restricting, that he was almost on the point of suggesting they try a different machine.

Then the same dial flickered again. Green and red. Then two more dials came to life. Blue and yellow. A white light flashed rapidly. The speed of the flashing grew faster and faster.

He heard a gurgling noise. A thump. The liquid in which he floated became darker and darker.

He felt pain (he had never really felt physical pain before). He screamed, but his voice was muffled.

He was on his way.

He fainted.

He woke up. He was being jolted horribly. The sphere seemed to have cracked. The fluid was rushing out of the crack and as a result his body was being bumped from side to side as the sphere rolled along. He opened his eyes. He closed them. He wailed.

Air hissed as the tube was wrenched from his face. The plastic lining of the machine began to sink until Jherek lay with his back against the metal of the wall, realising that the sphere had stopped rolling. He groaned. He was bruised everywhere. Still, he consoled himself, he *was* suffering now. No one could doubt that.

He looked at the jagged crack in the sphere. He would have to find another time machine, wherever he was, for this one had failed to take the strain of the trip. If he was in 1896 and could find Mrs Amelia Underwood (assuming that she, herself, had arrived back safely) he would have to approach an inventor and borrow a machine. Still, that was the slightest difficulty he would encounter, he was sure.

114

He tried to move his body and yelped as what had been a relatively dull pain turned, for a moment, into throbbing agony. The pain slowly died. He shivered as he felt the cold air blowing through the time machine's ruptured wall. It seemed to be dark beyond the crack.

He got up, wincing, and stripped off the suit. Underneath was his crumpled Victorian coat and trousers, in a delicate scarlet and purple. He checked that his power rings were still on his fingers and was satisfied. There was the ruby, there the emerald and there the diamond. The air, while cold, also smelled very strange, very thick. He coughed.

He edged his way to the crack and stepped through into the darkness. It was extremely misty. The machine seemed to have landed on some hard, man-made surface, on the edge of a stretch of water. A flight of stone steps led up through the mist and it was probable that the machine had bumped down these before it shattered. High above he could see a dim light, a yellow light, flickering.

He shivered.

This was not what he had expected. If he were in Dawn Age London, then the whole city was deserted! He had imagined it to be packed with people – with millions of people, for this was also the age of the Multitude Cultures.

He decided to make for the light. He stumbled towards the steps. He touched his face and felt the dampness clinging to it. Then he realised what it was he was experiencing and he gave an involuntary sigh of delight.

'Fog . . .'

It was fog.

Rather more cheerfully he felt his way up the steps and eventually struck his shoulder against a metal column. On the top of the column glowed a gas-lamp very similar to those Mrs Amelia Underwood had asked him to make for her. He patted the lamp. He was in the right period at least. Brannart Morphail had been unduly pessimistic.

But was it the right place. Was this Bromley? He looked back through the fog at the wide stretch of murky water. Mrs Underwood had spoken much of Bromley, but she had never mentioned a large river. Still, it could be London, which was near Bromley, and, if so, that river was the Thames. Something hooted from the depths of the fog. He heard a thin, distant shout. Then there was silence again.

He found himself in a narrow alley-way with an uneven, cobbled surface. There were sheets of paper pasted on the dark, brick walls on both sides of the alley. Jherek saw that the paper was covered in graphics and writing but, of course, he could not read anything. Even the translation pills, which worked their subtle engineering upon the brain cells, could not teach him to decipher a written language. He realised that he was still holding the pill My Lady Charlotina had given him. He would wait until he met someone before swallowing it. In his other hand was the crushed rose; all, for the present, that he had left of Mrs Amelia Underwood.

The alley opened onto a street and here the fog was a little lighter. He could see a few yards in both directions and there were several more lamps whose yellow light tried to penetrate the fog.

But still the place seemed deserted as he followed the street, looking with fascination at house after crumbling house as he passed. A few of the houses did have lights shining from behind the blinds at their windows. Once or twice he heard a muffled voice. For some reason, then, the population was staying inside. Doubtless he would find an answer to this mystery in time.

The next street he reached was wider still and here were taller houses (though in the same decrepit state) with their lower windows displaying a variety of objets d'art – here sewing machines, mangles, frying pans – there beds and chairs, tools and clothing. He paused every minute to glance in at these windows. The owners were right to display their treasures so proudly. And what a profusion! Admittedly some of the objects were a little smaller, a little darker, than he had imagined and many, of course, he could not recognise at all. However, when he and Mrs Underwood returned, he would be able to make her considerably more artefacts to please her and remind her of home.

Now he could see a more intense light ahead. And he saw human figures there, heard voices. He struck off across the street and at that moment his ears were filled by a peculiar clacking noise, a rattling noise. He heard a shout. He looked to his left and saw a black beast emerging from the fog. Its eyes rolled, its nostrils flared.

'A horse!' he cried. 'It is a horse!'

He had often made his own, of course, but it was not the same as seeing the original.

Again the shout.

He shouted back, cheering and waving his arms.

The horse was drawing something behind it – a tall black carriage on top of which was perched a man with a whip. It was the man who was shouting.

The horse stood up on its hind legs as Jherek waved. It seemed to him that the horse was waving back to him. Strange to be greeted by a beast upon one's first arrival in a century.

Then Jherek felt something strike him on the head and he fell down and to one side as the horse and carriage clattered past and disappeared into the fog.

Jherek tried to get up, but he felt faint again. He groaned. There were people running towards him now, from the direction of the bright light. Soon, as he raised himself to his hands and knees, he saw about a dozen men and women all like himself, dressed in period, standing in a circle around him. Their faces were heavy and serious. None of them spoke at first.

'What —?' He realised that they would not understand him. 'I apologise. If you wait one moment . . .'

Then they were all babbling at once. He raised the translation pill to his lips and swallowed it.

'Foreigner o' some kind. A Russian, most likely, round 'ere. Off one o' their boats . . .' he heard a man say.

'Have you any idea what happened to me just then?' Jherek asked him.

The man looked astonished and pushed his battered bowler hat onto the back of his head. 'I coulda swore you wos a foreigner!'

'You wos knocked darn by an 'ansom, that's wot 'appened to you, me ole gonoph,' said another man in a tone of great satisfaction. This man wore a large cloth cap shading his eyes. He put his hands into the pockets of his trousers and continued sagely: ''Cause you waved at the 'orse an' made it rear up, didn't you?'

'Aha! And one of its hoofs struck my head, eh?'

'Yus!' said the first man in a tone of congratulation, as if Jherek had just passed a difficult test.

One of the women helped Jherek to get to his feet. She seemed a bit wrinkled and she smelt very strongly of something Jherek could not identify. Her face was covered in a variety of paints and powders.

She leered at him.

Politely, Jherek leered back.

'Thank you,' he said.

'That's all right, lovey,' said the lady. ''Ad one too many meself, I reckon.' She laughed a harsh, cackling laugh and addressed the gathering in general. ''Aven't we all, at two o'clock in the morning? I can tell you're a toff,' she told him, looking him up and down. 'Bin to a party, 'ave you? Or maybe you're an artiste – a performer, eh?' She twitched her hips and made her long skirt swing.

'I'm sorry . . .' said Jherek. 'I don't . . .'

'There, there,' she said, planting a wet kiss on his moist and dirty face. 'Wanna warm bed for the night, do yer?' She snuggled her body against him, adding in a murmur for his ears alone. 'It won't cost yer much. I like the looks o' you.'

'You wish to make love to me?' he said, realisation dawning. 'I'm flattered. You are very wrinkled. It would be interesting. Unfortunately, however, I am —'

'Cheek!' She dropped her arm from his. 'Bleedin' cheek! Nasty drunken bastard!' She flounced off while all the others jeered after her.

'I offended her, I think,' said Jherek. 'I didn't mean to.'

'Somefink of an achievement, that,' said a younger man wearing a yellow jacket, brown trousers and a brown, curly-brimmed bowler. He had a thin, lively face. He winked at Jherek. 'Elsie *is* gettin' on a bit.'

The concept of age had never really struck Jherek before, though he knew it was a feature of this sort of period. Now, as he looked around him at the people and saw that they were in different stages of decay, he realised what it meant. They had not deliberately moulded their features in this way. They had no choice.

'How interesting,' he said to himself.

'Well, 'ave a *good* look,' said one of the men. 'Be my guest!'

Understanding that he was about to offend another one, Jherek quickly apologised. Then he pointed to the source of the light. 'I was on my way over there. What is it?'

'That's the coffee-stall,' said the young man in the yellow coat. 'The very hub of Whitechapel, that is. As Piccadilly is to the Empire, so Charley's coffee-stall is to the East End. You'd better 'ave a cup while you're at it. Charley's coffee'll kill or cure you, that's for certain!'

The young man led Jherek to a square van which was open on one side. From the opening a canvas awning extended for several feet and under this awning the customers were now reassembling. Inside the van were several large metal containers (evidently hot) a lot of white china cups and plates and a variety of different objects which were probably food of some kind. A big man with whiskers and the reddest face Jherek had ever seen stood in the van, his shirtsleeves rolled up, a striped apron over his chest, and served the other people with cups of liquid which he drew from the metal containers.

'I'll pay for this one,' said the young man generously.

'Pay?' said Jherek as he watched the young man hand some small brown discs to the bewhiskered one who served out the cups and plates. In exchange the young man received two china cups. He handed one to Jherek who gasped as the heat was absorbed by his fingers. Gingerly, he sipped the stuff. It was bitter and sweet at the same time. He quite liked it.

The young man was looking Jherek over. 'You speak good English,' he said.

'Thanks,' said Jherek, 'though really it's no reflection on my talents. A translation pill, you know.'

'Do what?' said the young man. But he didn't pursue the matter. His mind seemed to be on other things as he sipped his coffee and glanced absently around him. 'Very good,' he said. 'I'd have taken you for an English gent, straight. If it wasn't for the clothes, o' course – and that language you was speaking just after you was knocked down. Come off a ship, have you?' His eyes narrowed as he spoke.

'In a manner of speaking,' said Jherek. There was no point in mentioning the time machine at this stage. The helpful young man might want to take him to an inventor right away and get him a new one. His main interest at present was in finding Mrs Amelia Underwood. 'Is this 1896?' he asked.

'What, the year? Yes, of course. April Four, 1896. D'you reckon the dates different, then, where you come from?'

Jherek smiled. 'More or less.'

The other people were beginning to drift away, calling good night to one another as they left.

'Night night, Snoozer,' called a woman to the young man.

'Night, Meggo.'

'You're called Snoozer?' said Jherek.

'Right. Nickname.' Snoozer lifted the index finger of his right hand and laid it alongside his nose. He winked. 'What's your monnicker, mate?'

'My name? Jherek Carnelian.'

'I'll call you Jerry, eh? All right.'

'Certainly. And I'll call you Snoozer.'

'Well, about that —' Snoozer put down his empty cup on the counter. 'Maybe you could call me Mr Vine – which is by way of being my real name, see? I wouldn't mind, in the normal course of things, but where we're going "Mr Vine" would sound more respectable, see?'

'Mr Vine it is. Tell me, Mr Vine, is Bromley hereabouts?'

'Bromley in Kent?' Snoozer laughed. 'It depends what you mean. You can get to it fast enough on the train. Less than half-an-hour from Victoria Station – or is it Waterloo? Why, you got some relative there, have you?'

'My – um – betrothed.'

'Young lady, eh? English, is she?'

'I believe so.'

'Good for you. Well, *I'll* help you get to Bromley, Jerry. Not tonight, o' course, because it's too late. You got somewhere to stay, 'ave you?'

'I hadn't considered it.'

'Ah, well that's all right. How'd you like to sleep in a nice

120

hotel bed tonight – no charge at all? A comfortable bed in a posh West End hotel. At my expense.'

'You're very kind, Mr Vine.' Really, thought Jherek, the people of this age were extremely friendly. '*I am* rather cold and I am extremely battered.' He laughed.

'Yes, your clothes could do with a bit of a cleaning, eh?' Snoozer Vine fingered his chin. 'Well, I think I can help you there, too. Fix you up with a fresh suit of clothes and everything. And you'll need some luggage. Have you got any luggage?'

'Well, no. I —'

'Don't say another word. Luggage will be supplied. Supplied, Jerry, my friend, courtesy of Snoozer's suitcase emporium. What was your last name again?'

'Carnelian.'

'Carnell. I'll call you Carnell, if you don't mind.'

'By all means, Mr Vine.'

Snoozer Vine uttered a wild and cheerful laugh. 'I can see we're going to get on like old friends, Lord Carnell.'

'Lord?'

'*My* nickname for *you*, see? All right?'

'If it pleases you.'

'Good. Good. What a card you are, Jerry! I think our association's going to be very profitable indeed.'

'Profitable?'

He slapped Jherek heartily on the back. 'In what you might call a spiritual sense, I mean. A friendship, I mean. Come on, we'll get back to my gaff on the double and soon have you fitted up like the toff you most undoubtedly are!'

Bemused but beginning to feel more hopeful, Jherek Carnelian followed his young friend through a maze of dark and foggy streets until they came at last to a tall, black building which stood by itself at the end of an alley. Several of the windows were lit and from them came sounds of laughter, shouts and, Jherek thought, voices raised in anger.

'Is this your castle, Mr Vine?' he asked.

'Well —' Snoozer Vine grinned at Jherek. 'It is and it isn't, your lordship. I sometimes share it, you might say with one or two mates. Fellow craftsmen, sir.' He bowed low and gestured elaborately for Jherek to precede him up the broken steps to the main door, a thing of cracked wood and rusted metal, with peeling brown paint and, in its centre, a dirty brass knocker shaped like a lion's head.

They reached the top of the steps.

'Is this where we're to stay tonight, Mr Vine?' Jherek looked with interest at the door. It was marvellously ugly.

'No, no. We'll just fit ourselves up here and then go on – in a cab.'

'To Bromley?'

'Bromley later.'

'But I must get to Bromley as soon as possible. You see, I —'

'I know. Love calls. Bromley beckons. Rest assured, you'll be united with your lady tomorrow.'

'You are very certain, Mr Vine.' Jherek was pleased to have found such an omniscient guide in his quest. He was certain that his luck was changing at last.

'I am, indeed. If Snoozer Vine gives a promise, your lordship, it means something.'

'So this place is —?'

'You might call it a sort of extraordinary lodging house – for gentlemen of independent means, sir. For professional ladies. And for children – and others – bent on learning a trade. Welcome, your lordship, to Jones's Kitchen.'

And Snoozer Vine leaned past Jherek and rapped several times with the knocker upon the door.

But the door was already opening. A little boy stood in the shadows of the mephitic hallway. He was dressed entirely in what appeared to be strips of rag. His hair was greasy and long and his face was smeared with grime.

'Otherwise known,' said the boy, sneering up at the pair, 'as the Devil's Arsehole. 'Ello, Snoozer – who's yer mate?'

CHAPTER TWELVE

THE CURIOUS COMINGS AND GOINGS
OF SNOOZER VINE

Jones's Kitchen was hot and rich with odours, not all of which
Jherek found to his taste. It was packed with people, too. In the
long main room on the ground floor and in the gallery above it
which ran around the whole place there was crowded a
miscellaneous collection of benches, chairs and tables (none in
very good condition). Below the gallery and filling the length of
one wall was a big bar of stained deal. Opposite this bar, in a
huge stone grate, roared a fire over which was being roasted on
a spit the carcass of some animal. Dirty straw and offal, rags
and papers covered the flagstones of the floor and the floor also
swam with liquid of all kinds. Through the permanent drone of
voices came, at frequent intervals, great gusts of laughter,
bursts of song, whines of accusation and streams of oaths.

Soiled finery was evidently the fashion here tonight.

Powdered, painted ladies in elaborate, tattered hats wore gowns of green, red and blue silk trimmed with lace and embroidery and when they raised their skirts (which was often) they displayed layers of filthy petticoats. Some had the tops of their dresses undone. Men wore whiskers, beards or stubble and had battered top-hats or bowlers on their heads, loud check waistcoats, mufflers, caps, masher overcoats, yellow, blue and brown trousers, and many sported watch-chains or flowers in their button-holes. The girls and boys wore cut down versions of similar clothes and some of the children imitated their elders by painting their faces with rouge and charcoal. Glasses, bottles and mugs were in every hand, even the smallest, and there was a general scattering of plates and knives and forks and scraps of food on the tables and the floor.

Snoozer Vine guided Jherek Carnelian through this press. They all knew Snoozer Vine. 'Wot 'o, Snoozer!' they cried. ''Ow yer goin', Snooze,' and 'Give us a kiss, Snoozy!'

And Snoozer grinned and he nodded and he saluted as he steered Jherek through this Dawn Age crowd, these seeds from which would blossom a profusion of variegated plants which would grow and wilt, grow and wilt through a million or two years of history. These were his ancestors. He loved them all. He, too, smiled and waved and got, he was pleased to note, many a broad smile in return.

The little boy's question was frequently repeated.

''Oo's yer friend, Snoozer?'

'Wot's ther cove inna fancy dress?'

'Wot yer got there, Snooze?'

Once or twice, as he paused to peck a girl on the cheek, Snoozer would look up and answer:

'Foreign gent. Business acquaintance. Easy, easy, yer'll frighten 'im off. 'E's not familiar wiv our customs in this country.' And he would wink at the girl and pass on.

And once someone winked back at Snoozer. 'A new mark, eh? Har, har! You'll be buyin' ther rounds termorrer, eh?'

'Likely,' replied Snoozer, tapping the side of his nose as he had done before.

Jherek reflected that the translation pill was not working at full strength, for he could not understand much of the language, even now. Unfortunately what the pill had probably done was to translate his own vocabulary into 19th century English, rather than supplying him with their vocabulary. Still, he could get by well enough and make himself understood perfectly well.

''Ello, ducks,' said an old lady, patting his bottom as he went by and offering him something in a glass whose smell reminded him of the way the other lady had smelled. 'Want some gin? Want some fun, 'andsome?'

'Clear off, Nellie,' said Snoozer with equanimity. ''E's mine.'

Jherek noticed how Snoozer's voice had changed since he had entered the portals of Jones's Kitchen. He seemed almost to speak two different languages.

Several other women, men and children expressed their willingness to make love to Jherek and he had to admit that on another occasion in different circumstances he would have been pleased to have enjoyed the pleasures offered. But Snoozer dragged him on.

What *was* beginning to puzzle Jherek was that none of these people much resembled in attitude or even appearance Mrs Amelia Underwood. The horrifying possibility came to him that there might be more than one date known as 1896. Or different time-streams (Brannart Morphail had explained the theory to him once)? On the other hand, Bromley was known to Snoozer Vine. There were probably slightly different tribal customs applying in different areas. Mrs Underwood came from a tribe where dullness and misery were in vogue, whereas here the people believed in merrymaking and variety.

Now Snoozer led Jherek up a rickety staircase crowded with people and onto the gallery. A passage ran off the gallery and Snoozer entered it, pushing Jherek ahead of him until they came to one of several doors and Snoozer stopped, taking a key from his waistcoat pocket and opening one of the doors.

Going in, Jherek found himself in pitch darkness.

'Just a minute,' said Snoozer, stumbling around. A scratching sound was followed by a flash of light. Snoozer's face was illuminated by a little fire glowing at the tips of his fingers. He applied this fire to an object of glass and metal which stood on a table. The object began, itself, to glow and gradually brought a rather dim light to the whole small room.

The room contained a bed with rumpled grey sheets, a mahogany wardrobe, a table and two Windsor chairs, a large mirror and about fifty or sixty trunks and suitcases of various sizes. They were stacked everywhere, reaching to the ceiling, poking out from under the bed, teetering on top of the wardrobe, partially obscuring the mirror.

'You collect boxes, Mr Vine?' Jherek admired the trunks. Some were leather, some metal, some wooden. They all looked in excellent condition. Many had inscriptions which Jherek, of course, could not read, but the inscriptions seemed to be of a wide variety.

Snoozer Vine snorted and laughed. 'Yes,' he said. 'That's right, your lordship. My hobby, it is. Now, let's think about your kit.' He began to pace about the room, inspecting the cases, a frown of concentration upon his face. Every so often he would stop, perhaps wipe some dust off one of his trunks, to peer at the inscription or to test a handle. And then, at last, he pulled two leather travelling bags from under a pile and he stood them beside the lamp on the table, brushing away dust to reveal a couple of hieroglyphics. The bags were matched and the hieroglyphics were also the same.

'Perfect,' said Vine, fingering his sharp chin. 'Excellent, J.C. Your initials, eh?'

'I'm afraid I can't read . . .'

'Don't worry about that. I'll do all the readin' for you. Let's see, we'll need some clothes.'

'Ah!' Jherek was relieved that he could now help his friend. 'Say what you would care to wear, Mr Vine, and I will make it with one of my power rings.'

'Do what?'

'You probably don't have them here,' said Jherek, displaying his rings. 'But with these I can manufacture anything I please – from a – a handkerchief to – um – a house.'

'Come off it!' Snoozer Vine's eyes widened and became wary. 'You a conjurer by trade, then?'

'I can conjure what you want. Tell me.'

Snoozer uttered a peculiar laugh. 'All right. I'll have a pile o' gold – on that table.'

'At once.' With a smile Jherek visualised Snoozer's request and made the appropriate nerve in the appropriate finger operate his ruby power ring. 'There!'

And nothing appeared.

'You're having me on, ain't ya!' Snoozer offered Jherek a sideways look.

Jherek was astonished. 'How odd.'

'Odd's the word,' agreed Snoozer.

Jherek's brow cleared. 'Of course. No energy banks. The banks are a million years in the future.'

'Future?' Snoozer seemed frozen to the spot.

'I am from the future,' said Jherek. 'I was going to tell you later. The ship – well, it's a time machine, naturally. But damaged.'

'Come off it!' Snoozer cleared his throat several times. 'You're a Russian. Or something.'

'I assure you I speak the truth.'

'You mean you could spot the winners of tomorrow's races if I gave you a list tonight?'

'I don't understand.'

'Make predictions – like the fortune-tellers. Is that what you are. A gippo?'

'My predictions wouldn't have much to do with your time. My knowledge of your immediate future is sketchy to say the least.'

'You're a bloody loony,' said Snoozer Vine in some relief, having got over his astonishment. 'An escaped loony. Oh, just my luck!'

'I'm afraid I don't quite . . .'

'Never mind. You still want to get to Bromley?'

'Yes, indeed.'

'And you want to stay at a posh hotel tonight?'

'If that's what you think best.'

'Come on, then,' said Vine. 'We'd better get you the clobber.' He crossed to the wardrobe, shaking his head. 'Cor! You almost had me believing you, then.'

Jherek stood before the mirror and looked at himself with

127

some pleasure. He was dressed in a white shirt with a high, starched collar, a deep purple cravat with a pearl pin, a black waistcoat, black trousers, highly polished black boots, a black frock-coat and on his head a tall, black silk hat.

'The picture of an English aristocrat, though I say it meself,' said Snoozer Vine, who had selected the outfit. 'You'll pass, your lordship.'

'Thank you,' said Jherek, taking his friend's remarks for a compliment. He smiled and fingered the clothes. They reminded him of the clothes Mrs Amelia Underwood had suggested he wear. They cheered him up considerably. They seemed to bring her nearer to him. 'Mr Vine, my dear, they are *charming*!'

'Here, steady on,' said Snoozer, eyeing him with a certain amount of alarm on his thin, quick face. He, himself, was dressed in black, though the costume was not so fine as Jherek's. He picked up the two travelling bags which he had cleaned and filled with several smaller bags. 'Hurry up. The cab'll be here by now. They don't like to hang about long near Jones's.'

They went back through the throng, causing a certain amount of amusement and attracting plenty of cat-calls until they were outside in the cold night. The fog had cleared slightly and Jherek could see a cab waiting in the street. It was of the same type as the one which had knocked him over.

'Victoria Station,' Snoozer told the driver, who sat on a box above and behind the cab.

They got into the hansom and the driver whipped up the horse. They began to rattle through the streets of Whitechapel.

'It's a fair way,' Vine told Jherek, who was fascinated by the cab and what little he could see through the windows. 'We'll change there. Don't want to make the cabby suspicious.'

Jherek wondered why the driver should get suspicious, but he had become used to listening to Snoozer Vine without understanding every word.

Gradually the streets widened out and the gas-lamps became much more frequent. There was a little more traffic, too.

'We're getting near the centre of town,' Snoozer explained when Jherek questioned him. 'Trafalgar Square ahead. This is the Strand. We'll go down Whitehall and then down Victoria Street to the station.'

The names meant nothing to Jherek, but they all had a marvellous, exotic ring to them. He nodded and smiled, repeating the words to himself.

They disembarked outside a fairly large building of concrete and glass which had several tall entrances. Peering through one of the entrances Jherek saw a stretch of asphalt and beyond it a series of iron gates. Beyond the gates stood one or two machines which he recognised immediately as bigger versions of his own locomotive. He cried out in delight. 'A museum!'

'A bleeding railway station,' said Vine. 'This is where the trains go from. Haven't you got trains in your country?'

'Only the one I made myself,' said Jherek.

'Gor blimey!' said Snoozer and raised his eyes towards the glass roof which was supported on metal girders. He hurried Jherek through one of the entrances and across the asphalt so that they passed quite close to a couple of the locomotives.

'What are those other things behind it?' Jherek asked curiously.

'Carriages!' snorted Snoozer.

'Oh, I must make some as soon as I get back to my own time,' Jherek told him.

'Now,' said Snoozer ignoring him, 'you'll have to let me do all the talking. You keep quiet, all right – or you could get us both into trouble.'

'Very well, Snoozer.'

'It's Vine, if you have to address me by name at all. But try not to, see?'

Again, Jherek agreed. They went through an exit where several more cabs were waiting. Snoozer signalled the nearest and they climbed in.

'Imperial Hotel,' said Snoozer. He turned to Jherek who was, again, peering through the window at the romantic night. 'And don't forget what I told you, eh?'

'You are my guide,' Jherek assured him. 'I am in your hands – Vine.'

'Fine.'

And soon the cab had stopped outside a large house

whose lower windows blazed with light. There was an imposing entrance, of marble and granite, and a stone awning supported by marble pillars. As the cab drew up a middle-aged man in dark green, wearing a green top-hat taller than Jherek's, rushed from within the building and opened the door. A boy, also in green, but with a pill-box hat on his head, followed the man and took the two bags which the driver handed down.

'Good morning, sir,' said the middle-aged man to Jherek.

'This is Lord Carnell,' said Snoozer Vine. 'I am his man. We telegraphed from Dover to say we'd be arriving about now.'

The middle-aged man frowned. 'I don't recall no wire, sir. But maybe they'll know about it at the reception desk.'

Snoozer paid the driver and they followed the boy with the bags into the warmth of a wide lobby at the far end of which stood a highly polished bar. Behind the bar stood an old man dressed in a black frock-coat with a grey waistcoat. He looked faintly surprised and was leafing through a large book which rested on the bar before him. Jherek glanced about him as Vine approached the bar. There were lots of potted palms in the lobby and these, too, reminded him nostalgically of Mrs Underwood. He hoped he could leave for Bromley early tomorrow.

'Lord Carnell, sir?' the old man in the frock-coat was saying to Vine. 'No telegram, sir, I'm afraid.'

'This is extremely inconvenient,' Vine was saying in still another kind of voice. 'I sent the telegram myself as soon as the boat docked.'

'Not to worry, sir,' the old man soothed, 'we have plenty of unreserved accommodation as it happens. What will you require?'

'A suite,' said Snoozer Vine, 'for his lordship, with a room attached for my use.'

'Of course, sir.' Again the old man consulted the book. 'Number 26, facing the river, sir. A beautiful view.'

'That will do,' Vine said rather haughtily.

'And if you will sign the register, sir.'

Jherek was about to point out that he could not write when Vine picked up the pen, dipped it in the ink and made marks on the paper. Apparently it was not necessary for them both to sign.

They crossed soft, scarlet carpets to a cage of curling brass and iron and the boy pulled back a gate so that they could get in. Another old man stood inside the cage. 'Number 26,' said the boy.

Jherek looked around him. 'A strange sort of room,' he murmured. But Vine didn't reply. He looked steadily away from Jherek.

The old man pulled a rope and suddenly they were rising into the air. Jherek giggled with pleasure and then yelped as he fell against the wall when the cage stopped suddenly. The old man opened the gate.

'Aha,' said Jherek knowingly. This was a crude form of levitation. The gate opened onto a scarlet carpeted hallway. There was an air of great luxury about the whole place. It was more like home.

Jherek and Vine were almost immediately joined by the black-coated man and the boy with their bags. They were ushered a short distance along the hall and into a suite of large rooms. Windows looked out onto a stretch of gleaming water similar to that which Jherek had seen when he first arrived.

'Would you like some supper brought up, sir?' the man in the frock-coat asked Jherek. Jherek realised that he was beginning to feel hungry and he opened his mouth to agree with the suggestion when Snoozer Vine interrupted.

'No thank you. We have already dined – on the train up from Dover.'

'Then I'll bid you good night, your lordship.' The man in the frock-coat seemed to resent Snoozer Vine's speaking for Jherek. This last remark was directed pointedly at Jherek.

'Good night,' said Jherek. 'And thank you for putting the river there. I —'

'For the view. We've been away for some time. His lordship hasn't seen the good old Thames since last year,' hastily explained Snoozer Vine, herding the old man and the boy before him.

At last the door closed.

Vine gave Jherek a strange look and shook his head. 'Well, I mustn't complain. We're in. And when we go out we'll be a deal better off I shouldn't wonder. You'd better get some kip while you've got the chance. I'll nip into my own room now. Nightie night – your lordship.' Chuckling, Snoozer Vine left the main room and closed a door behind him.

Jherek had understood almost nothing of Vine's final remarks, but he shrugged and went to stare out at the river. He imagined himself in a punt on it with Mrs Amelia Underwood. He imagined Mrs Amelia Underwood here beside him now and he sighed. Even if he had difficulty getting back to his own time he was certain that he could settle here quite easily. Everyone was so kind to him. Perhaps Mrs Underwood would be kinder in her own time. Well, they would soon be reunited. Humming the tune of 'All Things Bright and Beautiful' he padded about the suite, exploring the bedroom, the sitting room, the dressing room and the bathrooms. He already knew about plumbing, but he was fascinated by the taps and the plugs and the chains involved in letting water into and out of various china containers. He played with them all for some time before tiring of it and going back into his gaslit bedroom. Perhaps he had better sleep, he thought. And yet, for all his adventures, his minor injuries, his excitement, he did not feel at all weary.

He wondered if Snoozer were tired. He opened the door to see if his friend had managed to sleep and was surprised to find Vine gone. The bed was empty. The two suitcases were open on the bed, but the smaller cases they had contained were also missing.

Jherek could think of no explanation for Snoozer's disappearance and neither could he imagine where Snoozer had taken the bags. He went back into his own room and regarded the Thames again, watching as a black craft chugged by before vanishing under the arch of one of the nearer bridges. The fog was so thin now that Jherek could see to the other side of the river, could see the outlines of the buildings and the glow of the gaslamps. Did Bromley lie in that direction?

He heard a movement from Snoozer's room. He turned. Snoozer had come back, creeping in and closing the outer door quietly behind him. He had two of the smaller bags held in one hand and they were full. They were bulging. He looked a little surprised when he saw Jherek watching him. He gave a weak grin. 'Oh, 'ello, your lordship.'

'Hello, Snoozer.' Jherek did not feel particularly curious about Snoozer's activities. He smiled back.

Snoozer misinterpreted the smile, it seemed. He nodded as he crossed to his bed and put the two small cases into the larger one. 'You guessed, ain't you?'

'About the bags?'

'That's right. Well, there's something in it for you, too.' Snoozer laughed. 'If it's only the fare to Bromley, eh?'

'Ah, yes,' said Jherek.

'Well, o' course, there'll be a cut. A quarter suit you? 'Cause I'm taking all the risks. Mind you, it's the best haul I've ever had. I've dreamed of getting in here for years. Any snoozer would. I needed someone like you who'd pass for a gent, see.'

'Oho,' said Jherek, still unable to get the drift of Snoozer's remarks. He smiled again.

'You're brighter than I thought, you are. I suppose they got hotel snoozers even where you come from, eh? Well, don't worry, as I say. Just keep mum. We'll leave here early in the morning before anyone else is up – and we'll be a lot richer than they'll be, eh?' Snoozer laughed. He winked. He opened his door and left again, closing the lock carefully.

Jherek went over to the bags. He had some difficulty in working out how they unfastened, but at last he got one open and looked inside. Snoozer seemed to be collecting watches and rings and gold discs. There were various other items in the bags, including some diamond pins very similar to one in Jherek's cravat (only his was a pearl), some small links for securing the cuffs of shirts, some thin cases which contained white paper tubes which in turn contained some kind of aromatic herb. There were some flasks, in silver and in gold, there were studs and chains and pendants, necklaces and a couple of tiaras and a fan with a frame of gold studded with emeralds. They were all quite pretty but Jherek could not see why Snoozer Vine needed so many things of that kind. He shrugged and closed the bag.

A little while later Snoozer returned with two more bags. He was elated. He was panting. His eyes shone.

'The biggest haul of my life. You wouldn't believe the swag what's here tonight. I couldn't have picked a better night in a hundred years. There's been a big ball in Belgravia somewhere. I saw a programme. And all the nobs from the country have come up – *and* people from abroad – in all their finest. There must be a million quid's worth of stuff lying around in their rooms. And them snoring away and me just taking me pick!' Snoozer removed a large bunch of keys from his pocket and rattled them in Jherek's face. From his other pocket he pulled a small object which reminded Jherek of the club Yusharisp had carried when disguised as a Piltdown Man. Only this one was smaller. 'And look at this! Found it on top of a jewel case. Pearl-handled pistol. I'll keep that for meself,' Snoozer laughed heartily, though very quietly, 'in case o' burglars, eh, Jerry?'

Jherek was glad to see his friend pleased. Other people's enthusiasms were often quite hard to appreciate and this was certainly one he could not share, but he smiled.

'In case 'o burglars!' Snoozer repeated in delight. He opened one of the cases and scooped several strands of pearls out, holding them up to the light. 'We'll pack all these away and be out of here while they're still sleeping off the effects of the bubbly. Ha, ha!'

Now Jherek did feel tired. He yawned. He stretched. 'Fine,' he said. 'Have you any objection if I sleep for an hour or two before we leave, Snoozer?'

'Sleep the sleep of the just, my old partner. You brought me luck and that's a fact. I can retire. I can get a stables and stock it with horses and become an Owner. Snoozer Vine, owner of the Derby winner. I can see it there.' He gestured with his hands. 'And I could buy a pub, somewhere out in the country. Hailsham way. Or Epsom, near the track.' He closed his eyes. 'Or go abroad. To Paris! Oo-la-la.' He chuckled to himself as he folded another bag and tucked it under his coat. And then he had left again.

Jherek lay down on his bed, having removed his coat and his silk hat. He was looking forward to dawn when, he hoped, Snoozer would set him on his way to Bromley and Number 23

Collins Avenue.

'Oh, Mrs Underwood,' he breathed. 'Do not fear. Even now your saviour is contemplating your rescue!'

He hoped that Mr Underwood would understand the position.

Jherek was awakened by Snoozer Vine shaking his shoulder. Snoozer had a look of heated rapture upon his face. There was sweat on his brow. His eyes glittered.

'Time to be off, Jerry, me boy. Back to Jones's. We'll have the stuff fenced by tonight and then it's me for the Continent for a bit.'

'Bromley?' said Jherek, sitting stiffly up.

'Bromley as soon as you like. I'll drop you off at the station. I'll get you a ticket. If I had the time I'd have a special bloody train laid on for you after what you've helped me do.'

Snoozer brandished Jherek's top hat and coat. 'Quick, into these. I've already told 'em we're leaving early – for your country estate. They don't suspect a thing. It's funny what a trusting lot o' buggers they are when they think you got a title.'

Jherek Carnelian struggled into the coat. There came a knock at the door. For an instant Snoozer looked wary and agitated and then he relaxed, grinning. 'That'll be the boy for our bags. We'll let him carry the swag out for us, eh?'

Jherek nodded absently. Again he was contemplating his re-union with Mrs Underwood.

The boy came in. He picked up their bags. He frowned as he found he had to struggle with them, as if he was remembering that they had not seemed so heavy the night before.

'Well, sir,' said Snoozer Vine to Jherek Carnelian in a loud voice, 'you'll be pleased to get back to Dorset, I shouldn't wonder.'

'Dorset?' As they followed the boy along the passage Jherek wondered why Vine was looking at him in such a strange way. 'Bromley,' he said.

'That's right, sir.' Anxiously Snoozer put a finger to his lips. They entered the cage and were borne to the ground floor. Vine's expression of elation was still on his face but he was doing his best to hide it, to compose his features into the somewhat

135

sterner lines of the previous night.

It was dawn outside; a grey, rainy dawn. Jherek waited near the door while another boy went to find a cab, for there were none waiting at this time in the morning. The same old man stood behind the reception desk. He was frowning slightly as he accepted the gold discs which Snoozer Vine handed to him.

'His lordship's eager to get back to the country,' Vine was explaining. 'Her ladyship hasn't been well. That is why we returned so suddenly from France.'

'I see.' The old man scribbled on a piece of paper and then handed the paper to Vine.

Jherek thought he detected a somewhat strained atmosphere in the hotel this morning. Everyone seemed to be looking at him with a slightly peculiar expression. He heard the clatter of a cab coming along the street and saw it appear with the green-suited boy clinging to the running board. The middle-aged man in the top hat opened the glass door. The boy picked up the bags as Snoozer crossed the lobby and joined Jherek.

'Good-bye, your lordship,' said the man at the desk.

'Good-bye,' said Jherek cheerfully. 'Thank you.'

'These bags are a weight, sir,' said the boy.

'Don't be cheeky, Herbert,' said the middle-aged man holding the door.

'Yes,' said Jherek conversationally, 'they're full of Snoozer's swag now.'

Snoozer gasped as the mouth of the middle-aged man dropped open.

At that moment a red-faced man in a nightshirt came running down the stairs pulling on a velvet dressing gown that Jherek would have liked to have worn himself.

'I've been robbed!' shouted the red-faced man. 'My wife's jewels. My cigarette case. Everything.'

'Stop!' shouted the old man at the desk.

The middle-aged man let the door go and threw himself at Jherek. The boy dropped the bags. Jherek fell over. He had never been attacked physically before. He laughed.

The middle-aged man turned on Snoozer Vine who was desperately trying to get the bags through the door and out to the cab, a look of profound agony on his thin face. He dropped

136

the bags when the middle-aged man tackled him.

'You can't,' he yelled. 'Not now!' He wriggled free, tugging something from his pocket. 'Stand back!'

'A snoozer!' growled the middle-aged man. 'I should have known. Don't threaten me. I'm an ex-sergeant-major.' And again he dived at Snoozer.

There was a fairly loud bang.

The middle-aged man fell down. Snoozer stared at him in surprise. The surprise was mirrored on the face of the middle-aged man who now had a huge red stain on the front of his green uniform. His top hat fell off. Snoozer waved something at the man in the dressing gown and the old man in the black coat. 'Pick up the bags, Jerry,' he said.

Bemused, Jherek bent and lifted the two heavy bags. The boy was hovering behind one of the potted palms, his cheeks sucked in and his eyes wide. Snoozer Vine's back was to the door but Jherek noticed that the cabby had climbed down from his cab and was running down the street waving to someone whom Jherek couldn't see. He heard a whistle sound.

'Through the door,' said Snoozer in a small, cold voice.

Jherek went through the door and out into the rainy street.

'Into the cab, quick,' said Snoozer. Now he waved the black and silver object at the cabby and another man, dressed in a suit of dark blue and wearing a hat with a rounded crown and no brim, who were running up the street towards them. 'Get back or I'll fire!'

Jherek found the whole thing extremely amusing. He had no idea what was going on but he was enjoying the drama. He looked forward to telling Mrs Amelia Underwood about it in a few hours. He wondered why Snoozer Vine was climbing onto the box of the cab and whipping up the horse. The cab shot off down the street. Jherek heard one more bang and then they had turned a corner and were dashing along another thoroughfare which had a number of people – mainly dressed in grey overcoats and flat hats – in it. All the people turned to stare at the cab as it flew past. Jherek waved gaily to some of them.

Full of elation, for he would soon be in Bromley, he began to sing. 'Jesus bids us shine with a pure, clear light . . .' he sang as he was jolted from side to side in the hurtling cab. 'Like a little candle burning in the night!'

They reached the entrance to Jones's Kitchen some time later, for Snoozer Vine had decided to leave the cab a good mile or so away. Jherek, who was carrying the bags, was quite tired when they got to the house and he wondered why Snoozer's manner had changed so markedly. The man kept snarling at him and saying things like 'You certainly turned good luck into bad in a hurry. I hope to Christ that feller didn't die. If he did it's as much your fault as mine.'

'Die?' Jherek had said innocently. 'But can't he be resurrected? Or is this too early?'

'Shut yer mouth!' Snoozer had told him. 'Well, if I swing so will you. I'd 'ave left yer behind if I 'adn't known you'd blab it all out in two minutes. I ought ter do you in, too.' He laughed bitterly. 'Don't forget yore an accomplice, that's all.'

'You said you'd get me to Bromley,' Jherek reminded him gently as they went up the steps to Jones's Kitchen.

'Bromley?' Snoozer Vine sneered. 'Ha! You'll be lucky if you don't wind up in Hell now!'

During the next few days Jherek began to understand, even more profoundly than before, what misery was. He found that he was growing a beard quite involuntarily and it itched terribly. He became infested with tiny insects of three or four different varieties and they bit him all over. The clothes which Snoozer Vine had originally given him were taken from him and he was given a few thin rags to wear instead. Snoozer occasionally left the room they both shared and went down to the ground floor, always returning very surly and unsteady and smelling of the stuff which the woman had offered Jherek on his first night in Jones's Kitchen. And it grew very cold. Snoozer would not allow Jherek to go downstairs and warm himself at the fire so Jherek, as he came to understand the nature of cold, came also to understand the nature of hunger and thirst. Initially he made the most of it, savouring every experience, but slowly it began to depress him. And slowly he found himself unable to respond to the novelty of it all. Slowly he was learning to know what fear was. Snoozer was teaching him that.

Snoozer would hiss at him sometimes, making incomprehensible threats. Snoozer would growl and snap and strike Jherek who still had no instinct to defend himself. Indeed, the very idea of defence was alien to him. And all the people who had been so friendly when he had first arrived now either ignored him or, like Snoozer, snarled at him if he ventured out of the room. He became thin and mean and dirty. He ceased to despair and began to forget Bromley and even Mrs Amelia Underwood. He began to forget that he had ever known any existence but the squalid, trunk-filled room above Jones's Kitchen.

And then, one morning, there came a great commotion below. Snoozer was still snoring on the bed, having come back in his usual unsteady, argumentative mood, and Jherek was sleeping in his usual place under the table. Jherek woke first, but his senses were too dulled by hunger, fatigue and misery for him to make any reaction to the noise. He heard yells, smashing sounds. Snoozer began to stir and open bleary eyes.

'What is it?' Snoozer said thickly. 'If only that bloody fence would turn up. All that stuff and nobody ter touch it 'cause o' that feller dying.' He swung his legs off the bed and swung a kick, automatically, at Jherek. 'Christ, I wish that bloody 'ansom 'ad killed yer that first bloody night.'

This was almost invariably his waking ritual. But this morning he cocked his head as it dawned on him that something was going on downstairs. He reached under his pillow and brought out his pistol. He got off the bed and went to the door. Cautiously, he opened the door, the pistol in his hand. Again he paused to listen. Loud voices. Oaths. Screams. Women's voices shouting in offended tones. A boy wailing. The deep, aggressive voices of men.

Snoozer Vine, looking little healthier than Jherek, began to pad along the passage. Jherek got up and watched from the doorway. He saw Snoozer reach the gallery just as two men, in the blue clothes he had seen on the other man as they left the hotel, rushed at him from both sides, as if they had been waiting for him. There was another shot. One of the men in blue staggered back. Snoozer broke free of the other's grasp, reached the rail of the gallery, hesitated and then leapt over it

139

to vanish from Jherek's sight.

Jherek began to shuffle along the passage to where one of the men in blue was helping the other get to his feet.

'Stand back!' shouted the one who was not wounded. But Jherek hardly heard him. He shuffled to the rail of the gallery and looked down. He saw Snoozer on the dirty flagstones of the ground floor. His head was bleeding. His whole face seemed covered in blood. He was spreadeagled at an awkward angle and he kept trying to raise himself on his hands and knees and failing. Slowly he was being surrounded by many other men, all dressed in the same blue suits with the same blue hats on their heads. They stood and looked at him, not trying to help him as he made effort after effort to raise himself up. And then he was still.

A fat man – one of the men who served behind the bar in Jones's Kitchen – appeared at the edge of the circle of men in blue. He looked down at Snoozer. He looked up at the gallery and saw Jherek. He pointed. 'That's 'im,' he said. 'That's the other one.'

Jherek felt a strong hand grip his thin shoulder. He was sensitive to pain, for Snoozer had raised a bruise on the same shoulder the night before. But the pain seemed to stimulate his memory. He turned to look up at the grim-faced man who held him.

'Mrs Amelia Underwood,' said Jherek in a small, pleading voice, '23 Collins Avenue, Bromley, Kent, England.'

He repeated the phrase over and over again as he was led down the steps of the gallery, through the deserted main room, out of the door into the morning light where a black waggon drawn by four black horses awaited him. Free from Snoozer, free from Jones's Kitchen, Jherek felt a mindless surge of relief.

'Thank you,' he told one of the men who had climbed into the waggon with him. 'Thank you.'

The man gave a thin smile. 'Don't thank me, lad. They'll 'ang you fer this one, certain.'

140

CHAPTER THIRTEEN

THE ROAD TO THE GALLOWS: OLD FRIENDS IN NEW GUISES

Better fed, better clothed, and better treated in prison than in Jones's Kitchen, Jherek Carnelian began to recover something of his previous state of mind. He particularly liked the grey baggy suit with the broad arrows stitched all over it and he determined, if he ever got back to his own age, to make himself one rather in the same fashion (though probably with orange arrows). The world of the prison did not have very much colour in it. It was mainly bleak greens and greys and blacks. Even the flesh of the other inmates was somewhat grey. And the sounds, too, had a certain monotony – clangs, cries and curses, for the most part. But the daily ritual of rising, eating, exercising, retiring had a healing effect on Jherek's mind. He had been accused of various crimes in the opening ritual and save for an occasional visitor who seemed sympathetic, had been left

141

pretty much to himself. He began to think clearly of Bromley again and Mrs Amelia Underwood. He hoped that they would let him out soon, or complete the ritual in whatever way they saw fit. Then he could continue his quest.

Every few days a man in a black suit with a white collar at his throat, carrying a black book, would visit Jherek's white-tiled cell and talk to Jherek about a friend of his who died and another friend of his who was invisible. Jherek found that listening to the man, whose name was Reverend Lowndes, had a pleasant soporific effect and he would smile and nod and agree whenever it seemed tactful to agree or shake his head whenever it seemed that Reverend Lowndes wanted him to disagree. This caused Reverend Lowndes to express great pleasure and smile a great deal and talk in his rather high-pitched and monotonous voice even more about his dead friend and the invisible friend who, it emerged, was the dead friend's father.

And once, upon leaving, Reverend Lowndes patted Jherek's shoulder and said to him:

'There is no question in my mind that your salvation is at hand.'

This cheered Jherek up and he looked forward to his release. The air outside the prison grew warmer, too, which was pleasant.

Jherek's other visitor was dressed in a black coat and had a silk hat, wing collar and black cravat. His waistcoat was also black, but his trousers were made up of thin grey stripes. He had introduced himself as Mr Griffiths, Defence Counsel. He had a large, dark head and huge, bushy black eyebrows which met near the bridge of his nose. His hands, too, were large and they were clumsy as they handled the documents which he removed from his small leather case. He sat on the edge of Jherek's hard bunk and leafed through the papers, puffing out his cheeks every so often and letting a loud sigh escape his lips from time to time. Then, at last, he turned to Jherek and pursed his lips again before speaking.

'We are going to have to plead insanity, my friend,' he said.

'Ah,' said Jherek uncomprehendingly.

'Yes, indeed. It appears you have admitted everything to the police. Several witnesses have positively identified you. You, indeed, recognised the witnesses before *other* witnesses. You have claimed no mitigating circumstances save that "you were not sure what was going on". That, in itself, is scarcely credible, from the rest of your statement. You saw the dead man, Vine, bringing in his "swag". You help him carry it about. You escaped with him after he had shot the porter. When questioned as to your name and origins you concocted some wild story about coming from the future in some sort of machine and you gave a name that was evidently invented but which you have insisted upon retaining. That is where I intend to begin *my* case – and that is what might well save your life. Now, you had best tell me, in your own opinion, what happened from the night that you met Alfred Vine until the morning when the police traced you both to Jones's Kitchen and Vine was killed while trying to escape...'

Jherek happily told his story to Mr Griffiths, since it passed the time. But Mr Griffiths blew out his cheeks a lot and rolled his eyes once or twice beneath his black eyebrows and once he clapped his hand to his forehead and let forth an oath.

'The only problem I have,' Mr Griffiths said, when he left the first time, 'is in convincing the Jury that a man as apparently sane as yourself in one way is without question a raving lunatic in another. Well, at least I am convinced of the truth of my case. Good-bye, Mr – um... good-bye.'

'I hope to see you again soon,' said Jherek politely as the guard let Mr Griffiths out of the cell.

'Yes, yes,' said Mr Griffiths hastily. 'Yes, yes.'

Mr Griffiths made a number of other visits, as did Reverend Lowndes. But whereas Reverend Lowndes always seemed to depart in an even happier mood than formerly, Mr Griffiths usually left with a wild, unhappy look upon his dark face and his manner was always flustered.

The Trial of Jherek Carnelian for his part in the murder of Edward Frank Morris, porter employed by the Imperial Hotel, Piccadilly, in the Borough of Westminster, London, on the morning of April 5th Eighteen Hundred and Ninety Six at approximately Six o'Clock, took place at the Old Bailey Number One Court at 10 a.m. on the 30th May. Nobody, including the Defendant, expected the trial to be a long one. The only speculation concerned the sentence and the sentence, even, did not seem to concern Jherek Carnelian, who had insisted on retaining the made up name in spite of all warnings that refusal to give his own name would go against him. Before the trial began Jherek was escorted to a wooden box in which he had to stand for the duration of the proceedings. He was rather amused by the box, which commanded a view of the rest of a comparatively large room. Mr Griffiths approached the box and spoke to Jherek urgently for a moment.

'This Mrs Underwood. Have you known her for long?'

'A fairly long time,' said Jherek. 'Strictly speaking of course – I *will* know her for a long time.' He laughed. 'I love these paradoxes, don't you?'

'I do not,' said Mr Griffiths feelingly. 'Would she be a respectable woman? I mean, would you say that she was – well – sane, for instance?'

'Eminently.'

'Hmph. Well, I intend to call her, if possible. Have her vouch for your peculiarities – your delusions and so on.'

'Call her? Bring her here, you mean?'

'Exactly.'

'That would be splendid, Mr Griffiths!' Jherek clapped his hands with pleasure. 'You are very kind, sir.'

'Hmph,' said Griffiths, turning away and going back to the table at which he sat with a number of other men all dressed like himself in black gowns and odd-looking false hair which was white and tightly curled with a little tuft hanging down behind. Further back were rows of seats in which sat a number of men in a variety of clothes, with no false hair on their heads. And above and behind Jherek was a gallery containing more people in their ordinary clothes. To his left was another series of tiered benches on which, as he watched, twelve people arranged themselves. All showed a marked interest in him. He was flattered to be the centre of attention. He waved and smiled but, oddly enough, nobody smiled back at him.

And then someone shouted something Jherek didn't catch and everyone suddenly began getting to their feet as another group of men in long robes and false hair filed into the room and

144

sat down behind a series of desks immediately opposite Jherek on the far side of the chamber. It was then that Jherek gasped in astonishment as he recognised the man who seemed to take pride of place, after himself, in the court.

'Lord Jagged of Canaria!' he cried. 'Have you followed me through time? What a friend you are, indeed!'

One of the men in blue who stood behind Jherek leaned forward and tapped him on the shoulder. 'Be quiet, lad. You speak when you're spoken to.'

But Jherek was too delighted to listen to him.

'Lord Jagged! Don't you recognise me?'

Everyone had begun to sit down again and Lord Jagged did not seem to have heard Jherek. He was leafing through some papers which someone had placed before him.

'Quiet!' said the man behind Jherek again.

Jherek turned with a smile. 'It's my friend,' he explained pointing.

'You'd better hope so,' said the man grimly. 'That's the Lord Chief Justice, that is. He's your Judge, lad – Lord Jagger. Don't get on the wrong side of him or you haven't a chance.'

'Lord *Jagged*,' said Jherek.

'Silence!' someone cried. 'Silence in court!'

Lord Jagged of Canaria looked up then. He had a peculiar, stern expression on his face and, as he looked at Jherek, he gave no sign that he recognised him.

Jherek was puzzled but guessed that this was some new game of Lord Jagged's. He decided to play it in the same way, so he made no further reference to the indisputable fact that the man opposite him, who seemed to command the respect of all, was his old friend.

The trial began and Jherek's interest remained lively throughout as a succession of people, most of whom he had seen at the hotel, came to tell what had happened on the night when Jherek and Snoozer Vine had arrived at the Imperial and what subsequently took place on the following morning. These people were questioned by a man called Sir George Freeman and then Mr Griffiths would question them again. By and large the people recounted the events pretty much as Jherek remembered them, but Mr Griffiths did not seem to believe them much of the time. Mr Griffiths was also interested in their view of Jherek. Had he behaved oddly? Did they notice anything strange about his face? What had he said? Some of the people remembered that Jherek had said some strange things – or at least things which they had not understood. They believed now that this was a thieves' code arranged between Jherek and Snoozer Vine. Men in blue uniforms were questioned, including the one whom Jherek had seen in the street when he left the hotel and several of the ones who had come to Jones's Kitchen later. Again these were closely questioned by Mr Griffiths. The Reverend Lowndes appeared to talk about Jherek and told everybody that he thought Jherek had 'repented'.

Then there was a break for lunch and Jherek was escorted back to a small, clean cell and given some unappetising food to eat. As he ate, Mr Griffiths came to see him again.

'There's every chance, I think, that the Jury will find you guilty but insane,' Mr Griffiths told him.

Jherek nodded absently. He was still thinking of the surprise at seeing Lord Jagged in the court. How had his friend managed to find him? How, for that matter, had he been able to get back through time? In another time machine? Jherek hoped so, for it would make everything much easier. As soon as all this was over he would take Mrs Amelia Underwood back with Lord Jagged in the new time machine. He would be quite glad to get back to his own age, for this one was, after a while, a bit tedious.

'Particularly,' Mr Griffiths went on, 'since you did not actually shoot the man. On the other hand, the prosecution seems out for blood and the Jury doesn't look too sympathetic. It'll probably be up to the Judge. Lord Jagger's got a reputation for leniency, I hear . . .'

'Lord *Jagged*,' Jherek told Mr Griffiths. 'That's his real name, at any rate. He's a friend of mine.'

'So that's what that was all about.' Mr Griffiths shook his head. 'Well, anyway, you're helping prove my case.'

'He's from my own period,' Jherek said. 'My closest friend in my own age.'

'He's rather well-known in *our* age,' said Mr Griffiths with a crooked smile. 'The most brilliant Q.C. in the Empire, the youngest Lord Chief Justice ever to sit on the bench.'

'So this is where he used to go on those long trips!' Jherek laughed. 'I wonder why he never mentioned it to me?'

'I wonder!' Mr Griffiths snorted and got up. 'Your lady friend is here, by the way. She had read about the case in the papers this morning and contacted me herself.'

'Mrs Underwood! This is wonderful. *Two* old friends. Oh, thank you, Mr Griffiths!' Jherek sprang to his feet as the door opened and revealed the woman he loved.

She was so beautiful in her dark velvet clothes. Her hat was quite plain with a little veil coming down in front of it through which he could see her lovely, heart-shaped face.

'Mrs Amelia Underwood!' Jherek moved forward to embrace her, but she withdrew.

'Sir!'

A warder made a gesture, as if to assist her.

'It's all right now,' said Mrs Underwood to the warder. 'Yes, it is he, Mr Griffiths.' She spoke very distantly and sadly as if she remembered a dream of which Jherek had been part.

'We can leave here and return very soon!' Jherek assured her. 'Lord Jagged is here. He must have a time machine. We can all go back in it.'

'I cannot go back, Mr Carnelian.' She spoke in a low voice, in the same remote tone. 'And until I saw you a moment ago I did not quite believe I had ever been there. How did you get here?'

'I followed you. In a time machine supplied by Brannart Morphail. I knew that you loved me.'

'Love? Ah . . .' She sighed.

'And you still love me, I can tell.'

'No!' She was shocked. 'I am married. I am . . .' She recovered herself. 'I did not come for this, Mr Carnelian. I came to see if it really were you and, if so, to plead for your life. I know that you would do nothing as wicked as take part in a murder – or even a robbery. I am sure you were duped. You were ever naïve in some ways. Mr Griffiths wants me to tell a lie to the court which, he thinks, might save your life.'

'A lie?'

'He wants me to say that I have known you for some time and

that you always displayed idiotic tendencies.'

'Must you say that? Why not tell them the truth?'

'They will not believe the truth. No one would!'

'I have noticed that they tend to ignore me when I tell them the truth and listen only when I repeat back to them what they have *told* me is the truth.'

Now Mr Griffiths was looking from Jherek to Mrs Amelia Underwood and back again and there was a miserable, haunted look on his face. 'You mean you both believe this wild nonsense about the future?'

'It is not nonsense, Mr Griffiths,' said Mrs Amelia Underwood firmly. 'But, on the other hand, I do not ask *you* to believe it. The important thing is to save Mr Carnelian's life – even if it means going against all my principles and uttering a perjury to the Court. It seems the only way, in this instance, to stop an injustice taking place!'

'Yes, yes,' said Mr Griffiths desperately. 'So you will go into the witness box and tell the jury that Mr – Carnelian – is mad. That is all I shall require.'

'Yes,' she whispered.

'You do love me,' said Jherek, also speaking softly. 'I can see it in your eyes, Mrs Underwood.'

She looked at him once, a look of longing, of agony. An imploring look. And then she turned and had left the cell.

'She does love me!' Jherek skipped around the cell. Mr Griffiths watched him skip. Mr Griffiths seemed tired. He had an air of fatalism about him as he, too, left the cell and Jherek began to sing at the top of his voice. 'All things bright and beautiful, all creatures great and small. All things wise and wonderful . . .'

After lunch everyone assumed their places again and the first person to appear was Mrs Amelia Underwood, looking even more strained than ever, in the role of Witness for the Defence.

Mr Griffiths asked her if she had known Jherek before. She said she had met him when travelling with her missionary father in South America, that he had caused her some embarrassment but that he was 'harmless'.

'An idiot, would you say, Mrs Underwood?'

'Yes,' murmured Mrs Underwood, 'an idiot.'

148

'Something of – um – an innocent, eh?'

'An innocent,' she agreed in the same voice. 'Yes.'

'Did he show any violent tendencies?'

'None. I do not believe he knows what violence is.'

'Very good. And crime? Would you say he had any notion of crime?'

'None.'

'Excellent.' Mr Griffiths turned towards the twelve men who were all leaning forward, concentrating on the exchange. 'I think, members of the jury that this lady – the daughter of a missionary – has successfully proved to you that not only did the defendant not *know* he was being involved in a crime by the deceased Alfred Vine but that he was incapable knowingly of committing any crime. He came to England to seek out the woman who had been kind to him in his own country – in the Argentine, as Mrs Underwood has told you. He was duped by unscrupulous rogues into aiding them in a theft. Knowing nothing of our customs . . .'

Lord Jagger leaned forward. 'I think we can save all this for the summing up, Mr Griffiths.'

Mr Griffiths bowed his head. 'Very well, m'lud. I apologise.'

And now it was Sir George Freeman's turn to question Mrs Underwood. He had small beady eyes, a red nose and an aggressive manner. He asked Mrs Underwood for particulars of where and when she had met Mr Carnelian. He produced arguments and evidence to show that no ship had docked in London from the Argentine on the date mentioned. He suggested that Mrs Underwood had misguidedly felt sorry for Mr Carnelian and had come forward to give evidence which was untrue in order to save him. Was she one of those who objected to capital punishment? He could understand that many good Christians were. He did not suggest that she was appearing in the witness box from anything but the best – if most misguided – of motives. And so on and so on until Mrs Underwood burst into tears and Jherek tried to climb out of his own box and go to her.

'Mrs Underwood!' he cried. 'Just tell them what really happened. Lord Jagged will understand! He will tell them that you are speaking the truth!'

And then everyone seemed to be springing up at once and there was a loud babble of voices and the rapping of a hammer against wood and a man crying loudly:

'Silence in court! Silence in court!'

'I shall have to have the court cleared in the event of a further demonstration of this kind,' said Lord Jagger drily.

'But she is only lying because these people will not believe the truth!' cried Jherek.

'Silence!'

Jherek looked wildly around him. 'They said that you would not believe the truth – that we met a million years in the future, that I followed her back here because I loved her – still do love her ...'

Lord Jagger ignored Jherek and instead leaned towards the men in the false hair below him. 'The witness may leave the box,' he said. 'She seems to be in distress. Do you have any further questions, gentlemen?'

Mr Griffiths shook his head in silent despair. Sir George Freeman seemed quietly pleased and also shook his head.

Jherek watched Mrs Underwood being led from the box. He saw her disappear and he had a terrible feeling that he would never see her again. He looked appealingly at Lord Jagger.

'Why did you let them make her cry, Jagged?'

'Silence!'

'I think I have successfully proven, m'lud, that the only witness for the defence was lying,' said Sir George Freeman.

'Have you anything to say to that, Mr Griffiths?' Lord Jagger asked.

Mr Griffiths had lowered his head. 'No, m'lud.' He turned and looked at Jherek, who was still agitated. 'Though I believe we have had ample proof of the defendant's unbalanced mental state today.'

'We shall decide on that later,' said Lord Jagger. 'And it is not, I should like to remind the jury, the defendant's mental condition *today* which is being examined. We are trying to discover whether he was mad on the morning of the murder.'

'Lord Jagged!' cried Jherek. 'I beg you. Finish this thing now. The charade might have been amusing to begin with, but it has caused Mrs Underwood genuine grief. Perhaps you do not understand how these people feel – but I do – I have experienced quite awful emotions and states of mind myself since I have been here.'

'Silence!'

'Lord Jagged!'

'Silence!'

'You will be able to speak in your own defence later, if you wish,' said Lord Jagger, without a flicker of humour, without a single sign of recognition. And Jherek at last began to doubt that this was his friend on the bench. Yet the face, the mannerisms, the voice were all the same – and the name was almost the same. It could not be a coincidence.

And then the thought occurred to him that Lord Jagged was taking some malicious pleasure in the proceedings – that he was not Jherek's friend at all. That he had engineered this entire fiasco from start to finish.

The rest of the trial seemed to take place in a flash. And when Lord Jagged asked Jherek if he wished to speak, he merely shook his head. He was too depressed to make any reaction, to try to convince them of the truth. He began to believe that, possibly, he was, indeed, quite mad.

But the thought almost made Jherek dizzy. It could not be! It could not be!

And then Lord Jagger made a short speech to the jury and they all left the court again. Jherek was taken back to his cell and was joined by Mr Griffiths.

'It looks grim,' said Mr Griffiths. 'You should have kept quiet, you know. Now they all think it was an elaborate trick to get you off. This could ruin me.'

He took something from his case and handed it to Jherek. 'Your friend, Mrs Underwood, asked me to give you this.'

Jherek took the paper. He looked at the marks on it and then handed it back to Mr Griffiths. 'You had better read it.'

Mr Griffiths squinted at the paper. He blushed. He coughed. 'It's rather personal.'

'Please read it,' said Jherek.

'Well, here goes – ahem – "I blame myself for what has happened. I know they will put you in prison for a long time, if they do not hang you. I fear that you have little hope now of acquittal and so I must tell you, Jherek, that I do love you, that I miss you, that I shall always remember you." Hmph. It's unsigned. Very wise. Most indiscreet to write it at all.'

Jherek was smiling again. 'I knew she loved me. I'll think of a way to rescue her, even if Lord Jagged will not help me.'

'My dear boy,' said Mr Griffiths solemnly, 'you must try to remember the seriousness of your position. It is very much on the cards that they will sentence you to be hanged.'

'Yes?' said Jherek. 'By the way, Mr Griffiths, what's involved in this "hanging", can you tell me?'

And Mr Griffiths sighed, got up and left the cell without a further word.

Jherek was escorted back to his box for the third time. As he mounted the steps he saw Lord Jagger and the others taking their places.

The twelve men came in and resumed their seats.

An oppressive silence now hung over the room.

One of the men in false hair began to read from a list of names and every time he read a name one of the twelve would answer 'Aye', until all twelve names had been read.

Then the man next to him got up and addressed the twelve. 'Gentlemen of the Jury, have you agreed upon your verdict?'

One of the twelve answered. 'Yes.'

'Do you find the prisoner at the bar guilty or not guilty?'

For a moment all twelve turned their eyes on Jherek whose attention was scarcely on the ritual at all.

'Guilty.'

Jherek was startled as the hands of two warders fell simultaneously upon his shoulders. He looked at each of their faces curiously.

Lord Jagger looked steadily into Jherek's eyes.

'Have you anything to say why sentence should not be passed upon you?'

Jherek said wearily: 'Jagged, I am tired of this farce. Let us take Mrs Amelia Underwood and go home.'

'I gather you have nothing to say,' said Lord Jagger, ignoring Jherek's suggestion.

One of the men near Lord Jagger handed Lord Jagger a

square of black cloth which he placed carefully on top of his white false hair. Reverend Lowndes appeared beside Lord Jagger. He was wearing a long black gown. He looked much sadder than usual.

'You have been found guilty of causing the cruel murder of an innocent employee of the hotel you sought to rob,' droned Lord Jagger, and for the first time Jherek thought he saw the light of humour in his friend's eyes. It was a joke after all. He smiled back. 'And therefore I must sentence you —'

'Ha! Ha!' shouted Jherek. 'It *is* you, Jagged!'

'Silence!' cried someone.

Lord Jagger's voice continued through the confusion, the faint murmur of voices in the court, until it concluded 'And may the Lord have mercy on your soul.'

And Reverend Lowndes said:

'Amen!'

And the warders tugged at Jherek to make him leave.

'I will see you later, Jagged!' he called.

But again Jagger ignored him, turning his back as he rose from his seat and muttering something to the Reverend Lowndes who nodded mournfully.

'No threats. They won't do any good,' said one of the warders. 'Come on, son.'

Jherek laughed as he let them lead him back to his cell. 'Really. I'm losing my sense of humour – my sense of drama. It must have been that terrible time in Jones's Kitchen. I will apologize to Jagged as soon as I meet him again!'

'You won't be meeting *him*,' said the warder with a jerk of his thumb backward, 'until he joins you down there!' And he pointed at the ground.

'Is that where you think the future lies?' asked Jherek with genuine curiosity.

But they said nothing more to him and in a moment he was alone in his cell fingering the note which Mrs Amelia Underwood had sent him, wishing he could read it, but remembering every word. She loved him. She had said so! He had never experienced such happiness before.

After he had been taken to yet another prison in another

black carriage, Jherek found that he was being treated with even more kindness than before. The warders who had spoken to him previously with a sort of good humour now spoke with sympathy and often patted him on the shoulder. Only on the matter of his release did they preserve a silence. One or two would tell him that they thought 'he ought to have got off' and that 'it wasn't fair', but he was never able to interpret the significance of their remarks. He saw Reverend Lowndes quite frequently and was able to make him happy enough. Sometimes they sang one or two hymns together and Jherek was reminded with greater clarity that he would soon be seeing Mrs Amelia Underwood again and singing those same hymns with her. He asked Reverend Lowndes if he had heard anything of Mrs Underwood, but Reverend Lowndes had not.

'She risked much to speak in your defence,' said Reverend Lowndes one day. 'It was in all the newspapers. It is possible that she has compromised herself. I understand that she is a married woman.'

'I understand that,' agreed Jherek. 'But I suppose she is waiting for me to arrange our transport back to my own time.'

'Yes, yes,' said Reverend Lowndes sadly.

'I would have thought that Lord Jagged would have contacted me by now, but perhaps his own time machine is in need of repair,' Jherek mused.

'Yes, yes, yes.' Reverend Lowndes opened his black book and began to read, his lips moving. Then he closed the book and looked up. 'It is tomorrow morning, you know.'

'Oh? You have heard from Lord Jagged?'

'Lord Jagger passed the sentence, if that is what you mean. He named the day as tomorrow. I am glad you are so composed.'

'Why should I not be? That is splendid news.'

'I am sure that the Lord knows how best to judge you.' Reverend Lowndes raised his grey eyes towards the roof. 'You have no need to fear.'

'None at all. Although the ride might be a rough one.'

'Yes indeed. I understand your meaning.'

'Ah!' Jherek leaned back on his bunk. 'I am looking forward to seeing all my friends again.'

'I am sure they will all be there.' Reverend Lowndes got up. 'I will come early tomorrow morning. If you find it hard to sleep, the warders will join you in your cell.'

'I shall sleep very well, I'm sure. So my release is due around dawn?'

'At eight o'clock.'

'Thank you for the news, Reverend Lowndes.'

Reverend Lowndes's eyes seemed to be watering, but he could not be crying, for there was a smile on his face. 'You do not know what this means to me, Mr Carnelian.'

'I am only too pleased to be able to cheer you up, Reverend Lowndes.'

'Thank you. Thank you.' The Reverend left the cell.

Next morning Jherek was given a rather heavy breakfast, which he ate with some difficulty so as not to offend the warders, who plainly thought they had brought him a special treat. All of them looked sad, however, and kept shaking their heads.

The Reverend Lowndes turned up early, as he had said he would.

'Are you ready?' he asked Jherek.

'More than ready,' Jherek replied cheerfully.

'Would you like to join me in a prayer?'

'If that is what you want, of course.' Jherek kneeled down with Reverend Lowndes as he had often knelt before and repeated the words which Reverend Lowndes spoke. This time the prayer seemed to go on for longer than usual and Reverend Lowndes's voice kept breaking. Jherek waited patiently every time this happened. After all, what did a few minutes mean when he would soon be reunited with the woman he loved (not to mention his dearest friend)?

And then they left the cell, with a warder on either side, and walked out into an unfamiliar forecourt which was surrounded on all sides by high blank walls. There was a sort of wooden dais erected in the forecourt and above this a tall beam supporting another horizontal beam. From the horizontal beam depended a thick rope with a loop at the bottom end. Another man, in stout black clothes, stood on the dais. Steps led up to it on one side. There was also a lever, near the man in black.

Several other people were already in the forecourt. They, too, looked sad. Doubtless they had grown to like Jherek (even though he could not remember having seen several of them before) and did not want him to leave their time.

'Is that the machine?' Jherek asked Reverend Lowndes. He had never expected to see a *wooden* time machine, but he supposed that they used wood for a lot of things in the Dawn Age cultures.

Silently, Reverend Lowndes nodded.

'I go up these steps, do I?'

'You do.'

Reverend Lowndes accompanied Jherek as he climbed the steps. The man in black drew Jherek's hands behind him and tied them securely.

'I suppose this is necessary?' Jherek remarked to the man in black, who had said nothing up to now. 'I had a rubber suit last time.'

The man in black did not reply but turned to Reverend Lowndes instead. 'He's a cool one. It's usually the foreigners scream and kick.'

Reverend Lowndes did not reply. He watched the man in black tie Jherek's feet.

Jherek laughed as the man in black put the rough rope loop over his head and tightened it around his neck. The strands of the loop tickled.

'Well,' he said. 'I'm ready. When are Lord Jagged and Mrs Underwood arriving?'

Nobody replied. Reverend Lowndes murmured something. One of the people in the small crowd below droned a few words.

Jherek yawned and looked up at the blue sky and the rising sun. It was a beautiful morning. He had rather missed the open air of late.

Reverend Lowndes took out his black book and began to read. Jherek turned to ask if Lord Jagged and Mrs Underwood would be long, but then the man in black placed a bag over his head and his voice was muffled and he could no longer see anyone. He shrugged. They would be along soon, he was sure.

He heard the Reverend Lowndes finish speaking. He heard a click and then the floor gave way beneath his feet. The sensation was not very different from that which he had had when travelling here in the time sphere. And then it seemed he was falling, falling, falling, and he ceased to think at all.

CHAPTER FOURTEEN

A FURTHER CONVERSATION WITH THE IRON ORCHID

The first thing Jherek considered as he came back to consciousness was that he had a very sore throat. He reached up to touch it, but his hands were still tied behind him. He disseminated the ropes and freed his hands and feet. His neck was chafed and raw. He opened his eyes and looked directly into the tattered multi-hued face of Brannart Morphail.

Brannart was grinning. 'I told you so, Jherek. I told you so! And the time machine didn't come back with you. Which means you've lost me an important piece of equipment!' His glee denied his accusations.

Jherek glanced about the laboratory. It was exactly the same as when he had left. 'Perhaps it broke up?' he suggested. 'It *was* made of wood, you know.'

'Wood? Wood? Nonsense. Why are you so hoarse?'

'There was a rope involved. A very primitive machine, all in all. Still, I'm back. Did Lord Jagged come to see you after I'd set off. Did he borrow another time machine?'

'Lord Jagged?'

My Lady Charlotina drifted over. She was wearing the same lily-coloured gown she had worn when he had left. 'Lord Jagged hasn't been here, Jherek, my juice. After all, you'd barely gone before you returned again.'

'It proves the Morphail Effect conclusively,' said Brannart in some satisfaction. 'If one goes back to an age where one does not belong, then so many paradoxes are created that the age merely spits out the intruder as a man might spit out a pomegranate pip which has lodged in his throat.'

Again, Jherek fingered his own throat. 'It took some time to spit me out, however,' he said feelingly. 'I was there for some sixty days.'

'Oh, come now!' Brannart glared at him.

'And Lord Jagged of Canaria was there, too. And Mrs Amelia Underwood. They seemed to have no difficulty in, as it were, sticking.' Jherek stood up. He was wearing the same grey suit with the broad black arrows on it. 'And look at this. They gave me this suit.'

'It's a beautiful suit, Jherek,' said My Lady Charlotina. 'But you *could* have made it yourself, you know.'

'Power rings don't work in the past. The energy won't transmit,' Jherek told her.

Brannart frowned. 'What was Jagged doing in the past?'

'Some scheme of his own, I take it, which hardly involved me. I understood that he would be returning with me.' Jherek inspected the laboratory, looking in every corner. 'They said Mrs Underwood would join me.'

'Well, she isn't here, yet.' My Lady Charlotina's couch drifted closer. 'Did you enjoy yourself in the Dawn Age?'

'It was often amusing,' Jherek admitted, 'though there were moments when it was quite dull. And other moments when . . .' And for the third time he fingered the marks on his throat. 'Do you know, Lady Charlotina, that many of their pastimes are not pursued from *choice* at all!'

'How do you mean?' She leaned forward to peer at his neck.

She reached out to touch the marks.

'Well, it is difficult to explain. Difficult enough to grasp. I didn't understand at first. They grow old – they decay, of course. They have no control over their bodies and barely any over their minds. It is as if – as if they dream perpetually, moved by impulses of which they have no objective understanding. Or, of course, that could be my subjective analysis of their culture, but I don't think so.'

My Lady Charlotina laughed. 'You'll never succeed in explaining it to me, Jherek. I have no brains, merely imagination. A good sense of drama, too.'

'Yes . . .' Jherek had forgotten the part she had played in bringing about the most recent events in his life. But so much time had passed for him that he could not feel any great bitterness towards her any more. 'I wonder when Mrs Amelia Underwood will come.'

'She said she would return?'

'I gathered that Lord Jagged was bringing her back.'

'Are you sure you saw Jagged there?' Brannart asked insistently. 'There has been no record of a time machine either coming or going.'

'There must be a record of one coming,' Jherek said reasonably. 'For *I* returned, did I not?'

'It wasn't really necessary for you to use a machine – the Morphail Effect dealt with you.'

'Well, I was sent in a machine.' Jherek frowned. He was beginning to review the most recent events of his own past. 'At least I *think* it was a time machine. I wonder if I misinterpreted what they were trying to tell me?'

'It is quite possible, I should think,' put in My Lady Charlotina, 'after all, you said yourself how difficult it was to grasp their conception of quite simple matters.'

A musing look crossed Jherek's face. 'But one thing is certain . . .' He took Mrs Amelia Underwood's letter from his pocket, remembering the words which Mr Griffiths had read out to him, 'I love you, I miss you, I shall always remember you.' He touched the crumpled paper to his lips. 'She wants to come back to me.'

'There is every chance that she *will*,' said Brannart

Morphail, 'whether she desires it or not. The Morphail Effect. It never fails.' He laughed. 'Not that she will necessarily come to this time again. You might have to search through the whole of the past million years for her. I don't advise that, of course. It could mean disaster for you. You've been very lucky to escape this time.'

'She will find me,' said Jherek happily. 'I know she will. And when she comes I will have built her a beautiful replica of her own age so that she need never pine for home.' He continued, confidentially, to tell Brannart Morphail of his plans. 'You see, I've spent a considerable amount of time in the Dawn Age. I'm intimately acquainted with their architecture and many of their customs. Our world will never have seen anything like the creations I shall make. It will amaze you all!'

'Ah, Jherek!' cried My Lady Charlotina in delight. 'You are beginning to sound like your old self again. Hurrah!'

Some days later Jherek had almost completed his vast design. It stretched for several miles across a shallow valley through which ran a sparkling river he had named the Thames. Glowing white bridges arched over the water at irregular intervals and the water was a deep, blue-green, to match the roses which climbed the pillars of the bridges. On both sides of the river stood a series of copies of Jones's Kitchen, Coffee Stalls, Prisons, Courts of Law and Hotels. Row upon row, they filled streets of shining marble and gold and quartz and at every inter-section was a tall statue, usually of a horse or a hansom cab. It was really very pretty. Jherek had taken the liberty of enlarging the buildings a little, to get variety. Thus a thousand-foot-high Coffee Stall loomed over a five-hundred-foot-high Hotel. Farther on, a tall Hotel dwarfed an Old Bailey, and so on.

Jherek was putting the finishing touches on his creation, which he simply called 'London, 1896', when he was hailed by a familiar, languid voice.

'Jherek, you are a genius and this is your masterpiece!'

Mounted upon a great hovering swan, swathed in quilted clothes of the deepest blue, a high collar framing his long, pale face, was Lord Jagged of Canaria, smiling his cleverest, most secret of smiles.

Jherek had been standing on the roof of one of his Prisons. He drifted over and perched on the statue of a hansom close to where Jagged hovered.

'It's a beautiful swan,' said Jherek. 'Have you brought Mrs Underwood with you?'

'So you know what I call her!'

Jherek frowned his puzzlement. 'What?'

'The swan! I thought, gentle Jherek, that you meant the swan. That is what I call the swan, Jherek. Mrs Amelia Underwood. In honour of your friend.'

'Lord Jagged,' said Jherek with a grin. 'You are deceiving me. I know your penchant for manipulation. Remember the world you built, which you peopled with microscopic warriors? This time you have been playing with love, with destiny – with the people you know. You encouraged me to pursue Mrs Amelia Underwood. And most of the details of the rest of that scheme were supplied by you – though you made me believe they were my ideas. I am sure you helped My Lady Charlotina concoct her vengeance. You might even have had something to do with my safe arrival in 1896. Further, it's possible you abducted Mrs Underwood and brought her to our age in the first place.'

Lord Jagged was laughing. He sent the great swan circling around the tallest buildings. He dived and he climbed and all the time he laughed. 'Jherek! You are intelligent! You *are* – you *are* the best of us!'

'But where is Mrs Amelia Underwood now, Lord Jagged?' Jherek Carnelian called, following after his friend, his pale grey suit (with the orange arrows) flapping as he moved through the air. 'I thought you sent a message that you were bringing her back with you!'

'I? A message? No.'

'Then where is she?'

'Why, in Bromley, I suppose. In Kent. In England. In 1896.'

'Oh, Lord Jagged, you are *cruel*!'

'To a degree.' Lord Jagged guided the swan back to where Jherek sat on the head of the statue which, in turn, rested its feet on the dome of the Old Bailey. It was an odd statue

– blindfolded, with a sword in one hand and a set of golden scales in the other. 'But did you not learn anything from your sojourn in the past, Jherek?'

'I experienced something, Lord Jagged, but I am not sure I *learned* anything.'

'Well, that is the best way to learn, I think.' Lord Jagged smiled again.

'It was you – the Lord Chief Justice – wasn't it?' Jherek said. The smile broadened.

'You must get Mrs Amelia Underwood back for me, Lord Jagged,' Jherek told him. 'If only so that she may see this.' He spread both his hands.

'The Morphail Effect,' said Lord Jagged. 'It is an indisputable fact. Brannart says so.'

'You know more.'

'I am flattered. Have you heard, by the by, what became of Mongrove and Yusharisp, the alien?'

'I have been busy. I've heard no gossip at all.'

'They succeeded in building a spaceship and have left together to spread Yusharisp's message throughout the universe.'

'So Mongrove has left us.' Jherek felt sad at hearing this news.

'He will tire of the mission. He will return.'

'I hope so.'

'And your mother, the Iron Orchid. Her liaison with Werther de Goethe is ended, I hear. She took up with the Duke of Queens, who had virtually retired from the world, and they are planning a party together. She will be the guiding spirit, so it should be successful.'

'I am glad,' said Jherek. 'I think I will go to see her soon.'

'Do. She loves you. We all love you, Jherek.'

'And I love Mrs Amelia Underwood,' said Jherek meaningly. 'Will I see her again, Lord Jagged?'

Lord Jagged patted the neck of his graceful swan. The bird began to flap away towards the East.

'Will I?' cried Jherek insistently.

And Lord Jagged called back over his shoulder: 'Doubtless you will. Much can happen yet. After all, there are at least a thousand years before the End of Time!'

The white swan soared higher into the blue sky. From its downy back Lord Jagged waved. 'Farewell, my fateful friend. Adieu, my time-tossed leaf, my thief, my grief, my toy! Jherek, my joy, good-bye!'

And Jherek saw the white swan turn its long neck once to look at him from enigmatic black eyes before it disappeared behind a single cloud which drifted in that bland, blind sky.

Dressed in various shades of pale green, the Iron Orchid and her son lay upon a lawn of deeper green which swept gently down to a viridian lake. It was late afternoon and a warm breeze blew.

Between the Iron Orchid and her slender son lay a cloth of greenish-gold and on this were jade plates bearing the remains of their picnic. There were green apples, green grapes and artichoke hearts; there was asparagus, lettuce, cucumber and watercress; little melons, celery and avocados, vine leaves and pears, and, at one corner of the cloth, there stared a radish.

The Iron Orchid's emerald lips opened slightly as she reached for an unpeeled almond. Jherek had been telling her of his adventures at the Dawn of Time. She had been fascinated but not altogether comprehending.

'And did you find out the meaning of "virtue", my bones?' She hesitated over the almond and now considered a cucumber.

He sighed. 'I must admit I am not sure. But I think it might have had something to do with "corruption".' He laughed and stretched his limbs upon the cool grass. 'One thing leads to another, mother.'

'How do you mean, my love, "corruption"?'

'It has something to do with not being in control of your own decisions, I think. Which in turn has something to do with the environment in which you choose to live – if you have a choice at all. Perhaps when Mrs Amelia Underwood returns she will be able to help me.'

'She will return here?' With a gesture of abandonment the Iron Orchid let her fingers fall upon the radish. She popped it into her mouth.

'I am certain of it,' he said.

'And then you will be happy!'

He looked at her in mild surprise. 'How do you mean, mother, "happy"?'

The end of the first volume

VOLUME TWO

The Hollow Lands

For Mike Harrison and
Diane Boardman

Let us go hence – the night is now at hand;
  The day is overworn, the birds all flown;
  And we have reaped the crops the gods have sown,
Despair and death; deep darkness o'er the land,
Broods like an owl; we cannot understand
  Laughter or tears, for we have only known
  Surpassing vanity: vain things alone
Have driven our perverse and aimless band.

Let us go hence, somewhither strange and cold,
  To Hollow Lands where just men and unjust
  Find end of labour, where's rest for the old,
Freedom to all from love and fear and lust.
  Twine our torn hands! O pray the earth enfold
Our life-sick hearts and turn them into dust.

Ernest Dowson
A Last Word
1899

Contents

CHAPTER ONE

IN WHICH JHEREK CARNELIAN CONTINUES TO BE IN LOVE

'You have begun another fashion I fear, my dear.' The
Iron Orchid slid the sable sheets down her smooth skin
and pushed them from the bed with her slender feet.

'I am so proud of you. What mother would not be?
You are a talented and tasty son!'

Jherek sighed from where he lay on the far side of the
bed, his face all but hidden in the huge downy pile of
pillows. He was pale. He was pensive.

'Thank you, brightest of blossoms, most revered of
metals.'

His voice was small.

'But you still pine,' she said sympathetically, 'for your

Mrs Underwood.'

'Indeed.'

'Few could sustain such a passion so well. The world still awaits, eagerly, expectantly, the outcome. Will you go to her? Will she come to you?'

'She said that she would come to me,' Jherek Carnelian murmured. 'Or so I understood. You know how difficult it is sometimes to make sense of a time traveller's conversation, and I must say that it was particularly confusing in 1896.' He smiled. 'It was wonderful, however. I wish you could have seen it, Iron Orchid. The Coffee Stalls, the Gin Palaces, the Prisons and all the other monuments. And so many people! One might doubt a sufficiency of air to give life to them!'

'Yes, dear.' Her response was not as lively as it might have been, for she had heard all this more than once. 'But your re-creation is there, for all of us to enjoy. And others now follow where you led.'

Realizing that he was in danger of boring her, he sat up in his pillows, stretching his fingers out before him and contemplating the shimmering power rings which adorned them. Pursing his perfect lips he made an adjustment to the ring on the index finger of his right hand. A window appeared on the far side of the room and through the window sunshine came leaping, warm and bright.

'What a beautiful morning!' exclaimed the Iron Orchid, complimenting him. 'How do you plan to spend it?'

He shrugged. 'I had not considered the problem. Have you a suggestion?'

'Well, Jherek, since you are the one who has set the fashion for nostalgia, I thought you might like to come with me to one of the old rotted cities.'

'You are most certainly in a nostalgic mood, Queen of imaginative mothers.' He kissed her softly upon the lids of her ebony eyes. 'We were last there together when I was a child – you are thinking of Shanalorm, of course?'

172

'Shanalorm, or whatever it's called. You were conceived there, too, as I remember.' She yawned. 'The rotted cities are the only permanency in this world of ours.'

'Some would say they *were* the world.' Jherek smiled. 'But they do not have the charm of the Dawn Age metropoli, ancient as they are.'

'I find them romantic,' she said reminiscently. She threw jet arms around him, kissing him upon the lips with her mouth of midnight blue, her dress (living purple poppies) undulating and sighing. 'What shall you wear, to go adventuring? Are you still in a mood for those arrowed suits?'

'I think not.' (Privately, he was disappointed that she still favoured blacks and dark blues, for it indicated that she had not completely forgotten her relationship with doom-embracing Werther de Goethe.) He considered the problem for a moment and then, with a twist of a power ring, produced flowing robes of white spider-fur. His intention was to create a contrast, and it pleased her. 'Perfect,' she purred. 'Come, let's board your carriage and be off.'

They left his ranch (which was purposely preserved much as it had been when he had tried to prepare a home for his lost love, Mrs Amelia Underwood, before she had been projected back to her own 19th century) and crossed the well-tended lawns, where his deer and his buffalo no longer roamed, through the rockeries, rose bowers and Japanese gardens which reminded him so poignantly of Mrs Underwood, to his landau of milky jade. The landau was upholstered inside with the skins of apricot-coloured vynyls (beasts now long extinct) and trimmed with green gold.

The Iron Orchid settled herself in the carriage and Jherek seated himself opposite, tapping a rail as a signal for the carriage to ascend. Someone (not himself) had produced a lovely, round yellow sun and gorgeous blue clouds, while below them rolled gentle grassy hills, woods of pine and clover-trees, rivers of amber and silver, rich and restful to the eye. There was miles and miles of it. They headed in a roughly southerly direction, towards Shanalorm.

They crossed a viscous white and foamy sea from which pink creatures, not unlike gigantic earthworms, poked either their heads or their tails (or both), and they speculated on its creator.

'Unfortunately, it is probably Werther,' said the Iron Orchid. 'How he strives against an ordinary aesthetic! Is this another example of his Nature, do you think? It certainly seems primitive.'

They were glad to have the white sea behind them. Now they floated over high salt crags which glittered in the light of a reddish orb which was probably the real sun. There was a silence in this landscape which thrilled them both and they did not speak until it was passed.

'Nearly there,' said the Iron Orchid, peering over the side of the landau (actually she had absolutely no clear idea where they were and had no need to know, for Jherek had given the carriage clear instructions). Jherek smiled, delighting in his mother's enthusiasms. She always enjoyed their outings together.

Caught by a gust of air, his spider-fur draperies lifted around him, all but obscuring his view. He patted them down so that their whiteness spread across the seat and at that moment, for a reason he could not define, he thought of Mrs Underwood and his brow clouded. It had been much longer than he had expected. He was sure that she would have returned by now if she could. He knew that soon he must visit the ill-tempered old scientist, Brannart Morphail, and beg him for the use of another time machine. Morphail had claimed that Mrs Underwood, subject as anyone else to the Morphail Effect, would soon be ejected from 1896 and might wind up in any period of time covered by the past million years, but Jherek was sure that she would return to this Age. After all, they were in love. She had admitted, at long last, that she loved him. Jherek wondered if Brannart, determined to prove his theory flawless, were actually blocking Mrs Underwood's attempts to get to him. He knew that the suspicion was unfair, but it was already obvious that both My Lady Charlotina and Lord Jagged of Canaria were playing complicated games involving his and Mrs Underwood's fates. He had taken this in good part so far, but he was beginning to wonder if the joke were not beginning to pall.

The Iron Orchid had noticed his change of mood. She leaned across and stroked his forehead. 'Melancholy, again, my love?'

'Forgive me, finest of flowers.' With an effort he cleared his face of lines. He smiled. He was glad when, at that moment, he noticed violet light pulsing on the horizon. 'Shanalorm looms. See!'

As she turned, her face was a black mirror reflecting the delicate radiation. 'Ah, at last!'

They entered a landscape that none chose to change; not merely because it was so fine, but also because it might have been unwise to tamper with the sources of their power. Cities like Shanalorm had been built over the course of many centuries and they were very old. It had been said that they were capable of converting the energy of the entire cosmos, that the universe could be created afresh by means of their mysterious engines, but no one had ever dared to test this pronouncement. Though few had bothered to do so in the past couple of millennia (it was currently considered vulgar) it was certainly possible to make any number of new stars or planets. The cities would last as long as Time itself (which was not that long, if Yusharisp, the little alien who had gone into space with Lord Mongrove, was to be believed).

Beneath its canopy of violet light, which did not seem to penetrate to the city itself, Shanalorm lay dreaming. Some of its bizarre buildings had melted and remained in a semi-liquid state, their outlines still discernible; other buildings were festering – machine mould and energy-moss undulated across their shells, bright yellow-green, bile-blue and reddish-brown, groaning and whispering as it sought fresh seepages from the power-reservoirs; peculiar little animals, indigenous to the cities, scuttled in and out of openings which might have been doors and windows, through shadows of pale blue, scarlet and mauve, cast by nothing visible; they swam through pools of glittering gold and turquoise, feasting off half-metallic plants which in turn were nurtured by queer radiations and cryptically structured crystals. And all the while Shanalorm sang to itself, a thousand interweaving songs, hypnotic harmonies. Once, it was said, the whole city had been sentient, the most intelligent being in the universe, but now it was senile and even its memories were fragmented. Images flickered here and there among the rotting jewel-metal of the buildings; scenes of Shanalorm's glories, of its inhabitants, of its history. It had had many names before it was called Shanalorm.

'Isn't it pretty, Jherek!' cried the Iron Orchid. 'Where shall we have our picnic?'

Jherek stroked part of the landau's rail and the carriage began to spiral very slowly down until it was floating between the towers, skimming just above the roofs of blocks and domes and globes which shone with a thousand indefinable shades. 'There?' He indicated a pool of ruby-coloured liquid overhung with old trees, their long, rusted branches touching the surface. A soft, red-gold moss crept down to the bank and tiny, tinkling insects made sparkling trails of amber and amethyst through the air.

'Oh, yes! It's perfect!'

As he landed the carriage and she stepped daintily out, she raised a finger to her lips, staring around at the scene with an expression of faint recognition.

'Is this...? Could it be...? Jherek, you know, I believe this is where you were *conceived*, my egg. Your father and I were walking' – she pointed at a complex of low buildings on the opposite shore, just visible through a drifting, yellow mist – 'over there! When the conversa-

176

tion turned, as it will in such places, to the customs of the ancients. I think we were discussing the Dead Sciences. As it happened, he had been studying some old text on biological restructuring, and we wondered if it was still possible to create a child according to Dawn Age practices.' She laughed. 'The mistakes we made at first! But eventually we got the hang of it and here you are – a creature of quality, the product of skilled craftsmanship. Possibly that is why I cherish you so deeply, with such pride.'

Jherek took her hand of gleaming jet. He kissed the tips of her fingers. Gently, he stroked her back. He could say nothing, but his hands were gentle, his expression tender. He knew her well enough to know that she was strangely excited.

They lay down together on the comfortable moss, listening to the music of the city, watching the insects dancing in the predominantly violet light.

'It is the peace, I believe, that I treasure most,' murmured the Iron Orchid, moving her head luxuriously against his shoulder, 'the antique peace. Have we lost something, do you think, that our forefathers possessed, some quality of experience? Werther believes that we have.'

Jherek smiled. 'It is my understanding, most glorious of blooms, that individuals are given to individual experiences. We can make of the past anything we choose.'

'And of the future?' said she dreamily, inconsequently.

'If Yusharisp's warnings are to be taken seriously, then the future fades; there is scarcely any left.'

But he had lost her attention. She got up and walked to the edge of the pool. Below the surface warm colours writhed and, entranced for the moment, she stared at them. 'I should regret...' she began, then paused, shaking her dusky hair. 'Ah, the *smells*, Jherek. Are they not sublime?'

He raised himself to his feet and went to join her, a billowing cloud of white as he moved. He took a deep breath of the chemical atmosphere and his body glowed.

He looked across the pool at the outline of the city, wondering how it had changed since it had been populated by humankind, when people had lived their lives among its engines and its mills, before it had become self-sufficient, no longer needing tending. Did it ever suffer loneliness, he thought, or miss what must have seemed to it, at last, the clumsy, affectionate attentions of the engineers who had brought it to life? Had Shanalorm's inhabitants drifted away from the city, or had the city rejected them? He put an arm around his mother's shoulders, but he realized that it was himself shivering, touched for a moment by an inexplicable chill.

'They are sublime,' he said.

'Not dissimilar, I suppose, to the one you visited – to London?'

'It is a city,' he agreed, 'and they do not alter much in their essentials.' And he felt another pang, so he laughed and said: 'What shall be the colours of our meal today?'

'Ice white and berry-blue,' she said. 'Those little snails with their azure shells – where are they from? And plums! What else? Aspirin in jelly?'

'Not today. I find it a trifle insipid. Shall we have a snow-fish of some sort?'

'Absolutely!' Removing her gown, she flicked it out over the moss and it became a silvery cloth. Together they arranged the food, seating themselves on opposite sides of the cloth.

But when it was ready Jherek did not feel hungry. To please his mother, he sampled some fish, a sip or two of mineral water, a morsel of heroin, and was glad when she herself became bored with the meal and suggested that they disseminate it. No matter how much he tried to give his whole heart to his mother's enthusiasm, he found that he still could not purge himself of a vague feeling of unease. He knew that he would like to be elsewhere but knew, too, that there was nowhere in the world he could go and be rid of his sense of dissatisfaction. He noticed that she was smiling.

'Jherek! You sag, my dear! You mope! Perhaps the time has come to forget your rôle – to give it up in favour of one which can be better realized?'

'I cannot forget Mrs Underwood.'

'I admire your resolution. I have told you so already. I merely remind you, from my own knowledge of the classics, that passion, like a perfect rose, must finally fade. Perhaps it is time to begin fading a little?'

'Never.'

She shrugged. 'It is your drama and you must be faithful to it, of course. I would be the first to question the wisdom of veering from the original conception. Your taste, your tone, your touch – they are exquisite. I shall argue no further.'

'It appears to go beyond taste,' said Jherek, picking at a piece of bark and making it thrum gently against the bole of the tree. 'It is difficult to explain.'

'What truly important work of art is not?'

He nodded. 'You are right, Iron Orchid. That is all it is.'

'It will soon resolve itself, fruit of my seed.' She linked her arm in his. 'Come, let us walk for a while through these tranquil streets. You might find inspiration here.'

He allowed her to lead him across the pool while she, still in a mood of fond reminiscence, talked of his father's love of this particular city and the profound knowledge he had had of its history.

'And you never knew who my father was?'

'No. Wasn't it delicious? He remained in disguise throughout. We were in love for weeks!'

'No clues?'

'Oh, well...' She laughed lightly. 'It would have spoiled it to have pursued the secret too fiercely, you know.'

Beneath their feet some buried transformer sighed and made the ground tremble.

CHAPTER TWO

PLAYING AT SHIPS

'I sometimes wonder,' said the Iron Orchid as Jherek's landau carried them away from Shanalorm, 'where all the current craze for Dawn Age discoveries is leading.'

'Leading, my life?'

'Artistically, I mean. Soon, largely because of the fashion you began, we shall have re-created that age down to the finest details. It will be like inhabiting the 19th century.'

'Yes, metallic magnificence?' He was polite but still unable to follow her drift.

'I mean, are we not in danger of taking Realism too far, Jherek? One's own imagination can become clogged,

180

after all. It was always your argument that travelling into the past rather spoiled one's conception – made the outlines fuzzy, as it were – inhibited creativity.'

'Perhaps,' he agreed. 'But I am not sure my "London" is harmed from being inspired by experience rather than fantasy. The fad could go too far, of course. In the case, for instance, of the Duke of Queens...'

'I know you rarely favour his work. It can be extravagant sometimes, a little, I suppose, empty, but ...'

'It is his tendency to vulgarize which disturbs me, to pile effect upon effect. I think he showed restraint in his "New York, 1930", for all the obvious influence of my own piece. Such influences might be good for him.'

'He, among others, could take it too far,' she said. 'That is what I meant.' Then she shrugged. 'But soon you'll set a fresh fashion, Jherek, and they will follow that.' She spoke almost wistfully, almost hopefully. 'You will guide them away from excess.'

'You are kind.'

'Oh, more!' Her raven face lit with humour. 'I am biased, my dear! You are my son!'

'I heard that the Duke of Queens had completed his "New York". Shall we go to see it?'

'Why not? And let us hope he'll be there, too. I am very fond of the Duke of Queens.'

'As am I, for all that I do not share his tastes.'

'He shares yours. You should be more generous.'

They laughed.

The Duke of Queens was delighted to see them. He stood some distance away from his design, admiring it with unashamed pleasure. He was dressed in a style of the 800th century, all crystal spirals and curlicues, beast eyes and paper bosses, with gauntlets which made his hands invisible. His sensitive face with its heavy black beard turned upwards as he called to Jherek and his mother:

'Iron Orchid, in all your swarthy beauty! And Jherek! I give you full credit, my dear, for your original inspiration. Regard this as a tribute to your genius!'

Jherek warmed to the Duke of Queens, as always. His taste might not have been all it could be, but his generosity was unquestionable. He determined to praise the Duke's creation, no matter what he thought of it privately.

It was, in fact, a relatively moderate affair.

'It is from the same period as your "London", as you can see. Very true to the original, I think.'

The Iron Orchid's hand tightened momentarily on Jherek's arm as they descended from the landau, as if to confirm the validity of her judgement.

'That tallest tower at the centre is the Empire State Apartments, in lapis lazuli and gold, built as the home of New York's greatest king (Kong the Mighty) who, as you know, ruled the city during its Golden Age. The bronze statue you see on the top of the building is Kong's...'

'He looks beautiful,' said the Iron Orchid, 'but almost inhuman.'

'It *was* the Dawn Age,' said the Duke. 'The building is just over a mile and a quarter high (I took the dimensions from an historical text-book) and a splendid example of the barbaric simplicity of typical architecture of the early Uranium Centuries – almost too early, some would say.'

Jherek wondered if the Duke of Queens were quoting whole from the text-book; his words had that ring to them.

'Are not the buildings crowded together rather?' said the Iron Orchid.

The Duke of Queens was not offended. 'Deliberately,' he told her. 'The epics of the time made constant references to the narrowness of the streets, forcing people to move crabwise – hence the distinctive "sidewalk" of New York.'

'And what are those?' said Jherek, pointing to a collection of picturesque thatched cottages. 'They seem untypical.'

'It is the village of Greenwich, a kind of museum frequented by sailors. A famous vessel was moored in the river. Can you see it?' He indicated something tied to a jetty, it glinted in the dark water of a lagoon.

'It appears to be a gigantic glass bottle,' said the Iron Orchid.

'So I thought, but somehow they managed to sail in them. Doubtless the secret of their locomotion has been lost, but I based the ship on a model of one I came across in a record. It is called the *Cutty Sark*.' The Duke of Queens permitted himself a smirk. 'And that, my dear Jherek, is where I have had the privilege of being imitated. My Lady Charlotina was so impressed that she has begun a reproduction of some other famous ship of the period.'

'I must say that your sense of detail is impressive,' Jherek complimented him. 'And have you populated the city?' He screwed up his eyes the better to see. 'Are those figures moving about in it?'

'They are! Eight million of them.'

'And what are those tiny flashes of light?' enquired the Iron Orchid.

'The muggers,' said the Duke of Queens. 'At that time New York attracted a good many artists, primarily photographers (called popularly "shooters", "muggers", or sometimes "mug-shotters") and what you see are their cameras in action.'

'You have a talent for thorough research,' said Jherek.

'I owe much to my sources, I admit,' agreed the Duke of Queens. 'And I found a time traveller in my menagerie who was able to help. He wasn't from exactly the same period, but close enough to have seen many records of the time. Most of the other buildings are in lurex and coloured perspex, favourite materials of Dawn Age craftsmen. The protective talismans are, of course, in neon, to ward off the forces of darkness.'

'Ah, yes,' said the Iron Orchid brightly. 'Gaf the Horse

183

in Tears had something similar in his "Canceropolis, 2215".'

'Really?' The Duke's tone was unintentionally distant. He was not fond of Gaf's work and had been known to describe it once as 'over-eager'. 'I must go to see it.'

'It's on the same theme as Argonheart Po's "Edible Birmingham, Undated", I believe,' said Jherek, to turn the subject a little. 'I tried it a day or two ago. It was delicious.'

'What he lacks in visual originality, he makes up for in culinary imagination.'

'Definitely a Birmingham of the mind,' agreed the Iron Orchid, 'and for the palate. Some of the buildings were blatant copies of My Lady Charlotina's "Rome, 1946".'

'A shame about the lions,' murmured the Duke of Queens sympathetically.

'They got out of control,' said the Iron Orchid. 'I warned her that they would. Not enough Christians. Still, I thought it drastic to disseminate it, merely because the population was eaten. But the flying elephants were lovely, weren't they?'

'I'd never seen a circus before,' said Jherek.

'I was just about to leave for Lake Billy the Kid, where some of the ships are being launched.' The Duke of Queens indicated his latest air car, a vast copy of one of the Martian flying machines which had attempted to destroy New York during the period in which he took an interest. 'Would you like to come?'

'A wonderful idea,' said the Iron Orchid and Jherek, thinking that one way of passing the time was as good as another, agreed.

'We shall follow in my landau,' he said.

The Duke of Queens gestured with one of his invisible hands. 'There is plenty of room in my air car, but just as you like.' He felt beneath his crystalline robes and produced a flying helmet and goggles. Donning them, he strode to his carriage, climbed with some difficulty up the smooth side and settled himself in the cock-pit.

184

Jherek watched in amusement as there came a roaring from the machine, a glow which was soon red-hot, a shower of sparks and a considerable amount of blue smoke, and then the contraption was lurching upwards. The Duke of Queens seemed to specialize in exceedingly unstable methods of transport.

Lake Billy the Kid had been enlarged for the occasion of the regatta (this, in itself, was unusual) and the surrounding mountains had all been moved back to accommodate the extra water. Small groups of people were gathered here and there on the shore, staring at the ships which had so far been presented. They made a fine collection.

Jherek and the Iron Orchid landed on the white ash of the beach and joined the Duke of Queens who was already talking to their hostess. My Lady Charlotina still wore several breasts and an extra pair of arms and her skin was a delicate blue; for decoration she had a collar from which trailed a few gauzy wisps of various colours. Her large eyes were alight with pleasure at seeing them.

'Iron Orchid, still in mourning I see. And Jherek Carnelian, most famous of metatemporal explorers. I had not expected you.'

Slightly put out, the Iron Orchid unostentatiously changed her skin colour to a more natural shade. Her gown became suddenly so blindingly white that they all blinked. She toned it down, murmuring apologies. 'Which of the boats is yours, dear?'

My Lady Charlotina pursed her lips in mock disapproval. '*Ships*, most venerable of plants. That one is mine.' She inclined her head in the direction of an immense reproduction of a woman, lying stomach-down in the water, her arms and legs spread out symmetrically, a crown of gold and diamonds upon her wooden head. 'The *Queen Elizabeth*.'

As they watched, a great gust of blackness billowed from the ears of the model and from the mouth (barely above the surface) there came a melancholy tooting.

'The one beside it is the *Monitor*, which carried off some virgins or something, did it not?' This was smaller than the *Queen Elizabeth*; the vessel's bulk representing a man's body, its back arched inwards, with a huge bull's head on its shoulders. 'O'Kala Incarnadine simply can't rid himself of his obsession with beasts. It's sweet, really.'

'Are they all of the same period?' asked the Duke of Queens. 'That one, for instance?' He pointed to a rather shapeless ship. 'It looks more like an island.'

'That's the S.S. *France*,' explained My Lady Charlotina. 'It's Grevol Lockspring's entry. The one just steaming towards it is the *Water Lily* – I'm sure it wasn't a real plant.' She named some of the other peculiarly wrought vessels. 'The *Mary Rose*. The *Hindenburg*. The *Patna*. And isn't that one beautiful – stately – The *Leningrad*?'

'They are all lovely,' said the Iron Orchid vaguely. 'What will they do when they are assembled?'

'Fight, of course,' said My Lady Charlotina in excitement. 'That's what they were built for, you see, in the Dawn Age. Imagine the scene – a heavy mist on the waters – two ships manoeuvring, each aware of the other, neither being able to find the other. It is, say, my *Queen Elizabeth* and Argonheart Po's *Nautilus* (I fear it will melt before the regatta is finished). The *Nautilus* sees the *Queen Elizabeth*, its foghorns disperse the mist, it focuses its funnels and – *whoosh!* – the *Queen Elizabeth* is struck by thousands of little belaying needles – she shudders and retaliates – from her forward ports (they must have been her breasts; that is where I've put them, at any rate) pour lethal tuxedos, wrapping themselves around the *Nautilus* and trying to drag it under. But the *Nautilus* is not so easily defeated ... Well, you can imagine the rest, and I will not spoil the actual regatta for you. Almost all the ships are here now. I believe there are a couple of entries to come, then we begin.'

'I cannot wait,' said Jherek absently. 'Is Brannart Morphail, by the by, still residing with you, My Lady Charlotina?'

'He has apartments at Below-the-Lake, yes. He is there now, I would guess. I asked him for help with the design of the *Queen Elizabeth*, but he was too busy.'

'Is he still angry with me?'

'Well, you did lose one of his favourite time machines.'

'It hasn't returned, then?'

'No. Are you expecting it?'

'I thought, perhaps, Mrs Underwood would use it to come back to us. You would tell me if she did?'

'You know that I would. Your relationship with her is my abiding interest.'

'Thank you. And have you seen Lord Jagged of Canaria recently?'

'He was supposed to come today. He half-promised to contribute a ship, but he is doubtless as lazy as ever and has forgotten. He might well be in one of those strange, unsociable moods of his. He retires, as you know, from society from time to time. Oh, Mistress Christia, what is this?'

The Everlasting Concubine fluttered long lashes over her wide, blue eyes. She was clad in filmy pink, with a pink hat perched on her golden hair. Her hands were dressed in pink gloves and she was presenting something which rested on her outstretched palms. 'It is not an entry, exactly,' she said, 'but I thought you might like it.'

'I do! What is it called?'

'The *Good Ship Venus*.' Mistress Christia smiled at Jherek. 'Hello, my dear. Does the flame of your lust burn as strongly as ever?'

'I am in love, these days,' he said.

'You draw a distinction.'

'I have been assured that there is one.' He kissed her upon her perfect nose. She tickled his ear.

'Where do you discover all these wonderful old emotions?' she asked. 'You must talk to Werther – he has the same interests, but does not pursue them with your panache, I am afraid. Has he told you about his "sin"?'

'I have not seen him since my return from 1896.'

My Lady Charlotina interrupted, placing a caressing hand upon Mistress Christia's thigh. 'Werther excelled himself – and so did you, Everlasting Concubine. Surely you aren't criticizing him?'

'How could I? I *must* tell you about Werther's "crime", Jherek. It all began on the day that I accidentally broke his rainbow...' And she embarked upon a story which Jherek found fascinating, not merely because it was really a very fine story, but also because it seemed to relate to some of the ideas he was himself mulling over. He wished that he found Werther better company, but every time he tried to have a conversation with the gloomy solitary, Werther would accuse him of being superficial or insensitive and the whole thing would descend into a series of puzzled questions on Jherek's part and recriminations on Werther's.

Mistress Christia and Jherek Carnelian strolled arm in arm along the shore while the Everlasting Concubine chatted merrily on. Out on Lake Billy the Kid the ships were beginning to take up their positions. The sun shone down on blue, placid water; from here and there came the murmur of animated conversation and Jherek found his good humour returning as Mistress Christia drew to the close of her tale.

'I hope Werther was grateful,' he said.

'He was. He *is* very sincere, Jherek, but in a different sort of way.'

'I need no convincing. Tell me, did he—?' And he broke off as he recognized a tall figure standing by the water's edge, deep in conversation with Argonheart Po (who was, as always, wearing his tall chef's cap). 'Excuse me, Mistress Christia. You will not think me rude if I speak to Lord Jagged?'

'You could never offend me, delicacy.'

'Lord Jagged!' called Jherek. 'How pleased I am to see you here.'

Handsome, weary, his long, pale face wearing just a shade of a smile, Lord Jagged turned. He wore scarlet silk, with one of his usual high, padded collars framing a head of shoulder-length near-white hair.

'Jherek, spice to my life! Argonheart Po was just giving me the recipe for his ship. He assures me that, contrary to the gossip, it cannot melt for at least another four hours. You will be as interested as I to hear how he accomplished the feat.'

'Good afternoon, Argonheart,' said Jherek with a nod to the fat and beaming inventor of, among other things, the savoury volcano. 'I was hoping, Lord Jagged, to have a word...'

Argonheart Po was already moving away, his hand held tightly by the ever tactful Mistress Christia.

'...about Mrs Underwood,' concluded Jherek.

'She is back?' Lord Jagged's aquiline features were expressionless.

'You know that she is not.'

Lord Jagged's smile broadened a fraction. 'You are beginning to credit me with prescience of some sort, Jherek. I am flattered, but I do not deserve the distinction.'

Disturbed because of this recent, subtle alteration in their old relationship, Jherek bowed his head. 'Forgive me, jaunty Jagged. I am full of assumptions. I am, in the words of the ancients, "over-excited".'

'Perhaps you have contracted one of those old diseases, my breath? The kind which could only be transmitted by word of mouth – which attacked the brain and made the brain attack the body...'

'Dawn Age science is your speciality, rather than mine, Lord Jagged. If you are making a considered diagnosis ...?'

Lord Jagged laughed one of his rare, hearty laughs and he flung his arm around his friend's shoulders.

'My luscious, loving larrikin, my golden goose, my grief, my prayer. You are healthy! I suspect that you are the only one of us that is!'

And, his usual, cryptic self, he refused to expand on this statement, drawing Jherek's attention, instead, to the regatta, which had begun at last. A vile yellow mist had been spread across the sparkling sea, making all murky; the sun had been dimmed, and great, shadowy shapes crept, honking, through the water.

Jagged arranged his collar about his face, but he kept his arm round Jherek's shoulders. 'They will fight to the death, I'm told.'

CHAPTER THREE

A PETITIONER AT THE COURT OF TIME

'What else is it but decadence,' said Li Pao, My Lady Charlotina's resident bore (and, like most time travellers, dreadfully literal-minded), 'when you spend your days in imitation of the past? And it is not as if you imitated the virtues of the past.' He brushed pettishly at his faded denim suit. He took off his denim cap and wiped his brow.

'Virtues?' murmured the Iron Orchid enquiringly. She had heard the word before.

'The best of the past. Its customs, its morals, its traditions, its standards...'

'Flags?' said Gaf the Horse in Tears, looking up from

191

an inspection of his new penis.

'Li Pao's words are always so hard to translate,' said My Lady Charlotina, their hostess. They had repaired to her vast palace under the lake and she was serving them with rum and hard tack. Every ship had been sunk. 'You don't really mean flags, do you, dear?'

'Only in a manner of speaking,' said Li Pao, anxious not to lose his audience. 'If by flags we refer to loyalties, to causes, to a sense of purpose.'

Even Jherek Carnelian, an expert in Dawn Age philosophies, could scarcely keep up with him. When the Iron Orchid turned to him in appeal to explain, he could only shrug and smile.

'My point,' said Li Pao, raising his voice a fraction, 'is that you could use all this to some advantage. The alien, Yusharisp...'

The Duke of Queens coughed in embarrassment.

'... had news of inescapable cataclysm. Or, at least, he thought it inescapable. There is a chance that you could save the universe with your scientific resources.'

'We don't really understand them any more, you see,' gently explained Mistress Christia, kneeling beside Gaf the Horse in Tears. 'It's a marvellous colour,' she said to Gaf.

'There are many here – prisoners of your whims, like myself – who, if given the opportunity, might learn the principles involved,' Li Pao went on, 'Jherek Carnelian, you are bent on rediscovering all the old virtues, surely you see my point?'

'Not really,' said Jherek. 'Why would you wish to save the universe? Is it not better to let it go its natural course?'

'There were mystics in my day,' said Li Pao, 'who considered it unwise to, as they put it, "tamper with nature". But if they had been listened to, you would not have the power you possess today.'

'We would still have been happy, doubtless,' O'Kala Incarnadine chewed patiently at his hard tack, his voice somewhat bleating in tone, owing to his having re-modelled his body into that of a sheep. 'One does not need power, surely, to be happy?'

'That was not exactly what I was trying to say.' Li Pao's lovely yellow skin had turned very slightly pink. 'You are immortal – yet you will still perish when the planet itself is destroyed. In perhaps two hundred years you will be dead. Do you want to die?'

My Lady Charlotina yawned. 'Most of us have died at some stage. Quite recently, Werther de Goethe hurled himself to his death on some rocks. Didn't you, Werther?'

Dark-visaged Werther sipped moodily at his rum. He gave a sigh of assent.

'But I speak of permanent death – without resurrection.' Li Pao sounded almost desperate. 'You must understand. None of you are unintelligent...'

'I am unintelligent,' said Mistress Christia, her pride wounded.

'So you say.' Li Pao dismissed her plea. 'Do you want to be dead for ever, Mistress Christia?'

'I have never considered the question that much. I suppose not. But it would make no difference, would it?'

'To what?'

'To me. If I were dead.'

Li Pao frowned.

'We would all be better off dead, useless eaters of the lotus that we are.' Werther de Goethe's jarring monotone came from the far side of the room. He glared down at his reflection in the floor.

'You speak only of postures, Werther,' the ex-member of the governing committee of the 27th century People's Republic admonished. 'Of poetic rôles. I speak of reality.'

'Is there nothing real about poetic rôles?' Lord Jagged of Canaria strolled across the room, admiring the flowers which grew from the ceiling. 'Was not your rôle ever poetic, Li Pao, when you were in your own time?'

'Poetic? Never. Idealistic, of course, but we were dealing with harsh facts.'

'There are many forms of poetry, I understand.'

'You are merely seeking to confuse my argument, Lord Jagged. I know you of old.'

'I thought I aimed at clarification. By metaphor, perhaps,' he admitted, 'and that does not always seem to clarify. Though it works very well for some.'

'I believe you deliberately oppose my arguments because you half-agree with them yourself.' Li Pao plainly felt he had scored a good point.

'I half-agree with *all* arguments, my dear!' Lord Jagged's smile seemed a touch weary. 'Everything is real. Or can be made real.'

'With the resources at your command, certainly.' Li Pao agreed.

'It is not exactly my meaning. You made your dream real, did you not? Of the Republic?'

'It was founded on reality.'

'My scanty acquaintance with your period does not allow me to dispute that statement with any fire, I fear. Whose dream, I wonder, laid those foundations?'

'Well, *dreams*, yes...'

'Poetic inspiration?'

'Well...'

Lord Jagged drew his great robe about him. 'Forgive me, Li Pao, for I realize that I *have* confused your argument. Please continue. I shall interrupt no further.'

But Li Pao had lost impetus. He fell into a sulking silence.

'There is a rumour, magnificent Lord Jagged, that you yourself have travelled in time. Do you speak from direct experience of Li Pao's period?' Mistress Christia raised her head from its contact with Gaf's groin.

'As a great believer in the inherent possibilities of the rumour as art,' said Lord Jagged gently, 'it is not for me to confirm or deny any gossip you might have heard, sweet Mistress Christia.'

'Oh, absolutely!' She gave her full attention back to Gaf's anatomy.

Not without difficulty, Jherek held back from taxing Lord Jagged further on that particular subject, but Jagged continued:

'There are some who would argue that Time does not really exist at all, that it is merely our primitive minds which impose a certain order upon events. I have heard it said that everything is happening, as it were, concurrently. Some of the greatest inventors of time machines have used that theory to advantage.'

Jherek, desperately feigning lack of interest, poured himself a fresh tot. When he spoke, however, his tone was not entirely normal.

'Would it be possible, I wonder, to make a new time machine? If Shanalorm's or some other city's memories were reliable...'

'They are not!' The querulous voice of Brannart Morphail broke in. He had added an inch or two to his hump since Jherek had last encountered him. His club foot was decidedly over-done. He came limping across the floor, his smock covered in residual spots of the various substances in his laboratories. 'I have visited every one of the rotted cities. They give us their power, but their wisdom has faded. I was listening to your discourse, Lord Jagged. It is a familiar theory, favoured by the non-scientist. I assure you, none the less, that one gets nowhere with Time unless one treats it as linear.'

'Brannart,' said Jherek hesitantly, 'I was hoping to see you here.'

'Are you bent on pestering me further, Jherek? I have not forgotten that you lost me one of my best time machines.'

'No sign of it, then?'

'None. My instruments are too crude to detect it if, as I suspect, it has gone back to some pre-Dawn period.'

'What of the cyclic theory?' Lord Jagged said. 'Would you give any credence to that?'

'So far as it corresponds to certain physical laws, yes.'

'And how would that relate to the information we were

195

given by the Duke's little alien?'

'I had hoped to ask Yusharisp some questions – and so I might have done if Jherek had not interfered.'

'I am sorry,' said Jherek, 'but ...'

'You are living proof of the non-mutability of Time,' said Brannart Morphail. 'If you could go back and set to rights the events brought about by your silly meddling, then you would be able to prove your remorse. As it is, you can't, so I would ask you to stop expressing it!'

Pointedly, Brannart Morphail turned to Lord Jagged, a crooked, insincere grin upon his ancient features. 'Now, dear Lord Jagged, you were saying something about the cyclic nature of Time?'

'I think you are a little hard on Jherek,' said Lord Jagged. 'After all, My Lady Charlotina knew, to some extent, the outcome of her joke.'

'We'll speak no more of that. You wondered if Yusharisp's reference to the death of the cosmos – of the universe ending one cycle and beginning another – bore directly upon the cyclic theory?'

'It was a passing thought, nothing more,' said Lord Jagged, looking back over his shoulder and winking at Jherek. 'You should be kinder, Brannart, to the boy. He could bring you information of considerable usefulness in your experiments, surely? I believe you feel angry with him because his experiences are inclined to contradict your theories.'

'Nonsense! It is his interpretation of his experiences with which I disagree. They are naïve.'

'They are true,' said Jherek in a small voice. 'Mrs Underwood said that she would join me, you know. I am sure that she will.'

'Impossible – or, at very least, unlikely. Time does not permit paradoxes. The Morphail Theory specifically shows that once a time traveller has visited the future he cannot return to the past for any length of time; similarly any stay in the past is limited, for the reason that if he did stay there he could alter the course of the future and therefore produce chaos. The Morphail Effect is my term to describe an actual phenomenon – the fact that no one has ever been able to move backwards in Time and *remain* in the past. Merely because your stay in the Dawn Age was unusually long you cannot insist that there is a flaw in my description. The chances of your 19th-century lady being returned to this point in time are, similarly, very slight – millions to one. You could search for her, of course, through the millennia, and, if you were successful, bring her back here. She has no time machine of her own and therefore cannot control her flight into her future.'

'They had primitive time machines in those days,' Jherek said. 'There are many references to them in the literature.'

'Possibly, but *we* have never encountered another from her period. How she got here at all remains a mystery.'

'Some other time traveller brought her, perhaps?' Jherek was tentative, glad, at last, to have Brannart's ear. Privately, he thanked Lord Jagged for making it possible. 'She once mentioned a hooded figure who came into her room shortly before she found herself in our Age.'

'Yet,' said Morphail agitatedly, 'I have told you repeatedly that I have no record of a time machine materializing during the phase in which you claim she arrived. Since I last spoke with you, Jherek, I checked carefully. You are in error – or she lied to you ...'

'She cannot lie to me, as I cannot to her,' said Jherek simply. 'We are in love, you see.'

'Yes, yes! Play whatever games amuse you, Jherek Carnelian, but not at the expense of Brannart Morphail.'

'Ah, my wrinkled wonder-worker, can you not bring yourself to display a little more generosity towards our venturesome Jherek? Who else among us would dare the descent into Dawn Age emotions?'

'I would,' said Werther de Goethe, no longer in the distance. 'And with a better understanding of what I was doing, I would hope.'

'But your moods are dark moods, Werther,' said Lord Jagged kindly. 'They do not entertain as much as Jherek's!'

'I do not care what the majority thinks,' Werther told him. 'A more select group of people, I am told, think rather more of my explorations. Jherek has hardly touched on "sin" at all!'

'I could not understand it, vainglorious Werther, even when you explained it,' Jherek apologized. 'I have tried, particularly since it is an idea which my Mrs Underwood shared with you.'

'Tried,' said Werther contemptuously, 'and failed. I have not. Ask Mistress Christia.'

'She told me. I was very admiring. She will confirm —'

'Did you envy me?' A light of hope brightened Werther's doomy eye.

'Of course I did.'

Werther smiled. He sighed with satisfaction. Magnanimously he laid a hand upon Jherek's arm. 'Come to my tower some day. I will try to help you understand the nature of sin.'

'You are kind, Werther.'

'I seek only to enlighten, Jherek.'

'You will find it difficult, that particular task,' said Brannart Morphail spitefully. 'Improve his manners, Werther, and I, for one, will be eternally grateful to you.'

Jherek laughed. 'Brannart, are you not in danger of taking your "anger" too far?' He made a movement towards the scientist, who raised a six-fingered hand.

'No further petitions, please. Find your own time machine, if you want one. Persist in the delusion that your Dawn Age woman will return, if you wish. But do not, I beg you Jherek, involve me any further. Your ignorance is irritating and since you refuse the truth, then I'll have no more of you. I have my work.' He paused. 'If, of course, you were to bring me back the time machine you lost, then I might spare you a few moments.' And, chuckling, he began to return to his laboratories.

'He is wrong in one thing,' Jherek murmured to Lord Jagged, 'for they did have time machines in 1896, as you know. It was upon your instructions that I was placed in one and returned here.'

'Ah,' said Lord Jagged, studying the cloth of his sleeve. 'So you said before.'

'I am disconsolate,' said Jherek suddenly. 'You give me no direct answers (it is your right, of course) and Brannart refuses his help. What am I to do, Jagged?'

'Take pleasure in the experience, surely?'

'I seem to tire so easily of my pleasures, these days. And when it comes to ways of enjoying current experiences, my imagination flags, my brain betrays me.'

'Could your adventures in the past have tired you more than you realize?'

'I am certain it was you, Jagged, in 1896. It has occurred to me that even you are not aware of it!'

'Oh, Jherek, my jackanapes, what juicy abstractions you hint at! How close we are in temperament. You must expand upon your theories. Unconscious temporal adventurings!' Lord Jagged took Jherek's arm and led him back to where the main party had gathered.

'I base my idea,' began Jherek, 'on the understanding that you and I are good friends and that therefore you would not deliberately —'

'Later. I will listen later, my love, when our duties as guests are done.'

And again Jherek Carnelian was left wondering if Lord Jagged of Canaria were not, under his worldly airs, quite as confused as himself.

CHAPTER FOUR

TO THE WARM SNOW PEAKS

Bishop Castle had arrived late. He made a splendid entrance, in his huge head-dress twice as tall as himself and modelled on a stone tower of the Dawn Age. He had great, bushy red brows and long fine hair to match; it framed his saturnine features and fell to his chest. He wore robes of gold and silver and held the huge ornamental gearstick of some 21st-century religious order. He bowed to My Lady Charlotina.

'I left my contribution overhead, most handsome of hostesses. There were no others there, merely some flotsam on the surface. Am I to assume that I have missed the regatta?'

'You must, I am afraid.' My Lady Charlotina came towards him and took his long hand. 'But you shall have some of our naval fare.' She drew him towards the barrels of rum. 'Hot or cold?' she asked.

As Bishop Castle sipped the rum My Lady Charlotina described the battles which had taken place that day on Lake Billy the Kid. 'And the way in which Lady Voiceless's *Bismarck* sank my own *Queen Elizabeth* was ingenious, to say the least.'

'Scuppered below decks!' said Sweet Orb Mace with a relish for words which were meaningless to her. 'Hoisted by her holds. Spliced in her mainbrace! Belayed across the bows!' Her bright yellow, furry face became animated. 'Rammed,' she added, 'under the water-line.'

'Yes, dear. Your knowledge of nautical niceties is admirable.'

'Admiral!' giggled Sweet Orb Mace.

'Try a little less of the rum and a little more of the hard tack, dear,' suggested My Lady Charlotina, leading Bishop Castle to her hammock. Not without difficulty, he seated himself beside her (his hat was inclined to topple him over if he were not singularly careful). Bishop Castle noticed Jherek and waved his gearstick in a friendly greeting.

'Still pursuing your love, Jherek?'

'As best I can, mightiest of mitres.' Jherek left Lord Jagged's side. 'How are your giant owls?'

'Disseminated, I regret to say. I had it in mind to make a Vatican City in the same period as your London – I am a slave to fashion, as you know – but the only references I could find placed it on Mars about a thousand years later, so I must assume that it was not contemporary. A shame. A Hollywood I began came to nothing, so I gave up my efforts to emulate you. But when you are leaving, take a look at my ship. I hope you will approve of my careful research.'

'What is it called?'

'The *Mae West*,' said Bishop Castle. 'You know it, I

assume.'

'I do not! That makes it even more interesting.'

The Iron Orchid joined them, her features almost invisible in their glaring whiteness. 'We were considering a picnic in the Warm Snow Peaks, Charlotina. Would you care to come?'

'An exquisite idea! Of course I shall come. I think we have had the best of this entertainment now. And you, Jherek, will you go?'

'I think so. Unless Lord Jagged...' He turned to look for his friend, but Jagged had disappeared. He shrugged, reconciling himself. 'I would love it. It's ages since I visited the peaks. I had no notion that they still existed.'

'Weren't they something Mongrove made, in a lighter vein than usual?' Bishop Castle asked. 'Has anyone heard from Mongrove, by the by?'

'Not since he rushed off into space with Yusharisp,' the Iron Orchid told him, glancing about the hall. 'Where is the Duke of Queens? I had hoped he would wish to come with us.'

'One of his time travellers – he calls them "retainers", I understand – came to him with a message. The message animated him. He left with his eyes bright and his face flushed. Perhaps another traveller entering our Age?'

Jherek refused to be moved by this news. 'Did Lord Jagged go with him?'

'I am not sure. I wasn't aware he had gone.' My Lady Charlotina raised her slender eyebrows. 'Odd that he did not pay his respects. All this rushing and mystery whets my curiosity.'

'And mine,' said Jherek feelingly, but he was determined to remain as insouciant as possible and bide his time. If Amelia Underwood had come back, he would know soon enough. He rather admired his own self-control; he was even faintly astonished by it.

'Isn't the scenery piquant?' said the Iron Orchid with something of a proprietorial air. On the slope where they

202

had laid their picnic they could see for scores of miles. Below, there were plains and rivers and lakes of a rich variety of gentle colours. 'So unspoiled. It hasn't been touched since Mongrove made it.'

'I must admit to a preference for his earlier work,' agreed Bishop Castle, running sensual fingers through the glittering snow which spread across the flanks of the great eminences. It was primarily white, with just the subtlest hint of pale blue. A few little flowers poked their delicate heads above the surface of the snow. They were mainly indigenous to this sort of alpine terrain – orange verdigris and yellow bottlewurt were two which Jherek had recognized, and another which he guessed was some kind of greenish St Buck's Buttons.

Sweet Orb Mace, who had insisted on accompanying them, was rolling down the slope in a flurry of warm snow, laughing and shouting and rather destroying the tranquillity of the scene. The snow clung to her fur as she tried to get up and instead she slipped and slid further, hanging, helpless with mirth, over a precipice which must have been at least a thousand feet high. Then, the snows gave way and with a startled yell she fell.

'What *could* have possessed Mongrove to go into space?' said My Lady Charlotina with a token smile in the general direction of the vanished Sweet Orb Mace. 'I cannot believe that she could possibly have been your father, you know, Jherek, however good the disguise.'

'It was a very strong rumour at one time,' the Iron Orchid said, stroking her son's hair and plucking little particles of snow from it. 'But I agree, Charlotina, it would not be quite in Sweet Orb Mace's style. Do you think she's all right?'

'Oh, of course. And if she forgot to use her gravity neutralizer, we can always resurrect her later. Personally, I am glad of the peace.'

'I understood from Mongrove that he regarded it as his destiny to accompany Yusharisp,' Bishop Castle said. 'To warn the universe of its peril.'

'I could never understand his pleasure in passing on such news,' said My Lady Charlotina. 'It could alarm some cultures, could it not? I mean, think of the timid creatures we have had to look after from time to time when they have visited us. Many of them are so frightened at seeing people who do not look like themselves that they rush off back to their own planets as soon as they can. If we do not, of course, select them for a menagerie. I suspect that Mongrove's motives were rather different. I suspect that he had become thoroughly bored with his gloomy rôle but was too proud to change.'

'An acute insight, sextupedal siren,' said Jherek. 'It is probably accurate.' He smiled, affectionately remembering the way in which he had tricked the giant when Mrs Amelia Underwood had belonged to Mongrove's menagerie. Then he frowned. 'Ah, those were pleasant days.'

'You are not happy with this outing, Jherek?' My Lady Charlotina was concerned.

'I can think of nowhere I would rather be in this whole world,' he said tactfully, producing a convincing smile.

Only the Iron Orchid was not entirely relieved to hear these words. She said quietly to him: 'I am inclined to regret the appearance both of Yusharisp from Space and your Mrs Underwood from Time. It could be imagination, but it seems to me at this moment that they introduced a certain flavour into our society which I find not entirely palatable. You were once the joy of us all, Jherek, because of the enthusiasm you carried with you...'

'I assure you, most considerate of mothers, that my enthusiasm burns within me still. It is merely that I have nothing on which to focus it at present.' He patted her hand. 'I promise to be more amusing just as soon as my inspiration returns.'

Relieved, she lay back in the snow, crying out almost immediately: 'Oh, look! It is the Duke of Queens!'

None could fail to recognize the air car which came lumbering over the peaks in their direction – a genuine ornithopter in the shape of a huge hen, clanking and clucking its way through the sky, sometimes dropping dangerously low and at other times soaring so high as to be almost invisible. Its wide wings beat mightily at the air, its mechanical head glared this way and that as if in horrible confusion. The beak opened and shut rapidly, producing a strange clashing noise. And there, just visible, was the Duke's head, adorned by a huge, wide-brimmed hat festooned with plumes, a hand waving a long silver spear, a scarlet cloak billowing about him. He saw them and, erratically, aimed his hen in their direction, coming in so close that they flung themselves into the snow so as to avoid being struck. The ornithopter spiralled upwards, then spiralled down again, landing, at last, a few yards away and waddling towards them.

The Duke's beard fairly bristled with excitement. 'It is a Hunt, my dears. Some of my beaters are not too far away. You must join me!'

'A Hunt, darling Duke – for what?' asked Bishop Castle, arranging his hat on his head.

'Another alien – same race as Yusharisp – spotted in these parts – spaceship and everything. We found the ship, but the alien had gone to ground somewhere. We'll find him soon. Bound to. Where's your car? Ah – Jherek's. That will do. Come along! The chase grows hot!'

They looked at one another enquiringly, laughingly. 'Shall we?' said My Lady Charlotina.

'It will be fun,' said the Iron Orchid. 'Will it not, Jherek?'

'Indeed, it will!' Jherek began to race towards his landau, the other three at his heels. 'Lead the way, hardiest of hunters. Into the air! Into the air!'

The Duke of Queens rattled his silver spear against his chicken's metal wattles. The chicken clucked and crowed and its wings began to beat again. 'Ha ha! What sport!'

The chicken rose a few feet and then came down again, after a false start. Snow blew about in clouds around the ornithopter and from out of this blizzard there came the sound of the Duke's exasperated tones mingling with the almost embarrassed voice of the chicken as it tried to lift its bulk skyward. Jherek's landau was already circling the air before the Duke had managed to take off.

'He always regretted letting me have Yusharisp,' said My Lady Charlotina. 'The alien did not seem much of an addition to a menagerie at the time. One can understand his pleasure at discovering another. I do hope he is successful. We must do our best to help him, everyone. We must take the Hunt seriously.'

'Without question!' said Jherek. More than the others, he welcomed the excitement.

'I wonder if this one bears the same dull tidings,' said the Iron Orchid. Only she did not seem to be as entertained by their escapade as much as she might have been.

CHAPTER FIVE

ON THE HUNT

From somewhere beyond a line of low, green hills there came the moan of a hunting harp.

The Duke's chicken was above and ahead of them, but they heard his thin voice crying:

'To the West! To the West!'

They saw him wave his spear in that direction, saw him desperately trying to turn his bird, which had begun to take on more than the suggestion of a list; so much that the Duke had great difficulty maintaining his seat.

A word from Jherek and the landau leapt forward, causing Bishop Castle to whistle with glee and hang hard onto his hat. The pleasure of the ladies was also keen;

they leant far over the sides, threatening to fall, as they sought the elusive alien.

'Be careful, my dears!' called Bishop Castle above the wail of the wind. 'Remember that these aliens can sometimes be dangerous. They have all sorts of *weapons*, you know!' He raised a cautioning hand. 'You could miss the fun, if killed or maimed, for there would not be time to resurrect you until the Hunt was finished.'

'We shall be careful, Bishop – oh, we *shall* be!' My Lady Charlotina chuckled as she almost lost her grip on the landau's rail.

'Besides, Jherek has a gun to protect us, haven't you, produce of my lust?' The Iron Orchid pointed at a rather large object on the floor of the landau. 'We were playing with it a day or two ago.'

'A deceptor-gun is not exactly a weapon,' said Bishop Castle, picking it up and squinting down its wide, bell-shaped funnel. 'All it can produce is illusions.'

'But they are very *real*, Bishop.'

The Bishop had taken an interest in the antique. 'One of the oldest examples I have seen. Notice that it even has its own independent power source – here, at the side.'

The others, having absolutely no interest in the Bishop's hobby, pretended that they had not heard him.

'Gone away!' came the Duke's distant drone. 'Gone away!'

'What *can* he mean?' said an astonished Lady Charlotina. 'Jherek, do you know?'

'I believe he means we have become too greatly separated,' Jherek offered. 'I have been deliberately keeping back, to give him the pleasure of the first sighting. It is his game, after all.'

'And quite a good one, really,' said My Lady Charlotina.

They passed the hills, drawing closer to the Duke of Queens.

'His ornithopter seems, as it were, on its last wings,' said Bishop Castle. 'Should we offer him a lift?'

'I don't think he would thank us,' said Jherek. 'We must wait until he crashes.'

They were flying over a landscape Jherek could not remember having seen before. It looked edible and was therefore probably something Argonheart Po had made. There were whole villages, after the Gentraxian fashion, set among wobbling clumps of golden trees.

'Mmm.' The Iron Orchid smacked her lips. 'I feel quite hungry again. Could we not taste ...?'

'No time,' Jherek told her. 'I think I heard the harp again.'

The sky suddenly darkened and they sped through absolute blackness for a moment. Below them, they could detect the sound of a savage sea.

'We must be quite close to Werther's tower,' My Lady Charlotina suggested, re-arranging one of her several breasts, which had come loose.

And sure enough when the sky lightened to reveal boiling black clouds, there was Werther's mile-high monument to his moody ego.

'Those are the rocks,' said My Lady Charlotina, pointing at the base of the tower, 'where we found his body – dashed to fragments. Lord Jagged resurrected him. It took ages to gather all the pieces.'

Jherek remembered Sweet Orb Mace. If she had really fallen off the precipice, they should not leave her too long before restoring her.

The sun was shining again; the downs were green. 'There's the Earl of Carbolic's "Tokyo, 1901",' cried the Iron Orchid. 'What beautiful colours.'

'All reproductions of the original sea-shells,' Bishop Castle murmured knowingly.

The landau, dutifully following the Duke of Queens, veered suddenly and began to head towards the ground.

'He's down!' shouted Bishop Castle. 'Near that forest over there.'

'Is he hurt, Bishop?' The Iron Orchid was on the far side of the car.

'No. I can see him moving. He does not seem to be in a very good temper. He's hitting the ornithopter.'

'Poor thing.' My Lady Charlotina gasped as the landau bumped suddenly to earth.

Jherek left the carriage and began to walk towards the Duke of Queens. The Duke's hat was askew and one of his leggings was torn, but he was now, in all other respects, his normal self. He cast the spear aside, pushed back his hat, placed his hands on his hips and grinned at Jherek. 'Well, it was a good chase, eh?'

'Very stimulating. Your ornithopter is useless?'

'Utterly.'

The Duke of Queens felt it a point of pride to fly, for the most part, only authentic reproductions of ancient machines. He had often been counselled against the idea, but remained adamant – and much bruised.

'Can we take you back to your castle?' My Lady Charlotina asked.

'I'm not giving up. I'll continue the Hunt on foot. He'll be in those woods somewhere.' The Duke inclined his head in the direction of the nearby elms, cedars and mahoganies. 'My beaters will bring him towards us, if we're lucky. Will you come with me?'

Jherek shrugged. 'Willingly.'

They all began to march towards the woods and had gone a fair way before Bishop Castle lifted the deceptor-gun he still held in his hand. 'I'm sorry, I still have your antique. Shall I take it back, Jherek?'

'Bring it with you,' said Jherek. 'It might be useful in snaring the alien if we see him.'

'Good thinking,' said the Duke of Queens approvingly.

The wood was silent but for the faintest rustle of the leaves and the soft sounds of their footfalls on green, glowing moss. The trees smelled rich and sweet.

'Oh, isn't it *eerie*?' said My Lady Charlotina in breathless delight. 'A genuine old-fashioned Magic Wood. I wonder who made it.'

Jherek noticed that the quality of the light had

changed subtly, so that it was now a late summer evening; also the wood seemed to extend much further than he had at first supposed.

'It must be Lord Jagged's.' Bishop Castle removed his hat and stood leaning against it for a moment. 'Only he can capture this particular quality.'

'It does have Jagged's touch,' agreed the Iron Orchid, and she passed her arm through her son's.

'Then we must watch for mythical beasts,' said the Duke of Queens. 'Kangaroos and the like, if I know Jagged.'

The Iron Orchid squeezed Jherek's arm. 'I think it's getting darker,' she whispered.

CHAPTER SIX

THE BRIGAND MUSICIANS

The foliage above their heads was now so thick that
hardly any light came through at all. The silence had
deepened and, scarcely realizing what they were doing,
they all crept as quietly as possible over the moss, gently
pushing aside the low branches which increasingly
blocked their way.

My Lady Charlotina took Jherek's other arm, murmuring animatedly: 'We are like the babes in the bush. Do
you think we will be *lost*, Jherek?'

'It would be wonderful if we were,' said the Iron
Orchid, but Jherek said nothing. For some reason, the
mysterious wood had a healing effect upon his emotions.

He felt much calmer; more at ease than he had been for a long while. He wondered why the thought had occurred to him that he was, in this wood, somehow much closer to Mrs Underwood. He peered through the shadowy gloom, half-expecting to see her in her grey dress and straw hat, standing beside the bole of a cedar or a pine, smiling at him, ready to continue where she had left off with what she termed his 'moral education'.

Only the Duke of Queens was unaffected by the atmosphere. He paused, tugging at his black beard, and he frowned.

'The beaters must have detected something,' he complained. 'Why haven't we heard them?'

'The forest does seem to be rather larger than we had at first supposed.' Bishop Castle tapped his fingers against the barrel of the deceptor-gun. 'Could we be walking in the wrong direction, I wonder?'

Jherek and the two ladies had also stopped. Jherek himself was in something of a trance. It had been in a wood not dissimilar to this one where Mrs Amelia Underwood had kissed him, admitting, at last, her love for him – and from a wood like this one she had been whisked away, back to her own time. For a moment he considered the notion that Lord Jagged and My Lady Charlotina had planned a surprise for him, but it was obvious from My Lady Charlotina's behaviour that she had known nothing about this wood before they had discovered it. Jherek took a deep breath of the air. The predominant smell, he supposed, was of earth.

'What was that?' The Duke of Queens cupped a hand to his ear. 'A harp, was it?'

Bishop Castle had abandoned his hat altogether now. He scratched his red locks, turning this way and that. 'I think you're right, my dear Duke. Music, certainly. But it could be birds.'

'The song of the rabbit,' gasped My Lady Charlotina, romantically clasping her various hands over her multitude of breasts. 'To hear it in these woods is to become

Primordial Man – experiencing the exact emotions He experienced all those millions of years ago!'

'You are in a lyrical mood indeed, my lady,' lazily suggested Bishop Castle, but it was obvious that he, too, was infected by the atmosphere. He raised the hand in which he held the heavy deceptor-gun. 'I think the sound came from that direction.'

'We must go extremely quietly,' said the Iron Orchid, 'to be sure not to disturb either the alien or any wild-life.' Jherek suspected that she did not care a jot about disturbing the animals – she merely desired the same uninterrupted peace which he had been enjoying. He confirmed her words by means of a grave nod.

A little later they detected a haze of dancing crimson light ahead of them and they proceeded with even greater caution.

And then the music began.

It dawned on Jherek, after a few moments, that this was the most beautiful music he had ever heard. It was profound, stately and very moving, it hinted at harmonies beyond the harmonies of the physical universe, it spoke of ideals and emotions which were magnificent in their sanity, their intensity and their humanity; it took him through despair and he no longer despaired, through pain and he no longer felt pain, through cynicism and he knew the exhilaration of hope; it showed him what was ugly and it was no longer ugly; he was dragged into the deepest chasms of misery only to be lifted higher and higher until his body, mind and feelings were in perfect balance and he knew an immeasurable ecstasy.

As he listened, Jherek, with the others, moved into the haze of crimson light; their faces were bathed in it, their clothing coloured by it, and they saw that it and the music emanated from a glade. The glade was occupied by a large machine and it was this which was the source of the crimson glow; it stood lopsidedly upon four or five spindly legs, one of which at least was evidently broken. The body was asymmetrical but essentially pear-shaped with little glassy protuberances, like flaws in a piece of ceramic, dotted about all over it; from an octagonal object at the tip, the crimson poured. Near the crippled machine stood or sat seven humanoid beings who were unmistakably space-travellers – they were small, scarcely half Jherek's size, and burly, with heads akin in shape to that of their ship, with one long eye containing three pupils which darted about, sometimes converging, sometimes equidistant, with large, elephantine ears, with bulbous noses. They were bewhiskered, unkempt and dressed in a variety of garments, none of which seemed congruent with another. And it was from these little men that the music came, for they held instruments of unlikely shapes, which they plucked or blew or sawed at with stumpy fingers. At their belts were knives and swords and on their wide, splayed feet were heavy boots; their heads were decorated with caps, scarves or metal helmets, adding to their practical appearance. Jherek found it difficult to equate the exquisite beauty of the music with the ruffians who produced it.

All were affected by the music, listening in awe, unnoticed by the players, as the symphony slowly reached a resolution of apparently clashing themes, ending in a concordance which was at once unimaginably complex and of an absolute simplicity. For a moment there was silence. Jherek realized that his eyes were full of tears and, glancing at the others, he saw that they had all been as moved as he had been. He drew a series of deep breaths, as a man near-drowned when he breaks at last to the surface of the sea, but he could not speak.

The musicians for their part threw aside their instruments and lay back upon the ground roaring with laughter. They giggled, they shrieked, they slapped their sides, they were nearly helpless with mirth – and their laughter was raucous, it was even crude, as if the musicians had been enjoying a sing-song of lewd lyrics rather than playing the most beautiful music in the universe. Gabbling in a harsh, grating language, they whistled parts of the melodies, nudging one another, winking and bursting into fresh fits of merriment, holding their sides and groaning as they shook.

Somewhat put out by this unexpected sequel, the Duke of Queens led his party into the glade. At his appearance the nearest alien looked up, pointed at him, snorted and fell into another series of convulsions.

The Duke, who had always made a fetish of inconvenience, flicked on his wrist translator (which had originally been intended for communicating with Yusharisp's colleague), an ornate, old-fashioned and rather bulky piece of equipment he favoured over simpler forms of translator. When the aliens' outburst had subsided and they sat asprawl, still tittering and giggling a little, the Duke bowed, presenting himself and his companions to them.

'Welcome to our planet, gentlemen. May we congratulate you on a performance which went beyond pleasure?'

As he drew closer, Jherek detected an odour he recognized from his sojourn in the 19th century; it was the smell of stale sweat. When one of the aliens stood up at last and came swaggering towards them, the odour grew decidedly stronger.

Grinning, the ruffian scratched himself and offered them a bow which was a mockery of the Duke's and sent his companions into a complaining, painful sequence of snorts and grunts.

'We were just having a bit of fun among ourselves,' the alien said, 'to pass the time. There seems precious little else to do on this tired old globe of yours.'

'Oh, I'm sure we can find ways of amusing you,' said My Lady Charlotina. She licked her lips. 'How long have you been here?'

The alien stood on one bandy leg and scratched at his calf. 'Not long. Sooner or later we'll have to see about repairing our ship, I suppose.' He offered her what seemed to be a crude wink. My Lady Charlotina sucked in her lower lip and sighed, while the Iron Orchid whis-

216

pered to Jherek:

'What marvellous additions they will make to a menagerie. I believe the Duke realizes it, too. He has first claim, of course. A shame.'

'And from what part of the cosmos have you come?' asked Bishop Castle politely.

'Oh, I doubt if you'd recognize the name. I'm not even sure it exists any more. Me and my crew are the last of our species. We're called the Lat. I'm Captain Mubbers.'

'And why do you travel the spaces between the stars?' The Iron Orchid exchanged a secret look with My Lady Charlotina. Their eyes sparkled.

'Well, you probably know that this universe is pretty much crapped out now. So we're drifting, really, hoping to find the secret of immortality and get a bit of fun along the way. When that's done – if we ever succeed – we're going to try to escape into another universe not subject to the same conditions.'

'A second universe?' said Jherek. 'Surely a contradiction?'

'If you like.' Captain Mubbers shrugged and yawned.

'The secret of immortality and a bit of fun!' exclaimed the Duke of Queens. 'We have both! You must be our guests!'

It was now quite plain to Jherek that the devious Duke intended to add the whole band to his collection. It would be a real feather in his cap to own such splendid musicians, and would more than make up for his gaff involving Yusharisp. However, Captain Mubbers' response was not quite what the Duke seemed to hope for. An expression of low cunning crossed his features and he turned to his crew.

'What do you think, lads? This gentleman says we can stay at his place.'

'Well,' said one, 'if he's *really* got the secret of immortality...'

'He's not just going to give it up, is he?' said another. 'What's in it for him?'

217

'We assure you, our motives are altruistic,' Bishop Castle insisted. 'It would give us pleasure to have you as our guests. Say that we enjoy your music. If you play some more for us, we will show our gratitude by making you immortal. *We* are all immortal, aren't we?' He turned for confirmation to his companions who chorused their agreement.

'Really?' mused Captain Mubbers. He fingered his jaw.

'Really,' breathed the Iron Orchid. 'Why I myself am some...' She cleared her throat, suddenly aware of My Lady Charlotina's affected lack of interest in her remarks. 'Well, quite a few hundred years old,' she concluded anticlimatically.

'I have lived two or three thousand years, at least,' said the Duke of Queens.

'Don't you get bored?' enquired one of the seated aliens. 'That's what we were wondering about.'

'Oh, no. No, no, no! We have our pastimes. We create things. We talk. We make love. We invent games to play. Sometimes we'll go to sleep for a few years, maybe longer, if we do tire of what we're doing, but you'd be surprised how swiftly the time goes when you're immortal.'

'I'd never even thought of it,' said Bishop Castle. 'I suppose it's because people have been immortal on this planet for millennia. You get used to it.'

'I've a better idea,' Captain Mubbers said with a grin. 'You will be *our* guests. We'll take you with us as we continue our ride through the universe. On the way you can tell us the secret of immortality.'

Nonplussed, the Duke shuddered. 'To space! Our nerves would not bear it, I regret!' He turned with a wan smile to Jherek, still addressing the alien. 'I thank you for your invitation, Captain Mubbers, but we have to refuse. Only Mongrove, who seeks discomfort in all forms, would ever contemplate venturing into *space*.'

'No,' said My Lady Charlotina sweetly. 'It is *our* duty to entertain you. We shall all go back to Below-the-Lake and have, oh, a party.'

'We were having a party when you turned up,' Captain Mubbers pointed out. He sniffed and rubbed at his bulbous nose. 'Mind you, I think I know what you mean. Eh?' And he sidled up to her and gave her a nudge in the thigh. 'We've been a long time in space, lady.'

'Oh, you poor things!' said My Lady Charlotina, putting two of her hands on either side of his face and twiddling his moustachios. 'Are there no females of your race now?'

'Not so much as a single old slag.' He raised his eyes piteously to contemplate the trees. 'It's been a very hard trip, you know. Why, I doubt if I've tickled an elbow in four or five years.' He darted a chiding glance at his companions who were leering to a man. Then, smirking, he reached up and put his hand on her bottom. 'Why don't you and me go inside the ship and talk about this some more?'

'It would be more comfortable if you returned with us,' insisted the Duke of Queens. 'You could have some food, a rest, a bath...'

'Bath?' Captain Mubbers started in alarm. 'Do what? Come off it, Duke. We've still got a long way to go. What are you trying to suggest?'

'I mean that we can supply anything you desire. We could even create females of your own species for you, reproduce exactly your own environment. It is easily within our power.'

'Ho!' said Captain Mubbers suspiciously. 'I bet!'

'I'd like to know what their game is.' One of the crew got up, picking his teeth (which were pointed and yellow). His three pupils darted this way and that, regarding the five Earth-people. 'You're too sodding eager to please, if you ask me.'

The Duke made a vague gesture with his hands. 'Surely you can't suspect our motives? As guests on our planet, it is your right to be entertained by us.'

'Well, you're the first lot who thought that,' said the crew member, putting his hand into his shirt and rubbing his chest. 'No, I agree with the skipper. You come with us.' The others nodded their approval of this proposal.

'But,' the Iron Orchid told them reasonably, 'my scrumptious little space-sailors, you fail to understand our absolute *loathing* of these vacuous reaches. Why, hardly anyone makes the trip to the nearer planets of our own system any more, let alone plunging willy-nilly into that chilly wilderness *between* the stars!' Her expression softened, she removed the cap of the one who had just approached. She stroked his bald spot. 'It is no longer in our natures to leave the planet. We are set in our ways. We are an old, old race, you see. Space bores us. Other planets irritate and frustrate us because good manners demand that we do not re-model them to our own tastes. What is there for us in your infinity? After all, save for minor differences, one star looks very much like another.'

The Lat snatched his hat from her hand and pulled it down over his head. 'Thrills,' he said. 'Adventures. Peril. New sensations.'

'There *are* no new sensations, surely?' said Bishop Castle, willing to hear of one if it existed. 'Just modifications of the old ones, I'd have thought.'

'Well,' said Captain Mubbers decisively, stooping to pick up his instrument. 'You're coming with us and that's that. I know a trap when I smell one.'

The Duke of Queens pursed his lips. 'I think it's time we left. Evidently, an impasse...'

'More like a *fait accompli*, chummy,' said the pugnacious alien, pointing his instrument in the Duke's general direction. 'Get 'em down and shove 'em up!'

By this time the other Lat had picked their horns and strings from the ground.

'I don't follow you?' the Duke told Captain Mubbers. 'Get what down? And shove what up?'

'The trousers and the hands in that order,' said Captain Mubbers. And he motioned with his instrument.

Bishop Castle laughed. 'I believe they are *menacing* us,

you know!'

My Lady Charlotina gave a squeal of delight. The Iron Orchid put fingers to her lips, her eyes widening.

'Are those weapons as well as musical instruments?' asked Jherek with interest.

'Spot on,' said Captain Mubbers. 'Watch this.' He turned away, directing the oddly shaped device at the nearby trees. 'Fire,' he said.

A howling, burning wind issued from the thing in his hands. It seared through the trees and turned them to smoking ash. It produced a tunnel of brightness through the gloom of the forest; it revealed a plain beyond, and a mountain beyond that. The wind did not stop until it reached the far-away mountain. The mountain exploded. They heard a faint bang.

'All right?' said Captain Mubbers, turning back to them enquiringly.

His companions smirked. One of them, in a metal helmet, said: 'You wouldn't get far, would you, if you tried to run for it?'

'Who would resurrect us?' said Bishop Castle. 'How curious? I haven't seen an actual weapon before.'

'You intend, then, to *kidnap* us!' said My Lady Charlotina.

'Mibix unview per?' said Captain Mubbers. 'Kroofrudi! Dyew oh tyae, hiu hawtquards!'

In despair, the Duke of Queens had switched off his translator.

CHAPTER SEVEN

A CONFLICT OF ILLUSIONS

'It is certainly not very much of an advantage,' said the
Duke of Queens miserably. They all sat together near the
spaceship while the Lat kneeled nearby, absorbed in
some kind of gambling game. The Iron Orchid and My
Lady Charlotina seemed to be the stakes. Only My Lady
Charlotina was getting impatient.

She sighed. 'I do wish they'd hurry up. They're lov-
able, but they're not very decisive.'

'You think not?' said Bishop Castle, picking at some
moss. 'They seemed to have reached the decision to kidnap us pretty quickly.'

Jherek was miserable. 'If they take us into space I'll

never see Mrs Amelia Underwood!'

'Try a disseminator ring on their weapons again,' suggested the Iron Orchid. 'Mine doesn't work, Bishop, but yours might.'

The Bishop concentrated, fiddling with his ring, but nothing at all happened. 'They are only effective on things we create ourselves. We could get rid of the rest of the trees, I suppose ...'

'There seems little point,' said Jherek. He sighed.

'Well,' said the Duke of Queens, an inveterate viewer of the bright side, 'we might see something interesting in space.'

'Our ancestors never did,' the Iron Orchid reminded him. 'Besides, how are we to get back?'

'Build a spaceship.' The Duke of Queens was puzzled by her apparent obtuseness. 'With a power ring.'

'If they work in the depths of the cosmic void. Do you recall any record of the rings themselves being used away from Earth?' Bishop Castle shrugged, not expecting a reply.

'Did they have power rings all those thousands and thousands of years ago? Oh, dear, I feel very sleepy.' My Lady Charlotina was unusually bored. She had gone off the whole idea of making love to the Lat, either singly or all together. 'Let's create an air car and go, shall we.'

Bishop Castle was grinning. 'I have a more amusing notion.' He waved the deceptor-gun. 'It should cheer us all up and make an exciting end to this adventure. Presumably the gun is conventionally loaded, Jherek?'

'Oh, yes.' Jherek nodded absently.

'Then it will fire illusions at random. I remember the craze for these toys. Two players each have a gun, not knowing which illusions will come out, but hoping that one illusion will counter another.'

'That's right,' said Jherek. 'I couldn't find anyone interested enough to play, however.'

Captain Mubbers had left his men and was swaggering towards them.

Hujo, ri fert glex min glex viel,' he barked, menacing them at musical instrument point.

They pretended to have no idea at all as to his meaning (which was fairly clear – he wanted the ladies to enter the spaceship).

'Kroofrudi!' said Captain Mubbers. 'Glem min glex viel!'

My Lady Charlotina dimpled prettily. 'My dear captain, we simply can't understand you. And you can't understand us now, can you?'

'Hrunt.' Shifting his grip on his instrument, Captain Mubbers smiled salaciously and placed a bold hand on her elbow. 'Hrunt glex, mibix?'

'Dog!' My Lady Charlotina blushed and fluttered her eyelashes at him. 'I suppose we should try the gun now, Bishop.'

There came a slight 'pop' and everything turned to blue and white. Blue and white birds and insects, delicate, languid, flitted through equally delicate willow trees – white against blue or blue against white, depending on their particular background.

Captain Mubbers was a little surprised. Then he shook his head and pushed My Lady Charlotina towards the ship.

'Perhaps we should allow him just a brief ravishment,' she said.

'Too late,' said Bishop Castle, and he fired again. 'Who loaded this gun, Jherek? We must hope for something a little less restrained.'

The second illusion now intruded upon the first. Into the delicate blue and white scenery there lumbered a monstrous ten-legged beast which was predominantly reptilian, with huge eyes which shot flames as it turned its fierce head this way and that.

Captain Mubbers yelled and aimed his instrument. He managed to destroy a fair amount of the wood beyond the blue and white landscape and the flame-eyed monster, but they were unaffected.

'I think it's time to slip away,' said Bishop Castle, pulling the trigger once more and introducing bright abstract patterns which whizzed erratically through the air, clashing horribly with the blue and white and making the reptilian beast irritable. The Lat were firing repeatedly at the monster, backing away from it as it advanced (by luck) towards them.

'Oh,' said the Iron Orchid in disappointment as Jherek took her by the arm and dragged her into the forest, 'can't we watch?'

'Can you remember where we left your air car, Jherek?' The Duke of Queens was panting and excited. 'Isn't this fun?'

'I think it was that way,' Jherek replied. 'But perhaps it would be wise to stop and make another?'

'Would that be sporting, do you think?' asked the Iron Orchid.

'I suppose not.'

'Come on then!' She raced off through the trees and had soon vanished in the gloom. Jherek followed her, with Bishop Castle close on his heels.

'Mother, I'm not sure it's wise to separate.'

Her voice drifted back to him. 'Oh, Jherek, you've become joyless, my juice!'

But soon he had lost her altogether and he stopped, exhausted, beside a particularly large old tree. Bishop Castle had kept up with him and now handed him the deceptor-gun. 'Would you mind holding this for a bit, Jherek. It's quite heavy.'

Jherek took it and tucked it into his clothes. He heard the sound of something large blundering through the forest. Trunks fell, branches cracked, fires started.

'It's particularly realistic, isn't it?' Bishop Castle seemed almost of the impression that he had made the monster himself. He winced as something howled past his nose and destroyed a line of trees. 'The Lat seem to be catching up with us.' He dived into the undergrowth, leaving Jherek still undecided as to the direction he should take.

And now, because he might be killed forever, before he could see Mrs Amelia Underwood again, he was filled by panic. It was a new emotion and part of his mind took an objective curiosity in it. He began to run. He was careless of the branches which struck his face. He ran on and on, through darkness, away from the sounds and the destruction. Danger was a wall which seemed to surround him, in escaping one source he encountered another. Once he bumped against someone in the dark and was about to speak when they said, 'Ferkit!' He moved away as quietly as possible and heard a blood-chilling shriek from somewhere else.

He ran, he fell, he crawled, got up and ran again. His chest was painful and his brain was useless. He thought that he might be sobbing and he knew that the next time he would fall and not have the will to rise.

He tripped. He lost his balance. He was reconciled to Death. He went sprawling down the sides of an old pit, bits of earth and rock falling with him, and was about to congratulate himself that he might after all have found relative safety when the bottom of the pit gave way and he was sliding down something which was smooth and plainly built for this purpose. Down and down he slid on the metal chute, feeling sick with the speed of his descent, unable to reach his power rings, unable to slow himself, until he must have been almost a mile underground. Then, at last, the chute came to an end and he landed, winded and dazed, on what appeared to be a pile of mildewed quilts.

The light was dim and it was artificial. After a while he sat up, feeling tenderly over his body for broken bones, but there were none. A peculiar sense of well-being filled him and he lay back upon the quilts with a yawn, hoping that his friends had managed to get back to the landau. He would rest and then consider the best method of joining them. A power ring would doubtless bore a tunnel upwards for him, then he could drift to the surface by means of counter-gravity. He felt extremely sleepy. He could hardly believe in the events which had just taken place. He was about to close his eyes when he heard a small, lisping voice saying:

'Welcome, sir, to Wonderland!'

He looked round. A small girl stood there. She had large blue eyes and blonde curly hair. Her expression was demure.

'You're very well made,' said Jherek admiringly. 'What are you, exactly?'

The small girl's expression was now one of disgust. 'I'm a little girl, of course. Aren't I?'

CHAPTER EIGHT

THE CHILDREN OF THE PIT

Jherek stood up and dusted at his white draperies, saying kindly: 'Little girls have been extinct for thousands of years. You're probably a robot or a toy. What are you doing down here?'

'Playing,' said the robot or toy; then it stepped forward and kicked his ankle, 'And I know what I am. And I know what you are. Nurse said we had to be careful of grown-ups – they're dangerous.'

'So are little girls,' said Jherek feelingly, rubbing an already battered leg. 'Where is your Nurse, my child?'

He had to admit he was surprised at how lifelike the creature was, but it could not be a child or he would have heard about it. Save for himself and Werther de Goethe, children had not been born on Earth for millennia. People were created, as the Duke of Queens had created Sweet Orb Mace, or re-created themselves, as King Rook had become Bishop Castle. Having children, after all, was rather a responsibility. Creating mature adults was difficult enough!

'Come on,' said the being, taking his hand. She led him down a tunnel of pink marble which, to Jherek's eye, had something in common with the style and materials of the ancient cities, though the tunnel seemed relatively new. The tunnel opened into a large room crammed with beautiful reproductions of antiques, some of which Jherek recognized as miniature whizz-mobiles, rocking horses, furry partridges, seasores, coloured quasimodos and erector sets. 'This is one of our play-rooms,' she told him. 'The school-room is through there. Nurse should be out soon with the others. *I'm* playing truant,' she added proudly.

Jherek admired his surroundings. Someone had gone to considerable trouble to reproduce an old nursery. He wondered if this, like the wood above, could be attributed to Lord Jagged. It certainly showed his finesse.

Suddenly a door opened and into the room poured a score of boys and girls, all of about the same apparent age, the boys in shirts and shorts, the girls in frilly dresses and aprons. They were shouting and laughing, but they stopped when they saw Jherek Carnelian. Their eyes widened, their mouths hung òpen.

'It's an adult,' said the self-styled child. 'I caught it in one of the corridors. It fell through the roof.'

'Do you think it's a Producer?' asked one of the boys, stepping up to Jherek and looking him over.

'They're fatter than that,' another girl said. 'Here comes Nurse, anyway. She'll know.'

Behind them loomed a tall figure, grim of visage, clothed in grey steel, humanoid and stern. A robot, much larger than Jherek, built to resemble a middle-aged

229

woman in the costume of the Late Multitude Cultures. Her voice, when she spoke, was a trifle rusty and her limbs were inclined to creak when they moved. Cold blue eyes glared from the steel face.

'What's this, Mary Wilde, playing truant again?' Nurse tut-tutted 'And who's this other little boy. Not one of mine by the look of him.'

'We think it's an adult, Nurse,' said Mary Wilde.

'Nonsense, Mary. Your imagination is running away with you again. There are no such things as adults any more.'

'That's what *he* said about children.' Mary Wilde put her hand to her mouth to suppress a giggle.

'Pull yourself together, Mary,' said Nurse. 'I can only conclude that this young man has also been playing truant. You will both be punished by having only bread and milk for supper.'

'I assure you that I *am* an adult, madam,' Jherek insisted. 'Although I have been a child in my time. My name is Jherek Carnelian.'

'Well, you're reasonably polite at any rate,' said Nurse. Her lips clashed as she drew them together. 'You had better meet the other little boys and girls. I really can't think why they've sent me an extra child. I'm already two over my quota.' The robot seemed a shade on the senile side, unable to accept new information. Jherek had the impression that she had been performing her tasks for a considerable length of time and had, as robots will in such conditions, become set in her ways. He decided, for the moment, to humour her.

'This is Freddie Fearless,' said Nurse, laying a gentle metal hand upon the brown curly locks of the nearest boy. 'And this is Danny Daring. Mick Manly and Victor Venture, here. Gary Gritt, Peter Pluck and Ben Bold, there. Kit Courage – Dick Dreadnought – Gavin Gallant. Say hello to your new friend, boys.'

'Hello,' they chorused obediently.

'What did you say your name was, lad?' asked Nurse.

'Jherek Carnelian, Nurse.'

'A strange, unlikely name.'

'Your children's names all seem to have a certain similarity, if I may say so...'

'Nonsense. Anyway, we'll call you Jerry – Jerry Jester, Always Playing the Fool, eh?'

Jherek shrugged.

'And these are the girls – Mary Wilde, you've already met. Betty Bold, Ben's sister. Molly Madcap. Nora Nosie.'

'I'm the school sneak,' announced Nora Nosie with undisguised pleasure.

'Yes, dear, and you're very good at it. This is Gloria Grande. Flora Friendly. Katie Kinde – Harriet Haughtie – Jenny Jolly.'

'I am honoured to meet you all,' said Jherek, with something of Lord Jagged's grace. 'But perhaps you could tell me what you are doing underground?'

'We're hiding!' whispered Molly Madcap. 'Our parents sent us here to escape the movie.'

'The movie?'

'Pecking Pa the Eighth's *The Great Massacre of the First-Born* – that's the working title, anyway,' Ben Bold told him.

'It's a remake about the birth of Christ,' said Flora Friendly. 'Pecking Pa is going to play Herod himself.'

This name alone meant something to Jherek. He knew that he had met a time traveller once who had fled from this same Pecking Pa, the Last of the Tyrant Producers, when he had been in the process of making another drama about the eruption of Krakatoa.

'But that was thousands of years ago,' Jherek said. 'You couldn't have been here all that time. Or could you?'

'We work to a weekly shift here,' said Nurse. She turned her eyes towards a chronometer on the wall. 'If we don't hurry, I shall be late with the recycling. That's the trouble with the parents – they've no thought for me – they send down another child without ever thinking about my schedules – and then they wonder why the routines are upset.'

'Do you mean you're recycling *time*?' asked Jherek in amazement. 'The same week over and over again.'

'Until the danger's over,' said Nurse. 'Didn't your parents tell you? We'll have to get you out of those silly clothes. Really, some mothers have peculiar ideas of how to dress children. You're quite a big boy, aren't you. It will mean making a shirt and shorts for a start.'

'I don't want to wear a shirt and shorts, Nurse! I'm not sure they'll suit me.'

'Oh, my goodness! You *have* been spoiled, Jerry!'

'I think the danger *is* over, Nurse,' said Jherek desperately, backing away. 'The Age of the Tyrant Producers has long since past. We're now very close to the End of Time itself.'

'Well, dear, that won't affect us here, will it? We operate a neat closed system. It doesn't matter what happens in the rest of the universe, we just go round and round through the same period. I do it all myself, you know, with no help from anyone else.'

'I think you've become a little fixed in your habits, Nurse. Have you considered limbering up your circuits?'

'Now, Jerry, I'll assume you're not being deliberately rude, because you're new here, but I'm afraid that if I hear any more talk like that from you I'll have to take strong measures. I'm kind, Jerry, but I'm firm.'

The great robot rumbled forward on her tracks, reaching out her huge metal arms towards him. 'Next, we'll undress you.'

Jherek bowed. 'I think I'll go now, Nurse. But as soon as I can I'll return. After all, these children can begin to grow up, the danger being over. They'll want to see the outside world.'

'Language, boy!' bellowed Nurse fiercely. 'Language!'

'I didn't mean to . . .' Jherek turned and bolted.

'Soldiers of the Guard!' roared Nurse.

Jherek found his way blocked by huge mechanical toy soldiers. They had expressionless faces and were not anything like as sophisticated as Nurse, but their metal bodies effectively blocked his escape.

Jherek yelped as he felt Nurse's strong hands fall on him. He was yanked into the air and flung over a cold steel knee. A metal hand rose and fell six times on his bottom and then he was upright again and Nurse was patting his head.

'I don't like to punish boys, Jerry,' said Nurse. 'But it is for their own good that they do not leave the nursery. When you are older you will understand that.'

'But I *am* older,' said Jherek.

'That's impossible.' Nurse began to strip his clothes from him and moments later he stood before her wearing the same kind of shirt and shorts and knee-socks as Kit Courage, Freddie Fearless and the others. 'There,' she said in satisfaction, 'now you're not so much of an odd boy out. I know how children hate to be different.'

Jherek, twice the height of his new chums, knew then that he was in the power of a moron.

CHAPTER NINE

NURSE'S SENSE OF DUTY

Jherek Carnelian sat at the far end of the dormitory, a bowl of bread and milk in his lap, an expression of hopeless misery upon his face, while Nurse stood by the door saying goodnight.

'I really should point out, Nurse, that, since your closed environment has been entered by an outsider, a variety of temporal paradoxes are likely to take place. They are sure to disrupt your way of life and mine probably much more than we should want.'

'Sleepy time now,' said Nurse firmly, for the sixth time since Jherek had arrived. 'Lights out, my little men!'

Jherek knew that it was useless to get up once he had

gone to bed. Nurse would detect him immediately and put him back again. At least it was easy to know how long he had been here. Each day measured exactly twenty-four hours and each hour had sixty minutes – it was all on the old non-malleable reckonings. The Age of the Tyrant Producers would have been one of the last to use them. Jherek knew that Nurse must have been programmed to act upon new information and to deal with it intelligently, but she had become sluggish over the centuries. His only hope was to keep insisting on what was self-evident truth, but it could take months. He wondered how the Iron Orchid and the others had fared on the surface. With any luck, when he was able to escape, he would find the Lat weapons neutralized (it was quite easy to do and had been done on several previous occasions) and the aliens returned to space.

'I think you should consider a re-programming, Nurse!' Jherek called into the darkness.

'Now, now, Jerry, you know I disapprove of cheeky children.' The door closed. Nurse rolled away down the corridor.

Jherek wondered if he had been right in believing that he had detected a faint uncertainty in Nurse's voice tonight.

Freddie Fearless said admiringly from the next bed. 'You can certainly keep it up, can't you Jerry? I don't know why the old girl lets you get away with it.'

'Perhaps, in her subconscious, she realizes that I'm an adult and doesn't like to admit it,' Jherek suggested.

This drew a ripple of laughter from the boys.

'That's Jerry Jester,' said Dick Dreadnought, 'always playing the fool! Life wouldn't be nearly so much fun without you, Jerry.' Like the others, he had accepted Jherek immediately and seemed to have forgotten that he had only recently entered the nursery.

With a sigh, Jherek turned over and tried to operate his power rings, as he had taken to doing every night, but plainly some protective device in the nursery blocked off the source of their energy. He still had the deceptor-gun, but he couldn't think of any use for it at present. He felt under his pillow. It was still there. With a sigh, he tried to go to sleep. It seemed to him that he was in an even more uncomfortable situation than when he had been Snoozer Vines' prisoner in Jone's Kitchen in 1896. He remembered that there, too, they had called him Jerry. Did all gaolers favour that name for him?

Jherek wakened and was surprised that the lights were not on, as they usually were; also he could not smell breakfast; moreover Nurse was not standing by the door ringing her bell and calling 'Wake up, sleeepyheads!' as was her wont.

From somewhere beyond the dormitory, however, there came various noises – yells, explosions, screams and bangs – and suddenly the door had sprung open, admitting light from the corridor.

'Berchoos ek!' said a familiar voice. 'Hoody?'

And Captain Mubbers, his whiskers bristling, his musical instrument in his hands, stood framed in the doorway. He glared at Jherek.

'Kroofrudi!' he said in recognition, and a nasty grin appeared on his face.

Jherek groaned. The Lat had found him and now the children were in danger.

'Ferkit! Jillip goff var heggo heg, mibix?'

'I still can't understand you, Captain Mubbers,' Jherek told the brigand-musician. 'However, I take it you would like me to accompany you and, of course, I shall. Hopefully you will then leave the rest of – I mean – leave the children alone.' With as much dignity as he could muster considering he was wearing a jacket and trousers of brightly striped flannel far too small for him, he rose from his bed, his hands in the air, and walked towards the Lat captain.

Captain Mubbers snorted with mirth. 'Shag uk fang dok pist kickle hrunt!' he yelled. His men gathered around him and they, too, joined in their leader's merriment. One even dropped his weapon, but was quick to recover it again. This made Jherek wonder if their own power source came from their spaceship or if the weapons, like his deceptor-gun, had independent cells. He supposed that there wasn't an easy way of finding out. He bore their laughter as manfully as he could.

Captain Mubbers' bulbous nose fairly glowed with the strain of his laughter. 'Uuuungh, k-k-kroofrudi! Uuuuuungh, k-kroofrudi!'

'What's this? What's this? More naughty boys from outside!' came Nurse's booming voice from down the corridor. 'And during the night, now! This will *never* do!'

Captain Mubbers and his men looked at one another with expressions of disbelieving surprise on their faces. Nurse rolled steadily on.

'You are nasty rough boys and you are disturbing my charges. Haven't you homes to go to?'

'Kroofrudi!' said Captain Mubbers.

'Ferkit!' said another.

'Ugh! Disgusting!' said Nurse. 'Where do you pick up such words!'

Captain Mubbers stepped to the head of his gang and menaced Nurse with his instrument. She ignored it completely. 'I have never seen such filthy little boys. And what have you got in your hands? Catapults, no doubt!'

Captain Mubbers aimed his instrument at Nurse and pulled the trigger. Howling fire left the muzzle and struck Nurse full on her chest. She made a fussy, brushing motion, then one of her arms extended and she snatched the instrument from Captain Mubbers' grasp.

'Naughty, naughty, naughty, little boy. I will not have such behaviour in the nursery!'

'Olgo glex mibix?' said Captain Mubbers placatingly. He tried to smile, but his eyes were glassy as he stared up at Nurse whose huge metal head looked down upon him. 'Frads kolek goj sako!'

'I will listen to no more of your nastiness. This is the only way to teach manners to the likes of you, young man.'

With great satisfaction, Jherek watched as Captain Mubbers was snatched yelling into the air, was thrown across Nurse's knee, was divested of his trousers and slapped soundly upon his bare and unlovely backside. Captain Mubbers shouted to his crew to help and they all began kicking at Nurse, tugging at her, swearing at her, to no avail. Sedately she completed the punishment of Captain Mubbers and then, one by one, gave similar treatment to his companions, confiscating their instruments at the same time.

Chastened, they all stood holding their bottoms, red-faced and tearful, while Jherek and the boys from the dormitory laughed delightedly.

Nurse began to roll down the corridor with an armful of alien instruments. 'You may have these back only when you leave the nursery,' she said. 'And you will not leave the nursery until you have learned some manners!'

'Kroofrudi,' said Captain Mubbers, glowering at the disappearing robot, but he spoke the word softly, nervously, more from bravado than anything else. 'Hrunt!'

Jherek felt almost sorry for the Lat, but he was glad that the children were safe.

'I heard you!' Nurse called chidingly. 'I shan't forget!'

Captain Mubbers caught her drift. He said no more.

Jherek grinned. It pleased him more than he would have guessed to see the Lat brought so low. 'Well,' he said, 'we're all in the same kettle of fish now, eh?'

'Mibix?' queried Captain Mubbers in a small, defeated voice.

'However, the idea of spending the same week, recycled through eternity, in the company of children, Lat and a senile robot is not entirely appealing,' said Jherek, in a critical and miserable mood for him. 'I really must think how I'm to effect my escape and achieve a reconciliation with Mrs Amelia Underwood.'

Captain Mubbers nodded. 'Greef cholokok,' he said, by way of affirmation.

Nurse was returning. 'I've locked your toys away,' she told Captain Mubbers and the others. 'And now it's straight to bed without any supper. Have you any idea how late it is?'

The Lat stared at her blankly.

'My goodness, I do believe they've sent me a party of mentally subnormals!' exclaimed Nurse. 'I thought they were going to be left behind to placate Pecking Pa.' She pointed at the row of empty beds down one side of the dormitory. 'In there,' she said slowly. 'Bed.'

The Lat shuffled towards the beds and stood looking stupidly down at them.

Nurse sighed and picked up the nearest alien, stripping off his clothing and plumping him down, pulling the bedding over his shivering body. The others hastily began to pull off their own clothes and climbed into bed.

'That's more like it,' said Nurse. 'You're learning.' She turned her hard, blue eyes on Jherek. 'Jerry, I think you'd better come to my sitting room. I'd like a word with you now.'

Meekly, Jherek followed Nurse down the corridor and into a room whose walls were covered in flock wallpaper, with landscape paintings and little ornaments. Elsewhere was a great deal of chintz and gingham. It reminded Jherek vaguely of the house he had furnished for Mrs Amelia Underwood.

Nurse rolled to one corner of the room. 'Would you like a cup of tea, Jerry?'

'No thank you, Nurse.'

'You are probably wondering why I asked you here, when it's long past your bed-time.'

'It had occurred to me, Nurse, yes.'

'Well,' she announced, 'my creative-thinking circuits are beginning to come back into play, I think. I've become rather set in my ways, as old robots will, particularly when involved in a temporal recycling operation

239

like this one. You follow me?'

'I do indeed.'

'You are older than the other children, so I think I can talk to you. Even,' Nurse made an embarrassed rumbling sound somewhere inside her steel chest, 'even ask your advice. You think I've become a bit of a stick in the mud, don't you?'

'Oh, not really,' Jherek told her kindly. 'We all develop habits, over the millennia, which are sometimes hard to lose when we no longer need them.'

'I have been thinking about one or two things which you've said this past week. You've been to the surface, evidently.'

'Um...'

'Come now, lad, tell the truth. I shan't punish you.'

'Yes, I have, Nurse.'

'And Pecking Pa is dead?'

'And forgotten.' Jherek wriggled uncomfortably in his too-tight pyjamas. 'It's been thousands of years since the Age of the Tyrant Producers. Things are much more peaceful these days.'

'And these outsiders – they are from the outside time-phase?'

'They are, more or less.'

'Which means that paradoxes begin to occur, if we're not careful.'

'I gather so, from what I have been told about the nature of Time.'

'You've been informed correctly. It means that I must think very carefully now. I knew this moment would come eventually. I have to worry about my children. They are all I have. They are the Future.'

'Well, the Past, at least,' said Jherek.

Nurse glared sternly at him. 'I'm sorry, Nurse,' he said. 'That was facetious of me.'

'My duty is to take them into an age where they will be in no danger,' Nurse continued. 'And it seems that we have reached that age.'

'I am sure they will be very welcome in my society,'
Jherek told her. 'I and one other are the only ones who
have been children. My people love children. I am proof
of that.'

'They are gentle?'

'Oh, yes, I think so. I'm not quite sure of the meaning –
you use words which are archaic to me – but I think
"gentle" is a fair description.'

'No violence?'

'There you've lost me altogether. What is "violence"?'

'I'm satisfied for the moment,' said Nurse. 'I must be
grateful to you, Jerry Jester. For all that you are always
acting the fool, you're made of decent stuff underneath.
You've re-awakened me to my chief responsibilities.'
Nurse seemed to simper (as much as a robot could simper). 'You are my Prince Charming, really. And I was the
Sleeping Beauty. It would seem that the danger to the
children is over and they can be allowed to grow normally. What sort of conditions exist in the outside world.
Will they find good homes?'

'Any kind they wish,' said Jherek.

'And the climate. Is it good?'

'Whatever one cares to make it.'

'Educational facilities?'

'Well,' he said, 'I suppose you could say that we believe
in self-education. But the facilities are excellent. The lib-
raries of the rotted cities are still more or less intact.'

'Those other children. They seemed to know you. Are
they from your time?' It was plain that Nurse was becoming increasingly intelligent with every passing second.

'They are aliens from another part of the galaxy,'
Jherek said. 'They were chasing me and some of my
friends.' He explained what had happened.

'Well, they must be expelled, of course,' said Nurse,
having listened gravely to his account. 'Preferably into
another period of time where they can do no more harm.
And here normal time must replace recycled time. That
is merely a question of stopping a process...' Nurse sank

into a thoughtful silence.

Jherek had begun to hope. 'Nurse,' he said. 'Forgive me for interrupting, but am I to understand that you have the power to pass people back and forth in Time?'

'Back is very difficult – they are not inclined to stick, in my experience. Forth is much easier. Recycling is,' a mechanical chuckle sounded in her throat, 'child's play, as it were.'

'So you could send me back, say, to the 19th century?'

'I could. But the chances of your staying there for long are poor...'

'I'm aware of the theory. We call it the Morphail Effect in this age. But you could send me back.'

'I could, almost certainly. I was programmed specifically for Time Manipulation. I probably know more about it than any other being.'

'You would not have to use a time machine?'

'There's a chamber in this complex, but it would not be a machine which moved physically through time. We've abandoned such devices. As a matter of fact, time travel itself, being so uncertain, was pretty much abandoned, too. It was only in order to protect the children that we built this place.'

'Would you send me back, Nurse?'

Nurse seemed hesitant. 'It's very dangerous, you know. I know that I owe you a favour. I feel stupid for having forgotten my duty. But sending you so far back...'

'I have been before, Nurse. I'm aware of the dangers.'

'That's as may be, young Jerry Jester. You were always a wild one – though I could never be as firm with you as I should have been. How I used to laugh, privately, here in my little sitting room, at your antics, at the things you said...'

'Nurse! I think you're slipping again,' Jherek warned her.

'Eh? Put another lump of coal on the fire, would you my boy?'

Jherek looked around, but could see no fire.

242

'Nurse?'

'Aha!' said Nurse. 'Send you to the 19th century. A long time ago. A long, long time ago. Before I was born. Before *you* were born, that's for certain. In those days there were oceans of light and cities in the skies and wild flying beasts of bronze. There were herds of crimson cattle that roared and were taller than castles. There were shrill...'

'To 1896 to be precise, Nurse. Would you do it for me? It would mean a great deal.'

'Magics,' she continued, 'phantasms, unstable nature, impossible events, insane paradoxes, dreams come true, dreams gone awry; nightmares assuming reality. It was a rich time and a dark time...'

'1896, Nurse.'

'Ah, sometimes, in my more Romantic moments, I wish that I had been some merchant governess; some great lady of Hong Kong, trading capital of the world, where poets, scholars and soldiers of fortune all congregated. The ships of a hundred nations at anchor in the harbours. Ships from the West, with cargoes of bearskins and exotic soaps; ships from the South, with crews of dark-visaged androids, bearing bicycles and sacks of grit; ships from the East...'

'Plainly we share an interest in the same century,' said Jherek desperately. 'Do not deny me my opportunity to go back there, dear Nurse.'

'How could I?' Her voice had become almost inaudible, virtually soft as nostalgia seized her. At that moment, Jherek felt a deep sympathy for the old machine; it was rare that one was privileged to witness the dreams of a robot. 'How could I refuse my Jerry Jester anything. He has made me live again.'

'Oh, Nurse!' Jherek was moved to tears. He ran forward and hugged the rigid body. 'And with your help I, too, shall come to life again!'

CHAPTER TEN

ON THE BROMLEY ROAD AGAIN

'Producing the time jump is relatively easy,' said Nurse, studying a bank of instruments in her laboratory as Jherek came rushing in (he had returned, briefly, to his ranch to get some translator pills and study his records in order to make himself a suit of clothes which would not set him apart from the denizens of 1896). 'Oh, that's yours, by the way. I found it under your pillow when I was making your bed.' The old robot pointed at the deceptor-gun resting on one of her benches. With a murmur of thanks, Jherek picked it up and slipped it into the pocket of his black overcoat. 'The problem is,' Nurse went on, 'in getting the spacial co-ordinates correctly fixed. A city called London (I'd never heard of it until you mentioned it) in an island called England. I've had to consult some pretty ancient memory banks, I can tell you, but I think it's sorted out now.'

'I can go?'

'You were always an impatient one, Jerry.' Nurse laughed affectionately. She still seemed to have it implanted in her that she had brought Jherek up since he had been a young boy. 'But – yes – I think you can set off soon. I do hope you're aware of the dangers, however.'

'I am, Nurse.'

'What on earth are you wearing, my boy? It looks like something I once saw in Tyrant Pecking Pa's remake of the classic *David Copperfield Meets the Wolf Man*. I considered it rather fanciful, then. But Pecking Pa always ran to *emotional* authenticity rather than period exactitude, I was told. At least, that's what he used to say. I met him once, you know. Some years ago, when his father was still alive. His father was so different; a gentleman. You wouldn't have known they were related. His father made all those wonderful, charming movies. They were a joy to live through. The whole society took part, of course. You'd be far too young to remember the pleasure of having even a small part in *Young Adolf Hitler* or *The Four Loves of Captain Marvel*. When Pecking Pa VIII came to power all the romance vanished. Realism became the rage. And someone suffers, every time, during a Realism period (I mean, who supplies the blood? Not the Tyrant himself!)'

Privately, Jherek Carnelian was very grateful to Pecking Pa VIII for his excesses in the name of Realism. Without them, Nurse would not be here now.

'The stories were pretty much the same, of course,' said Nurse, fiddling with some controls and making a screen turn to liquid gold, 'only more blood. There, that should do it. I hope there was just the one location for London on this island of yours. It's very *small*, Jerry.' She turned her great metal head to look at him. 'What I would call a

245

bit of a low-budget country.'

Jherek wasn't, as usual, following her too clearly. But he nodded and smiled.

'Still, small productions quite often produced interesting pictures,' said Nurse, with a touch of condescension. 'Hop into the box, Jerry, there's a good lad. I'll be sorry to see you go, but I suppose I'll have to get used to it, now. I wonder how many will remember their old Nurse in a few years time. Still, it's a fact of life I have to face. Starlets must become stars some day.'

Jherek stepped gingerly into the cylindrical chamber in the middle of the laboratory.

'Goodbye, Jerry,' said Nurse's voice from outside, before the buzzing became too loud, 'try to remember everything I taught you. Be polite. Listen for your cues. Keep away from casting couches. Camera! Action!'

And the cylinder seemed to begin to spin (though it might have been Jherek spinning). He clapped his hands to his ears to keep out the noise. He groaned. He fainted.

He moved through a country that was all soft, shifting colours and whose people were bodiless, kindly with sweet voices. He fell back and he was falling through the fabric of the ages, down and down to the very beginnings of mankind's long history.

He felt pain, as he had felt it before, but he did not mind it. He knew depressions such as he had never experienced, but they did not concern him. Even the joy which came to him was a joy he did not care about. He knew that he was borne upon the winds of Time and he knew, beyond any question, that at the end of this journey he would be reunited with his lost love, the beautiful Mrs Amelia Underwood. And when he reached 1896 he would not allow himself to be sidetracked from his great Quest for Bromley, as he has been sidetracked before by Snoozer Vines.

He heard his own voice calling, ecstatic and melodic. 'Mrs Underwood! Mrs Underwood! I am coming! Coming! Coming!'

And at last the sensation of falling had stopped and he opened his eyes, expecting to find himself still in the cylinder, but he was not. He was lying upon soft grass under a large, warm sun. There were trees and not far off the glint of water. He saw people walking about, all dressed in costumes appropriate to the late 19th century – men and women, children, dogs. In the distance he saw a carriage go by, drawn by horses. One of the inhabitants started to stroll slowly, purposefully towards him and he recognized the man's suit. He had seen many such during his previous stay in 1896. Quickly he slipped his hand in his pocket, took out a translator pill and popped it into his mouth. He began to stand up.

'Excuse me, sir,' said the man heavily, 'but I was wondering as to whether you could *read*.'

'As a matter of fact,' began Jherek, but was cut off.

'Because I was looking at that there notice, not four yards off, which plainly states, if I'm not mistaken, that you are requested not to set foot on this particular stretch of lawn, sir. Therefore, if you would kindly return to the public walk, I for one would be relieved to inform you that you had returned to the path of righteousness and were no longer breaking one of the byelaws of the Royal Borough of Kensington. Moreover, I must point out, sir, that if I was ever to catch you committing the same felony in this here park, I would be forced to take your name and address and see that a notice to appear in court on a particular date was served on you.' And the man laughed. 'Sorry, sir,' he said in a more natural tone, 'but you shouldn't really be on the grass.'

'Aha!' said Jherek. 'I follow. Thank you, um – officer – that's it, isn't it? It was inadvertent...'

'I'm sure it was, sir. You being a Frenchman, by your accent, wouldn't understand our ways. It's more free and easy over there, of course.'

Jherek stepped rapidly to the path and began to walk in the direction of a pair of large marble gate-posts he could see in the distance. The policeman fell in beside him, chatting casually about France and other foreign places he had read about. Eventually, he saluted and walked off down another path, leaving Jherek wishing that he had enquired the way to Bromley.

At least, thought Jherek, it was a relief not to be attracting quite so much attention as he had during his last trip to the Dawn Age. People still glanced at him from time to time and he felt rather self-conscious, as one might, but he was able to walk along the street and enjoy the sights without interruption. Carriages, hansoms, dairymen's drays, tradesmen's vans, all went by, filling the air with the creak of axles, the clopping of horses' hooves, the rattling of the wheels. The sun was bright and warm and the smells of the street had a very different quality to the one they had had during Jherek's previous stay. He realized that it must be summer now. He paused to smell some roses which were spilling over the wall of the park. They were beautiful. There was a *texture* to the scent which he had never been able to reproduce. He inspected the leaves of a cypress and here, too, found that his own work lacked a certain subtlety of detail which was difficult to define. He found himself delighting, even more than before, in the beauties of 1896. He stopped to stare as a two-storeyed omnibus went by, pulled by huge, muscular horses. On the open top deck be-ribboned straw hats nodded, sunshades twirled and blazers blazed; while below, through dusty windows and a confusion of advertisements, sat the dourer travellers, their eyes upon their newspapers and penny magazines. Once or twice a motor car would wheeze past, its exhaust mingling with the dust from the street, its driver swathed in a long coat and white cap, in spite of the heat, and Jherek would watch it in smiling wonderment.

He removed his top hat, wondering why his face seemed damp, and then he realized to his delight that he was *sweating*. He had witnessed this phenomenon before, in the inhabitants of this period, but had never dreamed of experiencing it personally. Glancing at the faces of the people who passed by – all in different stages of youth or decay, all male or female (without choice, he remembered, with a thrill of excitement) – he saw that many of them were sweating, too. It added to his sense of identification with them. He smiled at them, as if to say 'Look, I am like you,' but, of course, they did not understand. Some, indeed, frowned at him, while two ladies walking together giggled and blushed.

He continued along the road in a roughly eastward direction, noticing that the traffic grew thicker. The park ended on his left and a fresh one appeared on his right. Boys with bundles of newspapers and placards began to run about shouting, men with long poles began to poke them into lanterns which stood on thin, tall pedestals at regular intervals along the sides of the pavement, and the air became a little cooler, the sky a little darker.

Jherek, realizing that night was falling and that he had become so entranced by the atmosphere that he was, again, in danger of being deflected from his path, decided that it was time to make for Bromley. He remembered that Snoozer Vines had told him that he would need to take a train and that the trains left from somewhere called 'Victoria' or possibly 'Waterloo'.

He went up to a passer-by, a portly gentleman dressed rather like himself who was in the process of purchasing a newspaper from a small boy.

'Excuse me, sir,' said Jherek, raising his hat, 'I wonder if you would be good enough to help me.'

'Certainly, sir, if I can,' said the portly gentleman genially, replacing his money in his waistcoat pocket.

'I am trying to reach the town of Bromley, which is in Kent, and I wondered if you knew which train station I would need.'

'Well,' said the portly gentleman with a frown. 'It will either be Victoria or Waterloo, I should think. Or possibly London Bridge. Possibly all three. I would suggest that you purchase a railway guide, sir. I can see from the cut of your jib that you're a stranger to our shores – and an investment, if you intend to travel about this fair island, in a railway guide will pay you handsome dividends in the long run. I am sorry I cannot be of more assistance. Good evening to you.' And the portly gentleman rolled away, calling out:

'Cab! Cab!'

Jherek sighed and continued to walk up the busy street which seemed to become increasingly densely populated with every passing moment. He wished that he had mastered the logic of reading when he had had the chance. Mrs Underwood had tried to teach him, but she had never really explained the principles to his satisfaction. With the logic fully understood, a translation pill would do the rest for him, working its peculiar re-structuring effect upon his brain-cells.

He tried to stop several people, but they all seemed too busy to want to talk to him, and at last he reached an intersection crammed with traffic of every description. Bewildered he came to another stop, staring over the hansoms, four-wheelers and carts at the statue of a naked bowman with wings on his ankles, doubtless some heroic aviator who had taken part in the salvation of London during one of its periodic wars with other of the island's city-states. The noise was almost overwhelming, and now darkness added to his confusion. He thought he recognized some of the buildings and landmarks, from his last trip to the past, but he could not be sure. They were inclined to look very much alike. Across the street he saw the gold and crimson front of a house which seemed, for some reason, more as he had originally imagined 19th century houses to be. It had large windows with lace curtains from behind which poured warm gaslight. Other curtains, of red velvet held by cords of woven gold, were drawn back from the windows and from within there came a number of pleasant smells. Jherek decided that he would give up trying to stop one of the busy passers-by and ask for help, instead, at one of these houses. Nervously, he plunged into the traffic, was missed first by an

250

omnibus, then by a hansom cab, then by a four-wheeler, was cursed at roundly by almost everyone and arrived panting and dusty on the other side of the road.

Standing outside the gold and crimson building, Jherek realized that he was not sure of how to begin making his enquiry. He saw a number of people go through the doors as he watched, and concluded that some sort of party was taking place. He went to one of the windows and peered, as best he could, through the lace curtains. Men in black suits very much like his own, but wearing large white aprons around their waists, hurried about, bearing trays of food, while at tables, some large and some small, sat groups of men and women, eating, drinking and talking. It was definitely a party. Here, surely, would be someone who could help him.

As he stared, Jherek saw that at a table in the far corner sat a group of men, dressed in slightly different style to most of the others. They were laughing, pouring foaming wine from large green bottles, having an animated conversation. With a shock, Jherek thought that one of the men, dressed in a light yellow velvet jacket, a loose scarlet cravat covering a good deal of his shirt front, bore a startling resemblance to his old friend Lord Jagged of Canaria. He seemed to be on familiar terms with the other men. At first Jherek told himself that this could only be Lord Jagger, the judge at his trial, and decided that he could see points about the handsome, lazy face which distinguished him from Jagged, but he knew that he deceived himself. Obviously coincidence could explain the resemblance, both of name and features, but here was his opportunity to decide the truth. He left the windows and pushed open the doors of the house.

Immediately a small, dark man approached him.

'Good evening, sir? You have a table?'

'Not with me,' said Jherek in some astonishment.

The small man's smile was thin and Jherek knew enough to understand that it was not particularly friendly. Hastily, he said: 'My friends – over there!'

'Ah!' This seemed sufficient explanation. The small man was relieved. 'Your hat and coat, sir?'

Jherek realized that he was supposed to give these items of clothing to the man as some form of surety. Willingly, he dispensed with them, and made his way as quickly as possible to the table where he had seen Jagged.

But, somehow, Jagged had managed to disappear again.

A man with a coarse, good-natured face, adorned by a large black moustache, looked up at Jherek enquiringly. 'How d'ye do?' he said heartily. 'You'd be M. Fromental, from Paris? I'm Harris – and this is Mr Wells, whom you wrote to me about.' He indicated a narrow-faced, slight man, with a scrubby moustache and startlingly bright pale blue eyes. 'Wells, this is the agent chap Pinker mentioned. He wants to handle all your work over there.'

'I'm afraid . . .' began Jherek.

'Sit down my dear fellow and have some wine.' Mr Harris stood up, shaking his hand warmly, pressing him downwards into a chair. 'How are all my good friends in Paris? Zola? I was sorry to hear about poor Goncourt. And how is Daudet, at present? Madame Rattazzi is well, I hope.' He winked. 'And be sure, when you return, to give my regards to my old friend the Comtesse de Loynes . . .'

'The man,' said Jherek, 'who was sitting across the table from you. Do you know him, Mr Harris?'

'He's a contributor to the *Review* from time to time, like everyone else here. Name of Jackson. Does little pieces on the arts for us.'

'Jackson?'

'Do you know his stuff? If you want to meet him, I'll be glad to introduce you. But I thought your interest in coming to the Café Royale tonight was in talking to H. G. Wells here. He's a rather larger gun, these days, eh, Wells?' Mr Harris roared with laughter and slapped Mr Wells on the shoulder. The quieter man smiled wanly, but he was plainly pleased by Harris's description.

'It's a pity so few of our other regular contributors are here tonight,' Harris went on. 'Kipling said he'd come, but as usual hasn't turned up. A bit of a dour old dog, y'know. And nothing of Richards for weeks. We thought we were to be blessed by a visitation from Mr Pett Ridge, too, tonight. All we can offer are Gregory, here, one of our editors.' A gangling young man who grinned as, unsteadily, he poured himself another glass of champagne. 'And this is our drama critic, name of Shaw.' A red-bearded, sardonic looking man with eyes almost as arresting as Mr Wells's, dressed in a suit of tweeds which seemed far too heavy for the weather, acknowledged the introduction with a grave bow from where he was seated at the far end of the table looking over a bundle of printed papers and occasionally making marks on them with his pen.

'I am glad to meet all of you, gentlemen,' said Jherek Carnelian desperately. 'But it is the man — Mr Jackson, you called him — who I am anxious to speak to.'

'Hear that, Wells?' cried Mr Harris. 'He's not interested in your fanciful flights at all. He wants Jackson. Jackson!' Mr Harris looked rather blearily about him. 'Where's Jackson gone? He'll be delighted to know he's read in Paris, I'm sure. We'll have to put his rates up to a guinea an item if he gets any more famous.'

Mr Wells was frowning, staring hard at Jherek. When he spoke, his voice was surprisingly high. 'You don't look too well, M. Fromental. Have you recently come over?'

'Very recently,' said Jherek. 'And my name isn't Fromental. It's Carnelian.'

'Where on earth is Jackson?' Mr Harris was demanding.

'We're all a bit drunk,' said Mr Wells to Jherek. 'The last of the copy's gone off and Frank always likes to come here to celebrate.' He called to Mr Harris. 'Probably gone back to the office, wouldn't you say?'

'That's it,' said Mr Harris satisfied.

'Would you kindly refrain from making so much

damned noise, Harris!' said the red-headed man at the far end of the table. 'I promised these proofs back by tonight. And where's our dinner, by the way?'

Mr Wells leaned forward and touched Mr Harris on the arm. 'Are you absolutely sure this chap Fromental's turning up, Harris? I should have left by now. I've some business to attend to.'

'Turning up? He's here, isn't he?'

'This appears to be a Mr Carnelian,' said Mr Wells dryly.

'Oh, really? Well, Fromental will turn up. He's reliable.'

'I didn't think you knew him personally.'

'That's right,' Mr Harris said airily, 'but I've heard a lot about him. He's just the man to help you, Wells.'

Mr Wells seemed sceptical. 'Well, I'd better get off, I think.'

'You won't stay to have your supper?' Mr Harris was disappointed. 'There were one or two ideas I wanted to discuss with you.'

'I'll drop round to the office during the week, if that's all right,' said Mr Wells, rising. He took his watch from his waistcoat pocket. 'If I get a cab I ought to make it to Charing Cross in time for the nine o'clock train.'

'You're going back to Woking?'

'To Bromley,' said Mr Wells. 'Some business I promised to clear up for my parents.'

'To Bromley, did you say?' Jherek sprang from his chair. 'To Bromley, Mr Wells?'

Mr Wells was amused. 'Why, yes. D'you know it?'

'You are going now?'

'Yes.'

'I have been trying to get to Bromley for – well, for a very long time. Might I accompany you?'

'Certainly.' Mr Wells laughed. 'I never heard of anyone who was eager to visit Bromley before. Most of us are only too pleased to get away from it. Come on, then, Mr Carnelian. We'll have to hurry!'

CHAPTER ELEVEN

A CONVERSATION ON TIME MACHINES
AND OTHER TOPICS

Although Mr Wells's spirits seemed to have lifted considerably after he had left the Café Royale, he did not speak much until they had left the cab and were safely seated in a second class carriage which smelled strongly of smoke. At the ticket office Jherek had been embarrassed when he was expected to pay for his fare, but Wells, generously supposing him to have no English money, had paid for them both. Now he sat panting in one corner while Jherek sat opposite him in the other. Jherek took a wondering curiosity in the furnishings of the carriage. They were not at all as he had imagined them. He noted little stains and tears in the upholstery and assured himself that he would reproduce them faithfully at the next opportunity.

'I am extremely grateful to you, Mr Wells. I had begun to wonder if I should ever find Bromley.'

'You have friends there, have you?'

'One friend, yes. A lady. Perhaps you know her?'

'I know one or two people still, in Bromley.'

'Mrs Amelia Underwood?'

Mr Wells frowned, shook his head and began to pack tobacco into his pipe. 'No, I'm afraid not. What part does she live in?'

'Her address is 23 Collins Avenue.'

'Ah, yes. One of the newer streets. Bromley's expanded a lot since I was a lad.'

'You know the street?'

'I think so, yes. I'll put you on your way, don't worry.' Mr Wells sat back with his eyes twinkling. 'Typical of old Harris to confuse you with someone else he'd never met. For some reason he hates to admit that he doesn't know someone. As a result he claims to know people he's absolutely no acquaintance with, they hear that he's spoken of them as if they were his dearest friends, get offended and won't have anything to do with him!' Mr Wells's voice was high-pitched, bubbling, animated. 'I'm inclined to be a bit in awe of him, none the less. He's ruined half-a-dozen papers, but still publishes some of the best stuff in London – and he gave me a chance I needed. You write for the French papers do you, Mr Carnelian?'

'Well, no . . .' said Jherek, anxious not to have a repetition of his previous experience, when he had told the absolute truth and had been thoroughly disbelieved. 'I travel a little.'

'In England?'

'Oh, yes.'

'And where have you visited so far?'

'Just the 19th century,' said Jherek.

Mr Wells plainly thought he had misheard Jherek, then his smile broadened. 'You've read my book!' he said

256

ebulliently. 'You travel in time, do you, sir?'

'I do,' said Jherek, relieved to be taken seriously for once.

'And you have a time machine?' Mr Wells's eyes twinkled again.

'Not now,' Jherek told him. 'In fact, I'm looking for one, for I won't be able to use the method by which I arrived, to return. I'm from the future, you see, not the past.'

'I see,' said Mr Wells gravely. The train had begun to move off. Jherek looked at identical smoke-grimed roof after identical smoke-grimed roof illumined by the gas-lamps.

'The houses all seem to be very similar and closely packed,' he said. 'They're rather different to those I saw earlier.'

'Near the Café Royale? Yes, well you won't have slums in your age, of course.'

'Slums?' said Jherek. 'I don't think so.' He was enjoying the jogging motion of the train. 'This is great fun.'

'Not quite like your monorails, eh?' said Mr Wells.

'No,' said Jherek politely. 'Do you know Mr Jackson, Mr Wells? The man who left when I arrived.'

'I've seen him once or twice. Had the odd chat with him. He seems interesting. But I visit the *Saturday Review*'s offices very infrequently – usually when Harris insists on it. He needs to *see* his contributors from time to time, to establish their reality, I think.' Mr Wells smiled in anticipation of his next remark. 'Or perhaps to establish his own.'

'You don't know where he lives in London?'

'You'll have to ask Harris that, I'm afraid.'

'I'm not sure I'll have the chance now. As soon as I find Mrs Underwood we'll have to start looking for a time machine. Would you know where to find one, Mr Wells?'

Mr Wells's reply was mysterious. 'In here,' he said, tapping his forehead with his pipestem. 'That's where I found mine.'

'You built your own?'

'You could say that.'

'They are not common in this period, then?'

'Not at all common. Indeed, some critics have accused me of being altogether too imaginative in my claims. They consider my inventions not sufficiently rooted in reality.'

'So time machines are just starting to catch on?'

'Well, mine seems to be catching on quite well. I'm beginning to get quite satisfactory results, although very few people expected it to go at first.'

'You wouldn't be prepared to build me one, would you, Mr Wells?'

'I'm afraid I'm more of a theorist than a practical scientist,' Mr Wells told him. 'But if you build one and have any success, be sure to let me know.'

'The only one I travelled in broke. There was evidence, by the way, to suggest that it came from a period two thousand years before this one. So perhaps you are actually *re*-discovering time travel.'

'What a splendid notion, Mr Carnelian. It's rare for me to meet someone with your particular quality of imagination. You should write the idea into a story for your Parisian readers. You'd be a rival to M. Verne in no time!'

Jherek hadn't quite followed him. 'I can't write,' he said. 'Or read.'

'No true Eloi should be able to read or write.' Mr Wells puffed on his pipe, peering out of the window. The train now ran past wider-spaced houses in broader streets as if some force at the centre of the city had the power to condense the buildings, as clay is condensed by centrifugal force as it is whirled on the potter's wheel. Jherek was hard put to think of any explanation and finally dismissed the problem. How, after all, could he expect to understand Dawn Age aesthetics as it were overnight?

'It's a shame you aren't doing my translations, M. Carnelian, you'd do a better job, I suspect, than some.

258

You could even improve on the existing books!'

Again unable to follow the animated words of the young man, Jherek Carnelian gave up, merely nodding.

'Still, it wouldn't do to let oneself get too far-fetched, I suppose,' Mr Wells said thoughtfully. 'People often ask me where I get my incredible ideas. They think I'm deliberately sensational. They don't seem to realize that the ideas seem very *ordinary* to me.'

'Oh, they seem exceptionally ordinary to me, also!' said Jherek, eager to agree.

'Do you think so?' piped H. G. Wells a little coldly.

'Here we are, Mr Carnelian. This is your fabulous Bromley. We seem to be the only visitors at this time of night.' Mr Wells opened the carriage door and stepped out onto the platform. The station was lit by oil-lamps which flickered in a faint breeze. At the far end of the train a man in uniform put a whistle to his lips and blew a shrill blast, waving a green flag. Mr Wells closed the door behind them and the train began to move out of the station. They walked past boxes full of flowers, past a white-painted fence, until they came to the exit. Here an old man accepted the tickets Mr Wells handed him. They crossed the station precinct and entered a street full of two-storey houses. A few gas-lamps lit the street. From somewhere nearby a horse trotted past. A couple of children were playing around one of the lamps. Jherek and Mr Wells turned a corner.

'This is the High Street,' Mr Wells informed him. 'I was born here, you know. It hasn't changed that much, though Bromley itself has expanded. It's pretty much a suburb of London now.'

'Ah,' murmured Jherek.

'There's Medhurst's,' Mr Wells pointed towards a darkened shop-front, 'and that's where Atlas House used to be. It was never much of a success, my father's china shop. There's the old *Bell*, where most of the profits were spent. Cooper's the tailors, seems to have gone out of business.

Woodall's fish-shop...' He chuckled. 'For a time, you know, this was Heaven for me. Then it was Hell. Now, it's merely Purgatory.'

'Why have you come back, Mr Wells?'

'Business of my father's to clear up. I'll stop at the *Rose and Crown* and go back in the morning. It doesn't do any harm for a writer to take a look at his roots occasionally. I've come a long way since Bromley and Up Park. I've been very lucky, I suppose.'

'And so have I been lucky, Mr Wells, in meeting you.' Jherek was almost ecstatic. 'Bromley!' he breathed.

'You must be this town's first tourist, Mr Carnelian.'

'Thank you,' Jherek said vaguely.

'Now,' said Mr Wells, 'I'll put you on your way to Collins Avenue, then I'll head for the *Rose and Crown* before they begin to wonder what's happened to me.'

Mr Wells escorted him through several streets, where the hedges were extremely high and the houses much newer looking, until they paused on a corner of one tree-lined, gas-lit road. 'Here we are in darkest semi-detached land,' Mr Wells announced. 'Collins Avenue, see?'

He pointed out a sign which Jherek couldn't read.

'And where would Number Twenty Three be?'

'Well, I'd say about half-way up – let's see – on this side of the road. Yes – can you see it – right by that lamp.'

'You're very kind, Mr Wells. In a few moments I shall be re-united with my lost love! I have crossed thousands of centuries to be at her side! I have disproved the Morphail Theorem! I have dared the dangerous and surging seas of Time! At last, at last, I near the end of my arduous quest for Bromley!' Jherek took Mr Wells by the shoulders and kissed him firmly upon the forehead. 'And it is thanks to *you*, Mr Wells, my dear!'

Mr Wells backed away, perhaps a trifle nervously. 'Glad to have been of insistence – um – assistance to you, Mr Carnelian. Now I really must rush.' And he turned and began to walk rapidly back in the direction they had come from.

Jherek was too happy to notice any change in Mr Wells's manner. He strode with buoyant steps along the pavement of Collins Avenue. He reached a gate of curly cast iron. He jumped over it and walked up a crazy-paving path to the door of a red-brick Gothic villa not at all unlike the one Mrs Underwood had had him build for her at the End of Time.

He knew what to do, for she had trained him well. He found the bell. He tugged it. He removed his top hat, wishing that he had remembered to bring some flowers with him. He studied, in admiration, the stained glass lilies set into the top half of the door.

There came a movement from within the house and at last the door was opened, but not by Mrs Underwood. A rather young girl stood there. She wore black, with a white cap and a white apron. She looked at Jherek Carnelian with a mixture of surprise, curiosity and contempt.

'Yus?'

'This is Twenty Three Collins Avenue, Bromley, Kent, England, 1896?'

'It is.'

'The residence of the beautiful Mrs Amelia Underwood?'

'It's the Underwood residence right enough. What's your business?'

'I have come to see Mrs Underwood. Is she within?'

'What's the name?'

'Carnelian. Tell her that Jherek Carnelian is here to take her back to their love-nest.'

'Gor blimey!' said the young girl. 'It's a bloomin' loony!'

'I do not follow you.'

'You'd better not try, mister. Be off wiv yer! Garn! Mrs Underwood'll 'ave the p'lice on yer wiv talk like that!' She tried to close the door, but Jherek was already partly inside. 'Mrs Underwood's a respectable lady! Shove off – go *on*!'

261

'I am really at a loss,' said Jherek mildly, 'to understand why you should have become so excited.' Baffled, he still refused to budge. 'Please tell Mrs Underwood that I am here.'

'Oh, lor! Oh, lor!' cried the girl. '' Ave a bit o' sense, will yer! You'll get yerself arrested! There's a good chap – be on yer way and we'll say no more abart it.'

'I have come for Mrs Underwood,' Jherek said firmly. 'I don't know why you should wish to stop me from seeing her. Perhaps I have offended one of your customs? I was convinced that I had done everything right. If there is something I should do – some convention I should follow – point it out, point it out. I have no desire to be rude.'

'Rude! Oh, lor!' And turning her head she shouted back into the hall. 'Mum! Mum! There's a maniac outside. I can't 'old him all be meself!'

A door opened. The hallway grew lighter. A figure in a dress of maroon velvet appeared.

'Mrs Underwood!' cried Jherek. 'Mrs Amelia Underwood! It is I, Jherek Carnelian, returned to claim you for my own!'

Mrs Underwood was as beautiful as ever, but even as he watched she grew. gradually paler and paler. She leaned against the wall, her hand rising to her face. Her lips moved, but no sound issued from them.

'Help me, mum!' begged the maid, retreating into the hall. 'I can't manage 'im be meself. You know 'ow strong these loonies can be!'

'I have returned, Mrs Underwood. I have returned!'

'You—' He could barely hear the words. 'You – were *hanged*, Mr Carnelian. By the neck, until dead.'

'Hanged? In the time machine, you mean? I thought you said you would go with me. I waited. You were evidently unable to join me. So I came back.'

'C-came back!'

He pushed his way past the shivering maid. He stretched out his arms to embrace the woman he loved.

She put a pale hand to a pale forehead. There was a certain wild, distracted look in her eyes and she seemed to be talking to herself.

'My experiences – too much – knew I had not recovered properly – brain fever ...'

And before he could take her to him she had collapsed upon the red and black Moorish-patterned carpet.

CHAPTER TWELVE

THE AWFUL DILEMMA
OF MRS AMELIA UNDERWOOD

'*Now* look wot you've gorn an' done!' said the little maid accusingly. 'Ain't you ashamed of yerself?'

'How could I have made her swoon?'

'You frightened 'er somefink crool – jest like you frightened *me*! All that dirty talk!'

Jherek kneeled beside Mrs Amelia Underwood, patting ineffectually at her limp hands.

'You promise you won't do nuffink *nasty* an' I'll go an' get some water an' *sal volatile*,' said the girl, looking at him warily.

'Nasty? I?'

'Oo, yore a cool one!' The girl's tone was half-chiding,

264

half-admiring as she left the hall through a door under the staircase, but she no longer seemed to regard him as a complete menace. She returned very quickly, holding a glass of water in one hand and a small green bottle in the other. 'Stand back,' she said firmly. She joined Jherek on the floor, lifted Mrs Underwod's head under one arm and put the bottle to her nose. Mrs Underwood moaned.

'Yore very lucky indeed,' the maid said, 'that Mr Underwood's at 'is meeting. But 'e'll be back soon enough. *Then* you'll be in trouble!'

Mrs Underwood opened her eyes. When she saw Jherek, she closed them again. And again she moaned, but this time it seemed that she moaned with despair.

'Have no fear,' whispered Jherek. 'I will have you away from all this as soon as you have recovered.'

Her voice, when she managed to speak, was quite controlled. 'Where have you been, Mr Carnelian, if you were not hanged?'

'Been? In my own age, of course. The age you love. Where we were happy.'

'I am happy *here*, Mr Carnelian, with my husband, Mr Underwood.'

'Of course. But you are not as happy as you would be with me.'

She took a sip from the glass of water, brushed the smelling salts aside, and began to get to her feet. Jherek and the maid helped her. She walked slowly into the sitting room, a rather understated version of the one Jherek had created for her. The harmonium, he noticed, did not have nearly so many stops as the one he had made, and the aspidistra was not as vibrant; neither was the quality of the antimacassars all it could have been. But the smell was better. It was fuller, staler.

Carefully she seated herself in one of the large armchairs near the fireplace. Jherek remained standing. She said to the girl:

'You may go, Maude Emily.'

'Go, miss?'

'Yes, dear. Mr Carnelian, though a stranger to our customs, is not dangerous. He is from abroad.'

'Aeow!' said Maude Emily, considerably relieved and illumined, satisfied now that she had an explanation which covered everything. 'Well, I'm sorry about the mistake then, sir.' She made something of a curtsey and left.

'She's a good-hearted girl, but not very well trained,' said Mrs Underwood apologetically. 'You know the difficulties one has getting – but, of course, you would not know. She has only been with us a fortnight and has broken almost every scrap of china in the house, but she means well. We got her from a Home, you know.'

'A home?'

'A Home. A Girl's Home. Something like a Reformatory. The idea is not to punish them but to train them for some useful occupation in Life. Usually, of course, they go into Service.'

The word had a faintly familiar ring to it. 'Cannon fodder!' said Jherek. 'A shilling a day!' He felt at something of a loss.

'I had forgotten,' she said. 'Forgive me. You know so little about our society.'

'On the contrary,' he said. 'I know even more than before. When we return, Mrs Underwood, you will be surprised at how much I have learned.'

'I do not intend to return to your decadent age, Mr Carnelian.'

There was an icy quality in her voice which he found disturbing.

'I was only too happy to escape,' she continued. Then, a little more kindly, 'Not, of course, that you weren't the soul of hospitality, after your fashion. I shall always be grateful to you for that, Mr Carnelian. I had begun to convince myself that I had dreamed most of what took place...'

'Dreamed that you loved me?'

'I did not tell you I loved you, Mr Carnelian.'

'You indicated...'

'You misread my —'

'I cannot read at all. I thought you would teach me.'

'I mean that you misinterpreted something I might have said. I was not myself, that time in the garden. It was fortunate that I was snatched away before we ... Before we did anything we should both regret.'

He was not perturbed. 'You love me. I know you do. In your letter —'

'I love Mr Underwood. He is my husband.'

'I shall be your husband.'

'It is not possible.'

'Anything is possible. When I return, my power rings...'

'It is not what I meant, Mr Carnelian.'

'We could have real children,' he said coaxingly.

'Mr Carnelian!' Her colour had returned at last.

'You are beautiful,' he said.

'Please, Mr Carnelian.'

He sighed with pleasure. 'Very beautiful.'

'I shall have to ask you to leave. As it is, my husband will be returning shortly, from his meeting. I shall have to explain that you are an old friend of my father's – that he met your family when he was a missionary in the South Seas. It will be a lie, and I hate to lie. But it will save both our feelings. Say as little as possible.'

'You know that you love me,' he announced firmly. 'Tell him that. You will leave with me now.'

'I will do no such thing! Already there has been difficulty – my appearance in court – the potential scandal. Mr Underwood is not an over-imaginative man, but he became quite suspicious at one point...'

'Suspicious?'

'Of the story I was forced to concoct, to try to save you, Mr Carnelian, from the noose.'

'Noose of what?'

A note of desperation entered her voice. 'How, by the way, did you manage to escape death and come here?'

'I did not know death threatened! I suppose it is always a risk in time travel, though. I came here thanks to the help of a kindly, mechanical old creature called Nurse. I had been trying for some while to find a means of returning to 1896 so that we might be reunited. A happy accident led to a succession of events which finally resulted in my arrival here, in Collins Avenue. Do you know a Mr Wells?'

'No. Did he claim to know me?'

'No. He was on some business of his father's at the *Rose and Crown*. He was telling me that he invented time machines. A hobby, I gather. He does not manufacture them, but leaves that to others. I had meant to ask him for the name of a craftsman who could build one for us. It will make our return much easier.'

'Mr Carnelian, I *have* returned – for good. This is my home.'

He looked critically about him. 'It is smaller than *our* home. It has a trace or two more authenticity, I'll grant you, but it lacks a certain life, wouldn't you say? Perhaps I should not mention Mr Underwood's failings, but it would seem to me he could have given you a little more.' He lost interest in the subject and began to feel in his pockets, to see if he had brought something which could be a gift, but all he had was the deceptor-gun Nurse had handed back to him shortly before he had begun his journey. 'I know that you like bunches of flowers and water closets and so forth (you see, I have remembered every detail of what you told me) but I forgot to make some flowers, and a water closet, of course, might have proved too bulky an object to carry through time. However,' and he had a revelation as he began to tug off his nicest power ring, a ruby, 'if you would accept this, I would be more than happy.'

'I cannot accept gifts of any sort from you, Mr Carnelian. How should I explain it to my husband?'

'Explain that I had given you something? Would that be necessary?'

'Oh, please, please go!' She started as she heard a movement in the passage outside. 'It is he!' She stared wildly around the room. 'Remember,' she said in an urgent whisper, 'what I told you.'

'I will try, but I don't understand...'

The door of the sitting room opened and a man of average height entered.

Mr Underwood wore a pair of pince-nez upon his nose. His hay-coloured hair was parted firmly in the middle. His high, white collar pressed mercilessly into his pink neck and the knot of his tie was so tight and small as to be almost microscopic. He was unbuttoning his jacket with the air of a man removing protective clothing in an environment which might not be altogether safe. Precisely, he put down a black book he had carried in with him. Precisely, he raised his eyebrows and, with precision, brushed back a hair which had strayed loose from his perfectly symmetrical moustache. 'Good evening,' he said, with only a hint of enquiry. He acknowledged the presence of his wife. 'My dear.'

'Good evening, Harold. Harold, this is Mr Carnelian. He has just come from the Antipodes, where his father and mine, as you might recall, were missionaries.'

'Carnelian? An unusual name, sir. Yet, as I remember, the same as that felon's who...'

'His brother,' said Mrs Underwood. 'I was commiserating with him as you entered.'

'A dreadful business,' Mr Underwood glanced at a newspaper on the sideboard with the eye of a hunter who sees his quarry disappearing from bowshot. He sighed and perhaps he smiled. 'My wife was very brave, you know, in offering to speak for the defence. Great risk of scandal. I was only telling Mr Griggs, at the Bible Meeting tonight, that if we all had such courage in following the teachings of our conscience we might come considerably closer to the gates of the Kingdom of Heaven.'

'Ha, ha,' said Mrs Underwood. 'You are very kind, Harold. I only did my duty.'

'We do not all have your fortitude, my dear. She is an admirable woman, is she not, Mr Carnelian?'

'Without doubt,' said Jherek feelingly. He stared with unashamed curiosity at his rival. 'The most wonderful woman in your world – in any world, Mr Underwood.'

'Um, yes,' said Mr Underwood. 'You are, of course, grateful for the sacrifice she made. Your enthusiasm is understandable...'

'Sacrifice?' Jherek turned to Mrs Underwood. 'I was not aware that this society practised such rites? Whom did you...?'

'You have been away from England a long time, sir?' asked Mr Underwood.

'This is my second visit,' Jherek told him.

'Aha!' Mr Underwood seemed satisfied by the explanation. 'In the darkest depths of the jungle, eh? Bringing light to the savage mind.'

'I was in a forest...' said Jherek.

'He only recently heard of his brother's sad fate,' broke in Mrs Underwood.

Jherek could not understand why she kept interrupting them. He felt he was getting on quite well with Mr Underwood; getting on rather better, in truth, than he had expected.

'Have you offered Mr Carnelian some refreshment, my dear?' Mr Underwood's pince-nez glinted as he looked about the room. 'We are, needless to say, teetotallers here, Mr Carnelian. But if you would care for some tea...?'

Mrs Underwood pulled enthusiastically at a bell-rope. 'What a good idea!' she cried.

Maude Emily appeared almost immediately and was instructed to bring tea and biscuits for the three of them. She looked from Mr Underwood to Jherek Carnelian and back again. The look was significant and caused the faintest expression of panic in Mrs Underwood's otherwise resolutely set features.

'Tea!' said Jherek as Maude Emily left. 'I don't believe I've ever had it. Or did we —'

This time, inadvertently, Mr Underwood came to his wife's rescue. 'Never had tea, what? Oh, then this is a treat you cannot miss! You must spend most of your time away from civilization, Mr Carnelian.'

'From this one, yes.'

Mr Underwood removed his pince-nez. From his pocket he took a large, white handkerchief. He polished the pince-nez. 'I take your meaning, sir,' he said gravely. 'Who are we to accuse the poor savage of his lack of culture, when we live in such Godless times ourselves?'

'Godless? I was under the impression that this was a Religious Age.'

'Mr Carnelian, you are misinformed, I fear. Your faith is allowed to blossom unchecked, no doubt, as you sit in some far-off native hut, with only your Bible and Our Lord for company. But the distractions one has to contend with in this England of ours are enough to make one give up altogether and look to the consolations of the High Church. Why,' his voice dropped, 'I knew a man, a resident of Bromley, who came very close once to turning towards *Rome*.'

'He could not find Bromley?' Jherek laughed, glad that he and Mr Underwood were getting on so well. 'I had a great deal of trouble myself. If I had not met a Mr Wells at a place called, as I remember, the Café Royale, I should still be looking for it!'

'*The Café Royale!*' hissed Mr Underwood, in much the same tone as he had said 'Rome'. He replaced his pince-nez and stared hard at Jherek Carnelian.

'I had become lost...' Jherek began to explain.

'Who has not, before he enters the door of that gateway to the underworld?'

'... and met someone who had lived in Bromley.'

'No longer, I trust?'

'So I gathered.'

Mr Underwood breathed a sigh of relief. 'Mr Carnelian,' he said, 'you would do well to remember the fate of your poor brother. Doubtless he was as innocent as you

271

when he first came to London. I beg you to remember that not for nothing has it been called Satan's Own City!'

'Who would this Mr Satan be?' asked Jherek conversationally. 'You see, I was re-creating the city and it would be useful to have the advice of one who . . .'

'Maude Emily!' sang Mrs Underwood, as if greeting the sight of land after many days in an open boat. 'The tea!' She turned to them. 'The tea is here!'

'Ah, the tea,' said Mr Underwood, but he was frowning as he mulled over Jherek's latest words. Even Jherek had the idea that he had somehow said the wrong thing, in spite of being so careful – not that he felt there was very much point in Mrs Underwood's deception. All he needed to do, really, was to explain the problem to Mr Underwood (who plainly did not share his passion for Mrs Underwood) and Mr Underwood would accept that he, Jherek, was likely to be far happier with Mrs Underwood. Mr Underwood could remain here (with Maude Emily, perhaps) and Mrs Underwood would leave with him, Jherek.

As Maude Emily poured the tea and Mrs Underwood stood near the fireplace fiddling with a small lace handkerchief and Mr Underwood peered through his pince-nez as if to make sure that Maude Emily poured the correct amount of tea into each cup, Jherek said:

'I expect you are happy here, aren't you, Maude Emily, with Mr Underwood?'

'Yes, sir,' she said in a small voice.

'And you are happy with Maude Emily, Mr Underwood?'

Mr Underwood waved a hand and moved his lips, indicating that he was as happy with her as he felt he had to be.

'Splendid,' said Jherek.

A silence followed. He was handed a tea-cup.

'What do you think?' Mr Underwood had become quite animated as he watched Jherek sip. 'There are those who shun the use of tea, claiming that it is a stimulant we can

272

well do without.' He smiled bleakly. 'But I'm afraid we should not be human if we did not have our little sins, eh? Is it good, Mr Carnelian?'

'Very nice,' said Jherek. 'Actually, I have had it before. But we called it something different. A longer name. What was it, Mrs Underwood.'

'How should I know, Mr Carnelian.' She spoke lightly, but she was glaring at him.

'Lap something,' said Jherek. 'Sou something.'

'Lap-san-sou-chong! Ah, yes. A great favourite of yours, my dear, is it not? China tea.'

'There!' said Jherek beaming by way of confirmation.

'You have met my wife before, Mr Carnelian?'

'As children,' said Mrs Underwood. 'I explained it to you, Harold.'

'You surely were not given tea to drink as children?'

'Of course not,' she replied.

'Children?' Jherek's mind had been on other things, but now he brightened. 'Children? Do you plan to have any children, Mr Underwood.'

'Unfortunately.' Mr Underwood cleared his throat. 'We have not so far been blessed...'

'Something wrong?'

'Ah, no...'

'Perhaps you haven't got the hang of making them by the straightforward old-fashioned method? I must admit it took me a while to work it out. You know,' Jherek turned to make sure that Mrs Underwood was included in the conversation, 'finding what goes in where and so forth!'

'Nnng,' said Mrs Underwood.

'Good heavens!' Mr Underwood still had his tea-cup poised half-way to his lips. For the first time, since he had entered the room, his eyes seemed to live.

Jherek's body shook with laughter. 'It involved a lot of research. My mother, the Iron Orchid, explained what she knew and, in the long run, when we had pooled the information, was able to give me quite a lot of practical

273

experience. She has always been interested in new ideas for love-making. She told me that while genuine sperm had been used in my conception, otherwise the older method had not been adhered to. Once she got the thing worked out, however (and it involved some minor biological transformations) she told me that she had rarely enjoyed love-making in the conventional ways more. Is anything the matter, Mr Underwood? Mrs Underwood?'

'Sir,' said Mr Underwood, addressing Jherek with cool reluctance, 'I believe you to be mad. In charity, I must assume that you and your brother are cursed with that same disease of the brain which sent him to the gallows.'

'My brother?' Jherek frowned. Then he winked at Mrs Underwood. 'Oh, yes, my brother...'

Mrs Underwood, breathing heavily, sat down suddenly upon the rug, while Maude Emily had her lips together, had gone very red in the face, and was making strange, strangled noises.

'Why did you come here? Oh, why did you come here?' murmured Mrs Underwood from the floor.

'Because I love you, as you know,' explained Jherek patiently. 'You see, Mr Underwood,' he began confidentially, 'I wish to take Mrs Underwood away with me.'

'Indeed?' Mr Underwood presented to Jherek a peculiarly glassy and crooked grin. 'And what, might I ask, do you intend to offer my wife, Mr Carnelian?'

'Offer? Gifts? Yes, well,' again he felt in his pockets but again could find nothing but the deceptor-gun. He drew it out. 'This?'

Mr Underwood flung his hands into the air.

CHAPTER THIRTEEN

STRANGE EVENTS IN BROMLEY ONE
NIGHT IN THE SUMMER OF 1896

'Spare them,' said Mr Underwood. 'Take me, if you must!'

'But I don't want you, Mr Underwood,' Jherek said reasonably, gesturing with the gun. 'Though it is kind of you to offer. It is *Mrs* Underwood I want. She loves me, you see, and I love her.'

'Is this true, Amelia?'

Dumbly, she shook her head.

'You have been conducting a liaison of some sort with this man?'

'That's the word I was trying to think of,' said Jherek.

'I don't believe you are that murderer's brother at all.'

275

Mr Underwood remembered to keep his hands firmly above his head. 'Somehow you have escaped the gallows – and you, Amelia, seem to have played a part in thwarting justice. I felt at the time ...'

'No, Harold. I have nothing to be ashamed of – or, at least, very little ... If I tried to explain what had happened to me one night, when ...'

'One night, yes? When?'

'I was abducted.'

'By this man?'

'No, that came later. Oh, dear! I told you nothing, Harold, because I knew it would be impossible for you to believe. It would have put a burden upon you that I knew you should not have to bear.'

'The burden of truth, Amelia, is always easier to bear than the burden of deceit.'

'I was carried into our world's most distant future. How, I cannot explain. There I met Mr Carnelian, who was kind to me. I did not expect ever to return here, but return I did – to the same moment in which I had left. I decided that I had had a particularly vivid dream. Then I learned of Mr Carnelian's appearance in our time – he was being tried for murder.'

'So he is the same man!'

'I felt it my duty to help him. I knew that he could not be guilty. I tried to prove that he was insane so that his life, at least, would be spared. My efforts, however, were fruitless. They were not helped by Mr Carnelian's naïve insistence upon a truth which none could be expected to believe. He was sentenced to death. The last I knew, he had perished through the usual auspices of the Law.'

'Preposterous,' said Mr Underwood. 'I can see that I have been an absolute fool. If you are not as mad as he, then you are guilty of the most unholy deception ever practised by an erring wife upon her trusting husband.' Mr Underwood was trembling. He ran a hand across his head, disturbing his hair. He loosened his tie. 'Well, luckily the Bible is very clear on such matters. You must go, of course. You must leave my house, Amelia, and thank Our Lord Jesus Christ for the New Testament and its counsels. If we lived in Old Testament times, your punishment would not be so lenient!'

'Harold, please. You are distraught, I can see. If you will try to listen to Mr Carnelian's story...'

'Ha! Must I listen to his ravings any further, before he kills me?'

'Kill you?' said Jherek mildly. 'Is that what you want, Mr Underwood? I'd willingly do anything to help...'

'Oh!'

Jherek saw Maude Emily leaving the room. Perhaps she had become so bored with the conversation. He was certainly having quite a lot of difficulty understanding Mr Underwood, whose voice was shaking so much, and pitched so high at times, that the words were distorted.

'I will do nothing to stand in your way,' Mr Underwood told him. 'Take her and leave, if that is what you want. She has told you she loves you?'

'Oh, yes. In a letter.'

'A letter! Amelia?'

'I wrote a letter, but...'

'So you are foolish, as well as treacherous. To think that, under my own roof, I supported such a creature. I had thought you upright. I had thought you a true Christian. Why, Amelia, I *admired* you. Admired you, it seems, for what was merely your disguise, a cloak of hypocrisy.'

'Oh, Harold, how can you believe such things? If you knew the lengths to which I went to defend my —'

'Honour? Really, my dear, you must consider me a pretty poor sort of brain, if you think you can continue any further with your charade!'

'Well,' said Jherek cheerfully, wishing that Mr Underwood would make his meaning clearer, but glad that the main problem had been cleared up, 'shall we be off, Mrs Underwood?'

'I cannot, Mr Carnelian. My husband is not himself. The shock of your appearance and of your – your language. I know that you do not mean badly, but the disruption you are causing is much worse than I feared. Mr Carnelian – please put the gun back in your pocket!'

He slipped it into its old place. 'I was going to offer it in exchange. As I understood ...'

'You understand nothing at all, Mr Carnelian. It would be best if you left ...'

'Leave with him, Amelia. I insist upon it.' Mr Underwood lowered his hands, drew out his pocket handkerchief and, with a precise, thoughtful air, glancing often at the white cloth, mopped his brow. 'It is what you both want, is it not? Your freedom. Oh, I gladly give it to you. You pollute the sanctity of my home!'

'Harold, I can scarcely believe the vehemence – you have always preached charity. You are normally so *calm*!'

'Should I be calm, now?'

'I suppose not, but ...'

'All my life I have lived by certain principles – principles I understood you to share. Must I join you in throwing them aside? Your father, the Reverend Mr Vernon, once warned me that you were overly inclined to high spirits. When we married, I found no sign of that side of your character and assumed that the sober business of being a good wife had driven it from you. Instead, it was buried. And not very deeply, either!'

'I fear, Harold, that it is you who are mad!'

He turned his back on them. 'Go!'

'You will regret this, Harold. You know you will.'

'Regret my wife conducting a liaison under my own roof with a convicted murderer? Yes!' He laughed without humour. 'I suppose I shall!'

Jherek took Mrs Underwood's arm. 'Shall we be off?'

Her imploring eyes were still upon her husband, but she allowed Jherek to lead her to the door.

And then they were in the peace of Collins Avenue. Jherek realized that Mrs Underwood was disturbed by the parting.

'I think Mr Underwood accepted the situation very

278

well, don't you? There you are, you see, all your fears, Mrs Underwood, were groundless. The truth is always worth telling. Mr Underwood said as much. Perhaps he did not behave as gracefully as one might have hoped, but still...'

'Mr Carnelian, I know my husband. This behaviour is untypical, to say the least. You have been responsible for making him undergo greater strain than anyone should have to tolerate. I, too, am partly responsible...'

'Why are you speaking in a whisper, Mrs Underwood?'

'The neighbours.' She shook her head. 'We might as well walk a little, I suppose. It will give Harold time to think things over. These Bible Meetings of his sometimes take rather more out of him than one might expect. He is very dedicated. His people have been missionaries for generations. It was always his regret that he could not follow in his father's footsteps. His health, while not singularly poor, is badly affected by hot climates. He has been like it from a small child, his mother was telling me.' She checked her flow. 'I am babbling, I fear.'

'Babble on, beautiful Mrs Underwood!' Jherek's stride was light and long. 'We shall soon be where we both belong. I remember every word of the letter Mr Griffiths read to me. Particularly the last part: " – and so I must tell you, Jherek, that I do love you, that I miss you, that I shall always remember you." Oh, how happy I am. Now I know what happiness *is*!'

'Mr. Carnelian, I wrote that letter in haste.' She added resentfully, 'I thought you were about to die.'

'I can't understand why.'

A deep sigh escaped her and she did not explain further.

They walked through a number of streets very similar to Collins Avenue (Jherek wondered how the people could find their way to their individual dwellings) and after a while Jherek noticed that she was shivering. He, himself, had become conscious of an increased chill in the air. He removed his coat and put it around her shoulders.

She did not resist the gesture.

'Thank you,' she said. 'If I were not a sensible woman, Mr Carnelian, I might at this moment be thinking that I have been ruined. I prefer to think, however, that Harold will come to understand his error and that we may be reconciled.'

'He will live with Maude Emily,' Jherek told her. 'He indicated as much. She will comfort him.'

'Oh, dear. Oh, dear.' Mrs Underwood shook her head. The road had given way to a path which ran between first fences and then hedges. Beyond the hedges were open fields. The sky was clear and a large moon offered plenty of light.

'I think that we are probably going in the wrong direction for the *Rose and Crown*.'

'Why should you wish to visit a public house?'

'*Public* house?'

'Why do you want to go to the *Rose and Crown*, Mr Carnelian?'

'To see Mr Wells, of course, Mrs Underwood. To ask him the name of a good maker of time machines.'

'In my age, there are no such things as time machines. If this acquaintance of yours told you that, he was probably having some sort of joke with you.'

'Oh, no. Our conversation was most serious. He was one of the few people I have met in your world who seemed to know exactly what I was talking about.'

'He was doubtless humouring you. Where did this conversation take place?'

'On the train. And what a marvellous experience that was, in its own right. I shall be making plenty of modifications as soon as we return.'

'Then you have no means, as yet, of escaping to your original period?'

'Well, no, but I can't see any difficulty, really.'

'There could be difficulties for both of us if Maude Emily, as I suspect, went for a policeman. If my husband has not had time to calm down he will inform the policeman, when he arrives, that an escaped murderer and his female accomplice are even now in the vicinity of Bromley – and that the man is armed. What was that thing you were waving, anyway?'

'The deceptor-gun? Would you like me to demonstrate it?'

'I think not.'

From the distance the silence of the night was broken by the sound of a high-pitched whistling.

'The police!' gasped Mrs Underwood. 'It is as I feared.' She clutched his arm, then removed her hand almost immediately. 'If they find you, you are doomed!'

'Why so? You refer to the gentlemen with the helmets who helped me before. They will have access to a time machine. It was thanks to them, after all, that I was able to return to my own age on my previous visit.'

She ignored him, pushing him through a gate and into a field. It smelled sweet and he paused to take the scent into his lungs. 'There is no question,' he began, 'that I have much to learn. Smells, for instance, are generally missing in my reproductions, and when they do exist they lack subtlety. If there were only some way of recording ...'

'Silence!' she whispered urgently. 'See, they are coming this way.' She pointed back to the road. A number of small, dancing lights were in evidence. 'It is their bulls-eyes. The whole of the Bromley constabulary must be on your trail!'

Again a whistle sounded. They crouched behind the hedge, listening to the swish of bicycle tyres over the un-made road.

'They'll be making for the railway station, that's my guess,' said a gruff voice. 'They'd be fools to head for open countryside. We're on a wild-goose chase.'

'You can never be sure about madmen,' said another voice. 'I was part of the lot what tracked down the Lewisham Murderer three years ago. They found 'im cool as a cucumber in a boarding 'ouse not five streets away from the scene of the crime. 'E'd bin there for a fortnight, while we raced about half of Kent night and day catching nothing but colds in the 'ead.'

'I *still* think they'll try for a train. That bloke said 'e *came* on the train.'

'We're not entirely sure it was the same man. Besides, 'e said *two* men, obviously friends, got off the train. What 'appened to the other?'

'I don't believe 'e *did* come on the train.'

'What's 'e doin' in Bromley, any'ow?' said a third voice complainingly.

'Come back for 'is bit o' stuff – you know what some women're like – go 'ead over 'eels for that sort. I've seen it before – perficktly decent women brought low by a smooth-talking villain. If she ain't careful I'd say she'll be 'is next victim.'

'Often the way it goes,' another agreed.

They passed out of earshot. Mrs Underwood seemed to have a high colour again. 'Really!' she said. 'So I already have a reputation as the consort of criminals. Mud sticks, as they say. Well, Mr Carnelian, you will never understand the damage you have done, I know, but I am currently very much regretting that I allowed my better nature to take me to the Old Bailey in your defence! Even at the time, there was a hint of gossip – but now – well, I shall have to consider leaving the country. And poor Harold – why should he be made to suffer?'

'Leaving? Good.' He stood up, brushing pieces of straw from his trousers. 'Now, let's go and find Mr Wells.'

'Mr Carnelian – it is really far too dangerous. You heard those policemen. The station is being watched. They are combing Bromley for us!'

Jherek was still puzzled. 'If they wish to talk to us, why do we not let them? What harm can they do us?'

'Considerable harm, Mr Carnelian. Take my word for it.'

He shrugged. 'Very well, Mrs Underwood, I shall. However, there is still the question of Mr Wells . . .'

'I assure you, also, that this Mr Wells of yours can be

nothing but a charlatan. Time machines do not exist in this century.'

'I believe he has written a book on them.'

Understanding dawned. She frowned. 'There *was* a book. I read about it last year. A fantasy. Fiction. It was nothing but fiction!'

'What is "fiction"?'

'A made-up story – about things which are not real.'

'Everything, surely, is *real*?'

'About things which do not exist...' She was labouring, trying to find the right words.

'But time machines *do* exist. You know that, Mrs Underwood, as well as I do!'

'Not yet,' she said. 'Not in 1896.'

'Mr Wells suggested otherwise. Who am I to believe?'

'You love me?'

'You know that I do.'

'Then believe *me*,' she said firmly, and she took his hand and led him across the field.

Some time later, they lay in a dry ditch, looking at the outline of a building Mrs Underwood had described as a farmhouse. Once or twice they had seen the lights of the policemen's lanterns some way off, but now it seemed their pursuers had lost the trail. Jherek was still not entirely convinced that Mrs Underwood had interpreted the situation correctly.

'I distinctly heard one of them say they were looking for geese,' he informed her. She seemed tired from all the running about and her eyes kept closing as she tried to find a more comfortable position in the ditch. 'Geese, and not people.'

'We must get the assistance of some influential man, who will take up your case, perhaps be able to convince the authorities of the truth.' She had pointedly ignored almost all his comments since they had left the house. 'I wonder – this Mr Wells is a writer. You mentioned his reference to the *Saturday Review*? That is quite a respectable journal – or at least it used to be. I haven't seen

283

a copy for some time. If he could publish something – or if he has friends in the legal profession. Possibly it would be a good idea to try to see him, after all. If we hide in that barn during the night and leave early in the morning, we might be able to get to him after the police have decided we have made our escape.'

Wearily, she rose. 'Come along, Mr Carnelian.' She began to tramp across the field towards the barn.

In approaching the barn, they had to pass close to the farmyard and now several dogs began to bark excitedly. An upper window was flung open, a lantern blazed, a deep voice called: 'Who is it? What is it?'

'Good evening to you,' cried Jherek. Mrs Underwood tried to cover his mouth with her hand but it was too late. 'We are out for a stroll, sampling the joys of your countryside. I must congratulate you ...'

'By cracky, it's the lunatic!' explained the unseen man. 'The one we were warned was on the loose. I'll get my gun!'

'Oh, this is unbearable!' wept Mrs Underwood. 'And look!'

Three or four lights could be seen in the distance.

'The police?'

'Without doubt.'

From the farmhouse came a great banging about, shouts and barkings, and lights appeared downstairs. Mrs Underwood grabbed Jherek by the sleeve and drew him inside the first building. In the darkness something snorted and stamped.

'It's a horse!' said Jherek. 'They always delight me and I have seen so many now.'

Mrs Underwood was speaking to the horse, stroking its nose, murmuring to it. It became calmer.

From the farmyard there was a sudden report and the deep-voiced man yelled: 'Oh, damn! I've shot the pig!'

'We have one chance of escape now,' said Mrs Underwood, flinging a blanket over the horse's back. 'Pass me that saddle, Mr Carnelian, and hurry.'

He did not know what a 'saddle' was, but he gathered it must be a strange contraption made out of leather and brass which hung on the wall near to his head. It was heavy. As best he could, he helped her put it on the horse's back. Expertly she tightened straps and passed a ribbon of leather around the beast's head. He watched admiringly.

'Now,' she hissed, 'quickly. Mount.'

'Is this the proper time for such things, do you think'?

'Climb onto the horse, and then help me up.'

'I have no idea how...'

She showed him. 'Put your foot in this. I'll steady the animal. Fling your leg over the saddle, find the other stirrup – that's this – and take hold of the reins. We have no alternative.'

'Very well. This is great fun, Mrs Underwood. I am glad that your sense of pleasure is returning.'

Climbing onto the horse was much harder than he would have thought, but eventually, just as another shot rang out, he was sitting astride the beast, his feet in the appropriate metal loops. Hitching up her skirts, Mrs Underwood managed to seat herself neatly across the saddle. She took the reins, saying to him 'Hang on to me!' and then the horse was trotting swiftly out of its stall and into the yard.

'By golly, they've got the 'orse!' cried the farmer. He raised his gun, but could not fire. Plainly he was not going to risk a horse as well as a pig in his bid to nail the madman.

At that moment about half-a-dozen burly policemen came rushing through the gate and all began to grab for the reins of the horse while Jherek laughed and Mrs Underwood tugged sharply at the reins crying, 'Your heels, Mr Carnelian. Use your heels!'

'I'm sorry, Mrs Underwood, I'm not sure what you mean!' Jherek was almost helpless with laughter now.

Frightened by the desperate police officers, the horse reared once, whinnied twice, rolled its eyes, jumped the fence and was off at a gallop.

The last Jherek Carnelian heard of those particular policemen was: 'Such goings on in Bromley! Who'd a credited it!'

There was the sound of a third shot, but it did not seem aimed at them and Jherek thought that probably the farmer and one of the police officers had collided in the dark.

Mrs Underwood was shouting at him. 'Mr Carnelian! You will have to try to help. I have lost control!'

With one hand on the saddle and the other about her waist, Jherek smiled happily as he was jolted mightily up and down; he came close to losing his seat upon the back of the beast. 'Ah, Mrs Underwood, I am delighted to hear it. At last!'

CHAPTER FOURTEEN

A SCARCITY OF TIME MACHINES

A fresh dawn brightened Bromley. Taking his leave of the *Rose and Crown*, having risen early to complete his business and be as swiftly as possible on his way, Mr Wells entered the High Street with the air of a man who had, during the night, wrestled with a devil and thoroughly conquered it. This return to Bromley had been reluctant for two reasons; the first reason being his own identification of the place with everything unimaginative, repressive and stultifying about England; the second was that his business was embarrassing in that he came as something of a petitioner, to save his father from an appearance in the County Court by clearing up a small financial matter which had, for many months, apparently escaped his father's attention. It was because of this that he had not been able to condescend to Bromley quite as much as he would have liked – after all, these were his roots. His father, as far as Bromley was concerned, had been a Failure, but the son was now on his way to being a Great Success, with five books already published and several more due to appear soon. He would have preferred his return to have been greeted with more publicity – perhaps a brief interview in the *Bromley Record* – and to have arrived in greater style, but the nature of his business made that impossible. Indeed, he hoped that nobody would recognize him and that was his main reason for leaving the hostelry so early. And the reason for his air of self-congratulation – he felt he was On Top of Bromley. It held no further fears for him. Questions of minor debts, of petty scandals, could no longer plunge him into the depths of anxiety he had once known. He had escaped from Bromley and now, by returning, he had escaped from the ghosts he had taken with him.

Mr Wells gave his stick a twirl. He gave his small moustache a flick (it had never grown quite as thick as he had hoped it would) and he pursed his lips in a silent whistle. A great sense of well-being filled him and he looked with a haughty eye upon Bromley; at the milkman's float with its ancient horse dragging it slowly along, at the newspaper delivery boy as he cycled from door to door, doubtless blessing the dull inhabitants of this dull town with news of dull civic doings, at the blinds still closed over all the familiar shop windows, including the window of Atlas House where his mother and father, intermittently, had brought him up and where his mother had done her best to instill in him the basic principles of Remaining Respectable.

He grinned. These days, he didn't give a fig for their Respectability. He was his own man, making his own way, according to his own rules. And what different rules they were! His encounter on the previous evening, with that strange, foreign young man, had cheered him up quite a bit, now realized. Thinking over their conversation, it had occurred to him that *The Time Machine* had been taken for literal truth by the stranger. That, surely, was a Sign of Success, if nothing was!

Birds sang, milk-cans clinked, the sky above the roof-tops of Bromley was clear and blue, there was a fresh sort of smell in the air, a sense of peace. Mr Wells filled his lungs.

He expelled his breath slowly, alert and curious, now, to a new sound, a rather less peaceful sound, in the distance. He paused, expectantly, and then was astonished to see, rounding the bend in the High Street, a large plough-horse, lathered in sweat, foaming a little at the mouth, eyes rolling, galloping at full tilt in his direction. He stopped altogether as he saw that the horse had two riders, neither, it seemed, very securely mounted. In the front was a beautiful young woman in a maroon velvet dress covered in bits of straw, mud and leaves, her dark red curls in disarray. And behind her, with one hand about her waist, the other upon the reins, in his shirt-sleeves (his coat seemed to have slipped down between them and was flapping like an extra leg against the horse's side) was the young stranger, Mr Carnelian, whooping and laughing, for all the world like a stock-broker's clerk enjoying the fun of the roundabout ride at a Bank Holiday Fair. Its way partly blocked by the milk-man's float, the horse balked for a moment, and Mr Carnelian spotted Mr Wells. He waved cheerfully, lurching backwards and barely managing to recover his balance.

'Mr Wells! We were hoping to see you.'

Mr Wells's reply fell a little flat, even to his own ears: 'Well, here I am!'

'I was wondering if you knew who could make me a time machine?'

Mr Wells did his best to humour the foreigner and with a chuckle pointed with his stick to the bicycle supported in the hands of the gaping delivery boy. 'I'm afraid the nearest thing you'll find to a Time Machine hereabouts is that piece of ironmongery over there!'

Mr Carnelian took note of the bicycle and seemed ready to dismount, but then the horse was off again, with the young woman crying 'Woe! Woe!' or possibly 'Woah! Woah!' and her co-rider calling back over his shoulder: 'I am much obliged, Mr Wells! Thank you!'

Now five mud-drenched police constables on equally muddy cycles came racing round the corner and the leading officer was pointing at the disappearing pair, shouting:

'Collar 'im! It's the Mayfair Killer!'

Mr Wells watched in silence as the squadron went past, then he crossed the road to where the delivery boy was still standing, his jaw threatening to detach itself altogether from the rest of his face. Feeling in his waistcoat pocket, Mr Wells produced a coin. 'Would you care to sell me one of your papers?' he asked.

He had begun to wonder if Bromley had not ceased to be quite as dull as he remembered it.

Jherek Carnelian, with a bemused expression on his face, watched the oar drift away through the weed-strewn waters of the river. Mrs Underwood lay in fitful slumber at the other end of the boat (which they had requisitioned after the horse, on attempting to jump a fence a good ten miles from Bromley, had deposited them near the river).

Jherek had not had a great deal of success with the oars, anyway, and he was scarcely sorry to see the last one go. He leaned back, with one arm upon the tiller, and yawned. The day was extremely warm now and the sun was high in the sky. There came the lazy sounds of bees in the tall grass of the nearest bank and, on the other side of the river, white-clad ladies played croquet on a green and perfect lawn; the music of their tinkling laughter, the clack of mallets against balls, came faintly to Jherek's ears. This world was so *rich*, he thought, plucking a couple of small leaves off his battered jacket and inspecting them carefully. The texture, the detail, were all fascinating, and he wondered at the possibility of reproducing them when he and Mrs Underwood returned home.

Mrs Underwood stirred, rubbing at her eyes. 'Ah,' she said, 'I feel a little better for that.' She became aware of her surroundings. 'Oh, dear. We are adrift!'

'I lost the oars,' Jherek explained. 'See – there's one. But the current seems adequate. We are moving.'

She did not comment on this, but her lips curved in a smile which might have been described as philosophical rather than humorous.

'These time machines are much more common than you thought,' Jherek told her. 'I've seen several from the boat. People were riding them along the path beside the river. And those policemen had them, too. Probably thought they would follow us through Time.'

'Those are bicycles,' said Mrs Underwood.

'It's hard to tell them apart, I suppose. They all look very similar to me, but to your eye...'

'Bicycles,' she repeated, but without vehemence.

'Well,' he said, 'it all goes to show that your fears were groundless. We'll be back soon, you see.'

'Not by this method, I trust. In which direction are we heading?' She looked around her. 'Roughly westwards, I would say. We might easily be in Surrey. Ah, well, the police will find us eventually. I am reconciled.'

'In a world where Time seems so important,' Jherek mused, 'you'd think they would have more machines for manipulating it.'

'Time manipulates *us* in this world, Mr Carnelian.'

'As, of course, it will, according to Morphail. You see the reason I came so urgently to find you, Mrs Underwood, was that sooner or later we shall be plunged into the future, but the difference will be that we shall not be able to control our flight – we could land anywhere – we could be separated again.'

'I do not quite follow you, Mr Carnelian.' She dangled her hand in the water in a gesture which, for her, was almost abandoned.

'Once you have travelled into the future, you cannot remain for long in the past, lest a paradox result. Thus time itself ejects those whose presence in certain ages would lead to confusion, an alteration of history or something like that. How we have managed to remain so long in this period is a mystery. Presumably we have not yet begun to produce dangerous paradoxes. But I think that the moment we do, then we shall be on our way.'

'Are you suggesting that we shall have no choice?'

'I am. Thus we must make all speed to get back to *my* time, where you'll be happy. Admittedly, if we go into a future where time machines are less scarce, we should be able to make the journey in, as it were, several hops, but some of the periods between 1896 and the End of Time were exceptionally uncongenial and we could easily land in one of those.'

'You are trying to convince me, then, that I have no alternative?'

'It is the truth.'

'I have never known you to lie, Mr Carnelian.' She smiled that same smile again. 'I have often prayed that you would! Yet if I had remained in my own time and said nothing of what had happened to me, refused to act according to what I knew of the future, I might have remained here forever.'

'I suppose so. It might explain the instinct of some time travellers to speak as little of the future as possible and never to make use of their information. I have heard of these and it could be that they are "allowed" by Time to stay where they wish. By and large, however, few can resist talking of their adventures, making use of their information. Of course, we wouldn't really know about the ones who said nothing, would we? That could explain the flaw in the Morphail Theorem.'

'So – I shall say nothing and remain in 1896,' she said.

'By now Harold might have recovered his senses and if I tell the police that I was kidnapped by you I might not be charged as your accomplice. Moreover, if you disappear, then they'll never be able to prove you were the Mayfair Killer, somehow escaped from death. But we shall still need help.' She frowned.

There came a scraping sound from beneath them.

'Aha!' she said. 'We are in luck. The boat has run aground.'

They disembarked onto a narrow, sandy path. From the path ran a steep bank on which grew a variety of yellow, blue and scarlet flowers. At the top of the bank was a white fence.

While Mrs Underwood tidied her hair, using the river as a mirror, Jherek began to pick the flowers until he had quite a large bunch. His pursuit of a particularly fine specimen forced him to climb to the top of the bank so that he could then see what lay beyond the fence.

The bank went down to fields which were of a glowing green and oddly flat; and on the other side of the fields were a group of red-brick buildings, decorated with a number of rococo motifs in iron and stone. A tributary of the river ran alongside the buildings and in some of the more distant fields there were machines at work. The machines consisted of a heavy central cylinder from which extended about ten very long rods. As Jherek watched, the cylinders turned and the rods swung with them, distributing liquid evenly over the bright green fields. They were plainly agricultural robot workers; Jherek dimly remembered hearing about them in some malfunctioning record found in one of the rotted cities. He recalled that they had existed during the time of the Multitude Cultures, but he now knew enough about this particular period to be aware that they were still a rarity. This must then be something of an experimental project, he guessed. As such the buildings he could see could quite easily comprise a scientific establishment and, if so, there would be people there who would know how to go about procuring a time machine.

He was excited as he ran back down the bank, but he did not forget his priorities. He paused to arrange the flowers and, when she stood up from her toilet, turning towards him, he presented the bunch.

'A little late, I fear,' he said. 'But here they are! Your flowers, Mrs Underwood.'

She hesitated for a moment and then reached out to take them. 'Thank you, Mr Carnelian.' Her lips trembled.

He looked searchingly at her face. 'Your eyes –' he said – 'they seem wet. Did you splash some water into your face?'

She cleared her throat and put fingers first to one eye and then the other. 'I suppose I did,' she agreed.

'I believe that we are a little closer to our goal,' he told her, pointing back up the bank. 'It will not be long now before we are back in my own age and you can take up my "moral education" where you were forced to leave it, when you were snatched from my arms.'

She shook her head and her smile, now, seemed a little warmer. 'I sometimes wonder if you are *deliberately* naïve, Mr Carnelian. I have told you – my duty is to return to Harold and try to ease his mind. Think of him! He is not – not a flexible man. He must be in agony at this moment.'

'Well, if you wish to return, we will both go. I will explain to him in more detail...'

'That would not help. Somehow we must ensure your safety, then I will go to him on my own.'

'And after that, you will come to me?'

'No, Mr Carnelian.'

'Even though you love me?'

'Yes, Mr Carnelian. And, I say again. I have not confirmed what I said at a time when I was not altogether in my right senses. Besides, Mr Carnelian, what if I did love you? I have seen your world – your people play at real life – your emotions are the emotions of actors – sincere for the moment that they are displayed on stage before the public. Knowing this, how would I feel if I did love you? I would be aware that your love for me is nothing but a sentimental imposture, pursued, admittedly, with a certain persistence, but an imposture none the less.'

'Oh, no, no, no!' His large eyes clouded. 'How could you think that?'

They stood in silence upon the bank of the tranquil river. Her eyes were downcast as she looked at the flowers; her delicate hands stroked the petals; she breathed rapidly. He took a step towards her and then stopped. He thought for a moment, before he spoke.

'Mrs Underwood?'

'Yes, Mr Carnelian?'

'What *is* an imposture?'

She looked up in surprise and then she laughed. 'Oh, dear, Mr Carnelian! Oh dear! What are we to do?'

He took her hand and she did not resist him. He began to lead her up the bank. We'll go to the people who live in the laboratories I've just spotted. They'll help us.'

'Laboratories. How do you know?'

'Robot workers. You don't have many in 1896, do you?'

'We have none at all, as far as I've heard!'

'Then I am right. It is of an experimental nature. We shall find scientists there. And scientists will not only understand what I have to say – they'll be more than glad to be of assistance!'

'I am not at all sure, Mr Carnelian – Oh!' She had reached the fence, she was looking at the scene below them. First she blushed and then she laughed. 'Oh, Mr Carnelian, I'm afraid your hopes are unjustified. I wondered what the smell might be ...'

'Smell? Is it unusual?'

'A little. Oh, my goodness...'

'It is not an experimental farm, Mrs Underwood?' For the first time his spirits threatened to desert him.

'No, Mr Carnelian. It is what we call a sewage farm.' She leaned on the fence and as she laughed tears ran down her cheeks.

'What is "sewage"?' he asked.

'It is not something a lady could tell you, I fear!'

He sat down on the ground at her feet. He put his head in his hands and he became aware of a hint of despair in the back of his mind.

'Then how are we to find a time machine?' he said. 'Even an old one, even that broken one I left behind on my last visit – it would be *something*. Ah, Mrs Underwood, I think I have not planned this adventure as well as I might have done.'

'Perhaps that is why I am beginning to enjoy it,' she said. 'Cheer up, Mr Carnelian. My father always used to tell me that there was nothing like a good, solid, seemingly unsolvable problem to get one's teeth into and take one's mind off the usual silly anxieties which plague us. And this problem is huge – it certainly makes any others I might have had seem very trivial indeed! I must admit I had sunk into self-pity and that will never do. But I am over that now.'

'I suspect that I am only just beginning to discover what it is,' said Jherek feelingly. 'Does it involve a belief in an anthropomorphical and malevolent being called Fate?'

'I'm afraid it does, Mr Carnelian.'

He pulled himself slowly to his feet. She helped him on with his coat. He brightened at the next thought which occurred to him. 'Perhaps, however, it is furthering my "moral education"? Would that be the case, Mrs Underwood?'

They began to climb down the bank and back to the sandy path.

This time she took him by the hand. 'It's more in the nature of a side-effect, though I know I shouldn't sound so cynical. Mr Underwood has often said to me that there is nothing so unwelcome in the sight of the Lord than a cynical woman. And there are a great many of them about, I'm afraid, in these worldly and upsetting modern times of ours. Come along, let's see where this path takes us.'

'I hope,' he murmured, 'that it is not back to Bromley.'

296

CHAPTER FIFTEEN

ENTRAINED FOR THE METROPOLIS

The small sandy-haired man unscrewed the ebony and glass object from his right eye and sucked somewhat noisily at his teeth. 'Funny,' he said. 'It's a cut above yer usual paste. I'll give ya that much. But it's no more a real ruby than the kind ya kin by fer`a shillin' in the market. Settin's nice, though, I can't recognize the metal. Well, 'ow much d'yer wanna borrow on it?' He held out Jherek's power ring on the palm of his hand.

Mrs Underwood stood nervously beside Jherek at the counter. 'A sovereign?'

'I dunno.' He looked at it again. 'It's a curiosity, an' beautiful workmanship, I'll grant ... But what do I risk?

Fifteen bob?'

'Very well,' said Mrs Underwood. She accepted the money on Jherek's behalf. He was half-stupefied by the negotiations, having no clear idea of what was taking place. He didn't mind losing a power ring, for he could easily get another on his return and they were useless here, but he could not quite understand why Mrs Underwood was giving it to this man and why the man was giving her something in exchange. She accepted a ticket and tucked it into his top pocket.

They left the shop and entered a busy street. 'Luckily it's market day and we shan't be too noticeable,' said Mrs Underwood. 'Gypsies and so on will be about, as well.' Carts and carriages jammed the narrow roadway and a couple of motorcars added to the confusion, their fumes giving rise to a great deal of pointed coughing and loud complaints from those on foot. 'We'll have something to eat at the station buffet, while we are waiting for the train. Once in London, we'll go straight to the Café Royale and hope that one of your friends is there. It is our only chance.' She walked as rapidly as possible up the winding pavement of the country street, turning into an alley blocked by two posts; the alley became a series of stone steps. They climbed them and found themselves in a much quieter road. 'The station's this way, I believe,' she said. 'It is a stroke of luck that we were so close to Orpington.'

They approached a green and red building. It was indeed, the railway station and Mrs Underwood marched boldly to the ticket office and bought them two Second Class single tickets to Charing Cross. 'We have twenty minutes to wait,' she said, glancing at the clock over the ticket office, 'ample time for refreshments. And,' she added in an undertone, 'there are no police in evidence. We appear for the moment to have made good our escape.'

It was Jherek's first encounter with the cheese sandwich.

He found it rather hard going, but he made the most of the experience, telling himself that, after all, he might not have the chance again. He enjoyed the tea, finding it rather nicer than the beverage he had had at Mrs Underwood's, and when, at last, the train came steaming into the station he cried out in delight: 'It is just like my own little engine at home!'

Mrs Underwood seemed embarrassed. Some of the other people in the refreshment room were looking at Jherek and whispering among themselves. But Jherek hardly noticed. He was dragging Mrs Underwood eagerly through the doors and onto the platform.

'Orping*ton*,' called a thin man in a dark uniform. '*Or*pington!'

Jherek waited impatiently for some passengers to leave their carriage and he climbed in, nodding and smiling to those who were already seated.

'Isn't it splendid?' he said to her as they sat down. 'Ancient transport has always been one of my chief enthusiasms – as you know.'

'Please try to say as little as possible,' she begged him in a whisper. She had already warned him that the newspapers would have published reports of their adventures of the previous night. He apologized and settled back, but he could not resist peering animatedly out of the windows at the scenery as it went past.

Mrs Underwood seemed particularly distraught by the time they reached Charing Cross. Before leaving the carriage, she leaned out of the open window and then waited until all the other passengers had gone before saying to Jherek: 'I cannot see any sign that the police are waiting for us. But we must hurry.'

They joined the crowds making their way towards the barriers at the far end of the platforms and here even Jherek was conscious that they did not quite look the same as the others. Mrs Underwood's dress was muddy, crumpled and torn in a couple of places; also she wore no hat, whereas all the other ladies had hats, veils, sunshades and coats. Jherek's black coat was stained and as battered as Mrs Underwood's dress and he had a large hole in the knee of his left trouser leg. As they reached the gate and handed their tickets to the collector, they attracted some comment as well as disapproving glances. And it was Jherek who saw the policeman come walking ponderously towards them, his tongue thoughtfully stroking his lower lip, his hands clasped behind his back.

'Run, Mrs Underwood!' he shouted urgently.

And then it was too late for her to brazen out the confrontation for the policeman was saying: 'By Golly, it is them!' and was beginning to pull a whistle from his pocket.

They dashed for the exit, blundering first into a very large woman carrying a basket and leading a very small black and white dog on a piece of string, who cried ''ere, watch it!' rather too late; then into two maiden ladies who cackled like startled hens and said a great deal concerning the manners of the young; and lastly into a stout stockbroker in a hat of exaggerated height and sleekness, who grunted 'Bless my soul!' and sat down on a fruitstall so that the fruitstall collapsed and sent apples, grapefruit, oranges and pineapples rolling about in all directions, causing the policeman to interrupt his attempts to blow his whistle as he dodged a veritable Niagara of pears, calling after them: 'Stop there! Stop, I say, in the name of the Law!'

Outside the station they found themselves in the Strand and now Jherek saw something leaning against a wall on the corner of Villiers Street.

'Look!, Mrs Underwood – we are saved. A time machine!'

'That, Mr Carnelian, is a tandem bicycle.'

He already had his hands on it and was trying to straddle it as he had seen the others do.

'We would do better to hail a cab,' she said.

'Get aboard quickly. Can you see any controls?'

With a sigh, she took the remaining saddle, in the

front. 'We had best head for Regent Street. It is not far, happily. The other side of Piccadilly. At least this will prove to you, once and for all, that ...'

Her voice was lost as they hurtled into the press of the traffic, weaving between trams and omnibuses, between horses and motor cars and causing both to come to sudden stops and stand stock still in the middle of the road, panting and shuddering.

Jherek, expecting to see the scene vanish at any moment, paid little attention to the confusion happening around them. He was having a great deal of trouble keeping his balance upon the time machine.

'It will be soon!' he cried into her ear, 'it *must* be soon!' And he pedalled harder. All that happened was that the machine lurched onto the pavement, shot across Trafalgar Square at considerable speed, up the Haymarket, and was in Leicester Square almost before they had realized it. Here Jherek fell off the tandem, to the vast entertainment of a crowd of street urchins hanging about outside the doors of the Empire Theatre of Varieties.

'It doesn't seem to work,' he said.

Mrs Underwood informed him that she had told him so. She now had a large tear in the hem of her dress where it had caught in the chain. However, for the moment, they did not appear to have the police on their trail.

'Quickly,' she said, 'and let us pray to heaven that someone who knows you is in the Café Royale!'

Heads turned as they ran across Piccadilly Circus and arrived at last at the doors of the Café Royale which Jherek had last visited less than twenty-four hours before. Mrs Underwood pushed at the doors, but they would not budge. 'Oh goodness!' she said in despair. 'It's closed!'

'Closed?' said Jherek. He pressed his face to the glass. He could see people inside. He signed to them, but they shook their hands from side to side and pointed at the clock.

'Closed,' sighed Mrs Underwood. She uttered a funny, toneless laugh. 'Well, that's it! We're finished!'

'Hey!' called someone. They turned, ready to run, but it was not the police. From the great tide of traffic converging upon Piccadilly Circus they distinguished a hansom cab, its driver seated high in the rear of the vehicle, his face expressionless. 'Hi!' said a voice from within the cab.

'Mr Harris!' called Jherek, recognizing the face. 'We were hoping you would be in the Café Royale.'

'Get in!' hissed Harris. 'Hurry. Both of you.'

Mrs Underwood lost no time in accepting his offer and soon the three of them were crammed in the cab and it was jogging around the Circus and back towards Leicester Square.

'You *are* the young man I saw yesterday,' said Harris in triumph. 'I thought so. This is a bit of luck.'

'Luck for us, Mr Harris,' said Mrs Underwood, 'but not for you if your part in this is discovered.'

'Oh, I've bluffed my way out of worse situations,' he said. He laughed easily. 'Besides, I'm a journalist first and foremost -- and we newshounds are permitted a certain amount of leeway when obtaining a really tip-top story. I'm not just helping you out of altruism, you know. I read the papers today. They're saying that you're the Mayfair Killer come back from the dead to be re-united with your – um – paramour!' Mr Harris's eyes gleamed. 'What's your version? You certainly bear a striking resemblance to the Killer. I saw a drawing in one of the papers when the trial was taking place. And you, young lady, were a witness for the defence at the trial, were you not?'

She looked at Mr Harris a little suspiciously. It seemed to Jherek that she did not altogether like the bluff, rapid-speaking editor of the *Saturday Review*.

He saw that she hesitated and raised his hand. 'Say no more at this stage! What reason, after all, have you to trust me.' With his stick he opened a hatch at the top of the cab. 'I have changed my mind, cabby. Take us, instead, to Bloomsbury Square.' He let the flap fall back and turning to them said, 'I have rooms there where you will be safe for the moment.'

'Why are you helping us, Mr Harris?'

'I want an exclusive of your story, ma'am, for one thing. Also, there were facts about the Mayfair case which never seemed to fit right. I am curious to know what you can tell me.'

'You could help us with the Law?' Hope now overcame her caution.

'I have many friends,' said Mr Harris, stroking his chin with the head of his cane, 'in the Law. I am on intimate terms with several High Court Judges, Queen's Counsels – eminent lawyers of all descriptions. I think you could call me a man of influence, ma'am.'

'Then we may yet be saved,' said Mrs Underwood.

CHAPTER SIXTEEN

THE MYSTERIOUS MR JACKSON

After installing Mrs Underwood and Jherek Carnelian in his Bloomsbury rooms, Mr Harris left, telling them that he would return as soon as possible and that they were to make themselves comfortable. The rooms, it seemed, did not really meet with Mrs Underwood's approval, though Jherek found them extremely pleasant. There were numerous pictures of attractive young people upon the walls, there were thick velvet curtains at the windows, and deep-piled Turkish carpets upon the floors. There were porcelain figurines and a profusion of jade and amber ornaments. Looking through the books, Jherek found a great many elegant drawings of a kind he had not previously seen and he showed them to Mrs Underwood, hoping that they might cheer her up, but instead she closed the books with a bang, refusing to explain why she would not look at the pictures. He was disappointed, for he had hoped that she would help the time pass by reading to him from the books. He found some other books, with yellow paper covers, which did not have pictures, and handed one of these to her.

'Perhaps you could read this?'

She glanced at it and sniffed. 'It is *French*,' she said.

'You do not like it, either?'

'It is French.' She looked through into the bedroom, at the wide bed with its lavish coverings. 'This whole place reeks of the *fin de siècle*. Although Mr Harris has helped us, I do not have to approve of his morals. I am in no doubt as to his purposes in keeping these rooms.'

'Purposes? Does he not live in them?'

'Live? Oh, yes. To the full, it seems. But I suspect this is not the address at which he entertains his respectable friends.' She crossed to a window and flung it up. 'If he has any,' she added. 'I wonder how long we shall have to stay here.'

'Until Mr Harris has time to talk to a few people he knows and to take down our story,' said Jherek, repeating what Mr Harris had told them. 'There is a great sense of safety about this apartment, Mrs Underwood. Don't you feel it?'

'It has been designed to avoid ordinary public scrutiny,' she said, and she sniffed again. Then she stared into one of the long gilt mirrors and tried, as she had tried before, to tidy her hair.

'Aren't you tired?' Jherek walked into the bedroom. 'We could lie down. We could sleep.'

'So we could,' she said sharply. 'I suspect that there is more lying down than standing up goes on here, as a rule. Art nouveau everywhere! Purple plumes and incense. This is where Mr Harris entertains his actresses.'

'Oh,' said Jherek, having given up trying to understand

her. He accepted, however, that there was something wrong with the rooms. He wished that Mrs Underwood had been able to complete his moral education; if she had, he felt, he, too, might be able to enjoy sniffing and pursing his lips, for there was not much doubt that she *was* taking a certain pleasure in her activities: her cheeks were quite flushed, there was a light in her eyes. 'Actresses?'

'So-called.'

'There does not seem much in the way of food here,' he told her, 'but there are lots of bottles. Would you like something to drink?'

'No thank you, Mr Carnelian. Unless there is some mineral water.'

'You had better look for yourself, Mrs Underwood. I don't know which is which.'

Hesitantly, she entered the bedroom and surveyed the wide selection on a small sideboard set against the wall. 'Mr Harris appears to have a distaste for Adam's Ale,' she said. Her head lifted as there came a knocking upon the outer door. 'Who could that be?'

'Mr Harris returning earlier than expected?'

'Possibly. Open the door, Mr Carnelian, but have a care. I do not entirely trust your journalist friend.'

Jherek had some difficulty with the catch and the light knocking sounded again before he had the door open. When he saw who stood there, he grinned with relief and pleasure. 'Oh, Jagged, dear Jagged! At last! It is you!'

The handsome man in the doorway removed his hat. 'The name,' he said, 'is Jackson. I believe I saw you briefly last night at the Café Royale? You would be Mr Carnelian.'

'Come in, devious Jagged!'

With a slight bow to Mrs Underwood, who stood now in the centre of the sitting room, Lord Jagged of Canaria entered. 'You would be Mrs Underwood? My name is Jackson. I work for the *Saturday Review*. Mr Harris sent me to take some shorthand notes. He will join us later.'

'You are the judge!' she exclaimed. 'You are Lord Jagger, who sentenced Mr Carnelian to death!'

The man who claimed to be Mr Jackson raised his eyebrows as, with a delicate movement, he divested himself of his top-coat and laid it, together with his hat, gloves and stick, upon the table. 'Mr Harris warned me that you would still be a little agitated. It is understandable, madam, in the circumstances. I assure you that I am neither of the two men so far mentioned. I am merely Jackson – a journalist. My job is to put some basic questions to you. Mr Harris sent his regards and said that he is doing everything in his power to contact someone in high places – who must for the moment be nameless – in the hope that they will be able to assist you.'

'You bear a remarkable resemblance to the Lord Chief Justice,' she said.

'So I have been told. But I am neither as eminent nor as talented as that gentleman, to my regret.'

Jherek was laughing. 'Listen to him! Isn't he perfect!'

'Mr Carnelian,' she said, 'I think you are making a mistake. You will embarrass Mr Jackson.'

'No, no!' Mr Jackson dismissed the suggestion with a wave of his slender hand. 'We journalists are pretty hardy fellows, you know.'

Jherek shrugged. 'If you are not Jagged – and Jagged was not Jagger – then I must assume there are a number of Jaggeds, each playing different rôles, perhaps throughout history . . .'

Mr Jackson smiled and produced a notebook and a pencil. 'That's the stuff,' he said. 'We seem to have a rival to your friend Mr Wells, eh, Mrs Underwood?'

'Mr Wells is not my friend,' she said.

'You know him, however, don't you – Mr Jackson?' asked Jherek.

'Only slightly. We've had the odd conversation in the past. I've read a good many of his books, however. If your story is up to *The Wonderful Visit* and can be presented in the right way, then our circulation's assured!' He settled himself comfortably in a deep armchair. Jherek and Mrs Underwood sat on the edge of the ottoman opposite him. 'Now, I gather you're claiming to be the Mayfair Killer returned from the dead...'

'Not at all!' exclaimed Mrs Underwood. 'Mr Carnelian would not kill anyone.'

'Unfairly accused, then? Returned to vindicate the claim? Oh, this is splendid stuff!'

'I haven't *been* dead,' said Jherek. 'Not recently at any rate. And I don't understand about the rest.'

'You are on the wrong tack, I fear, Mr Jackson,' said Mrs Underwood primly.

'Where *have* you been, then, Mr Carnelian?'

'In my own time – in Jagged's time – in the distant future, of course. I am a time traveller, just as Mrs Underwood is.' He touched her hand, but she removed it quickly. 'That is how we met.'

'You honestly believe that you have travelled through time, Mr Carnelian?'

'Of course. Oh, Jagged, is there any point to this? You've already played this game once before!'

Mr Jackson turned his attention to Mrs Underwood. 'And you say that you visited the future? That you met Mr Carnelian there? You fell in love?'

'Mr Carnelian was kind to me. He rescued me from imprisonment.'

'Aha! And you were able to do the same for him here?'

'No. I am still not sure *how* he escaped death on the gallows, but escape he did – went back to his own time – then returned. Was it only last night? To Bromley.'

'Your husband then called the police.'

'Inadvertently, the police must have been called, yes. My husband was over-excited. Have you heard how he is, by the way?'

'I have only read the papers. He is quoted, in the more sensational sheets, as claiming that you have been leading a double-life – by day a respectable, God-fearing Bromley housewife – by night, an accomplice of thieves – "A

308

Female Charlie Peace" I believe you were termed in to-day's *Police Gazette*.'

'Oh, no! Then my reputation is gone for good.'

Mr Jackson inspected the cuff of his shirt. 'It would seem that it would take much, Mrs Underwood, to restore it. You know how the odour of scandal clings, long after the scandal itself is proved unfounded.'

She straightened her shoulders. 'It remains my duty to try to convince Harold that I am not the wanton creature he now believes me to be. It will cause him much grief if he thinks that I have been deceiving him over a period of time. I can still attempt to put his mind at rest on that issue.'

'Doubtless...' murmured Mr Jackson, and his pencil moved rapidly across the page of his notebook. 'Now, could we have a description of the future?' He returned his attention to Jherek. 'An Anarchist Utopia, is it, perhaps? You are an anarchist, are you not, sir?'

'I don't know what one is,' said Jherek.

'He certainly is not!' cried Mrs Underwood. 'A degree of anarchy might have *resulted* from his actions...'

'A Socialist Utopia, then?'

'I think I follow your meaning now, Mr Jackson,' said Mrs Underwood. 'You believe Mr Carnelian to be some kind of mad political assassin, claiming to be from an ideal future in the hope of propagating his message?'

'Well, I wondered...'

'Was this idea original to you?'

'Mr Harris suggested —'

'I suspected as much. He did not believe a word of our story!'

'He considered it a trifle over-coloured, Mrs Underwood. Would you not think so, if you heard it, say, from *my* lips!'

'I wouldn't!' smiled Jherek. 'Because I know who you are.'

'Do be quiet, please, Mr Carnelian,' said Mrs Underwood. 'You are in danger of confusing matters again.'

309

'You are beginning to confuse *me*, I fear,' said Mr Jackson equably.

'Then we are only reciprocating, joking Jagged, the confusion you have created in us!' Jherek Carnelian got up and strode across the room. 'You know that the Morphail Effect is supposed to apply in all cases of time travel to the past, whether by travellers who are returning to their own time, or those merely visiting the past from some future age.'

'I'm afraid that I have not heard of this "Morphail Effect"? Some new theory?'

Ignoring him, Jherek continued. 'I now suspect that the Morphail Effect only applies in the case of those who produce a sufficient number of paradoxes to "register" as it were upon the fabric of Time. Those who are careful to disguise their origins, to do little to make use of any information they might have of the future, are allowed to exist in the past for as long as they wish!'

'I'm not sure I entirely follow you, Mr Carnelian. However, please go on.' Mr Jackson continued to take notes.

'If you publish all this, Mr Carnelian will be judged thoroughly mad,' said Mrs Underwood quietly.

'If you tell enough people what I have told you – it will send us off into the future again, probably.' Jherek offered Mr Jackson an intelligent stare. 'Wouldn't it, Jagged?'

Mr Jackson said apologetically. 'I'm still not quite with you. However, just keep talking and I'll keep taking notes.'

'I don't think I'll say anything for a while,' said Jherek. 'I must think this over.'

'Mr Jackson *could* help us, if he would accept the truth,' said Mrs Underwood. 'But if he is of the same opinion as Mr Harris...'

'I am a reporter,' said Mr Jackson. 'I keep my theories to myself, Mrs Underwood. All I wish to do is my job. If you had some proof, for instance...'

'Show him that odd-looking gun you have, Mr Carnelian.'

Jherek felt in the pocket of his coat and pulled the deceptor-gun out. 'It's hardly proof,' he said.

'It is certainly a very bizarre design,' said Mr Jackson, inspecting it.

He was holding it in his hands when there came a knocking on the door and a voice bellowed:

'Open this door! Open in the name of the Law!'

'The police!' Mrs Underwood's hand went to her mouth. 'Mr Harris has betrayed us!'

The door shook as heavy bodies flung themselves against it.

Mr Jackson got up slowly, handing back the gun to Jherek. 'I think we had better let them in,' he said.

'You knew they were coming!' cried Mrs Underwood accusingly. 'Oh, we have been deceived on all sides.'

'I doubt if Mr Harris knew. On the other hand, you were brought here in an ordinary cab. The police could have discovered the address from the cabby. It's rather typical of Frank Harris to forget, as it were, those all-important details.'

Mr Jackson called out: 'Wait one moment, please. We are about to unlock the door!' He smiled encouragingly at Mrs Underwood as he undid the catch and flung the door wide. 'Good afternoon, inspector.'

A man in a heavy ulster, with a small bowler hat fixed rigidly upon the top of his rocklike head, walked with massive bovine dignity into the room. He looked about him, he sniffed rather as Mrs Underwood had sniffed; pointedly, he looked neither at Jherek Carnelian nor at Mrs Underwood. Then he said:

'Herr-um!'

He wheeled, a cunning rhino, his finger jutting forward like a menacing horn, until it was quite close to Jherek's nose. 'You 'im?'

'Who?'

'Mayfair Killer?'

'No.' Jherek inched backwards.

'Thought not.' He fingered a thoroughly well-waxed moustache. 'I'm Inspector Springer.' He brought bushy brows down over deep, brooding eyes. 'Of Scotland Yard,' he said. '*Heard* of me, 'ave you?'

'I'm afraid not,' said Jherek.

'I deal with politicals, with aliens, with disruptive forrin' elements – an' I deal with 'em extremely *firm*.'

'So you believe it, too!' Mrs Underwood rose. 'You are mistaken in your suspicions, inspector.'

'We'll see,' said Inspector Springer cryptically. He raised a finger and cocked it, ordering four or five uniformed men into the room. 'I *know* my anarchists, lady. All three of yer have that particular look abart yer. We're goin' to do some very thorough checkin' indeed. *Very* thorough.'

'You're on the wrong track, I think,' said Mr Jackson. 'I'm a journalist. I was interviewing these people and ...'

'So you say, sir. Wrong track, eh? Well, we'll soon get on the right one, never fear.' He looked at the deceptor-gun and stretched out his hand to receive it. 'Give me that there weapon,' he said. 'It don't look *English* ter *me*.'

'I think you'd better fire it, Jherek,' said Mr Jackson softly. 'There doesn't seem to be a lot of choice.'

'Fire it, Jagged?'

Mr Jackson shrugged. 'I think so.'

Jherek pulled the trigger. 'There's only about one charge left in it ...'

The room in Bloomsbury Square was suddenly occupied by fifteen warriors of the late Cannibal Empire period. Their triangular faces were painted green, their bodies blue, and they were naked save for bangles and necklaces of small skulls and finger-bones. In their hands were long spears with barbed, rusted points, and spiked clubs. They were female. As they grinned, they revealed yellow, filed teeth.

'I *knew* you was ruddy anarchists!' said Inspector Springer triumphantly.

His men had fallen back to the door, but Inspector Springer held his ground. 'Arrest them!' he ordered severely.

The green and blue lady warriors gibbered and seemed to advance upon him. They licked calloused lips.

'This way,' whispered Mr Jackson, leading Jherek and Mrs Underwood into the bedroom. He opened a window and climbed out onto a small balcony. They joined him as he balanced for a moment on one balustrade and then jumped gracefully to the next. A flight of steps had been built up to this adjoining balcony and it was an easy matter to descend by means of the steps to the ground. Mr Jackson strolled through a small yard and opened a gate in a wall which led into a secluded, leafy street.

'Jagged – it *must* be you. You knew what the deceptor-gun would do!'

'My dear fellow,' said Mr Jackson coolly, 'I merely realized that you possessed a weapon and that it could be useful to us in our predicament.'

'Where do we go now?' Mrs Underwood asked in a small, pathetic voice.

'Oh, Jagged will help us get back to the future,' Jherek told her confidently. 'Won't you, Jagged?'

Mr Jackson seemed faintly amused. 'Even if I were this friend of yours, there would be no reason to assume, surely, that I can skip back and forth through time at will, any more than can you!'

'I had not considered that,' said Jherek. 'You are merely an experimenter, then? An experimenter little further advanced in your investigations than am I?'

Mr Jackson said nothing.

'And are we part of that experiment, Lord Jagged?' Jherek continued. 'Are my experiences proving of help to you?'

Mr Jackson shrugged. 'I could enjoy our conversations better,' he said, 'if we were in a more secure position.

313

Now we are, all three, "on the run". I suggest we repair to my rooms in Soho and there review our situation. I will contact Mr Harris and get fresh instructions. This, of course, will prove embarrassing for him, too!' He led the way through the back streets. It was evening and the sun was beginning to set.

Mrs Underwood fell back a step or two, tugging at Jherek's sleeve. 'I believe that we are being duped,' she whispered. 'For some reason, we are being used to further the ends of either Mr Harris or Mr Jackson or both. We might stand a better chance on our own, since obviously the police do not believe, any longer, that you are an escaped murderer.'

'They believe me an anarchist, instead. Isn't that worse?'

'Luckily, not in the eyes of the Law.'

'Then where can we go?'

'Do you know where this Mr Wells lives?'

'Yes, the Café Royale. I saw him there.'

'Then we must try to get back to the Café Royale. He does not *live* there, exactly, Mr Carnelian – but we can hope that he spends a great deal of his time there.'

'You must explain the difference to me,' he said.

Ahead of them Mr Jackson was hailing a cab, but when he turned to tell them to get in, they were already in another street and running as fast as their weary legs would carry them.

CHAPTER SEVENTEEN

A PARTICULARLY MEMORABLE NIGHT
AT THE CAFÉ ROYALE

It was dark by the time Mrs Underwood had managed to find her way to the Café Royale. They had kept to the back streets after she had, in a second-hand clothing shop near the British Museum, purchased a large, tattered shawl for herself and a moth-eaten raglan to cover Jherek's ruined suit. Now, she had assured him, they looked like any other couple belonging to the London poor. It was true that they no longer attracted any attention. It was not until they tried to go through the doors of the Café Royale that they found themselves once again in difficulties. As they entered a waiter came rushing up. He spoke in a quiet, urgent and commanding voice.

'Shove off, the pair of yer! My word, I never thought I'd see the day beggars got so bloomin' bold!'

There were not many customers in the restaurant, but those who were there had begun to comment.

'Shove off, will yer!' said the waiter in a louder voice. 'I'll git the peelers on yer...' He had gone quite red in the face.

Jherek Carnelian ignored him, for he had seen Frank Harris sitting at a small table in the company of a lady of exotic appearance. She wore a bright carmine dress, trimmed with black lace, a black mantilla, and had several silver combs in her raven hair. She was laughing in a rather high-pitched, artificial way at something Mr Harris had just said.

'Mr Harris!' called Jherek Carnelian.

'Mr *Harris*!' Mrs Underwood said fiercely. Undaunted by the agitated waiters, she began to stalk towards the table. 'I should appreciate a word with you, sir!'

'Oh, my God!' Mr Harris groaned. 'I thought you were still ... How? Oh, my God!'

The lady in carmine turned to see what was happening. Her lips matched her dress. In a rather frigid tone she said: 'This lady is a friend of yours, Mr Harris?'

He clutched for his companion's hand. 'Donna Isobella, I assure you – two people I gave my protection to – um...'

'Your *protection*, Mr Harris, seems worth very little.' Mrs Underwood looked Donna Isobella up and down. 'Is this, then, the highly placed person with whom I understood you to be in conference?'

There came a chorus of complaints from other tables. The waiter seized Jherek Carnelian by the arm. Jherek, mildly surprised, stared down at him. 'Yes?'

'You *must* leave, sir. I can see now that you are a gentleman – but you are improperly dressed...'

'It is all I have,' said Jherek. 'My power rings, you see, are useless here.'

'I don't understand...'

316

Kindly, Jherek showed the waiter his remaining rings. 'They all have slightly different functions. This one is chiefly used for biological restructuring. This one...'

'Oh, my God!' said Mr Harris again.

A new voice interrupted. It was excited and loud. 'There they are! I told you we should find them in this sinkhole of iniquity!'

Mr Underwood did not appear to have slept for some time. He still wore the suit Jherek had seen him in the previous night. His hay-coloured hair was still in disarray. His pince-nez clung lopsidedly to his nose.

Behind Mr Underwood stood Inspector Springer and his men. They looked a little dazed.

Several customers got up and called for their hats and coats. Only Mr Harris and Donna Isobella remained seated. Mr Harris had his head in his hands. Donna Isobella was staring brightly around her smiling at everyone now. Silver flashed; carmine rustled. She seemed pleased by the interruption.

'Seize them!' demanded Mr Underwood.

'Harold,' began Mrs Underwood, 'there has been a terrible mistake! I am not the woman you believe me to be!'

'To be sure, madam! To be sure!'

'I mean that I am innocent of the sins with which you charge me, my dear!'

'Ha!'

Inspector Springer and his men began to weave their way somewhat warily towards the small group on the far side of the restaurant, while Harold Underwood brought up the rear.

Mr Harris was trying to recover his position with Donna Isobella. 'My connection with these people is only of the most slender, Donna Isobella.'

'No matter how slender, I wish to meet them,' she said. 'Introduce us, please, Frank!'

It was when the Lat brigand-musicians materialized that many of the waiters left with the few customers who

317

had remained.

Captain Mubbers, his instrument at the ready, stared distractedly around him. The pupils of his single eye began slowly to focus. 'Ferkit!' he growled belligerently, at no one in particular. 'Kroofrudi!'

Inspector Springer paused in his stride and stared thoughtfully down at the seven small aliens. With the air of a man who is on the brink of discovering a profound truth, he murmured: 'Ho!'

'Smakfrub, glex mibix cue?' said one of Captain Mubbers' crew-members. And with his instrument he feinted at Inspector Springer's legs. Evidently they had the same problem, in that their weapons could not work at this distance from their power source, or else the charges had run out.

The Lat's three pupils crossed alarmingly and then fled apart. He mumbled to himself, turning his back on Inspector Springer. His ears shrugged.

'The rest of your anarchist gang, eh?' said Inspector Springer. 'And even more desperate-looking than the last lot. What's the lingo? Some kind a' Roossian, is it?'

'They are the Lat,' said Jherek. 'They must have got caught in the field Nurse set up. Now we *do* have a paradox. They're space-travellers,' he explained to Mrs Underwood, 'from my own time...'

'Any of you speak English?' enquired Inspector Springer of Captain Mubbers.

'Hawtyard!' Captain Mubbers growled.

''Ere, I say, steady on!' expostulated Inspector Springer. 'Ladies,' he said, 'at least of sorts, are in the company.'

One of his men, indicating the striped flannel suits which each of the Lat wore, suggested that they might have escaped from prison – for all that the suits resembled pyjamas.

'Those are not their normal clothes,' said Jherek. 'Nurse put them into those when...'

'Nobody *arsked* you, sir, if you don't mind,' said In-

318

spector Springer haughtily. 'We'll take your statement in a moment.'

'Those are the ones you must arrest, officer!' insisted Harold Underwood, still shaking with rage. He indicated his wife and Jherek.

'It's astonishing,' said Mrs Underwood half to herself, 'how you can live with someone for such a long time without realizing the heights of passion to which they are capable of rising.'

Inspector Springer reached towards Captain Mubbers. The Lat's bulbous nose seemed to pulse with rage. Captain Mubbers looked up at Inspector Springer and glared. The policeman tried to lay his hand on Captain Mubbers' shoulder. Then he withdrew the hand sharply.

'Eouw!' he exclaimed, nursing the injured limb. 'Little beggar bit me!' He turned in desperation to Jherek. 'Can you talk their lingo?'

'I'm afraid not,' said Jherek. 'Translation pills are only good for one language at a time and currently I am talking and hearing yours...'

Inspector Springer appeared to dismiss Jherek from his mind for the moment. 'The others just vanished,' he said, aggrievedly, convinced that someone had deliberately deceived him.

'*They* were illusions,' Jherek told him. '*These* are real – space-travellers...'

Again Inspector Springer made a movement towards Captain Mubbers. 'Jillip goff!' Captain Mubbers demanded. And he kicked Inspector Springer sharply in the shins with one of his hoof-like feet.

'Eouw!' said Inspector Springer again. 'All right! Yer arsked fer it!' And his expression became ugly.

Captain Mubbers pushed aside a table. Silver-ware clattered to the floor. Two of his crew, their attention drawn to the knives and forks, fell upon their knees and began to gather the implements up, chattering excitedly as if they had just discovered buried treasure.

'Leave that cutlery alone!' bellowed Inspector Springer.

319

'All right, men! Charge 'em!'

To a man, the constables produced their truncheons, and were upon the Lat, who fought back with the table-ware as well as their powerless instrument-weapons.

Mr Jackson came strolling in. There were now no waiters to be seen. He hung up his own hat and coat, taking only a mild interest in the mêlée at the centre of the restaurant, and crossed to where Frank Harris sat moaning softly to himself, Donna Isobella sat clapping her hands and giggling, and Jherek Carnelian and Mrs Underwood stood wondering what to do. Harold Under-wood was waving his fists, leaping around the periphery of the fight shouting at Inspector Springer to do his duty (he did not seem to believe that the inspector's duty had much to do with arresting three-foot high brigand-musi-cians from a distant galaxy).

'Good evening to you,' said Mr Jackson affably. He opened a slender gold case and extracted an Egyptian cigarette. Inserting it into a holder, he lit it with a match and, leaning against a pillar, proceeded to watch the fight. 'I thought I'd find you here,' he added.

Jherek was quite enjoying himself. 'And I might have guessed that you would come, Jagged. Who would want to miss this?'

It seemed that none of his friends wished to do so, for now, their costumes blazing and putting to shame the opulence of the Café Royale, the Iron Orchid, the Duke of Queens, Bishop Castle and My Lady Charlotina appeared.

The Iron Orchid, in particular, was delighted to see her son, but when she spoke he discovered that he could not understand her. Feeling in his pockets, he produced the rest of his translation pills and handed them to the four newcomers. They were quick to realize the situation and each swallowed a pill.

'I thought at first it was another illusion from your deceptor-gun,' the Iron Orchid told him, 'but actually we are back in the Dawn Age, are we not, with you?'

320

'You are, indeed, tenderest of blooms. You see, I am re-united with Mrs Underwood.'

'Good evening,' said Mrs Underwood to Jherek's mother in a tone which might have contained a hint of coolness.

'Good evening, my dear. Your costume is beautiful. It is contemporary, I suppose?' The Iron Orchid turned in a swirl of fiery drapery. 'And Jagged is here, too! Greetings to you, languid Lord of Canaria!'

Mr Jackson smiled faintly in acknowledgement.

Bishop Castle gathered his blue gown about him and sat down next to Mr Harris and Donna Isobella. 'I am glad to be out of that wood, at any rate,' he said. 'Are you residents of this age, or visitors like myself?'

Donna Isobella beamed at him. 'I am from Spain,' she said. 'I dance. Exotically, you know.'

'How delightful. Are the Lat causing you much trouble?'

'The little beast-men? Oh, no. They and the police are entertaining themselves quite cheerfully, I think.'

With a shaking hand, Mr Harris poured himself a large glass of champagne. He did not offer any to the others. He drank rapidly.

My Lady Charlotina kissed Mrs Underwood upon the cheek. 'Oh, you can scarcely know the excitement you have caused us all, pretty ancestress. But your own age seems not without its diversions!' She went to join Bishop Castle at the table.

The Duke of Queens was exclaiming with great pleasure about the plush and gilt decor of the restaurant. 'I am determined to make one,' he announced. 'What did you say it was called, Jherek?'

'The Café Royale.'

'It shall flourish again, five times the size, at the End of Time!' proclaimed the Duke.

From the middle of the room came muffled cries of 'Ferkit!' and 'Eouw!' Neither Inspector Springer's team, nor Captain Mubbers', seemed to be getting the upper hand. More tables were turned over.

The Duke of Queens took careful note of the police uniforms. 'Does this happen every evening? Presumably the Lat are a new addition to the programme?'

'I think the best they've done in the past are drunken revels of the conventional sort,' said Mr Jackson. 'Though they are not so very different in essence, I suppose.'

'The Café is well known,' Donna Isobella was explaining to an intensely interested Bishop Castle, 'for its Bohemian clientele. It is rather less formal than most restaurants of its class.'

There came a queer whizzing noise now and a flash of light which blinded them all, then Brannart Morphail was hanging near the ceiling in a harness of pulsing yellow, with what appeared to be two rapidly spinning discs upon his back, threatening to collide with a large crystal chandelier. His medical boot waved back and forth in an agitated way as he slapped at part of the harness near his shoulder, evidently finding difficulty in controlling the machine.

'I warned you! I warned you!' he cried from on high. His voice was crackling, improperly modulated, as if he were using an inferior translator. It rose and fell. 'All this manipulation of time is creating havoc! No good will come of it! Beware! Beware!'

Even the police and the Lat paused in their battle to stare up at the apparition.

Brannart Morphail, with a yell, began to float upon his back, his arms waving, his feet kicking. 'It's the damned special co-ordinates every time!' he complained. He slapped the harness again and flipped over so that he was staring down at them, floating on his stomach. From the discs, the loud whizzing noise grew higher and more erratic. 'Only machine I could get working to come here. Some stupid 95th-century idea of economy! Argh!' And he was on his back again.

Mr Underwood had become very suddenly calm. He

stood regarding Brannart Morphail through his pince-nez, his face very white, his body rigid. Occasionally his lips moved.

'It's all your doing. Jherek Carnelian!' One of the discs stopped working altogether and Brannart Morphail began to drift lopsidedly across the ceiling, banging against the chandeliers and making them ring. 'You can't make these uncontrolled jaunts here and there through time without causing the most appalling eddies in the mega-flow! Look what's happened now. I came to stop you, to warn you – aaah!' The scientist kicked savagely, trying to extricate himself from a velvet pelmet near the window.

In a low, unsteady voice, Mr Harris was talking to My Lady Charlotina who was stroking his head. 'All my life,' he was saying, 'I've been accused of telling tall stories. Who's going to believe this one?'

'Brannart's right, of course,' said Mr Jackson, still leaning comfortably against the pillar. 'I wonder if the risks will be worth it?'

'Risks?' said Jherek, watching as Mrs Underwood went towards her husband.

'I can't understand why the Effect has not begun to take place!' complained Brannart Morphail, floating freely again, but still unable to get the second disc working. He noticed Mr Jackson for the first time. 'What's your part in this, Lord Jagged? Something whimsical and cunning, no doubt.'

'My dear Brannart, I assure you...'

'Bah! Oof!' The disc began to whirl and the scientist was wrenched upwards and to one side. 'Neither Jherek nor that woman should still be here – nor should you, Jagged! Go against the Logic of Time and you bring doom to all!'

'Doom...' murmured Mr Underwood, unaware that his wife had reached him and was shaking his shoulder.

'Harold! Speak to me!'

He turned his head and he was smiling gently. 'Doom,' he said again. 'I should have realized. It is the Apocalypse. Do not worry, my dear, for *we* shall be saved.' He patted her hand. She burst into tears.

Mr Jackson approached Jherek who was watching this scene with anxious interest. 'I think, perhaps, it would be wise to leave now,' said Mr Jackson.

'Not without Mrs Underwood,' said Jherek firmly.

Mr Jackson sighed and shrugged. 'Of course not. Anyway, it is important that you remain together. You are so rare...'

'Rare?'

'A figure of speech.'

Mr Underwood began to sing, oblivious of his wife's tears. He sang in a surprisingly rich tenor voice. 'Jesu, lover of my soul./ Let me to thy bosom fly./ While the nearer waters roll,/ While the tempest still is high;/ Hide me, O my Saviour, hide,/ Till the storm of life is past;/ Safe into the haven guide/ O receive my soul at last.'

'How lovely!' cried the Iron Orchid. 'A primitive ritual, such as the rotted cities recall!'

'I suspect is it more of a sorcerous summoning,' said Bishop Castle, who took a special interest in such ancient customs. 'We might even say some sort of holey ghost.' He explained kindly to a rapt Donna Isobella: 'So-called because they could be seen only imperfectly. They were partly transparent, you know.'

'Aren't we all on such occasions?' said Donna Isobella. She smiled winningly at Bishop Castle who leaned over and kissed her on the lips.

'Beware!' groaned Brannart Morphail, but they had all lost interest in him. The Lat and the constables had resumed their fight.

'I must say I *like* your little century,' said the Duke of Queens to Jherek Carnelian. 'I can see why you come here.'

Jherek was flattered, in spite of his usual scepticism concerning the Duke's taste. 'Thank you, darling Duke. I didn't make it, of course.'

324

'You discovered it, however. I should like to come again. Is it all like this?'

'Oh, no, there's a great deal of variety.' He spoke a little vaguely, his eyes on Mr and Mrs Underwood. Mrs Underwood, still weeping, held her husband's hand and joined in the song. 'Cover my defenceless head/ With the shadow of thy wing.' Her descant was a perfect counterpart to his tenor. Jherek found himself oddly moved. He frowned. 'There's leaves, and horses, and sewage farms.'

'How do they grow sewage?'

'It's too complicated to explain.' Jherek was reluctant to admit his ignorance, particularly to his old rival.

'Perhaps, if you have a moment, you could take me on a short tour of the main features?' suggested the Duke of Queens hesitantly. 'I would be extremely grateful, Jherek.' He spoke in his most ingratiating voice and Jherek realized that, at long last, the Duke of Queens was acknowledging his superior taste. He smiled condescendingly at the Duke. 'Of course,' he said, 'when I have a moment.'

Mr Harris had fallen head down onto the table-cloth. He had begun to snore rather violently.

Jherek took a step or two towards Mrs Underwood, but then thought better of it. He did not know why he hesitated. Bishop Castle looked up. 'Join us, jaunty Jherek, please. After all, you *are* our host!'

'Not exactly,' said Jherek, but he seated himself on the other side of Donna Isobella.

The Lat had been driven into the far corner of the Café Royale, but they were putting up a spirited resistance. Not a policeman taking part in the fray was short of at least one bitten hand and bruised shin.

Jherek found himself unable to pay any attention at all to the conversation at the table. He wondered why Mrs Underwood wept so copiously as she sang. Mr Underwood's face, in contrast, was full of joy.

Donna Isobella moved a fraction closer to Jherek and he caught the mingled scents of violets and Egyptian cigarettes. Bishop Castle had begun to kiss her hand, the nails of which were painted to match her dress.

The whizzing noise from overhead grew louder again and Brannart Morphail drifted in, chest once more towards the floor. 'Get back to your own times, while you may!' he called. 'You will be stranded – marooned – abandoned! Take heed! Take hee-ee-eeeed!' And he vanished. Jherek, for one, was glad to see him go.

Donna Isabella flung back her head and flashed a bright smile at Jherek, apparently replying to something Bishop Castle had said, but addressing Jherek. 'Love love, my love,' she announced, 'but *never* commit the error of loving a person. The abstraction offers all the pleasure and nothing whatsoever of the pain. Being *in* love is so much preferable to loving *someone*.'

Jherek smiled. 'You sound a bit like Lord Jagged over there. But I'm afraid I am already trapped.'

'Besides,' said Bishop Castle, insistently keeping his hold of the lady's hand, 'who is to say which is sweeter – melancholia or mindless ecstasy?'

They both looked at him in mild astonishment.

'I have my own preferences,' she said, 'I *know*.' She returned her full attention to Jherek, saying huskily: 'But there – you are so much *younger* than I.'

'Is that so?' Jherek became interested. He had understood that, through no choice of their own, these people had extremely short life-spans. 'Well, then, you must be at least five hundred years old.'

Donna Isabella's eyes blazed. Her lip curled. She made to speak and then changed her mind. She turned her back on him. She laughed rather harshly at something Bishop Castle murmured.

He noticed, on the far side of the room, a shadowy figure whom he did not recognize. It was clad in some kind of armour, and stared about in consternation.

Lord Jagged had noticed it, too. He drew his fine brows together and puffed thoughtfully on his cigarette.

The figure disappeared almost immediately.

'Who was that, Jagged?' enquired Jherek.

'A warrior from a period six or seven centuries before this one,' said Mr Jackson. 'I can't be mistaken. And look!'

A small child, the outline of her body flickering a little, stared about her in wonderment, but was there for only a matter of seconds before she had vanished.

'Seventeenth century,' said Jagged. 'I am beginning to take Brannart's warnings seriously. The whole fabric of Time is in danger of diffusing completely. I should have been more careful. Ah, well...'

'You seem concerned, Jagged.'

'I have reason to be,' said Lord Jagged. 'You had better collect Mrs Underwood immediately.'

'She is singing, at present, with Mr Underwood.'

'So I see.'

There came a chorus of whistlings from the street and into the restaurant burst a score of uniformed policemen, their truncheons drawn. The leader presented himself to Inspector Springer and saluted. 'Sergeant Sherwood, sir.'

'In the nick of time, sergeant.' Inspector Springer re-arranged his ulster and placed his battered bowler hard upon his head. 'We're cleaning up a den of forrin' anarchists 'ere, as you can observe. Are the vans outside?'

'Plenty of vans for this little lot, inspector.' Sergeant Sherwood cast a loathing eye upon the assembled company. 'I allus *knew* wot they said abart this place was true!'

'An' worse. I mean, *look* at 'em.' Inspector Springer indicated the Lat who had given up the fight and were sitting sulkily in a corner, nursing their bruises. 'You'd 'ardly believe they was yuman, would yer?'

'Ugly customers, right enough. Not English, o' course.'

'Nar! Latvians. Typical Eastern European political troublemakers. They breed 'em like that over there.'

'Wot? Special?'

'It's somefin' to do with the diet,' said Inspector

Springer. 'Curds an' so forth.'

'Oo-er. I wouldn't 'ave your job, inspector, for a million quid.'

'It *can* be nasty,' agreed Inspector Springer. 'Right. Let's get 'em all rounded up.'

'The – um – painted women, too?'

'By all means, sergeant. Every one of 'em. We'll sort out 'oo's 'oo at the Yard.'

Mr Jackson had been listening to this conversation and now he turned to Jherek with a shrug. 'I fear there is little we can do for the moment,' he said philosophically. 'We are all about to be carried off to prison.'

'Oh, really?' Jherek cheered up.

'It will be nice to be a prisoner again,' he said nostalgically. He identified gaol with one of his happiest moments, when Mr Griffiths, the lawyer, had read to him Mrs Amelia Underwood's declaration of her love. 'Perhaps they'll be able to furnish us with a time machine, too.'

Lord Jagged did not seem quite as cheerful as Jherek. 'We shall be needing one very much,' he said, 'if our problems are not to be further complicated. In more ways than one, I would say, time is running out.'

There was a sudden click and Jherek Carnelian looked down at his wrists. A newly arrived constable had snapped a pair of handcuffs on them. ''Ope you like the bracelets, sir,' said the constable with a sardonic grin.

Jherek laughed and held them up. 'Oh, they're beautiful!' he said.

In a general babble of excited merriment, the party filed out of the Café Royale and into the waiting police vans. Only Mr Harris was left behind. His snores had taken on a puzzled, melancholy note.

The Iron Orchid giggled. 'I suppose this happens to *you* all the time,' she said to Donna Isobella, whose lips seemed a little set. 'It's a rare treat for me, however.'

Mr Underwood beamed at the policemen as Mrs Underwood led him through the doors.

'Be of good cheer,' he told Inspector Springer, 'for the Lord is with us.'

Inspector Springer shook his head and sighed. 'Speak for yourself,' he said. He was not looking forward to the night ahead.

CHAPTER EIGHTEEN

TO THE TIME MACHINE, AT LAST!

'The 'Ome Secretary,' declared Inspector Springer importantly, ''as bin informed.' He stood with his fists upon his hips in the centre of the large cell. He looked about him at his prisoners with the self-satisfied expression of a farmer who has made a good purchase of livestock. 'I should not be surprised,' he continued, 'if we 'ave not uncovered the biggest load of conspirators against the Crown since the Gunpowder Plot. And, 'opefully, we shall in the next few days flush a few more from their foxholes.' He gave his particular attention now to Captain Mubbers and his crew. 'We shall also discover 'ow the likes o' you are smuggled inter this country.'

'Groonek, wertedas,' mumbled Captain Mubbers, staring up placatingly at Inspector Springer. 'Freg nusher, tunightly, mibix?'

'So you say, my lad! We'll let an English jury decide *your* fate!'

Captain Mubbers abandoned his attempts to reason with Inspector Springer and, with a muttered 'Kroofrudi!' retired to the company of his crew in the corner.

'We'll need a translator, inspector,' said Sergeant Sherwood, from where he stood by the door, taking down details on a clipboard. 'I couldn't get their names. All the rest,' he continued, 'seem pretty foreign, with the exception of those three.' With his pencil he indicated Mr and Mrs Underwood and the man who had given his name as 'Mr Jackson'.

'I have a pill left,' offered Jherek. 'You could take that and it would enable you to converse with them, if you were on your own...'

'Pills? You stand there and offer me, an officer of the Law, *drugs*?' He turned to Sergeant Sherwood. 'Drugs,' he said.

'That explains it.' Sergeant Sherwood nodded soberly. 'I wonder wot 'appened to that other one you mentioned. ''Im with the flying machine.'

''Is whereabouts will come to light in time,' said Inspector Springer.

'Absolutely,' said Jherek. 'I hope he got back all right. The distortion seems to have subsided, wouldn't you say, Jagged?'

'Jackson,' said Jagged, but he was not very emphatic. 'Yes, but it won't last unless we act quickly.'

Mr Underwood had stopped singing and instead was shaking his head from side to side a good deal. 'The tensions,' he was saying, 'the strain – as you say, my dear.' Mrs Underwood was soothing him. 'I apologize for my outbursts – for everything – it was un-Christian – I should have listened – if you love this man...'

'Oh, Harold!'

'No, no. I would rather you went with him. I need a rest, anyway – in the country. Perhaps I could go to stay with my sister – the one who runs the Charity House at Whitehaven. A divorce...'

'Oh, *Harold*!' She clutched his arm. 'Never. It is all right, I will stay with you.'

'What?' said Jherek. 'Don't listen to her, Mr Underwood.' But then he wished that he had not spoken. 'No, you must listen to her, I suppose...'

Mr Underwood said more firmly. 'It is not merely for your sake, Amelia. The scandal...'

'Oh, Harold. I am sorry.'

'Not your fault, I'm sure.'

'You will sue *me*?'

'Well, naturally. You could not ...'

'Harold!' This time her tears seemed to be of a different quality. 'Where would I go?'

'With – with Mr Carnelian, surely?'

'You cannot realize what that means, Harold.'

'You are used to foreign climes. If you left England, set up a new home somewhere...'

She wiped her eyes, staring accusingly at Jherek. 'This is all your doing, Mr Carnelian. Now see what has happened.'

'I can't quite see...' he began, but then gave up, for she had given her attention back to Mr Underwood.

Another policeman entered the cell. 'Aha,' said Inspector Springer. 'Sorry to get you out of bed, constable. I jest wanted to clear somefin' in my mind. You were at the execution, I believe, of the Mayfair Killer?'

'I wos, sir.'

'And would you say this chap's the one that got 'anged?' He pointed at Jherek.

'Bears a resemblance, sir. But I saw the Killer go. With a certain amount o' dignity, as wos remarked upon at the time. Couldn't be the same.'

'You saw the body – after?'

'No, sir. In fac', sir, there was a bit of a rumour went

rahnd – well ... No, sir – 'e looks sort o' different –
shorter – different colour 'air an' complexion...'

'I've changed them, since you –' began Jherek helpfully, but Inspector Springer said: 'Quiet, you!' He
seemed satisfied. 'Thank you, constable.'

'Thank you, sir.' The constable left the cell.

Inspector Springer approached Mr Underwood. 'Feel-
in' calmer now, eh?'

'A little,' agreed Mr Underwood warily. 'I hope, I
mean, you don't think I...'

'I think you wos mistaken, that's all. 'Aving 'ad a
chance ter – well – see you in different circumstances – I
would say – well – that you wos a bit 'ighly-strung – not
quite right in the – um –' He began again, almost kindly.
'With your missus runnin' off, an' all that. Besides, I'm
grateful to yer, Mr Underwood. Not knowing, like, you
'elped me unmask this vicious gang. We've bin 'earing
abaht a plan to assassinate 'Er Majesty, but the clews 'ave
bin a bit thin on the ground – now we've got somefin' ter
work on, see?'

'You mean, these people ...? Amelia – were you
aware ...?'

'Harold!' She gestured imploringly to Jherek. 'We
have told you the truth. I am sure that nobody here
knows anything about such a terrible plot. They are all
from the future!'

Again Inspector Springer shook his head. 'The problem will be,' he said to Sergeant Sherwood, 'in sortin' the
out an' out loonies from the conscious criminals.'

The Iron Orchid yawned. 'I must say, my dear,' she
murmured to Jherek, 'that you have your dull moments
as well as your amusing ones in the Dawn Age.'

'It's not often like this,' he apologized.

'Therefore, sir,' said Inspector Springer to Mr Underwood, 'you can go. We'll need you as a witness, of course,
but I don't think, as things stand, we want to keep you
up any longer.'

'And my wife?'

'She must stay, I'm afraid.'

Mr Underwood allowed Sergeant Sherwood to lead him from the cell. 'Goodbye, my dear,' he said.

'Goodbye, Harold.' She did not seem very moved now.

The Duke of Queens drew off his magnificent hunting hat and brushed at its plumes. 'What is this stuff?' he asked Mr Jackson.

'Dust,' said Jackson. 'Grime.'

'How interesting. How do you make it?'

'There are many ways of manufacturing it in the Dawn Age,' Mr Jackson told him.

'You must tell me some of them, Jherek.' The Duke of Queens replaced his hat on his head. His voice dropped to a whisper. 'And what are we waiting for now?' he enquired eagerly.

'I am not quite sure,' Jherek said. 'But you're bound to enjoy it. I enjoy everything here.'

'Who could fail to, O banisher of boredom!' The Duke of Queens beamed benignly upon Inspector Springer. 'And I *do* love your characters, Jherek. They are in perfect key.'

Sergeant Sherwood returned with a stately-looking middle-aged man in a black tailcoat and a tall black hat. Recognizing him, Inspector Springer saluted. ''Ere they are for you, sir. I don't mind admitting it took some doing to nab 'em, but nabbed they are!'

The stately man nodded and cast a cold eye, on Lat, on Jherek, heaving a sigh. He allowed no expression to come to his face as he inspected the Iron Orchid, the Duke of Queens, Bishop Castle, My Lady Charlotina, Donna Isobella and Mrs Underwood. It was only when he took a close glance at Mr Jackson's face that he breathed a barely heard: 'Good heavens!'

'Good evening, Munroe – or is it morning, yet?' Jagged seemed amused. 'How's the Minister?'

'Is it you, Jagger?'

'I'm afraid so.'

'But, how —?'

334

'Ask the inspector here, my dear chap.'

'Inspector?'

'A friend of yours, sir?'

'You do not recognize Lord Charles Jagger?'

'But ...' said Inspector Springer.

'I *told* you it was,' said Jherek in triumph to Mrs Underwood, but she silenced him.

'Did you explain anything to the inspector, Jagger?'

'It's not really his fault, but he was so convinced we were all mixed up in this business that there was no point in trying to get through to him. I thought it best to wait.'

Munroe smiled sourly. 'And got me from my bed.'

'There's the Latvians, sir,' said Inspector Springer eagerly, 'at least.'

Munroe made a stately turn and looked sternly at the Lat. 'Ah, yes. Not friends of yours, are they Jagger?'

'Not at all. Inspector Springer has done a good job there. The rest of us – all my guests – were dining at the Café Royale. As you know, I take an interest in the arts...'

'Of course. There is no more to be said.'

'So you're not even a bloomin' anarchist?' complained Inspector Springer moodily to Jherek. 'Just a well-connected loony.' And he uttered a deep sigh.

'Inspector!' admonished the stately gentleman.

'Sorry, sir.'

'Ferkit!' said Captain Mubbers from his corner. He seemed to be addressing Munroe. 'Gloo, mibix?'

'Ugh,' said Munroe.

None of the Lat seemed to have taken their imprisonment well. They sat in a sad little group on the floor of the cell, picking their huge noses, scratching their oddly shaped heads.

'Did you have any reason to suspect Lord Jagger and his friends, inspector?' asked Munroe distantly.

'Well, no, sir, except – well, even that wasn't ... these green and blue women, sir –' Inspector Springer subsided. 'No, sir.'

'They have not been charged?'

'Not yet – er, no, sir.'

'They can go?'

'Yes, sir.'

'There you are, Jagger.'

'Thank you, Munroe.'

'This other business,' said Munroe, waving his stick at the disconsolate aliens, 'can wait until morning. I hope you have plenty of evidence for me, inspector.'

'Oh, yes, sir,' said Inspector Springer. In his eyes there was no light of pleasurable anticipation in the future. He stared hopelessly at the Lat. 'They're definitely forrin', sir, for a start.'

As they all entered the wide avenue of Whitehall, Lord Jagged's friend Munroe lifted his hat to the ladies. 'My compliments on your costumes,' he said. 'It must have been a marvellous ball if they were all as fine. See you at the club, perhaps, Jagger?'

'Perhaps tomorrow,' said Jagged.

Munroe made his stately way up Whitehall.

Light began to touch the tall buildings.

'Oh, look!' cried My Lady Charlotina. 'It's a proper old-fashioned dawn. A real one!'

The Duke of Queens clapped Jherek on the shoulder. 'Beautiful!'

Jherek still felt he had earned the Duke's esteem rather cheaply, considering that he had done nothing at all to produce the sun-rise, but he could not help indulging an immensely satisfying sense of identification with the wonders of the 19th century world, so again he shook his head modestly, but allowed the Duke to continue with his praise.

'Smell that air!' exclaimed the Duke of Queens. 'A thousand rich scents mingle in it! Ah!' He strode ahead of the others who followed him as he turned along the embankment, admiring the river with its flotsam, its barges, its sheen of oil, all grey in the early dawn.

Jherek said to Mrs Underwood. 'Will you now admit

that you love me, Mrs Underwood? I gather that your connection with Mr Underwood is at an end?'

'He seems to think so.' She sighed. 'I did my best.'

'Your singing was marvellous.'

'He must have been fairly unstable to begin with,' she said. 'However, I must blame myself for what happened.'

She seemed unwilling to speak further and, tactfully, Jherek shared her silence.

A tug-boat hooted from the river. Some gulls flapped upwards into a sky of soft and glowing gold, the trees lining the embankment rustled as if awakening to the new day. The others, some distance in front of Jherek and Mrs Underwood, commented on this aspect and that of the city.

'What a perfect ending to our picnic,' said the Iron Orchid to Lord Jagged. 'When shall we be going back, do you know?'

'Soon,' he said, 'I would think.'

Eventually, they left the embankment and turned into a street Jherek knew. He touched Mrs Underwood's arm. 'Do you recognize the building?'

'Yes,' she murmured, her mind evidently on other things, 'it is the Old Bailey, where they tried you.'

'Look, Jagged!' called Jherek. 'Remember?'

Lord Jagged, too, seemed abstracted. He nodded.

Laughing and chattering, the party passed the Old Bailey and paused to wonder at the next aspect of the period which had caught their fancy.

'St Paul's Cathedral,' said Donna Isobella, clinging to Bishop Castle's arm. 'Haven't you seen it before?'

'Oh, we *must* go in!'

It was then that Lord Jagged lifted his sensitive head and paused, like a fox catching wind of its hunters. He raised a hand, and Jherek and Mrs Underwood hesitated, watching as the others ran up the steps.

'A remarkable –' Bishop Castle vanished. The Iron Orchid began to laugh and then she, too, vanished. My Lady Charlotina took a step backward, and vanished.

And then the Duke of Queens, his expression amused and expectant, vanished.

Donna Isobella sat down on the steps and screamed.

They could hear Donna Isobella's screams from several streets away as Lord Jagged led them hurriedly into a maze of little cobbled alleys. 'We'll be next, if we're not lucky,' he said. 'Morphail Effect bound to manifest itself. My own fault – absolutely my own fault. Quickly...'

'Where are we going, Jagged?'

'Time machine. The one you originally came in. Repaired. Ready to go. But the fluctuations caused by recent comings and goings could have produced serious consequences. Brannart knew what he was talking about. Hurry!'

'I am not sure,' said Mrs Underwood, 'that I wish to accompany either of you. You have caused me considerable pain, you know, not to mention ...'

'Mrs Underwood,' said Lord Jagged of Canaria softly, 'you have no choice. The alternative is dreadful, I assure you.'

Convinced by his tone, she said nothing further for the moment.

They came to an alley full of bleak, festering buildings close to the river. At the far end of the alley, a few men were beginning to move boxes onto a cart. They could see the glint of the dirty Thames water.

'I feel faint,' complained Mrs Underwood. 'I cannot keep up this pace, Mr Jackson. I have had no sleep to speak of in two nights.'

'We are there,' he said. He took a key from his pocket and inserted it into the lock of a door of mouldering oak. The door creaked as he pushed it inward. Lord Jagged closed the door, reached up to take an oil lamp from a hook. He struck a match and lit the lamp.

As the light grew brighter, Jherek saw that they stood in quite a large room. The floor was stone and the whole placed smelled of mildew. He saw rats running swiftly along the beams in the roof.

Jagged had crossed to a great pile of rags and debris and began to pull them to the ground. He had lost some of his composure in his haste.

'What *is* your part in this, Mr Jackson?' said Mrs Underwood, averting her eyes from the rats. 'I am right, am I not, in believing that you have to an extent manipulated the destinies of myself and Mr Carnelian?'

'Subtly, I hope, madam,' said Jagged, still tugging at the heap. 'For so abstract a thing, Time keeps a severe eye upon our activities. I had to be careful. It is why I adopted two main disguises in this world. I have travelled in Time a great deal, as you have probably guessed. Both to the past – and the future, such as it exists at all in my world. I knew about the "End of Time" before ever Yusharisp brought the news to our planet. I also discovered that there are certain people who are, by virtue of a particular arrangement of genes, not so prone to the Morphail Effect as are others. I conceived a means of averting disaster for some of us...'

'Disaster, Jagged?'

'The end of all of us, dear Jherek. I could not bear to think that, having achieved such balance, we should perish. We had learned, you see, how to live. And it was for nothing. Such an irony was unbearable to me, the lover of ironies. I spent many, many years in this century – the furthest back I could go in my own machine – running complicated checks, taking a variety of people into the future, seeing how, as it were, they "took" when returned to their own time. None did. I regret their fate. Only Mrs Underwood stayed, apparently virtually immune to the Morphail Effect!'

'So you, sir, were my abductor!' she cried.

'I am afraid so. There!' He pulled the last of the coverings free, revealing the spherical time machine which Brannart Morphail had loaned to Jherek on his first trip to the Dawn Age.

'I am hoping,' he continued, 'that some of us will sur-

339

vive the End of Time. And you can help me. This time machine can be controlled. It will take you back to our own age, Jherek, where we can continue with our experiments. At least,' he added, 'it should. The instability of the megaflow at present is worrying. But we must hope. We must hope. Now, the two of you, enter the machine. There are breathing masks for both.'

'Mr Jackson,' said Mrs Underwood. 'I will not be bullied any further.' She folded her arms across her bosom. 'Neither will I allow myself to be mesmerized by your quasi-scientific lecturings!'

'I think he is right, Mrs Underwood,' said Jherek hesitantly. 'And the reason I came to find you was because you *are* prone to the Morphail Effect. At least in a time machine we stand a chance of going to an age of our choice.'

'Remember how Jherek escaped hanging,' said Lord Jagged. He had by now opened the circular outer door of the time machine. 'That was the Morphail Effect. It would have been a paradox if he had died in that particular way in this age. I knew it. That was why I lent myself to what appeared to you, Mrs Underwood, to be his destruction. There is proof of my good-will. He is not dead.'

Reluctantly, she began to move with Jherek towards the time machine. 'I shall be able to return?' she asked.

'Almost certainly. But I am hoping that you will not wish to when you have heard me out.'

'You will accompany us?'

'My own machine is not a quarter of a mile from here. I must use it, for I cannot afford to abandon it. It is a very sophisticated model. It does not even register on Brannart's instruments. As soon as you are on your way, I will go to it and follow you. I promise you, Mrs Underwood, that I am not deceiving you. I will reveal all I know upon our return to the "End of Time".'

'Very well.'

'You will not find the interior of the machine pleasant,'

Jherek told her as he helped her into the airlock. 'You must hold your breath for a moment.' They crouched together in the cylinder. He handed her a breathing mask. 'Fit this over your head, like so ...'

He smiled as he heard her muffled complaints.

'Fear not, Mrs Underwood. Our great adventure is almost ended. Soon we shall be back in our own dear villa, with roses climbing round the door, with our pipes and our slippers and our water closets! King Darby and Queen Joan in Camelot!' The rest of his effusion was muffled, even to his own ears, by the necessity of putting on his mask as the airlock began to fill with milky fluid. Jherek wished that there had been rubber suits of the kind normally used in the machine, for the stuff felt unpleasant and was soaking rapidly through their clothes. There was a look of outraged disgust, in fact, in Mrs Underwood's eyes.

The machine filled rapidly and they drifted into the main chamber. Here certain instruments were already flashing green and red alternately, swimming about his head. They floated, unable to control their movements, in the thick liquid. As his body turned slowly, he saw that Mrs Underwood had shut her eyes. Blue and yellow lights began to flash. The liquid became increasingly cloudy.

Figures, which he could not read, began to register on the display panels. A white light throbbed and he knew that the machine was on the very brink of beginning its journey into the future. He relaxed. Happiness filled him. Soon he would be home.

The white light burned his eyes. He became dizzy. Pain began to nag at his nerves and he stopped himself from screaming, for fear that she would hear him and be troubled.

The liquid grew dark until it was the colour of blood. His senses fled him.

He woke up knowing that the journey must be over. He tried to turn himself round so that he could see if Mrs

Underwood were awake. He could feel her body resting against his leg.

But then, surprisingly, the process began again. The green lights gave way to red, to blue and to yellow. The white light shrieked. The pain increased, the liquid became dark again.

And again he fainted.

He woke up. This time he stared directly into Mrs Underwood's pale, unconscious face. He tried to reach out to take her hand and, as if this action were enough to begin it, the process started again. The green and red alternating lights, the blue and yellow lights, the blinding whiteness, the pain, the loss of his awareness. He woke up. The machine was shuddering. From somewhere there came a grating whine.

This time he screamed, in spite of himself, and he thought that Mrs Underwood was also screaming. The white light throbbed. Suddenly it was totally black. Then a green light flickered. It went out. A red light flickered and went out. Blue and yellow lights flashed.

And then Jherek Carnelian knew that Lord Jagged's fears had been realized. There had been too many attempts at once to manipulate Time – and Time was refusing further manipulation. They were adrift. They were shifting back and forth at random on the timeflow. They were as much victims of the Morphail Effect as if they had never entered the time machine. Time was taking its vengeance on those who had sought to conquer it.

Jherek's one consolation, as he fainted again, was that at least he and Mrs Underwood were together.

CHAPTER NINETEEN

IN WHICH JHEREK CARNELIAN
AND MRS AMELIA UNDERWOOD DEBATE
CERTAIN MORAL PROBLEMS

'Mr Carnelian! please, Mr Carnelian, try to wake up!'

'I am awake,' he groaned, but he did not open his eyes. His skin felt pleasantly warm. There was a delicious smell in his nostrils. There was silence.

'Then open your eyes, please, Mr Carnelian,' she demanded. 'I need your advice.'

He obeyed her. He blinked. 'What an extraordinarily deep blue,' he said of the sky. 'So we are back, after all. I became a trifle pessimistic, I must admit, when the machine seemed to be malfunctioning. How did we get out?'

'I pulled you out, and it was as well I did.' She made a gesture. He looked and saw that the time machine was in even worse condition than when he had landed in the 19th century. Mrs Underwood was brushing sand from her tattered dress of maroon velvet. 'That awful stuff,' she said. 'Even when it dries it makes everything stiff.'

He sat up, smiling. 'It will be the work of a moment to supply you with fresh clothes. I still have most of my power rings. I wonder who made this. It is ravishing!'

The scenery stretched for miles, all waving fern-like plants of a variety of sizes, from the small ones carpeting the ground to very large ones as big as poplars; and not far from the beach on which they lay was a lazy sea, stretching to the horizon. In the far distance behind them was a line of low, gentle hills.

'It is a remarkable reproduction,' she agreed. 'Rather better in detail than most of those made by your people.'

'You know the original?'

'I studied such things once. My father was of the modern school. He did not reject Darwin out of hand.'

'Darwin loved him?' Jherek's thoughts had returned to his favourite subject.

'Darwin was a scientist, Mr Carnelian,' she said impatiently.

'And he made a world like this?'

'No, no. It isn't anything really to do with him. A figure of speech.'

'What is a "figure of speech"?'

'I will explain that later. My point was that this landscape resembles the world at a very early age of its geological development. It is tropical and typical ferns and plants are in evidence. It is probably the Ordovician period of the Paleozoic, possibly the Silurian. If this were a perfect reproduction those seas you observe would team with edible life. There would be clams and so on, but no large beasts. Everything possible to sustain life, and nothing very much to threaten it!'

'I can't imagine who could have made it,' said Jherek. 'Unless it was Lady Voiceless. She built a series of early worlds a while ago – the Egyptian was her best.'

'Such a world as this would have flourished millions of years before Egypt,' said Mrs Underwood, becoming lyrical. 'Millions of years before Man – before the dinosaurs, even. Ah, it is paradise! You see, there are no signs at all of animal life as we know it.'

'There hasn't actually been any animal life, as such, for a good while,' said Jherek. 'Only that which we make for ourselves.'

'You aren't following me very closely, Mr Carnelian.'

'I am sorry. I will try. I want my moral education to begin as soon as possible. There are all sorts of things you can teach me.'

'I regard *that*,' she said, 'as my duty. I could not justify being here otherwise.' She smiled to herself. 'After all, I come from a long line of missionaries.'

'A new dress?' he said.

'If you please.'

He touched a power ring; the emerald.

Nothing happened.

He touched the diamond and then the amethyst. And nothing at all happened. He was puzzled. 'I have never known my power rings to fail me,' he said.

Mrs Underwood cleared her throat. 'It is becoming increasingly hot. Suppose we stroll into the shade of those ferns?'

He agreed. As they walked, he tried his power rings again, shaking his head in surprise.

'Strange. Perhaps when the time machine began to go awry . . .'

'It went wrong, the time machine?'

'Yes. Plainly shifting back and forth in time at random. I had completely despaired of returning here.'

'Here?'

'Oh, dear,' he said.

'So,' she said, seating herself upon a reddish-coloured rock and staring around her at the mile upon mile of Silurian ferns, 'we could have travelled backwards, could we, Mr Carnelian?'

'I would say that we could have, yes.'

'So much for your friend Lord Jagged's assurances,' she said.

'Yes.' He sucked his lower lip. 'But he was afraid we had left things too late, if you recall.'

'He was correct.' Again she cleared her throat.

Jherek cleared his. 'If this is the age you think it is, am I to gather there are no people to be found here at all?'

'Not one. Not a primate.'

'We are at the beginning of Time?'

'For want of a better description, yes.' Her lovely fingers drummed rapidly against the rock. She did not seem pleased.

'Oh dear,' he said, 'we shall never see the Iron Orchid again!'

She brightened a little at this. 'We'll have to make the best of it, I suppose, and hope that we are rescued in due course.'

'The chances are slight, Mrs Underwood. Nobody has ever gone this far back. You heard Lord Jagged say that your age was the furthest he could reach into the past.'

She straightened her shoulders rather as she had done that time when they stood upon the bank of the river. 'We must build a hut, of course – preferably *two* huts – and we must test which of the life, such as it is, is edible. We must make a fire and keep it lit. We must see what the time machine will give us that is useable. Not much I would assume.'

'You are certain that this is the period...?'

'Mr Carnelian! Your power rings do not work. We have no other evidence. We must assume that we are marooned in the Silurian.'

'The Morphail Effect is supposed to send us into the future,' he said, 'not the past.'

'This is certainly no future we might expect from 1896, Mr Carnelian.'

'No.' A thought came to him. 'I was discussing the

possibility of the cyclic nature of Time with Brannart Morphail and Lord Jagged quite recently. Could we have plunged so far into the future that we are, as it were, at the start again?'

'Such theories cannot mean a great deal to us,' she told him, 'in our present circumstances.'

'I agree. But it would explain *why* we are in them, Mrs Underwood.'

She plucked a frond from over her head and began to fan herself, deliberately ignoring him.

He drew a deep breath of the rich Silurian (or possibly Ordovician) air. He stretched himself out luxuriously upon the ground. 'You yourself described this world as Paradise, Mrs Underwood. In what better place could two lovers find themselves?'

'Another abstract idea, Mr Carnelian? You surely do not refer to yourself and myself?'

'Oh, but I do!' he said dreamily. 'We could begin the human race all over again! A whole new cycle. This time we shall flourish *before* the dinosaurs. This is Paradise and we are Adolf and Eva! Or do I mean Alan and Edna?'

'I think you refer to Adam and Eve, Mr Carnelian. If you do, then you blaspheme and I wish to hear no more!'

'Blas-what?'

'Pheme.'

'Is that also to do with Morality?'

'I suppose it is, yes.'

'Could you explain, perhaps, a little further,' he asked enticingly.

'You offend against the Deity. It is a profanity to identify yourself with Adam in that way.'

'What about Eve?'

'Eve, too.'

'I am sorry.'

'You weren't to know.' She continued to fan herself with the frond. 'I suppose we had best start looking for food. Aren't you hungry?'

347

'I am hungry for your kisses,' he said romantically, and he stood up.

'Mr Carnelian!'

'Well,' he said, 'we can "marry" now, can't we? Mr Underwood said as much.'

'We are not divorced. Besides, even if I were divorced from Mr Underwood, there is no reason to assume that I should wish to give myself in marriage to you. Moreover, Mr Carnelian, there is nobody in the Silurian Age *to* marry us.' She seemed to think she had produced the final argument, but he had not really understood her.

'If we were to complete my moral education,' he said. 'Would you marry me then?'

'Perhaps – if everything else was properly settled – which seems unlikely now.'

He walked slowly back to the beach again and stared out over the sluggish sea, deep in thought. At his feet a small mollusc began to crawl through the sand. He watched it for a while and then, hearing a movement behind him, turned. She was standing there. She had made herself a hat of sorts from fern-leaves. She looked extremely pretty.

'I am sorry if I upset you, Mr Carnelian,' she said kindly. 'You are rather more direct than I have been used to, you see. I know that your manner is not deliberately offensive, that you are, in some ways, more innocent than I. But you have a way of saying the wrong thing – or sometimes the right thing in the wrong way.'

He shrugged. 'That is why I am so desperate for my moral education to begin. I love you, Mrs Amelia Underwood. Perhaps it was Lord Jagged who encouraged me to affect the emotion in the first place, but since then it has taken hold of me. I am its slave. I can console myself, of course, but I cannot stop loving you.'

'I am flattered.'

'And you have *said* that you loved me, but now you try to deny it.'

'I am still *Mrs* Underwood,' she pointed out gently.

The small mollusc began, tentatively, to crawl onto his foot. 'And I am still Jherek Carnelian,' he replied.

She noticed the mollusc. 'Aha! Perhaps this one is edible.'

As she reached down to inspect it, he stopped her with his hand on her shoulder. 'No,' he said. 'Let it go.'

She straightened up, smiling gently at him. 'We cannot afford to be sentimental, Mr Carnelian.'

His hand remained for an instant on her shoulder. The worn, stiffened velvet was beginning to grow soft again. 'We cannot afford not to be, I think.'

Her grey eyes were serious; then she laughed. 'Oh, very well. Let us wait, then, until we are *extremely* hungry.' Gaily, with her black buttoned boots kicking at the fine sand of that primordial shore, she began to stride along beside the thick and salty sea.

'All things bright and beautiful,' she sang, 'all creatures great and small./ All things wise and wonderful: / The Lord God made them all!'

There was a certain defiance in her manner, a certain spirited challenge to the inevitable, which made Jherek gasp with devotion.

'Self-denial, after all,' she called back over her shoulder, 'is good for the soul!'

'Ah!' He began to run after her and then slowed before he had caught up. He stared around him at the calm, Silurian world, struck suddenly by the freshness of it all, by the growing understanding that they really were the only two mammals on this whole planet. He looked up at the huge, golden sun and he blinked in its benign glare. He was full of wonder.

A little later, panting, sweating, laughing, he fell in beside her. He noticed that her expression was almost tender as she turned to look at him.

He offered her his arm.

After a second's hesitation, she took it.

349

They strolled together through the hot, Silurian afternoon.

'Now, Mrs Underwood,' he said contentedly, 'what *is* "self-denial"?'

The end of the second volume

VOLUME THREE

The End of All Songs

For John Clute
– and Tom Disch

The fire is out, and spent the warmth thereof,
(This is the end of every song man sings!)
The golden wine is drunk, the dregs remain,
Bitter as wormwood and as salt as pain;
And health and hope have gone the way of love
Into the drear oblivion of lost things,
Ghosts go along with us until the end;
This was a mistress, this, perhaps, a friend.
With pale, indifferent eyes, we sit and wait
For the dropt curtain and the closing gate:
This is the end of all the songs man sings.

Ernest Dowson
Dregs
1899

Contents

Acknowledgements

Apart from Alfred Austin's, all verses quoted in the text are the work of Ernest Wheldrake. The majority are from *Posthumous Poems*, published in 1881 and never reprinted.

IN WHICH JHEREK CARNELIAN AND MRS AMELIA UNDERWOOD COMMUNE, TO SOME DEGREE, WITH NATURE

'I really do think, Mr Carnelian, that we should at least *try* them raw, don't you?'

Mrs Amelia Underwood, with the flat of her left hand, stroked thick auburn hair back over her ear and, with her right hand, arranged her tattered skirts about her ankles. The gesture was almost petulant; the glint in her grey eye was possibly wolfish. There was, if nothing else, something over-controlled in the manner in which she perched primly upon her block of virgin limestone and watched Jherek Carnelian as he crouched, elbows and knees pressed in the sand of a Palaeozoic beach, and sweated in the heat of the huge Silurian (or possibly Devonian) sun.

Perhaps for the thousandth time he was trying to strike two of his power-rings together to make a spark to light the heap of half-dried ferns he had, in a mood of ebullience long since dissipated, arranged several hours before.

'But you told me,' he murmured, 'that you could not bear to consider ... There! Was that a spark? Or just a glint?'

'A glint,' she said, 'I think.'

'We must not despair, Mrs Underwood.' His optimism

was uncharacteristically strained. Again he struck ring against ring.

Around him were scattered the worn and broken fragments of fronds which he had earlier tried to rub together at her suggestion. As power-ring clacked on power-ring, Mrs Underwood winced. In the silence of this Silurian (if it was Silurian) afternoon the sound had an effect upon her nerves she would not previously have credited; she had never seen herself as one of those over-sensitive women who populated the novels of Marie Corelli. She had always considered herself robust, singularly healthy. She sighed. Doubtless the boredom contributed something to her state of mind.

Jherek echoed her sigh. 'There's probably a knack to it,' he admitted. 'Where are the trilobites?' He stared absently around him at the ground.

'Most of them have crawled back into the sea, I think,' she told him coldly. 'There are two brachiopods on your coat.' She pointed.

'Aha!' Almost affectionately he plucked the molluscoidea from the dirty black cloth of his frock-coat. Doubtfully, he peered into the shells.

Mrs Underwood licked her lips. 'Give them to me,' she commanded. She produced a hat-pin.

His head bowed, Pilate confronting the Pharisees, he complied.

'After all,' she told him as she poised the pin, 'we are only missing garlic and butter and we should have a meal fit for a French gourmet.' The utterance seemed to depress her. She hesitated.

'Mrs Underwood?'

'Should we say grace, I wonder?' She frowned. 'It might help. I think it's the colour . . .'

'Too beautiful,' he said eagerly. 'I follow you. Who could destroy such loveliness?'

'That greenish, purplish hue pleases you?'

'Not you?'

'Not in *food*, Mr Carnelian.'

358

'Then in what?'

'Oh ...' Vaguely. 'In – no, not even in a picture. It brings to mind the excesses of the Pre-Raphaelites. A morbid colour.'

'Ah.'

'It might explain your affinities ...' She abandoned the subject. 'If I could conquer ...'

'A yellow one?' He tried to tempt her with a soft-shelled creature he had just discovered in his back pocket. It clung to his finger; there was the sensation of a kiss.

She dropped molluscs and hat-pin, covered her face with her hands and began to weep.

'Mrs Underwood!' He was at a loss. He stirred the pile of fronds with his foot. 'Perhaps if I were to use a ring as a prism and direct the rays of the sun through it we could ...'

There came a loud squeak and he wondered at first if one of the creatures were protesting. Another squeak, from behind him. Mrs Underwood removed her fingers to expose red eyes which now widened in surprise.

'Hi! I say – Hi, there!'

Jherek turned. Tramping through the shallows, apparently oblivious of the water, came a man dressed in a seaman's jersey, a tweed Norfolk jacket, plus-fours, heavy woollen stockings, stout brogues. In one hand he clutched a stick of a peculiarly twisted crystalline nature. Otherwise he appeared to be a contemporary of Mrs Underwood's. He was smiling. 'I say, do you speak English of any kind?' He was bronzed. He had a full moustache and signs of a newly sprouting beard. He beamed at them. He came to a stop, resting his knuckles on his hips. 'Well?'

Mrs Underwood was confused. 'We speak English, sir. Indeed we are – at least I am – English, as you must be.'

'Beautiful day, isn't it?' The stranger nodded at the sea. 'Nice and calm. Must be the early Devonian, eh? Have you been here long?'

'Long enough, sir.'

'We are marooned,' Jherek explained. 'A malfunction

of our time-craft. The paradoxes were too much for it, I suspect.'

The stranger nodded gravely. 'I've sometimes experienced similar difficulties, though happily without such drastic results. You're from the nineteenth century, I take it.'

'Mrs Underwood is. I hail from the End of Time.'

'Aha!' The stranger smiled. 'I have just come from there. I was fortunate enough to witness the complete disintegration of the universe – briefly, of course. I, too, am originally from the nineteenth century. This would be one of my regular stops, if I were journeying to the past. The peculiar thing is that I was under the impression I was going forward – beyond, as it were, the End of Time. My instruments indicate as much. Yet here I am.' He scratched his sandy hair, adding, in mild disappointment, 'I was hoping for some illumination.'

'You are on your way, then, to the future?' Mrs Underwood asked. 'To the nineteenth century?'

'It seems that I must be. When did you leave?'

'1896,' Mrs Underwood told him.

'I am from 1894. I was not aware that anyone else had hit upon my discovery during that period ...'

'There!' exclaimed Jherek. 'Mr Wells was right!'

'Our machine was from Mr Carnelian's period,' she said. 'Originally, I was abducted to the End of Time, under circumstances which remain mysterious. The motives of my abductor continue to be obscure, moreover. I ...' She paused apologetically. 'This is of no interest to you, of course.' She moistened her lips. 'You would not, I suppose, have the means of lighting a fire, sir?'

The stranger patted the bulging pockets of his Norfolk jacket. 'Somewhere. Some matches. I tend to carry as many necessities as possible about my person. In the event of being stranded ... Here we are.' He produced a large box of vestas. 'I would give you the whole box, but ...'

'A few will do. You say you are familiar with the early Devonian.'

'As familiar as one can be.'

'Your advice, then, would be welcome. The edibility of the molluscs, for instance?'

'I think you'll find the *myalina subquadrata* the least offensive, and very few are actually poisonous, though a certain amount of indigestion is bound to result. I, myself, am a slave to indigestion.'

'And what do these *myalina* look like?' Jherek asked.

'Oh, like mussels, really. You have to dig for them.'

Mrs Underwood took five matches from the box and handed it back.

'Your time-craft, sir, is functioning properly?' Jherek said.

'Oh, yes, perfectly.'

'And you are returning to the nineteenth century?'

'To 1895, I hope.'

'Then you could take us with you?'

The stranger shook his head. 'It's a single-seater. The saddle barely accommodates me, since I began to put on weight. Come, I'll show you.' He turned and began to plod through the sand in the direction from which he had come. They followed.

'Also,' added the stranger, 'it would be unwise for me to try to take people from 1896 to 1895. You would meet yourselves. Considerable confusion would result. One can tamper just a little with the Logic of Time, but I hesitate to think what would happen if one went in for such blatant paradoxes. It would seem to me that if you have been treating the Logic so cavalierly it is no wonder – I do not moralize, you understand – that you find yourselves in this position.'

'Then you verify the Morphail Theory,' Jherek said, trudging beside the time-traveller. 'Time resists paradox, adjusting accordingly – refusing, you might say, to admit a foreign body to a period to which it is not indigenous?'

'If a paradox is likely to occur. Yes. I suspect that it is all to do with consciousness, and with our *group* understanding of what constitutes Past, Present and Future.

361

That is, Time, as such, does not exist ...'

Mrs Underwood uttered a soft exclamation as the stranger's craft came in sight. It consisted of an open frame of tubular lengths of brass and ebony. There was ivory here and there, as well as a touch or two of silver, copper coils set into the top of the frame, immediately above a heavily sprung leather saddle of the sort normally seen on bicycles. Before this was a small board of instruments and a brass semi-circle where a lever might normally fit. Much of the rest of the machine was of nickel and crystal and it showed signs of wear, was much battered, dented and cracked in places. Behind the saddle was strapped a large chest and it was to this that the stranger made at once, undoing the brass buckles and pushing back the lid. The first object he drew out of the trunk was a double-barrelled shot-gun which he leaned against the saddle; next he removed a bale of muslin and a solar topee, and finally, using both hands, he hauled up a large wickerwork basket and dumped it in the sand at their feet.

'This might be useful to you,' he said, replacing the other objects in the trunk and securing the straps. 'It's the best I can offer, short of passage home. And I've explained why that's impossible. You wouldn't want to come face to face with yourselves in the middle of Waterloo Circus, would you?' He laughed.

'Don't you mean Piccadilly Circus, sir?' enquired Mrs Underwood with a frown.

'Never heard of it,' said the time-traveller.

'I've never heard of Waterloo Circus,' she told him. 'Are you sure you're from 1894?'

The stranger fingered the stubble on his chin. He seemed a little disturbed. 'I thought I'd merely gone full circle,' he murmured. 'Hm – perhaps this universe is not quite the same as the one I left. Is it possible that for every new time-traveller a new chronology develops? Could there be an infinite number of universes?' He brightened. 'This is a fine adventure, I must say. Aren't you hungry?'

Mrs Amelia Underwood raised her beautiful brows.

The stranger pointed at the basket. 'My provisions,' he said. 'Make what use of them you like. I'll risk finding some food at my next stop – hopefully 1895. Well, I must be on my way.'

He bowed, brandishing his quartz rod significantly. He climbed onto his saddle and placed the rod in the brass groove, making some adjustments to his other controls.

Mrs Underwood was already lifting the lid of the hamper. Her face was obscured, but Jherek thought he could hear her crooning to herself.

'Good luck to you both,' said the stranger cheerfully. 'I'm sure you won't be stuck here forever. It's unlikely, isn't it? I mean, what a find for the archeologists, ha, ha! Your bones, that is!'

There came a sharp click as the stranger moved his lever a notch or two and almost immediately the time machine began to grow indistinct. Copper glowed and crystal shimmered; something seemed to be whirling very rapidly above the stranger's head and already both man and machine were semi-transparent. Jherek was struck in the face by a sudden gust of wind which came from nowhere and then the time-traveller had gone.

'Oh, look, Mr Carnelian!' cried Mrs Amelia Underwood, brandishing her trophy. 'Chicken!'

CHAPTER TWO

IN WHICH INSPECTOR SPRINGER TASTES
THE DELIGHTS OF THE SIMPLE LIFE

For the following two days and nights a certain tension, dissipating before the advent of the time-traveller but since restored, existed between the lovers (for they *were* lovers – only her upbringing denied it) and they slept fitfully, the pair of them, on either side of a frond-fondled limestone rock, having to fear nothing but the inquisitive attentions of the little molluscs and trilobites whose own lives now were free from danger, thanks to the hamper, crammed with cans and bottles enough to sustain a good-sized expedition for a month. No large beasts, no unexpected turn of the weather, threatened our Adam and our Eve; Eve, alone, knew inner conflict: Adam, simple bewilderment; but then he was used to bewilderment, and sudden moods or twists of fate had been the stuff of his existence until only recently – yet his spirits were not what they had been.

They rose somewhat, those spirits, at dawn this morning – for the beauty, in its subtlety, excelled any creation of *fin de cosmos* artifice. A huge half-sun filled the horizon line so that the sky surrounding it shone a thousand shades of copper, while its rays, spread upon the sea, seemed individually coloured – blues, ochres, greys, pinks – until they reached the beach and merged again, as if at apex, to make the yellow sand glare rainbow white, turn the limestone to shimmering silver and make individual leaves and stems of the fronds a green that seemed near-sentient, it was so alive; and there was a human figure at the core of this vision, outlined against the pulsing semi-circle of dark scarlet, the velvet dress murky red amber, the auburn hair a-flame, the white hands and neck reflecting the hues, delicate hint of the palest of poppies. And there was music, sonorous – it was her voice; she declaimed a favourite verse, its subject a trifle at odds with the ambience.

> *Where the red worm woman wailed for wild revenge,*
> *   While the surf surged sullen 'neath moon-silver'd*
> *   sky,*
> *Where her harsh voice, once a sweet voice, sang,*
> *   Now was I.*
> *And did her ghost on that grey, cold morn,*
> *   Did her ghost slide by?*

Rapt, Jherek straightened his back and pushed aside the frock-coat which had covered him through the night; to see his love thus, in a setting to match the perfection of her beauty, sent all other considerations helter-skelter from his head; his own eyes shone: his face shone. He waited for more, but she was silent, tossing back her locks, shaking sand from her hem, pursing those loveliest of lips.

'Well?' he said.

Slowly, through iridescence, the face looked up, from shadow into light. Her mouth was a question.

'Amelia?' He dared the name. Her lids fell.

'What is it?' she murmured.

'Did it? Was it her ghost? I await the resolution.'

The lips curved now, perhaps a touch self-consciously, but the eyes continued to study the sand which she stirred with the sharp toe of her partly unbuttoned boot. 'Wheldrake doesn't say. It's a rhetorical question ...'

'A very sober poem, is it not?'

A sense of superiority mingled with her modesty, causing the lashes to rise and fall rapidly for a moment. 'Most good poems are sober, Mr Carnelian, if they are to convey – significance. It speaks of death, of course. Wheldrake wrote much of death – and died, himself, prematurely. My cousin gave me the *Posthumous Poems* for my twentieth birthday. Shortly afterwards, she was taken from us, also, by consumption.'

'Is all good literature, then, about death?'

'Serious literature.'

'Death is serious?'

'It is final, at any rate.' But she shocked herself, judging this cynical, and recovered with: 'Although really, it is only the beginning – of our real life, our eternal life ...'

She turned to regard the sun, already higher and less splendid.

'You mean, at the End of Time? In our own little home?'

'Never mind.' She faltered, speaking in a higher, less natural tone. 'It is my punishment, I suppose, to be denied, in my final hours, the company of a fellow Christian.' But there was some insincerity to all this. The food she had consumed during the past two days had mellowed her. She had almost welcomed the simpler terrors of starvation to the more complex dangers of giving herself up to this clown, this innocent (oh, yes, and perhaps this noble, manly being, for his courage, his kindness went without question). She strove, with decreasing success, to recreate that earlier, much more suitable, mood of resigned despondency.

'I interrupted you.' He leaned back against his rock. 'Forgive me. It was so delicious, to wake to the sound of your voice. Won't you go on?'

She cleared her throat and faced the sea again.

What will you say to me, child of the moon,
When by the bright river we stand?

When forest leaves breathe harmonies to the night
        wind's croon.
    Will you give me your hand, child of the moon?
Will you give me your hand?

But her performance lacked the appropriate resonance,
certainly to her own ears, and she delivered the next verse
with even less conviction.

Will you present your pyre to me, spawn of the sun,
        While the sky is in full flame?
While the day's heat the brain deceives, and the
        drugged bees hum.
    Will you grant me your name, spawn of the sun?
Will you grant me your name?

Jherek blinked. 'You have lost me entirely, I fear . . .' The
sun was fully risen, the scene fled, though pale gold light
touched sky and sea still, and the day was calm and sultry.
'Oh, what things I could create with such inspiration, if
only my power rings were active. Vision upon vision, and
all for you, Amelia!'

'Have you no literature, at the End of Time?' she asked.
'Are your arts only visual?'

'We converse,' he said. 'You have heard us.'

'Conversation has been called an art, yet . . .'

'We do not write it down,' he said, 'if that is what you
mean. Why should we? Similar conversations often arise –
similar observations are made afresh. Does one discover
more through the act of making the marks I have seen you
make? If so, perhaps I should . . .'

'It will pass the time,' she said, 'if I teach you to write
and read.'

'Certainly,' he agreed.

She knew the questions he had asked had been innocent,
but they struck her as just. She laughed. 'Oh, dear, Mr
Carnelian. Oh, dear!'

He was content not to judge her mood to but to share

it. He laughed with her, springing up. He advanced. She awaited him. He stopped, when a few steps separated them. He was serious now, and smiling.

She fingered her neck. 'There is more to literature than conversation, however. There are stories.'

'We make our own lives into stories, at the End of Time. We have the means. Would you not do the same, if you could?'

'Society demands that we do not.'

'Why so?'

'Perhaps because the stories would conflict, one with the other. There are so many of us – there.'

'Here,' he said, 'there are but two.'

'Our tenancy in this – this Eden – is tentative. Who knows when ...?'

'Logically, if we are torn away, then we shall be borne to the End of Time, not to 1896. And what is there, waiting, but Eden, too?'

'No, I should not call it that.'

They stared, now, eye to eye. The sea whispered. It was louder than their words.

He could not move, though he sought to go forward. Her stance held him off; it was the set of her chin, the slight lift of one shoulder.

'We could be alone, if we wished it.'

'There should be no choice, in Eden.'

'Then here, at least ...' His look was charged, it demanded; it implored.

'And take sin with us, out of Eden?'

'No sin, if by that you mean that which give your fellows pain. What of me?'

'We suffer. Both.' The sea seemed very loud, the voice faint as a wind through ferns. 'Love is cruel.'

'No!' His shout broke the silence. He laughed. 'That is nonsense! Fear is cruel! Fear alone!'

'Oh, I have so much of that!' She called out, lifting her face to the sky, and she began to laugh, even as he seized her, taking her hands in his, bending to kiss that cheek.

Tears striped her; she wiped them clear with her sleeve, and the kiss was forestalled. Instead she began to hum a tune, and she placed a hand on his shoulder, leaving her other hand in his. She dipped and led him in a step or two. 'Perhaps my fate is sealed,' she said. She smiled at him, a conspiracy of love and pain and some self-pity. 'Oh, come, Mr Carnelian, I shall teach you to dance. If this is Eden, let us enjoy it while we may!'

Brightening considerably, Jherek allowed her to lead him in the steps.

Soon he was laughing, a child in love and, for the moment, not the mature individual, the man whose command could conquer.

Disaster (if it was disaster) delayed, they pranced, beside the Palaeozoic seaside, an improvised polka.

But it was only delayed. Both were expectant, fulfillment, consummation, hovered. And Jherek sang a wordless song; within moments she would be his bride, his pride, his celebration.

The song was soon to die on his lips. They rounded a clump of flimsy vegetation, a pavement of yellow rock, and came to a sudden and astounded stop. Both glared, both felt vitality flow from them to be replaced by taut rage. Mrs Underwood, sighing, withdrew into the stiff velvet of her dress.

'We *are* fated,' she murmured. 'We *are*!'

They continued to glare at the unwitting back of the one who had frustrated their idyll. He remained unaware of their wrath, their presence.

The shirtsleeves and trousers rolled up to elbow and knee respectively, the bowler hat fixed firmly on the heavy head, the briar pipe between the lips, the newcomer was paddling contentedly in the amniotic ocean.

As they watched, he took a large white handkerchief from the pocket of his dark, serge trousers (waistcoat and jacket, shoes and socks, lay neat and incongruous on the beach behind), shook it out, tied a small knot at each corner, removed his hat and spread the handkerchief over his cropped and balding scalp. This accomplished, he began to hum – 'Pom te pom, pom pom pom, te pom pom' – wading a little further through the shallow water, pausing to raise a red and goose-pimpled foot and to brush at two or three wheat-coloured trilobites which had begun to climb his leg.

'Funny little beggars,' he was heard to mutter, but did not seem to mind their curiosity.

Mrs Underwood was pale. 'How is it possible?' A vicious whisper. 'He has pursued us through Time!' With one hand, she unclenched the other. 'My respect for Scotland Yard, I suppose, increases ...'

Forgetting his private disappointment in favour of his social responsibilities (he had developed proprietorial feelings toward the Palaeozoic) Jherek called:

'Good afternoon, Inspector Springer.'

Mrs Underwood reached a hand for his arm, as if to forestall him, but too late. Inspector Springer, the almost seraphic expression fading to be replaced by his more familiar stern and professional mask, turned unwillingly.

Bowler forgotten in his left hand, he removed his pipe from his lips. He peered. He blinked. He heaved a sigh, fully the equal of their own most recent sighs. Happiness fled away.

'Good 'eavens!'

'Heavens, if you prefer.' Jherek welcomed correction, for he still studied the mores of the nineteenth century.

'I *thought* it was 'eaven.' Inspector Springer's slap at an exploring trilobite was less tolerant than before. 'But now I'm beginning to doubt it. More like 'ell ...' He remembered the presence of Mrs Underwood. He stared mournfully at a wet trouser leg. 'The other place, I mean.'

There was a tinge of pleased malice in her tone: 'You think yourself dead, Inspector Springer?'

'The deduction fitted the facts, madam.'

Not without dignity, he placed the bowler on top of the knotted handkerchief. He peered into the pipe and, satisfied that it had gone out, slipped it into a pocket. Her irony was wasted; he became a trifle more confidential.

'An 'eart-attack, I presumed, brought about by the stress of recent events. I was jest questioning them foreigners – the little anarchists with only one eye – or three, if you look at it another way – when it seemed to me they vanished clear away.' He cleared his throat, lowered his voice a fraction. 'Well, I turned to call me sergeant, felt a bit dizzy meself, and the next thing I knows, 'ere I am in 'eaven.' He seemed, then, to recall his previous relationship with the pair. He straightened, resentful. 'Or so I deduced until you turned up a minute ago.' He waded forward until he stood on glinting sand. He began to roll down his trousers. He spoke crisply. 'Well then,' he demanded, 'what is the explanation? Briefly, mind. Nothing fancy.'

'It is simple enough.' Jherek was glad to explain. 'We have been hurled through Time, that is all. To a pre-Dawn Age. That is, to a period before Man existed at all. Millions of years. The Upper or —?' He turned to Mrs Underwood for help.

'Probably the Lower Devonian,' she said. She was off-hand. 'The stranger confirmed it.'

'A warp in Time,' Jherek continued. 'In which you were caught, as we were. Admitting no large paradoxes, Time ejected us from your period. Doubtless, the Lat were so ejected. It was unfortunate that you were in the proximity ...'

Inspector Springer covered his ears, heading for his boots as if towards a haven. 'Oh, Gawd! Not again. It *is* 'ell! It *is*!'

'I am beginning to share your view, Inspector.' Mrs Underwood was more than cool. She turned on her heel and started to walk in the direction of the frond forest at the top of the beach. Normally her conscience would sharply rule out such obvious tricks, but she had been thwarted; she had become desperate – she gave Jherek the impression that he was to blame for Inspector Springer's arrival, as if, perhaps, by speaking of sin he had called forth Satan into Eden.

Frozen, Jherek was trapped by the manoeuvre as neatly as any Victorian beloved. 'Amelia,' was all he could pipe.

She did not, of course, reply.

Inspector Springer had reached his boots. He sat down beside them; he pulled free, from one of them, a grey woollen sock. He addressed the sock as he tried to pull it over his damp foot. 'What I can't work out,' he mused, 'is whether I'm technically still on duty or not.'

Mrs Underwood had come to the frond forest. Determinedly she disappeared into the rustling depths. Jherek made up his mind to stumble in wretched pursuit. The host in him hesitated for only a second:

'Perhaps we'll see you again, Inspector?'

'Not if I —'

But the high-pitched scream interrupted both. A glance was exchanged. Inspector Springer forgot differences, obeyed instincts, leapt to his feet, hobbling after Jherek as he flung himself forward, racing for the source of the scream.

But already Mrs Underwood was flying from the forest, outrage and horror remoulding her beauty, stopping with a gasp when she saw salvation; mutely, she pointed back into the agitated foliage.

The fronds parted. A single eye glared out at them, its three pupils fixed steadily, perhaps lecherously, upon the panting form of Mrs Underwood.

'Mibix,' said a guttural, insinuating voice.

'Ferkit,' replied another.

CHAPTER THREE

A LOWER DEVONIAN TEA

Swaggering, in torn and mephitic striped pyjamas, a three foot high humanoid, with a bulbous nose, pear-shaped head, huge protuberant ears, facial whiskers, a silver dinner-fork in one hand and a silver dinner knife in the other, emerged from the ferns.

Jherek, too, had once worn the pyjamas of the Nursery; had suffered the regime of that robot survivor from the Late Multitude Cultures. He recognized Captain Mubbers, leader of the Lat brigand-musicians. He had seen him twice since the Nursery – at the Café Royal, and later, in custody together, at Scotland Yard.

Captain Mubbers grunted at Jherek with something like grudging neutrality, but when his three pupils focussed on Inspector Springer he uttered an unpleasant laugh.

Inspector Springer would accept no nonsense, even when five more Lat joined their leader and shared his amusement. 'In the name of Her Majesty the Queen,' he began. But he hesitated; he was off-guard.

'Ood ja shag ok gongong pish?' Captain Mubbers was contemptuous. 'Klixshat efang!'

Inspector Springer was used to this sort of thing; he

remained apparently impassive, saying ponderously:

'That's insulting behaviour to a police officer. You're doing yourself no good at all, my lad. The sooner you understand that English law ...' Abruptly, he was baffled. 'This still would be England, wouldn't it?' Mrs Underwood was enlisted.

'I'm not altogether sure, Inspector.' She spoke without sympathy, almost with relish. 'I haven't recognized anything.'

'It's a bit too warm for Bognor, certainly. I could be outside my jurisdiction.' Inspector Springer sensed escape. The notebook he had begun to extract from his back pocket was now returned. Beneath his disturbed moustache there appeared a strained grin. It was weak. He had lost the day to the Lat. He continued, lame. 'You think yourself lucky, my lad. If you ever set foot in the Metropolitan area again —'

'Hrunt!' Derisively, Captain Mubbers waved his remaining man forward. He came cautiously from the bushes, pupils a-dart for Springer's forces. And Jherek relaxed a fraction, knowing the Lat would be wary of decisive action until they were convinced the three were without allies.

Inspector Springer seemed ill at ease with his new and self-appointed diplomatic status. 'By the looks of it,' he told the Lat, 'we're all in the same boat. It's no time to be raking up old scores, lads. You can see the sense of that, surely?'

Questioningly, Captain Mubbers looked up at Jherek and Mrs Underwood. 'Kaprim ul shim mibix clom?' he asked, with a nod of his head in the policeman's direction.

Jherek shrugged. 'I'm inclined to agree with the inspector, Captain Mubbers.'

'Ferkit!' exclaimed one of the other Lat. 'Potkup mef rim chokkum! Shag ugga?' He started forward, brandishing a fish-fork marked with the prominent 'N' of the Café Royal.

'Thurk!' commanded Captain Mubbers. He leered unctuously at Mrs Underwood; he offered her an unwhole-some bow. He took a step closer, murmuring: 'Dwap ker niknur, fazzy?'

'Really!' Mrs Underwood lost all her carefully restored composure. 'Mr Carnelian! Inspector Springer! How can such suggestions ...? Oh!'

'Kroofrudi.' Captain Mubbers was unrepentant. Significantly, he patted his elbow. 'Kwot-kwot?' He glanced back at the frond forest. 'Nizzle uk?'

Inspector Springer's sense of decency was offended. He listed forward, one boot still in his hand. 'Law or no law ...'

'Fwik hrunt!' spat Captain Mubbers. The others laughed, repeating the witticism to one another; but the policeman's objection had lowered the tension.

Mrs Underwood said firmly: 'They are probably hungry. We have some biscuits back at our camp. If we were to lead them there ...'

'At once,' said Jherek, and he began to walk. She linked her arm in his, an action which served to confuse both Jherek and Captain Mubbers.

Inspector Springer kept step with them. 'I must say, I could do with a nice Rich Tea!'

'I think I've eaten most of those.' Jherek was regretful. 'But there's a whole box of Fig Rolls.'

'Ho, ho!' Inspector Springer performed a cryptic wink. 'We'll let *them* 'ave the Fig Rolls, eh?'

Puzzled, but temporarily passive, the Lat trailed behind.

Relishing the delicate touch of her arm against his rib, Jherek wondered if a police inspector and seven aliens could constitute the 'society' Mrs Underwood claimed as the influence upon the 'morality' and 'conscience' thwarting the full expression of his love for her. He felt, in his heart, that she would so define the group. Resignation, once more, slid into the space so recently left by anticipation.

They reached the rock and the hamper; their home. Kettle in hand, he set off for the spring they had discovered. Mrs Underwood prepared the primus.

Alone for a moment, Jherek reflected that their provisions would soon expire, with eight fresh mouths to fill. He foresaw, indeed, a dispute in which the Lat would attempt to gain possession of the food. It would mean some relief, at least. He smiled. It might even mean a War.

A little later, when the primus stove had been pumped and lit and the kettle settled on its flame, he studied the Lat. It seemed to him that their attitude towards Mrs Underwood had altered a fraction since they had first seen her in the frond forest. They sat in a semi-circle on the sand, a short distance away from the rock in whose shadow the three humans crouched. Their manner, while still what she would probably have called 'insulting', was tinged with caution; perhaps awe; perhaps they were daunted by the easy way in which she had taken command of events. Could it be that she reminded them of that invulnerable old robot, Nurse? They had learned to fear Nurse. Certainly their position – cross-legged, hands on knees – recalled Nurse's demands upon her charges.

The kettle began to steam. Inspector Springer, with a courtly gesture to Mrs Underwood, reached for the handle. Accepting the metal tea-pot from his hostess, he poured on the water. The Lat, like witnesses at a religious ritual (for Inspector Springer certainly conveyed this mood – he the priest, Mrs Underwood the priestess) were grave and wary. Jherek, himself, shared some of their feelings as the ceremony advanced with formal grace.

There were three tin cups and a tin basin. These were laid out on the top of the hamper (which contained many such comforts). A can of milk was set beside them, and a box of sugar, with a spoon.

'A minute or two to let it brew,' intoned Inspector Springer. In an aside, he told Jherek: 'It's what I've been missing most of all.'

Jherek could not guess if he meant the tea itself or the ritual involved.

From a box at her side, Mrs Underwood made a selection of biscuits, arranging them in a pattern upon a tin plate.

And at length the tea was poured. The milk was added. The sugar was added.

Inspector Springer was the first to sip.

'Ah!' The sense of occasion remained. 'That's better, eh?'

Mrs Underwood handed the large bowl to Captain Mubbers. He sniffed it, blew at it, then sucked up half the contents in a single inhalation.

'Gurp?' he enquired.

'Tea,' she told him. 'I hope it's to your taste. We have nothing stronger.'

'Tee-ee!' Captain Mubbers, quick to mine innuendo from the least promising vein, glanced sidelong (with two of his pupils) at his companions. They sniggered. 'Kroofrudi.' He held out the cup for more.

'That's for all of you to share,' she said firmly. She waved, to indicate his men. 'All of you.'

'Frit hrunti?' He seemed unwilling.

She took the bowl from him and gave it to the man next to him.

'Grotchit snirt.' Captain Mubbers snorted and touched his comrade's elbow with his own. 'Nootchoo?'

The Lat was amused. The tea burbled as he exploded with laughter.

Inspector Springer cleared his throat. Mrs Underwood averted her eyes. Jherek, feeling a need to extend some sort of friendship to the Lat, bubbled his tea and laughed with them.

'Not you, Mr Carnelian,' she said. 'You, surely, know better. Whatever else, you are not a savage.'

'They offend your morality?'

'Morality, no. Merely my sensibilities.'

'It strikes you as unaesthetic.'

'Your analysis is accurate.'

She had withdrawn from him again. He swallowed the stuff down. To him, it seemed crude, in taste and texture.

But he accepted her standard; to serve it, and to win her approval, was all he desired.

The biscuits, one by one, were consumed.

Inspector Springer was the first to finish; he withdrew a large white handkerchief from his pocket and dabbed at his moustache. He was thoughtful. He voiced Jherek's concern of a short while before:

'Of course,' he said, 'this grub isn't going to last for ever now, is it?'

'It will not last very long at all,' said Mrs Underwood.

'And the Lat will try to steal it,' added Jherek.

'They'll 'ave a job there.' Inspector Springer spoke with the quiet confidence of the professional protector of property. 'Being English, we're more fair-minded, and therefore we'll keep strict control of the supplies. Not, I suppose, that we can let them starve. We shall 'ave to eke 'em out – learn to live off the land. Fish and stuff.'

'Fish?' Mrs Underwood was uncertain. 'Are there fish?'

'Monsters!' he told her. ' 'Aven't you seen 'em? Sort of sharks, though a bit smaller. Catch one o' those beggars and we could eat for a fortnight. I'll put me mind to it.' He had brightened again and seemed to be enjoying the challenges offered by the Lower Devonian. 'I think I spotted a bit o' line in the 'amper. We could try using snails for bait.'

Captain Mubbers indicated that his bowl was empty.

'Crotchnuk,' he said ingratiatingly.

'No more,' she said firmly. 'Tea-time is over, Captain Mubbers.'

'Crotchnuk mibix?'

'All gone,' she said, as if to a child. She took the lid from the pot and showed him the sodden leaves. 'See?'

His hand was swift. It seized the pot. The other dived into the opening, scooping out the tea-leaves, cramming them into his mouth. 'Glop-pib!' he spluttered approvingly. 'Drexy glop-pib!'

Fatalistically, Mrs Underwood allowed him to complete his feast.

378

CHAPTER FOUR

A FRESH QUEST – ON THE TRAIL
OF THE HAMPER

'But, Inspector, you told us that the hamper could not be removed without bringing you instantly to wakefulness!' Mrs Amelia Underwood was within an ace of tapping her foot; there was a note to her voice which Jherek recognized.

Inspector Springer also recognized it. He blushed as he held up the wrist to which was attached a severed thong. 'I tied it to the 'amper,' he said lamely. 'They must o' cut it.'

'How long have you been asleep, Inspector?' Jherek asked.

''Ardly at all. A few winks 'ere, a few there. Nothin' to speak of.'

'They were hearty winks!' She drew in a sharp breath as she stared around her in the grey pre-dawn. 'Judging by your snores. I heard them all night.'

'Oh, come now, ma'am ...'

'They could be miles away,' said Jherek. 'You should see them run, when they want to. You did not sleep well either, Mrs Underwood?'

'Only the inspector, it seems, enjoyed a satisfying rest.'

She glared at the policeman. 'If you want your house burgled, tell the police you're going on holiday. That's what my brother always used to say.'

'That's 'ardly fair, ma'am ...' he began, but he knew he was on shaky ground. 'I took every precaution. But these foreigners – with their *knives* —' again he displayed the severed thong – 'well, 'ow can you anticipate ...?'

She inspected the surrounding sand, saying mournfully. '*Look* at all these footprints. Do you remember, Mr Carnelian, when we would rise in the morning and go down to the sea and there wouldn't be a mark on the beach? Not a sign of another soul! It's so *spoiled* now.' She was pointing. 'There – a fresh trail. Leading inland.'

Certainly, the ground was disturbed. Jherek detected the broad footprints of the departing Lat.

'They'll be carrying the 'amper,' offered Inspector Springer, 'so they'll be slowed down a bit.' He clutched his midriff. 'Ooh, I 'ate to start the day on an empty stomach.'

'That,' she said with satisfaction, 'is entirely your fault, Inspector!'

She led the way forward while Jherek and Inspector Springer, tugging on their coats, did their best to keep pace with her.

Even before they had entered a large stretch of frond-forest and were labouring uphill, Mrs Underwood's quick eye detecting a broken branch or a crushed leaf as sign-posts to the route of the thieves, the sun had risen, splendid and golden, and begun to beat its hottest. Inspector Springer made much use of his handkerchief on the back of his neck and his forehead, but Mrs Underwood would not let them pause.

The hill grew steeper. It was virtually sheer. Still she led; still she allowed them no rest. They panted – Jherek cheerfully and Inspector Springer with loud resentment. At two stages he was heard to breathe the word 'Women' in a desperate, incantatory fashion, and at a third he appended another word, in a voice which was entirely inaudible. Jherek, in contrast, was enjoying the exertion, the sense of adventure, though he had no belief that they could catch Captain Mubbers and his men.

She was a score of yards ahead of them, and higher. 'Nearly at the top,' she called.

Inspector Springer was not encouraged. He stopped, leaning against the stem of a fern which rose fifteen feet over his head and rustled as it took the weight of his bulky frame.

'It would be best,' Jherek said, passing him, 'if we were to remain as close together as possible. We could so easily become separated.'

'She's a bloomin' mad woman,' grunted the inspector. 'I knew it all along.' But he laboured after Jherek, even catching him up as he clambered over a fallen trunk which left a smear of green on the knees of his trousers. Jherek sniffed. 'Your smell! I wondered – I haven't quite smelt anything like it before? It *is* you. Very odd. Pleasant, I suppose . . .'

'Gur!' said Inspector Springer.

Jherek sniffed again, but continued to climb, now using his hands and his feet, virtually on all fours. 'Certainly pungent . . .'

'Cor! You cheeky little b —'

'Excelsior!' It was Mrs Underwood's voice, though she could no longer be seen. 'Oh, it's magnificent!'

Inspector Springer caught hold of Jherek's ankle. 'If you've any further personal comments, I'd be more than grateful if you'd keep them to yourself.'

'I'm sorry, Inspector.' Jherek tried to free his foot. He frowned. 'I certainly meant no offence. It's simply that such smells – perspiration, is it? – are uncommon at the End of Time. I love it. Really.'

'Ugh!' Inspector Springer let go of Jherek's foot. 'I 'ad you marked right from the start, too. Bloomin' cream puff. Café Royal – Oscar Wilde – should 'ave trusted me own judgement . . .'

'I can see them!' Mrs Underwood's voice again. 'The

381

quarry's in sight!'

Jherek pressed past a low branch and saw her through the dappled fronds.

'Ouch!' said Inspector Springer from behind him. 'Cor! If I ever get back to London and if I ever lay 'ands on you ...'

The belligerence seemed to give him energy, enabling him, once more, to catch up. They arrived, shoulder to shoulder, to stand at Mrs Underwood's side. She was flushed. Her eyes shone. She pointed.

They stood on the edge of a cliff that was almost sheer, its sides dotted with clumps of vegetation. Some hundreds of feet below them the cliff levelled out to a broad, stony beach, touching the wide, placid waters of a creek whose brilliant blue, reflecting the sky, was in beautiful and harmonious contrast with the browns, greens and yellows of the flanking cliffs.

'It is simple,' she said, 'and it is magnificent! Look, Mr Carnelian! It goes on forever. It is the world! So much of it. All virgin. Not even a wild beast to disturb its vast serenity. Imagine what Mr Ruskin would say to all this. Switzerland cannot compare ...' She was smiling now at Jherek. 'Oh, Mr Carnelian – it *is* Eden. It is!'

'Hm,' said Inspector Springer. 'It's pretty enough scenery. But where's our little friends? You said —'

'There!'

Tiny figures could be seen on the beach. There was activity. They were at work.

'Making something, by the look of it,' murmured Inspector Springer. 'But what?'

'A boat, probably.' She spread an arm. 'You'll observe there is just a small area of beach – a sort of cove, really. The only way to continue is across the water. They will not turn back, for fear of our pursuit.'

'Aha!' Inspector Springer rubbed his hands together. 'So we've got 'em, ripe. We'll nab 'em before they can ever —'

'They are seven,' she reminded him. 'We are three. And

one of us a woman.'

'Yes,' he said. 'That's true.' He lifted his bowler between thumb and forefinger, scratching his head with his little finger. 'But we're bigger. And we 'ave the advantage of surprise. Surprise is often worth more than any amount of 'eavy artillery ...'

'So I gather from the *Boys' Own Paper*,' she said sourly. 'But I would give much, at this moment, for a single revolver.'

'Not allowed to carry them in the ordinary way, ma'am,' he said portentously. 'If we had received information ...'

'Oh, really, Inspector!' She was exasperated. 'Mr Carnelian? Have you any suggestions?'

'We might frighten them off, Mrs Underwood, long enough for us to regain the hamper.'

'And have them chase and overwhelm us? No. Captain Mubbers must be captured. With a hostage, we can hope to return to our camp and bargain with them. I had hoped to maintain civilized behaviour. However ...'

She inspected the cliff edge. 'They descended here. We shall do the same.'

'I've never 'ad much of an 'ead for 'eights.' Inspector Springer watched dubiously as she swung herself over the edge and, clinging to tufts of foliage and outcroppings of rock, began to climb downwards. Jherek, concerned for her safety, yet acknowledging her leadership, watched her carefully, then he followed her. Grumbling, Inspector Springer blundered in the rear. Little showers of stones and loose earth fell on Jherek's head.

The cliff was not so steep as Jherek had imagined, and the descent became noticeably easier after the first thirty feet so that at times they could stand upright and walk.

It seemed to Jherek that the Lat had seen them, for their activity became more frenetic. They were building a large raft, from the stems of the bigger ferns which grew near the water, using strips of their torn up pyjamas to hold the rather fleshy trunks together. Jherek knew little of such matters, but it seemed to him that the raft would quickly become water-logged and sink. He wondered if the Lat could swim. Certainly, he could not.

'Ah! We are too late!' Mrs Underwood began to let herself slide down the cliff, ripping her already tattered dress in several places, careless of modesty, as she saw Captain Mubbers order their hamper placed in the middle of the raft. The six Lat, under the command of their captain, lifted the raft and began to bear it towards the brackish waters of the creek.

Jherek, anxious to remain close to her, copied her example, and was soon sliding without control after her.

'Stop!' she cried, forgetting her plans to capture Captain Mubbers. 'We wish to bargain!'

Startled, perhaps, by the wild descent, the Lat began to run with their raft until they were up to their waists in water. Captain Mubbers jumped aboard. The raft tilted. He flung himself upon the hamper, to save it. The raft swung out at an angle and the Lat began to flounder after it, pulling themselves aboard as best they could, but two were left behind. Their shrieks could be heard by the human beings, who had almost reached the bottom of the cliff.

'Ferkit!'

'Kroofrudi!'

'Nukgnursh!'

Captain Mubbers and his men had left their paddles on the beach. With their hands, they tried to force the raft back towards the land.

'Quickly!' cried Mrs Underwood, a general still. 'Seize them. There are our hostages!'

The raft was now many yards from the shore, though Captain Mubbers seemed determined not to abandon his men.

Jherek and Inspector Springer waded into the shallows and grabbed at the two Lat, who were now almost up to their necks in the waters of the creek. They splashed; they tried to kick, but were gradually herded back to where Mrs Underwood, blazing and determined, awaited them

384

(it was evident that they were much more nervous of Mrs Underwood than of those they recognized as her minions).

'Knuxfelp!' cried Captain Mubbers to his men. 'Groo hrunt bookra!' His voice grew fainter.

The two Lat reached the beach, dodged past Mrs Underwood, and began to make for the cliff. They were in a state of panic.

'Blett mibix gurp!' screamed one of the hysterical Lat as he fell over a stone. His comrade helped him to his feet, glaring behind him at the drifting raft. It was then that he suddenly transfixed – all three pupils focussed on the raft. He ignored Jherek and Inspector Springer as they ran up and laid hands on him. Jherek was the first to look back.

There was something in the water, besides the raft. A glittering green, insect-like body, moving very rapidly.

'Gawd!' breathed Inspector Springer. 'It must be over six feet long!'

Jherek glimpsed antennae, white-grey claws, spiny and savage, a rearing, curling tail, armed with brown tusks, paddle-shaped back legs, all leaping half-out of the thick waters, attacking the raft.

There were two loud snapping noises, close together, and the front claws had each grasped a Lat. They struggled and screamed. The tusky tail swung up and round, clubbing them unconscious. Then the gigantic scorpion (for it resembled nothing else) had returned to the depths, leaving debris behind, a bobbing wickerwork hamper, green pulpy logs to which the surviving Lat clung.

Jherek saw a trail in the distant water, near the middle of the creek. He knew that this must be another such beast; he waded forward, offering his arms to the desperate Lat and shouting:

'Oh, what a jolly adventure, after all! The Duke of Queens could not have arranged a more sensational display! Just think, Mrs Underwood – none of this was engineered. It is all happening spontaneously – quite naturally. The scorpions! Aren't they superbly sinister, sweet sister of the sphynx?'

'Mr Carnelian!' Her voice was more than urgent. 'Save yourself. More of the creatures come from all sides!'

It was true. The surrounding water was thick with gigantic scorpions. They converged.

Jherek drew Captain Mubbers and another Lat back to the shore. But a third was too slow. He had time to cry one last 'Ferkit!' before the claws contracted and the great tail thumped and he became a subject of contention between the scorpion who had caught him and those of the scorpion's comrades who were disappointed at their own lack of success.

Mrs Underwood reached his side. There was alarm and disapproval on her features. 'Mr Carnelian – you frightened me so. But your bravery . . .'

He raised both eyebrows.

'It was superb,' she said. Her voice had softened, but only momentarily. She remembered the hamper. It was the only thing left afloat, and apparently was without interest for the scorpions, who continued to dispute the ownership of the rapidly disintegrating corpse which occasionally emerged above the surface of the creek. There was foam, and there was blood.

The hamper bobbed up and down in the eddy created by the warring water scorpions; it had almost reached the middle of the creek.

'We must follow its drift,' she said, 'and hope to catch up with it later. Is there a current? Inward or outward? Where is the sea?'

'We must watch,' said Jherek. 'With luck, we can plot its general course at least.'

Something fishy appeared above the surface near the hamper. A brown, glistening back, with fins, slid from view almost immediately.

'The sharks,' said Inspector Springer. 'I told you about them.'

The hamper, which made this world a true Eden, rose under the back of at least one large finny creature. It turned over.

'Oh!' cried Mrs Underwood.

They saw the hamper sink. They saw it rise again. The lid had swung open, but still it bobbed.

Quite suddenly, Mrs Underwood sat down on the shingle and began to cry. To Jherek, the sound diminished all those which still issued from that savage Lower Devonian creek. He went to her. He seated himself beside her and he put a slim arm around her lonely shoulders.

It was then that a small power-boat, its motor whining, rounded the headland. It contained two black-clad figures, one seated at the wheel, the other standing up with a boathook in its hands. The craft made purposefully for the hamper.

CHAPTER FIVE

AT THE TIME CENTRE

Mrs Underwood stopped crying and began to blink.

'It's getting to be like bloomin' Brighton,' said Inspector Springer disapprovingly. 'It seemed so unspoiled at first. What a racket that boat makes!'

'They have saved the hamper,' said she. The two figures were hauling it aboard. The boat was rocked by the squirming movements of the large fish. A few objects fell from the hamper. The two figures seemed abnormally anxious to recover the objects, taking great trouble to pursue and scoop up a tin mug which had gone adrift. This done, the boat headed in their direction.

Jherek had seen nothing quite like the costumes of the newcomers; though they bore some resemblance to certain kinds of garments sometimes worn by space-travellers; they were all of a piece, shining and black, pouched and quilted, belted with broad bands containing what were probably tools. They had tight-fitting helmets of the same material, with goggles and ear-pieces, and there were black gauntlets on their hands.

'I don't like the look of 'em,' muttered the inspector. 'Divers, ain't they?' He glanced back at the hills. 'They could be up to no good. Why 'aven't they showed themselves before?'

'Perhaps they didn't know we were here,' said Jherek reasonably.

'They're showing an uncommon interest in our 'amper. Could be the last we'll see of it.'

'They are almost upon us,' said Mrs Underwood quietly. 'Let us not judge them, or their motives, until we have spoken. Let us hope they have some English, or at worst French.'

The boat's bottom crunched on the shingle; the engine was cut off; the two passengers disembarked, pulling the little vessel clear of the water, removing the hamper and carrying it between them to where Mrs Underwood, Jherek Carnelian, Inspector Springer, Captain Mubbers and the three surviving Lat awaited them. Jherek noted that they were male and female, but of about the same height. Little of their faces could be seen above the high collars and below the goggles. When they were a couple of yards away they stopped and lowered the hamper. The female pushed back her goggles, revealing a heart-shaped face, large blue-grey eyes, as steady as Mrs Underwood's, and a full mouth.

It was unsurprising that Mrs Underwood took her for French.

'*Je vous remercie bien . . .*' she began.

'Aha!' said the woman, without irony, 'You are English, then.'

'Some of us are,' said Inspector Springer heavily. 'These little ones are Latvians.'

'I am Mrs Persson. May I introduce Captain Bastable.' The man saluted; he raised his own goggles. His face was tanned and handsome; his blue eyes were pale.

'I am Mrs Underwood. This is Mr Carnelian, Inspector Springer, Captain Mubbers – I'm afraid I've no idea of the other names. They do not speak English. I believe they are space-travellers from the distant future. Are they not, Mr Carnelian?'

389

'The Lat,' he said. 'We were never entirely clear about their origins. But they did come in a space-ship. To the End of Time.'

'You are from the End of Time, sir?' Captain Bastable spoke in the light, clipped tones familiar to Jherek as being from the nineteenth century.

'I am.'

'Jherek Carnelian, of course,' said Mrs Persson. 'A friend of the Duke of Queens, are you not? And Lord Jagged?'

'You know them?' He was delighted.

'I know Lord Jagged slightly. Oh, I remember – you are in love with this lady, your – Amelia?'

'My Amelia!'

'I am not "your Amelia", Mr Carnelian,' she said firmly. And she became suspicious of Mrs Persson.

Mrs Persson was apologetic. 'You are from 1896. I was forgetting. You will forgive me, I hope, Mrs Underwood. I have heard so much about you. Your story is one of the greatest of our legends. I assure you, we are honoured to meet you in the flesh.'

Mrs Underwood frowned, guessing sarcasm, but there was none.

'You have heard —?'

'We are only a few, we gossip. We exchange experiences and tales, as travellers will, on the rare occasions when we meet. And the Centre, of course, is where we all congregate.'

The young man laughed. 'I don't think they're following you, Una.'

'I babble. You will be our guests?'

'You have a machine here?' said Mrs Underwood, hope dawning.

'We have a base. You have not heard of it? You are not yet members of the Guild, then?'

'Guild?' Mrs Underwood drew her eyebrows together. 'No.'

'The Guild of Temporal Adventurers,' explained Captain Bastable. 'The GTA?'

'I have never heard of it.'

'Neither have I,' said Jherek. 'Why do you have an association?'

Mrs Persson shrugged. 'Mainly so that we can exchange information. Information is of considerable help to those of us whom you could call "professional time-travellers".' She smiled self-deprecatingly. 'It is such a risky business, at best.'

'Indeed it is,' he agreed. 'We should love to accept your invitation. Should we not, Mrs Underwood?'

'Thank you, Mrs Persson.' Mrs Underwood was still not at ease, but she had control of her manners.

'We shall need to make two trips. I suggest, Oswald, that you take the Lat and Inspector Springer back with you and then return for us three.'

Captain Bastable nodded. 'Better check the hamper first. Just to be on the safe side.'

'Of course. Would you like to look, Mrs Underwood, and tell me if anything is missing?'

'It does not matter. I really think —'

'It is of utmost importance. If anything is lost from it, we shall search meticulously until it is found. We have instruments for detecting almost everything.'

She peered in. She sorted. 'Everything here, I think.'

'Fine. Time merely tolerates us, you know. We must not offend.'

Captain Bastable, the Lat and Inspector Springer, were already in their boat. The motor whined again. The water foamed. They were away.

Mrs Persson watched it disappear before turning back to Jherek and Mrs Underwood. 'A lovely day. You have been here some while?'

'About a week, I would say,' Mrs Underwood smoothed at her ruined dress.

'So long as one avoids the water, it can be very beautiful. Many come to the Lower Devonian simply for the rest. If it were not for the eurypterids – the water scorpions – it would be perfect. Of all Palaeozoic periods, I find it the nicest. And, of course, it is a particularly friendly age, permitting more anachronism than most. This is your first visit?'

'The first,' said Mrs Underwood. Her expression betrayed what propriety restrained her from stating, that she hoped it would be the last.

'It can be dull.' Mrs Persson acknowledged the implication. 'But if one wishes to relax, to re-plot one's course, take bearings – there are few better at this end of Time.' She yawned. 'Captain Bastable and I shall be glad to be on our way again, as soon as our caretaking duties are over and we are relieved. Another fortnight should see us back in some twentieth century or other.'

'You seem to suggest that there are more than one?' said Jherek. 'Do you mean that different methods of recording history apply, or —?'

'There are as many versions of history as there are dedicated time-travellers.' Mrs Persson smiled. 'The difficulty lies in remaining in a consistent cycle. If one cannot do so, then all sorts of shocks are likely – environmental readjustment becomes almost impossible – madness results. How many fashions in insanity, do you think, have been set by mentally disturbed temporal adventures? We shall never know!' She laughed. 'Captain Bastable, for instance, was an inadvertent traveller (it sometimes happens), and was on the borders of madness before we were able to rescue him. First one finds it is the future which does not correspond, and this is frightening enough, if you are not expecting it. But it is worse when you return – to discover that your past has changed. You two, I take it, are fixed to a single band. Count yourselves lucky, if you do not know what to expect of multiversal time-travelling.'

Jherek could barely grasp the import of her words and Mrs Underwood was lost completely, though she fumbled with the notion: 'You mean that time-traveller we met, who referred to Waterloo Circus, was not from my time at all, but one which corresponded ...?' She shook her head.

'You cannot mean it. My time no longer exists, because . . .?'

'Your time exists. Nothing ever perishes, Mrs Underwood. Forgive me for saying so, but you seem singularly ill-prepared for temporal adventuring. How did you come to choose the Lower Devonian, for instance?'

'We did not choose it,' Jherek told her. 'We set off for the End of Time. Our ship was in rather poor condition. It deposited us here – although we were convinced we went forward.'

'Perhaps you did.'

'How can that be?'

'If you followed the cycle round, you arrived at the end and continued on to the beginning.'

'Time is cyclic, then?'

'It can be.' She smiled. 'There are spirals, too, as it were. None of us understands it very well, Mr Carnelian. We pool what information we have. We have been able to create some basic methods of protecting ourselves. But few can hope to understand very much about the nature of Time, because that nature does not appear to be constant. The Chronon Theory, for instance, which was very popular in certain cultures, has been largely discredited – yet seems to apply in societies which accept the theory. Your own Morphail Theory has much to recommend it, although it does not allow for the permutations and complications. It suggests that Time has, as it were, only one dimension – as if Space had only one. You follow me, Mr Carnelian?'

'To some extent.'

She smiled. 'And "to some extent" is all I follow myself. One thing the Guild always tells new members – "There are no experts where Time is concerned". All we seek to do is to survive, to explore, to make occasional discoveries. Yet there is a particular theory which suggests that with every one discovery we make about Time, we create two new mysteries. Time can never be codified, as Space can be, because our very thoughts, our information

393

about it, our actions based on that information, all contribute to extend the boundaries, to produce new anomalies, new aspects of Time's nature. Do I become too abstract? If so, it is because I discuss something which is numinous – unknowable – perhaps truly metaphysical. Time is a dream – or a nightmare – from which there is never any waking. We who travel in Time are dreamers who occasionally share a common experience. To retain one's identity, to retain some sense of meaning in one's own life, that is all the time-traveller can hope for – it is why the Guild exists. You are lucky that you are not adrift in the multiverse, as Captain Bastable was, for you can become like a drowning man who refuses to float, but flounders – and every wave which you set up in the Sea of Time has a habit of becoming a whole ocean in its own right.'

Mrs Underwood had listened, but she was disturbed. She lifted the lid of the hamper and opened an air-tight tin, offering Mrs Persson a brandy-snap.

They munched.

'Delicious,' said Mrs Persson. 'After the twentieth, the nineteenth century has always been my favourite.'

'From what century are you originally?' Jherek asked, to pass the time.

'The twentieth – mid-twentieth. I have a fair bit to do with that ancestor of yours. And his sister, of course. One of my best friends.' She saw that he was puzzled. 'You don't know him? Strange. Yet, Jagged – your genes ...' She shrugged.

He was, however, eager. Here could be the answer he had sought from Jagged.

'Jagged has refused to be frank with me,' he told her, 'on that very subject. I would be grateful if you could enlighten me. He has promised to do so, on our return.'

But she was biting her lip, as if she had inadvertently betrayed a confidence. 'I can't,' she said. 'He must have reasons – I could not speak without first having his permission ...'

'But there is a motive,' said Mrs Underwood sharply: 'It seems that he deliberately brought us together. We have had more than a hint – that he could be engineering some of our misfortunes ...'

'And saving us from others,' Jherek pointed out, to be fair. 'He insists disinterest, yet I am certain ...'

'I cannot help you speculate,' said Mrs Persson. 'Here comes Captain Bastable with the boat.'

The small vessel was bouncing rapidly towards them, its engine shrieking, the water foaming white in its wake. Bastable made it turn, just before it struck the beach, and cut off the engine. 'Do you mind getting a bit wet? There are no scorpions about.'

They waded to the boat and pulled themselves aboard after dumping the hamper into the bottom. Mrs Underwood scanned the water. 'I had no idea creatures of that size existed ... Dinosaurs, perhaps, but not insects – I know they are not really insects, but ...'

'They won't survive,' said Captain Bastable as he brought the engine to life again. 'Eventually the fish will wipe them out. They're growing larger all the time, those fish. A million years will see quite a few changes in this creek.' He smiled. 'It's up to us to ensure we make none ourselves.' He pointed back at the water. 'We don't leave a trace of oil behind which isn't detected and cleaned up by one of our other machines.'

'And that is how you resist the Morphail Effect,' said Jherek.

'We don't use that name for it,' interjected Mrs Persson, 'but, yes – Time allows us to remain here as long as there are no permanent anachronisms. And that includes traces which might be detected by future investigators and prove anachronistic. It is why we were so eager to rescue that tin cup. All our equipment is of highly perishable material. It serves us, but would not survive in any form after about a century. Our existence is tentative – we could be hurled out of this age at any moment and find ourselves not only

395

separated, perhaps for ever, but in an environment incapable, even in its essentials, of supporting human life.'

'You run great risks, it seems,' said Mrs Underwood. 'Why?'

Mrs Persson laughed. 'One gets a taste for it. But, then, you know that yourself.'

The creek began to narrow, between lichen-covered banks, and, at the far end, a wooden jetty could be seen. There were two other boats moored beside it. Behind the jetty, in the shadow of thick foliage, was a dark mass, man-made.

A fair-haired youth, wearing an identical suit to those worn by Mrs Persson and Captain Bastable, took the mooring rope Mrs Persson flung to him. He nodded cheerfully to Jherek and Mrs Underwood as they jumped onto the jetty. 'Your friends are already inside,' he said.

The four of them walked over lichen-strewn rock towards the black, featureless walls ahead; these were tall and curved inward and they had a warm, rubbery smell. Mrs Persson took off her helmet and shook out her short dark hair; she had a pleasant, boyish look. Her movements were graceful as she touched the wall in two places, making a section slide back to admit them. They stepped inside.

There were several box-shaped buildings in the compound, some quite large. Mrs Persson led them towards the largest. There was little daylight, but a continuous strip of artificial lighting ran the entire circumference of the wall. The ground was covered in the same slightly yielding black material and Jherek had the impression that the entire camp could be folded in on itself within a few seconds and transported as a single unit. He imagined it as some large time-ship, for it bore certain resemblances to the machine in which he had originally travelled to the nineteenth century.

Captain Bastable stood to one side of the entrance allowing first Mrs Persson and then Mrs Underwood to enter. Jherek was next. Here were panels of instruments, screens, winking indicators, all of the primitive, fascinating kind which Jherek associated with the remote past.

'It's perfect,' he said. 'You've made it blend so well with the environment.'

'Thank you.' Mrs Persson's smile was for herself. 'The Guild stores all its information here. We can also also detect the movements of time-vessels along the megaflow, as it's sometimes termed. We did not, incidentally, detect yours. Instead there was a sort of rupture, quickly healed. You did not come in a ship?'

'Yes. It's somewhere on the beach where we left it, I think.'

'We haven't found it.'

Captain Bastable unzipped his overalls. Underneath them he wore a simple grey military uniform. 'Perhaps it was on automatic return,' he suggested. 'Or if it was malfunctioning, it could have continued on, moving at random, and be anywhere by now.'

'The machine was working badly,' Mrs Underwood informed him. 'We should not, for instance, be here at all. I would be more than grateful, Captain Bastable, if you could find some means of returning us – at least myself – to the nineteenth century.'

'That wouldn't be difficult,' he said, 'but whether you'd stay there or not is another matter. Once a time-traveller always a time-traveller, you know. It's our fate, isn't it?'

'I had no idea ...'

Mrs Persson put a hand on Mrs Underwood's shoulder. 'There are some of us who find it easier to remain in certain ages than others – and there are ages, closer to the beginnings or the ends of Time, which rarely reject those who wish to settle. Genes, I gather, have a little to do with it. But that is Jagged's speciality and he has doubtless bored you as much as he has bored us with his speculations.'

'Never!' Jherek was eager.

Mrs Persson pursed her lips. 'Perhaps you would care

for some coffee,' she said.

Jherek turned to Mrs Underwood. He knew she would be pleased. 'Isn't that splendid, dear Mrs Underwood. They have a stall here. Now you must really feel at home!'

CHAPTER SIX

DISCUSSIONS AND DECISIONS

Captain Mubbers and his men were sitting in a line on a kind of padded bench; they were cross-legged and tried to hide their knees and elbows, exposed since they had destroyed their pyjamas; all were blushing a peculiar plum colour and averted their eyes when the party containing Mrs Persson and Mrs Underwood entered the room. Inspector Springer sat by himself in a sort of globular chair which brought his knees close to his face; he tried to sip from a paper cup, tried to rise when the ladies came in, succeeded in spilling the coffee on his serge trousers; his grumble was half-protest, half-apology; he subsided again. Captain Bastable approached a black machine, marked with letters of the alphabet. 'Milk and sugar?' he asked Mrs Underwood.

'Thank you, Captain Bastable.'

'Mr Carnelian?' Captain Bastable pressed some of the letters. 'For you?'

'I'll have the same, please.' Jherek looked around the small relaxation room. 'It's not like the stalls they have in London, is it, Captain Bastable?'

'Stalls?'

'Mr Carnelian means coffee stalls,' explained Mrs Underwood. 'I think it's his only experience of drinking coffee, you see.'

'It is drunk elsewhere?'

'As is tea,' she said.

'How crude it is, my understanding of your subtle age.' He accepted a paper cup from Captain Bastable, who had already handed Mrs Underwood her own. He sipped conscientiously, expectantly.

Perhaps they noticed his expression of disappointment. 'Would you prefer tea, Mr Carnelian?' asked Mrs Persson. 'Or lemonade? Or soup?'

He shook his head, but the smile was weak. 'I'll forgo fresh experience for the moment. There are so many new impressions to assimilate. Of course, I know that this must seem familiar and dull to you – but to me it is marvellous. The chase! The scorpions! And now these huts!' He glanced towards the Lat. 'The other three are not, then, back yet?'

'The others ...?' Captain Bastable was puzzled.

'He means the ones the scorpions devoured,' Mrs Underwood began. 'He believes ...'

'That they will be reconstituted!' Mrs Persson brightened. 'Of course. There is no death, as such, at the End of Time.' She said apologetically to Jherek: 'I am afraid we lack the necessary technology to restore the Lat to life, Mr Carnelian. Besides, we do not possess the skills. If Miss Brunner or one of her people were on duty during this term – but, no, even then it would not be possible. You must regard your Lat as lost forever, I fear. As it is, you can take consolation that they have probably poisoned a few scorpions. Happily, there being so many scorpions, the balance of nature is not noticeably changed, and thus we retain our roots in the Lower Devonian.'

'Poor Captain Mubbers,' said Jherek. 'He tries so hard and is forever failing in his schemes. Perhaps we could arrange some charade or other – in which he is monumentally successful. It would do his morale so much good.

Is there something he could steal, Captain Bastable? Or someone he could rape?'

'Not here, I'm afraid.' But Captain Bastable blushed as he controlled his voice, causing Mrs Persson to smile and say, 'We are not very well equipped for the amusement of space-travellers, I regret, Mr Carnelian. But we shall try to get them back to their original age – your age – as near to their ship as possible. They'll soon be pillaging and raping again with gusto!'

Captain Bastable cleared his throat. Mrs Underwood studied a cushion.

Mrs Persson said: 'I forgot myself. Captain Bastable, by the way, Mrs Underwood, is almost a contemporary of yours. He is from 1901. It *is* 1901, isn't it, Oswald?'

He nodded, fingering his cuff. 'Thereabouts.'

'What puzzles me, more than anything,' continued Mrs Persson, 'is how so many people arrived here at the same time. The heaviest traffic in my experience. And two parties without machines of any kind. What a shame we can't speak to the Lat.'

'We could, if we wished,' said Jherek.

'You know their language?'

'Simpler. I have a translation pill, still. I offered them before, but no one seemed interested. At the Café Royal. Do you remember, Inspector?'

Inspector Springer was as sullen as Captain Mubbers. He seemed to have lost interest in the conversation. Occasionally a peculiar, self-pitying grunt would escape his throat.

'I know the pills,' said Mrs Persson. 'Are they independent of your cities?'

'Oh, quite. I've used them everywhere. They undertake a specific kind of engineering, I gather, on those parts of the brain dealing with language. The pill itself contains all sorts of ingredients – but entirely biological, I'm sure. See how well I speak *your* language!'

Mrs Persson turned her eyes upon the Lat. 'Could they give us any more information than Inspector Springer?'

'Probably not,' said Jherek. 'They were all ejected at about the same time.'

'I think we'll keep the pill, therefore, for emergencies.'

'Forgive me,' said Mrs Underwood, 'if I seem insistent, but I should like to know our chances of returning to our own periods of history.'

'Very poor, in your own case, Mrs Underwood,' said Captain Bastable. 'I speak from experience. You have a choice – inhabit some period of your future, or "return" to a present which could be radically changed, virtually unrecognizable. Our instruments have been picking up all kinds of disruptions, fluctuations, random eddies on the megaflow which suggest that heavier than usual distortions and re-creations are occurring. The multiversal planes are moving into some sort of conjunction —'

'It's the Conjunction of the Million Spheres,' said Mrs Persson. 'You've heard of it?'

Jherek and Mrs Underwood shook their heads.

'There's a theory that the conjunction comes when too much random activity occurs in the multiverse. It suggests that the multiverse is, in fact, finite – that it can only sustain so many continua – and when the maximum number of continua is attained, a complete re-organization takes place. The multiverse puts its house in order, as it were.' Mrs Persson began to leave the room. 'Would you care to see some of our operations?'

Inspector Springer continued to sulk and the Lat were still far too embarrassed to move, so Amelia Underwood and Jherek Carnelian followed their hosts down a short connecting tunnel and into a room filled with particularly large screens on which brilliantly coloured display models shifted through three dimensions. The most remarkable was an eight-arrowed wheel, constantly altering its size and shape. A short, swarthy, bearded man sat at the console below this screen; occasionally he would extend a moody finger and make an adjustment.

'Good evening, Sergeant Glogauer.' Captain Bastable

402

bent over the bearded man's shoulder and stared at the instruments. 'Any changes?'

'Chronoflows three, four and six are showing considerable abnormal activity,' said the sergeant. 'It corresponds with Faustaff's information, but it contradicts his automatic reconstitution theory. Look at number five prong!' he pointed to the screen. 'And that's only measuring crude. We can't plot the paradox factors on this machine – not that there would be any point in trying at the rate they're multiplying. That kind of proliferation is going on everywhere. It's a wonder *we're* not affected by it. Elsewhere, things are fairly quiescent at present, but there's a lot more activity than I'd like. I'd propose a general warning call – get every Guild member back to sphere, place and century of origin. That might help stabilization. Unless it's got nothing at all to do with us.'

'It's too late to know,' said Mrs Persson. 'I still hold with the reaction theory on the Conjunction, but where it leaves us – how we'll be affected – is anyone's guess.' She shrugged and was cheerful. 'I suppose it helps to believe in reincarnation.'

'It's the sense of insecurity that I mind,' said Glogauer.

Jherek made a contribution. 'They're very pretty. It reminds me of some of the things the rotting cities still do.'

Mrs Persson turned back from where she was inspecting a screen. 'Your cities, Mr Carnelian, are almost as bewildering as Time itself.'

Jherek agreed. 'They are almost as old, I suppose.'

Captain Bastable was amused. 'It suggests that Time approaches senility. It's an attractive metaphor.'

'We can do without metaphors, I should have thought,' Sergeant Glogauer told him severely.

'It's all we have.' Captain Bastable permitted himself a small yawn. 'What would be the chances of getting Mrs Underwood and Mr Carnelian here back to the nineteenth century?'

'Standard line?'

Captain Bastable nodded.

'Almost zero, at present. If they didn't mind waiting . . .'

'We are anxious to leave.' Mrs Underwood spoke for them both.

'What about the End of Time?' Captain Bastable asked Glogauer.

'Indigenous? Point of departure?'

'More or less.'

The sergeant frowned, studying surrounding screens. 'Pretty good.'

'Would that suit you?' Captain Bastable turned to his guests.

'It was where we were heading for, originally,' Jherek said.

'Then we'll try to do that.'

'And Inspector Springer?' Mrs Underwood's conscience made her speak. 'And the Lat?'

'I think we'll try to deal with them separately – they arrived separately, after all.'

Una Persson rubbed her eyes. 'If there were any means of contacting Jagged, Oswald. We could confer.'

'There is every chance he has returned to the End of Time,' Jherek told her. 'I would willingly bear a message.'

'Yes,' she said. 'Perhaps we will do that. Very well. I suggest you sleep now, after you've had something to eat. We'll make the preparations. If everything goes properly, you should be able to leave by morning. I'll see what the power situation is like. We're a bit limited, of course. Essentially this is only an observation post and a liaison point for Guild members. We've very little spare equipment or energy. But we'll do what we can.'

Leaving the charting room, Captain Bastable offered Mrs Underwood his arm. She took it.

'I suppose this all seems a bit prosaic to you,' he said. 'After the wonders of the End of Time, I mean.'

'Scarcely that,' she murmured. 'But I do find it rather confusing. My life seemed so settled in Bromley, just a few months ago. The strain . . .'

'You *are* looking drawn, dear Amelia,' said Jherek from behind them. He was disturbed by Captain Bastable's attentions.

She ignored him. 'All this moving about in Time cannot be healthy,' she said. 'I admire anyone who can appear as phlegmatic as you, Captain.'

'One becomes used to it, you know.' He patted the hand which enfolded his arm. 'But you are bearing up absolutely wonderfully, Mrs Underwood, if this is your first trip to the Palaeozoic.'

She was flattered. 'I have my consolations,' she said. 'My prayers and so on. And my Wheldrake. Are you familiar with the poems of Wheldrake, Captain Bastable?'

'When a boy, they were all I read. He can be very apt. I follow you.'

She lifted her head and, as they moved along that black, yielding corridor, she began to speak in slow, rounded tones:

> For once I looked on worlds sublime,
>   And knew pure Beauty, free from Time,
> Knew unchained Joy, untempered Hope;
>   And coward, then, I fled!

Captain Bastable had been speaking the same words beneath his breath. 'Exactly!' he said, adding:

> Detected now beneath the organ's note,
>   The organ's groan, the bellows' whine;
> And what the Sun made splendid,
>   Bereft of Sun is merely fine!

Listening, Jherek Carnelian felt a peculiar and unusual sensation. He had the impulse to separate them, to interrupt, to seize her and to carry her away from this handsome Victorian officer, this contemporary who knew so much better than did Jherek how to please her, to comfort her. He was baffled.

405

He heard Mrs Persson say: 'I do hope our arrangements suit you, Mr Carnelian. Is your mind more at ease?'

He spoke vaguely. 'No,' he said, 'it is not. I believe I must be "unhappy".'

CHAPTER SEVEN

EN ROUTE FOR THE END OF TIME

'The capsule has no power of its own,' Una Persson explained. Morning light filtered through the opening in the wall above them as the four stood together in the Time Centre's compound and inspected the rectangular object, just large enough for two people and resembling, as Mrs Underwood had earlier remarked, nothing so much as a sedan chair. 'We shall control it from here. It is actually safer than any other kind of machine, for we can study the megaflow and avoid major ruptures. We shall keep you on course, never fear.'

'And be sure to remind Lord Jagged that we should be glad of his advice,' added Captain Bastable. He kissed Mrs Underwood's hand. 'It has been a very great pleasure, ma'am.' He saluted.

'It has been a pleasure for me to meet a gentleman,' she replied, 'I thank you, sir, for your kindness.'

'Time we were aboard, eh?' Jherek's joviality was of the false and insistent sort.

Una Persson seemed to be enjoying some private glee. She hugged one of Oswald Bastable's arms and whispered in his ear. He blushed.

Jherek climbed into his side of the box. 'If there's anything I can send you from the End of Time, let me know,' he called. 'We must try to keep in touch.'

'Indeed,' she said. 'In the circumstances, all we time-travellers have is one another. Ask Jagged about the Guild.'

'I think Mr Carnelian has had his fill of adventuring through time, Mrs Persson.' Amelia Underwood was smiling and her attitude towards Jherek had something possessive about it, so that Jherek was bewildered even more.

'Sometimes, once we have embarked upon the exercise, we are not allowed to stop,' Una Persson said. 'I mention it, only. But I hope you are successful in settling, if that is what you wish. Some would have it that Time creates the human condition, you know – that, and nothing else.'

They had begun to shout, now that a loud thrumming filled the air.

'We had best stand clear,' said Captain Bastable. 'Occasionally there is a shock wave. The vacuum, you know.' He guided Mrs Persson towards the largest of the black huts. 'The capsule finds its own level. You have nothing to fear on that score. You won't be drowned, or burned, or compressed.'

Jherek watched them retreat. The thrumming grew louder and louder. His back pressed against Mrs Underwood's. He turned to ask her if she were comfortable but before he could speak a stillness fell and there was complete silence. His head felt suddenly light. He looked to Mrs Persson and Captain Bastable for an answer, but they were gone and only a shadowy, flickering ghost of the black wall could be seen. Finally this, too, disappeared and foliage replaced it. Something huge and heavy and alive moved towards them, passed through them, it seemed, and was gone. Heat and cold became extreme, seemed one. Hundreds of colours came and went, but were pale, washed out, rainy. There was dampness in the air he breathed; little tremors of pain ran through him but were past almost before his brain could signal their presence.

Booming, echoing sounds – slow sounds, deep and sluggish – blossomed in his ears. He swung up and down, he swung sideways, always as if the capsule were suspended from a wire, like a pendulum. He could feel her warm body pressed to his shoulders, but he could not hear her voice and he could not turn to see her, for every movement took infinity to consider and perform, and he appeared to weigh tons, as though his mass spread through miles of space and years of time. The capsule tilted forward, but he did not fall from his seat; something pressed him in, securing him: grey waves washed him; red rays rolled from toe to head. The chair began to spin. He heard his own name, or something very like it, being called by a high, mocking voice. Words piped at him; all the words of his life.

He breathed in and it was as if Niagara engulfed him. He breathed out; Vesuvius gave voice.

Scales slipped by against his cheek and fur filled his nostrils and flesh throbbed close to his lips, and fine wings fluttered, great winds blew; he was drenched by a salty rain (he became the History of Man, he became a thousand warm-blooded beasts, he knew unbearable tranquillity). He became pure pain and was the universe, the big slow-dancing stars. His body began to sing.

In the distance:

'*My dear – my dear – my dearest dear ...*'

His eyes had shut. He opened them.

'My dear!'

Was it Amelia?

But, no – he could move – he could turn and see that she was slumped forward, insensible. Still the pale colours swam. They cleared.

Green oak trees surrounded a grassy glade; cool sunlight touched the leaves.

He heard a sound. She had tumbled from the capsule and lay stretched, face-forward, upon the ground. He climbed from his seat, his legs trembling, and went to her, even as the capsule made a wrenching noise and was gone.

'Amelia!' He touched soft hair, stroked the lovely neck, kissed the linen exposed by the torn velvet of her sleeve. 'Oh, Amelia!'

Her voice was muffled. 'Even these circumstances, Mr Carnelian, do not entitle you to liberties. I am not unconscious.' She moved her head so that her steady grey eyes could see him. 'Merely faint. Perhaps a trifle stunned. Where are we?'

'Almost certainly at End of Time. These trees are of familiar workmanship.' He helped her to her feet. 'I think it is where we originally came across the Lat. It would be logical to return me here, for Nurse's sanctuary is not far distant.' He had already recounted his adventures to her. 'The Lat spaceship is probably also nearby.'

She became nervous. 'Should we not seek out your friends?'

'If they have returned. Remember, the last we saw of them was in London, 1896. They vanished – but did they return? Our destinations were the same. Almost certainly the Morphail Effect sent them home – but we know that Brannart's theories do not apply to all the phenomena associated with Time.'

'We'll not be served by further speculation,' she pointed out. 'You have your power-rings, still?'

He was impressed by her sense. 'Of course!' He stroked a ruby, turning three of the oaks into a larger version of the power-boat of the Palaeozoic, but translucent, of jade. 'My ranch awaits us – rest or roister, as we will!' He bowed low as, with a set expression upon her beautiful features, she advanced towards the boat. He brought up the rear. 'You do not think the jewelled propeller vulgar?' He was eager for her praise. 'It seemed a refinement.'

'It is lovely,' said she, distantly. With considerable dignity, she entered the vessel. There were benches, quilted with cloth-of-gold. She chose one near the centre of the craft. Joining her, he lounged in the prow. A wave of a hand and the boat began to rise. He laughed. He was his old self again. He was Jherek Carnelian, the son of a

410

woman, the darling of his world, and his love was with him.

'At last,' he cried, 'our aggravations and adventures are concluded. The road has been a weary one, and long, yet at its end what shall we find but our own little cottage complete with cat and kettle, cream, crumpets, cranberries, kippers, cauliflower, crackers, custard, kedgeree for tea, sweet, my dear Amelia, sweet tranquillity! Oh, you shall be happy. You shall!'

Stiffly though she sat, she seemed more amused than insulted. She seemed pleased to recognize the landscapes streaming by below, and she did not chide him for his use of her Christian name, nor for his suggestions which were, of course, improper.

'I knew it!' he sang. 'You have learned to love the End of Time.'

'It does have certain attractions,' she admitted, 'after the Lower Devonian.'

CHAPTER EIGHT

ALL TRAVELLERS RETURNED: A CELEBRATION

The jade air-car reached the ranch and hovered. 'You see,' said Jherek, 'it is almost exactly as you last saw it, before you were torn away from me and tumbled back through Time. It retains all the features you proposed, familiar comforts of your own dear Dawn Age. You will be happy, Amelia. And anything else you wish, it shall be yours. Remember – my knowledge of your needs, your age, is much more sophisticated now. You will not find me the náive who courted you so long, it seems, ago!'

'It is the same,' she said, and her voice was wistful, 'but we are not.'

'I am more mature,' he agreed, 'a better mate.'

'Ah!' She smiled.

He sensed ambiguity. 'You do not love another? Captain Bastable ...'

She became wicked. 'He is a gentleman of excellent manners. And his bearing – so soldierly ...' But her eyes laughed at her words. 'A match any mother would approve. Were I not already married, I should be the envy of Bromley – but I am married, of course, to Mr Underwood.'

Jherek made the car spiral down towards the rose-gardens and the rockeries he had created for her, and he said with some nervousness: 'He said he would – what? – "divest" you!'

'Divorce. I should have to appear in court – millions of years from here. It seems,' (turning so that he should not see her face), 'that I shall never be free.'

'Free? Free? No woman was ever more free. Here is humanity triumphant – Nature conquered – all desires may be fulfilled – of enemies, none. You can live as you please. I shall serve you. Your whims shall be mine, dearest Amelia!'

'But my conscience,' she said. 'Can I be free from that?'

His face fell. 'Oh, yes, of course, your conscience. I was forgetting it.' The car sank to the lawn. 'You did not leave it, then, behind? In Eden?'

'There? I had greater need of it, did I not?'

'I thought you suggested otherwise.'

'Then condemn me as fickle. All women are so.'

'You contradict yourself, but apparently without relish.'

'Ha!' She was the first to leave the craft. 'You refuse to accuse me, Mr Carnelian? You will not play the game? The old game?'

'I did not know there was a game, Amelia. You are disturbed? The set of your shoulders reveals it. I am confused.'

She rounded on him, but her face was softening. Her eyes held disbelief, fast fading. 'You do not try me for my femininity? I am not accused of womanliness?'

'All this is meaningless.'

'Then perhaps there is a degree of freedom here, at the End of Time, mixed with all your cruelties.'

'Cruelties?'

'You keep slaves. Casually, you destroy anything which bores you. Have you no consideration for these time-travellers you capture? Was I not captured so – and put in a menagerie? And Yusharisp – bartered for me. Even in my age such barbarities are banished!'

413

He accepted her admonishment. He bowed his head. 'Then you must teach me what is best,' he said. 'Is this "morality"?'

She was overwhelmed, suddenly, by the enormity of her responsibility. Was it salvation she brought to Paradise, or was it merely guilt? She hesitated. 'We shall discuss it, in the fullness of time,' she told him.

They set foot upon the crazy paving of the path, between low yew-hedges. The ranch – Gothic red brick reproduction of her ideal Bromley villa – awaited them. A parrot or two perched on chimneys and gables; they seemed to flute a welcome.

'It is as you left it,' he said. He was proud. 'But, elsewhere, I have built for you a "London", so that you shall not be homesick. It still pleases you, the ranch?'

'It is as I remember it.'

He understood that he read disappointment in her tone. 'You compare it now with the original, I suppose.'

'It has the essentials of the original.'

'But remains a "mere copy", eh? Show me . . .'

She had reached the porch, ran a hand over the painted timber, fondled a still-blooming rose (for none had faded since she had vanished), touched the flower to her nose. 'It has been so long,' she murmured. 'I needed familiarity, then.'

'You do not need it now?'

'Ah, yes. I am human. I am a woman. But perhaps there are other things which come to mean more. I felt, in those days, that I was in hell – tormented, mocked, abused – in the company of the mad. I had no perspective.'

He opened the door, with its stained-glass panels. Potted plants, pictures, carpets of Persian design, dark paint, were revealed in the gloom of the entrance hall.

'If there are additions . . .' he began.

'Additions!' She was half amused. She inspected the what-nots and the aspidistras with a disdainful eye. 'No more, I think.'

'Too cluttered, now?' He closed the door and caused

414

light to blossom.

'The house could be bigger. More windows, perhaps. More sun. More air.'

He smiled. 'I could remove the roof.'

'You could, indeed!' She sniffed. 'Yet it is not as musty as I supposed it would be. How long is it since you departed it?'

'That's difficult. We can only find out by conferring with our friends. They will know. My range of scents has much improved since I visited 1896. I agree that it was an area in which I was weak. But my palette is altogether enriched.'

'Oh, this will do, Mr Carnelian. For the present, at any rate.'

'You cannot voice your disquiet?'

She turned kind eyes on him. 'You possess a sensitivity often denied by your behaviour.'

'I love you,' he said simply. 'I live for you.'

She coloured. 'My rooms are as I left them? My wardrobe remains intact?'

'Everything is there.'

'Then I will rejoin you for lunch.' She began to mount the stairs.

'It will be ready for you,' he promised. He went into the front parlour, staring around him at this Collins Avenue of the mind, peering through the windows at the gentle green hills, the mechanical cows and sheep with their mechanical cow-boys and shepherds, all perfectly reproduced to make her feel at home. He admitted to himself that her response had bewildered him. It was almost as if she had lost her taste for her own preferred environment. He sighed. It had seemed so much easier, when her ideas were definite. Now that she herself found them difficult to define, he was at a loss. Antimacassars, horsehair furniture, red, black and yellow carpets of geometrical pattern, framed photographs, thick-leaved plants, the harmonium with which she had eased her heart, all now (because she seemed to have disapproved) accused him as a brute who

415

could never please any woman, let alone the finest woman who had ever breathed. Still in the stained rags of his nineteenth-century suit, he slumped into an armchair, head on hand, and considered the irony of his situation. Not long since, he had sat in this house with Mrs Underwood and made tentative suggestions for its improvement. She had forbidden any change. Then she had gone and all that he had left of her was the house itself. As a substitute, he had come to love it. Now it was she who suggested improvements (of almost exactly the kind he had proposed) and he felt a deep reluctance to alter a single potted palm, a solitary sideboard. Nostalgia for those times when he had courted her and she had tried to teach him the meaning of virtue, when they had sung hymns together in the evenings (it had been she, again, who had insisted upon a daily time-scale similar to that which she had known in Bromley), filled him – and with nostalgia came trepidation, that his hopes were doomed. At every stage, when she had been close to declaring her love for him, to giving herself to him, she had been thwarted. It was almost as if Jagged watched them, deliberately manipulating every detail of their lives. Easier to think that, perhaps, than to accept an arbitrary universe.

He rose from the chair and, with an expression of defiance (she had always insisted that he follow her conventions) created a hole in the ceiling through which he might pass and enter his own room, a haven of glittering white, gold and silver. He restored the floor to completeness and his ruby ring cleansed his body of Palaeozoic grime, placed wafting robes of white spider-fur about him, brought ease to his mind as it dawned on him that his old powers (and therefore his old innocence) were restored to him. He stretched himself and laughed. There was certainly much to be said for being at the mercy of the primeval elements, to be swept along by circumstances one could not in any way control, but it was good to return, to feel one's identity expand again, unchecked. Creatively, he knew that he would be capable of the best entertainments he had yet given his world. He felt the need for company, for old friends to whom he could retail his adventures. Had his mother, the magnificent Iron Orchid, yet returned to the End of Time? Was the Duke of Queens as vulgar as ever, or had his experiences taught him taste? Jherek became eager for news.

In undulating white, he left his room and began to cross the landing, crammed with nooks which in turn were crammed with little china figurines, china vases, china flowers, china animals, to the stairs. His emerald power-ring brought him delicate scents, of Lower Devonian ferns, of nineteenth-century streets, of oceans and of meadows. His step grew lighter as he descended to the dining room. 'All things bright and beautiful,' he sang, 'all creatures great and small . . .'

A turn of his amber ring and an ethereal orchestra accompanied him. The amethyst – and peacocks stepped behind him, his train in their prim beaks, their feathers at full flourish. He passed an embroidered motto – he still could not read it, but she had told him its sense (if sense it were!): 'What Mean These Stones?' he carolled. 'What Mean These – tra-la-la – Stones?'

His spider-fur robes began to brush ornaments from the shelves at the side of the stairs. With scarcely any feelings of guilt at all, he widened the steps a little, so that he could pass more freely.

The dining room, dark, with heavy curtains and brown, gloomy furniture, dampened his spirits for only a second. He knew what she had once demanded – partially burned animal flesh, near-tasteless vegetables – and he ignored it. If she no longer dictated her pleasures, then he would offer his own again.

The table bloomed exotic. A reminder of their recent adventures – a spun-sugar water-scorpion glittering as a centre-piece – two translucent scarlet jellies, two feet high, in the image, to the life, of Inspector Springer. A couple of herds of animated marzipan cows and sheep (to satisfy her relish for fauna) grazing, in miniature, at the bases of the jellies. Everywhere: fronds of yellow, blue, pink, white, lilac and purple, of savoury, brittle pastry. Not a typical table, for Jherek usually chose for colour and preferred to limit himself to two, with one predominating – perhaps not a tasteful table, even – but a jolly one, that he hoped she would appreciate. Great green pools of gravy; golden mounds of mustards; brown, steaming custards, and pies in a dozen pastel shades; bowls of crystals – cocaine in the blue, heroin in the silver, sugar in the black – and tottering pyramids of porridge – a dish for any mood, to satisfy every appetite. He stood back, grinning his pleasure. It was unplanned, it was crowded, but it had a certain zest, he felt, that she would appreciate.

He struck the nearby gong. Her feet were already upon the stairs.

She entered the room. 'Oh!'

'Lunch, my lovely Amelia. Flung together, I fear, but all quite edible.'

She eyed the little marzipan ruminants.

He beamed. 'I knew you'd like those. And Inspector Springer? Does he not amuse you?'

Fingers flew to lips; a sound escaped her nostrils. The bosom rose and then was slow to fall; she was almost as red as the jelly.

'You are distressed.'

Eruption. She doubled, gasping.

'Fumes?' He stared wildly. 'Something poisonous?'

'Oh, ho, ho ...' She straightened, hand at back of hip. 'Oh, ho, ho!'

He relaxed. 'You *are* amused.' He pulled back her chair, as she had trained him to do. She slumped down, still shaking, picking up a spoon. 'Oh, ho, ho ...'

He joined in. 'Oh, ho, ho.'

It was thus, before they had put a morsel to their mouths, that the Iron Orchid found them. They saw her in the doorway, after some time. She was smiling. She was resplendent.

'Dear Jherek, wonder of my womb! Astonishing Amelia,

ancestress without compare! Do you hide from us all? Or are you just returned? If so, you are the last. All travellers are back – even Mongrove, you know. He has returned from space – gloomier, if anything, than before. We speculated. We expected your return. Jagged was here – he said that he sent you on, but that only the machine arrived, bereft of passengers. Some would have it – Brannart Morphail in particular – that you were lost forever in some primitive age – destroyed. I disbelieved, naturally. There was talk, earlier, of an expedition, but nothing came of it. Today, at My Lady Charlotina's, there was a rumour of a fluctuation – a time-machine had been sensed for a second or two on one of Brannart's instruments. I knew it must be you!'

She had chosen red for her chief colour. Her crimson eyes glittered with maternal joy at her son restored to her. Her scarlet hair curled itself here and there about her face, as if in ecstasy, and her poppy-coloured flesh seemed to vibrate with pleasure. As she moved, her perspex gown, almost the colour of clementines, creaked a little.

'You know there is to be a celebration?' she said. A party so that we may all hear Mongrove's news. He has consented to appear, to speak. And the Duke of Queens, Bishop Castle, My Lady Charlotina – we shall be there to give our tales. And now you and Mrs Underwood? Where have you been, you rogues? Hiding here, or adventuring through History?'

Mrs Underwood began: 'We have had a tiring experience, Mrs Carnelian, and I think ...'

'Tiring? Mrs What? Tiring? I'm not certain of the meaning. But Mrs Carnelian – that is excellent. I never thought – yes, excellent. I must tell the Duke of Queens.' She cruised for the door. 'But I'll interrupt your meal no longer. The theme for the celebration is of course 1896 —' a gesture to Mrs Underwood – 'and I know you will both surpass yourselves! Farewell!'

Mrs Underwood implored him: 'We are not going?'

'We must!'

419

'It is expected?'

He knew secret glee in his own cunning. 'Oh, indeed it is,' he said.

'Then, of course, I shall go with you.'

He eyed her crisp cream dress, her pinned auburn hair. 'And the beauty of it is,' he said, 'that if you go as you are, the purity of your conception will outshine all others!'

She snapped a branch from a savoury frond.

CHAPTER NINE

THE PAST IS HONOURED: THE FUTURE REAFFIRMED

First there came a broad plane, a vast, level carpet of pale green; the jade power-boat sped low over this – then avenues approached – spaced to have their entrances arranged around the perimeter of a semi-circle; each avenue leading inwards to a hub. The air-car selected one. Cypresses, palms, yews, elders, redwoods, pines, shoe and plane trees, sped by on either side – their variety proclaiming that the Duke of Queens had not lost his vulgar touch (Jherek wondered, now, if he would have it otherwise). The focus became visible, ahead, but they heard the music before they recognized details of the Duke's display.

'A waltz!' cried Mrs Underwood (she had renounced the sensible day dress for fine blue silk, white lace, a flounce or two, even the suggestion of a bustle, and the hat she wore was two feet across at the brim; on her hands, lace gloves, and in them a blue and white parasol). 'Is it Strauss, Mr Carnelian?'

In the tweeds she had helped him make, he leaned back against the side of the car, his face half-shaded by his cap. One hand fingered his watch-chain, the other steadied the briar-wood pipe she had considered fitting ('a manlier, more mature air, altogether,' she had murmured with satisfaction, after the brogues were on his feet and the cravat adjusted, 'your figure would be envied anywhere' and then she had become a fraction confused). He shook his head. 'Or Starkey, or Stockhausen. I was never as familiar as I should have been with the early primitives. Lord Jagged would know. I hope he is there.'

'He became almost garrulous at our departure,' she said. 'I wonder if he regrets that now, as people sometimes do. I remember once that the brother of a girl I knew at school kept us company for an entire vacation. I thought he disliked me. He seemed disdainful. At the end of the holiday he drove me to the station, was taciturn, even surly. I felt sorry for him, that he should be burdened. I entered the train. He remained on the platform. As the train left, he began to run beside it. He knew that I should probably never see him again. He was red as a raspberry as he shouted his parting remark.' She inspected the silver top of her parasol.

He could see that there was a small, soft smile on her lips, which was all that was visible to him of her face, beneath the brim of the hat.

'His remark?'

'Oh!' She looked up and, for an instant, the eye which met his was merry. 'He said "I love you, Miss Ormont", that was all. He could only declare himself when he knew I should not be able to confront him again.'

Jherek laughed. 'And, of course, the joke was that you were not this Miss Ormont. He confused you with another.'

He wondered why both tone and expression changed so suddenly, though she remained, it seemed, amused. She gave her attention back to the parasol. 'My maiden name was Ormont,' she said. 'When we marry, you see, we take the name of our betrothed.'

'Excellent! Then I may expect, one day, to be Jherek Underwood?'

'You are devious in your methods of clinging to your

points, Mr Carnelian. But I shall not be trapped so simply. No, you would not become Jherek Underwood.'

'Ormont?'

'The idea is amusing, even pleasant.' She checked herself. 'Even the hottest of radicals has never suggested, to my knowledge, such a reversal.' Smiling, she chewed her underlip. 'Oh, dear! What dangerous thoughts you encourage, in your innocence!'

'I have not offended?'

'Once, you might have done so. I am shocked at myself, for not feeling shocked. What a bad woman I should seem in Bromley now!'

He scarcely followed, but he was not disturbed. He sank back again and made the pipe come alight for the umpteenth time (she had not been able to tell him how to keep it fuming). He enjoyed the Duke's golden sunshine, the sky which matched, fortuitously, his loved one's dress. Other air-carriages could be seen in other avenues, speeding for the hub – red and gold, plush and gilt, a fanciful reproduction of the Duke's only prolonged experience with the nineteenth century.

Jherek touched her hand. 'Do you recognize it, Amelia?'

'It is overpoweringly huge.' The brim of the hat went up and up, a lace glove touched her chin. 'It disappears, look, in clouds.'

She had not seen. He hinted: 'But if the proportions were reduced ...'

She tilted her head, still craning. 'Some sort of American Building?'

'You have been there!'

'I?'

'The original is in London.'

'Not the Café Royal?'

'Don't you see – he has taken the décor of the Café Royal and added it to your Scotland Yard.'

'Police headquarters – with red plush walls!'

'The Duke comes near, for once, to simplicity. You do not think it too spare?'

423

'A thousand feet high! It is the tallest piece of plush, Mr Carnelian, I may ever hope to see. And what is that at the roof – now the clouds part – a darker mass?'

'Black?'

'Blue, I think.'

'A dome. Yes, a hat, such as your policemen wear.'

She seemed out of breath. 'Of course.'

The music grew louder. He waved his pipe in time. But she was puzzled. 'Isn't it a little slow – a little drawn out – for a waltz. It's as if it were played on those Indian instruments – or were they Arabic? More than a flavour of the Oriental, at any rate. High-pitched, too, in a way.'

'The tapes are from one of the cities, doubtless,' said Jherek. 'They are old – possibly faulty. This is not authentic, then?'

'Not to my time.'

'We had best not tell the Duke of Queens. It would disappoint him, don't you think?'

She shrugged compliance. 'Yet it has a rather grating effect. I hope it does not continue throughout the entire reception. You do not know the instruments used?'

'Electronics or some such early method of music-making. You would know better ...'

'I think not.'

'Ah.'

A degree of awkwardness touched the atmosphere and, for a moment, both strove to find a new subject and restore the mood of relaxation they had been enjoying till now. Ahead, at the base of the building, was a wide, shadowy archway, and into this other air-cars were speeding – fanciful vehicles of every description, and most based on Dawn Age technology or mythology: Jherek saw a hobby-horse, its mechanical copper legs making galloping motions in the air, a Model T, its owner seated on the section where the long vertical bar joined the short horizontal one, and he heard the distinctive sound of a clipper ship, but it had disappeared before he could see it properly. Some of the vessels moved with considerable speed, others made more stately progress, like the large, grey and white car – it could be nothing else but a London Pigeon – immediately in front of them as the archway loomed.

'It seems the whole world attends,' said Jherek.

She fingered the complicated lace on her bodice. She smoothed a pleat. The music changed; the sound of slow explosions and of something being dragged through sand surrounded them as their car entered a great hall, its ceiling suported by fluted arches, in which, evidently, they were to park. Elaborately dressed figures floated from their own air-cars towards a doorway into the hall above; voices echoed.

'It dwarfs King's Cross!' exclaimed Mrs Underwood. She admired the mosaics, finely detailed, multicoloured, on walls and arches. 'It is hard to believe that it has not existed for centuries.'

'In a sense it has,' said Jherek, aware that she made an effort to converse. 'In the memories of the cities.'

'This was made by one of your cities?'

'No, but the advice of the cities is sought on such matters. For all that they grow senile, they still remember a great deal of our race's history. Is the interior familiar to you?'

'It resembles nothing so much as the vault of a Gothic cathedral, much magnified. I do not think I know the original, if one exists. You must not forget, Mr Carnelian, that I am no expert. Most aspects of my own world, most areas of it, are unknown to me. My experiences of London were not so varied, I would gather, as yours have been. I led a quiet life in Bromley, where the world is small.' She sighed as they left the car. 'Very small,' she said, almost under her breath. She adjusted her hat and tossed her head in a manner he found delightful. At that moment she seemed at once more full of life and of melancholy than he had ever seen her. He hesitated for a fraction of a second before offering her his arm, but she took it readily, smiling, the sadness melting, and together they ascended to

425

the doorway above.

'You are glad, now, that you have come?' he murmured.

'I am determined to enjoy myself,' she told him.

Then she gasped, for she had not expected the scene they entered. The entire building was filled not by separated floors, but by floating platforms and galleries, rising higher and higher into the distance, and in these galleries and upon these platforms stood groups of people, conversing, eating, dancing, while other groups, or individuals, drifted through the air, from one platform to another, as, in her own world, people might cross the floor of a ballroom. High, high above, the furthest figures were tiny, virtually invisible. The light was subtle, supplying brilliance and shade, and shifting almost imperceptibly the whole time; the colours were vibrant, of every possible shade or tone, complementing the costumes of the guests, which ranged from the simplest to the most grotesque. Perhaps by some clever manipulation of the acoustics of the hall, the voices rose and fell in waves, but were never loud enough to drown any particular conversation, and, to Mrs Underwood, seemed orchestrated, harmonized into a single yet infinitely variegated chorus. Here and there, along the walls, people stood casually, their bodies at right angles to those of the majority, as they used power-rings to adjust their gravity, enabling them to convert the dimensions of the hall (or at least their experience of those dimensions) to an impression of length rather than height.

'It reminds one of a medieval painting,' she said. 'Italian, are they? Of heaven? My father's house ... Though the perspective is better ...' Aware that she babbled, she subsided with a sigh, looking at him with an expression showing amusement at her own confusion.

'It pleases you, though?' He was solicitous, yet he could see that she was not unhappy.

'It is wonderful.'

'Your morality is not offended?'

'For today, Mr Carnelian, I have decided to leave a

great deal of my morality at home.' Again, she laughed at herself.

'You are more beautiful than ever,' he told her. 'You are very fine.'

'Hush, Mr Carnelian. You will make me self-conscious. For once, I feel in possession of myself. Let me enjoy it. I will –' she smiled – 'permit the occasional compliment – but I should be grateful if you will forgo declarations of passion for this evening.'

He bowed, sharing her good humour. 'Very well.'

But she had become a goddess and he could not help it if he were astonished. She had always been beautiful in his eyes, and admirable, too. He had worshipped her, in some ways, for her courage in adversity, for her resistance to the ways of his own world. But that had been bravery under siege and now, it seemed, she single-handedly gave siege to that same society which, a few months before, had threatened to engulf and destroy her identity. There was a determination in her bearing, a lightness, an air of confidence, that proclaimed to everyone what he had always sensed in her – and he was proud that his world should see her as the woman he knew, in full command of herself and of her situation. Yet there was, as well, a private knowledge, an intimate understanding between them, of the resources of character on which she drew to achieve that command. For the first time he became conscious of the depth of his love for her and, although he had always known that she had loved him, he became confident that her emotion was as strong as his own. Like her, he required no declaration; her bearing was declaration enough.

Together, they ascended.

'Jherek!'

It was Mistress Christia, the Everlasting Concubine, clad in silks that were almost wholly transparent, they were so fine, and plainly influenced by the murals she had had described to her by one of those who had visited the Café Royal. She had let her body fill out, her limbs had

427

rounded and she was slightly, deliciously, plump.

'May it be Amelia?' she asked of Mrs Underwood, and looked to both for confirmation.

Mrs Underwood smiled assent.

'I have been hearing of all your adventures in the nineteenth century. I am so jealous, of course, for the age seems wonderful and just the sort of period I should like to visit. This costume is not of my own invention, as you have guessed. My Lady Charlotina was going to use it, but thought it more suitable for me. Is it, Amelia, authentic?' She whirled in the air, just above their heads.

'Greek . . ?' Amelia Underwood hesitated, unwilling to contradict. Then, it seemed, she realized the influence. 'It suits you perfectly. You look lovely.'

'I would be welcome in your world?'

'Oh, certainly! In many sections of society you would be the centre of attention.'

Mistress Christia beamed and bent, with soft lips, to kiss Mrs Underwood upon her cheek, murmuring, 'You look magnificent, of course, yourself. Did you make the dress or did you bring it from the Dawn Age? It must be an original.'

'It was made here.'

'It is still beautiful. You have the advantage over us all! And you, too, Jherek look the very picture of the noble, Dawn Age hero. So manly! So desirable!'

Mrs Underwood's hand tightened a fraction on Jherek's arm. He became almost euphoric.

Yet Mistress Christia was sensitive, too. 'I shall not be the only one to envy you today, Amelia.' She permitted herself a wink. 'Or Jherek, either.' She looked beyond them. 'Here is our host!'

The Duke of Queens had been a soldier, during his brief stay in 1896. But never had there been a scarlet tunic so thoroughly scarlet as the one he sported, nor buttons so golden, nor epaulettes so bright, nor belt and boots so mirror-gleaming. He had doffed his beard and assumed Dundreary sidewhiskers; there was a shako a-tilt on his massive head; his britches were dark blue and striped with yellow. His gloves were white and one hand rested upon the pommel of his sword, which dripped with braid. He saluted and bowed. 'Honoured you could attend,' he said.

Jherek embraced him. 'You have been coached, dear friend! You look so handsome!'

'All natural,' declared the Duke with some pride. 'Created through exercise, you know, with the help of some time-travellers of a military persuasion. You heard of my duel with Lord Shark?'

'Lord Shark! I thought him a misanthrope entirely. To make Mongrove seem as gregarious as Gaf the Horse in Tears. What lured him from his grey fortress?'

'An affair of honour.'

'Indeed?' said Amelia Underwood. 'Insults, was it, and pistols at dawn?'

'I offended him. I forget how. But I was remorseful at the time. We settled with swords. I trained for ages. The irony was, however ...'

He was interrupted by Bishop Castle, in full evening dress, copied from Mr Harris, doubtless. His handsome, rather ascetic, features were framed by a collar that was perhaps a little taller than normally fashionable in 1896. He had disdained black and the coat and trousers were, instead, bottle-green; the waistcoat brown, the shirt cream-coloured. His tie matched his coat and the exaggeratedly high top-hat on his head.

'Jesting Jherek, you have been hidden too long!' His voice was slightly muffled by the collar covering his mouth. 'And your Mrs Underwood! Gloom vanishes. We are all united again!'

'Is it mannerly to compliment your costume, Bishop Castle?' A movement of her parasol.

'Compliments are the colour of our conversation, dear Mrs Underwood. We are fulfilled by flattery; we feed on praise; we spend our days in search of the perfect peal of persiflage that will make the peacock in us preen and say

429

"Behold – I beautify the world!" In short, exquisite butterfly in blue, you may so compliment me and already do. May I in turn honour your appearance; it has detail which, sadly, few of us can match. It does not merely attract the eye – it holds it. It is the finest creation here. Henceforth there is no question but that you shall lead us all in fashion. Jherek is toppled from his place!'

She lifted an appreciative eyebrow; his bow was sweeping and all but lost him his hat, while his head virtually disappeared from view for a moment. He straightened, saw a friend, bowed again, and drifted away. 'Later,' he said to them both, 'we must reminisce.'

Jherek saw amusement in her eyes as she watched Bishop Castle rise to a nearby gallery. 'He is a voluble cleric,' she said. 'We have bishops not unlike him in 1896.'

'You must tell him, Amelia. What greater compliment could you pay?'

'It did not occur to me.' She hesitated, her self-assurance gone for a second: 'You do not find me callow?'

'Ha! You rule here already. Your good opinion is in demand. You have the authority both of bearing and of background. Bishop Castle spoke nothing but the truth. Your praise warmed him.'

He was about to escort her higher when the Duke of Queens, who had been in conversation with Mistress Christia, turned back to them. 'Have you been long returned, Jherek and Amelia, to the End of Time?'

'Hardly a matter of hours,' said she.

'So you remained behind in 1986. You can tell us what became of Jagged?'

'Then he is not yet back?' She glanced to Jherek with some alarm. 'We heard ...'

'You did not meet him again in 1896? I assumed that was his destination.' The Duke of Queens frowned.

'He could be there,' said Jherek, 'for we have been adventuring elsewhere. At the very Beginning of Time, in fact.'

'Lord Jagged of Canaria conceals himself increasingly,'

430

complained the Duke, brushing at a braid. 'When challenged, he proves himself a master of sophistry. His mysteries cease to entertain because he confuses them so.'

'It is possible,' said Amelia Underwood, 'that he has become lost in Time; that he did not plan this disappearance. If we had not been fortunate, we should still be stranded now.'

The Duke of Queens was embarrassed by his own pettishness. 'Of course. Oh, dear – Time has become such a talking point and it is not one, I fear, which interests me greatly. I have never had Lord Jagged's penchant for the abstract. You know what a bore I can be.'

'Never that,' said Jherek affectionately. 'And even your vulgarities are splendid.'

'I hope so,' he said with modesty. 'I do my best. You like the building, Jherek?'

'It is a masterpiece.'

'More restrained than usual?'

'Much.'

The Duke's eye brightened. 'What an arbiter we make of you, Jherek! It is only because of your past innovations, or because we respect your experience, too?'

Jherek shrugged. 'I have not considered it. But Bishop Castle claims that art has a fresh leader.' He bowed to his Amelia.

'You like my Royal Scotland Yard, Mrs Underwood?' The Duke was eager.

'I am most impressed, Duke of Queens.' She appeared to be relishing her new position.

He was satisfied. 'But what is this concerning the Beginning of Time? Shall you bring us more ideas, scarcely before we can assimilate the old ones?'

'Perhaps,' said Jherek. 'Molluscs, you know. And ferns. Rocks. Hampers. Water-scorpions. Time Centres. Yes, there would be enough for a modest entertainment of some sort.'

'You have tales for us, too!' Mistress Christia had returned. 'Adventures, eh?'

Now more of the guests had sighted them and began to drift towards them.

'I think some, at least, will amuse you,' said Amelia Underwood. Jherek detected a harder edge to her voice as she prepared to face the advancing crowd, but she had lost that quality when she next spoke. 'We found many surprises there.'

'Oh, this is delightful!' cried Mistress Christia. 'What an enviable pair you are!'

'And brave, too, to risk the snares and vengeances of Time,' said the Duke of Queens.

Gaf the Horse in Tears, a Gibson Girl to the life, a Sailor hat upon his up-pinned hair, leaned forward. 'Brannart told us you were doomed, gone forever. Destroyed, even.'

Sharp-featured Doctor Volospion, in a black, swirling cape and a black, wide-brimmed hat, his eyes glittering from the shadows of his face, said softly: 'We did not believe him, of course.'

'Yet our time-travellers disappear – vanishing from our menageries at an astonishing rate. I lost four Adolf Hitlers alone, just recently.' Sweet Orb Mace was splendid in rubashka, tarboosh, pantaloons and high, embroidered boots. 'And one of them, I'm sure, was real. Though rather old, admittedly ...'

'Brannart claims these disappearances as proof that Time is ruptured.' Werther de Goethe, a saturnine Sicilian brigand, complete with curling moustachios which rather contradicted the rest of the impression, adjusted his cloak. 'He warns that we stand upon a brink, that we shall all, soon, plunge willy-nilly into disordered chronological gulfs.'

There was a pause in the babble, for Werther's glum drone frequently had this effect, until Amelia said:

'His warnings have some substance, it would seem.'

'What?' The Duke of Queens laughed heartily. 'You are living denials of the Morphail Effect!'

'I think not.' She was modest, looked to Jherek to speak,

432

but he gave her the floor. 'As I understand it, Brannart Morphail's explanations are only partial. They are not false. Many theories describe Time – and all are provable.'

'An excellent summary,' said Jherek. 'My Amelia relates what we have learned, darling of Dukes, at the Beginning of Time. More scientists than Brannart concern themselves with investigating Time's nature. I think he will be glad of the information I bring. He is not alone in his researches, he'll be pleased to know.'

'You are certain of it?' asked Amelia, who had flickered an eye at his recent 'my' (though without apparent displeasure).

'Why should he not be?'

She shrugged. 'I have only encountered the gentleman in dramatic circumstances, of course ...'

'He is due?' asked Jherek of the Duke.

'Invited – as is the world. You know him. He will come late, claiming we force him against his will.'

'Then he might know the whereabouts of Jagged.' He appraised the hall, as if mention of the name would invoke the one he most wished to see. Many he recognized, not famous for their gregariousness, were here, even Lord Shark (or one of his automata, sent in his place) who styled himself 'The Unknown'; even Werther de Goethe, who had sworn never to attend another party. Yet, so far, that last member of the End of Time's misanthropic triumvirate, Lord Mongrove, the bitter giant, in whose honour this celebration was being held, was not in evidence.

Her arm was still in his. A touch drew his attention. 'You are concerned for Jagged's safety?' she asked.

'He is my closest friend, devious though he seems. Could he not have suffered our fate? More drastically?'

'If so, we shall never know.'

He drove this worry from his mind; it was not his business, as a guest, to brood. 'Look,' he said, 'there is My Lady Charlotina!'

She had seen them, from above, and now flew to greet

433

them, her golden robe-de-style, with its crystal beads, its ribbons and its roses, fluttering with the speed of her descent.

'Our hero and heroine happily restored to us. Is this the final scene? Are sleigh-bells to ring, blue-bloods to sing, catharsis achieved, tranquillity regained? I have missed so much of the plot. Refresh me – regale us all. Oh, speak, my beauties. Or are we to witness a re-enactment?'

Mrs Underwood was dry. 'The tale is not yet finished, I regret, My Lady Charlotina. Many clues remain to be un-ravelled – threads are still to be woven together – there is no clearly seen pattern upon the fabric – and perhaps there never will be.'

My Lady Charlotina's disbelieving laughter held no rancour. 'Nonsense – it is your duty to bring about reso-lution soon. It is cruel of you both to keep us in such suspense. If your timing is not exact, you will lose your audience, my dears. First there will be criticism of fine points, and then – you could not risk this – uninterest. But you must bring me up to date, before I judge. Give me merely the barest details, if that is what you wish, and let gossip colour the tale for you.'

Smiling broadly, Amelia Underwood began to tell of their adventures at the Beginning of Time.

CHAPTER TEN

IN WHICH THE IRON ORCHID
IS NOT QUITE HERSELF

Jherek still sought for Jagged. Leaving Amelia to spin a yarn untangled by his interruptions, he drifted a good distance roofward, until his love and the circle surrrounding her were a pattern of dots below.

Jagged alone could help him now, thought Jherek. He had returned expecting revelation. If Jagged had been playing a joke on them, then the joke should be made clear; if he manipulated a story for the world's entertainment – then the world, as My Lady Charlotina had said, was entitled to a resolution. The play continued, it seemed, though the author had been unable to write the final scenes. He recalled, with a trace of rancour, that Jagged had encouraged him to begin this melodrama (or was it a farce and he a sad fool in the eyes of all the world? Or tragedy, perhaps?) and Jagged therefore should provide help. Yet if Jagged were vanished forever, what then?

'Why,' said Jherek to himself, 'I shall have to complete the play as best I can. I shall prove that I am no mere actor, following a road laid by another. I shall show I am a playwright, too!'

Li Pao, from the twenty-seventh century, had overheard him. Insistently clad in blue overalls, the ex-member of the People's Governing Committee, touched Jherek to make him turn.

'You consider yourself an actor in a play, Jherek Carnelian?'

'Hello, Li Pao. I spoke confused thoughts aloud, that is all.'

But Li Pao was greedy for a discussion and would not be guided away from the subject. 'I thought you controlled your own fate. This whole love-story business, which so excites the woman, did it not begin as an affectation?'

'I forget.' He spoke the truth. Emotions jostled within him, each in conflict with the other, each eager for a voice. He let none speak.

'Surely,' Li Pao smiled, 'you have not come to believe in your rôle, as the ancient actors were said to do, and think your character's feelings are your own? That would be most droll.' Li Pao leaned against the rail of his drifting gallery. It tilted slightly and began to sink. He brought it back until he was again level with Jherek.

'However, it seems likely,' Jherek told him.

'Beware, Jherek Carnelian. Life becomes serious for you. That would never do. You are a member of a perfectly amoral society: whimsical, all but thoughtless, utterly powerful. Your actions threaten your way of life. Do I see a ramshackle vessel called Self-Destruction heaving its battered bulwarks over the horizon? What's this, Jherek? Is your love genuine, after all?'

'It is, Li Pao. Mock me, if you choose, but I'll not deny there's truth in what you say. You think I conspire against my own peace of mind?'

'You conspire against your entire society. What your fellows could see as your morbid interest in morality actually threatens the status quo – a status quo that has existed for at least a million years, in this form alone! Would you have all your friends as miserably self-conscious as me?' Li Pao was laughing. His lovely yellow face

436

shone like a small sun. 'You know my disapproval of your world and its pleasures.'

'You have bored me often enough ...' Jherek was amiable.

'I admit that I should be sad to see it destroyed. It is reminiscent of that Nursery you discovered, before you disappeared. I should hate to see these children face to face with reality.'

'All this –' the sweep of an arm – 'is not "reality"?'

'Illusion, every scrap. What would happen to you all if your cities were to close down in an instant, if your heat and your light – the simplest of animal needs – were taken from you? What would you do?'

Jherek could see little point in the question. 'Shiver and stumble,' he said, 'until death came. Why do you ask?'

'You are not frightened by the prospect?'

'It is no more real than anything else I experience or expect to experience. I would not say that it is the most agreeable fate. I should try to avoid it, of course. But if it became inevitable, I hope I should perish with good grace.'

Li Pao shook his head, amused. 'You are incorrigible. I hoped to convince you, now that you, of all here, have rediscovered your humanity. Yet perhaps fear is no good thing. Perhaps it is only we, the fearful, who attempt to instil our own sense of urgency into others, who avoid reality, who deceive others into believing that only conflict and unhappiness lead us to the truth.'

'It is a view expressed even at the End of Time, Li Pao.' The Iron Orchid joined them, sporting an oddly wrought garment, stiff and metallic and giving off a glow; it framed her face and her body, which was naked and of a conventional, female shape. 'You hear it from Werther de Goethe. From Lord Shark. And, of course, from Mongrove himself.'

'They are perverse. They adopt such attitudes merely to provide contrast.'

'And you, Li Pao?' asked Jherek. 'Why do you adopt them?'

'They were instilled into me as a child. I am conditioned, if you like, to make the associations you describe.'

'No instincts guide you, then?' asked the Iron Orchid. She laid a languid arm across her son's shoulders. Apparently absent-minded, she stroked his cheek.

'You speak of instincts? You have none, save the seeking of pleasure.' The little Chinese shrugged. 'You have need of none, it could be said.'

'You do not answer her question.' Jherek Carnelian found himself a fraction discomfited by his mother's attentions. His eyes sought for Amelia, but she was not in sight.

'I argue that the question is meaningless, without understanding of its import.'

'Yet ...?' murmured the Iron Orchid, and her finger tickled Jherek's ear.

'My instincts and my reason are at one,' said Li Pao. 'Both tell me that a race which struggles is a race which survives.'

'We struggle mightily against boredom,' she said. 'Are we not inventive enough for you, Li Pao?'

'I am unconvinced. The prisoners in your menageries – the time-travellers and the space-travellers – they condemn you. You exploit them. You exploit the universe. This planet and perhaps the star around which it circles draws its energy from a galaxy which, itself, is dying. It leeches on its fellows. Is that just?'

Jherek had been listening closely. 'My Amelia said something not dissimilar. I could understand her little better, Li Pao. Your world and hers seem similar in some respects and, from what I know of them, menageries are kept.'

'Prisons, you mean? This is mere sophistry, Jherek Carnelian, as you must realize. We have prisons for those who transgress against society. Those who occupy them are there because they gambled – normally they staked

438

their personal freedom against some form of personal gain.'

'The time-travellers often believe they stake their lives, as do the space-travellers. We do not punish them. We look after them.'

'You show them no respect,' said Li Pao.

The Iron Orchid pursed her lips in a kind of smile. 'Some are too puzzled, poor things, to understand their fate, but those who are not soon settle. Are *you* not thoroughly settled, Li Pao? You are rarely missed at parties. I know many other time-travellers and space-travellers who mingle with us, scarcely ever taking up their places in the menageries. Do we use force to keep them there, my dear? Do we deceive them?'

'Sometimes.'

'Only as we deceive one another, for the pleasure of it.'

Once more, Li Pao preferred to change ground. He pointed a chubby finger at Jherek. 'And what of "your Amelia"? Was she pleased to be manipulated in your games? Did she take pleasure in being made a pawn?'

Jherek was surprised. 'Come now, Li Pao. She was never altered physically – and certainly into nothing fishy.'

Li Pao put his finger to a tooth and sighed.

The Iron Orchid pulled Jherek away, still with her arm about his shoulders. 'Come, fruit of my loins. You will excuse us, Li Pao?'

Li Pao's bow was brief.

'I have seen Mrs Underwood,' the Iron Orchid said to Jherek, as they flew higher to where only a few people drifted. 'She looks more beautiful than ever. She was good enough to compliment me on my costume. You recognize the character?'

'I think not.'

'Mrs Underwood did, when I reminded her of the legend. A beautiful little story I had one of the cities tell me. I did not hear all the story, for the city had forgotten much, but enough was gained to make the costume. It is the tale of Old Florence and the Night of Gales and of

the Lady in the Lamp, who tended to the needs of five
hundred soldiers in a single day! Imagine! Five hundred!'
She licked purple lips and grinned. 'Those ancients! I
have it in mind to re-enact the whole story. There are
soldiers here, too, you know. They arrived fairly recently
and are in the menagerie of the Duke of Queens. But
there are only twenty or so.'

'You could make some of your own.'

'I know, flesh of my flesh, but it would not be quite
the same. It is your fault.'

'How, maternal, eternal flower?'

'Great stock is placed on authenticity, these days. Reproductions, where originals can be discovered, are an
absolute anathema. And they become scarcer, they vanish
so quickly.'

'Time-travellers?'

'Naturally. The space-travellers remain. But of what use
are they?'

'Morphail has spoken to you, headiest of blooms?'

'Oh, a little, my seed. But all is Warning. All is Proph-
ecy. He rants. You cannot hear him; not the words. I
suppose Mrs Underwood shall be gone soon. Perhaps then
things will return to a more acceptable pattern.'

'Amelia remains with me,' said Jherek, detecting, he
thought, a wistful note in his mother's voice.

'You keep her company exclusively,' said the Iron
Orchid. 'You are obsessed. Why so?'

'Love,' he told her.

'But, as I understand it, she makes no expression of love.
You scarcely touch!'

'Her customs are not as ours.'

'They are crude, then, her customs!'

'Different.'

'Ah!' His mother was dismissive. 'She inhabits your
whole mind. She affects your taste. Let her steer her own
course, and you yours. Who knows, later those courses
might again cross. I heard something of your adventures.
They have been furious and stunning. Both of you need to

drift, to recuperate, to enjoy lighter company. Is it you, bloom of my womb, keeping her by your side, when she would run free?'

'She is free. She loves me.'

'I say again – there are no signs.'

'I know the signs.'

'You cannot describe them?'

'They lie in gesture, tone of voice, expression in the eyes.'

'Ho, ho! This is too subtle for me, this telepathy! Love is flesh touched against flesh, the whispered word, the fingernail drawn delicately down the spine, the grasped thigh. There is no throb, Jherek, to this love of yours. It is pale – it is mean, eh?'

'No, giver of life. You feign obtuseness, I can tell. But why?'

Her glance was intense, for her, but cryptic.

'Mother? Strongest of orchids?'

But she had twisted a power-ring and was falling like a stone, with no word of reply. He saw her drop and disappear into a large crowd which swarmed at about the halfway point, below.

He found his mother's behaviour peculiar. She exhibited moods he had never encountered before. She appeared to have lost some of her wit and substituted malice (for which she had always had a delicious penchant, but the malice needed the wit to make it entertaining); she appeared to show a dislike for Amelia Underwood which she had not shown earlier. He shook his head and fingered his chin. How was it, that she could not, as she had always done in the past, delight in his delight? With a shrug, he aimed himself for a lower level.

A stranger sped to greet him from a nearby gallery. The stranger was clad in sombrero, fancy vest, chaps, boots and bandoliers, all in blinding red.

'Jherek, my pod, my blood! Why fly so fast?'

Only the eyes revealed identity, and even this confused him for a second before he realized the truth.

'Iron Orchid. How you proliferate!'

'You have met the others, already?'

'One of them. Which is the original?'

'We could all claim that, but there is a programme. At a certain time several vanish, one remains. It matters not which, does it? This method allows one to circulate better.'

'You have not yet met Amelia Underwood?'

'Not since I visited you at your ranch, my love. She is still with you?'

He decided to avoid repetition. 'Your disguise is very striking.'

'I represent a great hero of Mrs Underwood's time. A bandit king – a rogue loved by all – who came to rule a nation and was killed in his prime. It is a cycle of legend with which you must be familiar.'

'The name?'

'Ruby Jack Kennedy. Somewhere ...' she cast about ... 'you should find me as the treacherous woman who, in the end, betrayed him. Her name was Rosie Lee.' The Iron Orchid dropped her voice. 'She fell in love, you know, with an Italian called "The Mouser", because of the clever way he trapped his victims ...'

He found this conversation more palatable and was content to lend an ear, while she continued her delighted rendering of the old legend with its theme of blood, murder and revenge and the curse which fell upon the clan because of the false pride of its patriarch. He scarcely listened until there came a familiar phrase (revealing her taste for it, for she was not to know that one of her alter egos had already made it): 'Great stock is placed on authenticity, these days. Do you not feel, Jherek, that invention is being thwarted by experience? Remember how we used to stop Li Pao from giving us details of the ages we sought to recreate? Were we not wiser to do so?'

She had only half his attention. 'I'll admit that our entertainments lack something in savour for me, since I journeyed through Time. And, of course, I myself could be said to be the cause of the fashion you find distressing.'

She, in her own turn, had given his statements no close attention. She glared discontentedly about the hall. 'I believe they call it "social realism",' she muttered.

'My "London" began a specific trend towards the recreation of observed reality . . .' he continued, but she was waving a hand at him, not because she disagreed, but because he interrupted a monologue.

'It's the spirit, my pup, not the expression. Something has changed. We seem to have lost our lightness of touch. Where is our relish for contrast? Are we all to become antiquarians and nothing more? What is happening to us, Jherek. It is – darkening . . .'

This particular Iron Orchid's mood was very different from that of the other mother, already encountered. If she merely desired an audience while she rambled, he was happy to remain one, though he found her argument narrow.

Perhaps the argument was the only one held by this facsimile, he thought. After all, the great advantage of self-reproduction was that it was possible to hold as many different opinions as one wished, at the same time.

As a boy, Jherek remembered, he had witnessed some dozen Iron Orchids in heated debate. She had enjoyed a phase where she found it easier to divide herself and argue, as it were, face to face, than to attempt to arrange her thoughts in the conventional manner. This facsimile, however, was proving something of a bore (always the danger, if only one opinion were held and rigorously maintained), though it had that quality which saves the bore from snubs or ostracism – and, unfortunately, encourages it to retain the idea that it is an interesting conversationalist – it had a quality of pathos.

Pathos, thought Jherek, was not normally evident in his mother's character. Had he detected it in the facsimile he had previously encountered? Possibly . . .

'I worship surprises, of course,' she continued. 'I embrace variety. It is the pepper of existence, as the ancients said. Therefore, I should be celebrating all these new events. These "time-warps" of Brannart's, these disappearances, all these comings and goings. I wonder why I should feel – what is it? – "disturbed"? – by them. Disturbed? Have you ever known me "disturbed", my egg?'

He murmured: 'Never ...'

'Yes, I am disturbed. But what is the cause? I cannot identify it. Should I blame myself, Jherek?'

'Of course not ...'

'Why? Why? Joy departs; Zest deserts me – and is this replacement called Anxiety? Ha! A disease of time-travellers, of space-voyagers to which we, at the End of Time, have always been immune. Until now, Jherek ...'

'Softest of skins, strongest of wills, I do not quite ...'

'If it has become fashionable to rediscover and become infected by ancient psychoses, then I'll defy fashion. The craze will pass. What can sustain it? This news of Mongrove's? Some machination of Jagged's? Brannart's experiments?'

'Symptoms both, the latter two,' he suggested. 'If the universe is dying ...'

But she had been steering towards a new subject, and again she revealed the obsession of her original. Her tone became lighter, but he was not deceived by it. 'One may also, of course, look to your Mrs Underwood as an instigator ...'

The statement was given significant emphasis. There was the briefest of pauses before the name and after it. She goaded him to defend her or deny her, but he would not be lured.

Blandly he replied. 'Magnificent blossom, Li Pao would have it that the cause of our confusion lay within our own minds. He believes that we hold Truth at bay whilst embracing Illusion. The illusion, he hints, begins to reveal itself for what it is. That is why, says Li Pao, we know concern.'

She had become an implacable facsimile. 'And you, Jherek. Once the gayest of children! The wittiest of men! The most inventive of artists! Joyful boy, it seems to me that you turn dullard. And why? And when? Because Jagged encouraged you to play Lover! To that primitive...'

'Mother! Where is your wit? But to answer, well, I am sure that we shall soon be wed. I detect a difference in her regard for me.'

'A conclusion? I exult!'

Her lack of good humour astonished him. 'Firmest of metals, do not, I pray, make a petitioner of me. Must I placate a virago when once I was assured of the good graces of a friend?'

'I am more than that, I hope, blood of my blood.'

It occurred to him that if he had rediscovered Love, then she had rediscovered Jealousy. Could the one never exist without the presence of the other?

'Mother, I beg you to recollect ...'

A sniff from beneath the sombrero. 'She ascends, I see. She has her own rings, then?'

'Of course.'

'You think it wise, to indulge a savage —?'

Amelia hovered close to, in earshot now. A false smile curved the lips of the shade, this imperfect doppelganger. 'Aha! Mrs Underwood. What beautiful simplicity of taste, the blue and white!'

Amelia Underwood took time to recognize the Iron Orchid. Her nod was courteous, when she did so, but she refused to ignore the challenge. 'Overwhelmed entirely by the brilliant exoticism of your scarlet, Mrs Carnelian.'

A tilt of the brim. 'And what rôle, my dear, do you adopt today?'

'I regret we came merely as ourselves. But did I not see you earlier, in that box-like costume, then later in a yellow gown of some description? So many excellent disguises.'

'I think there is one in yellow, yes. I forget. Sometimes I feel so full of rich ideas, I must indulge more than one. You must think me coarse, dear ancestor.'

'Never that, lushest of orchids.'

Jherek was amused. It was the first time he had heard

445

Mrs Underwood use such language. He began to enjoy the encounter, but the Iron Orchid refused further sport. She leaned forward. Her son was blessed with an ostentatious kiss; Amelia Underwood was pecked. 'Brannart has arrived. I promised him an account of 1896. Surly he might be, but rarely dull. For the moment, then, dear children.'

She began to pirouette downwards. Jherek wondered where she had seen Brannart Morphail, for the hunchbacked, club-footed scientist was not in evidence.

Amelia Underwood settled on his arm again. 'Your mother seems distraught. Not as self-contained as usual.'

'It is because she divides herself too much. The substance of each facsimile is a little thin.' He explained.

'Yet it is clear that she regards me as an enemy.'

'Hardly that. She is not, you see, herself ...'

'I am complimented, Mr Carnelian. It is a pleasure to be taken seriously.'

'But I am concerned for her. She has never been serious in her life before.'

'And you would say that I am to blame.'

'I think she is perturbed, sensing a loss of control in her own destiny, such as we experienced at the Beginning of Time. It is an odd sensation.'

'Familiar enough to me, Mr Carnelian.'

'Perhaps she will come to enjoy it. It is unlike her to resist experience.'

'I should be glad to advise her on how best to cope.'

He sensed irony, at last. He darted a glance of enquiry. Her eyes laughed. He checked a desire to hug her, but he touched her hand, very delicately, and was thrilled.

'You have been entertaining them all,' he said, 'down there?'

'I hope so. Language, thanks to your pills, is no problem. I feel I speak my own. But ideas can sometimes be difficult to communicate. Your assumptions are so foreign.'

'Yet you no longer condemn them.'

'Make no mistake – I continue to disapprove. But nothing is gained by blunt denials and denunciations.'

446

'You triumph, as you know. It is that which the Iron Orchid finds uncomfortable.'

'I appear to be enjoying some small social success. That, in turn, brings embarrassment.'

'Embarrassment?' He bowed to O'Kala Incarnadine, as Queen Britannia, who saluted him.

'They ask me my opinion. Of the authenticity of their costumes.'

'The quality of imagination is poor.'

'Not at all. But none is authentic, though most are fanciful and many beautiful. Your people's knowledge of my age is sketchy, to say the least.'

By degrees, they were drifting towards the bottom of the hall.

'Yet it is the age we know most about,' he said. 'Mainly because I have studied it and set the fashion for it, of course. What is wrong with the costumes?'

'As costumes, nothing. But few come close to the theme of "1896". There is a span, say, of a thousand years between one disguise and another. A man dressed in lilac ducks and wearing a crusty (and I must say delicious looking) pork pie upon his head announced that he was Harald Hardrede.'

'The prime minister, yes?'

'No, Mr Carnelian. The costume was impossible, at any rate.'

'Could he have been this Harald Hardrede, do you think? We have a number of distinguished temporal adventurers in the menageries.'

'It is unlikely.'

'Several million years have passed, after all, and so much now relies on hearsay. We are entirely dependent upon the rotting cities for our information. When the cities were younger, they were more reliable. A million years ago, there would have been far fewer anachronisms at a party of this kind. I have heard of parties given by our ancestors (your descendants, that is) which drew on all the resources of the cities in their prime. This masque must be

447

feeble in comparison. There again, it is pleasant to use one's own imagination to invent an *idea* of the past.'

'I find it wonderful. I do not deny that I am stimulated by it, as well as confused. You must consider me narrow-minded . . .'

'You praise us too much. I am overjoyed that you should find my world at last acceptable, for it leads me to hope that you will soon agree to be my —'

'Ah!' she exclaimed suddenly, and she pointed. 'There is Brannart Morphail. We must give him our news.'

CHAPTER ELEVEN

A FEW QUIET MOMENTS IN THE MENAGERIE

'... And thus it was, mightiest of minds, that we returned,' concluded Jherek, reaching for a partridge tree which drifted past – he picked two fruits, one for himself and one for Mrs Underwood, at his side. 'Is the information enough to recompense for my loss of your machine?'

'Scarcely!' Brannart had added another foot or two to his hump since they had last met. Now it towered, taller than his body, tending to overbalance him. Perhaps to compensate, he had increased the size of his club foot. 'A fabrication. Your tale defies logic. Everywhere you display ignorance of the real nature of Time.'

'I thought we brought fresh knowledge, um, Professor,' said she, half-distracted as she watched a crocodile of some twenty boys and girls, in identical dungarees, float past, following yet another Iron Orchid, a piping harlequin, towards the roof. Argonheart Po, huge and jolly, in a tall white chef's hat (he had come as Captain Cook), rolled in their wake, distributing edible revolvers. 'It would suggest, for instance, that it is now possible for me to return to the nineteenth century, without danger.'

'You still wish to return, Amelia?' What was the lurch

in the region of his navel? He dissipated the remainder of his partridge.

'Should I not?'

'I assumed you were content.'

'I accept the inevitable with good grace, Mr Carnelian – that is not necessarily contentment.'

'I suppose it is not.'

Brannart Morphail snorted. His hump quivered. He began to tilt, righted himself. 'Why have you two set out to destroy the work of centuries? Jagged has always envied me my discoveries. Has he connived with you, Jherek Carnelian, to confuse me?'

'But we do not deny the truth of your discoveries, dear Brannart. We merely reveal that they are partial, that there is not one Law of Time, but many!'

'But you bring no proof.'

'You are blind to it, Brannart. We are the proof. Here we stand, immune to your undeniably exquisite but not infallible Effect. It is a fine Effect, most brilliant of brains, and applies in billions, at least, of cases – but occasionally...'

A large green tear rolled down the scientist's cheek. 'For millennia I have tried to keep the torch of true research alight, single-handed. While the rest of you have devoted your energies to phantasies and whimsicalities, I have toiled. While you have merely exploited the benefits built up for you by our ancestors, I have striven to carry their work further, to understand that greatest mystery of all...'

'But it was already fairly understood, Brannart, most dedicated of investigators, by members of this Guild I mentioned...'

'... but you would thwart me even in that endeavour, with these fanciful tales, these sensational anecdotes, these evidently concocted stories of zones free from the influence of my beloved Effect, of groups of individuals who prove that Time has not a single nature but several ... Ah Jherek! Is such cruelty deserved, by one who has sought to be only a servant of learning, who has never interfered

450

– criticized a little, perhaps, but never interfered – in the pursuits of his fellows?'

'I sought merely to enlighten ...'

My Lady Charlotina went by in a great basket of lavender, only her head visible in the midst of the mound. She called out as she passed. 'Jherek! Amelia! Luck for sale! Luck for sale!' She had made the most, it was plain, of her short spell of temporal tourism. 'Do not bore them too badly, Brannart. I am thinking of withdrawing my patronage.'

Brannart sneered. 'I play such charades no longer!' But it seemed that he did not relish the threat. 'Death looms, yet still you dance, making mock of the few who would help you!'

Mrs Underwood understood. She murmured: 'Wheldrake knew, Professor Morphail, when he wrote in one of his last poems —

> Alone, then, from my basalt height
> I saw the revellers rolling by –
> Their faces all bemasked,
> Their clothing all bejewelled –
> Spread cloaks like paradise's wings in flight,
> Gowns grown so hell-fire bright!
> And purple lips drained purple flasks,
> And gem-hard eyes burned cruel.
> Were these old friends I would have clasped?
> Were these the dreamers of my youth?
> Ah, but old Time conquers more than flesh!
> (He and his escort Death.)
> Old Time lays waste the spirit, too!
> And Time conquers Mind,
> Time conquers Mind –
> Time Rules!'

But Brannart could not respond to her knowing, sympathetic smile. He looked bemused.

'It is very good,' said Jherek dutifully, recalling Captain

451

Bastable's success. 'Ah, yes ... I seem to recall it now.' He raised empty, insincere eyes towards the roof, as he had seen them do. 'You must quote me some of Wheldrake's verses, too, some day.'

The sidelong look she darted him was not unamused.

'Tcha!' said Brannart Morphail. The small floating gallery in which he stood swung wildly as he shifted his footing. He corrected it. 'I'll listen to nonsense no longer. Remember, Jherek Carnelian, let your master Lord Jagged know that I'll not play his games! From henceforth I'll conduct my experiments in secret! Why should I not? Does he reveal his work to me?'

'I am not sure that he is with us at the End of Time. I meant to enquire ...'

'Enough!'

Brannart Morphail wobbled away from them, stamping impatiently on the floor of his platform with his monstrous boot.

The Duke of Queens spied them. 'Look, most honoured of my guests! Wakaka Nakooka has come as a Martian Pastorellan from 1898.'

The tiny black man, himself a time-traveller, turned with a grin and a bow. He was giving birth to fledgeling hawks through his nose. They fluttered towards the floor, now littered with at least two hundred of their brothers and sisters. He swirled his rich cloak and became a larger than average Kopps' Owl. With a flourish, off he flew.

'Always birds,' said the Duke, almost by way of apology. 'And frequently owls. Some people prefer to confine themselves by such means, I know. Is the party entertaining you both?'

'Your hospitality is as handsome as ever, most glamorous of Dukes.' Jherek floated beside his friend, adding softly: 'Though Brannart seems distraught.'

'His theories collapse. He has no other life. I hope you were kind to him, Jherek.'

'He gave us little opportunity,' said Amelia Underwood. Her next remark was a trifle dry. 'Even my quotation from

Wheldrake did not seem to console him.'

'One would have thought that your discovery, Jherek, of the Nursery and the children would have stimulated him. Instead, he ignores Nurse's underground retreat, with all its machinery for the control of Time. He complains of trickery, suggests we invented it in order to deceive him. Have you seen your old school-chums, by the by?'

'A moment ago,' Jherek told him. 'Are they enjoying their new life?'

'I think so. I give them less discipline than did Nurse. And, of course, they begin to grow now that they are free of the influence of the Nursery.'

'You have charge of them?'

The Duke seemed to swell with self-esteem. 'Indeed I have – I am their father. It is a pleasant sensation. They have excellent quarters in the menagerie.'

'You keep them in your menagerie, Duke?' Mrs Underwood was shocked. 'Human children?'

'They have toys there – playgrounds and so on. Where else would I keep them, Mrs Underwood?'

'But they grow. Are not the boys separated from the girls?'

'Should they be?' The Duke of Queens was curious. 'You think they will breed, eh?'

'Oh!' Mrs Underwood turned away.

'Jherek.' The Duke put a large arm around his friend's shoulders. 'While on the subject of menageries, may I take you to mine, for a moment – at least until Mongrove arrives? There are several new acquisitions which I'm sure will delight you.'

Jherek was feeling overwhelmed by the party, for it had been a good while since he had spent so much time in the company of so many. He accepted the Duke's suggestion with relief.

'You will come too, Mrs Underwood?' The Duke asked from politeness, it appeared, not enthusiasm.

'I suppose I should. It is my duty to inspect the conditions under which those poor children are forced to live.'

'The nineteenth century had certain religious attitudes towards children, I understand,' said the Duke conversationally to her as he led them through a door in the floor. 'Were they not worshipped and sacrificed at the same time?'

'You must be thinking of another culture,' she told him. She had recovered something of her composure, but there was still a trace of hostility in her manner towards her flamboyant host.

They entered a classic warren of passages and halls, lined with force-bubbles of varying sizes and shapes containing examples of thousands of different species, from a few viruses and intelligent microcosmic life to the gigantic two-thousand-foot-long Python Person whose spaceship had crashed on Earth some seven hundred years before. The cages were well-kept and reproduced, as exactly as was possible, the environments of those they contained. Mrs Underwood had, herself, experience of such cages. She looked at these with a mixture of disgust and nostalgia.

'It seemed so simple, then,' she murmured, 'when I thought myself merely damned to Hell.'

The Duke of Queens brushed at his fine Dundrearies. 'My homo-sapiens collection is somewhat sparse at present, Mrs Underwood – the children, a few time-travellers, a space-traveller who claims to be descended from common stock (though you would not credit it!). Perhaps you would care to see it after I have shown you my latest non-human acquisitions?'

'I thank you, Duke of Queens, but I have little interest in your zoo. I merely wished to reassure myself that your children are reasonably and properly looked after; I had forgotten, however, the attitudes which predominate in your world. Therefore, I think I shall —'

'Here we are!' Proudly the scarlet duke indicated his new possessions. There were five of them, with globular bodies into which were set a row of circular eyes (like a

454

coronet, around the entire top section of the body) and a small triangular opening, doubtless a mouth. The bodies were supported by four bandy limbs which seemed to serve as legs as well as arms. The colour of these creatures varied from individual to individual, but all were nondescript, with light greys and dark browns proliferating.

'Is it Yusharisp and some friends?' Jherek was delighted to recognize the gloomy little alien who had first brought them the news of the world's doom. 'Why has not Mongrove ...?'

'These are from Yusharisp's planet,' explained the Duke of Queens, 'but they are not him. They are five fresh ones! I believe they came to look for him. In the meantime, of course, he has been home and returned here.'

'He is not aware of the presence of his friends on our planet?'

'Not yet.'

'You'll tell him tonight?'

'I think so. At an appropriate moment.'

'Can they communicate?'

'They refuse to accept translation pills, but they have their own mechanical translators, which are, as you know, rather erratic.'

Jherek pressed his face against the force-bubble. He grinned at the inmates. He smiled. 'Hello! Welcome to the End of Time!'

China-blue eyes glared vacantly back at him.

'I am Jherek Carnelian. A friend of Yusharisp's,' he told them agreeably.

'The leader, the one in the middle, is known as Chief Public Servant Shashurup,' the Duke of Queens informed him.

Jherek made another effort. He waved his fingers. 'Good afternoon, Chief Public Servant Shashurup!'

'Why-ee (skree) do you continue-oo too-too-to tor(roar)-ment us?' asked the CPS. 'All we a(kaaar)sk(skree) is (hiss) that-tat-tat you do-oo-oo us(ushush) the cour(kur-kur-kur)-tesy-ee of com-com-communicat(tate-tate)ing our requests

455

to your representat(tat-tat)ives!' He spoke wearily, without expectation of answer.

'We have no "representatives", save ourselves,' said Jherek. 'Is there anything wrong with your environment? I'm sure that the Duke of Queens would be only too pleased to make any adjustments you saw fit ...'

'Skree-ee-ee,' said CPS Shashurup desperately. 'It is not(ot-ot) in our nat(tate-tate)ure to (skree) make(cake-cake) threat(et-et-et)s, but we must warn you (skree) that unless we are re(skree)lea(skree)sed our peo(pee-pee)ple will be forced to take steps to pro(pro-pro)tect us and secure(ure-ure) our release. You are behaving childishly! It is imposs(oss-oss)ible to believe(eve-eve-eve) that a race grown so old can still(ill-ill) skree-skree yowl eek yaaaarrrrk!'

Only Mrs Underwood showed any genuine interest in the Chief Public Servant's attempts to communicate with them. 'Shouldn't you release them, Duke of Queens?' she asked mildly. 'I thought it was argued that no life-form was kept here against its will.'

'Ah,' said the Duke, dusting at his braid, 'that is so, by and large. But if I let them go immediately, some rival will acquire them. I have not yet had time to display them as mine, you see.'

'Then how long must they remain prisoners?'

'Prisoners? I do not understand you, Mrs Underwood. But they'll stay here until after this party for Mongrove, at least. I'll conceive a special entertainment later, at which I may display them to full advantage.'

'Irr-re-re-sponsible oaf(f-f-f)!' cried CPS Shashurup, who had overheard some of this. 'Your people already suck(uck-uck) the universe dry and we do not complain(ain-ain-ain). Oh, but we shall see (skree-skree-skree) a change when we are free (ee-ee-ee-ee)!'

The Duke of Queens glanced at his index-finger's nail, in which a small, perfect picture formed. It showed him the party above.

'Ah, Mongrove has arrived at last. Shall we return?'

CHAPTER TWELVE

IN WHICH LORD MONGROVE REMINDS US
OF INEVITABLE DOOM

'Truly, my dear friends, I, too, disbelieved, as you do ...'
moaned Mongrove from the centre of the hall, '... but
Yusharisp showed me withered planets, exhausted stars –
matter collapsing, disintegrating, fading to nothing ...
Ah, it is bleak out there. It is bleak beyond imagining.'
His great, heavy head dropped towards his broad, bulky
chest and a monstrous sigh escaped him. Massive hands
clasped themselves together just above his mighty stomach.
'All that is left are ghosts and even the ghosts fade. Civilizations that, until recently, spanned a thousand star-
systems, have become merely a whisper of static from a
detector screen. Gone without trace. Gone without trace.
As *we* shall go, my friends.' Mongrove's gaze upon them
was a mixture of sympathy and accusation. 'But let my
guide Yusharisp, who risked his own life to come to us, to
warn us of our fate, and to whom none but I would listen,
tell you in his own words.'

'Scarce(skree)ly – scarcely any life survives in the universe,' said the globular alien. 'The process of collapse
continues faster than (roar) I predicted. This is partially
(skree) the fault of the people of this planet. Your cities

457

(yelp) draw their energy from the easiest available (skree-skree) source. Now they (roar) suck raw energy from disintegrating novae, from already (skree) dying suns. It is the only reason why (skree) you still (yelp) survive!'

Bishop Castle stood at Jherek's left shoulder. He leaned to murmur: 'In truth I become quickly bored with boredom. The Duke of Queens' efforts to make entertainment from that alien are surely useless, as even he must see now.' But he lifted his head and dutifully cried: 'Hurrah! Hurrah!' and applauded.

Mongrove lifted a hand. 'Yusharisp's point is that we are contributing to the speed with which the universe perishes. If we were to use less energy for pursuits like – like this party – we could slow down the rate of collapse. It is all running out, dear friends!'

My Lady Charlotina said, in a loud whisper, 'I thought Mongrove shunned what he called "materialism". This talk smacks of it, if I'm not mistaken. But, then, I probably am.' She smiled to herself.

But Li Pao said firmly: 'He echoes only what I have been saying for years.'

An Iron Orchid, in red and white checks and a simple red and white domino, linked arms with Bishop Castle. 'The world does grow boring, I agree, most concise of clerics. Everyone seems to be repeating themselves.' She giggled. 'Especially me!'

'It is even in our power, thanks to our cities, to preserve this planet,' continued Mongrove, raising his voice above what had become a general babble of conversation. 'Yusharisp's people sent us their finest minds to help. They should have arrived by now. When they do, however, there is just a chance that there will still be time to save our world.'

'He must be referring to those we have just seen in the Duke's menagerie,' said Mrs Underwood. She gripped Jherek's arm. 'We must tell Lord Mongrove where they are!'

Jherek patted her hand. 'We could not. It would be in

very bad taste to spoil the Duke's surprise.'

'Bad taste?'

'Of course.'

She subsided, frowning.

Milo de Mars went by, leaving a trail of perfectly symmetrical gold six-pointed stars in her wake. 'Forgive me, Lord Mongrove,' she fluted, as the giant petulantly brushed the metallic things aside.

'Oh, what self-satisfied fools you are!' cried Mongrove.

'Should we not be? It seems an excellent thing to be,' said Mistress Christia in surprise. 'Is it not what, we are told, the human race has striven for, all these millions of years? Is it not contentment?' She twirled her Grecian gown. 'Is that not what we have?'

'You have not earned it,' said Li Pao. 'I think that is why you will not make efforts to protect it.'

Amelia smiled approval, but Jherek was puzzled. 'What does he mean?'

'He speaks of the practical basis of the morality you were so anxious to understand, Mr Carnelian.'

Jherek brightened, now that he realized they touchd upon a subject of interest. 'Indeed? And what is this practical basis?'

'In essence – that nothing is worth possessing unless it has been worked for.'

He said, with a certain slyness, 'I have worked hard to possess you, dearest Amelia.'

Again amusement threatened to get the better of her. The struggle showed on her face for only a moment before she was once more composed. 'Why, Mr Carnelian, will you always insist on confusing the issue with the introduction of personal matters?'

'Are such matters less important?'

'They have their place. Our conversation, I thought was a trifle more abstract. We discussed morality and its usefulness in life. It was a subject dear to my father's heart and the substance of many a sermon.'

'Yet your civilization, if you'll forgive me saying so, did

not survive for any great length of time. A couple of hundred years saw its complete destruction.'

She was nonplussed, but soon found an answer: 'It is not to do with the survival of civilizations, as such, but with personal satisfaction. If one leads a moral life, a useful life, one is happier.'

He scratched his head beneath the tweed cap. 'It seems to me that almost everyone at the End of Time is happier, however, than were those I encountered in your Dawn Age era. And morality is a mystery to us, as you know.'

'It is a mindless happiness – how shall it survive the disaster Lord Mongrove warns us about?'

'Disaster, surely, is only that if one believes it to be important. How many here, would you say, believe in Mongrove's doom?'

'But they will.'

'Are you certain?'

She cast an eye about her. She could not say that she was certain.

'But are you not afraid, even a little?' she asked him.

'Afraid? Well, I would regret the passing of all this variety, this wit. But it has existed. Doubtless something like it will exist again.'

She laughed and she took his arm. 'If I did not know you better, Mr Carnelian, I should mistake you for the wisest and most profound of philosophers.'

'You flatter me, Amelia.'

Mongrove's voice continued to boom from the babble, but the words were indistinct. 'If you will not save yourselves, think of the knowledge you could save – the inherited knowledge of a million generations!'

An Iron Orchid, in green velvet and brocade, glided by beside Brannart Morphail, who was discoursing along lines very similar to Mongrove's, though it was evident he did not listen to the gloomy giant. With some alarm, Jherek heard her say: 'Of course, you are completely right, Brannart. As a matter of fact, I have it in mind to take a trip through time myself. I know you would disapprove, but it is possible that I could be of use to you . . .'

Jherek heard no more of his mother's remarks. He shrugged, dismissing them as the expression of a passing foible.

Sweet Orb Mace was making love to Mistress Christia, the Everlasting Concubine, in a most interesting fashion. Their intertwined bodies drifted amongst the other guests. Elsewhere, Orlando Chombi, Kimick Rentbrain and O'Kala Incarnadine linked hands in a complicated aerial dance, while the recently re-styled Countess of Monte Carlo extended her substance until she was thirty feet tall and all but invisible; this, it seemed, for the entertainment of the Nursery children, who gathered around her and laughed with delight.

'We have a duty to our ancestors!' groaned Mongrove, now, for the moment, out of sight. Jherek thought he was buried somewhere in the sudden avalanche of blue and green roses tipped from Doctor Volospion's Pegasus-drawn platform. 'And to those (skree) who follow us . . .' added a piping but somewhat muffled voice.

Jherek sighed. 'If only Jagged would reveal himself, Amelia! Then, I am sure, any confusion would be at an end.'

'He might be dead,' she said. 'You feared as much.'

'It would be a difficult loss to bear. He was my very best friend. I have never known anyone, before, who could not be resurrected.'

'Mongrove's point – that no one shall be resurrected after the apocalypse.'

'I agree the prospect is more attractive, for then none should feel a loss.' They drifted towards the floor, still littered with the feebly fluttering fledgeling hawks. Many had already expired, for Wakaka Nakooka had forgotten to feed them. Absently, Jherek dissipated them, so that they might descend and stand there, looking up at a party grown less sedate than when first they had arrived.

'I thought you were of the opinion that we should live forever, Amelia?' he said, still peering upwards.

'It is my *belief*, not my opinion.'

He failed to distinguish the difference.

'In the Life Beyond,' she said. She tried to speak with conviction, but her voice faltered, adding to herself: 'Well, yes, perhaps there is still a Life Beyond, hard though it is to imagine. Ah, it is so difficult to retain one's ordinary faith ...'

'It is the end of everything!' continued Mongrove, from somewhere within the mountain of roses. 'You are lost! Lost! You will not listen! You will not understand! Beware! Oh, beware!'

'Mr Carnelian, we should try to make them listen to Lord Mongrove, surely!'

Jherek shook his head. 'He has nothing very interesting to say, Amelia. Has he not said it before? Is not Yusharisp's information identical to that which he first brought, during the Duke's African party. It means little ...'

'It means much to me.'

'How so?'

'It strikes a chord. Lord Mongrove is like the prophet to whom none would listen. In the end his words were vindicated. The Bible is full of such stories.'

'Then surely, we have no need for more?'

'You are deliberately obtuse!'

'I assure you that I am not.'

'Then help Mongrove.'

'His temperament and mine are too dissimilar. Brannart will comfort him, and Werther de Goethe, too. And Li Pao. He has many friends, many who will listen. They will gather together and agree that all but themselves are fools, that only they have the truth, the right to control events and so on. It will cheer them up and they'll doubtless do little to spoil the pleasure of anyone else. For all we know, their antics will prove entertaining.'

'Is "entertainment" your only criterion?'

'Amelia, if it pleases you, I'll go this moment to Mongrove and groan in tune with him. But my heart will not be in it, love of my life, joy of my existence.'

She sighed. 'I would not have you live a lie, Mr Carnelian. To encourage you towards hypocrisy would be a sin, I know.'

'You have become somewhat sober again, dearest Amelia.'

'I apologize. Evidently, there is nothing to be done, in reality. You think Mongrove postures?'

'As do we all, according to his temperament. It is not that he is insincere, it is merely that he chooses one particular rôle, though he knows many other opinions are as interesting and as valuable as his own.'

'A few short years are left ...' came Mongrove's boom, more distant now.

'He does not wholly believe in what he says?'

'Yes and no. He chooses wholly to believe. It is a conscious decision. Tomorrow, he could make an entirely different decision, if he became bored with this rôle (and I suspect he *will* become bored, as he realizes how much he bores others).'

'But Yusharisp is sincere.'

'So he is, poor thing.'

'Then there is no hope for the world.'

'Yusharisp believes that.'

'You do not?'

'I believe everything and nothing.'

'I never quite understood before ... is that the philosophy of the End of Time?'

'I suppose it is.' He looked about him. 'I do not think we shall see Lord Jagged here, after all. Lord Jagged could explain these things to you, for he enjoys discussing abstract matters. I have never much had the penchant. I have always preferred to make things rather than to talk. I am a man of action, you see. Doubtless it is something to do with being the product of natural childbirth.'

Her eyes, when next she looked at him, were full of warmth.

CHAPTER THIRTEEN

THE HONOUR OF AN UNDERWOOD

'I am still uncertain. Perhaps if we began again?'

Amiably, Jherek disintegrated the west wing.

They were rebuilding his ranch. The Bromley-Gothic redbrick villa had vanished. In its place stood something altogether larger, considerably lighter, having more in common with the true Gothic of medieval France and Belgium, with fluted towers and delicately fashioned windows.

'It is all, I think, a trifle too magnificent,' she said. She fingered her fine chin. 'And yet, it would only seem grandiose in Bromley, as it were. Here, it is almost simple.'

'If you will try your own amethyst power-ring ...' he murmured.

'I have still to trust these things ...' But she twisted and thought at the same time.

A fairy-tale tower, the ideal of her girlhood, stood there. She could not bring herself to disseminate it.

He was delighted, admiring its slender hundred-and twenty-feet, topped by twin turrets with red conical roofs. It glittered. It was white. There were tiny windows.

'Such an elegant example of typical Dawn Age architecture!' he complimented her.

'You do not find it too fanciful?' She was shy of her achievement, but pleased.

'A model of utility!'

'Scarcely that ...' She blushed. Her own imagination, made concrete, astonished her.

'More! You must make more!'

The ring was turned again and another tower sprang up, connected to its fellow by a little marble bridge. With some hesitation she disseminated the original building he had made at her request, replacing it with a main hall and living apartments above. She gave her attention to the landscape around. A moat appeared, fed by a sparkling river. Formal gardens, geometric, filled with her favourite flowers, stretched into the distance, giving place to rose bowers and undulating lawns, a lake, with cypresses and poplars and willows. The sky was changed to a pale blue and the small clouds in it were never whiter; then she added subtle colours, pinks and yellows, as of the beginnings of a sunset. All was as she had once dreamed of, not as a respectable Bromley housewife, but as a little girl, who had read fairy stories with a sense that she consulted forbidden texts. Her face shone as she contemplated her handiwork. A new innocence bloomed there. Jherek watched, and revelled in her pleasure.

'Oh, I should not ...'

A unicorn now grazed upon the lawn. It looked up, its eyes mild and intelligent. Its golden horn caught the sunlight.

'It is everything I was told could never be. My mother admonished me, I remember, for entertaining silly fancies. She said no good would come of them.'

'And so you still think, do you not?'

She glanced his way. 'So I *should* think, I suppose.'

He said nothing.

'My mother argued that little girls who believed in fairy tales grew up to be shallow, vain and, ultimately, disappointed, Mr Carnelian. The world, I was told, was harsh and terrible and we were put into it in order that we should be tested for our worthiness to dwell in Heaven.'

'It is a reasonable belief. Though unrewarding, I should have thought, in the long run. Limiting, at least.'

'Limitations were regarded as being good for one. I have expressed that opinion myself.'

'So you have.'

'Yet there are no more cruelties here than there were in my world.'

'Cruelties?'

'Your menageries.'

'Of course.'

'But you do not, I now understand, realize that you are cruel. You are not hypocrites in that particular way.'

He was euphoric. He was enjoying listening to her voice as he might enjoy the peaceful buzz of an insect. He spoke only to encourage her to continue.

'We keep more prisoners in my society, when you think of it,' she said. 'How many wives are prisoners of their homes, their husbands?' She paused. 'I should not dare think such radical ideas at home, much less utter them!'

'Why not?'

'Because I would offend others. Disturb my friends. There are social checks to one's behaviour, far greater than any legal or moral ones. Have you learned that, yet, from my world, Mr Carnelian?'

'I have learned something, but not a great deal. You must continue to teach me.'

'I saw the prisons, when you were incarcerated. How many prisoners are there through no fault of their own? Victims of poverty. And poverty enslaves so many more millions than you could ever contain in your menageries. Oh, I know. I know. You could have argued that, and I should not have been able to deny it.'

'Ah?'

'You are kind to humour me, Mr Carnelian.' Her voice grew vague as she looked again upon her first creation. 'Oh, it is so beautiful!'

He came to stand beside her and when he put an arm about her shoulder, she did not resist.

Some time went by. She furnished their palace with simple, comfortable furniture, refusing to clutter the rooms. She made tapestries and brocades for floors and walls. She re-introduced a strict pattern of day and night. She created two large, long-haired black and white cats, and the parklands around the palace became populated with deer, as well as unicorns. She longed for books, but he could find her none, so in the end she began to write one for herself and found this almost as satisfactory as reading. Yet, still, he must court her. Still she refused the fullest expression of her affections. When he proposed marriage, as he continued to do, frequently, she would reply that she had given an oath in a ceremony to remain loyal to Mr Underwood until death should part them.

He returned, time after time, to the reasonable logic that indeed Mr Underwood was dead, had been dead for many millennia, that she was free. He began to suspect that she did not care a fig for her vows to Mr Underwood, that she played a game with him, or, failing that, waited for him to take some action. But as to what the action should be, she gave him no clue.

This idyll, pleasurable though it was, was marred not only by his frustration, but also by his concerns for his friend, Lord Jagged of Canaria. He had begun to realize to what extent he had relied on Jagged to guide him in his actions, to explain the world to him, to help him shape his own destiny. His friend's humour, his advice, indeed, his very wisdom, were much missed. Every morning, upon awaking, he hoped to see Lord Jagged's air-car upon the horizon, and every morning he was disappointed.

One morning, however, as he lounged alone upon a balcony, while Mrs Underwood worked at her book, he saw a visitor arrive, in some kind of Egyptianate vessel of ebony and gold, and it was Bishop Castle, his high crown nodding on his handsome head, a tall staff in his left hand, his three golden orbs bobbing at his belt, stepping gracefully from air-car to balcony and kissing him lightly upon the forehead, complimenting him on the white linen suit made for him by Mrs Underwood.

'Things have settled, since the Duke's party,' the bishop informed him. 'We return to our old lives with some relief. A great disappointment, Mongrove, didn't you think?'

'The Duke of Queens sets great store by his entertainment value. I cannot think why.'

'He is out of touch with everyone else's taste. Scarcely a recommendation in one who desires to be the most popular of hosts.'

'It is not,' Jherek added, 'as if he were himself interested in this alien's prophecies. He probably hoped that Mongrove would have had some adventures on his trip through the universe – something with a reasonable amount of sensation in it. Yet Mongrove may be relied upon to ruin even the best anecdote.'

'It is why we love him.'

'To be sure.'

Mrs Underwood, in rose-pink and yellow, entered the room behind the balcony. She extended a hand. 'Dear Bishop Castle. How pleasant to see you. You will stay for lunch?'

'If I do not inconvenience you, Mrs Underwood.' It was plain that he had done much research.

'Of course not.'

'And what of my mother, the Iron Orchid?' asked Jherek. 'Have you seen her of late?'

Bishop Castle scratched his nose with his crook. 'You had not heard, then? She seeks to rival you, Jherek, I am sure. She somehow inveigled Brannart Morphail into allowing her the use of one of his precious time-craft. She has gone!'

'Through time?'

468

'No less. She told Brannart that she would return with proof of his theories, evidence that you manufactured the tales you told him! I am surprised no one has yet informed you.' Bishop Castle laughed. 'She is so original, your beautiful mother!'

'But she may be killed,' said Mrs Underwood. 'Is she aware of the risks?'

'Fully, I gather.'

'Oh!' cried Jherek. 'Mother!' He put his hand to his lips; he bit the lower one. 'It is you, Amelia, she seeks to rival. She thinks she is outdone by you!'

'She spoke of a time for her return?' Mrs Underwood asked Bishop Castle.

'Not really. Brannart might know. He controls the experiment.'

'Controls! Ha!' Jherek put his head in his hands.

'We may only pray – excuse me – hope – that she returns safely,' said Mrs Underwood.

'Time cannot defeat the Iron Orchid!' Bishop Castle laughed. 'You are too gloomy. She will be back soon – doubtless with news of exploits to rival yours – which is what she hopes for, I am sure.'

'It was luck, only, that saved us both from death,' Mrs Underwood told him.

'Then the same luck will come to her aid.'

'You are probably right,' said Jherek. He was despondent. First his best friend gone, and now his mother. He looked at Mrs Underwood, as if she would once again vanish before his eyes, as she had done before, when he had first tried to kiss her, so long ago.

Mrs Underwood spoke rather more cheerfully, in Jherek's view, than the situation demanded. 'Your mother is not one to perish, Mr Carnelian. For all you know, it was merely a facsimile that was sent through time. The original could still be here.'

'I am not sure that is possible,' he said. 'There is something to do with the life essence. I have never properly understood the theory concerning transmigration. But I do not think you can send a doppelganger through time, not without accompanying it.'

'She'll be back,' said Bishop Castle with a smile.

But Jherek, worrying for Lord Jagged, becoming convinced that he had perished, lapsed into silence and was a poor host during lunch.

Several more days passed, without incident, with the occasional visit from My Lady Charlotina or the Duke of Queens or Bishop Castle, again. The conversation turned often to speculation as to the fate of the Iron Orchid, as was inevitable, but if Brannart Morphail had news of her he had passed none of it on, even to My Lady Charlotina who still chose to play patron to him and give him his laboratories in her own vast domicile at Below-the-Lake. Neither would Brannart tell anyone the Iron Orchid's original destination.

In the meanwhile, Jherek continued to pay court to Amelia Underwood. He learned the poems of Wheldrake (or at least, those she could remember) from her and found that they could be interpreted in reference to their own situation – 'So close these lovers were, yet was their union sundered by the world' – 'Cruel Fortune did dictate that they/Should ever singly pass that way', and so on – until she professed a lack of interest in he who had been her favourite poet. But it seemed to Jherek Carnelian that Amelia Underwood began to warm to him a little more. The occasional sisterly kiss became more frequent, the pressure of a hand, the quality of a smile, all spoke of a thaw in her resolve. He took heart. Indeed, so settled had become their domestic routine, that it was almost as if they were married. He hoped that she might slip, almost accidentally, into consummation, given time.

Life flowed smooth and, save for the nagging fear at the back of his mind that his mother and Lord Jagged might never return, he experienced a tranquillity he had not enjoyed since he and Mrs Underwood had first shared a house together; and he refused to remember that whenever he had come to accept such peace, it had always been interrupted by some new drama. But, as the uneventful days continued, his sense of inevitable expectation increased, until he began to wish that whatever it was that was going to happen would happen as soon as possible. He even identified the source of the next blow – it would be delivered by the Iron Orchid, returning with sensational information, or else by Jagged, to tell them that they must go back to the Palaeozoic to complete some overlooked task.

The blow did come. It came one morning, about three weeks after they had settled in their new home. It came as a loud and repetitive knocking on the main door. Jherek stumbled from his bed and went to stand on his balcony, leaning over to see who was disturbing them in this peculiar manner (no one he knew ever used that door). On the bijou drawbridge was grouped a party of men all of whom were familiar. The person knocking on the main door was Inspector Springer, wearing a new suit of clothes and a new bowler hat indistinguishable from his previous ones; gathered around him was a party of burly police officers, some ten or twelve; behind the police officers, looking self-important but a little wild-eyed, stood none other than Mr Harold Underwood, his pince-nez on his nose, his hay-coloured hair neatly parted in the middle, wearing a suit of good, dark worsted, an extremely stiff, white collar and cuffs, a tightly knotted tie and black, polished boots. In his hand he held a hat, similar to Inspector Springer's. Behind this party, a short distance away, in the ornamental garden, there buzzed a huge contraption consisting of a number of inter-connected wheels, ratchets, crystalline rods and what seemed to be padded benches – an open, box-like structure, but bearing a close similarity to the machine Jherek had first seen in the Palaeozoic. At the controls sat the bearded man in plus-fours and Norfolk jacket who had given them his hamper. He was the first to see Jherek. He waved a greeting.

From a nearby balcony there came a stifled shriek: 'Harold!'

Mr Underwood looked up and fixed a cold eye upon his wife, in negligee and slippers of a sort not normally associated with a Bromley housewife.

'Ha!' he said, his worst fears confirmed. Now he saw Jherek, peering down at him. 'Ha!'

'Why are you here?' croaked Jherek, before he realized he would not be understood.

Inspector Springer began to clear his throat, but Harold Underwood spoke first.

'Igrie gazer,' he seemed to say. 'Rijika batterob honour!'

'We had better let them in, Mr Carnelian,' said Mrs Underwood in a faint voice.

CHAPTER FOURTEEN

VARIOUS ALARUMS, A GOOD DEAL
OF CONFUSION, A HASTY EXCURSION

'I 'ave, sir,' said Inspector Springer with heavy satisfaction, 'been invested with Special Powers. The 'Ome Secretary 'imself 'as ordered me to look into this case.'

'The new machine – my, um, Chronomnibus – was requisitioned,' said the time-traveller apologetically from the background. 'As a patriot, though strictly speaking not from this universe ...'

'Under conditions of utmost secrecy,' continued the Inspector, 'we embarked upon our Mission ...'

Jherek and Mrs Underwood stood on their threshold and contemplated their visitors.

'Which is?' Mrs Underwood was frowning pensively at her husband.

'To place the ringleaders of this plot under arrest and return forthwith to our own century so that they – that's you, of course, among 'em – may be questioned as to their motives and intentions.' Inspector Springer was evidently quoting specifically from his orders.

'And Mr Underwood?' Jherek asked politely. 'Why is he here?'

''E's one o' the few 'oo can identify the people we're

after. Anyway, 'e volunteered.'

She said, bemusedly: 'Have you come to take me back, Harold?'

'Ha!' said her husband.

Sergeant Sherwood, sweating and, it seemed, only barely in control of himself, fingering his tight, dark blue collar, emerged from the ranks of his constables (who, like him, seemed to be suffering from shock) and, saluting, stood beside his leader.

'Shall we place these two under arrest, sir?'

Inspector Springer licked his lips contemplatively. ''Ang on a mo, sergeant, before putting 'em in the van.' He reached into his jacket pocket and produced a document, turning to Jherek. 'Are you the owner of these premises?'

'Not exactly,' said Jherek, wondering if the translation pills he and Amelia had taken were doing their job properly. 'That is to say, if you could explain the meaning of the term, perhaps I could ...'

'Are you or are you not the owner ...'

'Do you mean did I create this house?'

'If you built it, too, fair enough. All I want to know ...'

'Mrs Underwood created it, didn't you, Amelia?'

'Ha!' said Mr Underwood, as if his worst suspicions were confirmed. He glared coldly at the fairy-tale palace.

'This lady built it?' Inspector Springer became pettish. 'Now, listen 'ere ...'

'I gather you are unfamiliar with the methods of building houses at the End of Time, Inspector,' said Mrs Underwood, making some effort to save the situation. 'One has power-rings. They enable one —'

Inspector Springer raised a stern hand. 'Let me put it another way. I 'ave 'ere a warrant to search your premises or, indeed, any premises I might regard as 'avin' upon them evidence in this matter, or 'arbourin' suspected criminals. So, if you will kindly allow me and my men to pass ...'

'Certainly.' Jherek and Amelia stepped aside as Inspector Springer led his men into the hall. Harold Underwood hesitated a moment, but at last crossed the threshold, as if into the netherworld, while the time-traveller hung back, his cap in his hands, murmuring disconnected phrases. 'Awfully embarrassing ... had no idea ... a bit of a joke, really ... regret the inconvenience ... Home Secretary assured me ... can see no reason for intrusion ... would never have agreed ...' But at Jherek's welcoming gesture, he joined the others. 'Delightful house ... very similar to those structures one finds in the, um ... fifty-eighth century, is it? ... Glad to find you arrived back safely ... am still a trifle at sea, myself ...'

'I have never seen such a large time-machine,' said Jherek, hoping to put him at ease.

'Have you not?' The time-traveller beamed. 'It is unusual, isn't it? Of course, the commercial possibilities have not escaped me, though since the Government took an interest, everything has been shrouded in secrecy, as you can imagine. This was my first opportunity to test it under proper conditions.'

'It would be best, sir, I think,' cautioned Inspector Springer, 'to say no more to these people. They are, after all, suspected alien agents.'

'Oh, but we have met before. I had no idea, when I agreed to help, that these were the people you meant. Believe me, Inspector, they are almost undoubtedly innocent of any crime.'

'That's for me to decide, sir,' reproved the policeman. 'The evidence I was able to place before the 'Ome Secretary upon my return was sufficient to convince 'im of a plot against the Crown.'

'He seemed somewhat bewildered by the whole affair. His questions to me were not exactly explicit ...'

'Oh, it's *bewildering*, right enough. Cases of this kind often are. But I'll get to the bottom of it, given time.' Inspector Springer fingered his watch-chain. 'That's why there is a police force, sir. To solve bewildering cases.'

'Are you certain that you are within your jurisdiction,

Inspector ...' began Mrs Underwood.

'I 'ave ascertained from the gentleman 'ere,' Inspector Springer indicated the time-traveller, 'that we are still on English soil. Therefore ...'

'Is it really?' cried Jherek. 'How wonderful!'

'Thought you'd get away with it, eh?' murmured Sergeant Sherwood, eyeing him maliciously. 'Made a bit of a mistake, didn't you, my lad?'

''Ow many others staying 'ere?' Inspector Springer enquired as he and his men tramped into the main hall. He looked with disgust upon the baskets of flowers which hung everywhere, upon the tapestries and the carpets and the furniture, which was of the most decadent sort of design.

'Only ourselves.' Mrs Underwood glanced away from the grim eye of her husband.

'Ha!' said Mr Underwood.

'We have separate apartments,' she explained to the inspector, upon whose ruddy features there had spread the suggestion of a leer.

'Well, sir,' said Sergeant Sherwood, 'shall we take this pair back first?'

'To the nineteenth century?' Jherek asked.

'That is what he means,' the time-traveller replied on the sergeant's behalf.

'This would be your opportunity, Amelia.' Jherek's voice was small. 'You said that you wished, still, to return ...'

'It is true ...' she began.

'Then ...?'

'The circumstances ...'

'You two 'ad better stay 'ere,' Inspector Springer was telling two of the constables, 'to keep an eye on 'em. We'll search the premises.' He led his men off towards a staircase. Jherek and Amelia sat down on a padded bench.

'Would you care for some tea?' Amelia asked her husband, the time-traveller and the two constables.

'Well ...' said one of the constables.

'I think that'd be all right, ma'am,' said the other.

Jherek was eager to oblige. He turned a power-ring and produced a silver tea-pot, six china cups and saucers, a milk-jug and a hot-water jug, a silver tea-strainer, six silver spoons and a primus stove.

'Sugar, I think,' she murmured, 'but not the stove.'

He corrected his error.

The two police constables sat down together quite suddenly, goggling at the tea. Mr Underwood remained standing, but seemed rather more stiff than he had been. He muttered to himself. Only the time-traveller reacted in a normal fashion.

Mrs Underwood seemed to be suppressing amusement as she poured the tea and handed out the cups. The constables accepted the tea, but only one of them drank any. The other merely said, 'Gord!' and put his cup on the table, while his companion grinned weakly and said: 'Very good, very good,' over and over again.

From above there came a sudden loud cracking sound and a yell. Puzzled, Jherek and Amelia looked up.

'I do hope they are not damaging ...' began the time-traveller.

There was a thunder of boots and Inspector Springer, Sergeant Sherwood and their men came tumbling, breathless, back into the hall.

'They're attacking!' cried Sergeant Sherwood to the other two policemen.

''Oo?'

'The enemy, of course!' Inspector Springer answered, running to peer cautiously out of the window. 'They must know we've occupied these premises. They're a cunning lot, I'll grant you that.'

'What happened up there, Inspector?' asked Jherek, carrying forward a cup of tea for his guest.

'Something took the top off the tower, that's all!' Automatically the inspector accepted the tea. 'Clean off. Some kind of 'igh-powered naval gun, I'd say. 'Ave you got any sea near 'ere?'

'None, I fear. I wonder who could have done that.' Jherek looked enquiringly at Amelia. She shrugged.

'The Wrath of God!' announced Mr Underwood helpfully, but nobody took much notice of his suggestion.

'I remember once, some flying machine of the Duke of Queens' crashed into my ranch,' Jherek said. 'Did you notice a flying machine, Inspector?'

Inspector Springer continued to peer through the window. 'It was like a bolt from the blue,' he said.

'One minute the roof was there,' added Sergeant Sherwood, 'the next it was gone. There was this explosion – then – bang! – gone. It got very 'ot for a second, too.'

'Sounds like some sort of ray,' said the time-traveller, helping himself to another cup of tea.

Inspector Springer proved himself a reader of the popular weeklies by the swiftness with which he accepted the notion. 'You mean a Death Ray?'

'If you like.'

Inspector Springer fingered his moustache. 'We were fools not to come armed,' he reflected.

'Ah!' Jherek remembered his first encounter with the brigand-musicians in the forest. 'That's probably the Lat returned. They had weapons. They demonstrated one. Very powerful they were, too.'

'Those Latvians. I might 'ave guessed!' Inspector Springer crouched lower. ''Ave you any means of telling 'em you're our prisoners?'

'None at all, I fear. I could go and find them, but they could be hundreds of miles away.'

''undreds? Oh, Lor!' exclaimed Sergeant Sherwood. He looked at the ceiling, as if he expected it to fall in on him. 'You're right, Inspector. We should've put in for some pistols.'

'The Day of Doom is here!' intoned Harold Underwood, raising a finger.

'We must introduce him to Lord Mongrove,' Jherek said, inspired. 'They would get on very well, don't you think, Amelia?'

But she did not reply. She was staring with a mixture of sympathy and resignation at her poor, mad husband. 'I am to blame,' she said. 'It is all my doing. Oh, Harold, Harold.'

There came another loud report. Cracks began to appear in the walls and ceiling. Jherek turned a power-ring and re-formed the palace. 'I think you'll find the roof's back on, Inspector, should you wish to continue your tour.'

'I'll receive a medal for this, if I ever get back,' said Inspector Springer to himself. He sighed.

'I'd suggest, sir,' said his sergeant, 'that we make the most of what we've got and return with these two.'

'You're probably right. We'll do a dash for it. Better put the gyves on 'em, eh?'

Two constables produced their handcuffs and advanced towards Jherek and Amelia.

At that moment an apparition appeared at the window and drifted through. It was Bishop Castle, completely out of breath, looking extremely excited, his huge mitre askew. 'Oh, the adventures, my dears! The Lat have returned and are laying waste to *everything*! Murder, pillage, rape! It's marvellous! Ah, you have company ...'

'I believe you've met most of them,' Jherek said. 'This is Inspector Springer, Sergeant Sherwood ...'

Bishop Castle subsided slowly to the floor, nodding and smiling. Blinking, the constables backed away.

'They have taken *prisoners*, too. Just as they took us prisoner, that time. Ah, boredom is banished, at last! And there has been a *battle* – the Duke of Queens magnificent, in charge of our aerial fleet (it did not last more than a few seconds, unfortunately, but it did look pretty), and My Lady Charlotina as an amazon, in a *chariot*. Amusement returns to our dull world! Dozens, at least, are *dead*!' He waved his crook apologetically at the company. 'You must forgive the interruption. I am so sorry. I forget my manners.'

'I know you,' said Inspector Springer significantly. 'I

arrested you before, at the Café Royal.'

'So pleased to see you again, Inspector.' It was plain that Bishop Castle had not understood a word that Inspector Springer had said. He popped a translation pill into his mouth. 'You decided to continue your party, then, at the End of Time?'

'End of Time?' said Harold Underwood, showing fresh interest. 'Armageddon?'

Amelia Underwood went to him. She tried to sooth him. He shook her off.

'Ha!' he said.

'Harold. You're being childish.'

'Ha!'

Despondently, she remained where she was, staring at him.

'You should see the *destruction*,' continued Bishop Castle. He laughed. 'Nothing at all is left of Below-the-Lake, unless Brannart's laboratories are still there. But the menagerie is completely gone, and all My Lady Charlotina's apartments – the lake itself – all gone! It'll take her hours to replace them.' He tugged at Jherek's sleeve. 'You must return with me and see the spectacle, Jherek. That's why I came away, to make sure you did not miss it all.'

'Your friends aren't going anywhere, sir. And neither, I might add, are you.' Inspector Springer signalled his constables forward.

'How wonderful! You'd take us prisoners, too! Have you any weapons, like the Lats? You must produce something, Inspector, to rival their effects, unless you wish to be absolutely outshone!'

'I thought these Latvians were on your side,' said Sergeant Sherwood.

'Indeed, no! What would be the fun of that?'

'You say they're destroying everything. Rape, pillage, murder?'

'Exactly.'

'Well, I never . . .' Inspector Springer scratched his head.

'So you're merely the foils of these people, instead o' the other way about?'

'I think there's a misunderstanding, Inspector,' said Mrs Underwood. 'You see . . .'

'Misunderstanding!' Suddenly Harold Underwood lurched towards her. 'Jezebel!'

'Harold!'

'Ha!'

There came another boom, louder than the previous ones, and the ceiling vanished to reveal the sky.

'It can only be the Lat,' said Bishop Castle, with the air of an expert. 'You really must come with me. Jherek and Amelia, unless you want to be destroyed before you have enjoyed any of the fun.' He began to lead them towards his air-car at the window. 'There'll be nothing left of our world, at this rate!'

'Do they really mean to destroy you all?' asked the time-traveller, as they went by.

'I gather not. They originally came for prisoners. Mistress Christia, of course,' this to Jherek, 'is now a captive. I think it's their habit to go about the galaxy killing the males and abducting the females.'

'You'll let them?' Mrs Underwood enquired.

'What do you mean?'

'You won't stop this?'

'Oh, eventually, I suppose we'll have to. Mistress Christia wouldn't be happy in space. Particularly if it has become as bleak as Mongrove reports.'

'What do you say, Amelia? Shall we go and watch? Join in?' Jherek wanted to know.

'Of course not.'

He suppressed his disappointment.

'Perhaps you wish *me* to be abducted by those creatures?' she said.

'Indeed, no!'

'Perhaps it would be better to return in my Chronomnibus,' suggested the time-traveller, 'at least until —'

'Amelia?'

She shook her head. 'The circumstances are too shameful for me. Respectable society would be closed to me now.'

'Then you will stay, dearest Amelia?'

'Mr Carnelian, this is no time to continue with your pesterings. I will accept that I am an outcast, but I still have certain standards of behaviour. Besides, I am concerned for Harold. He is not himself. And for that, we are to blame. Well, perhaps not you, really – but I must accept a large share of guilt. I should have been firmer. I should not have admitted my love –' and she burst into tears.

'You do admit it, then, Amelia!'

'You are heartless, Mr Carnelian,' she sobbed, 'and scarcely tactful ...'

'Ha!' said Harold Underwood. 'It is just as well that I have already begun divorce proceedings ...'

'Excellent!' cried Jherek.

Another boom.

'My machine!' exclaimed the time-traveller, and ran outside.

'Take cover, men.' Inspector Springer called. They all lay down.

Bishop Castle was already in his air-car, surrounded by a cloud of dust. 'Are you coming, Jherek?'

'I think not. I hope you enjoy yourself, Bishop Castle.'

'I shall. I shall.' The air-car began to rise, Charon's barge, into the upper atmosphere.

Only Mr and Mrs Underwood and Jherek Carnelian remained standing, in the ruins of the palace. 'Come,' said Jherek to them both, 'I think I know where we can find safety.' He turned a power-ring. His old air-car, the locomotive, materialized. It was in gleaming red and black now, but lime-coloured smoke still puffed from its stack. 'Forgive the lack of invention,' he said to them, 'but as we are in haste ...'

'You would save Harold, too?' she said, as Jherek helped her husband aboard.

'Why not? You say you are concerned for him.' He grinned cheerfully, while overhead a searing, scarlet bolt of pure energy went roaring by, 'Besides, I wish to hear the details of this divorce he plans. Is that not the ceremony that must take place before we can be married?'

She made no reply to this, as she joined him on the footplate. 'Where are we going, Mr Carnelian?'

The locomotive began to puff skyward. 'I'm full of old smokies,' he sang, 'I'm covered in dough. I've eaten blue plovers and I'm snorting up coke!' Mr Underwood clutched the rail and stared down at the ruins they left behind. His knees were shaking. 'It's a railroad song, from your own time,' Jherek explained. 'Would you like to be the fireman?'

He offered Mr Underwood the platinum shovel. Mr Underwood accepted the shovel without a word and, mechanically, began to stoke coal into the fire-chamber.

'Mr Carnelian! Where are we going?'

'To certain safety, dearest Amelia. To certain safety, I assure you.'

CHAPTER FIFTEEN

IN WHICH JHEREK CARNELIAN AND MRS UNDERWOOD FIND SANCTUARY OF SORTS, AND MR UNDERWOOD MAKES A NEW FRIEND

'You are not disturbed, dearest Amelia, by this city?'

'I find the place improbable. I failed to realize, listening only to talk of such settlements, how vast and how, well, how unlike cities they were!'

Mr Underwood stood some distance away, on the other side of the little plaza. Green globes of fuzzy light, about the size of tennis balls, ran up and down his outstretched arms; he watched them with childlike delight; behind him the air was black, purple, dark green shot with crimson, as chemicals expanded and contracted in a kind of simulation of breathing, giving off their vapours; bronze sparks showered nearby, pinkish energy arced from one tower to another; steel sang. The city murmured to itself, almost asleep, certainly drowsy. Even the narrow rivulets of mercury, criss-crossing the ground at their feet, seemed to be running slowly.

'The cities protect themselves,' Jherek explained. 'I have seen it before. No weapon can operate within them, no weapon can harm them from without, because they can always command more energy than any weapon brought against them, you see. It was part of their original design.'

'This resembles a manufactory more than it does a township,' she remarked.

'It is actually,' he told her, 'more in the nature of a museum. There are several such cities on the planet; they contain what remains of our knowledge.'

'These fumes – are they not poisonous?'

'Not to Man. They could not be.'

She accepted his assurance, but continued wary, as he led them from the plaza, through an arcade of lurid yellow and mauve metallic fronds, faintly reminiscent of those they had seen in the Palaeozoic; a strange greyish light fell through the fronds and distorted their shadows. Mr Underwood wandered some distance behind them, softly singing.

'We must consider,' she whispered, 'how Harold is to be saved.'

'Saved for what?'

'From his insanity.'

'He seems happier in the city.'

'He believes himself in Hell, no doubt. Just as I once believed. Inspector Springer should never have brought him.'

'I am not altogether sure that the inspector is quite himself.'

'I agree, Mr Carnelian. All this smacks of political panic at home. There is thought to be considerable interest in Spiritualism and Freemasonry among certain members of the Cabinet, at the present time. There is even some talk that the Prince of Wales . . .'

She continued in this vein for a while, mystifying him entirely. Her information, he gathered, was gleaned from a broadsheet which Mr Underwood had once acquired.

The arcade gave way to a chasm running between high, featureless buildings, their walls covered with chemical stains and peculiar semi-biological growths, some of which palpitated; ahead of them was something globular, glowing and dark, which rolled away from them as they advanced and, as they reached the end of the chasm, vanished. Here the vista widened and they could see across a plain littered with half-rotted metal relics to where, in the distance, angry flames spread themselves against an invisible wall.

'There!' he said. 'That must be the Lat's weapons at work. The city throws up its defences. See, I told you that we should be safe, dear Amelia.'

She glanced over her shoulder to where her husband sat upon a structure that seemed part of stone and part of some kind of hardened resin. 'I wish you would try to be more tactful, Mr Carnelian. Remember that my husband is within earshot. Consider his feelings, if you will not consider mine!'

'But he has relinquished you to me. He said as much. By your customs that is sufficient, is it not?'

'He divorces me, that is all. I have a right to choose or reject any husband I please.'

'Of course. But you choose me. I know.'

'I have not told you that.'

'You have, Amelia. You forget. You have mentioned more than once that you love me.'

'That does not mean – would not mean – that I would necessarily marry you, Mr Carnelian. There is still every chance that I may return to Bromley – or at least to my own time.'

'Where you will be an outcast. You said so.'

'In Bromley. Not everywhere.' But she frowned. 'I can imagine the scandal. The newspapers will have published something, to be sure. Oh, dear.'

'You seemed to be enjoying life at the End of Time.'

'Perhaps I would continue to do so, Mr Carnelian, were I not haunted, very definitely, by the Past.' Another glance over her shoulder. 'How is one ever to relax?'

'This is a fluke. It is the first time anything like it has ever occurred here.'

'Besides, I would remind you that, according to Bishop Castle (not to mention the evidence of our own eyes) your world is being destroyed about your ears.'

'For the moment, only. It can soon be replaced.'

'Lord Mongrove and Yusharisp would have us believe otherwise.'

'It is hard to take them seriously.'

'For you, perhaps. Not for me, Mr Carnelian. What they say makes considerable sense.'

'*Opportunities for redemption must therefore be few in such an ambience as you describe,*' said quite another voice, a low, mellow, slightly sleepy voice.

'There are none,' said Mr Underwood, 'at least that I know of.'

'*That is interesting. I seem to recall something of the theory, but most of the information I would require was stored elsewhere, in a sister city, whose co-ordinates I cannot quite recollect. I am of a mind to believe, however, that you are either a manifestation of this city's delusions (which proliferate notoriously, these days) or else that you are deluded yourself, a victim of too much morbid fascination with ancient mythologies. I could be mistaken — there was a time when I was infallible, I think. I am not sure that your description of this city tallies with the facts which remain at my command. You could argue, I know, that I myself am deluded as to the truth, yet my evidence would seem to tally with my instincts, whereas you, yourself, make intellectual rather than instinctive assumptions; that at least is what I gather from the illogicalities so far expressed in your analysis. You have contradicted yourself at least three times since you sat down on my shell.*'

It was the compound of rock and resin that spoke. 'One form of memory bank,' murmured Jherek. 'There are so many kinds, not always immediately recognizable.'

'*I think,*' continued the bank, '*that you are still confused and have not yet ordered your thoughts sufficiently to communicate properly with me. I assure you that I will function much more satisfactorily if you phrase your remarks better.*'

Mr Underwood did not seem offended by this criticism.

'I think you are right,' he said. 'I am confused. Well, I am mad, to be blunt.'

'*Madness may only be the expression of ordinary emotional confusion. Fear of madness can cause, I believe, a retreat into the very madness one fears. This is only superficially a paradox. Madness may be said to be a tendency to simplify, into easily grasped metaphors, the nature of the world. In your own case, you have plainly been confounded by unexpected complexities, therefore you are inclined to retreat into simplification – this talk of Damnation and Hell, for instance – to create a world whose values are unambivalent, unequivocal. It is a pity that so few of my own ancestors survive for they, by their very nature, would have responded better to your views. On the other hand it may be that you are not content with this madness, that you would rather face the complexities, feel at ease with them. If so, I am sure that I can help, in a small way.*'

'You are very kind,' said Mr Underwood.

'*Nonsense. I am glad to be of service. I have had nothing to do for the best part of a million years. I was in danger of growing "rusty". Luckily, having no mechanical parts, I can remain dormant for a long time without any especially deleterious effects. Though, as part of a very complex system, there is much information I can no longer call upon.*'

'Then you are of the opinion that this is not the afterlife, that I am not here as punishment for my sins, that I shall not be here for eternity, that I am not, as it were, dead.'

'*You are certainly not dead, for you can still converse, feel, think and experience physical needs and discomforts ...*'

The bank had a penchant for abstract conversation which seemed to suit Mr Underwood, though Jherek and Amelia became quickly bored listening to it. 'It reminds me of an old schoolmaster I once had,' she whispered, and she grinned. 'It is just what Harold needs really, at present.'

The vivid splashes of light no longer spread across the horizon and the scene darkened. No sun could be observed in the lurid sky, across which clouds of queerly coloured gases perpetually drifted. Behind them, the city seemed to stir, shuddering with age and strain, groaning almost complainingly.

'What would happen to you if your cities collapsed?' she asked him.

'That is impossible. They are self-perpetuating.'

'There is no evidence of that.' Even as she spoke, two of the metallic structures fell into the dust and became dust themselves.

'Yet they are,' he told her. 'In their own way. They have been like this for millennia, somehow surviving. We see only the surface. The essence of the cities is not so tangible, and that is as robust as ever.'

She accepted what he said with a shrug. 'How long must we remain here, then?'

'You sought escape from the Lat, did you not? We remain here until the Lat leave the planet.'

'You do not know when that will be?'

'It will be soon, I am sure. Either they will become bored with the game or we will. Then the game will end.'

'With how many dead?'

'None, I hope.'

'You can resurrect everyone?'

'Certainly.'

'Even the denizens of your menageries?'

'Not all. It depends how solidly they have made an impression on our own memories, you see. Our rings work from our minds, to achieve the reconstructions.'

She did not pursue the topic. 'We seem as thoroughly marooned now at the End of Time as we did at the Beginning,' she said moodily. 'How few are our moments of ordinary living . . .'

'That will change. These are particularly agitated days.

Brannart explained that the chronological fluctuations are unusually persistent. We must all agree to stop travelling through time for a while, then everything will be back to normal.'

'I admire your optimism, Mr Carnelian.'

'Thank you, Amelia.' He began to walk again. 'This is the very city where I was conceived, the Iron Orchid told me. With some difficulty, it seems.'

She looked back. Mr Underwood still sat upon the memory bank, deep in conversation. 'Should we leave him?'

'We can return for him later.'

'Very well.'

They stepped upon thin silver surfaces which creaked as they crossed, but did not crack. They ascended a flight of ebony stairs, towards an ornamental bridge.

'It would seem fitting,' said Jherek, 'if I were to propose formally to you here, Amelia, as my father proposed to my mother.'

'Your father?'

'A mystery my mother chooses to perpetuate.'

'So you do not know who —'

'I do not.'

She pursed her lips. 'In Bromley such a fact would be sufficient to put a complete bar on marriage, you know.'

'Truly?'

'Oh, yes.

'But we are not in Bromley,' she added.

He smiled. 'Indeed, we are not.'

'However ...'

'I understand.'

'Please, continue ...'

'I was saying that it would seem fitting that I should ask you, here in this city where I was conceived, for your hand in marriage.'

'Should I ever be free to give it, you mean?'

'Exactly.'

'Well, Mr Carnelian, I cannot say that this is sudden. But . . .'

'Mibix dug frishy hrunt!' said a familiar voice, and across the bridge came marching Captain Mubbers and his men, armed to the teeth and looking not a little put out.

CHAPTER SIXTEEN

THE SKULL BENEATH THE PAINT

When Captain Mubbers saw them he stopped suddenly, aiming his instrument-weapon at Jherek.

Jherek was almost pleased to see him. 'My dear Captain Mubbers . . .' he began.

'Mr Carnelian! He is armed!'

Jherek could not quite understand the point of her excitement. 'Yes. The music they produce is the most beautiful I have ever heard.'

Captain Mubbers plucked a string. There came a grinding noise from the bell-shaped muzzle of his weapon; a slight fizzle of blue sparks appeared for a moment around the rim. Captain Mubbers uttered a deep sigh and threw the thing to the flagstones of the bridge. Similar grindings and fizzlings came from the other instruments held by his men.

Popping a translation pill into his mouth (he had taken to carrying them everywhere just recently) Jherek said:

'What brings you to the city, Captain Mubbers?'

'Mind your own smelly business, sonny jim,' said the leader of the space-invaders. 'All we armjoint want to do now is find a shirt-elastic way out!'

'I can't understand why you wanted to come in, though ...' He glanced apologetically at Mrs Underwood, who could not understand anything that was being said. He offered her a pill. She refused. She folded her arms in an attitude of resignation.

'Spoils,' said another of the Lat.

'Shut it, Rokfrug,' Captain Mubbers ordered.

But Rokfrug continued:

'The knicker-patch place seemed so rotten-well protected that we thought there was bound to be something worth having here. Just our shirt-elastic luck —'

'I said shut it, arse-brain!'

But Captain Mubbers' men seemed to be losing faith in his authority. The crossed their three eyes in a most offensive manner and made rude gestures with their elbows.

'Weren't you already sufficiently successful elsewhere?' Jherek asked Rokfrug. 'I thought you were doing extremely well with the destruction, the rape and so on ...'

'Pissing right we were, until ...'

'Cork your hole, bum-face!' shouted his leader.

'Oh, elbow-off!' retorted Rokfrug, but seemed aware that he had gone too far. His voice became a self-pitying mumble as Captain Mubbers gazed disapprovingly back at him. Even his fellows plainly thought Rokfrug's language had put him beyond the pale.

'We're under a bit of a strain,' said one of them, by way of apology.

'Who wouldn't be?' Captain Mubbers kicked petulantly at his abandoned weapon. 'All the farting trouble we went to to get knicker-patching back to our ship in the first place ...'

'... and everything we laid waste to crapping re-appearing,' complained Rokfrug, evidently glad to find a point of agreement with his captain.

'... and all our puking prisoners suddenly disappearing ...' added another.

'What's the point of it?' Captain Mubbers asked Jherek

plaintively. 'When we sighted this planet we thought looting it'd be as easy as wiping your bum.'

'Ever since,' said Rokfrug, 'we've been buggered about. These people haven't got the shirt-elastic they were born with. No common sense. How can you terrorize people who keep laughing at you? Besides, the scenery keeps changing ...'

'It's a Planet of Illusions,' said Captain Mubbers portentously. His pupils darted about in his single eye. 'I mean, this is probably another of their traps.' He focussed on Jherek. 'Is it? You seem a decent sort of bugger, basically. Is it?'

'I don't think anyone's been deliberately misleading you,' Jherek told him. 'In fact, there seems to have been an effort to accommodate you. What exactly happened? Who stopped you?'

'Well, it was half-and-half. Partly we just ran out of farting steam,' Rokfrug said. 'Then these soppy little round buggers arrived. They —'

Mrs Underwood was tapping Jherek urgently on the arm.

He turned, at last, to look at her. Plodding up the steps behind them, grim-faced and triumphant, was Inspector Springer, Sergeant Sherwood and the party of constables.

'Gee noo fig tendej vega!' said Inspector Springer.

'Flow hard!' exclaimed Mrs Underwood.

It was time for Jherek to swallow a fresh pill.

'Led us straight to 'em, didn't you?' Inspector Springer waved his men forward. 'Shackle 'em, lads!'

The constables, moving like automata, pressed forward to arrest the unresisting Lat.

'I knew you'd arrange a meeting sooner or later,' Inspector Springer told Jherek. 'That's why I let you get away.'

'But how were you able to follow us, Inspector?' Mrs Underwood asked.

'Commandeered a vehicle,' Sergeant Sherwood told her importantly.

'Whose?'

'Oh – 'is . . .' A thumb was jerked backward.

Both Jherek and Amelia turned and looked below. There stood the Duke of Queens, wearing a bright pastel blue uniform not dissimilar in cut to Sergeant Sherwood's. As they saw him he gave a cheerful wave of his bright yellow truncheon and blew his silver whistle.

'Good heavens!' she exclaimed.

'We've made 'im an honorary constable, 'aven't we, Inspector?' said Sergeant Sherwood.

'There's no 'arm in 'umorin' 'em, sometimes.' Inspector Springer smiled to himself. 'If it's to your advantage.'

'Kroofrudi hrunt!' said Captain Mubbers as he was led away.

The city shuddered and groaned. A sudden darkness came and went. Jherek noticed that everyone's skins seemed ghastly pale, almost blue, and the light gave their eyes a peculiar flat sheen, so that they were like the eyes of statues.

'Cripes,' said Sergeant Sherwood. 'What was that?'

'The city —' Mrs Underwood whispered. 'It is so still. So silent.' She moved closer to Jherek. She gripped his arm. He was pleased to comfort her. 'Does this often happen?'

'To my knowledge, no . . .'

Everyone had stopped moving, even the Duke of Queens, below. The Lat grunted nervously to one another. The mouths of the majority of the constables hung open.

Another great shudder. Somewhere in the distance a piece of metal rattled and then fell with a crash, but that was the only sound.

Jherek pressed her towards the stair. 'We had better get to the ground, I think. If that *is* the ground.'

'An earthquake?'

'The world is too old for earthquakes, Amelia.'

They hurried down the steps and their action lent motion to the others, who followed.

'Harold must be found,' said Mrs Underwood. 'Is there danger, Mr Carnelian?'

'I do not know.'

'You said the city was safe.'

'From the Lat.' He could scarcely bear to look at her deathly-pale skin. He blinked, as if blinking would dispel the scene, but the scene remained.

They reached the Duke of Queens. The Duke stroked his beard, which had gone a seedy sort of purple colour. 'I stopped by at your palace, Jherek, but you had gone on. Inspector Springer told me that he, too, was looking for you, so we followed in your wake. It took a while to find you. You know what these cities are like.' He fingered his whistle. 'Wouldn't you say this one was behaving a bit oddly, at present, though?'

'Collapsing?'

'Possibly – or undergoing some sort of radical change. The cities are said to be capable of restoring themselves. Could that be it?'

'There is no evidence . . .'

The Duke nodded. 'Yet it can't be breaking down. The cities are immortal.'

'Breaking down superficially, perhaps.'

'One hopes that is all it is. You do look sickly, Jherek, my darling.'

'We all do, I think. The light.'

'Indeed.' The Duke replaced his whistle in his pocket. 'Those aliens of mine escaped, you know. While the Lat were on the rampage. They got to their own ship, with Yusharisp and Mongrove.'

'They've left?'

'Oh, no! They're spoiling everything. The Lat must be annoyed. They look a bit annoyed, don't they? Yusharisp and company have taken over!' The Duke laughed, but the sound was so unpleasant, even to his own ears, that he stopped. 'Ha, ha . . .'

The city seemed to lurch, as if the entire structure slipped downhill. They recovered their balance.

496

'We'd better proceed to the nearest exit,' said one of the constables in a hollow voice. 'Walking, not running. As long as nobody panics, we'll be able to evacuate the premises in no time at all.'

'We've got what we came for,' agreed Sergeant Sherwood. His uniform had turned a luminous grey. He kept brushing at it, as if he thought the colour was dust clinging to the material.

'Where did we leave the whatsit?' Inspector Springer removed his bowler hat and wiped the inner band with a handkerchief. He looked enquiringly at the Duke of Queens. 'Attention there, Special Constable!' His grin was unspontaneous and horrible. 'The airship thing?' There had never been jocularity so false.

For a moment the Duke of Queens was so puzzled by the inspector's manner that he merely stared.

'The airship, ho, ho, ho, what brought us 'ere!' Inspector Springer replaced his hat and swallowed rapidly two or three times.

The Duke was vague. 'Over there, I think.' He rotated slowly, gesturing with his truncheon (which had turned brown), seeking his bearings. 'Or was it that way?'

'Cor blimey!' said Inspector Springer in disgust.

'Mibix?' Captain Mubbers spoke absently, as one whose mind is on other things. He returned to chewing on the metal of his hand-cuffs.

The ground made a moaning sound and shivered.

'Harold.' Mrs Underwood plucked at Jherek's sleeve. He noticed that the white linen of his suit had become a patchy green. 'We must find him, Mr Carnelian.'

As Jherek and Amelia began to run back to where they had left her husband Inspector Springer also broke into a trot, closely followed by his men, carrying the muttering but unresisting Lat between them, and lastly by the Duke of Queens who was beginning to cheer up at the prospect of action. Action, sensation, was his lifeblood; he wilted without it.

As Jherek and Amelia ran, they heard the piercing eery

tones of the Duke's whistle and his lusty voice crying:
'Halloo! View halloo!'

Tiny whispering noises issued from the ground, with
each step that they made. Something hot and organic
seemed at one point to be pulsing beneath their feet. They
reached the plain of rotting metal. Harold Underwood
could be distinguished through the murky semi-darkness,
still deep in conversation with his friend, the rock. He
looked up. 'Ha!' His tone was kindlier. 'So you are all
here, now. It says something, does it not, for our earthly
hypocrisies?' Evidently the rock had made no real impression on his convictions.

The plain gasped, gave way and became a mile-wide pit.

'I think I'd better make a new air-car,' said the Duke of
Queens, coming to a sudden halt.

Harold Underwood crossed to the lip of the pit and
stared down. He scratched his hay-coloured hair, disturbing the parting. 'So there's another level, at least,' he
mused. 'I suppose one should be relieved.' He made to investigate further but did not demur when his wife gently
drew him back.

The Duke of Queens was twisting all his rings. 'Do our
rings not work in the city itself?' he asked Jherek.

'I can't remember.'

At their backs a building silently burst. They watched
the debris float by overhead. Jherek noticed that all their
skins now had a mottled, glossy appearance, like mother-
of-pearl. He moved closer to Amelia, who still clutched her
husband (the only member of the party who seemed
serene). They began to move away from the pit, skirting
the city proper.

'It is rare that the city's power is overtaxed,' said Harold
Underwood's rocky confidante. 'Who could need such
energy?'

'You know what is causing this upheaval, then?' Jherek
enquired of it.

'No, no. A conversion problem, perhaps. Who can say?
You could try the central philosophy department. Except

498

I believe I am all that is left of it. Unless I am the whole of it. Who is to say which is a fragment and which the whole? And is the whole contained in every fragment or a fragment in the whole, or are whole and fragment different, not in terms of size or capacity, but in essential qualities . . .?

Regretting his impoliteness, Jherek continued on past the rock. 'It would be wonderful to discuss these points,' he apologized, 'but my friends . . .'

'The circle is the circle,' Harold Underwood said. 'We shall be back again, no doubt. Farewell, for the moment.' Humming to himself, he allowed Jherek and Amelia to lead him off.

'Indeed, indeed. The nature of reality is such that nothing can, by definition, be unreal, if it exists, and since anything can exist if it can be conceived of, then all that we say is unreal is therefore real . . .'

'Its arguments are sometimes very poor,' Harold Underwood said in an undertone, as if apologizing. 'I do not believe that it has quite the authority it claims. Well, well, well, who would have believed that Dante, a Catholic, could have been so accurate, after all!' He smiled at them. 'But then, I suppose, we must forget these sectarian differences now. Damnation certainly broadens the mind, eh?'

Mrs Underwood gasped. 'Was that a joke, Harold?'

He beamed.

Something alive, perhaps an animal, ran swiftly across their path and into the heart of the city.

'We are at the edge,' said the Duke of Queens. 'Yet nothing but blackness seems to exist beyond. Perhaps it is some optical trick? A malfunctioning force-screen?'

'No,' said Jherek, who was ahead of him. 'The city still sheds a little light. I can see – but it is a wasteland.'

'There is no sun.' Amelia peered forward. 'There are no stars. That is what it is.'

'The planet is dead, do you mean?' The Duke of Queens joined them. 'Yes, it is a desert out there. What can have become of our friends?'

'I suppose it is too late to say that I, of course, forgive you everything, Amelia,' Harold Underwood said suddenly.

'What, Harold?'

'It does not matter now. You were, of course, this man's mistress. You did commit adultery. It is why you are both here.'

With some reluctance, Amelia Underwood withdrew her gaze from the lifeless landscape. She was frowning.

'I was right, was I not?' her husband continued.

Dazed, she glanced from Jherek Carnelian to Harold Underwood. Jherek was turning, a bemused half-smile on his lips.

She gestured helplessly. 'Harold, is this the time ...?'

'She loves me,' said Jherek.

'Mr Carnelian!'

'And you are his mistress?' Harold Underwood put a gentle hand to her face. 'I do not accuse you, Amelia.'

She gave a deep sigh and tenderly touched her husband's wrist. 'Very well, Harold. In spirit, yes. And I do love him.'

'Hurrah!' cried Jherek. 'I knew. I knew! Oh, Amelia. This is the happiest day of my life.'

The others all turned to stare at them. Even the Duke of Queens seemed shocked.

And from somewhere in the sky overhead a booming voice, full of gloomy satisfaction, shouted:

'I told you so. I told you all. See – it is the end of the world!'

CHAPTER SEVENTEEN

SOME CONFUSION CONCERNING THE EXACT NATURE OF THE CATASTROPHE

The large, black egg-shaped air-boat containing, in an indentation at the top, Lord Mongrove settled to the ground nearby. A look of profound and melancholy gratification lay upon the giant's heavy features. In robes of funereal purple he stepped from the boat, his right hand drawing their attention to the desolation beyond the city, where not even a wind whispered or stirred the barren dust to a semblance of vitality.

'It has all gone,' intoned Mongrove. 'The cities no longer sustain our follies. They can barely sustain themselves. We are the last survivors of humanity – and there is some question as to whether *we* shall continue to exist for much longer. Well, at least most of the time-travellers have been returned and the space-travellers given ships, for all the good it will do them. Yusharisp and his people did their best, but they could have done much more, Duke of Queens, if you had not been so foolish as to trap them for your menagerie . . .'

'I wanted to surprise you,' said the Duke somewhat lamely. He was unable to take his eyes away from the desolation. 'Do you mean that it's completely lifeless out there?'

'The cities are oases in the desert that is our Earth,' Mongrove confirmed. 'The planet itself crumbles imminently.'

Jherek felt Mrs Underwood's hand seeking his. He took it, grasping it firmly. She smiled bravely up at him.

The Duke continued to fiddle with his useless powerrings. 'I must say one feels a certain sense of loss,' he said, half to himself. 'Is My Lady Charlotina gone? And Bishop Castle? And Sweet Orb Mace? And Argonheart Po? And Lord Shark the Unknown?'

'Everyone, save those here.'

'Werther de Goethe?'

'Werther, too.'

'A shame. He would have enjoyed this scene so much.'

'Werther flirts with Death no longer. Death grew impatient. Death took him, perforce.' Lord Mongrove uttered a great sigh. 'I am meeting Yusharisp and the others here, shortly. We shall know, then, how much longer we have.'

'Our time is limited, then?' said Mrs Underwood.

'Probably.'

'Gord!' said Inspector Springer, upon whom the import of Mongrove's words was just beginning to dawn. 'What bad luck!' He removed his bowler again. 'I suppose there's no chance at all of getting back now? You wouldn't 'ave seen a large time-machine about, eh? We *were* 'ere on official business ...'

'Nothing exists beyond the cities,' Mongrove reiterated. 'I believe your time-travelling colleague was prevailed upon to help in the general exodus. We thought you dead, you see.'

For an instant, at their backs, the city shrieked, but subsided quickly. Scarlet clouds, like blood in water, swirled into the atmosphere. It was as if the city had been wounded.

'So he's returned ...' continued Inspector Springer. 'That's for sure, eh?'

'I regret that the evidence would suggest as much. If he

was unlucky, he might have been caught up in the general destruction. It happened very quickly. Atoms, you know, dissipating. As our atoms will doubtless dissipate, eventually. As the city's will. And the planet's. Joining the universe.'

'Oo, blimey!' Sergeant Sherwood screwed up his face.

'Hm.' Inspector Springer rubbed his moustache. 'I don't know what the 'Ome Secretary's going to say. There's nobody to explain ...'

'And we'll never know, either,' Sergeant Sherwood pointed out. 'This is a fine turn up.' He seemed to be accusing the inspector. 'What price promotion now?'

'I think it's high time you reconciled yourselves to your fate,' suggested Harold Underwood. 'Earthly ambition should be put aside. We are, after all, here for eternity. We must begin considering repentance.'

'Do be quiet, Mr Underwood, there's a good chap.' Inspector Springer's shoulders had slumped somewhat.

'It could be that there is still a chance of salvation, Inspector.'

''Ow do you mean, sir?' asked Sergeant Sherwood. 'Salvation?'

'I have been considering the possibility that one may be granted the Kingdom of Heaven, even after one has been consigned here, if one can work out, satisfactorily, exactly why one was placed here ...'

''Ere?'

'In Hell.'

'You think this is —'

'I know it, Sergeant!' Harold Underwood's smile was radiant. Never had he been so relaxed. It was plain that he was absolutely happy. Amelia Underwood contemplated him with some relief and affection.

'I am reminded of John Bunyan's uplifting moral tale, *The Pilgrim's Progress*,' began Mr Underwood, flinging a friendly arm around Sergeant Sherwood's shoulders. 'If you recall the story ...' They wandered off together, along the perimeter.

'Would that we were all so deluded, at this moment,' said Mrs Underwood. 'Shall there be no chance of escape, ultimately, Lord Mongrove?'

'Yusharisp and his people are currently looking into the problem. It could be that, with careful use of the resources at our command, we could keep a small artificial vessel of some kind going, for a few hundred years. We should have to ration all provisions most carefully. It might even be that some would not be able to join the vessel, that a selection would have to be made of those most likely to survive ...'

'A sort of new Ark, then?' she suggested.

The reference was meaningless to Lord Mongrove, but he was polite. 'If you like. It would entail living in the most rigorous and uncomfortable conditions. Self-discipline would be all-important, of course, and there would be no place for amusement of any sort. We would use what we could from the cities, store the information we could glean, and wait.'

'For what?' asked the Duke of Queens, appalled.

'Well, for some kind of opportunity ...'

'What kind?'

'We cannot be sure. No one knows what will happen after the dissipation. Perhaps new suns and planets will begin to form. Oh, I know it is not very hopeful, Duke of Queens, but it is better than complete extinction, is it not?'

'Indeed,' said the Duke of Queens with some dignity, 'it is not! I hope you have no intention of selecting *me* for this – this drifting menagerie!'

'The selection will be arranged justly. I shall not be the arbiter. We must draw lots, I suppose.'

'This is *your* plan, Lord Mongrove?' asked Jherek.

'Well, mine and Yusharisp's.'

'It appeals to you?'

'It is not a question of what appeals, Jherek Carnelian. It is a question of realities. There are no more options. Will you not understand that? *There are no more op-*

tions!' Mongrove became almost kindly. 'Jherek, your childhood is over. Now it is time for you to become an adult, to understand that the world is no longer your cockle.'

'Don't you mean oyster?' Inspector Springer asked.

'I think he does,' agreed Mrs Underwood, with some distaste. The thought of sea-food was still inclined to make her feel queasy.

'It would help,' said Mongrove sternly, 'if I were not interrupted. I speak of the most serious matters. We may be moments away from total obliteration!' He looked up. 'Ah, here are our saviours.'

With a sort of wheezing noise the familiar asymmetrical mound that was Yusharisp's spaceship started to descend, to land near to Mongrove's egg. Almost immediately a tiny squeaking began and a mould-covered door opened in the side of the ship. From the door issued Yusharisp (at least, it was probably Yusharisp) followed by his colleagues.

'So(skree) many sur(skree)vivors!' exclaimed Yusharisp. 'I suppose (skree) that we (roar) should be grateful! We, the survivors of (skree) Pweeli, greet (roar) you, and are glad to kreee yelp mawk ...' Yusharisp lifted one of his feet and began to fiddle with something at the side of his body.

Another Pweelian (probably CPS Shashurup) said: 'I take it (skree) that Lord Mongrove (roar) has informed you that the end (skree) is with us and that (roar) you must now (skree) place yourselves under our discipline (skree) if you wish to (roar) extend your chances of living (skree) (roar) ...'

'A most distasteful idea,' said the Duke of Queens.

The Pweelian said, with a note of satisfaction in his voice: 'It is not (skree) long since, Duke (roar) of Queens, that we were (roar) forced to subject ourselves to your will without (skree) any justification whatso(skree)ever!'

'That was entirely different.'

'Indeed(skree) it was!'

The Duke of Queens subsided into a sulk.

'As far (skree) as we can ascertain (skree),' continued Yusharisp, 'your cities are still continuing to (roar) function, though they have been hard-pressed. Indeed, surprisingly, there is (skree) every evidence that (yelp) they will remain functional long enough (roar) to (skree) allow us good time in which to prepare evacuation (yelp). If a means of harnessing their energies can be found ...'

Helpfully, Jherek lifted a hand on which power-rings gleamed. 'These harness the energies of the city, Yusharisp. We have used them for a good many millions of years, I believe.'

'Those toys (yelp) are not (skree) what we need now, Jherek Car(roar)nelian.'

'This encounter becomes boring,' said Jherek in Amelia's ear. 'Shall we seek privacy? I have much to say.'

'Mr Carnelian – the Pweelians hope to help us!'

'But in such a dull way, Amelia. Would you belong to yet another menagerie?'

'It is not quite the same thing. As they say, we have no choice.'

'But we have. If the cities live, so may we live in them, at least for a while. We shall be free. We shall be alone.'

'You do not fear annihilation, still? For all that you have seen that wasteland – out there?'

'I am still not entirely sure what "fear" is. Come, we'll walk a little way and you can try to explain to me.'

'Well – a little way ...' Her hand was still in his. They began to leave.

'Where (skree) are you going?' shrieked Yusharisp in astonishment.

'Perhaps we'll rejoin you later,' Jherek told him. 'We have something we wish to discuss.'

'There is no time! (Roar). There is no (yelp) time left!'

But Jherek ignored him. They headed for the city, where Harold Underwood and Sergeant Sherwood had already disappeared, not long since.

'This is (skree) insane!' cried Yusharisp. 'Do you reject

our (roar) help, after all our efforts? After all we have (yelp) *forgiven* you!'

'We are still a little confused,' Jherek said, remembering his manners, 'as to the exact nature of the catastrophe. So—'

'Confused! Isn't it (skree) obvious?'

'You seem a trifle insistent that there is only one answer.'

'I warned you, Jherek,' said Mongrove. 'There are no more options!'

'Aha.' Jherek continued to draw Amelia towards the city.

'It is the very End of Time. The End of Matter!' Mongrove had gone a very odd colour. 'There may be only a few seconds left!'

'Then I think we should like to spend them as peacefully as possible,' Jherek told him. He put his arm round his Amelia's shoulders. She moved closer to him. She smiled up into his face. He bent to kiss her, as they turned a corner of a ruined building.

'Oh, there you are, at last,' said an amiable voice. 'I'm not too late, after all.'

This time, Jherek did not respond to the newcomer until he had kissed Amelia Underwood warmly upon her welcoming lips.

CHAPTER EIGHTEEN

IN WHICH TRUTHS ARE REVEALED AND CERTAIN RELATIONSHIPS ARE DEFINED

A burst of red, flickering light threw the figure of the time-traveller (for it was he) into silhouette. The city gibbered for a moment, as if, in its senility, it had just become aware of danger. Voices began to sound from a variety of places as memory banks were activated, one by another. The near querulous babble became quite disturbing before it subsided. Amelia's kiss at length betrayed awareness of her surroundings, of an observer. Their lips withdrew, they smiled and shared a glance, and then they moved their heads to acknowledge the time-traveller, who waited, nonchalantly studying some detail of a lichen-covered structure, until they had finished.

'Forgive us,' said Jherek, 'but with the uncertainty of our future ...'

'Of course, of course.' The time-traveller had not heard Jherek's words. He waved an airy hand. 'I must admit I did not know if – phew – you'll never believe the devil of a job I had to get those passengers back before coming on here. It couldn't be more than a couple of hours, eh? A pretty fine balance. Has everyone else turned up?'

Jherek could tell by Amelia's expression that she disapproved of the time-traveller's insouciance. 'The world ends, did you know, sir? In a matter of minutes, we gather.'

'Um.' He nodded an acknowledgement but did not judge the statement interesting.

'The Duke of Queens is here.' Jherek wondered at a sudden fresh breeze bearing the scent of hyacinths. He sought the source, but the breeze subsided. 'And Yusharisp, from space, and Inspector Springer, and Lord Mongrove, and Captain Mubbers and the rest.'

Almost blankly, the time-traveller frowned. 'No, no – Society people I mean.'

'Society?' enquired Mrs Underwood, for the moment back in Bromley. Then she realized his meaning. 'The Guild! They are due here? They hope to save something of the world?'

'We arranged a meeting. This seemed the most convenient spot. On an ordinary course one can, after all, go no further!' The time-traveller walked the few yards to where his large and somewhat battered machine rested, its crystalline parts smouldering with dark, shifting colours, its brass reflecting the red light from the city. 'Heaven knows what damage this jockeying about has done to my machine. It was never properly tested, you see. My main reason for being here is to get information from some Guild member, both as regards the obtaining of spare parts and so that I may, with luck, get back into my own universe.' He tapped the ebony framework. 'There's a crack there that will last no more than another couple of long journeys.'

'You do not come to witness the End of the World, then?' Jherek wished that his power-rings were working and that he could make himself a warmer coat. He felt a chill enter his bones.

'Oh, no, Mr Carnelian! I've seen that more than once!' The time-traveller was amused. 'This is merely a convenient "time-mark", if you take my meaning.'

'But you could rescue Inspector Springer and his men,

509

and my husband — take them back, surely?' Mrs Underwood said. 'You did, after all, bring them here.'

'Well, I suppose that morally I have contributed to their predicament. However, the Home Secretary requisitioned my machine. I was unwilling to use it. Indeed, Mrs Underwood, I was intimidated. I never thought to hear such threats from the lips of British Civil Servants! And it was Lord Jagged who gave me away. I was working in secret. Of course, recognizing him, I confided something of my research to him.'

'You recognized Lord Jagged?'

'As a fellow time-traveller, yes.'

'So he is still in the nineteenth century!'

'He was. He vanished shortly after I was contacted by the Home Secretary. I think initially he had hoped to requisition my machine for his own use, and took advantage of his acquaintance with various members of the government. His own machine had failed him, you see.'

'Yet he was no longer in 1896 when you left?' Jherek became eager for news of his friend's safety. 'Do you know where he went?'

'He had some theory he wanted to test. Time-travel without machinery. I thought it dangerous and told him as much. I don't know what he was plotting. I must say I didn't care for the fellow. An unhealthy sort of chap. Too full of himself. And he did *me* no good, involving me in his complicated schemes, as he did.'

Jherek would not listen to this criticism. 'You do not know him well. He has been a great help to me on more than one occasion.'

'Oh, I'm sure he has his virtues, but they are of the proud sort, the egocentric sort. He plays at God, and that's what I can't abide. You meet the odd time-traveller like that. Generally speaking, they come to a sticky end.'

'You think Lord Jagged is dead, then?' Mrs Underwood asked him.

'More than likely.'

Jherek was grateful for the hand she slipped into his. 'I

believe this sensation must be very close to the "fear" you were talking about, Amelia. Or is it "grief", I wonder?'

She became remorseful. 'Ah, it is my fault. I teach you of nothing but pain. I have robbed you of your simple joyfulness!'

He was surprised. 'If joy flees, Amelia, it is in the face of experience. I love you. And it seems there is a price to pay for that ecstasy I feel.'

'Price! You never mentioned such things before. You accepted the good and had no understanding of the evil.' She spoke in an undertone, conscious of the time-traveller's proximity.

Jherek raised her hand to his lips, kissing the clenched fingers. 'Amelia, I mourn for Jagged, and perhaps my mother, too. There is no question...'

'I became emotional,' she said. 'It is hard to know whether such a state of mind is suitable to the occasion...' And she laughed, though her eyes blinked at tears. She cleared her throat. 'Yes, this is mere hysteria. However, not knowing if death is a heartbeat hence or if we are to be saved...'

He drew her to him. He kissed her eyes. Very quickly, then, she recovered herself, contemplating the city with a worried, unhappy gaze.

The city had every appearance of decline, and Jherek himself no longer believed the assurances he had given her, that the changes in it were merely superficial. Where once it had been possible to see for distances of almost a mile, down vistas of statuary and buildings, now there was only sufficient light (and that luridly unpleasant) to see a hundred yards or so. He began to entertain thoughts of begging the time-traveller to rescue them, to take them back to 1896, to risk the dangers of the Morphail Effect (which, anyway, did not seem to operate so savagely upon them as it did upon others).

'All that sunshine,' she said. 'It was false, as I told you. There was no real sun ever in your sky – only that which the cities made for you. They kept a shell burning and

511

this barren cinder of a planet turning about it. Your whole world, Jherek, it was a lie!'

'You are too critical, Amelia. Man has an instinct to sustain his own environment. The cities were created in response to that instinct. They served it well.'

Her mood changed. She started away from him. 'It is so cruel that they should fail us now.'

'Amelia . . .' he moved to follow.

It was then that the sphere appeared, without warning, a short distance from the time-traveller's 'Chronomnibus'. It was black, and distorted images of the surrounding city could be seen in its gleaming hull.

Jherek joined her and together they watched as a hatch whirled and two black-clad figures emerged, pushing back their breathing-apparatus and goggles to become recognizable as Mrs Una Persson and Captain Oswald Bastable.

Captain Bastable smiled as he saw them. 'So you did arrive safely. Excellent.'

The time-traveller approached, shaking hands with the young captain. 'Glad you were able to keep the rendezvous, old man. How do you do, Mrs Persson? How pleasant to see you again.'

Captain Bastable was in high spirits. 'This should be worth witnessing, eh?'

'You have not been present at the end before?'

'No, indeed!'

'I was hoping that you could give me some advice.'

'Of course, if we can help. But the man you really need is Lord Jagged. It was he who —'

'He is not here.' The time-traveller placed both hands in the pockets of his Norfolk. 'There is some doubt that he survives.'

Una Persson shook out her short hair. She glanced idly around as a building seemed to dance a few feet towards her and then collapsed in on itself, rather like a concertina. 'I've never much cared for these places. Is this Tanelorn?'

'Shanalorm, I think.' Jherek held back, though he was

desperate for news of his friend.

'Even the names are confusing. Will it take long?'

Believing that he interpreted her question, Jherek told her: 'Mongrove estimates a matter of moments. He says the very planet crumbles.'

Mrs Persson sighed and rubbed at a weary eye. 'We have Shifter co-ordinates which require working out, Captain Bastable. The conditions are so good. Such a pity to waste —'

'The information we stand to gain ...' Evidently Captain Bastable had wanted to keep this appointment more than had she. He shrugged apologetically. 'It isn't every day we have the chance to see something as interesting ...'

She gestured with a gauntleted hand. 'True. Pay no attention to me. I'm not quite recovered.'

'I am trying to get back to my own universe,' began the time-traveller. 'It was suggested to me that you could help, that you have experience of such problems.'

'It's a matter of intersections,' she told him. 'That was why I wanted to concentrate on the Shifter. Conditions are excellent.'

'You can still help?'

'Hopefully.' She did not seem ready to discuss the matter. Politely, yet reluctantly, the time-traveller checked his eagerness and became silent.

'You are all taking this situation very casually.' Amelia Underwood cast a critical eye over the little group. 'Even selfishly. There is a possibility that at least some of those here could be evacuated, taken back through time. Have you no sense of the import – of the tragedy taking place. All the aspirations of our race vanishing as if they had never existed!'

Una Persson seemed to express a certain weary kindness when she replied. 'That is, Mrs Underwood, a somewhat melodramatic interpretation ...'

'Mrs Persson, the situation seems to be rather more than "melodramatic". This is extinction!'

'For some, possibly.'

513

'Not for you time-travellers, perhaps. Will you make no effort to help others?'

Mrs Persson did her best to stifle a yawn. 'I think our perspectives must be very different, Mrs Underwood. I assure you that I am not without a social conscience, but when you have experienced so much, on such a scale, as we have experienced, issues take on a different colouring. Besides, I do not think – Good heavens! What is that?'

They all followed her gaze towards a low line of ruins; recently crumbled. In the semi-darkness there bobbed, apparently along the top of the ruins, a procession of about a dozen objects, roughly dome-shaped. They were immediately familiar to Jherek and Amelia as the helmets of Inspector Springer's constables. They heard the faint sound of a whistle.

Within a few seconds, as a break appeared in the ruins, it was apparent to all that they witnessed a chase. The Lat were attempting to escape their captors. Their little pear-shaped bodies scuttled rapidly over the fallen masonry, but Springer's men were not far behind. They could hear the cries of the Lat and the police quite clearly now.

'Hrunt mibix ferkit!'

'Stop! Stop in the name of the law! Collar 'im, Weech!'

The Lat stumbled and fell, but managed to keep ahead of their pursuers, for all that most of them, save Captain Mubbers and perhaps Rokfrug, still wore handcuffs.

The whistles shrilled again. There was a great waving of truncheons. The Lat disappeared from view, but emerged again not far from Mrs Persson's time-sphere, saw the group of humans and hesitated before dodging off in the opposite direction.

The policemen, who would remain solidly conscious of their duty until the Crack of Doom sounded at last, and the very ground fell away from beneath their pounding boots, continued implacably after their prey.

Soon both Lat and police were out of sight and earshot again, and the conversation could resume.

Mrs Persson lost something of her weary manner and

seemed amused by the incident. 'I had no idea there were others here! Were not those the aliens we sent on? I would have thought that they would have left the planet by now.'

'They wanted to loot and rape everything first,' Jherek explained. 'But then the Pweelians stopped them. The Pweelians seem to take pleasure in stopping almost everyone from doing almost everything! This is their hour of triumph, I suppose. They have waited for it for a long time, of course, so it seems niggardly to criticize ...'

'You mean there is still another race of space-travellers in the city?' Captain Bastable asked.

'Yes. The Pweelians, as I said. They have some sort of plan for survival. But I did not find it agreeable. The Duke of Queens ...'

'He is here!' Mrs Persson brightened. Captain Bastable frowned a little circumspectly to himself.

'You know the Duke?'

'Oh, we are old friends.'

'And Lord Mongrove?'

'I have heard of him,' said Mrs Persson, 'but I have never had the pleasure of meeting him. However, if there is an opportunity ...'

'I should be delighted to introduce you. Always assuming that this little oasis, as Mongrove called it, doesn't disintegrate before I have the chance.'

'Mr Carnelian!' Amelia tugged at his sleeve. 'I would remind you that this is no time for social chat. We must attempt to prevail upon these people to rescue as many of those here as is possible!'

'I was forgetting. It is so nice to know that Mrs Persson is a friend of the Duke of Queens. Do you not think, dearest Amelia, that we should try to find him. He would be glad to resume the acquaintance, I am sure!'

Mrs Amelia Underwood shrugged her beautiful shoulders and sighed a really rather shallow sigh. She was beginning to lose interest, it seemed, in the whole business.

CHAPTER NINETEEN

IN WHICH DIFFERENCES OF OPINION ARE
EXPRESSED AND RELATIONSHIPS FURTHER
DEFINED

Becoming aware of Amelia's displeasure, and seeking to respond to events as she wished, Jherek recalled some Wheldrake.

> *Thus is the close upon us*
> *(Corpse calls to corpse and chain echoes chain).*
> *Now the bold paint flakes upon the cheek*
> *(And our pain lends point to pain).*
> *Now there are none among us*
> *Need seek for Death's domain ...*

Captain Bastable joined in the last line, looking for approval not to Jherek but to Mrs Underwood.

'Ah, Wheldrake,' he began, 'ever apt ...'

'Oh, bother Wheldrake!' said Mrs Underwood, and she stalked off in the direction from which she and Jherek had originally come, but she paused suddenly as a cheerful voice called out:

'There you are, Amelia! Sergeant Sherwood and I were just on the point of Woman's contribution to Sin. It would be worth having any comments, from the horse's mouth, as you might say.'

'And damn you, Harold!'

She gasped at her own language. Then she grinned. 'Oh, dear ...'

If Harold had noticed he doubtless accepted her oath as further evidence of their situation. He smiled vaguely at her. 'Well, perhaps later ...' His pince-nez glittered so that his eye-sockets appeared to contain flame. Chatting, he and the police sergeant strolled on.

Jherek caught up with her. 'I have offended you, my dear. I thought ...'

'Perhaps I, too, am mad,' she told him. 'Since nobody else is taking the end of the world seriously, then it is evident that I should not, either.' But she was not convinced.

'Yusharisp and the Pweelians take it seriously, dearest Amelia. And Lord Mongrove. But it seems to me that you have no real leaning in their direction.'

'I do what I think is right.'

'Yet it conflicts with your temperament, you would admit?'

'Oh, this is unfair!' She paced on. Now they could see the Pweelian spacecraft where they had left it. Inspector Springer and the Duke of Queens held their hands in the air.

Standing on three legs, Yusharisp, or one of his comrades, held an object in his fourth foot (or hand) with which he menaced Inspector Springer and the Duke of Queens.

'My goodness!' Amelia hesitated. 'They are using force! Who would have suspected it?'

Lord Mongrove seemed put out by the turn of events. He stood to one side, muttering to himself. 'I am not sure. I am not sure.'

'We have decided (skree) to act for your own (roar) good,' Yusharisp told the two men. 'The others will be rounded up in time. Now, if you will kindly, for the moment, board the spaceship ...'

517

'Put that gun away!' The ringing command issued from the lips of Amelia Underwood. Even she seemed surprised by it. 'Does the end of the world mean the end of the Rule of Law? What point is there in perpetuating intelligent life if violence is to be the method by which we survive? Are we not above the beasts?'

'I think (skree) madam that you (yelp) fail to understand the urgency (skree) of the situation (roar).' Yusharisp was embarrassed. The weapon wavered. Seeing this the Duke of Queens immediately lowered his hands.

'We (skrrreee) did not intend to continue to threaten anyone (roar) after (yelp) the immediate danger was (skree) avoided,' said another Pweelian, probably CPS Shushurup. 'It is not in (skree) our nature to approve of (skree) violence or (roar) threats.'

'You have been threatening everyone since you arrived!' she told them. 'Bullying us not, until now, with weapons, but with moral arguments which begin to seem increasingly specious to me and which have never convinced the denizens of this world (it is not mine, I might add, and I do not approve of their behaviour any more than do you). Now you give us evidence of the weakness of your arguments – you bring forth your guns and your bald threats of violence!'

'It is not (skree) anything like so (roar) simple, madam. It is a question of (yelp) survive or die ...'

'It seems to me,' she said calmly, 'that it is you who simplify, Mr Yusharisp.'

Jherek looked admiringly on. As usual, the arguments were inclined to confuse him, but he thought Amelia's assumption of authority was magnificent.

'I would suggest,' she continued, 'that you leave these people to their own solutions to their problems, and that you do, for yourselves, whatever you think best.'

'Lord Mongrove (yelp) invited our (skree) help,' said CPS Shushurup in an aggrieved whine. 'Do not listen (skree) to her (yelp), Yusharisp. We must continue (roar) with our work!'

The limb holding the gun became steadier. Slowly, the Duke of Queens raised his hands, but he winked at Jherek Carnelian.

Lord Mongrove's gloomy boom interrupted the dispute. 'I have, I must admit, Yusharisp, been having second thoughts ...'

'*Second thoughts!*' Yusharisp was beside himself. 'At this (skree) stage!'

The little alien gestured with his weapon. 'Look (skree) out there at that – that (roar) nothingness. Can you not feel (yelp) the city breaking apart? Lord Mongrove, of all (skree) people, I would have thought that you (roar) could not change your mind. Why (skree) – why?'

The giant shuffled his feet in the rust and the dust. He scratched his huge head. He fingered the collar of his robe of funereal purple. 'As a matter of fact, Yusharisp, I, too, am becoming just a jot bored with this – um – drama.'

'Drama! Skrrreeeee! It is not a game (yelp) Lord Mongrove. You, yourself, said as (skree) much!'

'Well, no ...'

'There, you see, Sergeant Sherwood. It cannot be argued any longer, I think, that there are no devils in Hell. Look at those chaps there. Devils, if ever I saw some!' It was Harold Underwood, emerging from behind the Pweelian's spaceship. 'So much for the sceptics, eh? So much for the Darwinians, hm? So much, Sergeant Sherwood, for your much vaunted Science! Ha!' He approached Yusharisp with some curiosity. He inspected him through his pince-nez. 'What a distortion of the human body – revealing, of course, the distortion of the spirit within.' He straightened up, linking arms, again, with his disciple. 'With luck, Sergeant Sherwood, we shall soon get a look at the Arch Fiend Himself!' Nodding to those of the company he recognized, Harold Underwood wandered off again.

Mrs Underwood watched her husband disappear. 'I must say, I have never known him so agreeable. What a shame he could not have been brought here before.'

'I wash my (skree) feet of you all!' said Yusharisp. He

appeared to be sulking as he went to lean against the noxious side of his spaceship. 'Most of them have run away, already.'

'Shall we lower our hands?' asked the Duke of Queens.

'Do what you (skree) like ...'

'I wonder if my men 'ave caught them Latvians yet,' said Inspector Springer. 'Not, I suppose, that it matters a lot now. On the other 'and, I 'ate to leave things unfinished. Know what I mean, Duke?' He looked at his watch.

'Oh, I do, very much, Inspector Springer. I had plans for a party that would have made all other parties seem drab, and I was about to embark on my new project – a life-size reproduction of the ancient planet, Mars, complete with reproductions of all its major cities, and a selection of different cultures from its history. But with things as they are ...' He contemplated the blackness of infinity beyond the city, he contemplated the ruin within. 'There aren't the materials any longer, I suppose.'

'Or the means,' Mongrove reminded him. 'Are you sure, Duke, that you don't want to take part in this Salvation scheme?'

The Duke sat down upon a half-melted metal cube. 'It doesn't have much to recommend it, dear Mongrove. And one cannot help feeling, well, interfered with ...'

The cube on which he sat began to grumble. Apologetically he stood up.

'It is Fate which interferes with your useless idyll!' said Yusharisp, in some exasperation. 'Not (skree) the people of Pweeli. We acted (roar) from the noblest of motives.'

Once more losing interest in the conversation, Jherek made to lead Amelia away. She resisted his tugging hand for only a moment before going with him.

'The time-travellers and the space-travellers do not, as yet, seem to be aware of one another's presence,' she said. 'Should we tell them? After all, only a few yards separate them!'

'Let us leave them all, Amelia. Initially we sought privacy.'

Her expression softened. She moved closer to him. 'Of course, dear Jherek.'

He swelled with pleasure.

'It will be so sad,' she said a little later, in a melancholy tone, 'to die, when we have at last both admitted our feelings.'

'To die, Amelia?'

Something like a dead tree, but made of soft stone, started to flicker. A screen appeared in its trunk. The image of a man began to speak, but there was no sound. They watched it for a little while before continuing.

'To die?' he said.

'Well, we must accept the inevitable, Jherek.'

'To be called by my first name! You do not know, Amelia, how happy you make me!'

'There seemed no further point in refusing you the true expression of my feelings, since we have such a short time together.'

'We have eternity!'

'In one sense, possibly. But all are agreed that the city must soon perish.'

As if to deny her words, a steady throbbing began to pulse beneath their feet. It had strength and signified the presence of considerable energy, while the glow from the surrounding ruins suddenly took on a healthier colour, a sort of bright blue.

'There! The city recovers!' Jherek exclaimed.

'No. Merely the appearance of recovery which always precedes death.'

'What is that golden light over there?' He pointed beyond a line of still rotating cylinders. 'It is like sunshine, Amelia!'

They began to run towards the source of the light. Soon they could see clearly what lay ahead.

'The city's last illusion,' said Jherek. They were both overawed, for the vision was so simple yet so much at odds with its surroundings. It was a little grassy glade, full of wild flowers, warm and lovely in the sun, covering a space of only thirty feet or so, yet perfect in every detail, with butterflies, bees, and a bird perching in a delicate elm. They could hear the bird singing. They could smell the grass.

Hand in hand, they stepped into the illusion.

'It is as if the city's memory conjures up a final image of Earth at her loveliest,' said Amelia. 'A sort of monument.'

They seated themselves on a hillock. The ruins and the livid lights were still plainly visible, but they were able to ignore them.

Mrs Underwood pointed a little way ahead to where a red and white chequered cloth had been spread on the grass, under the tree. On the cloth were plates, flasks, fruits, a pie. 'Should we see if the picnic is edible?'

'In a moment.' He leaned back and breathed the air. Perhaps the scent of hyacinths he had detected earlier had come from here.

'It cannot last,' she reminded him. 'We should take advantage of it while we may.' She stretched herself, so that her head lay in his lap. He stroked her hair and her cheek. He stroked her neck. She breathed deeply and luxuriously, her eyes closed as she listened to the insects, feeling the warmth of that invisible, non-existent sun upon her skin. 'Oh, Jherek ...'

'Amelia.' He bent his head and kissed her tenderly upon the lips for the second time since they had come to the city, and without hesitation she responded, and his touch upon her bared shoulder, her waist, only made her cling to him the closer and kiss him more deeply.

'I am like a young girl,' she said, after a while. 'It is as it should have been.'

He was baffled by this reference, but he did not question her. He merely said : 'Now that you have called me by my first name, Amelia, does that mean that we are married, that we can ...'

She shook her head sadly. 'We can never – never be husband and wife. Not now.'

'No?'

'No, Jherek, dear. It is too late for that.'

'I see.' Wistfully, he pulled up a blade of grass.

'The divorce, you see, has not taken place. And no ceremony binds us. Oh, there is much I could explain, but let us not waste the minutes we have.'

'These – these conventions. They are important enough to deny us the expression of our love?'

'Oh, do not mistake me, my dear. I know now that those conventions are not universal – that they have no usefulness here – but you forget – for years I have obeyed them. I cannot, in my own self, rebel against them in so short a time. As it is, I quell a tide of guilt that threatens to flood through me.'

'Guilt, again?'

'Yes, dearest. If I went so suddenly against my training, I suspect that I should break down completely. I should not be the Amelia Underwood you know!'

'Yet, if there were more time ...'

'Oh, I know that eventually I should have been able to overcome the guilt ... That is the awful irony of it all!'

'It is ironic,' he agreed. He rose, helping her to her feet. 'Let us see what the picnic can offer us.'

The song of the bird (it was some sort of macaw) continued to sound from the tree as they approached the red and white chequered cloth, but another noise began to break through, a sort of shrilling which was familiar to both of them. Then, bursting from the gloom of the city into the sunlight of the illusion, Captain Mubbers, Rokfrug and the other Lat appeared. They were badly out of breath and sweating; they had something of the appearance of bright red, animated turnips. Their three pupils rolled wildly in their eyes as they sighted Jherek and Amelia and came to a confused halt.

'Mibix?' said Rokfrug, recognizing Jherek. 'Drexim flug roodi?'

523

'You are still, I take it, pursued by the police.' Amelia was impatient, more than cool towards the intruders. 'There is nowhere to hide here.'

'Hrunt krufroodi.' Captain Mubbers glanced behind him as there came a thundering of boots and the dozen identically clad police officers, evidently as weary as the Lat, burst into the pastoral illusion, paused, blinked, and began to advance towards their quarry, whereupon Captain Mubbers uttered a strangled 'Ferkit!' and turned at bay, ready to do battle against their overwhelming numbers.

'Oh, really!' cried Amelia Underwood. 'Officer, this will not do!' She addressed the nearest policeman.

The policeman said steadily: 'You're all under arrest. You might as well come quietly.'

'You intend to arrest us, as well?' Mrs Underwood bridled.

'Strictly speakin', ma'am, you've been under arrest from the start. All right, lads ...' But he hesitated when two loud popping noises sounded, close together, and Lord Jagged of Canaria, the Iron Orchid upon his arm, materialized on the hillock.

Lord Jagged was resplendent in his favourite pale yellow robes, his tall collar framing his patrician features. He seemed in high spirits. The Iron Orchid, at her most stately and beautiful, wore billowing white of an untypical cut and was as happy as her escort.

'At last!' said Lord Jagged, apparently in some relief. 'This must be the fiftieth attempt!'

'The forty-ninth, indefatigable Jagged,' crooned the Orchid. 'I intended to give up on the fiftieth.'

Jherek ran towards his friend and his mother. 'Oh, Jagged! Cryptic, magnificent, darling Jagged! We have worried about you so much! And Iron Orchid, you are delicious. Where, where have you been?'

The kiss from Jagged's lips on Jherek's was less than chaste and was equalled by the Iron Orchid's. Standing back from them, Mrs Underwood permitted herself a sniff, but came forward reluctantly as the radiant Orchid beckoned.

'My dears, you will be so delighted by our news! But you seem distraught. What has been happening to you?'

'Well,' said Mrs Underwood with some pleasure, 'we are currently under arrest, although the charge is not altogether clear.'

'You seem to have a penchant, you two, for falling foul of the law,' said Jagged, casting a languid eye over the company. 'It's all right, constable. I think you know who I am.'

The leading constable saluted, but stood his ground. 'Yes, sir,' he said uncertainly. 'Though we do 'ave orders, direct from the 'Ome Secretary ...'

'The Home Secretary, constable, takes his advice from me, as no doubt you are aware ...'

'I 'ad 'eard something to that effect, sir.' He fingered his chin. 'What about these Latvians?'

Lord Jagged shrugged. 'I don't think they offer a threat to the Crown any longer.'

Jherek Carnelian was overjoyed by his friend's performance. 'Excellent, dear Jagged! Excellent!'

'And then, sir, there's some question about it being the end o' the world,' continued the constable.

'Don't concern yourself with that, my good man. I'll look into it, the first chance I get.'

'Very well, sir.' As one in a dream, the policeman signed to his colleagues. 'We'd better be getting back, then. Shall we tell Inspector Springer you're in charge now, sir?'

'You might as well, constable.'

The policemen wandered out of the illusion and disappeared in the darkness of the city, leaving the Lat somewhat nonplussed. Captain Mubbers looked enquiringly up at Lord Jagged but received a dismissive glance.

Rokfrug had found the food and was cramming his mouth with pie. 'Groodnix!' he said. 'Trimpit dernik, queely!'

The rest of the Lat seated themselves around the cloth and were soon feasting with gusto.

'So, most miraculous of mothers, you knew all along where to find Lord Jagged!' Jherek hugged her again. 'You played the same game, eh?'

'Not at all!' She was offended. 'We met quite by accident. I had, it is true, grown so bored with our world that I sought one which would prove more agreeable and some, I'll admit, were interesting, but the Morphail Effect gave me difficulties. I kept being thrown out of one era and into another almost before I knew it. Brannart had warned me, but your experiences had caused me to disbelieve him.' She inspected her son from head to foot and her look towards Amelia Underwood was not as critical as it had once been. 'You are both pale. You need to replenish your bloom.'

'Now we bloom, opulent Orchid! We feared so much for your well-being. Oh, and since you have been gone the world has grown dark ...'

'Death, we are told, has come to the universe,' put in Amelia, returning the Iron Orchid's glance.

Lord Jagged of Canaria smiled a wide, soft smile. 'Well, so we are returned at an opportune moment.'

'It depends what you mean by opportune, Lord Jagged.' Amelia Underwood pointed out into the darkness. 'Even the city dies now.'

'Of all our friends,' Jherek continued sorrowfully, 'only Lord Mongrove and the Duke of Queens survive. The rest are memories only!'

'Memories are sufficient, I think,' said Jagged. 'They will do.'

'You are callous, sir!' Mrs Underwood adjusted a button at her throat.

'Call me so.'

'We expected you to be waiting for us, Jagged,' said Jherek Carnelian, 'when we returned to the End of Time. Did you not promise to be here – to explain?'

'I arrived, but had to leave again almost at once.

Through no fault of my own, I was delayed. My machine failed me. I had to make some experiments. It was in the course of these experiments that I happened to meet your mother and she prevailed upon me to satisfy a whim.'

'A whim?' Mrs Underwood turned away in disgust.

'We are married,' said the Iron Orchid almost demurely. 'At last.'

'Married. I envy you! How did this come about?'

'It was a simple ceremony, Jherek, my juice.' She stroked the white material of her gown. It seemed that she blushed.

Curiosity made Amelia Underwood turn back.

'It was in the fifty-eighth century, I think,' the Iron Orchid said. Their customs are very moving. Simple, yet profound. The sacrifice of the slaves had, happily, become optional by the middle of what I believe they called the "Wet Prince" period. We had little else to do, you see, since we were waiting for the right moment to try to transfer ...'

'Sans machine,' said Jagged, with a certain quiet pride. 'We have learned to travel, perforce, without gadgetry. It was always theoretically possible.'

'By a coincidence difficult to credit,' she continued, 'Lord Jagged found me a prisoner of some extra-terrestrial creatures temporarily in control of the planet —'

'The Flerpian Conquests of 4004–6,' explained Jagged in an aside.

'— and was able to rescue me before I could experience an interesting method of torture they had devised, where the shoulders are exposed to —' She broke off. 'But I digress. From there we continued to move forward as best we could, by a series of stages. I could not, of course, have done it on my own. And some of the natives were obstructive. But your father handled them so well. He is very good with natives, don't you think?'

Jherek said in a small voice. 'My father?'

'Lord Jagged, of course! You must have guessed!' She laughed fulsomely. 'You must have guessed, my egg!'

'I thought there was a rumour concerning Sweet Orb Mace ...'

'Your father wished to make a secret of it, for reasons of his own. It was so long ago. He had some scientific obsession, then, concerning his own genes and how best to perpetuate them. He thought this method the most satisfactory.'

'As it proved.' Lord Jagged put a slim-fingered hand upon his son's head and affectionately ruffled his hair. 'As it proved.'

Again, Jherek embraced Lord Jagged. 'Oh, I am so pleased, Jagged, that it is you! This news is a gift that makes all the waiting worthwhile.' He reached to take his shy Amelia's hand. 'This is, indeed, the happiest of days!'

Mrs Underwood was reserved, though she did not deny him her hand. She stood in that smiling company and she tried to speak. She failed, and now the Iron Orchid hugged her. 'Tell me, dearest Amelia, that you are to be our new daughter!'

'As I explained to Jherek, it might have been possible.'

'In the past?'

'You seem to forget, Iron Orchid, that there is nothing *but* the past. There is no future left to us.'

'No future?'

'She is quite right.' Lord Jagged took his hands from his son's shoulders.

'Oh!' A knuckle rose to Amelia's mouth. 'I had hoped you brought a reprieve. It was foolish ...'

Arranging his yellow robes about him, Lord Jagged of Canaria seated himself upon the hillock, indicating that they should join him. 'The information I have is probably not altogether palatable,' he began, 'but since I promised an explanation when last we parted, I feel obliged to fulfil that promise. I trust I will not bore you.' And he began to speak.

CHAPTER TWENTY

IN WHICH LORD JAGGED OF CANARIA EXHIBITS A FRANKNESS NOT PREVIOUSLY DISPLAYED

'I suppose, my dears, that I had best begin by admitting that I was not originally from the End of Time,' said Lord Jagged. 'My origins are not too far from your own, Amelia (if I may call you Amelia) – in the twenty-first century, to be exact. After a number of adventures, I arrived here, some thousand or so years ago and, not wishing to spend my life in a menagerie, set myself up as a self-created personality. Thus, though trapped by the Morphail Effect, I was able to continue my research and experiments into the Nature of Time, discovering, in fact, that I could, by exercising certain disciplines, remain for long periods in one era. It even became apparent that I could, if I wished, settle in certain unpopulated periods. During the course of these experiments, I met other time-travellers, including Mrs Persson (perhaps the most experienced chrononaut we have), and was able to exchange information, concluding, at last, that I was something of a sport, for no other time-traveller was as little influenced as was I by the Morphail Effect. At last I concluded that I was, under certain conditions, impervious to the Effect so long as I took particular precautions (which included settling very thoroughly in one period and producing no anachronisms whatsoever). Further research showed that my ability had only so much to do with self-discipline and a great deal to do with my particular genes.'

'Aha!' said Jherek. 'Others spoke of genes to us.'

'Quite so. Well, in the course of my various expeditions through the millennia I became aware, long before that alien brought the news to us, that the End of Time was close. Having learned so much, it seemed to me then that I might be able to save something of our culture and, indeed, ensure the survival of our race, by making a kind of loop. It must be obvious to you what I hoped to do – to take certain people from the End of Time and put them at the Beginning, with all their knowledge (or as much as could be taken) and their civilization intact. Science would build us new cities, I thought, and we should have billions more years ahead of us. However, one factor emerged very early and that concerned the Morphail Effect. It would not permit my plan, no matter how far back in Time I went. Only those with genes like mine might colonize the past. Therefore I modified my scheme. I would find a new Adam and Eve, who could breed together and produce a race unfettered by Time (or at least the irritating Morphail Effect). To do this I had to find a man and a woman who shared the same characteristics as myself. At length I gave up my search, discovered, through experiments, that your mother, Jherek, the Iron Orchid, was the only creature I had ever found who had genes even beginning to resemble mine. That was when I put to her, without her knowledge of my intentions, that we should conceive a child together.'

'It seemed such an amusing idea,' said the Iron Orchid. 'And no one had done anything like it for millennia!'

'Thus, after some difficulties, you were born, my boy. But I still needed to find a wife for you, one who could remain, say, in the Palaeozoic (where a station, as I think you now know, already exists) without suddenly being whisked out of it again. I searched from the beginning of

530

history, trying subject after subject, until at last, Amelia Underwood, I found my Eve – you!'

'If you had consulted me, sir . . .'

'I could tell you nothing. I have explained that I had to work in secrecy, that my method of countering the Morphail Effect was so delicate that I could not, then, afford a single tiny anachronism. To consult you, would have been to reveal something of my own identity. An impossibility then – a dangerous thought! I had to kidnap you and bring you here. Then I had to introduce you to Jherek, then I had to hope that you would be attracted to one another. Everything in fact seemed to go reasonably well. But I reckoned without the complications – My Lady Charlotina, you'll recall, interfered, piqued by the manner in which she had been deceived by us.'

'And when I went to seek your help, you were not there, Jagged! You were about your temporal adventurings, then!'

'Exactly, Jherek. By bad chance I was not able to forestall your going to Brannart, borrowing a machine and returning to the nineteenth century. I was, I assure you, as surprised to encounter you there as you were surprised to see me! Luckily, in one of my rôles, as High Court Judge, I arranged to preside at your trial . . .'

'. . . and you could not acknowledge me, because of the Morphail Effect!'

'Yes. But I did arrange for the Effect to work at the very moment of your apparent execution. This led me to make other discoveries about the Nature of Time, but I could not afford, even then, to tell you of my plans. Mrs Underwood had to remain where she was (itself regarded as an impossibility by Brannart) while I worked. I returned here, as soon as possible, desperately trying to remedy matters but gradually learning more and more things which conflicted with Brannart's theories. I was able to contact Mrs Persson and she was of considerable help to me. I arranged to meet her here, by the by . . .'

'She has arrived,' Amelia Underwood told him.

'I am very pleased. She wishes to watch – but I move ahead of myself. The next thing I learned, on my return, was that you had again vanished, Jherek. But you had made a discovery which was to alter my whole research. I had heard rumours about a method of recycling Time, but had dismissed them. The Nursery you discovered not only proved that it was possible, but showed *how* it was possible. It meant that much of what I had been doing was no longer necessary. But you, of course, were still stranded. I risked much to return and rescue you all, exposing myself to the Morphail Effect and, indeed, suffering from it. I became stranded in the nineteenth century, and if it had not been for that time-travelling fellow, what's-his-name, arriving out of the blue, I might never have hit upon the solution to my problem. He was able to give me a great deal of information about alternate time-cycles – he was from one himself, of course – and I regret that, in order to save myself embarrassment (for by then I had exposed myself too far and my disguises, as it were, were wearing rather thin) I had to go along with the Home Secretary's scheme for commandeering his time-craft and sending it after you. I did not imagine the complications I have witnessed ...'

'It seems to me, Lord Jagged,' murmured Amelia Underwood, 'that your problems would not have arisen at all, had you anticipated certain ordinary human factors ...'

'I bow to your criticism, Amelia. I deserve it. But I was a man obsessed – and needing to act, I thought, with great urgency. All the various fluctuations created in the mega-flow – largely because of me, I'll admit – were actually contributing to the general confusion. The present condition of this universe would not have manifested itself for a while yet, but for the energy used by the cities in our various schemes. But all that will change now, with luck.'

'Change? You say it is too late.'

'Did I give you that impression? I am sorry. I wish that you had not had to suffer so much, particularly since it now appears that my whole experiment was pointless.'

'Then we cannot settle in the past, as you planned?' said Jherek.

'Pointless!' Amelia gasped with indignation.

'Well, yes and no.'

'Did you not deliberately place us in the Palaeozoic as part of your experiment, Lord Jagged?'

'No, Amelia. I was not deceiving you. I thought I sent you here.'

'Instead we went back.'

'That is what I am coming to. You did not, strictly speaking, go back. You went *forward*, and thus countered the Morphail Effect at core!'

'How so?'

'Because you completed a circle. If Time is a circle (and it is only one way of looking at it) and we travel it round, we go, of course, from the End to the Beginning quite swiftly, do you see? You overshot the End – you went completely round and back to the Beginning.'

'And deceived the Morphail Effect!' said Jherek, clapping his hands together.

'In a word, yes. It means that we can, if we so desire, all escape the End of Time merely by jumping forward to the Beginning. The disadvantages, however, are considerable. We should not, for one thing, have the power of the cities ...'

But Jherek's excitement dismissed these quibbles. 'And so, like Ovid, you return to lead us from Time's captivity into the promised land – forward, as you might put it, Jagged, into the past!'

'Not so.' His father laughed. 'There is no need for any of us to leave this planet or this period.'

'But final destruction looms, if it is not already upon us.'

'Nonsense – what has given you that impression?'

'Come,' said Jherek beginning to rise, 'I'll show you.'

'But I have much more to tell you, my son.'

'Later – when you have seen.'

'Very well.' With a swirl of his robes, Lord Jagged of Canaria helped first Amelia, then his wife, to their feet. 'It would probably be a good idea, anyway, to seek out Mrs Persson and the others. But really, Jherek, this uncharacteristic alarmism is scarcely called for.'

From their picnic Captain Mubbers and Rokfrug looked up. 'Trorf?' said the leader of the Lat through a mouthful of plumcake; but his lieutenant calmed him. 'Grushfalls, hrunt fresha.' They gave their attention back to the food and scarcely noticed as the four humans stepped carefully out of the little pastoral glade and into the lurid, flickering light of that vast expanse of ruins whose very atmosphere, it now seemed to Jherek, gave off a faint, chilly scent of death.

CHAPTER TWENTY-ONE

A QUESTION OF ATTITUDES

'I must say,' Jagged paused in his rapid, stately stride, 'the city suffers a certain lassitude ...'

'Oh, Jagged, you understate!' His son was beside him, while the ladies, in conference, came a little way behind.

Streamers of half-metallic, half-organic matter, of a dusty lavender shade, wriggled across their path as if withdrawn by the squat building on their right. In the gloom, it was impossible to tell their nature.

'But it revives,' Jagged said. 'Look there, is that not a newly created conduit?' The pipe he indicated, running to left and right of them, did seem new, though very ordinary.

'It is no sign, paternal Jagged. The illusions proliferate.'

His father was insouciant. 'If you'll have it so.' There was a glint in his eye. 'Youth was ever obstinate.'

Jherek Carnelian detected irony in his father, his friend. 'Ah, sardonic Jagged, it is so good to have your companionship again! All trepidation vanishes!'

'Your confidence warms me.' Jagged's gesture was expansive. 'What, after all, is a father for but to give comfort to his children?'

'Children?'

A casual wave. 'One forms attachments, here and there, in Time. But you, Jherek, are my only heir.'

'A song?'

'A son, my love.'

As they advanced through the glowing semi-darkness, Jherek, infected by Jagged's apparently causeless optimism, sought for signs which would indicate that the city came back to life. Perhaps there were indeed signs of this revivification: that light which, as he had seen, glowed a robust blue, and light which now burned steady crimson; moreover, the regular pounding from beneath his feet put him in mind of the beat of a strengthening heart. But, no. How could it be?

Fastidious as ever, Lord Jagged folded back one of his sleeves so that it should not trail in the fine rust which lay everywhere upon the ground. 'We can rely upon the cities,' he said, 'even if we cannot ever hope fully to understand them.'

'You speculate, Jagged. The evidence is all to the contrary. Their sources of power have dissipated.'

'The sources exist. The cities have discovered them.'

'Even you, Jagged, cannot be so certain.' But Jherek spoke now to be denied.

'You are aware, then, of all the evidence?' Jagged paused, for ahead of them was darkness. 'Have we reached the outskirts?'

'It seems so.'

They waited for the Iron Orchid and Amelia Underwood, who had fallen some distance behind. To Jherek's surprise the two women appeared to be enjoying one another's company. No longer did they glare or make veiled attacks. They might have been the oldest of friends. He wondered if he would ever come to understand these subtle shifts of attitude in women; yet he was pleased. If all were to perish, it would be as well to be on good terms at the end. He hailed them.

Here the city shed a wider shaft of light into the landscape beyond: a pale, cracked, barren expanse no longer deserving the appellation 'earth'; a husk that might crumble to invisible dust at a touch.

The Iron Orchid twisted a white pleat. 'Dead.'

'And in the last stages of decay.' Amelia was sympathetic.

The Orchid put her back to the scene. 'I cannot accept,' she said levelly, 'that this is my world. It was so vital.'

'It's vitality was stolen, so Mongrove says.' Jherek contemplated the darkness which his mother refused.

'That's true of all life, in a sense.' Lord Jagged touched, for a second, his wife's hand. 'Well, the core remains.'

'Is it not already rotten, Lord Jagged?' Perhaps Amelia regretted her remorselessness as she glimpsed the Orchid's face.

'It can be revived, one supposes.'

'It is cold ... complained the Iron Orchid, moving further away, towards the interior.

'We drift, surely,' Jherek said. 'There is no sun. Not another star survives. Not a single meteorite. We drift in eternal darkness – and that darkness must, dear parent, shortly engulf us, too!'

'You over-dramatize, my boy.'

'Possibly he does not.' The Orchid's voice lacked timbre.

They followed her and, almost immediately, came upon the machines used by the time-traveller and by Mrs Persson and Captain Bastable.

'But where are our friends?' mused Lord Jagged.

'They were here not long since,' Jherek told him. 'The Morphail Effect?'

'Here!' Lord Jagged's look was frankly sceptical.

'Could they be with Yusharisp and the others?' Jherek smiled vaguely at Amelia and his mother, who had linked arms. He was still puzzled by the change in them. It had something to do, he felt, with the Iron Orchid's marriage to Lord Jagged, this banishment of the old tension. 'Shall we seek them out, venturesome Jagged?'

'You know where to look?'

'Over there.'

'Then lead on, my innocent!' Lord Jagged, as had often been his way in the old days, appeared to be relishing a private joke. He stood aside for Jherek.

The light from the city glittered, for a moment sharp rather than murky, and a building that had been a ruin now seemed whole to Jherek, but elsewhere there were creakings and murmurings and groanings, all suggestive of the city's decline. Again they emerged at the edge, and here the light was very dim indeed. It was not until he heard a sound that Jherek was able to advance.

'If (skree) you would take back to their (yelp) own time this (skree) group, it would at least (roar) reduce the problem to tidier proportions, Mrs (yelp) Persson.'

They were all assembled, now, about the Pweelian spacecraft – Inspector Springer and his constables, the Duke of Queens, huge, melancholy Mongrove, the time-traveller in his Norfolk jacket and plus-fours, Mrs Persson and Captain Bastable in their black uniforms, gleaming like sealskin. Only Harold Underwood, Sergeant Sherwood and the Lat were missing. Against the mould-like exterior of the Pweelian spaceship the Pweelians themselves were hard to distinguish. Beyond the group lay the now-familiar blackness of the infinite void.

They heard Mrs Persson. 'We made no preparations for passengers. As it is, we are anxious to return to our base to begin certain important experiments needed to verify our understanding of the multiverse's intersections ...'

Lord Jagged, his pale yellow robes in contrast to the general nocturnal colouring of his surroundings, strolled into the group, leaving Jherek and the two women to follow. Jagged's private mirth was unabated. 'You are as anxious as ever, my dear Yusharisp.' Though it must have been some time since last he had seen the alien, Jagged had no difficulty in identifying him. 'And so you persist in taking the narrower view?'

The little creature's many eyes glared distastefully at

the newcomer. 'I should have (roar) thought, Lord Jagged, that no broader view (yelp) existed!' He became suspicious. 'Have you (skree) been here all along?'

'Only recently returned.' Lord Jagged performed a brief bow. 'I apologize. There were difficulties. A fine judgement is required, so close to the end of all things, if one is to arrive with matter beneath one's feet or find oneself in absolute vacuum!'

'At least (roar) you'll admit ...'

'Oh, I don't think we need disagree, Mr Yusharisp. Let us accept the fact that we shall always be temperamentally at odds. This is the moment for realism, is it not?'

Yusharisp, whilst remaining suspicious, subsided.

CPS Shushurup intervened. 'Everything is settled (skree). We intend to requisition (skree) whatever we can salvage from the (roar yelp) city in order to further our survival plans. If you wish to (yelp) help, and share the subsequent benefit (skree) of our work ...'

'Requisition? Salvage?' Lord Jagged raised a cool eyebrow. It seemed that his tall collar quivered. 'Why should that be necessary?'

'We have (skree) not the time to (roar) spare to (skree) explain again!'

Lord Mongrove lifted his heavy head, contemplating Jagged through dismal eyes, his voice as doom-laden as ever, though he spoke as if he had never associated himself with the extra-terrestrials. 'They have this scheme, equivocal Jagged, to build a self-contained environment which will outlast the final collapse of the cities.' He was a bell, tolling the futility of struggle. 'It has certain merits.'

Lord Jagged was openly dismissive. He was dry. He was contemptuous. 'I am sure it would suit the Pweelian preference for tidiness as opposed to order. For simplification as opposed to multiplicity of choice.' The patrician features displayed stern dismay. 'But they have no business, Lord Mongrove, interfering with the workings of our city (which I am sure they understand poorly).'

'Do any of us ...?' But Mongrove was already quelled.

'Besides,' continued the chrononaut, 'it is only recently that I installed my own equipment here. I should be more than a little upset if, however inadvertently, it were tampered with.'

'What?' The Duke of Queens was lifted from apathy. He stared about him, as if he would see the machinery. He became hopeful and expectant. 'Your own equipment, sagacious Jagged? Oho!' He stroked his beard and, as he stroked, a smile began to appear. 'Aha!'

They formed an audience for the lord in yellow. He gave them his best, all subtlety and self-control, with just a hint of self-mockery, enough to win the full attention of even the mistrustful time-traveller.

'Installed not long since with the help of your friend, Jherek, who enabled you to reach the nineteenth century on your last visit.'

'Nurse?' Affection warmed him.

'The same. She was invaluable. Her programmes contained every scrap of information needed. It was merely a question of refreshing her memory. She is the most sophisticated of any ancient automaton I have ever encountered. I was soon able to put our problem to her and suggest the solution. Much of the rest of the work was hers.'

The Iron Orchid evidently knew nothing of this. 'The work, heroic husband?'

'Needed to install the equipment I mentioned. You will have noticed that, of late, the city has been conserving its power, in unison with all our other cities.'

'Con(skree)serving! Bah (roar)!' Yusharisp's translation box uttered something resembling a bitter laugh. 'Ex(skree)pending its last (roar), you mean!'

Lord Jagged of Canaria ignored the Pweelian, turning instead to the Duke of Queens. 'It was fortunate that when I returned to the End of Time, seeking Jherek and Amelia, I heard of the discovery of the Nursery and was able to invite Nurse to Castle Canaria.'

'So that is where she disappeared to – she's in your

menagerie, devious Jagged!'

'Not exactly. I doubt if much of my menagerie, such as it was, survives. Nurse is now in one of the other cities. She should be finishing off a few minor adjustments.'

'You have a plan, then, to save a whole city?' Lord Mongrove glanced behind him. 'Surely not this one. See how it perishes, as we watch!'

'This is needless pessimism, Lord Mongrove. The city transforms itself, that is all.'

'But the light . . .' began the Duke of Queens.

'Conserved, as I said.'

'And out there?' Mongrove gestured towards the void.

'You could populate it. There is room for a good-sized sun.'

'You see, Jagged,' explained the Duke of Queens, 'our power-rings do not work. It suggests that the city cannot give us the energy we require.'

'You have tried?'

'We have.'

'Not two hours since,' said Amelia Underwood.

'While the city was in flux. But now?'

'They will not work, Lord Jagged.' Lord Mongrove stroked the dark stones on his fingers. 'Our inheritance is spent forever.'

'Oh, you are too doleful, all of you. It is merely a question of attitude.' Lord Jagged stretched his left hand out before him and with his right he began to twist a ruby, staring into the sky the while, still half-conscious of his audience.

Overhead there appeared what might have been a small, twinkling star; but it was already growing. It became a fiery comet, turning the stark landscape jet black and glaring white. It grew again and it was a sun illuminating the featureless world for as far as their wincing eyes could see.

'That will do, I think.' Jagged was quietly satisfied. 'The conventional orbit.' Another touch of the same ring. 'And a turning world.'

Amelia murmured: 'You are the Master Conjuror, dear

Lord Jagged. A veritable Mephistopheles. Is that sun the size of the old one?'

'A trifle smaller, but it is all we need.'

'Skree,' said Yusharisp in alarm, all his eyes slitted to resist the glare. 'Skree, skree, skree!'

Jagged chose to take the remark as a compliment. 'Just a simple beginning or two,' he murmured modestly. He swirled the great yellow cloak about him. He touched another ring and the glare became less blinding, diffused as it was, now, by the shimmering atmosphere existing everywhere beyond the city. The sky became a greenish blue and the white landscape, with its deep, black fissures, became a dull grey, seamed with brown cracks; yet still it stretched to every horizon.

'How unsightly is our Earth without its images.' The Iron Orchid was disdainful.

As if apologizing for it, Jagged said: 'It is a very old planet, my dear. But you must all regard it as a new canvas. Everything you wish for can be re-created. New scenes can be created, just as it has always been. Rest assured that the cities will not fail us.'

'So Judgement Day is resisted, after all.' The time-traveller had his head on one side as he looked, with new eyes, at Lord Jagged of Canaria. 'I congratulate you, sir. You command enormous power, it seems.'

'I borrow the power,' said Jagged, to him, his voice soft. 'It comes from the cities.'

CPS Shushurup cried: 'It cannot be real! This man confounds us with an illusion (skree)!'

Lord Jagged affected not to hear him and turned, instead, to Mrs Persson who watched him, her expression analytical. 'The cities conserved their energies because I need them for what, I am confident, will be a successful experiment. Of course, not everyone will consider my plan a perfect one, but it is a beginning. It is what I mentioned to you, Mrs Persson.'

'It is why we are here.' Her smile was for Captain Bastable. 'To see if it should work. Certainly I am convinced by the preliminaries.'

The huge and healthy sun shone down on them all, its light spreading through the city, casting great, mellow shadows. The city continued to throb quietly and steadily; an engine waiting to be used.

'It's extremely impressive, sir,' said Bastable. 'When do you intend to make the loop?'

'In about a month.'

'You cannot,' said Mrs Persson, 'sustain this state indefinitely?'

'It would be preferable, of course, but uneconomic.'

They shared amusement.

CPS Shushurup waddled up, waving a leg. 'Do not let (skree) yourselves be (roar) convinced by this (skree) illusion. For (roar) illusion is all that it is!'

Lord Jagged said mildly: 'It depends, does it not, upon your interpretation of the word "illusion"? It is a warming sun, a breathable atmosphere, the planet turns on its orbit, it circles that sun.'

Yusharisp joined the Chief Public Servant. The bright sunlight emphasized the warts and blotches on his little round body. 'It is illusion (skree), Lord Jagged, because (roar) it cannot last the (yelp) disintegration (skree) of the universe!'

'I think it will, Mr Yusharisp.' Lord Jagged made to address his son, but the Pweelians refused to content themselves with his answer.

'Energy (skree) is needed to produce (roar) such "miracles" – you will (skree) agree to that?'

Lord Jagged inclined his head.

'There must (roar) therefore be a source (skree) – perhaps a planet (skree) or two which (yelp) have escaped the (skree) catastrophe. That source (roar) will be used up soon (yelp) enough!'

It seemed that Lord Jagged of Canaria spoke to everyone but his questioner. He retained the same mild, but slightly icy, expression. 'I fear that you cannot draw satisfaction even from that idea, my dear Yusharisp. Morals may be drawn, but by a more liberal intelligence.'

'Morals (skree)! You know (roar) nothing of such (yelp) things!'

Lord Jagged continued to speak to them all, now more directly than before. 'Such is the character of one prone to morbid anxiety that he would rather *experience* the worst of things than *hope* for the best. It is a particular and puritanical mentality, and one to which I can respond with scant sympathy. Why have such conclusions been drawn? Because that kind of mentality would prefer to bring on catastrophe rather than live forever in fear of its *possibility*. Suicide rather than uncertainty.'

'You are not (roar) suggesting that (skree) this problem was merely (yelp) in our own (skree) minds, Lord Jagged?' Again the strange, mechanical laughter from CPS Shushurup.

'Was it not the people of Pweeli who took it upon themselves to spread the bad news throughout the galaxy? Did you not preach your despair wherever you could find hearers? The facts were plain enough to all, but your response to them was scarcely positive. Therefore, yes – to some degree the problem was merely in your own minds. You have not investigated all the possibilities. Your case depends, for one thing, upon a firm belief in a finite universe, with finite resources. However, as the time-traveller here will tell you and as Mrs Persson and Captain Bastable will confirm, the universe is not finite.'

'Words (skree) and nothing more ...'

The time-traveller spoke earnestly. 'I may not agree with Lord Jagged in most things, but he speaks the truth. There are a multiplicity of dimensions to the universe which you, Mrs Persson, refer to I believe as "the multiverse". This is merely one such dimension, although, indeed, all experience the same fate as this one, but not simultaneously.'

Lord Jagged acknowledged the time-traveller's support. 'Therefore, by drawing its resources from any part of the multiverse at any point in time – *which will not be a parallel point* – this planet can be sustained forever, if need be.'

'The notion (yelp) is quite without foundation,' said Yusharisp dismissively.

Lord Jagged drew his high collar about his face and stretched an elegant hand towards the sun. 'There is my proof, gentlemen.'

'Illusion,' said Yusharisp obstinately, '(yelp).'

'Pseudo-science (skree),' agreed Shushurup.

Lord Jagged made an acquiescent gesture and would respond no more, but Mrs Persson remained sympathetic to the aliens in their great distress. 'We have discovered,' she said gently, 'that the "real" universe is infinite. Infinite, timeless and still. It is a tranquil pool which will reflect any image we conceive.'

'Meta(skree)physical poppy(roar)cock!'

Captain Bastable came to her aid. 'It is *we* who populate the universe with what we call Time and Matter. Our intelligence moulds it; our activities give it detail. If, sometimes, we imprison ourselves, it is perhaps because our humanity is at fault, or our logic ...'

'How can we (skree) take seriously such notions?' Yusharisp's many eyes blinked contemptuously. 'You people make a playground of the universe and justify your actions with arguments so (roar) preposterous that no (skree) intelligent being (yelp) could believe them for a moment. You deceive (skree) yourselves so that you may (yelp) remain unembarrassed by any morality ...'

Lord Jagged seemed more languid than ever and his voice was sleepy. 'The infinite universe is just that, Yusharisp. It is all a playground.' He paused. 'To "take it seriously" is to demean it.'

'You will (roar) not respect the very stuff of (skree) life?'

'To respect it is quite another thing to "taking it seriously".'

'There is (skree) no difference!' The alien was smug; his comrades seemed to congratulate him.

'Ah,' said Lord Jagged, his smile small. 'You emphasize the very difference in our viewpoints, by insisting on this difference.'

'Bah (skree)!' Yusharisp glowered.

As if apologizing for his one-time friend, Lord Mongrove droned: 'I think he is upset because he places such importance on the destruction of the universe. Its end confirmed his moral understanding of things. I felt much as he did, at one stage. But now I grow weary of the ideas.'

'Turn(yelp)coat!' said CPS Shushurup. 'It was on your invitation (skree) Lord Mongrove that (yelp) we came (skree) here!'

'There was surely nowhere else to go.' Mongrove was faintly astonished. 'This is, after all, the only bit of matter left in the universe.'

With dignity, CPS Shushurup raised an admonishing hand (or foot). 'Come, Yusharisp, fellow Pweelians. There is (skree) no more use in (roar) trying to do (yelp) anything (roar) more for these fools!' The entire deputation, the Last of the Pweelians, began to waddle back in single-file into their unwholesome spacecraft.

Mongrove, remorseful, made to follow. 'Dear friends – fellow intelligences – do nothing drastic, please ...' But the hatch squelched shut in his melancholy face and he uttered a lugubrious sigh. The ship did not take-off. It remained exactly where it had landed, in silent accusation. Moodily Mongrove began to pick at a piece of mould on its surface. 'Oh, this is truly a Hell for the serious-minded!'

Inspector Springer removed his bowler hat to wipe his forehead in a characteristic gesture. 'It *'as* become rather warm, sir, all of a sudden. Nice to see the sun again, though, I suppose.' He turned to his sweltering men. 'You can loosen your collars, lads, if you wish. 'E's quite right. As 'ot as 'ell. I'm beginning to believe it meself.' The constables began to unbutton the tops of their tunics. One or two went so far as to remove their helmets and were not admonished.

A moment later, Inspector Springer removed his jacket.

'And the preliminaries are now complete. There is a sun, an atmosphere, the planet revolves.' Una Persson's words were clipped as she spoke to Lord Jagged.

Lord Jagged had been lost in thought. He raised his eyes and smiled. 'Ah, yes. As I said. They are over. The rest must be dealt with later, when I activate my equipment.'

'You said you are certain of success.' The time-traveller was cool, still critical. He was not disposed to support Lord Jagged's view of himself. 'The experiment seems somewhat grandiose to me.'

Lord Jagged accepted the criticism. 'I make no claims, sir. The technology is not of my invention, as I said. But it will do its job, with Nurse's help.'

'You will re-cycle Time!' exclaimed Captain Bastable. 'I do hope we can return in order to witness that stage of the experiment.'

'It will be safe enough, during the first week,' said Jagged.

'Is that how you intend to preserve the planet, Jagged?' Jherek asked in excitement. 'To use the equipment I found in the Nursery?'

'It is similar equipment, though more complex. It should preserve our world for eternity. I shall make a loop of a seven-day period. Once made, it will be inviolable. The cities will become self-perpetuating; there will be no threats either from Time or from Space, for the world will be closed off, re-living the same seven days over and over again.'

'We shall re-live the same short period for eternity?' The Duke of Queens shook his head. 'I must say, Jagged, that your scheme has no more attraction than Yusharisp's.'

Lord Jagged was grave. 'If you are conscious of what is happening, then you will not repeat your actions during that period. But the time will remain the same, even though it seems to change.'

'We shall not be trapped – condemned to a mere week

547

of activity which we shall not be able to alter?'

'I think not.' Lord Jagged looked out across the miles and miles of wasteland. 'Ordinary life, as we know it at the End of Time, can continue as it has always done. The Nursery itself was deliberately limited – a kind of temporal deep-freeze to preserve the children.'

'How quickly one would become bored, if one had the merest hint that that was happening.' The Iron Orchid did her best to hide any anxiety she might display.

'Again, it is a question of attitudes, my dear. Is the prisoner a prisoner because he lives in a cage or because he *knows* that he lives in a cage?'

'Oh, I shall not attempt to discuss such things!'

He spoke fondly. 'And there, my dear, lies your salvation.' He embraced her. 'And now there is one more thing I must do here. The equipment must be supplied with energy.'

While they watched, he walked a little way into the city and stood looking about him. His pose was at once studied and casual. Then he seemed to come to a decision and placed the palm of his right hand across all the rings on his left.

The city gave out one high, almost triumphant, yell. There came a pounding roar as every building shook itself. Blue and crimson light blended in a brilliant aura overhead, blotting the sun. Then a deep sound, comforting and powerful, issued from the very core of the planet. There was a rustling from the city, familiar murmurings, the squeak of some half-mechanical creature.

Then the aura began to grow dim and Jagged became tense, as if he feared that the city could not, after all, supply the energy for his experiment.

There came a whining noise. The aura grew strong again and formed a dome-shaped cap hovering a hundred feet or more over the whole of the city. Then Lord Jagged of Canaria seemed to relax, and when he turned back to them there was a suggestion of self-congratulation in his features.

548

Amelia Underwood was the first to speak as he returned. 'Ah, Mephistopheles. Are you capable, now, of creation?'

He was flattered by the reference this time. He shared a private glance. 'What's this, Mrs Underwood? Manicheanism?'

'Oh, dear! Perhaps!' A hand went to her mouth, but she parodied herself.

He added: 'I cannot create a world, Amelia, but I can revive an existing one, bring the dead to life. And perhaps I once hoped to populate another world. Oh, you are right to think me prideful. It could be my undoing.'

On Jagged's right, from behind a gleaming ruin of gold and steel, came Harold Underwood and Sergeant Sherwood. They sweated, both, but seemed unaware of the heat. Mr Underwood indicated the sunny sky, the blue aura. 'See Sergeant Sherwood, how they tempt us now.' He pushed his pince-nez more firmly onto his nose as he approached Lord Jagged who towered over him, his extra height given emphasis by his face-framing collar. 'Did I hear right, sir?' said Mr Underwood. 'Did my wife – perhaps my ex-wife, I am not sure – refer to you by a certain name?'

Lord Jagged, smiling, bowed.

'Ha!' said Harold Underwood, satisfied. 'I must congratulate you, I suppose, on the quality of your illusions, the variety of your temptations, the subtlety of your torments. This present illusion, for instance, could well deceive some. What seemed to be Hell now resembles Heaven. Thus, you tempted Christ, on the mountain.'

Even Lord Jagged was nonplussed. 'The reference was a joking one, Mr Underwood ...'

'Satan's jokes are always clever. Happily, I have the example of my Saviour. Therefore, I bid you good-day, Son of the Morning. You may have claimed my soul, but you shall never own it. I trust you are thwarted as often as possible in your machinations.'

'Um ...' said Lord Jagged.

Harold Underwood and Sergeant Sherwood began to head towards the interior, but not before Harold had addressed his wife: 'You are doubtless already Satan's slave, Amelia. Yet I know we can still be saved, if we are genuinely repentant and believe in the Salvation of Christ. Be wary of all this, Amelia. It is merely a semblance of life.'

'Very convincing, on the surface, though, isn't it, sir?' said Sergeant Sherwood.

'He is the Master Deceiver, Sergeant.'

'I suppose 'e is, sir.'

'But –' Harold flung an arm around his disciple – 'I was right in one thing, eh? I said we should meet Him eventually.'

Amelia sucked at her lower lip. 'He is quite mad, Jherek. What should we do for him? Can he be sent back to Bromley?'

'He seems very much at ease here, Amelia. Perhaps so long as he receives regular meals which the city, after all, can be programmed to provide, he could stay here with Sergeant Sherwood.'

'I should not like to abandon him.'

'We can come and visit him from time to time.'

She remained dubious. 'It has not quite impinged upon me,' she said, 'that it is not the end of the world!'

'Have you ever seen him more relaxed?'

'Never. Very well, let him stay here, for the moment at least, in his – his Eternal Damnation.' She uttered a peculiar laugh.

Inspector Springer approached Lord Jagged with due deference. 'So things are more or less back to normal then, are they sir?'

'More or less, Inspector.'

Inspector Springer sucked at a tooth. 'Then I suppose we'd better get on with the job then, sir. Roundin' up the suspects and that ...'

'Most of them are in the clear now, Inspector.'

'The Latvians, Lord Jagged?'

'I suppose you could arrest them, yes.'

'Very good, sir.' Inspector Springer saluted and returned his attention to his twelve constables. 'All right, lads. Back on duty again. What's Sherwood up to? Better give 'im a blast on your whistle, Reilly, see if 'e answers.' He mopped his forehead. 'This *is* a very peculiar place. If I was a dreamin' man, I'd be 'alf inclined to think I was in the middle of a bloomin' nightmare. Har, har!' The answering laughter of some of his men as they plodded behind him was almost hollow.

Una Persson glanced at one of several instruments attached to her arm. 'I congratulate you, Lord Jagged. The first stages are a great success. We hope to be able to return to witness the completion.'

'I would be honoured, Mrs Persson.'

'Forgive me, now, if I get back to my machine. Captain Bastable . . .'

Bastable hovered, evidently reluctant to go.

'Captain Bastable, we really must —'

He became attentive. 'Of course, Mrs Persson. The Shifter and so forth.' He waved a cheerful hand to them all. 'It's been an enormous pleasure. And thank you so much, Lord Jagged, for the privilege . . .'

'Not at all.'

'I suppose, unless we do return just before the loop is finally made, we shall not be able to meet —'

'Come along, Oswald!' Mrs Persson was marching through the mellow sunshine to where they had left their machine.

'Oh, I don't know.' Lord Jagged waved in reply. 'A pleasant journey to you.'

'Thanks most awfully, again.'

'Captain Bastable!'

'— because of the drawbacks you mentioned,' shouted Bastable breathlessly, and ran to join his co-chrononaut.

When they had gone, Amelia Underwood looked almost suspiciously at the man Jherek one day hoped to make her father-in-law. 'The world is definitely saved, is it, Lord Jagged?'

'Oh, definitely. The cities have ample energy. The time-loop, when it is made, will re-cycle that energy. Jherek has told you of his adventures in the Nursery. You understand the principle.'

'Sufficiently, I hope. But Captain Bastable spoke of drawbacks.'

'I see.' Lord Jagged pulled his cloak about him. Now Mongrove and the Duke of Queens, the time-traveller and the Iron Orchid, Jherek and Amelia were all that remained of his audience. He spoke more naturally. 'Not for all, Amelia, those drawbacks. After a short period of re-adjustment, say a month, in which Nurse and I will test our equipment until we are satisfied with its functioning, the world will be in a perpetually closed circuit, with both past and future abolished. A single planet turning about a single sun will be all that remains of this universe. It will mean, therefore, that both time-travel and space-travel will be impossible. The drawback will be (for many of us) that there is no longer any intercourse between our world of the End of Time and other worlds.'

'That is all?'

'It will mean much to some.'

'To me!' groaned the Duke of Queens. 'I do wish you had told me, Jagged. I'd hoped to re-stock my menagerie.' He looked speculatively at the Pweelian spaceship. He fingered a power-ring.

'A few time-travellers may yet arrive, before the loop is made,' comforted Jagged. 'Besides, doleful Duke, your creative instincts will be fulfilled for a while, I am sure, by helping in the resurrection of all our old friends. There are dozens. Argonheart Po ...'

'Bishop Castle. My Lady Charlotina. Mistress Christia. Sweet Orb Mace. O'Kala Incarnadine. Doctor Volospion.' The Duke brightened.

'The long-established time-travellers, like Li Pao, may also still be here – or will re-appear, thanks to the

552

Morphail Effect.'

'I thought you had proved that a fallacy, Lord Jagged.'
Mongrove spoke with interest.

'I have proved it a Law – but not the only Law – of
Time.'

'We shall resurrect Brannart and tell him!' said the
Iron Orchid.

Amelia was frowning. 'So the planet will be completely
isolated, for eternity, in time and space.'

'Exactly,' said Jagged.

'Life will continue as it has always done,' said the Duke
of Queens. 'Who shall you resurrect first, Mongrove?'

'Werther de Goethe, I suppose. He is no real fellow
spirit, but he will do for the moment.' The giant cast a
glance back at the Pweelian spaceship as he began to move
his great bulk forward. 'Though it will be a travesty, of
course.'

'What do you mean, melancholy Mongrove?' The Duke
of Queens turned a power-ring to rid himself of his uniform and replace it with brilliant multicoloured feathers
from head to foot, a coxcomb in place of his hair.

'A travesty of life. This will be a stagnant planet, forever cycling a stagnant sun. A stagnant society, without
progress or past. Can you not see it, Duke of Queens?
Shall we have been spared death only to become the living dead, dancing forever to the same stale measures?'

The Duke of Queens was amused. 'I congratulate you,
Lord Mongrove. You have found an image with which to
distress yourself. I admire your alacrity!'

Lord Mongrove licked his large lips and wrinkled his
great nose. 'Ah, mock me, as you always mock me – as you
all mock me. And why not? I am a fool! I should have
stayed out there, in space, while suns flickered and faded
and whole planets exploded and became dust. Why remain here, after all, a maggot amongst maggots?'

'Oh, Mongrove, your gloom is of the finest!' Lord
Jagged congratulated him. 'Come – you must all be my
guests at Castle Canaria!'

'Your castle survives, Jagged?' Jherek asked, putting his arm round his Amelia's waist.

'As a memory, swiftly restored to reality – as shall be the entire society at the End of Time. That is what I meant, Amelia, when I told you that memories would suffice.'

She smiled a little bleakly. She had been listening intently to Mongrove's forebodings. It took some little while before she could rid herself of her thoughts and laugh with the others as they said farewell to the time-traveller, who intended, now that he had certain information from Mrs Persson, to make repairs to his craft and return to his own world if he could.

The Duke of Queens stood on the grey, cracked plain and admired his handiwork. It was a great squared-off monster of a vehicle and it bobbed gently in the light wind which stirred the dust at their feet.

'The bulk of it is the gas-container – the large rear-section,' he explained to Jherek. 'The front is called, I believe, the cab.'

'And the whole?'

'From the twentieth century. An articulated truck.'

The Iron Orchid sighed as she tripped towards it, gathering up the folds of her wedding dress. 'It looks most uncomfortable.'

'Not as bad as you'd think,' the Duke reassured her. 'There is breathing equipment inside the gas-bag.'

CHAPTER TWENTY-TWO

INVENTIONS AND RESURRECTIONS

Soon all would be as it had always been, before the winds of limbo had come to blow their world away. Flesh, blood and bone, grass and trees and stone would flourish beneath the fresh-born sun, and beauty of every sort, simple or bizarre, would bloom upon the face of that arid, ancient planet. It would be as if the universe had never died; and for that the world must thank its half-senile cities and the arrogant persistence of that obsessive temporal investigator from the twenty-first century, from the Dawn Age, who named himself for a small pet singing bird fashionable two hundred years before his birth, who displayed himself like an actor, yet disguised himself and his motives with all the consummate cunning of a Medici courtier; this fantastico in yellow, this languid meddler in destinies, Lord Jagged of Canaria.

They had already witnessed the rebuilding of Castle Canaria, at first a glowing mist, opaque and coruscating, modelled upon a wickerwork cage, some seventy-five feet high; and then its bars had become pale gold and within could be seen the floating compartments, each a room, where Jagged chose to live in certain moods (though he had had other moods, other castles). They had watched while Lord Jagged had spread the sky with tints of pink-tinged amber and cornflower blue, so that the orb of the sun burned a dull, rich red and cast shadows through the bars of that great cage so that it seemed the surrounding dust was criss-crossed by lattice: but then the dust itself was banished and turf replaced it, sparkling as it might after a shower, and there were hedges, too, and trees, and a pool of clear water, all standing in contrast to the surrounding landscape, thousands and thousands of miles of featureless desert. And they had been fired by this experience to begin their own creations at once and Mongrove went off to build his black mountains, his cold, cloud-cloaked halls, his gloomy heights; and the Duke of Queens went in another direction to erect first mosaic pyramids, then flower-hung ziggurats, then golden moondomes and etoliated Towers of Mercury, then an ocean, as large as the Mediterranean, on which floated monstrous, baroque fish, each fish an apartment. Meanwhile the Iron Orchid, content for the moment to share her husband's quarters, caused forests of slightly metallic blossoms to spring up from fields of silver snow, where cold birds, bright as steel, but electric green and engine red, clashed beaks and wings and sang human songs in the voices of machines, where robot foxes lurked and automata in scarlet, mounted on mechanical horses, hunted them – acre upon acre of ingenious animated gadgetry.

Jherek Carnelian and Amelia Underwood were more modest in their creations; first they chose an area and surrounded it with great breaks of poplars, cypresses and willows, so that the wasteland beyond could not be seen. Her fanciful palace was forgotten; she wished for a low Tudor house, with thatch and beams, whitewashed. A few of the windows she allowed for stained-glass, but the majority were as large as possible and leaded. Flower-beds surrounded the house and in these she put roses, holly-hocks and a variety of old, half-wild English flowers. There was a paved area, a pathway, a vegetable garden, shaded arbours of yew and climbing roses, a pond with a fountain in the centre, and goldfish, and everywhere high hedges, as if she would shield her house from the rest of the world. He admired it, but had little to do with its creation. Within were oak tables and chairs, bookcases (though the books themselves defeated her powers of creation, just as her attempts to recreate paintings failed badly – Jherek consoled her: no one could make such things, at the End of Time); there were comfortable armchairs, carpets, polished boards, vases of flowers, tapestries, figurines, candlesticks, lamps; there was a large kitchen, with tapped water, and every modern utensil, including knife-polishers, a gas-copper and a gas-stove, though she knew she would have little use for them. The kitchen looked out onto the vegetable garden where her runner-beans and cabbages already flourished. On the top floor of the house she created two sets of apartments for them, with a bedroom, dressing room, study and sitting room each. And when she had finished she looked to her Jherek for his approval and, ever enthusiastic, he gave it.

Elsewhere the creation continued: a superabundance of inventiveness. A summoning of certain particles by the Iron Orchid, and Bishop Castle, complete with crook and mitre, was born again, joining her to recreate first My Lady Charlotina of Below-the-Lake, a little bemused and her memory not what it was, and then Mistress Christia, the Everlasting Concubine, Doctor Volospion, O'Kala Incarnadine, Argonheart Po, Sweet Orb Mace, all restored to life and ready to add their own themes to the reconstructed world, to resurrect their particular friends. And Mongrove, in his rainy, thunder-haunted crags, let gloomy, romantic Werther de Goethe look on the world again and mourn, while Lord Shark the Unknown, resentful, unbelieving, contemptuous, stayed in Mongrove's domain for only a few moments before flinging himself from a cliff, to be restored by a solicitous Mongrove, who had assumed that he was not yet quite himself, and fussed over until, in a pet, he summoned his plain grey air-car and sailed away, to build again his square living quarters with their square rooms, each one of exactly the same proportions, and to populate them with his automata, each one exactly in his image (not to satisfy his ego but because Lord Shark was a being devoid of any sort of imagination). Lord Shark, once his residence and his servants were re-established, created nothing further, allowed the grey, cracked ground to be his only view, while in all other quarters of the planet whole ranges of mountains were flung up, great rivers rolled across lush plains, seas heaved, woods proliferated; hills and valleys, meadows and forests were filled with life of every description.

Argonheart Po made perhaps his most magnificent contribution to his world, a detailed copy of one of the ancient cities, each ruined tower and whispering dome subtly delicious to taste and smell, each chemical lake a soup of transporting exquisiteness, each jewel a bon-bon of mouth-watering delicacy, each streamer a noodle of previously undreamed of savouriness. The Duke of Queens built a fleet of flying trucks, causing them to perform complex aerobatics in the skies above his home, while below he prepared for a party on the theme of Death and Destruction, searching the memory-banks of the cities for fifty of the most famous ruins in history: Pompeii existed again on the slopes of Krakatoa, Alexandria, built all of books, burned afresh, while every few minutes a new mushroom cloud blossomed over Hiroshima, showering mushrooms almost fit to match Argonheart's culinary marvels. The grave-pits of Brighton, reduced to miniatures because of the huge amount of space needed to contain them, were heaped with tiny bodies, some of which still moved, mewling and touchingly pathetic; but perhaps his most effective creation was his liquidized Minneapolis, frozen, viscous, still recognizable, with its inhabitants turning to semi-transparent jelly even as they tried to flee the Swiss holocaust.

It was, as Bishop Castle proposed, a Renaissance. Lord

Jagged of Canaria was a hero; his exploits were celebrated. Only Brannart Morphail saw Jagged's interference as unwelcome; indeed Brannart remained sceptical of the whole theory behind the method of salvation. He looked with a jaundiced eye upon the carolling sculptures surrounding the green feather palace of My Lady Charlotina (she had renounced the underworld since the flood which had swept her from her halls), upon the pink pagodas of Mistress Christia and the ebony fortress of Werther de Goethe, warning all that the destruction had merely been averted for a little while, but none of them chose to listen to him. Doctor Volospion, a scarecrow in flaring, tattered black, his body black, his eyes red flames, made a Martian sarcophagus some thousand feet high, with a reproduction on its lid of the famous Revels of Cha'ar in which four thousand boys and girls died of exhaustion and seven thousand men and women flogged one another to death. Doctor Volospion found his home 'pretty' and filled it inside with lunatic manikins given to biting him or laying little vicious traps for him whenever they could, and this he found 'amusing'. Bishop Castle's own laser-beam cathedral, whose twin steeples disappeared in the sky, was unpretentious in comparison, though the music which the beams produced was ethereal and moving: even Werther de Goethe, impressed by but disapproving of Doctor Volospion's dwelling, congratulated Bishop Castle on his sonorous melodies, and Sweet Orb Mace actually copied the idea for (she was feminine again) her blue quartz Old New Old Old New New Old New Old New New New Old New New Versailles, which had flourished in her favourite period (the Integral Seventh Worship) on Sork, a planet of some Centauri or Beta, vanished long-since, the whole structure based on certain favourite primitive musical forms from the fiftieth century. O'Kala Incarnadine simply became a goat and trotted about in what remained of the wastelands bleating to anyone who would give him an ear that he preferred the planet unspoiled; the idea seemed to give him considerable pleasure, but he set no fashion. Indeed the only positive response he received at all was from Li Pao (who had not enjoyed, it emerged, his brief return to 2648) who judged his rôle a subtle metaphor, and from Gaf the Horse in Tears who derived much mindless glee from bleating back at him, hovering overhead in his aerial sampan and occasionally pelting him with the fruit he won from one of the thirty or so machines dotted about on the boat's fifth tier.

The time-traveller had become frustrated, for it had materialized that he still needed someone who could help him with the repairs he must make to his machine before he would risk a cross-dimension time-leap. He had found Lord Jagged too concerned with his own experiments to be helpful and Brannart Morphail now refused to speak to anyone, having been snubbed so badly in the first few days of the resurrection. For a short time he fell in with another time-traveller, returned, like Li Pao, by the Morphail Effect, calling himself Rat Oosapric, but it turned out that the man was an escaped criminal from the thirty-sixth century Stilt Cities and knew nothing at all about the principles of time-travel; he merely tried to steal the time-traveller's machine and was restrained from so doing by the fortunate arrival of My Lady Charlotina who froze him with a power-ring and sent him drifting into the upper atmosphere for a while. My Lady Charlotina, deprived of Brannart Morphail, was trying to convince the time-traveller that she should be his patron, that he should become her new Scientist. The time-traveller considered the idea but found her terms too restricting. It was My Lady Charlotina who returned from the old city, leaving the time-traveller to his brooding, with the news that Harold Underwood, Inspector Springer, Sergeant Sherwood, the twelve constables, and the Lat all seemed healthy and relatively cheerful, but that the Pweelian spacecraft had vanished. This caused the Duke of Queens to reveal his secret a little earlier than he had planned. He had re-started his menagerie and the

Pweelians were his prize, though they did not know it. He had allowed them to build their own environment – the closed one they had planned to escape the End of Time – and they now believed that they were the only living creatures in the entire universe. Anyone who wished to do so could visit the Duke's menagerie and watch them moving about in their great sphere, completely unaware that they were observed, involved in their curious activities. Even Amelia Underwood went to see them and agreed with the Duke of Queens that they seemed completely at ease and if anything rather happier than they had originally been.

This visit to the Duke was the first time Jherek and Amelia had emerged into society since they had built their new house. Amelia was astonished by the rapid changes: there were only a few small areas no longer altered, and there was a certain freshness to everything which made even the most bizarre inventions almost charming. The air itself, she said, had the sweet sharpness of a spring morn. On the way home they saw Lord Jagged of Canaria in his great flying swan, a yellowish white, with another tall figure beside him. Jherek brought his locomotive alongside and hailed him, at once recognizing the other occupant of the swan.

'My dear Nurse! What a pleasure to meet you again! How are your children?'

Nurse was considerably more coherent than she had been when Jherek had last seen her. She shook her old steel head and sighed. 'Gone, I fear. Back to an earlier point in Time – where I still operate the time-loop, where they still play as, doubtless, they will always play.'

'You sent them back?'

'I did. I judged this world too dangerous for my little ones, young Jerry. Well, I must say, you're looking well. Quite a grown man now, eh? And this must be Amelia, whom you are to marry. Ah, I am filled with pride. You have proved yourself a fine boy, Jerry.' It seemed that she still had the vague idea that Jherek had been one of her

original charges. 'I expect "daddy" is proud of you, too!'
She turned her head a full ninety degrees to look fondly
at Lord Jagged, who pursed his lips in what might have
been an embarrassed smile.

'Oh, very proud,' he said. 'Good morning Amelia.
Jherek.'

'Good morning, Sir Machiavelli.' Amelia relished his
discomfort. 'How go your schemes?'

Lord Jagged relaxed, laughing. 'Very well, I think.
Nurse and I have a couple of modifications to make to a
circuit. And you two? Do you flourish?'

'We are comfortable,' she told him.

'Still – engaged?'

'Not yet married, Lord Jagged, if that is what you ask.'

'Mr Underwood still in the city?'

'So we hear from My Lady Charlotina.'

'Aha.'

Amelia looked at Lord Jagged suspiciously, but his
answering expression was bland.

'We must be on our way.' The swan began to drift clear
of the locomotive. 'Time waits for no man, you know.
Not yet, at any rate. Farewell!'

They waved to him and the swan sailed on. 'Oh, he is
so devious,' she said, but without rancour. 'How can a
father and son be so different?'

'You think that?' The locomotive began to puff towards
home. 'And yet I have modelled myself on him for as long
as I can remember. He was ever my hero.'

She was thoughtful. 'One seeks for signs of corruption
in the son if one witnesses them in the father, yet is it not
fairer to see the son as the father, unwounded by the
world?'

He blinked but did not ask her to elaborate as, with
pensive eye, she contemplated the variegated landscape
sweeping by below.

'But I suppose I envy him,' she said.

'Envy Jagged? His intelligence?'

'His work. He is the only one upon the whole planet

who performs a useful task.'

'We made it beautiful again. Is that not "useful", Amelia?'

'It does not satisfy me, at any rate.'

'You have scarcely begun, however, to express your creativity. Tomorrow, perhaps, we shall invent something together, to delight our friends.'

She made an effort to brighten. 'I suppose that you are right. It is a question, as your father said, of attitude.'

'Exactly.' He hugged her. They kissed, but it seemed to him that her kiss was not as wholehearted as, of late, it had become.

From the next morning it was as if a strange fever took possession of Amelia Underwood. Her appearance in their breakfast room was spectacular. She was clad in crimson silk, trimmed with gold and silver, rather oriental in influence. There were curling slippers upon her feet; there were ostrich and peacock feathers decorating her hair and it was evident that she had painted or otherwise altered her face, for the eyelids were startling blue, the eyebrows plucked and their length exaggerated, the lips fuller and of astonishing redness, the cheeks glowing with what could only be rouge. Her smile was unusually wide, her kiss unexpectedly warm, her embrace almost sensual; scent drifted behind her as she took her place at the other end of the table.

'Good morning, Jherek, my darling!'

He swallowed a small piece of toast. It seemed to stick in his throat. His voice was not loud. 'Good morning, Amelia. You slept well?'

'Oh, I did! I woke up a new woman. *The* new woman, if you would have it. Ha, ha!'

He tried to clear the piece of toast from his throat. 'You seem very new. The change in appearance is radical.'

'I would scarcely call it that, dear Jherek. Merely an

563

aspect of my personality I have not shown you before. I determined to be less stuffy, to take a more positive view of the world and my place in it. Today, my love, we *create*!'

'Create?'

'It is what you suggested we do.'

'Ah, yes. Of course. What shall we create, Amelia?'

'There is so much.'

'To be sure. As a matter of fact, I had become fairly settled – that is, I had not intended ...'

'Jherek, you were famous for your invention. You set fashion after fashion. Your reputation demands that you express yourself again. We shall build a scene to excel all those we have so far witnessed. And we shall have a party. We have accepted far too much hospitality and offered none until now!'

'True, but ...'

She laughed at him, pushing aside her kedgeree, ignoring her porridge. She sipped at her coffee, staring out through the window at her hedges and her gardens. 'Can you suggest anything, Jherek?'

'Oh – a small "London" – we could make it together. As authentic as anything.'

'"London"? You would not repeat an earlier success, surely?'

'It was an initial suggestion, nothing more.'

'You are admiring my new dress, I see.'

'Bright and beautiful.' He recalled the hymn they had once sung together. He opened his lips and took a deep breath, to sing it, but she forestalled him.

'It is based on a picture I saw in an illustrated magazine,' she told him. 'An opera, I think – or perhaps the music hall. I wish I knew some music hall songs. Would the cities be able to help?'

'I doubt if they can remember any.'

'They are concerned these days, I suppose, with duller things. With Jagged's work.'

'Well, not entirely ...'

564

She rose from the table, humming to herself. 'Hurry, Jherek dear. The morning will be over before we have begun!'

Reluctantly, as confused by this rôle as he had been confused when first they had met, he got up, almost desperately trying to recapture a mood which had always been normal to him, until, it seemed, today.

She linked her arm in his, her step rather springier than usual, perhaps because of the elaborate boots she wore, and they left the house and entered the garden. 'I think now I should have kept my palace,' she said. 'You do not find the cottage dull?'

'Dull? Oh, no!'

He was surprised that she gave every hint of disapproving of his remark. She cast speculative eyes upon the sky, turned a power-ring, and made a garish royal blue tint where a moment ago there had been a relatively subdued sunrise. She added broad streaks of bright red and yellow. 'So!'

Beyond the willows and the cypresses was what remained of the wasteland. 'Here,' she said, 'is what Jagged told us was to be our canvas. It can contain anything – any folly the human mind can invent. Let us make it a splendid folly, Jherek. A vast folly.'

'What?' He began to cheer, though forebodings remained. 'Shall we seek to outdo the Duke of Queens?'

'By all means!'

He was dressed in modest dove-grey today; a frock-coat and trousers, a waistcoat and shirt. He produced a tall hat and placed it, jaunty, on his head. Hand went to ring. Columns of water seemed to spring from the ground, as thick as redwoods, and as tall, forming an arch that in turn became a roof through which the sun glittered.

'Oh, you are too cautious, Jherek!' Her own rings were used. Great cliffs surrounded them and over every cliff gushed cataracts of blood, forming a sea on which bobbed obsidian islands filled with lush, dark vegetation; and now the sun burned almost black above and peculiar sounds came to them across the ocean of blood, from the islands.

'It is very grand,' said Jherek, his voice small. 'But I should not have believed ...'

'It is based on a nightmare I once had.'

'A horse?'

'A dream.'

Something dark reared itself from the water. There was a brief flash of teeth, reminiscent of the creatures they had encountered in the Palaeozoic, of a snake-like and powerful body, an unpleasant rushing sound as it submerged again. He looked to her for an explanation.

'An impression,' she said, 'of a picture I saw as a girl, at the Crystal Palace I think. Oh, you would not believe some of the nightmares I had then. Until now I had forgotten them almost completely. Does the scene please you, Jherek? Will it please our friends?'

'I think so.'

'You are not as enthusiastic as I had hoped you would be.'

'I am. I am enthusiastic, Amelia. Astonished, however.'

'I am glad I astonish you, Jherek dear. It means, then, that our party has every chance of success, does it not?'

'Oh, yes.'

'I shall make a few more touches but leave the rest until later. Let us go into the world now.'

'To —?'

'To offer invitations.'

He acquiesced and called for his locomotive. They boarded her, setting course for Castle Canaria where they hoped to find the Iron Orchid.

CHAPTER TWENTY-THREE

AMELIA UNDERWOOD TRANSFORMED

'The Lat are still with us?' Mistress Christia, the Everlasting Concubine, licked lush lips and widened her already very wide blue eyes to assume that particular look of heated innocence so attractive to those who loved her (and who did not?). 'Oh, what splendid news, Iron Orchid! They raped me, you know, an enormous number of times. You cannot see them now, since my resurrection, but my elbows were both bright red!' Her dress, liquid crystal, coruscated as she lifted her arms. They walked together through the dripping, glassy passage in one of Mrs Underwood's obsidian islands; at the far end of the tunnel was reddish light, reflected from the bloody sea beyond. 'The atmosphere is rather good here, don't you think?'

'A trifle reminiscent of something of Werther's.'

'None the worse for that, dearest Orchid.'

'You have always found his work more attractive than I have.' (They had been rivals once, however, for sighing de Goethe.)

The light was blocked. My Lady Charlotina rustled towards them, in organdie and tulle of clashing greens. She staggered for a second as a wave struck the island, and it tilted, then righted itself. 'Have you seen the *beasts*? One has eaten poor O'Kala.' She giggled. 'They are fond of goats, it seems.'

'I thought the beasts good,' agreed her friend. The Orchid had retained white as her main effect, but had added a little pale yellow (Jagged's colours) here and there. The yellow looked well on her lips, against the pallor of her skin. 'And the smell. So heavy.'

'Not too sweet?' asked Mistress Christia.

'For me, no.'

'And your *marriage*, oracular Orchid,' breathed My Lady Charlotina, giving her ears a pinch, to increase the size of the lobes. She added earrings. 'I have just heard. But should we call you Orchid still? Is it not Lady Jagged now?'

They moved back towards the opening in the passage.

'I had not considered it.' The Iron Orchid was the first to reach the open. Her son was there, leaning against a dark green palm, staring into the depths of the crimson ocean.

'With Jherek,' said My Lady Charlotina enviously, from behind her, 'you begin a dynasty. Imagine that!'

All three women emerged now and saw him. He looked up, as if he had thought himself alone.

'We interrupt a reverie ...' said Mistress Christia kindly.

'Oh, no ...' He still wore clothes his Amelia had considered suitable – a straw boater, a bright blazer, white shirt and white flannels.

'Well, Jherek?' His mother approached closer, amused. 'Shall you be presenting us with a son, you and your Amelia?'

'An air?'

'A boy, my boy!'

'Aha! I rather doubt it. We cannot marry, you see.'

'Your father and I, Jherek, were not formally married when ...'

'But she has reservations,' he told her gloomily. 'Her

568

husband, who is still in the city, haunts us. But perhaps she changes ...'

'Her inventions indicate as much.'

A sigh. 'They do.'

'You do not find this lake, these cliffs, these beasts, magnificently realized?'

'Of course I do.' He raised his head to watch the blood as it roared from every edge. 'Yet I am disturbed, mother.'

'Resentful of her hidden talent, you mean!' The Iron Orchid chided him.

'Where is she?' My Lady Charlotina cast about. 'I must congratulate her. All her work, Jherek? Nothing yours?'

'Nothing.'

'Exquisite!'

'She was with Li Pao when I last saw her,' Jherek said. 'On one of the farther islands.'

'I was glad Li Pao returned in time,' the Iron Orchid said. 'I should miss him. But so many others are gone!'

'And nothing for a menagerie, save what we make ourselves,' complained My Lady Charlotina. She produced a sunshade (the fashion had been set by Amelia) and twirled it. 'We live in difficult days, audacious Orchid.'

'But challenging.'

'Oh, yes.'

'The Duke of Queens has those round aliens,' said Mistress Christia.

'By rights,' My Lady Charlotina told her bitterly, with a glance at Jherek, 'at least one of those is mine. Still, not very much of an acquisition, by any real standards. I suppose they'll be prized now, however.'

'He remains very proud of them.' Mistress Christia moved to hug Jherek. 'You seem sad, handsomest of heroes.'

'Sad? Is that the emotion? I am not sure I am enjoying it, Mistress Christia.'

'Why sad?'

'I am not at all sure.'

'You seek to rival Werther, that is it. You are in competition!'

'I had not thought of Werther.'

'Here he is!' The Iron Orchid and My Lady Charlotina pointed together. Werther had seen them from above and came circling down on his coffin-shaped car. His cape and hood were black and white checks and he had removed all the flesh from his face so that his skull was revealed and only his dark eyes, in the recesses of the sockets, gave it life. 'Where is Mrs Underwood, Jherek?' said Werther. 'I must honour her. This is the most beautiful creation I have seen in a millennium!'

They were slow to answer. Only Jherek pointed to a distant island.

'Oho!' said Mistress Christia, and she winked at the Iron Orchid. 'Amelia makes another conquest.'

Jherek kicked at a piece of rock. It resisted his foot. Again, he sighed. His boater fell from his head. He stooped and picked it up.

The women linked arms and rose together into the air. 'We go to Amelia,' called back the Iron Orchid. 'Shall you join us, Jherek?'

'In a moment.'

He had only recently escaped the press of guests who flocked about his intended bride, for she was at the centre and all congratulated her on her creation, her costume, her comportment and if they spoke to him, it was to praise Amelia. And over there on the other island, she chattered, she was witty, she held them but – and he could define it no better – she was not his Amelia.

He turned, at the sound of a footfall, and it was the time-traveller, hands in pockets, looking quite as glum as he did himself. 'Good afternoon to you, Jherek Carnelian. My Lady Charlotina passed on your invitation. Lord Mongrove brought me. This is all very fanciful. You must have journeyed further inland, during your stay in the Palaeozoic, than I realized.'

'To the creek?'

'Beyond the creek there are landscapes very similar to this – wild and beautiful, you know. I assumed this to be a perverse version. Ah, to see again the rain falling through sunshine on a Palaeozoic morning, near the great waterfalls, with the ferns waving in a light wind which ripples the waters of the lake.'

'You make me envious.' Jherek stared at his reflection, distorted in the blood. 'I sometimes regret our return, though I know now we should have starved.'

'Nonsense. With decent equipment and a little intelligence one could live well in the Palaeozoic.' The time-traveller smiled. 'So long as one resisted the urge to swim in the creeks. That fish, by the by, is very tasty. Sweet, you know. Like a kind of ham.'

'Um,' said Jherek, looking towards the island where Amelia Underwood held court.

'It seems to me,' murmured the time-traveller after a pause, 'that all the romance has gone out of time-travel since I first began. I was one of the first, you know. Perhaps the very first.'

'A pioneer,' Jherek confirmed.

'Quite so. It would be a terrible irony indeed if I were to be marooned here, when your Lord Jagged puts his time-recycling plan into operation. I crossed eons, crossed the barriers between the worlds, and now I am threatened with being imprisoned forever in the same week, repeated over and over again, throughout eternity.' He uttered something resembling a staccato snort. 'Well, I shall not allow it. If I cannot get help with repairs to my craft, I shall risk the journey back and ask for the support of the British Government. It will be better than this.'

'Brannart refuses his aid?'

'He is involved, I gather, in building a machine of his own. He refuses to accept Lord Jagged's theories or his solutions.'

Jherek's smile was faint. 'For thousands of years Brannart was the Lord of Time. His Effect was one of the few laws known to that imprecise science. Suddenly he is

571

dethroned, without authority. It is no wonder that he became so agitated recently, that he still utters warnings. Yet there would be much he could continue to do. Your Guild would welcome his knowledge, would it not?'

'Possibly. He is not what I would call a true scientist. He imposes his imagination upon the facts, rather than using that imagination to investigate. It is probably not his fault, for you all do that, and with considerable success. In most cases you are in the position to alter all the Laws of Nature which, in my own time, were regarded as unalterable.'

'I suppose that's so.' Jherek saw more new arrivals heading for Amelia's island.

'Enviable, of course. But you have lost the scientific method. You solve problems by changing the facts. Magic, we'd call it.'

'Very kind of you.' Absently.

'Fundamentally different attitudes. Even your Lord Jagged is to some extent infected.'

'Infected?' He saw Argonheart Po's shortcake space-shuttle spiralling above the cliffs. It, too, made for the island which had his attention.

'I employed the word without criticism. But for someone like myself used to getting to grips with a problem by means of analytical method . . .'

'Naturally.'

'Natural to me. I was trained to despise any other method.'

'Aha.' It was useless to hold himself in check any longer. He twisted a power-ring. He rose into the air. 'Forgive me – social commitments – perhaps we'll have a chance to chat later.'

'I say,' said the time-traveller urgently, 'you couldn't give me a lift, I suppose? I have no means of crossing . . .'

But Jherek was already out of earshot, leaving the time-traveller abjectly staring at the pink-flecked foam washing the rocking obsidian shore, stranded until some other guest arrived to help him to the mainland. Something

572

black and somewhat phallic pushed itself above the surface of the crimson sea and stared at him, smacking its tiny
lips before losing interest and swimming away in the
direction Jherek had taken. Removing his hands from his
pockets, the time-traveller turned, seeking the highest
point of the island where, with luck, he would be safe
from the beasts and be able to signal for help.

She was surrounded. Jherek could just see her head and
shoulders at the centre of the crowd; she was struggling
with a cigarette. In imitation, Sweet Orb Mace, all mauve
fluff, puffed smoke from her ears, while Bishop Castle
decorously swung his huge headdress back to avoid
collision with the holder. The Iron Orchid, Mistress
Christia, My Lady Charlotina and Werther de Goethe
were closest to her and their words came to Jherek through
the general babble.

'Even you, Amelia, would admit that the nineteenth
century is rather passé ...'

'Oh, but you have proven it, my love, with all this.
It is so wonderfully original ...'

'And yet so simple —'

'The best ideas, Mistress Christia, are always simple ...'

'Truly, sweetest Orchid – the ones you wish you'd conceived yourself, but never did ...'

'But *serious*, withal. If Man were still mortal – ah,
and what he loses! – what a comment on that mortality!'

'I see it merely as beauty, Werther, and nothing more.
Surely, Amelia, the creation is not intended ...'

'There was no conscious intention.'

'You must have planned for days —?'

'It came spontaneously.'

'I knew it! It's so vital ...'

'And the monsters! Poor O'Kala ...'

'We must remember to revive him.'

'At the end. Not before.'

'Our first post-Resurrection resurrection! Here's the Duke of Queens.'

'Come to pay my compliments. I bow to a master. Or should it be mistress?'

'Master will do, Duke of Queens.'

'Mistress of my heart!'

'Really Werther, you embarrass me!' A burst of laughter such as she had never uttered before. Jherek pushed forward.

'Oh, Amelia, but if you would give me just the smallest encouragement ...'

'Jherek! Here at last!'

'Here,' he said. A silence seized him. It threatened to spread through the throng, for it was that kind, but Bishop Castle wagged his crook.

'Oho, Werther. You were overheard. Will this mean a duel, I wonder?'

'A *duel*!' The Duke of Queens saw an opportunity to strike a pose. 'I will advise you. My own skill with the foil is considered not unremarkable. I am sure Lord Shark would agree ...'

'Boasting Duke!' The Iron Orchid put a pale yellow hand upon Amelia's naked shoulder and a white one upon Jherek's Joseph-coat. 'I am sure that we are as tired of the fashion for duelling as we are of the nineteenth century. Amelia must have seen enough of such sport in her native Burnley.'

'Bromley,' said Jherek.

'Forgive me. Bromley.'

'Oh, but the idea is appealing!' cawed Doctor Volospion, his pointed chin thrust forward from beneath the brim of his hat. He cocked an eye first at Jherek, then at Werther. 'The one so fresh and healthy, the other so stale and deathly. It would suit you, Werther, eh? With your penchant for parable. A duel between Life and Death. Whoever shall win shall decide the fate of the planet!'

'I could not undertake such a responsibility, Doctor Volospion.' It was impossible to tell either from Werther's tone or from his expression (a skull's are limited at the best of times) if he jested or was in earnest.

Jherek, who had never much cared for Doctor Volospion (the doctor's jealousy of Lord Jagged was notorious), affected not to have heard. His suspicion of Volospion's motives was confirmed with the next remark.

'Is it only Jagged then who is allowed to decide Man's fate?'

'We choose our own!' Jherek defended his absent father. 'Lord Jagged merely supplies us with the means of choice. We should have none at all without him!'

'So the old dog is barked for by the pup.' Doctor Volospion's malice was at its sharpest.

'You forget, Doctor Volospion,' said the Iron Orchid sweetly, 'that the bitch is here, too.'

Volospion bowed to this; a withdrawal.

In a loud voice Amelia Underwood declared: 'Shall we repair to the largest island? Refreshment awaits us.'

'I anticipate inspiration,' said Argonheart Po, with weighty gallantry.

The guests became airborne.

For a second Jherek and Amelia were left alone, confronting one another. His face was a question which she ignored. He made a movement towards her, certain that he saw pain and bewilderment behind those painted, unblinking eyes.

'Amelia . . .'

She was already rising.

'You punish me!' His hand went up, as if to catch at her fluttering gown.

'Not you, my love.'

CHAPTER TWENTY-FOUR

THE VISION IN THE CITY

'We hear you have command of so many ancient arts, Mrs Underwood. You read I understand?' Agape, Gaf the Horse in Tears, all foliage save for his face, one of Amelia's swiss rolls filling the twigs at the end of his left bough, rustled with enthusiasm. 'And write, eh?'

'A little.' Her amusement was self-conscious.

'And play an instrument?'

She inclined an artificial curl or two. 'The harmonium.'

The guests, each with a costume more outrageous than the next, filed in to stand on both sides of the long trestle tables, sampling the cups of tea, the cucumber sandwiches, the roast ham, the cold sausages, the strawberry flan, the battenbergs, the ginger cakes, the lettuce and the cress, all under the shade of the tall red and white striped marquee. Jherek, in a corner of the tent, nibbled a pensive teacake, ignored by all save Li Pao, who was complaining of his treatment during his brief return home. 'They called *me* decadent, you know ...'

'And you sew. Embroider, is it?' Bishop Castle carefully replaced a rattling, scarcely tasted, cup upon the trestle.

'I used to. There is little point, now . . .'

'But you must demonstrate these arts!' The Iron Orchid signalled to Jherek. 'Jherek. You told us Amelia *sang*, did you not?'

'Did I tell you that? She does.'

'You must persuade her to give us an air.'

'A son?'

'A song, my seed!'

He looked miserably over to where Amelia gesticulated, laughing with Doctor Volospion. 'Will you sing a hymn for us, Amelia?'

Her answering smile chilled him. 'Not now, I think.' The crimson-clad arms spread wide. 'Has everyone enough tea?'

A murmur of satiation.

Werther advanced again, hovering, a white hand holding a silver cake-stand from which he helped himself, popping one pastry at a time into his clacking jaws. 'Queen of Melancholy, come with me to my Schloss Dolorous, my dear and my darling to be!'

She flirted. At least, she attempted to flirt. 'Oh, chivalrous Knight of Death, in whose arms is eternal rest – would that I were free.' The eyelids fluttered. Was there a tear? Jherek could bear no more. She was glancing towards him, perhaps to test his reaction, as he bowed and left the tent.

He hesitated outside. The red cascades continued to fall from all sides into the lake. The obsidian islands slowly drifted to the centre, some of them already touching. In the distance he could see the time-traveller gingerly leaping from one to another.

He had a compulsion to seek solitude in the old city, where he had sought it as a boy. It was possible that he would find his father there and could gain advice.

'Jherek!'

Amelia stood behind him. There was a tear on either scarlet cheek. 'Where are you going? You are a poor host today.'

577

'I am ignored. I am extraneous.' He spoke as lightly as he could. 'Surely I am not missed. All the guests join your entourage.'

'You are hurt?'

'I merely had it in mind to visit the city.'

'Is it not bad manners?'

'I do not understand you fully, Amelia.'

'You go now?'

'It occurred to me to go now.'

She paused. Then: 'I would go with you.'

'You seem content' – a backward look at the marquee – 'with all this.'

'I do it to please you. It was what you wanted.' But she accused him. The tears had fallen: no more followed.

'I see.'

'And you find my new rôle unattractive?'

'It is very fine. It is impressive. Instantly, you rank with the finest of fashion-setters. The whole of society celebrates your talents, your beauty. Werther courts you. Others will.'

'Is that not how life is led, at the End of Time – with amusements, flirtations?'

'I suppose that it is.'

'Then I must learn to indulge in such things if I am to be accepted.' Again that chilling smile. 'Mistress Christia would have you for a lover. You have not noticed?'

'I want only you. You are already accepted. You have seen that today.'

'Because I play the proper game.'

'If you'll have it so. You'll stay here, then?'

'Let me and I'll come with you. I am unused to so much attention. It has an effect upon the nerves. And I would satisfy myself that Harold fares well.'

'Oh, you are concerned for him.'

'Of course.' She added: 'I have yet to cultivate that particular insouciance characteristic of your world.'

Lord Jagged's swan was drifting down. The pale yellow draperies billowed; he was somewhere amongst them –

they heard his voice.

'My dears. How convenient. I did not wish to become involved with your party, but I did want to make a brief visit, to congratulate you upon it. A beautiful ambience, Amelia. It is yours, of course.'

She acknowledged it. The swan began to hover, Lord Jagged's face now distinct, faintly amused as it often was, looking down on them. 'You are more at ease, I see, with the End of Time, Amelia.'

'I begin to understand how one such as I might learn to live here, Mephistopheles.'

The reference brought laughter, as it always did. 'So you have not completely committed yourself. No wedding, yet?'

'To Jherek?' She did not look at Jherek Carnelian, who remained subdued. 'Not yet.'

'The same reasons?'

'I do my best to forget them.'

'A little more time, that is all you need, my dear.' Jagged's stare gained intensity, but the irony remained.

'I gather there is only a little left.'

'It depends upon your attitude, as I say. Life will continue as it has always done. There will be no change.'

'No change,' she said, her voice dropping. 'Exactly.'

'Well, I must continue about my work. I wish you well, Amelia – and you, my son. You have still to recover from all your adventures. Your mood will improve, I am sure.'

'Let us hope so, Lord Jagged.'

'Hi! I say there. Hi!' It was the time-traveller, from a nearby island. He waved at Jagged's swan. 'Is that you, Jagged?'

Lord Jagged of Canaria turned a handsome head to contemplate the source of this interruption. 'Ah, my dear chap. I was looking for you. You need help, I gather.'

'To get off this damned island.'

'And to leave this damned era, too, do you not?'

'If you are in a position ...'

'You must forgive me for my tardiness. Urgent problems. Now solved.' The swan began to glide towards the time-traveller, settling on the rocky shore so that he could climb aboard. They heard the time-traveller say: 'This is a great relief, Lord Jagged. One of the quartz rods requires attention, also two or three of the instruments need adjusting ...'

'Quite so,' came Jagged's voice. 'I head now for Castle Canaria where we shall discuss the matter in full.'

The swan rose high into the air and disappeared above one of the cliffs, leaving Jherek and Amelia staring after it.

'Was that Jagged?' It was the Iron Orchid, at the entrance to the tent. 'He said he might come. Amelia, everyone is remarking on your absence.'

Amelia went to her. 'Dearest Orchid, be hostess for a little while. I am still inexperienced. I tire. Jherek and I would rest from the excitement.'

The Iron Orchid was sympathetic. 'I will give them your apologies. Return soon, for our sakes.'

'I will.'

Jherek had already summoned the locomotive. It awaited them, blue and white steam drifting from its funnel, emeralds and sapphires winking.

As they climbed into the air they looked down on the scene of Amelia's first social creation. Against the surrounding landscape it resembled some vast and terrible wound; as if the Earth were living flesh and a gigantic spear had been driven into its side.

Shortly, the city appeared upon the horizon, its oddly shaped, corroded towers, its varicoloured halo, its drifting streamers and clouds of chemical vapour, its little grumblings and murmurings, its peculiar half-organic, half-metallic odour, filling them both with a peculiar sense of nostalgia, as if for happier, simpler days.

They had not spoken since they had left; neither, it seemed, was capable of beginning a conversation; neither could come to terms with feelings which were, to Jherek at least, completely unfamiliar. He thought that for all her gaudy new finery he had never known her so despairing. She hinted at this despair, yet denied it when questioned. Used to paradox, believing it the stuff of existence, he found this particular paradox decidedly unwelcome.

'You will look for Mr Underwood?' he asked, as they approached the city.

'And you?'

He knew foreboding. He wished to volunteer to accompany her, but was overwhelmed by unusual and probably unnecessary tact.

'Oh, I'll seek the haunts of my boyhood.'

'Isn't that Brannart?'

'Where?' He peered.

She was pointing into a tangle of ancient, rotten machinery. 'I thought in there. But he has gone. I even glimpsed one of those Lat, too.'

'What would Brannart want with the Lat?'

'Nothing, of course.'

They had flown past, but though he looked back, he saw no sign either of Brannart Morphail or the Lat. 'It would explain why he did not attend the party.'

'I assumed that was pique, only.'

'He could never resist an opportunity in the past to air his portentous opinions,' said Jherek. 'I am of the belief that he still works to thwart our Lord Jagged, but that he cannot be successful. The time-traveller was explaining to me, as I recall, why Brannart's methods fail.'

'So Brannart is out of favour,' said she. 'He did much to help you at first.' She chided him.

'By sending you back to Bromley? He forgets, when he berates us for our meddling with Time, that a great deal of what happened was because of his connivance with My Lady Charlotina. Waste no sympathy on Brannart, Amelia.'

'Sympathy? Oh, I have little of that now.' She had returned to her frigid, sardonic manner.

This fresh ambiguity caused further retreat into his own thoughts. He had surprised himself with his criticisms,

581

having half a notion that he did not really intend to attack Brannart Morphail at all. He was inexpert in this business of accusation and self-immolation: a novice in the expression of emotional pain, whereas she, it now seemed, was a veteran. He floundered, he who had known only extrovert joy, innocent love; he floundered in a swamp which she in her ambivalence created for them both. Perhaps it would have been better if she had never announced her love and retained her stern reliance upon Bromley and its mores, left him to play the gallant, the suitor, with all the extravagance of his world. Were his accusations really directed at her, or even at himself? And did she not actually rack her own psyche, all aggression turned upon herself and only incidentally upon him, so that he could not react as one who is threatened, must thresh about for an object, another person, upon whom to vent his building wrath, as a beaten dog snaps at a neutral hand, unable to contemplate the possibility that it is its master's victim?

All this was too much for Jherek Carnelian. He sought relief in the outer world; they flew across a lake whose surface was a rainbow swirl, bubbling and misty, then across a field of lapis lazuli dotted with carved stone columns, the remnants of some peculiar two hundred thousandth-century technology. He saw, ahead, the mile-wide pit where not long since they had awaited the end of the world. He made the locomotive circle and land in the middle of a group of ruins wreathed in bright orange fire, each flame an almost familiar shape. He helped her from the footplate and they stood in frozen attitudes for a second before he looked deliberately into her kohl-circled eyes to see if she guessed his thoughts, for he had no words to express them; the vocabulary of the End of Time was rich only in hyperbole. He reflected then that it had been his original impulse to expand his own vocabulary, and consequently his experience, that had led him to this present pass. He smiled.

'Something amuses you?' she said.

'Ah, no, Amelia. It is only that I cannot say what I wish to say —'

'Do not be constrained by good manners. You are disappointed in me. You love me no longer.'

'You wish me to say so?'

'It is true, is it not? You have found me out for what I am.'

'Oh, Amelia, I love you still. But to see you in such misery — it makes me dumb. The Amelia I now see is not what you are!'

'I am learning to enjoy the pleasures of the End of Time. You must allow me an apprenticeship.'

'You do not enjoy them. You use them to destroy yourself.'

'To destroy my old-fashioned notions. Not myself.'

'Perhaps those notions are essential. Perhaps they *are* the Amelia Underwood I love, or at least part of her ...' He subsided; words again failed him.

'I think you are mistaken.' Did she deliberately put this distance between them? Was it possible that she regretted her declaration of love, felt bound by it?

'You love me, still ...?'

She laughed. 'All love all at the End of Time.'

With an air of resolve, she broke the ensuing silence. 'Well, I will look for Harold.'

He pointed out a yellow-brown metal pathway. 'That will lead you to the place where you left him.'

'Thank you.' She set off. The dress and the boots gave her a hobbling motion; her normal grace was almost entirely gone. His heart went to her, but his throat remained incapable of speech, his body incapable of movement. She turned a corner, where a tall machine, its casing damaged to expose complicated circuits, whispered vague promises to her as she passed but became inaudible, a hopeless whore, quickly rebuffed by her lack of interest.

For a moment Jherek's attention was diverted by the sight of three little egg-shaped robots on caterpillar tracks trundling across a nearby area of rubble deep in a conversation held in a polysyllabic, utterly incomprehensible language; he looked back to the road. She was gone.

He was alone in the city, but the solitude was no longer palatable. He wanted to pursue her, to demand her own analysis of her mood, but perhaps she was as incapable of expressing herself as was he. Did Bromley supply a means of interpreting emotion as readily as it supplied standards of social conduct?

He began to suspect that neither Amelia's society nor his, for all their differences, concerned themselves with anything but the surface of things. Now that he was in the city it might be that he could find some still functioning memory bank capable of recalling the wisdom of one of those eras, like the Fifth Confucian or the Zen Commonwealth, which had placed rather exaggerated emphasis on self-knowledge and its expression. Even the strange, neurotic refinements of that other period with which he had a slight familiarity, the Saint-Claude Dictatorship (under which every citizen had been enjoined to supply three distinctly different explanations as to their psychological motives for taking even the most minor decisions), might afford him a clue to Amelia's behaviour and his own reactions. It occured to him that she might be acting so strangely because, in some simple way, he was failing to console her. He began to walk through the ruins, in the opposite direction to the one she had taken, trying to recall something of Dawn Age society. Could it be that he was supposed to kill Mr Underwood? It would be easy enough to do. And would she permit her husband's resurrection? Should he, Jherek, change his appearance, to resemble Harold Underwood as much as possible? Had she rejected his suggestion that he change his name to hers because it was not enough? He paused to lean against a carved jade post whose tip was lost in chemical mist high above his head. He seemed to remember reading of some ritual formalizing the giving of oneself into another's power. Did she pine because he did not perform it? Or did the reverse apply? Did kneeling have something to do with it, and if so who knelt to whom?

'Om,' said the jade post.

'Eh?' said Jherek, startled.

'Om,' intoned the post. 'Om.'

'Did you detect my thoughts, post?'

'I am merely an aid to meditation, brother. I do not interpret.'

'It is interpretation I need. If you could direct me . . .'

'Everything is as everything else,' the post told him. Everything is nothing and nothing is everything. The mind of man is the universe and the universe is the mind of man. We are all characters in God's dreams. We are all God.'

'Easily said, post.'

'Because a thing is easy does not mean that it is difficult. Because a thing is difficult does not mean that it is easy.'

'Is that not a tautology?'

'The universe is one vast tautology, brother, yet no one thing is the same as another.'

'You are not very helpful. I sought information.'

'There is no such thing as information. There is only knowledge.'

'Doubtless,' said Jherek doubtfully. He bade good day to the post and retreated. The post, like so many of the city's artefacts, seemed to lack a sense of humour, though probably, if taxed, it would – as others here did – claim a 'cosmic sense of humour' (this involved making obvious ironies about things commonly observed by the simplest intelligence).

In the respect of ordinary, light conversation, machines, including the most sophisticated, were notoriously bad company; more literal-minded even than someone like Li Pao. This thought led him, as he walked on, to ponder the difference between men and machines. There had once been very great differences, but these days there were few, in superficial terms. What were the things which distinguished a self-perpetuating machine, capable of almost any sort of invention, from a self-created human being, equally capable? There *were* differences – perhaps emotional. Could it not be true that the less emotion the entity possessed the poorer its sense of humour – or the more emotion it repressed the weaker its capacity for original irony?

These ideas were scarcely leading him in the direction he wished to go, but he was beginning to give up hope of finding any solution to his dilemma in the city, and at least he now felt he understood the jade post better.

A chromium tree giggled at him as he entered a paved plaza. He had been here several times as a boy. He had a great deal of affection for the giggling tree.

'Good afternoon,' he said.

The tree giggled as it had giggled without fail for at least a million years, whenever addressed or approached. Its function seemed merely to amuse. Jherek smiled, in spite of the heaviness of his thoughts.

'A lovely day.'

The tree giggled, its chromium branches gently clashing.

'Too shy to speak, as usual?'

'Tee hee hee.'

The tree's charm was very hard to explain, but it was unquestionable.

'I believe myself, old friend, to be "unhappy" – or worse!'

'Hee hee hee.' The tree seemed helpless with mirth. Jherek began to laugh, too. Laughing, he left the plaza, feeling considerably more relaxed.

He had wandered close to the tangle of metal where, from above, Amelia had thought she had seen Brannart Morphail. Curiosity led him on, for there were, indeed, lights moving behind the mass of tangled girders, struts, hawsers, cables and wires, though they were probably not of human origin. He approached closer, but cautiously. He peered, thinking he saw figures. And then, as a light flared, he recognized the unmistakable shape of Brannart Morphail's quaint body, an outline only, for the light half-blinded him. He recognized the scientist's voice, but it was not speaking its usual tongue. As he listened, it dawned on Jherek that Brannart Morphail was, however, using a language familiar to him.

'Gerfish lortooda, mibix?' said the scientist to someone beyond the pool of light. 'Derbi kroofrot!'

Another voice answered and it was equally unmistakable as belonging to Captain Mubbers. 'Hrunt, arragak fluzi, grodsink Morphail.'

Jherek regretted that he no longer habitually carried his translation pills with him, for he was curious to know why Brannart should be conspiring with the Lat, for conspiring he must be – there was a considerable air of secrecy to the whole business. He resolved to mention his discovery to Lord Jagged as soon as possible. He considered attempting to see more of what was going on but decided not to risk revealing his presence; instead he turned and made for the cover of a nearby dome, its roof cracked and gaping like the shell of an egg.

Within the dome he was delighted to find brilliantly coloured pictures, all as fresh as the day they were made, and telling some kind of story, though the voices accompanying them were distorted. He watched the ancient programme through until it began again. It described a method of manufacturing machines of the same sort as the one on which Jherek watched the pictures, and there were fragments, presumably demonstrating other programmes, of scenes showing a variety of events – in one a young woman in a kind of luminous net made love underwater to a great fish of some description, in another two men set fire to themselves and ran through what was probably the airlock of a spaceship, making the spaceship explode, and in another a large number of people wearing rococo metal and plastic struggled in free fall for the possession of a small tube which, when one of them managed to take hold of it, was hurled towards one of several circular objects on the wall of the building in which they floated. If the tube struck a particular point on the circular object there would be great exultation from about half the people and much despondency displayed by the other half, but Jherek was particularly interested in the fragment which seemed to be demonstrating how a man and a woman might copulate, also in free fall. He found the ingenuity involved extremely touching and left the dome in a rather more positive and hopeful spirit than when he had entered it.

It was in this mood that he determined to seek out Amelia and try to explain his discomfort with her own behaviour and his. He sought for the way he had come, but was already lost, though he knew the city well; but he had an idea of the general direction and he began to cross a crunching expanse of sweet-smelling green and red crystals, almost immediately catching sight of a landmark ahead of him – a curving, half-melted piece of statuary suspended, without visible support, above a mechanical figure which stretched imploring arms to it, then scooped little golden discs in its hands and flung them into the air, repeating these motions over and over again, as they had been repeated ever since Jherek could remember. He passed the figure and entered an alley poorly illuminated with garish amber and cerise; from apertures on both sides of the alley little metal snouts emerged, little machine-eyes peered inquisitively at him, little silver whiskers twitched. He had never known the function of these platinum rodents, though he guessed that they were information-gatherers of some kind for the machines housed in the great smooth radiation-splashed walls of the alley. Two or three illusions, only half tangible, appeared and vanished ahead of him – a thin man, eight feet tall, blind and warlike; a dog in a great bottle on wheels, a yellow-haired porcine alien in buff-coloured clothing – as he hurried on.

He came out of the alley and pushed knee-deep through soft black dust until the ground rose and he stood on a hillock looking down on pools of some glassy substance, each perfectly circular, like the discarded lenses of some gigantic piece of optical equipment. He skirted these, for he knew from past experience that they were capable of movement and could swallow him, subjecting him to hallucinatory experiences which, though entertaining, were time-consuming, and a short while later he saw ahead the pastoral illusion where they had met Jagged on his return. He crossed the illusion, noticing that a fresh picnic had been laid and that there was no trace of the Lat having been here (normally they left a great deal of litter behind them), and would have continued on his way towards the mile-wide pit had he not heard the sound, to his left, of voices raised in song.

> *Who so beset him round*
> *With dismal stories,*
> *Do but themselves confound —*
> *His strength the more is.*

He crossed an expanse of yielding, sighing stuff, almost losing his balance so that on several occasions he was forced to take to the air as best he could (there was still some difficulty, it seemed, with the city's ability to transmit power directly to the rings). Eventually, on the other side of a cluster of fallen arcades, he found them, standing in a circle around Mr Underwood, who waved his arms with considerable zest as he conducted them — Inspector Springer, Sergeant Sherwood and the twelve constables, their faces shining and full of joy as they joined together for the hymn. It was not for some moments that Jherek discovered Mrs Underwood, a picture of despairing bewilderment, her oriental dress all dusty, her feathers askew, seated with her head in her hand, watching the proceedings from an antique swivel chair, the remnant of some crumbled control room.

She lifted her head as he approached, on tip-toe, so as not to disturb the singing policemen.

'They are all converted now,' she told him wearily. 'It seems they received a vision shortly before we arrived.'

The hymn was over, but the service (it was nothing less) continued.

'And so God came to us in a fiery globe and He spoke to us and He told us that we must go forth and tell the world of our vision, for we are all His prophets now. For he has given us the means of grace and the hope of glory!' cried Harold Underwood, his very pince-nez aflame with fervour.

'Amen,' responded Inspector Springer and his men.

'For we were afraid and in the very bowels of Hell, yet still He heard us. And we called unto the Lord — Our help is in the name of the Lord who hath made heaven and earth. Blessed be the name of the Lord; henceforth, world without end. Lord, hear our prayers; and let our cry come unto thee.'

'And He heard us!' exulted Sergeant Sherwood, the first of all these converts. 'He heard us, Mr Underwood!'

'Hungry and thirsty: their soul fainted in them,' continued Harold Underwood, his voice a holy drone:

'So they cried unto the Lord in their trouble: and he delivered them forth from their distress.

He led them forth by the right way: that they might go to the city where they dwelt.

O that men would therefore praise the Lord for His goodness; and declare the wonders that he doeth for the children of men!

For He satisfieth the empty soul: and filleth the hungry soul with goodness.

Such as sit in darkness, and in the shadow of death: being fast bound in misery and iron;

Because they rebelled against the words of the Lord: and lightly regarded the counsel of the most Highest.'

'Amen,' piously murmured the policemen.

'Ahem,' said Jherek.

But Harold Underwood passed an excited hand through his disarranged hay-coloured hair and began to sing again.

'Yea, though I walk in death's dark vale,
yet will I fear none ill ...'

'I must say,' said Jherek enthusiastically to Mrs Underwood, 'it makes a great deal of sense. It is attractive to me. I have not been feeling entirely myself of late, and have noticed that you —'

'Jherek Carnelian, have you no conception of what has happened here?'

'It is a religious service.' He was pleased with the precision of his knowledge. 'A conspiracy of agreement.'

'You do not find it strange that all these police officers should suddenly become pious – indeed, fanatical! – Christians?'

'You mean that something has happened to them while we have been away?'

'I told you. They have seen a vision. They believe that God has given them a mission, to return to 1896 – though how they intend to get there Heaven alone knows – to warn everyone of what will happen to them if they continue in the paths of sinfulness. They believe that they have *seen* and *heard* God Himself. They have gone completely mad.'

'But perhaps they have had this vision, Amelia.'

'Do you believe in God now?'

'I have never disbelieved, though I, myself, have never had the pleasure of meeting Him. Of course, with the destruction of the universe, perhaps He was also destroyed ...'

'Be serious, Jherek. These poor people, my husband amongst them (doubtless a willing victim, I'll not deny) have been duped!'

'Duped?'

'Almost certainly by your Lord Jagged.'

'Why should Jagged – you mean that Jagged is God?'

'No. I mean that he plays at God. I suspected as much. Harold has described the vision – they all describe it. A fiery globe announcing itself as "The Lord thy God" and calling them His prophets, saying that He would release them from this place of desolation so that they could return to the place from which they had come to warn others – and so on and so on.'

'But what possible reason would Jagged have for deceiving them in that way?'

'Merely a cruel joke.'

'Cruel? I have never seen them happier. I am tempted to join in. I cannot understand you, Amelia. Once you tried to convince me as they are convinced. Now I am prepared to be convinced, you dissuade me!'

'You are deliberately obtuse.'

'Never that, Amelia.'

'I must help Harold. He must be warned of the deception.'

They had begun another hymn, louder than the first.

> *There is a dreadful Hell,*
> *And everlasting pains;*
> *There sinners must with devils dwell*
> *In darkness, fire, and chains.*

He tried to speak through it, but she covered her ears, shaking her head and refusing to listen as he implored her to return with him.

'We must discuss what has been happening to us ...' It was useless.

> *O save us, Lord, from that foul path,*
> *Down which the sinners tread;*
> *Consigned to flames like so much chaff;*
> *There is no greater dread.*

Jherek regretted that this was not one of the hymns Amelia Underwood had taught him when they had first lived together at his ranch. He should have liked to have joined in, since it was not possible to communicate with her. He hoped they would sing his favourite – *All Things Bright and Beautiful* – but somehow guessed they would

592

not. He found the present one not to his taste, either in tune (it was scarcely more than a drone) or in words which, he thought, were somewhat in contrast to the expressions on the faces of the singers. As soon as the hymn was over, Jherek lifted up his head and began to sing in his high, boyish voice:

> 'O Paradise! O Paradise!
> Who doth not crave for rest?
> Who would not seek the happy land
> Where they that loved are blest;
> Where loyal hearts and true
> Stand ever in the light,
> All rapture through and through,
> In God's most holy sight.
>
> O Paradise! O Paradise!
> The world is growing old;
> Who would not be at rest and free
> Where love is never cold ...'

'Excellent sentiments, Mr Carnelian.' Harold Underwood's tone denied his words. He seemed upset. 'However, we were in the middle of giving thanks for our salvation ...'

'Bad manners? I am deeply sorry. It is just that I was so moved ...'

'Ha!' said Mr Underwood. 'Though we have witnessed a miracle today, I cannot believe that it is possible to convert one of Satan's own hierarchy. You shall not deceive us now!'

'But you *are* deceived, Harold!' cried his wife. 'I am sure of it!'

'Listen not to temptation, brothers,' Harold Underwood told the policemen. 'Even now they seek to divert us from the true way.'

'I think you'd better be getting along, sir,' said Inspector Springer to Jherek. 'This is a private meeting and I shouldn't be surprised if you're not infringing the Law of

Trespass. Certainly you could be said to be Causing a Disturbance in a Public Place.'

'Did you really see a vision of God, Inspector Springer?' Jherek asked him.

'We did, sir.'

'Amen,' said Sergeant Sherwood and the twelve constables.

'Amen,' said Harold Underwood. 'The Lord has given us the Word and we shall take the Word unto all the peoples of the world.'

'I'm sure you'll be welcome everywhere.' Jherek was eager to encourage. 'The Duke of Queens was saying to me only the other day that there was a great danger of becoming bored, without outside stimulus, such as we used to get. It is quite possible, Mr Underwood, that you will convert us all.'

'We return to our own world, sir,' Sergeant Sherwood told him mildly, 'as soon as we can.'

'We have been into the very bowels of Hell and yet were saved!' cried one of the constables.

'Amen,' said Harold Underwood absently. 'Now, if you'll kindly allow us to continue with our meeting ...'

'How do you intend to return to 1896, Harold?' implored Mrs Underwood. 'Who will take you?'

'The Lord,' her husband told her, 'will provide.' He added, in his old, prissy voice: 'I see you appear at last in your true colours, Amelia.'

She blushed as she stared down at her dress. 'A party,' she murmured.

He pursed his lips and looked away from her so that he might glare at Jherek Carnelian. 'Your master still has power here, I suppose, so I cannot command you ...'

'If we're interrupting, I apologize again.' Jherek bowed. 'I must say, Mr Underwood, that you seemed rather happier, in some ways, before your vision.'

'I have new responsibilities, Mr Carnelian.'

'The 'ighest sort,' agreed Inspector Springer.

'Amen,' said Sergeant Sherwood and the twelve constables. Their helmets nodded in unison.

'You are a fool, Harold!' Amelia said, her voice trembling. 'You have not seen God! The one who deceives you is closer to Satan!'

A peculiar, self-congratulatory smile appeared on Harold Underwood's features. 'Oh, really? You say this, yet you did not experience the vision. We have been chosen, Amelia, by God to warn the world of the terrors to come if it continues in its present course. What's this? Are you jealous, perhaps, that you are not one of the chosen, because you did not keep your faith and failed to do your duty?'

She gave a sudden cry, as if physically wounded. Jherek took her in his arms, glaring back at Underwood. 'She is right, you know. You are a cruel person, Harold Underwood. Tormented, you would torment us all!'

'Ha!'

'Amen,' said Inspector Springer automatically. 'I really must warn you again that you're doing yourself no good if you persist in these attempts to disrupt our meeting. We are empowered, not only by the 'Ome Secretary 'imself, but by the 'Osts of 'Eaven, to deal with would-be troublemakers as we see fit.' He gave the last few words special emphasis and placed his fists on his waistcoated hips (his jacket was not in evidence, though his bowler hat was still on his head). 'Get it?'

'Oh, Jherek, we must go!' Amelia was close to tears. 'We must go home.'

'Ha!'

As Jherek led her away the new missionaries stared after them for only a moment or two before returning to their service. They walked together up the yellow-brown metal pathway, hearing the voices raised again in song:

> *Christian! seek not yet repose,*
> *Hear thy guardian Angel say;*
> *Thou art in the midst of foes;*
> *Watch and pray.*

595

Principalities and powers,
Mustering their unseen array,
Wait for thy unguarded hours;
Watch and pray.

Gir'd thy heavenly armour on,
Wear it ever night and day;
Ambush'd lies the evil one;
Watch and pray . . .

They came to where they had left the locomotive and, as
she clambered onto the footplate, her hem in tatters, her
clothes stained, she said tearfully. 'Oh, Jherek, if there is a
Hell, then surely I deserve to be consigned there . . .'

'You do not blame yourself for what has happened to
your husband, Amelia?'

'Who else shall I blame?'

'You were blaming Jagged,' he reminded her.

'Jagged's machinations are one thing; my culpability is
another. I should never have left him. I have betrayed
him. He has gone mad with grief.'

'Because he loses you?'

'Oh, no – because his pride is attacked. Now he finds
consolation in religious mania.'

'You have offered to stay with him.'

'I know. The damage is done, I suppose. Yet I have a
duty to him, perhaps more so, now.'

'Aha.'

They began to rise up over the city. Another silence
had grown between them. He tried to break it:

'You were right, Amelia. In my wanderings I found
Brannart. He plots something with the Lat.'

But she would not reply. Instead, she began to sob.
When he went to comfort her, she shrugged him away.

'Amelia?'

She continued to sob until the scene of her party came
in sight. There were still guests there, Jherek could see,
but few. The Iron Orchid had not been sufficient to make

them stay – they wanted Amelia.

'Shall we rejoin our guests . . .?'

She shook her head. He turned the locomotive and made for the thatched roof of their house, visible behind the cypresses and the poplars. He landed on the lawn and immediately she ran from the locomotive to the door. She was still sobbing as she ran up the stairs to her apartment. Jherek heard a door close. He sat at the bottom of the stairs pondering on the nature of this new, all-consuming feeling of despair which threatened to rob him of the ability to move, but he was incapable of any real thought. He was wounded, he knew self-pity, he grieved for her in her pain and he, who had always expressed himself in terms of action (her wish had ever been his command, even if he had misinterpreted her occasionally), could think of nothing, not the simplest gesture, which might please her and ease their mutual misery.

After some time he went slowly to his bed.

Outside, beyond the house, the great rivers of blood still fell with unchecked force over the black cliffs, filling the swirling lake where cryptic monsters swam and on which obsidian islands still bobbed, their dark green fleshy foliage rustling in a hot, sweet wind; but Mrs Amelia Underwood's pièce-de-résistance had been abandoned long since by her forgotten guests.

CHAPTER TWENTY-FIVE

THE CALL TO DUTY

For the first time in his long life Jherek Carnelian, whose body could always be modified so that it did not need sleep, knew insomnia. Oblivion was his only demand, but it refused to come. Line after line of thought developed in his brain and each line led nowhere and had to be cut off. He considered seeking Jagged out, yet something stopped him. It was Amelia, only Amelia – Amelia was the only company he desired and yet (he must admit this to himself, here in the dark) presently he feared her. Thus in his mind he performed a forward step only, immediately thereafter, to take a backward – forward, backward – a horrid little dance of indecision which brought, in due course, his first taste of self-disgust. He had always followed his impulses, without a grain of self-consciousness, without the suggestion of a question, as did his peers at the End of Time. Yet now it seemed he had two impulses; he was caught like a steel ball between magnets, equidistant. His identity and his actions had hitherto been one – so now his identity came under siege. If he had two impulses, why, he must be two people. And if he were two people, then which was the worthwhile one, which should be abandoned as soon as possible? So Jherek discovered the old night-game of see-saw, in which a third Jherek, none too firm in his resolves, tried to hold judgement on two others, sliding first this way, then the other – 'I shall demand from her ...' and 'She deserves better than I ...' were two beginnings new to Jherek, though doubtless familiar to many of Mrs Underwood's contemporaries, particularly those who were frustrated in their relationships with the object of their affections, or were in a position of having to choose between old loyalties and fresh ones, between an ailing father, say, and a handsome suitor or, indeed, between an unlovable husband and a lover who offered marriage. It was halfway through this exercise that Jherek discovered the trick of transference – what if she experienced these torments, even as he experienced them? And immediately self-pity fled. He must go to her and comfort her. But no – he deceived himself, merely wishing to influence her, to focus her attention on to his dilemma. And so the see-saw swung again, with the judging Jherek poorly balanced on the pivot.

And so it might have continued until morning, had not she softly opened his door with a murmured query as to his wakefulness.

'Oh, Amelia!' He sat up at once.

'I have done you an injury,' she whispered, though there was none to overhear. 'My self-control deserted me today.'

'I am not quite sure what it is that you describe,' he told her, turning on the lamp by his bed so that it shed just a fraction more light and he could see her haggard face, red with crying, 'but you have done me no injury. It is I who have failed. I am useless to you.'

'You are brave and splendid – and innocent. I have said it before, Jherek: I have robbed you of that innocence.'

'I love you,' he said. 'I am a fool. I am unworthy of you.'

'No, no, my dear. I am a slave to my upbringing and I know that upbringing to be narrow, unimaginative, even brutalizing – ah, and it is essentially cynical, though I could never have admitted it. But you, dearest, are without a grain of cynicism, though I thought at first you and your world were nothing else but cynical. And now I see I am on the verge of teaching you my own habits – cynicism, hypocrisy, fear of emotional involvement disguised as self-denial – ah, there is a monstrous range . . .'

'I asked you to teach me these things.'

'You did not know what you asked.'

He stretched a hand to her and she took it, though she remained standing. Her hand was cold, and it shook a little.

'I am still unable to understand all that you say,' he told her.

'I pray that you never shall, my dear.'

'You love me? I was afraid I had done something to destroy your love.'

'I love you, Jherek.'

'I wish only to change for you, to become whatever you wish me to be . . .'

'I would not have you change, Jherek Carnelian.' A little smile appeared.

'Yet, you said . . .'.

'You accused me, earlier, of not being myself.' With a sigh she sat down upon the edge of his bed. She still wore the tattered oriental dress, but she had removed her feathers from her hair, which was restored to its natural colour, though not its original cut. Most of the paint was gone from her face. It was evident to him that she had slept no better than had he. His hand squeezed hers and she sighed for a second time. 'Of not being your Amelia,' she added.

'Not accused – but I was confused . . .'

'I tried, I suppose, to please you, but could not please myself. It seemed so wicked . . .' This smile was broader and it mocked her own choice of words. 'I have been trying so hard, Jherek, to enjoy your world for what it is. Yet I am constantly haunted first by my own sense of duty, which I have no means of expressing, and second by the knowledge of what your world is – a travesty, artificially maintained, denying mortality and therefore defying destiny.'

'Surely that is only one way of seeing it, Amelia.'

'I agree completely. I describe only my emotional response. Intellectually I can see many sides, many arguments. But I am, in this, as in so many other things, Jherek, a child of Bromley. You have given me these power-rings and taught me how to use them – yet I am filled with a desire to grow a few marigolds, to cook a pie, to make a dress – oh, I feel embarrassed as I speak. It seems so silly, when I have all the power of an Olympian god at my disposal. It sounds merely sentimental, to my own ears. I cannot think what you must feel ...'

'I am not sure what sentimentality is, Amelia. I wish you to be happy, that is all. If that is where fulfilment lies for you, then do these things. They will delight me. You can teach me these arts.'

'They are scarcely arts. Indeed, they are only desirable when one is denied the opportunity to practise them.' Her laughter was more natural, though still it shook. 'You can join in, if you wish, but I would not have you miserable. You must continue to express yourself as you wish, in ways that fulfil your instincts.'

'As long as I can express myself the means is unimportant, Amelia. It is that frozen feeling that I fear. And it is true that I live for you, so that what pleases you pleases me.'

'I make too many demands,' she said, pulling away. 'And offer nothing.'

'Again you bewilder me.'

'It is a bad bargain, Jherek, my dear.'

'I was unaware that we bargained, Amelia. For what?'

'Oh ...' she seemed unable to answer. 'For life itself, perhaps. For something ...' She gasped, as if in pain, but then smiled again, gripping his hand tighter. 'It is as if a tailor visits Eden and sees an opportunity for trade. No,

I am too hard upon myself, I suppose. I lack the words ...'

'As do I, Amelia. If only I could find adequate phrases to tell you what I feel! But of one thing you must be certain. I love you absolutely.' He flung back the bedclothes and sprang up, taking her hand to his breast. 'Amelia, of that you must be assured!'

He noticed that she was blushing, trying to speak, swallowing rapidly. She made a gulping noise.

'What is it, my dear?'

'Mr Carnelian – Jherek – you – you ...'

'Yes, my love?' Solicitously.

She broke free, making for the door. 'You seem unaware that you are – Oh, heavens!'

'Amelia!'

'You are quite naked, my dear.' She reached the door and sped through. 'I love you, Jherek. I love you! I will see you in the morning. Goodnight.'

He sat down heavily upon his bed, scratching his knee and shaking his head, but he was smiling (if somewhat bewilderedly) when he stretched out again and pulled the sheets over himself and fell into a deep sleep.

In the morning they breakfasted and were happy. Both had slept well, both chose to discuss little of the previous day's events, although Amelia expressed an intention of trying to discover if, in any museum in any of the old cities, there might be preserved seeds which she could plant. Jherek thought that there were one or two likely places where they could look.

Shortly after breakfast, as she boiled water to wash the dishes, two visitors arrived. The Iron Orchid – in a surprisingly restrained gown of dark blue silk against which living butterflies beat dark blue wings, upon the arm of the bearded time-traveller, dressed, as always, in his Norfolk jacket and tweed plus-fours. That Amelia had set more than one fashion was obvious from the way in which the Iron Orchid demurely knocked upon the door and waited until Amelia, her hands quickly dried, her sleeves rolled down, answered it and smilingly admitted them to the sitting room.

'I am so sorry, Iron Orchid, for yesterday's rudeness,' began Amelia. 'An instinct, I suppose. I was worried about Harold. We visited the city and were longer than we expected.'

The Iron Orchid listened patiently and with a hint of sardonic pleasure while Amelia's apologies ran their course.

'My dear, I told them nothing. Your mysterious disappearance only served to give greater spice to a wonderful creation. I see that you have not yet disseminated it . . .'

'Oh, dear. I shall do so presently.'

'Perhaps it should be left? A kind of monument?'

'So close to the garden? I think not.'

'Your taste cannot be questioned. I merely suggested . . .'

'You are very kind. Would you care for some tea?'

'Excellent!' said the time-traveller. He appeared to be in fine spirits. He rubbed his hands together. 'A decent cup of English tea would be most welcome, dear lady.'

They waited expectantly.

'I will put the kettle on.'

'The kettle?' The Iron Orchid looked questioningly at the time-traveller.

'The kettle!' he breathed, as if the words had mystic significance for him. 'Splendid.'

In poorly disguised astonishment (for she had expected the tea to appear immediately), the Iron Orchid watched Amelia Underwood leave for the kitchen, just as Jherek came in.

'You are looking less pensive today, my boy.'

'Most maternal of blossoms, I am completely without care! What a pleasure it is to see you. Good morning to you, sir.'

'Morning,' said the time-traveller. 'I am staying, presently, at Castle Canaria. The Iron Orchid suggested that I accompany her. I hope that I do not intrude.'

'Of course not.' Jherek was still in a woollen dressing gown and striped nightshirt, with slippers on his feet. He signed for them to sit down and sat, himself, upon a near-by sofa. 'Do the repairs to your craft progress well?'

'Very well! I must say – for all my reservations – your Lord Jagged – your father, that is – is a brilliant scientist. Understood exactly what was needed. We're virtually finished and just in time it seems – just waiting to test a setting. That's why I decided to drop over. I might not have another chance to say goodbye.'

'You will continue your travels?'

'It has become a quest. Captain Bastable was able to give me a few tips, and if I get the chance to return to the Palaeozoic, where they have a base, I gather they'll be able to supply me with further information. I need, you see, to get back onto a particular track.' The time-traveller began to describe complicated theories, most of them completely hypothetical and absolutely meaningless to Jherek. But he listened politely until Amelia returned with the tea-tray; he rose to take it from her and place it upon the low table between them and their guests.

'We have yet to solve the servant problem,' Amelia told them as she poured the tea.

The Iron Orchid, to her credit, entered into the spirit of the thing. 'Jherek had – what did you call them, dear? – serbos.'

'Servos – mechanical servants in human form. But they were antiques, or at least of antique design.'

'Well,' said Amelia, handing out the cups, 'we shall manage for a while, at any rate. All we had in Bromley was a maid and a cook (and she did not live in) and we coped perfectly.' As the time-traveller accepted his cup she said, 'It would be such a pleasure for me to be able to return your kindness to us, when we were stranded. You must, at least, come to dinner soon.'

He was cheered as well as embarrassed. 'Thank you, dear lady. You cannot, I think, realize what a great con-solation it is for me to know that there are, in this peculiar world, at least a few people who maintain the old-fashioned virtues. However, as I was saying to Mr Carnelian, I shall soon be on my way.'

'Today?'

'Tomorrow morning, probably. It must be so, I fear, for Lord Jagged completes the circuit shortly and then it will be impossible either to leave or to return to this world.'

She sipped and reflected. 'So the last brick of the gaol is about to be cemented in place,' she murmured.

'It is unwise to see it in those terms, dear lady. If you are to spend eternity here ...'

She drew a deep breath. Jherek was disturbed to see something of a return to yesterday's manner.

'Let us discuss a different topic,' he suggested brightly.

'It is scarcely a prison, dear,' said the Iron Orchid pinching, with finger and thumb, the wing of a straying butterfly tickling her chin.

'Some would call it Heaven,' tactfully said the time-traveller. 'Nirvana.'

'Oh, true. Fitting reward for a dead Hindu! But I am a live Christian.' Her smile was an attempt to break the atmosphere.

'Speaking of that,' said the time-traveller, 'I am able to do one last favour for Lord Jagged, and for you all, I dare say.' He laughed.

'What is it?' said Jherek, grateful for the change of subject.

'I have agreed to take Mr Underwood and the policemen back to 1896 before I continue on my journey.'

'What?' It was almost a breath from Amelia, slow and soft.

'You probably do not know that something happened in the city quite recently. They believe that God appeared to them and are anxious to return so that they might ...'

'We have seen them,' Jherek told him anxiously.

'Aha. Well, since I was responsible for bringing them

605

here, when Lord Jagged suggested that I take them
back —'

'Jagged!' exclaimed Amelia Underwood rising. 'This
is all his plot.'

'Why should Jagged "plot"?' The Iron Orchid was
astonished. 'What interest has he in your husband, my
dear?'

'None, save where it concerns me.' She turned upon the
disconcerted Jherek. 'And you, Jherek. It is an extension
of his schemings on our behalf. He thinks that with
Harold gone I shall be willing to —' she paused. 'To
accept you.'

'But he has abandoned his plans for us. He told us as
much, Amelia.'

'In one respect.'

Mildly the Orchid interjected. 'I think you suspect
Jagged of too much cunning, Amelia. After all, he is much
involved with a somewhat larger scheme. Why should he
behave as you suggest?'

'It is the only question for which I have no ready
answer.' Amelia raised fingers to her forehead.

A knock at the front door. Jherek sprang to answer,
glad of respite, but it was his father, all in voluminous
lemon, his features composed and amused. 'Good morning
to you, my boy.'

Lord Jagged of Canaria stepped into the sitting room
and seemed to fill it. He bowed to them all and was stared
at.

'Do I interrupt? I came to tell you, sir,' addressing the
time-traveller, 'that the quartz has hardened satisfactorily.
You can leave in the morning, as you planned.'

'With Harold and Inspector Springer and the rest!'
almost shouted Amelia.

'Ah, you know.'

'We know everything –' her colour was high, her eyes
fiery – 'save why you arranged this!'

'The time-traveller was good enough to say that he
would transport the gentlemen back to their own period.

It is their last chance to leave. No other will arise.'

'You made sure, Lord Jagged, that they should wish to leave. This ridiculous vision!'

'I fear that I do not follow your reasoning, beautiful Amelia.' Lord Jagged looked questioningly at Jherek.

Amelia sank to the sofa, teeth in knuckles.

'It seems to us,' Jherek loyally told his father, 'that you had something to do with Harold Underwood's recent vision in which God appeared to him in a burning sphere and ordered him to return to 1896 with a mission to warn his world of terrors to come.'

'A vision, eh?' Jagged smiled. 'But he will be considered mad if he tries to do that. Are they all so affected?'

'All!' mumbled Amelia viciously from behind her fist.

'They will not be believed, of course.' Jagged seemed to muse, as if all this news were new.

'Of course!' Amelia removed her knuckles from her mouth. 'And thus they will be unable to affect the future. Or, if they are caught by the Morphail Effect, it will be too late for them to return here. This world will be closed to them. You have staged everything perfectly, Lord Jagged.'

'Why should I stage such scenes?'

'Could it be to ensure that I stay with Jherek?'

'But you *are* with him, my dear.' Innocent surprise.

'You know what I mean, I think, Lord Jagged.'

'Are you concerned for your husband's safety if he returns?'

'I think his life will scarcely change at all. The same might not be said for poor Inspector Springer and his men, but even then, considering what has already happened to them, I have no particular fears. Quite likely it is the best that could happen. But I object to your part in arranging matters so – so suitably.'

'You do me too much credit, Amelia.'

'I think not.'

'However, if you think it would be best to keep Harold Underwood and the policemen in the city, I am sure that

607

the time-traveller can be dissuaded ...'

'You know it is too late. Harold and the others want nothing more than to return.'

'Then why are you so upset?'

Jherek interposed. 'Ambiguous parent, if you are the author of all this – if you have played God as Amelia suggests – then be frank with us.'

'You are my family. You are all my confidants. Frankness is not, admittedly, my forte. I am not prone to making claims or to denying accusations. It is not in my nature, I fear. It is an old time-travelling habit, too. If Harold Underwood experienced a vision in the city and it was not a hallucination – and you'll all admit the city is riddled with them, they run wild there – then who is to argue that he has not seen God?'

'Oh, this is the rankest blasphemy!'

'Not quite that, surely,' murmured the time-traveller. 'Lord Jagged has a perfectly valid point.'

'It was you, sir, who first accused him of playing at God!'

'Ah. I was upset. Lord Jagged has been of considerable help to me, of late ...'

'So you have said.'

As the voices rose, only the Iron Orchid remained where she had been sitting, watching the proceedings with a degree of quiet amusement.

'Jagged,' said his son desperately, 'do you categorically deny —'

'I have told you, my boy, I am incapable of it. I think it is a kind of pride.' The lord in yellow shrugged. 'We are all human.'

'You would be more, sir, it seems!' accused Amelia.

'Come now, dear lady. You are over-excited. Surely the matter is not worth ...' The time-traveller waved his hands helplessly.

'My coming seems to have created some sort of tension,' said Lord Jagged. 'I only stopped by in order to pick up my wife and the time-traveller, to see how you were settling down, Amelia ...'

'I shall settle down, sir – if I do – in my own way and in my own time, without help from you!'

'Amelia,' Jherek implored, 'there is no need for this!'

'You will calm me, will you!' Her eyes were blazing on them all. All stepped back. 'Will you?'

Lord Jagged of Canaria began to glide towards the door, followed by his wife and his guest.

'Machiavelli!' she cried after him. 'Meddler! Oh, monstrous, dandified Prince of Darkness!'

He had reached the door and he looked back, his eyes serious for a fraction of a moment. 'You honour me too much, madam. I seek only to correct an imbalance where one exists.'

'You'll admit your part in this?'

Already his shoulder had turned and the collar hid his face. He was outside, floating to where his great swan awaited him. She watched from the window. She was breathing heavily, was reluctant, even, to let Jherek take her hand.

He tried to excuse his father. 'It is Jagged's way. He means only good ...'

'He can judge?'

'I think you have hurt his feelings, Amelia.'

'I hurt his? Oho!' She removed the hand from his grasp and folded both under her heaving breast. 'He makes fools of all!'

'Why should he wish to? Why should he, as you say, play God?'

She watched the swan as it disappeared in the pale blue sky. 'Perhaps he does not know, himself,' she said softly.

'Harold can be stopped. Jagged said so.'

She shook her head and moved back into the room. Automatically, she began to gather up the cups and place them on the tray. 'He will be happier in 1896, without question. Now, at any rate. The damage is done. And he has a mission. He has a duty to perform, as he sees it. I envy him.'

He followed her reasoning. 'We shall go to seek for seeds today. As we planned. Some flowers.'

She shrugged. 'Harold believes he saves the world. Jagged believes the same. I fear that growing flowers will not satisfy my impulses. I cannot live, Jherek, unless I feel my life is useful.'

'I love you,' was all he could answer.

'But you do not need me, my dear.' She put down the tray and came to him. He embraced her.

'Need?' he said. 'In what respect?'

'It is the woman that I am. I tried to change, but with poor success. I merely disguised myself and you saw through that disguise at once. Harold needed me. My world needed me. I did a great deal of charitable work, you know. Missionary work, of sorts, too. I was not inactive in Bromley, Jherek.'

'I am sure that you were not, Amelia, dearest ...'

'Unless I have something more important than myself to justify—'

'There is nothing more important than yourself, Amelia.'

'Oh, I understand the philosophy which states that, Jherek —'

'I was not speaking philosophically, Amelia. I was stating fact. You are all that is important in my life.'

'You are very kind.'

'Kind? It is the truth!'

'I feel the same for you, as you know, my dear. I did not love Harold. I can see that I did not. But he had certain weaknesses which could be balanced by my strengths. Something in me was satisfied that is satisfied no longer. In your own way, in your very confidence, your innocence, you are strong ...'

'You have – what is it? – character? – which I lack.'

'You are free. You have a conception of freedom so great that I can barely begin to sense it. You have been brought up to believe that nothing is impossible, and your experience proves it. I was brought up to believe that almost everything was impossible, that life must be suffered, not enjoyed.'

'But if I have freedom, Amelia, you have conscience. I give you my freedom. In exchange, you give me your conscience.' He spoke soberly. 'Is that not so?'

She looked up into his face. 'Perhaps, my dear.'

'It is what I originally sought in you, you'll recall.'

She smiled. 'True.'

'In combination, then, we give something to the world.'

'Possibly.' She returned to her tea-cups, lifting the tray. He sprang to open the door. 'But does this world want what, together, we can give it?'

'It might need us more than it knows.'

She darted him an intelligent look as he followed her into the kitchen. 'Sometimes, Jherek Carnelian, I come close to suspecting that you have inherited your father's cunning.'

'I do not understand you.'

'You are capable of concocting the most convincing of arguments, on occasion. Do you deliberately seek to mollify me?'

'I stated only what was in my mind.'

She put on a pinafore. She was thoughtful as she washed the tea-cups, handing them to him as each one was cleaned. Unsure what to do with them, he made them weightless so that they drifted up to the ceiling and bobbed against it.

'No,' she said at last, 'this world does not need me. Why should it?'

'To give it texture.'

'You speak only in artistic terms.'

'I know no others. Texture is important. Without it a surface quickly loses interest.'

'You see morality only as texture?' She looked about for the cups, noted them on the ceiling, sighed, removed her pinafore.

'The texture of a painting is its meaning.'

'Not the subject?'

'I think not. Morality gives meaning to life. Shape at any rate.'

'Texture is not shape.'

'Without texture the shape is barren.'

'You lose me. I am not used to arguing in such terms.'

'I am scarcely used to arguing at all, Amelia!'

They returned to the sitting room, but she would advance into the garden. He went with her. Many flowers sweetened the air. She had recently added insects, a variety of birds to sing in the trees and hedges. It was warm; the sun relaxed them both. They went hand-in-hand along a path between rose trellises, much as they had wandered once in their earliest days together. He recalled how she had been snatched from him, as he had been about to kiss her. A hint of foreboding was pushed from his mind. 'What if these hedges were bare,' he said, 'if there was no smell to the roses, no colour to the insects, they would be unsatisfying, eh?'

'They would be unfinished. Yet there is a modern school of painting – was such a school, in my time – that made a virtue of it. Whistlerites, I believe they were called. I am not too certain.'

'Perhaps the leaving out was meant to tell us something too, Amelia? What was important was what was absent.'

'I don't think these painters said anything to that effect, Jherek. I believe they claimed to paint only what the eye saw. Oh, a neurotic theory of art, I am sure ...'

'There! Would you deny this world your common sense? Would you let it be neurotic?'

'I thought it so, when first I came. Now I realize that what is neurotic in sophisticated society can be absolutely wholesome in a primitive one. And in many respects, I must say, your society shares much in common with some of those our travellers experienced when first landing upon South Sea islands. To be sinful, one must have a sense of sin. That is my burden, Jherek, and not yours. Yet, it seems, you ask me to place that burden on you, too. You see, I am not entirely selfish. I do you little good.'

'You give meaning to my life. It would have none without you.' They stood by a fountain, watching her goldfish swimming. There were even insects upon the surface of the water, to feed them.

She chuckled. 'You can argue splendidly, when you wish, but you shall not change my feelings so quickly. I have already tried to change them myself for you. I failed. I must think carefully about my intentions.'

'You consider me bold, for declaring myself while your husband is still in our world?'

'I had not quite considered it in those terms.' She frowned. She drew away from him, moving around the pool, her dress dappled with bright spots of water from the fountain. 'I believe you to be serious, I suppose. As serious as it is possible for you to be.'

'Ah, you find me superficial.' He was saddened.

'Not that. Not now.'

'Then —?'

'I remain confused, Jherek.'

They stood on opposite sides of the pool, regarding each other through the veil of falling silvery water. Her beauty, her auburn hair, her grey eyes, her firm mouth, all seemed more desirable than ever.

'I wish only to honour you,' he said, lowering his eyes.

'You do so, already, my dear.'

'I am committed to you. Only to you. If you wished, we could try to return to 1896 . . .'

'You would be miserable there.'

'Not if we were together, Amelia.'

'You do not know my world, Jherek. It is capable of distorting the noblest intentions, of misinterpreting the finest emotions. You would be wretched. And I would feel wretched, also, to see one such as you transformed.'

'Then what is to be the answer?'

'I must think,' she said. 'Let me walk alone for a while, my dearest.'

He acknowledged her wish. He strode for the house, driving back the thoughts that suggested he would never see her again, shaking off the fear that she would be snatched from him, as she had been snatched once before, telling himself that it was merely association and that circumstances had changed. But how radically, he wondered, had they changed?

He reached the house. He closed the door behind him. He began to wander from room to room, avoiding only her apartments, the interior of which he had never seen, though he retained a deep curiosity about them, had often restrained an impulse to explore.

It came to him, as he entered his own bedroom and lay down upon the bed, still in his nightshirt and dressing gown, that perhaps all these new feelings were new only to him. Jagged, he felt sure, had known such feelings in the past – they had made him what he was. He vaguely recollected Amelia saying something about the son being the father, unwounded by the world. Did he grow more like Jagged? The thoughts of the previous night came back to him, but he refused to let them flourish. Before long, he had fallen asleep.

He was awakened by the sound of her footfall as she came slowly upstairs. It seemed to him that, on the landing, she paused at his door before her own door opened and she entered her rooms. He lay still for a little while, perhaps hoping that she would return. He got up, disseminating his night-clothes, naked as he listened; she did not come back. He used one of his power-rings to make a loose blouse and long kilt, in dark green. He left the bedroom and stood on the landing, hearing her moving about on the other side of the wall.

'Amelia?'

There was no reply.

He had grown tired of introspection. 'I will return soon, my dear,' he called.

Her voice was muffled. 'Where do you go?'

'Nowhere.'

He descended, passing through the kitchen and into the garden at the back, where he normally kept his locomotive. He boarded the craft, whistling the tune of *Carrie Joan*, feeling just a hint of nostalgia for the simpler days before he had met Amelia at the party given by the Duke of Queens. Did he regret the meeting? No.

The locomotive steamed into the sky, black, silver and gold now. He noticed how strange the two nearby scenes looked – the thatched house and its gardens, the lake of blood. They clashed rather than contrasted with each other. He wondered if she would mind if he disseminated the lake, but decided not to interfere.

He flew over transparent purple palaces and towering, quivering pink and puce mounds of unremarkable workmanship and imprecise invention, over a collection of gigantic prone figures, apparently entirely made of chalk, over a half-finished forest, and under a black thunderstorm whose lightning, in his opinion, was thoroughly overdone, but he refused to let the locomotive bear him back towards the city, to which his thoughts constantly went these days, perhaps because it was the city of his conception, perhaps because Lord Jagged and Nurse worked there (if they did), perhaps because he might study the man who remained his rival, at least until the next morning. He had no inclination to visit any of the friends whose company would normally give him pleasure; he considered going to Mongrove's rainy crags, but Mongrove would be of no help to him. Perhaps, he thought, he should choose a site and make something, to exercise his imagination in some ordinary pursuit, rather than let it continue to create impossible emotional dilemmas for him. He had just decided that he would try to build a reproduction of the Palaeozoic seashore and had found a suitable location when he heard the voice of Bishop Castle above him.

The bishop rode in a chariot whose wheels rotated, red and flaming, but which was otherwise of ordinary bronze, gold and platinum. His hat, one of his old crenellated kind, was immediately visible over the side of the chariot,

but it was a moment before Jherek noticed his friend's
face.

'I am so glad to see you, Jherek. I wished to congratulate
you – well, Amelia, really – on yesterday's party.'

'I will tell her, ebullient Bishop.'

'She is not with you?'

She remains at home.'

'A shame. But you must come and see this, Jherek. I
don't know what Brannart has been trying, but I would
say it had gone badly wrong for him. Would you be
amused for a few minutes?'

'I can think of nothing I should want more.'

'Then follow me!'

The chariot banked away, flying north, and obediently
Jherek set a course behind it.

In a moment Bishop Castle was laughing and shouting,
pointing at the ground. 'Look! Look!'

Jherek saw nothing but a patch of parched, unused
earth. Then dust swirled and a conical object appeared,
its outer casing whirling counter to another within. The
whirling stopped and a man emerged from the cone. For
all that he wore breathing equipment and carried a large
bag, the man was recognizable as Brannart Morphail by
his hump and his club foot. He turned, as if to tell the
other occupants of the cone not to leave, but already a
number of small figures had tumbled out and stood there,
hands on hips, looking around them, glaring through
their goggles. It was Captain Mubbers and the remnants
of his crew. He gesticulated at Brannart, tapping his elbow
several times. Wet, smacking noises could be heard, even
from where Jherek and Bishop Castle hovered watching.

At length, after an argument, they all crowded back
into the cone. The two shells whirled again and the cone
vanished. Bishop Castle was beside himself with laughter,
but Jherek could not see why he was so amused.

'They have been doing that for the past four hours, to
my knowledge!' roared Bishop Castle. 'The machine appears. It stops. They disembark, argue, and get back in

again. All exactly the same. Wait . . .'

Jherek waited and, sure enough, the dust swirled, the cone reappeared, Brannart and then Captain Mubbers and his men got out, they argued and returned to the ship. Each movement had been the same.

'What is happening, Bishop?' Jherek asked, as soon as the next wave of laughter had subsided.

'Some sort of time-loop, evidently. I wondered what Brannart was up to. He schemed, I gather, with the Lat – offering to take them back to a period when their space-ship – and space – still existed – if they would help him. He swore me to secrecy, but it cannot matter now.'

'What did he plan?' In the confusion Jherek realized he had forgotten to warn Jagged of what he had seen.

'Oh, he was not too clear. Wished to thwart Jagged in some way, of course. Go back in time and change events.'

'Then what has happened to him now?'

'Isn't it obvious? Ho, ho, ho!'

'Not to me.'

'He's hoist by his own petard – caught in a particularly unpleasant version of the Morphail Effect. He arrives in the past, certainly, but only to be flung back to the present immediately. As a result he's stuck. He could go round and round for ever, I suppose . . .'

'Should we not try to rescue him?'

'Jagged is the only one qualified to do that, Jherek, I'd say. If we tried to help we might find ourselves caught in the loop, too.'

Jherek watched as the cone appeared for the third time and the figures went through their set ritual. He tried to laugh, but he could not find it as amusing as did his friend.

'I wonder if Jagged knew of this,' continued Bishop Castle, 'and trapped Brannart into the situation. What a fine revenge, eh?'

Everyone, it seemed, suspected his father of a scheme. However, Jherek was not in a mood to defend Lord Jagged again today.

Bishop Castle brought his chariot closer to Jherek's locomotive. 'By the by, Jherek, have you seen Doctor Volospion's latest? It's called "The History of the World in Miniature" – the entire history of mankind from start to finish, all done with tiny reproductions at incredible speed – it can be slowed down to observe details of any particular millennium – it lasts a full week!'

'It is reminiscent, is it not, of something of Jagged's?'

'Is it? Well, Volospion always saw himself as a rival to Jagged, and perhaps hopes to fill his shoes, now that he is occupied with other things. O'Kala Incarnadine has been safely resurrected, by the by, and has lost interest in being a goat. He has become some kind of leviathan, with his own lake. Now that *is* a copy – of Amelia's creation. Well, if you'll forgive me, I'll be on my way. Others will want to see this.'

For the fourth time, the whirling cone appeared, Brannart and the Lat emerged. As Bishop Castle flew off Jherek dropped closer. He was still unable to understand them.

'Hrunt!' cried Captain Mubbers.

'Ferkit!' declared Brannart Morphail.

Blows were exchanged. They returned to the craft.

Jherek wondered if he should not continue on to Castle Canaria and tell Lord Jagged what was happening, but the sight had distressed him too much and he did not relish a further encounter with his father and mother today. He decided to return with the news to Amelia.

It was almost twilight as he directed the locomotive home. The darkness seemed to come quicker than usual and it was beneath a starless, moonless sky that he eventually located the house where only one light burned at a single window.

He was surprised, as he landed, to note that the window was not Amelia's but his own. He did not recall leaving a light there. He felt alarm as he entered the house and ran upstairs. He knocked at her door. 'Amelia! Amelia!' There was no reply. Puzzled, he opened his door and went in. The lamp burned low, but there was sufficient light to

618

see that his Amelia occupied the bed, her face turned away from him, the great sable sheet drawn tightly around her body so that only her head was visible.

'Amelia?'

She did not turn, though he could see that she was not asleep. He could do nothing but wait.

Eventually, she spoke in a small, unsteady voice. 'As a woman, I shall always be yours.'

'Are we —? Is this marriage?'

She looked up at him. There were tears in her eyes; her expression was serious. Her lips parted.

He kneeled upon the bed; he took her head in his hands. He kissed her eyes. She moved convulsively and he thought he alarmed her until he realized that she was struggling free of the sheet, to open her arms to him, to hold him, as if she feared to fall. He took her naked shoulders in his arm, he stroked her cheek, experiencing a sensation at once violent and tender – a sensation he had never felt before. The smell of her body was warm and sweet.

'I love you,' he said.

'I shall love you for ever, my dear,' she replied. 'Believe me.'

'I do.'

Her words seemed subtly inappropriate and the old sense of foreboding came and went. He kissed her. She gasped and her hands went beneath his blouse; he felt her nails in his flesh. He kissed her shoulder. She drew him to her.

'It is all I can give you ...' She seemed to be weeping.

'It is everything.'

She groaned. With a touch of a power-ring he disrobed, stroking the tears on her cheek, kissing her trembling shoulder, until at last he drew back the sheet and pressed himself upon her.

'The lamp,' she said. He caused it to vanish and they were in complete darkness.

'Always, Jherek.'

'Oh, my dearest.'

She hugged him. He touched her waist. 'Is this what you do?' he asked. 'Or is it this?'

Then they made love; and in the fullness of time they slept.

The sun had risen. He felt it upon his eyelids and he smiled. At last the future, with its confusion and its fears, was banished; nothing divided them. He turned, so that his first sight of the morning would be of her; but even as he turned the foreboding came back to him. She was not there. There was a trace of her warmth, little more. She was not in the room. He knew that she was not in the house.

'Amelia!'

This was what she had decided. He recalled her anecdote of the young man who had only dared declare his love when he knew he would never see her again. All his instincts had told him, from that moment by the fountain, that it was her intention to answer her Victorian conscience, to go back with Harold Underwood to 1896, to accept her responsibilities. It was why she had said what she said to him last night. As a woman, she would always be his, but as a wife she was committed to her husband.

He plunged from his bed, opening the window, and, naked, flung himself into the dawn sky, flying as rapidly as his power-rings could carry him, rushing towards the city, her name still on his lips, like the mad cry of a desolate seabird.

'Amelia!'

Once before he had followed her thus, coming too late to stop her return to her own time. Every sensation, every thought was repeated now, as the air burned his body with the speed of his flight. Already he planned how he might pursue her back to Bromley.

He reached the city. It seemed to sleep, it was so still.

And near the brink of the pit he saw the great open structure of the time-machine, the chronomnibus. Aboard he could see the time-traveller at the controls, and the policemen, all in white robes, with their helmets upon their heads, and Inspector Springer, also in white, wearing his bowler, and Harold Underwood with his hay-coloured hair and his pince-nez twinkling in the early sun. And he glimpsed Amelia, in her grey suit, seemingly struggling with her husband. Then the outlines of the machine grew faint, even as he descended. There was a shrill sound, like a scream, and the machine faded away and was gone.

He reached the ground, staggering.

'Amelia.' He could barely see for his tears; he stood hopeless and trembling, his heart pounding, gasping for air.

He heard sobbing and it was not his own sobbing. He lifted his head.

She lay there, in the black dust of the city, her face upon her arm. She wept.

Half-sure that this was a terrible illusion, merely a recollection from the city's memory, he approached her. He fell on his knees beside her. He touched her grey sleeve.

She looked up at him. 'Oh, Jherek! He told me that I was no longer his wife ...'

'He has said as much before.'

'He called me "impure". He said that my presence would taint the high purpose of his mission, that even now I tempted him ... Oh, he said so many things. He threw me from the machine. He hates me.'

'He hates sanity, Amelia. I think it is true of all such men. He hates truth. It is why he accepts the comforting lie. You would have been of no use to him.'

'I was so full of my resolve. I loved you so much. I fought so hard against my impulse to stay with you.'

'You would martyr yourself in response to the voice of Bromley? To a cause you know to be at best foolish?' He was surprised by his words and it was plain that he surprised her, also.

'*This* world has no cause at all,' she told him, as he held her against him. 'It has no use for one such as me!'

'Yet you love me. You trust me?'

'I trust you, Jherek. But I do not trust your background, your society – all this . . .' She stared bleakly at the city. 'It prizes individuality and yet it is impossible to feel oneself an individual in it. Do you understand?'

He did not, but he continued to comfort her.

He helped her to her feet.

'I can see no future for us here,' she told him. She was exhausted. He summoned his locomotive.

'There is no future,' he agreed, 'only the present. Surely it is what lovers have always wished for.'

'If they are nothing but lovers, Jherek, my dear.' She sighed deeply. 'Well, there is scarcely any point to my complaints.' Her smile was brave. 'This is my world and I must make the best of it.'

'You shall, Amelia.'

The locomotive appeared, puffing between high, ragged towers.

'My sense of duty —' she began.

'To yourself, as I said. My world esteems you as Bromley never could. Accept that esteem without reserve; it is given without reserve.'

'Blindly, however, as children give. One would wish to be respected for – for noble deeds.'

He saw clarity, at last. 'Your going to Harold – that was "noble"?'

'I suppose so. The self-sacrifice . . .'

' "Self-sacrifice" – another. And is that "virtuous"?'

'It is thought so, yes.'

'And "modest"?'

'Modesty is often involved.'

'Your opinion of your own actions is "modest"?'

'I hope so.'

'And if you do nothing save what your own spirit tells you to do – that is "lazy", eh? Even "evil"?'

'Scarcely evil, really, but certainly unworthy . . .'

The locomotive came to a rest beside them, where the chronomnibus had lately been.

'I am enlightened at last!' he said. 'And to be "poor", is that frowned upon by Bromley.'

She began to smile. 'Indeed, it is. But I do not approve of such notions. In my charity work, I tried to help the poor as much as I could. We had a missionary society, and we collected money so that we could purchase certain basic comforts . . .'

'And these "poor" ones, they exist so that you might exercise your own impulses towards "nobility" and "self-sacrifice". I understand!'

'Not so, Jherek. The poor – well, they just *exist*. I, and others like me, tried to ease their conditions, tried to find work for the unemployed, medicine for their sick.'

'And if they did not exist? How, then, would you express yourself?'

'Oh, there are many other causes, all over the world. Heathen to be converted, tyrants to be taught justice, and so on. Of course, poverty is the chief source of all the other problems . . .'

'I could perhaps create some "poor" for you.'

'That would be terrible. No, no! I disapproved of your world before I understood it. Now I do not disapprove – it would be irrational of me. I would not change it. It is I who must change.' She began to weep again. 'I who must try to understand that things will remain as they are throughout eternity, that the same dance will be danced over and over again and that only the partners will differ . . .'

'We have our love, Amelia.'

Her expression was anguished. 'But can't you see, Jherek, that it is what I fear most! What is love without time, without death?'

'It is love without sadness, surely.'

'Could it be love without purpose?'

'Love is love.'

'Then you must teach me to believe that, my dear.'

623

CHAPTER TWENTY-SIX

WEDDING BELLS AT THE END OF TIME

She was to be Amelia Carnelian; she insisted upon it. They found seeds and bulbs, preserved by the cities, and they planted them in her gardens. They began a new life, as man and wife. She was teaching him to read again, and to write, and if Jherek felt contentment she, at least, felt a degree more secure; his assurances of fidelity became credible to her. But though the sun shone and the days and nights came and went with a regularity unusual at the End of Time, they were without seasons. She feared for her crops. Though she watered them carefully, no shoots appeared, and one day she decided to turn a piece of ground to see how her potatoes fared. She found that they had gone rotten. Elsewhere not a single seed had put out even the feeblest root. He came upon her as she dug frantically through her vegetable garden, searching for one sign of life. She pointed to the ruined tubers.

'Imperfectly preserved, I suppose,' he suggested.

'No. We tasted them. These are the same. It is the earth that ruins them. It is not true soil at all. It is without goodness. It is barren, Jherek, as everything is fundamentally barren in this world.' She threw down the spade; she

624

entered the house. With Jherek at her heels, she went to sit at a window looking out towards her rose-garden.

He joined her, feeling her pain but unable to find any means of banishing it.

'Illusion,' she said.

'We can experiment, Amelia, to make earth which will allow your crops to grow.'

'Oh, perhaps . . .' She made an effort to free herself from her mood, then her brow clouded again. 'Here is your father, like an Angel of Death come to preside at the funeral of my hopes.'

It was Lord Jagged, stepping with jaunty tread along the crazy paving, waving to her.

Jherek admitted him. He was all bustle and high humour. 'The time comes. The circuit is complete. I let the world run through one more full week, to establish the period of the loop, then we're saved forever! My news displeases you?'

Jherek spoke for Amelia. 'We do not care to be reminded of the manner in which the world is maintained, Father!'

'You will notice no outward effects.'

'We shall have the *knowledge* of what has happened,' she murmured. 'Illusions cease to satisfy, Lord Jagged.'

'Call me Father, too!' He seated himself upon a chaise-longue, spreading his limbs. 'I should have guessed you very happy by now. A shame.'

'If one's only function is to perpetuate illusion, and one has known real life, one is inclined to fret a little,' said she with ungainly irony. 'My crops have perished.'

'I follow you, Amelia. What do you feel, Jherek?'

'I feel for Amelia,' he answered. 'If she were happy, then I would be happy.' He smiled. 'I am a simple creature, father, as I have often been told.'

'Hm,' said Lord Jagged. He eased himself upward and was about to say more when, in the distance, through the open windows, they heard a sound.

They listened.

'Why,' said Amelia, 'it is a band.'

'Of what?' asked Jherek.

'A musical band,' his father told him. He swept from the house. 'Come, let's see!'

They all ran through the walks and avenues until they reached the white gate in the fence Amelia had erected around the trees. The lake of blood had long since vanished and gentle green hills replaced it. They could see a column of people, far away, marching towards them. Even from here, the music was distinct.

'A brass band!' cried Amelia. 'Trumpets, trombones, tubas —!'

'And a silver band!' declared Lord Jagged, with unfeigned enthusiasm. 'Clarinets, flutes, saxophones!'

'Bass drums – hear!' For the moment her miseries were gone. 'Snare drums, tenor drums, timpani ...'

'A positive profusion of percussion!' added Jherek, wishing to include himself in the excitement. 'Ta-ta-ta-*ta*! Hooray!' He made a cap for himself, so that he might fling it into the air. 'Hooray!'

'Oh, look!' Amelia had forgotten her distress entirely, for the moment at least. 'So many! And is that the Duke of Queens?'

'It is!'

The band – or rather the massed bands, for there must have been at least a thousand mechanical musicians – came marching up the hill towards them, with flags flying, plumes nodding, boots and straps shining, scarlet and blue, silver and black, gold and crimson, green and yellow.

Father, son and wife hung over the white gate like so many children, waving to the Duke of Queens, who marched at the front, a long pole whirling in the air above him, two others whirling on either side, a baton in one hand, a swagger-cane in the other, a huge handle-bar moustache upon his face, and a monstrous bearskin tottering on his head, goose-stepping so high that he almost fell backwards with every movement of his legs. And the band had grown so loud, though it remained in perfect time,

626

that it was utterly impracticable to try to speak, either to the Duke of Queens or to one another.

On and on it marched, with its sousaphones, its kolaphones, its brownophones, its telophones and its gramophones, performing intricate patterns, weaving in and out of itself, making outrageously difficult steps coupled with peculiar time-signatures; with its euphoniums and harmoniums, pianos and piccolos, its banjos, its bongos and its bassoons, saluting, marking time, forming fours, bagpipes skirling, bullroarers whirling, ondes Martenot keening, cellos groaning, violins wailing, Jew's harps boinging, swannee whistles, wailing, tubular bells tolling, calliopes wheezing, guitars shrieking, synthesizers sighing, ophicleides panting, gongs booming, organs grinding, sweet potatoes warbling, xylophones clattering, serpents blaring, bones rattling, glockenspiels tinkling, virginals whispering, bombardons moaning, until it had marshalled itself before the gate. And then it stopped.

'Haydn, eh?' said Lord Jagged knowledgeably as the proud Duke approached.

'*Yellow Dog Charlie*, according to the tape reference.' The Duke of Queens was beaming from beneath his bearskin. 'But you know how mixed up the cities are. Something from your period again, Mrs Un —'

'Carnelian,' she murmured.

'– derwood. We simply can't leave it alone, can we? I've seen a craze last a thousand years, unabated.'

'Your enthusiasms always tend to prolong themselves beyond the capabilities of your contemporaries, ebullient bandsman, most carefree of capellmeisters, most glorious of gleemen!' congratulated Lord Jagged. 'Have you marched far?'

'The parade is to celebrate my first venture into connubial harmony!'

'Music?' enquired Jherek.

'Marriage.' A wink at Jherek's father. 'Lord Jagged will know what I mean.'

'A wedding? laconically supplied Jagged.

'A wedding, yes! It is all the rage. Today – I think it's today – I am joined in holy matrimony (admit my grasp of the vocabulary!) to the loveliest of ladies, the beautiful Sweet Orb Mace.'

'And who conducts the rites?' asked Amelia.

'Bishop Castle. Who else? Will you come, and be my best men and women?'

'Well . . .'

'Of course we'll come, gorgeous groom.' Lord Jagged leapt the gate to embrace the Duke before he departed. 'And bring gifts, too. Green for a groom and blue for a bride!'

'Another custom?'

'Oh, indeed.'

Amelia pursed her lips and frowned at Lord Jagged of Canaria. 'It is astonishing that so many of our old customs are remembered, sir.'

His patrician head moved to meet her eyes; he wore the faintest of smiles. 'Oh, didn't you know? In the general confusion, with the translation pills and so forth, it seems that we are all talking nineteenth-century English. It serves. It serves.'

'You arranged this?'

Blandly, he replied. 'I am constantly flattered by your suggestions, Amelia. I admire your perceptions, though it would seem to me that you are inclined to over-interpret, on occasion.'

'If you would have it so, sir.' She curtsied, but her expression was hardly demure.

Fearful of further tension between the two, Jherek said: 'So we are again to be guests at the Duke of Queens.' You are not disturbed by the prospect, Amelia?'

'We have been invited. We shall attend. If it be a mock marriage, it will certainly be an extravagant one.'

Lord Jagged of Canaria was looking at her through perceptive eyes and it was as if his mask had fallen for a moment.

She was baffled by this sudden sincerity; she avoided

that eye.

'Very well, then,' said Jherek's father briskly, 'We shall meet again soon, then?'

'Soon,' she said.

'Farewell,' he said, 'to you both.' He strode for his swan which swam on a tiny pond he had manufactured for parking purposes. He was soon aloft. A wave of yellow froth and he was gone.

'So marriage is the fashion now,' she said as they walked back to the house.

He took her hand. 'We are already married,' he said.

'In God's eyes, as we used to say. But God looks down on this world no longer. We have only a poor substitute. A poseur.'

They entered the house. 'You speak of Jagged again, Amelia?'

'He continues to disturb me. It would seem he has satisfied himself, seen all his schemes completed. Yet still I am wary of him. I suppose I shall always be wary, through eternity. I fear his boredom.'

'Not your own?'

'I have not his power.'

He let the matter rest.

That afternoon, with Jherek in morning dress and Amelia in grey and blue stripes, they set off for the wedding of the Duke of Queens.

Bishop Castle (it was evidently his workmanship) had built a cathedral specially for the ceremony, in classical subtlety, with great stained glass windows, Gothic spires and masonry, massive and yet giving the impression of lightness, and decorated on the outside primarily in orange, purple and yellow. Surrounding the area was the band of the Duke of Queens, its automata at rest for the moment. There were tall flag-masts, flying every conceivable standard still existing in the archives; there were tents and booths dispensing drinks and sweetmeats, games of chance and of skill, exhibitions of antique entertainments, through which moved the guests, laughing and talking, full of merriment.

'It's a lovely scene,' said Jherek, as he and Amelia descended from their footplate. 'A beautiful background for a wedding.'

'Yet still merely a scene,' she said. 'I can never rid myself of the knowledge that I am playing a part in a drama.'

'Were ceremonies different, then, in your day?'

She was silent for a moment. Then: 'You must think me a cheerless creature.'

'I have seen you happy, Amelia, I think.'

'It is a trick of the mind I was never taught. Indeed, I was taught to suspect an open smile, to repress my own. I try, Jherek, to be carefree.'

'It is your duty,' he told her as they joined the throng and were greeted, at once, by their friends. 'Why, Mistress Christia, the last time I saw your companions they were trapped in a particularly unpleasant dilemma, battling with Brannart.'

Mistress Christia, the Everlasting Concubine, laughed a tinkling laugh, as was her wont. She was surrounded by Captain Mubbers and his men, all dressed in the same brilliant powder-blue she wore, save for strange balloon-like objects of dull red, on elbows and knees. 'Lord Jagged rescued them, I gather, and I insisted that they be my special guests. We are to be married, too, today!'

'You – to them all!' said Amelia in astonishment. She blushed.

'They are teaching me their customs.' She displayed the elbow balloons. 'These are proper to a married Lat female. The reason for their behaviour, where women were concerned, was the conviction that if we did not wear knee- and elbow-balloons we were – um?' She looked enquiringly at her nearest spouse, who crossed his three pupils and stroked his whiskers in embarrassment. Jherek thought it was Rokfrug. 'Dear?'

'Joint-sport,' said Rokfrug almost inaudibly.

'They are so contrite!' said Mistress Christia. She moved intimately to murmur to Amelia. 'In public, at least, dear.'

'Congratulations, Captain Mubbers,' said Jherek. 'I hope you and your men will be very happy with your wife.'

'Fill it, arse-lips,' Captain Mubbers said, sotto voce, even as they shook hands. 'Sarcy fartin' knicker-elastic hole-smeller.'

'I intended no irony.'

'Then wipe it and button it, bumface, Nn?'

'You have given up any intention of going into space again?' Amelia said.

Captain Mubbers shrugged his sloping shoulders. 'Nothing there for us, is there?' He offered her a knowing look which took her aback.

'Well —' she drew a breath — 'I am sure, once you have settled down to married life ...' She was defeated in her efforts.

Captain Mubbers grunted, eyeing her elbow, visible through the silk of her dress.

'Flimpoke!' Mistress Christia had noticed. 'Well!'

'Sorry, my bone.' He stared at the ground.

'Flimpoke?' said Jherek.

'Flimpoke Mubbers,' Mistress Christia told him, with every evidence of pride. 'I am to be Mrs Mubbers, and Mrs Rokfrug, and Mrs Glopgoo ...'

'And we are to be Mr and Mr Mongrove-de Goethe!' It was Werther, midnight blue from head to toe. Midnight blue eyes stared from a midnight-blue face. It was rather difficult to recognize him, save for his voice. Beside him lounged in an attitude of dejected satisfaction the great bulk of Lord Mongrove, moody monarch of the weeping cliffs.

'What? You marry? Oh, it is perfect.'

'We think so,' said Werther.

'You considered no one else?'

'We have so little in common with anyone else,' droned Mongrove. 'Besides, who would have me? Who would spend the rest of his life with this shapeless body, this colourless personality, this talentless brain ...?'

'It is a good match,' said Jherek hastily. Mongrove was inclined, once started, to gather momentum and spend an hour or more listing his own drawbacks.

'We decided, at Doctor Volospion's fairground, when we fell off the carousel together, that we might as well share our disasters ...'

'An excellent scheme.' A scent of dampness wafted from Mongrove's robes as he moved; Jherek found it unpleasant. 'I trust you will discover contentment ...'

'Reconciliation, at least,' said Amelia.

The two moved on.

'So,' said Jherek, offering his arm. 'We are to witness three weddings.'

'They are too ludicrous to be taken seriously,' she said, as if she gave her blessing to the proceedings.

'Yet they offer satisfaction to those taking part, I think.'

'It is so hard for me to believe that.'

They found Brannart Morphail, at last, in unusual finery, a mustard-coloured cloak hanging in pleats from his hump, tassels swinging from the most unlikely places on his person, his medical boot glittering with spangles. He seemed in an almost jolly mood as he limped beside My Lady Charlotina of Above-the-Ground (her new domicile).

'Aha!' cried Brannart, sighting the two. 'My nemesis, young Jherek Carnelian!' The jocularity, if forced, was at least well-meant. 'And the *cause* of all our problems, the beautiful Amelia Underwood.'

'Carnelian, now,' she said.

'Congratulations! You take the same step, then?'

'As the Duke of Queens,' agreed Jherek amicably, 'and Mistress Christia. And Werther and Lord Mongrove ...'

'No, no, no! As My Lady Charlotina and myself!'

'Ah!'

My Lady Charlotina fluttered lashes fully two inches long and produced a winsome smile. In apple-green tupperware crinoline and brown slate bonnet she had some difficulty moving even at the relatively slow pace of her husband-to-be.

'You proposed rapidly enough, you dog!' said Jherek to the scientist.

'She proposed,' Brannart grunted, momentarily returned to his usual mood. 'I owe my rescue to her.'

'Not to Jagged?'

'It was she who went to get Jagged's help.'

'You were attempting a jump backwards through time, eh?' Jherek said.

'I did my best. Given half a chance, I might have improved this disastrous situation. But I tried to move within too limited a period and, as always happens, I got caught in a kind of short-circuit. Proving, irrefutably, of course, the truth of Morphail's Law.'

'Of course,' they both consented.

'I suppose the Law still applies, at present,' Amelia suggested.

'At present, and always.'

'Always?'

'Well –' Brannart rubbed his warted nose – 'in essence. If Jagged re-cycles a seven-day period, then the Law will probably apply to the time contained within that span, d'you see.'

'Aha.' Amelia was disappointed, though Jherek did not know why. 'There is no other means of leaving this world, once the circuit is completed?'

'None at all. Isolated chronologically as well as spacially. By rights this planet has no business existing at all.'

'So we gather,' said Jherek.

'It defies all logic.'

'You have ever made a practice of that, have you not?' said Amelia.

'Have we, dear?' said My Lady Charlotina of Above-the-Ground.

'What I was taught to call logic, at any rate.' Amelia swiftly compromised.

'This will mean the death of Science,' said Brannart

cheerfully. 'Oh, yes. The death of Science, right enough. No more enquiry, no more investigation, no more analysis, no more interpretation of phenomena. Nothing for me to do.'

'There are functions of the cities which might be restored,' said Amelia helpfully.

'Functions?'

'Old sciences which could be re-discovered. There are all kinds of possibilities, I should have thought.'

'Hm,' said Brannart. Gnarled fingers crossed a pitted chin. 'True.'

'Memory banks which need their wits sharpening,' Jherek told him. 'It would take a brilliant scientist to restore them ...'

'True,' repeated Brannart. 'Well, perhaps I can do something in that direction, certainly.'

My Lady Charlotina patted his pleated hump. 'I shall be so proud of you, Brannart. And what a contribution you could make to social life, if some of those machines could be got to reveal their secrets.'

'Jagged will be so jealous!' Amelia added.

'Jealous?' Brannart brightened still further. 'I suppose he will.'

'Hideously,' said Jherek.

'Well, you of all people would know, Jherek.' The scientist seemed to do a little jig on his spangled boot. 'You think so?'

'Without question!'

'Hm.'

A small irascible voice said from just behind Jherek: 'Ah! There you are posterior-visage. I've been looking for you!'

It was Rokfrug. He continued heavily: 'If the ladies will excuse us, I'd like a middle-of-the-leg word with you, sediment-nostril.'

'I have already apologized, Lieutenant Rokfrug,' Brannart Morphail told him. 'I see no reason to go on with this —'

'You offered me rapine, loot, arson, toe-pillage, and all I get is to be a member of a smelly male harem ...'

'It was not my fault. You did not have to agree to the marriage!' Brannart began to back away.

'If it's the only way to get a bit of jointing hoo-hoo, what else am I supposed to do? Come here!'

Brannart broke into a hobbling run, pursued by Lieutenant Rokfrug who was quickly tripped by the passing Lord Jagged, who picked him up, dusted him down, pointed him in the wrong direction and continued towards them.

Brannart, followed by his bride-to-be, disappeared behind a cluster of booths, while Rokfrug vanished into a candy-striped tent. Lord Jagged seemed content.

'So the peace is kept.' He smiled at Jherek and Amelia. 'And a certain balance is maintained.'

'Perhaps I should have dubbed you "Solomon",' said Amelia acidly.

'You *must* call me "Father", my dear.' A bow to a passing O'Kala Incarnadine, recognizable only from the face at the top of the giraffe neck. For reasons best known to himself, Lord Jagged had discarded his usual robes and collars and wore, like Jherek, a simple grey morning suit, with a grey silk hat upon his noble head, a silver-topped cane in one gloved hand. The only touch of yellow was the primrose in his button-hole. 'And here is my own spouse. Iron Orchid, as delicious as only you can be!'

The Orchid acknowledged the compliment. She wore her name-flower today – orchids of every possible hue and variety clustered over her body, hugging themselves close to her as if she were the only substantial thing remaining in the universe. The scents were so strong, in combination, that they threatened to overwhelm everyone within a radius of twenty feet. Orchids formed a hood around her head, from which she peered. 'Husband mine! And dear children! All together, again. And for such a beautiful occasion! How many weedings take place today?' Her question was for Jherek.

'Weddings, mama. Three – no four – to my knowledge.'

'About twenty in all,' said Jagged. 'You know how quickly these things catch on.'

'Who else?' said Jherek.

'Doctor Volospion weds the Platinum Poppy.'

'Such a pleasant, empty creature,' sniffed the Iron Orchid, 'at least, before she changed her name.'

'And Captain Marble is to be spliced to Soola Sen Sun. And Lady Voiceless, I gather, gives herself in marriage to Li Pao.'

The Iron Orchid seemed displeased by this announcement, but she said nothing.

'And how long, I wonder, will these "marriages" last,' said Amelia.

'Oh, I should think as long as the various parties wish them to last,' murmured Lord Jagged. 'The fashion could remain with us for a thousand years, or even two. One never knows. It all depends upon the ingenuity, surely, of the participants. Something else might come along to fire society's imagination . . .'

'Of course,' she said. She had become subdued. Noticing this, Jherek pressed her arm, but she was not comforted.

'I should have thought, Amelia, that you would have been pleased by this development.' Lord Jagged's lips curved a fraction. 'A tendency towards social stability, is it not?'

'I cannot rise to your jesting today, Lord Jagged.'

'You still grieve for your perished potatoes, then?'

'For what is signified by their destruction.'

'Later, we must put our heads together. There could be a solution to the problem . . .'

'There can be no solution, sir, to the abiding dilemma of one who would not be a drone in a world of drones.'

'You are too hard on yourself, and on us. See it, instead, as a reward to the human race for all its millions of years of struggle.'

'I have not been part of that struggle.'

'Surely, in one sense . . .'

636

'In one sense, sir, we have all been involved. In another, we have not. It is, as you would agree, I know, not what *is*, but how one looks at what is.'

'You will change.'

'I fear that I shall.'

'You fear cynicism in yourself?'

'Perhaps it is that.'

'Some would consider your attitude cowardly.'

'*I* consider it cowardly, Lord Jagged, you may be sure. Let us terminate this conversation. It excludes too many; it discomforts all. My problems are my own responsibility.'

'You claim more than you should, Amelia. Have I had no part in creating those problems?'

'I suppose that you would be offended if I disagreed with you on that point.'

His voice was very quiet and only for her ears. 'I have a conscience, too, Amelia. All that I have done might be seen as the result of possessing an exaggerated sense of duty.'

Her lips parted; her chin lifted a fraction. 'If I could believe that, I think I should be more reconciled to my situation.'

'Then you must believe it.'

'Oh, Jagged! Amelia is right. We become bored with all this listless talk. It lacks colour, my dears.' The Iron Orchid drew close to her husband.

Lord Jagged of Canaria raised his hat to Amelia. 'Perhaps we can continue with this later. I have a proposal of my own, which you might find satisfactory.'

'You must not concern yourself,' she said, 'with our affairs.'

Jherek made to speak, but an ear-splitting fanfare came suddenly from all directions and an unnaturally loud, somewhat distorted voice – almost certainly that of the Duke of Queens – cried from the air:

'The weddings begin!'

They joined the crowd moving towards the cathedral.

637

CHAPTER TWENTY-SEVEN

CONVERSATIONS AND CONCLUSIONS

Dusty varicoloured light fell from brilliant windows through the lofty shadows of the cathedral; rainbow patterns littered the marble floors, the dark oak stalls, the cool vaulted galleries, the golden pulpits, the brass and ceramic choirs; they filtered through the silver-framed squints, dappling the extravagant costumes of brides, grooms and celebrants who, together, were the whole complement of this world at the End of Time and would remain its sole denizens for eternity. At the great altar, against the radiance from the circular stained glass behind him, wearing vestments of black and red silk trimmed with woven ribbons of white and grey, a magnificent mitre swaying on his head, his aluminium crook in one gloved hand, his other hand raised to give a blessing, stood Bishop Castle, impressive and grave as through the high doors, admitting a sweep of sunshine into the main aisle, sounded the blare of a thousand instruments voicing a single note. Then there came a silence from without while the cathedral echoed, transformed the note, seeming to answer. Bishop Castle let the echoes fade before signalling Sweet Orb Mace, on the arm of Lord Jagged himself, to proceed towards the altar; then came the Duke of Queens, in uniform still, striding until he stood beside his bride-to-be, who wore white – hair, eyebrows, lashes, lips, gown bobbysox and boots. The altar itself was already piled with blue and green gifts of every description. From the chancel Jherek, Amelia and the Iron Orchid watched as, with due ceremony, Bishop Castle handed the Duke of Queens a black curved bow and a single arrow, enjoining the groom to 'show yourself worthy of this woman'. The Iron Orchid whispered that Amelia would be familiar with the ritual and would doubtless be a trifle blasé, but she, the Orchid, was thrilled. Bishop Castle motioned and twenty palm trees sprang up in the main aisle, standing, one behind each other, in a perfectly straight line. The Duke of Queens placed the arrow upon the string, drew it back, and shot at the first palm tree. The arrow pierced the tree through, entered the next and pierced that, going on to the next and the next until all twenty trees were pierced. There came a yell from the distance (it seemed that Li Pao had been standing behind the last palm tree and had received the arrow directly in his eye and had been killed; with as little fuss as possible he was resurrected – meanwhile the ceremony continued), but the Duke of Queens was already handing the bow back to Bishop Castle while intoning a reference to Sugriva, Jata-yus and Disney the Destroyer and calling upon the Buddha to strike him bald if his love for Sweet Orb Mace ever faltered. This ritual progressed for some time, giving great satisfaction to the central participants, as is the nature of ritual, but tending to drag a little so far as the audience was concerned, though many admitted that the spoken parts were moving. Bishop Castle gradually brought the wedding to its conclusion. '... until such time as the afore-mentioned Parties shall deem this Agreement void and that any disputes arising from this Agreement, or the per-formance thereof, shall be determined by arbitration in the Heavenly City or its Dependencies in accordance with the rules then obtaining of the High, Middle and Low

Courts of Chance and Arbitrary Union and judgement on
the award rendered may be entered in any court having
jurisdiction thereof, in the name of God the Father, God
the Mother or God the Next of Kin, God Bless, Good
Luck and Keep Smiling.' The ceremonial chain of iron
was locked about Sweet Orb Mace's neck; the huge jewelled truss was fitted onto the lower part of the Duke of
Queens' torso, thumbs were cut and blood mingled,
halos were exchanged, two goats were slaughtered, and a
further fanfare announced that the marriage was duly
sanctified. Next came Werther de Goethe and Lord Mongrove, who had chosen a shorter but rather gloomier ceremony, followed by Mistress Christia, the Everlasting Concubine, and her little group of grooms, then Doctor
Volospion with Platinum Poppy (a clever, but obvious
copy of the Iron Orchid, to the smallest feature). It was at
this point that Lord Jagged slipped away. Probably,
Jherek thought, it was because his father was quickly
bored by such things and also because (it was rumoured)
he had no liking for the envious Volospion. Not a few of
the others had chosen group marriages, which, save for
the naming of the names, took somewhat less time to complete. Amelia was becoming restless, as was the Iron
Orchid; the two women whispered together and occasionally made remarks which caused one or both to repress
laughter and, on certain occasions, under cover of some
loud report, for instance, from a Wedding Cannon, or
Clare Cyrato's perfect rising contralto shriek as her labia
were pierced, or the Earl of Carbolic's nine hundredth-
century bull-bellow, allowed themselves to giggle quite
openly. Jherek did not feel excluded; he was relieved that
their friendship flourished, though every so often he
noticed a look of disapproval cross Amelia's features, as if
she found her own behaviour reprehensible. Sometimes
she would join in the applause which began to fill the
cathedral, as more and more people, on the spur of the
moment, rushed towards the tasteful web of neon that was
the altar, and married one another. The proceedings

were becoming extremely chaotic and Bishop Castle, who had lost his air of gravity, was waving his mitre around his head, making up more and more extravagant rituals and, like the ringmaster, putting his brides and his grooms through increasingly ludicrous paces, so that laughter now sounded from every corner of the great cathedral, bursts of clapping greeted quite unremarkable exercises (such as the four ladies who insisted on being married whilst standing on their hands). As the Iron Orchid remarked: 'The wittiest of us are already wedded – these give us only low comedy!'

They prepared to leave.

'Bishop Castle should not lend himself to such sport,' said the Orchid. 'I note that most of these people are largely of immigrant origin who have been returned, just recently, by the Morphail Effect. Is that not boorish Pereg Tralo – there in the blazing crown, with all those little girls? But what is Gaf the Horse in Tears doing to that other time-traveller, the one bending down – there?'

Amelia turned away.

The Iron Orchid patted her padded shoulder. 'I agree, my dear, it is most distasteful.'

The remaining celebrants were dancing now, in a long line which wandered in and out of the arches, up and down the stairs, along the high galleries, through deep shadows and into sudden sunlight, while Bishop Castle urged them on, his mitre swinging in time to the music of the Duke's band which came faintly from beyond the doors. 'Bless you!' he cried. 'Bless you!'

Fire bloomed now as brands were added, at the insistence, it seemed, of Trixitroxi Ro, dethroned queen of a decadent court who had been exiled, by successful revolutionaries, to the future, and who had, for hundreds of years, only one idea for a successful party – to set fire to everything.

The Iron Orchid, Jherek and Amelia, began to make their way towards the doors, moving against the crowd.

'These are the very worst aspects of the world's infancy,'

protested the Orchid as she was jostled by a brand-bearing cat-masked spring-footed Holy Electrician from a period which had prospered at least a million years before.

'You become a snob, Iron Orchid!' Amelia's mockery was good-natured.

'You relished such scenes once, Mother, it is true,' agreed Jherek.

'Oh, perhaps I grow old. Or some quality leaves life at the End of Time. I find it hard to describe.'

The doors were still a good distance from them. The dancing crowd had separated into several interweaving sections. Screams of laughter mingled with snatches of song, with shrieks and guffaws and the sound of stamping feet; bizarre masks grinned through the hagioscopes in walls and pillars, bodies, painted and unpainted, natural and remodelled, writhed on steps, in choirs, pews, pulpits and confessionals; feathers waved, spangles glittered, silks scraped on satins, jewelled cloaks and boots reflected torchlight and seemed to blaze of their own accord; skins, yellow and green and brown and red and pink and black and blue and orange, glistened; and everywhere the eyes they saw were burning, the mouths were hot.

Of the three, only Jherek laughed. 'They enjoy themselves, mother! It is a festival.'

'Danse macabre,' murmured Amelia. 'The damned, the dead, the doomed – they dance to forget their fate ...'

This was a trifle too much even for the Orchid in her abnormal despondency. 'It is certainly vulgar,' she said, 'if nothing else. The Duke of Queens is to blame, of course. It is typical of him to allow a perfectly entertaining event to degenerate into – ah!' she fell to the flagging, bowled down by a squirming couple over whom she had tripped.

Jherek helped her up. He was smiling. 'You used to chide me for my criticisms of the Duke's taste. Well, I am vindicated at last.'

She sniffed. She noticed the face of one of the people on the ground. 'Gaf! How can you lend yourself to this?'

'Eh?' said Gaf the Horse in Tears. He extricated himself

from under his partner. 'Iron Orchid! Oh, your perfume, your petals, your delicate stamen – let them consume me!'

'We are leaving,' she said pointedly, casting a hard eye over the black and white fur which Gaf sported. 'We find the proceedings dull.'

'Dull, dearest Orchid? It is an experience. Experience of any sort is sufficient to itself!' Gaf thought she joked. From where he lay, he extended a hand. 'Come. Join us. We —'

'Perhaps another time, weeping stallion.' She perceived an opening in the throng and made towards it, but it had closed before any of them could reach it.

'They seem drunk with the prospect of their own damnation ...' began Amelia before her voice was lost in the yell of the throng. She held herself as she had when Jherek had first seen her, her mouth set, her eyes contemptuous, and all his love swept over him so that he was bound to kiss her. But her cheek was cold. She plunged away, colliding with the crowd which caught her and began to bear her from him. She was as one who had fallen into a torrent and feared drowning. He ran to her rescue, dragging her clear of the press; she gasped and sobbed against him. They were on the edge of the sunlight from the doors; escape was near. They could hear the band still playing outside. She was shouting to him, but her words were indistinct. The Iron Orchid plucked at Jherek's arm, to lead them from the cathedral and at that moment darkness descended.

The sun was gone; no light entered the doors or fell through the windows; the music died; there was silence outside. It was cold. Yet many of the revellers danced on, their way illuminated by the guttering flames of the flambeaux in their hands; many still laughed or shouted. But then the cathedral itself began to tremble. Metal and glass rattled, stone groaned.

The doors, now a black gap, could still be seen, and towards them the three fled, with Iron Orchid crying in astonishment: 'Jagged has failed us. The world ends, after all!'

Into the coldness they rushed. Behind them firelight flickered from the many windows of the building, but it was too feeble to brighten the surrounding ground, though it was possible to identify the whereabouts of the stalls and booths and tents from the voices, some familiar, calling out in bewilderment. Jherek expected the air to give way to vacuum at any moment. He clutched Amelia and now she hugged him willingly. 'If only there had been some way to live,' she said. 'And yet I think I am glad for this. I could never have changed. I would have become a hypocrite and you would have ceased to love me.'

'Never that,' he said. He kissed her. Perhaps because the surrounding air was so cold, she seemed very warm to him, almost feverish.

'What an unsatisfactory conclusion,' came the voice of the Iron Orchid. 'For once, it seems, Jagged has lost his sense of timing! Still, there'll be no one to criticize in a moment or two ...'

Beneath their feet, the ground shook. From within the cathedral a single voice was raised in a high, sustained scream. Something fell with a rush and a crash to the ground; several of the cathedral's bells tolled, crazy and dissonant. Two or three figures, one with a brand that was now scarcely more than an ember, came to the door and stood there uncertainly.

Jherek thought he heard a howling, far off, as if of a distant hurricane, but it did not approach; instead it seemed to die away in another direction.

They all awaited death with reconciliation, trepidation, amusement, relish or incredulity, according to their temperaments. Here and there people could be heard chatting with complete lack of concern, while others moaned, crying out for impossible succour.

'At least Harold is safe,' she said. 'Did Jagged know that this could happen, do you think?'

'If he did, he made sure we should not suspect.'

644

'He certainly said nothing to *me*.' The Iron Orchid did not bother to hide her petulance. 'I am his wife, after all.'

'He cannot help his secretive nature, Mother,' said Jherek Carnelian in defence.

'Just as you cannot help possessing an open one, my child. Where are you? Over there, eh?'

'Here,' said Amelia.

The blind hand found her. 'He is so easily deceived,' confided the Orchid to her daughter-in-law. 'It made him entertaining, of course, before all this began – but now ... I blame myself for lacking forethought, certain sorts of perception ...'

'He is a credit to you, Mother.' Amelia wished to comfort. 'I love him for what you made him.'

Jherek was amused. 'It is always the way of women, as I was discovering, to regard men as some sort of blank creature into which one woman or another has instilled certain characteristics. This woman has made him shy – this woman has made him strong – another has driven such and such an influence (always a woman's of course) from him ... Am I merely no more than an amalgamation of women's creative imaginations? Have I no identity of my own?'

'Of course, dear.' Amelia spoke. 'Of course. You are completely yourself! I spoke only figuratively.'

The Iron Orchid's voice came again. 'Do not let him bully you, Amelia. That is his father's influence!'

'Mother, you remain as adamant as always!' Jherek said affectionately. 'A flower that can never be bent by even the strongest of winds!'

'I trust you are only jesting, Jherek. There is none more malleable than I!'

'Indeed!'

Amelia was forced to join in Jherek's laughter. The Iron Orchid, it seemed, sulked.

Jherek was about to speak again when the ground beneath his feet began to undulate violently, in tiny waves.

They held fast to one another to stop themselves from falling. There was a briny smell in the air and, for a second, a flash of violet light on the horizon.

'It is the cities,' said the Iron Orchid. 'They are destroyed!' She moved closer to Amelia.

'Do you find it colder?' his mother asked.

'Somewhat,' replied Amelia.

'Certainly,' said Jherek.

'I wonder how long . . .'

'We have already had longer than I expected,' Jherek said to her.

'I do wish it would finish. The least Jagged could do for us . . .'

'Perhaps he struggles with his machinery, still trying to save something,' suggested Jherek.

'Poor man,' murmured Amelia. 'All his plans ruined.'

'You sympathize now?' Jherek was confounded.

'Oh, well – I have always felt for the loser, you know.'

Jherek contented himself with squeezing her shoulder.

There came another flash of violet light, some distance away from the first, and this lasted just a fraction longer.

'No,' said the Iron Orchid, 'it is definitely the cities. I recognize the locations. They explode.'

'It is strange that the air is still with us,' Jherek said. 'One city must continue to function, at least, to create the oxygen.'

'Unless we breathe only what is left to us,' suggested Amelia.

'I am not sure that this is the end, at all,' Jherek announced.

And, as if in response to his faith, the sun began to rise, dull red at first and then increasingly brighter until it filled the blue sky with streaks of yellow and mauve and crimson; and everywhere was cheering. And life resumed.

Only Amelia seemed discontented with this reprieve. 'It is madness,' she said. 'And I shall soon be mad myself, if I am not mad already. I desired nothing but death and now even that hope has been dashed!'

The shadow of a great swan fell across her and she looked up through red-rimmed, angered eyes. 'Oh, Lord Jagged! How you must enjoy all these manipulations!'

Lord Jagged was still in his morning suit, with his tall hat on his head. 'Forgive me, for the darkness and so on,' he said. 'It was necessary to start the first week's cycle from scratch, as we mean to begin. It is running smoothly now, as it will run for ever.'

'You do not offer even the slightest possibility that it will collapse?' Amelia was not facetious; she seemed desperate.

'Not the slightest, Amelia. It is in its nature to function perfectly. It could not exist if it were not perfect, I assure you.'

'I see ...' She began to move away, a wretched figure, careless of where she walked.

'There is an alternative, however,' said Lord Jagged laconically. 'As I mentioned.' He threw himself elegantly from his swan and landed near her, his hands in his pockets, waiting for his words to register with her. She came about slowly, like a tacking schooner, looking from Jagged to Jherek, who had approached his father.

'An alternative?'

'Yes, Amelia. But you might not find it any more to your liking and Jherek would probably consider it completely distasteful.'

'Tell me what it is!' Her voice was strained.

'Not here.' He glanced around him, withdrawing one hand from a pocket so that he might signal to his swan. The air-car moved obediently and was beside him. 'I have prepared a simple meal in pleasant surroundings. Be my guests.'

She hesitated. 'I can take little more of your mystification, Lord Jagged.'

'If decisions are to be reached, you will want to make them where you may be sure to be free of interruption, surely.'

Bishop Castle, swaying a little beneath the weight of his mitre, leaning for support upon his crook, stepped from the cathedral. 'Jagged – was this your doing?' He was bemused.

Lord Jagged of Canaria bowed to his friend. 'It was necessary. I regret causing you alarm.'

'Alarm! It was splendid. What a perfect sense of drama you have!' Yet Bishop Castle was pale and his tone was achieved with a certain difficulty.

The old half-smile crossed Lord Jagged's perfect lips. 'Are all the weddings duly solemnized?'

'I think so. I'll admit to being carried away – a captive audience, you know, easily pleased – we forget ourselves.'

From the cluster of booths came the Duke of Queens. He signalled to his band to play, but after a few seconds of the din he thought better of his decision and made the band stop. He stepped up, with Sweet Orb Mace prettily clinging to his arm. 'Well, at least my marriage wasn't interrupted, illusive Jagged, elusive Lord of Time, though I believe such interruptions were once traditional.' He chuckled. 'What a joke. I was convinced that you had blundered.'

'I had more faith,' said Sweet Orb Mace, brushing black curls from her little face. 'I knew that you would not wish to spoil the happiest day of my life, dear Jagged.'

She received a dry bow from Jherek's father.

'Well,' briskly said the Duke, 'we leave now to our honeymoon (scarcely more than an asteroid, really), and so must say farewell.'

Amelia, with a gesture Jherek found almost shocking, it was so untypical, threw her arms about the jolly Duke and kissed him on his bearded cheek. 'Farewell, dear Duke of Queens. You, I know, will always be happy.' Sweet Orb Mace, in turn, was kissed. 'And may your marriage last for a long, long while.'

The Duke seemed almost embarrassed, but was pleased by her demonstration. 'And may you be happy, too, Mrs Under —'

'Carnelian.'

'– wood. Aha! Here are our wings, my dear.' Two automata carried two large pairs of white feathered wings. The Duke helped his bride into her harness and then slipped into his own, stretching his arms to catch the loops. 'Now, Sweet Orb Mace, the secret lies in taking a good, fast run *before* you commence to beat. See!' He began to race across the ground, followed by his mate. He stumbled once, righted himself, started to flap the great wings and, eventually, succeeded in becoming wildly airborne. His wife imitated him and soon she, too, was a few feet in the air, swaying and flapping. Thus, erratically, they disappeared from view, two huge, drunken doves.

'I hope,' said Amelia gravely, 'that they do not get those wings too sticky.' And she smiled at Jherek, and she winked at him. He was glad to see that she had recovered her spirits.

Mistress Christia ran past, tittering with glee, pursued by four Lat, including Captain Mubbers who grunted happily: 'Get your balloons down, you beautiful bit of bone, you!'

She had already allowed her knee-balloons to slip enticingly half-way towards her calves.

'Cor!' retorted Lieutenant Rokfrug. 'What a lovely pair!'

'Save a bit for us!' begged the Lat furthest in the rear.

'Don't worry,' panted the second furthest, 'there's enough for everyone!'

They all rushed into the cathedral and did not emerge again.

Now, in small groups, the brides, the grooms and the guests were beginning to go their ways. Farewells were made. My Lady Charlotina and Brannart Morphail passed overhead in a blue and white enamel dish-shaped boat, but Charlotina was oblivious of them all and the only evidence of Brannart being with her was his club-foot waving helplessly over the rim of the air-car.

'What do you say, Amelia?' softly asked Lord Jagged. 'Will you accept my invitation?'

She shrugged at him. 'This is the last time I intend to trust you, Lord Jagged.'

'It could be the last time you will have to, my dear.'

The Iron Orchid mounted the swan first, with Amelia behind her, then Jherek and lastly Jagged. They began to rise. Below them, near the cathedral and amongst the tents and booths, a few determined revellers continued to dance. Their voices, thin and high, carried up to the four who circled above. Amelia Carnelian began to quote from Wheldrake's longest and most ambitious poem, unfinished at his death, *The Flagellants*. Her choice seemed inappropriate to Jherek, but she was looking directly at Lord Jagged and seemed to be addressing him, as if only he would understand the significance of the words.

> *So shall they dance, till the end of time,*
> *Each face a mask, each mark a sign*
> *Of pride disguised as pain.*
> *Yet pity him who must remain,*
> *His flesh unflayed, his soul untried:*
> *His pain disguised as pride.*

Lord Jagged's face was impassive, yet he gave a great shrug and looked away from her, seemingly in annoyance. It was the only occasion Jherek had ever detected that kind of anger in his father. He frowned at her, questioning her, wondering at the peculiar smile on her lips – a mixture of sympathy and triumph, and of bitterness – but she continued to stare at Jagged, even though the lord in yellow refused to meet that gaze. The swan sailed over forests now, but Amelia continued with her Wheldrake.

> *I knew him when he offered all,*
> *To God, and Woman, too,*
> *His faith in life was strong,*
> *His trust in Christ was pure ...*

Jagged's interruption was, for him, quite abrupt. 'They can be delightfully sentimental, those Victorian versifiers, can they not? Are you familiar with Swinburne, Amelia?'

'Swinburne? Certainly not, sir!'

'A shame. He was once a particular favourite of mine. Was he ever Laureate?'

'There was some talk – but the scandal. Mr Kipling refused, I heard. Mr Alfred Austin is – was – our new Poet Laureate. I believe I read a book of his about gardens.' She chatted easily, but there remained an edge to her voice, as if she knew he changed the subject and she refused to be diverted. 'I am not familiar with his poetry.'

'Oh, but you should look some out.' And in turn, Lord Jagged quoted:

> But the world has wondrously changed, Granny, since
>   the days when you were young;
> It thinks quite different thoughts from then, and
>   speaks with a different tongue.
> The fences are broken, the cords are snapped, that
>   tethered man's heart to home;
> He ranges free as the wind or the wave, and changes
>   his shore like the foam.
> He drives his furrows through fallow seas, he reaps
>   what the breakers sow,
> And the flash of his iron flail is seen mid the barns of
>   the barren snow.
> He has lassoed the lightning and led it home, he has
>   yoked it unto his need,
> And made it answer the rein and trudge as straight as
>   the steer or steed.
> He has bridled the torrents and made them tame, he
>   has bitted the champing tide,
> It toils as his drudge and turns the wheels that spin
>   for his use and pride.
> He handles the planets and weights their dust, he
>   mounts on the comet's car,

*And he lifts the veil of the sun, and stares in the eyes
of the uttermost star ...*

'Very rousing,' said Amelia. The swan dipped and seemed
to fly faster, so that her hair was blown about her face.
'Though it is scarcely Wheldrake. A different sort of verse
altogether. Wheldrake writes of the spirit, Austin, it
seems, of the world. Sometimes, however, it is good for
those who are much in the world to spend a few quiet
moments with a poet who can offer an insight or two as to
the reasons why men act and think as they do ...'

'You do not find Wheldrake's preoccupations morbid,
then?'

'In excess, yes. You mentioned Swinburne ...'

'Aha! Goes too far?'

'I believe so. We are told so. The fleshly school, you
know ...'

Lord Jagged pretended (there was no other word) to
notice the bemused, even bored, expressions of the Iron
Orchid and Jherek Carnelian. 'Look how we distress our
companions, our very loved ones, with this dull talk of
forgotten writers.'

'Forgive me. I began it – with a quotation from Wheldrake I found apt.'

'Those we have left are not penitents of any sort,
Amelia.'

'Perhaps so. Perhaps the penitents are elsewhere.'

'Now I lose your drift entirely.'

'I speak without thinking. I am a little tired.'

'Look. The sea.'

'It is a lovely sea, Jagged!' complimented the Iron
Orchid. 'Have you only just made it?'

'Not long since. On my way back. He turned to Jherek.
'Nurse sends her regards, by the way. She says she is glad
to hear that you are making a sensible life for yourself
and settling down and that it is often the wild ones who
make the best citizens in the end.'

'I hope to see her soon. I hold her in great esteem and

affection. She re-united me with Amelia.'

'So she did.'

The swan had settled; they disembarked onto a pale yellow beach that was lapped by white foam, a blue sea. Forming a kind of miniature cove was a semi-circle of white rocks, most of them just a little taller than Jherek, apparently worn almost to spikes by the elements. The smell of brine was strong. White gulls flapped here and there in the sky, occasionally swooping to catch black and grey fish. The pale yellow beach, of fine sand, with a few white pebbles, was spread with a dark brown cloth. On pale yellow plates was a variety of brown food – buns, biscuits, beef, bacon, bread, baked potatoes, pork pies, pickles, pemmican, peppercorns, pattercakes and much more – and there was brown beer or sarsaparilla or tea or coffee to drink.

As they stretched out, one at each station of the cloth, Amelia sighed, evidently glad to relax, as was Jherek.

'Now, Lord Jagged,' Amelia began, ignoring the food, 'you said there was an alternative ...'

'Let us eat quietly for a moment,' he said. 'You will admit the common sense of becoming as calm as possible after today's events, I know.'

'Very well.' She selected a prune from a nearby dish. He chose a chestnut.

Conscious that the encounter was between Jagged and Amelia, Jherek and the Iron Orchid said little. Instead they munched and watched the seabirds wheeling while listening to the whisper of the waves on the shore.

Of the four, the Iron Orchid, in her orchids, supplied the only brilliant colour to the scene; Jherek, Amelia and Lord Jagged were still in grey. Jherek thought that his father had chosen an ideal location for the picnic and smiled drowsily when his mother remarked that it was like old times. It was as if the world had never been threatened, as if his adventures had never taken place, yet now he had gained an entire family. It would be pleasant, he thought, to make a regular habit of these picnics; surely even Amelia must be enjoying the simplicity, the sunshine, the relative solitude. He glanced at her. She was thoughtful and did not notice him. As always, he was warmed by feelings of the utmost tenderness as he contemplated her grave beauty, a beauty which showed itself at its best when she was unaware of attention, as now, or when she slept. He smiled, wondering if she would agree to a ceremony, not public or grandiose as the ones they had recently witnessed but private and plain, in which they should be properly married. He was sure that she yearned for it.

She looked up and met his eyes. She smiled briefly before speaking to his father: 'And now, Lord Jagged – the alternative.'

'It is within my power,' said Jagged, responding to her briskness, 'to send you into the future.'

She became instantly guarded again. 'Future? There is none.'

'Not for this world – and there will be none at all, when this week has passed. But we are still capable of moving back and forth in the conventional time-cycle – just for the next seven days. When I say "the future" I mean, of course, "the past" – I can send you forward to the Palaeozoic, as I originally hoped. You would go forward and therefore not be at all subject to Morphail's Law. There is a slight danger, though I would not say much. Once in the Palaeozoic you would not be able to return to this world and, moreover, you would become mortal.'

'As Olympians sent to Earth,' she said.

'And denied your god-like powers,' he added. 'The rings will not work in the Palaeozoic, as you already know. You would have to build your own shelters, grow and hunt your own food. There are no material advantages at all, though you would have the advice and help of the Time Centre, doubtless, if it remains. That, I must remind you, *is* subject to the Morphail Effect. If you intended to bear children . . .'

'It would be unthinkable that I should not,' she told

654

him firmly.

'... you would not have the facilities you have known in 1896. There would be a risk, though probably slight, of disease.'

'We should be able to take tools, medicines and so forth?'

'Of course. But you would have to learn to use them.'

'Writing materials?'

'An excellent idea. There would be no problem, I think I have an *Enquire Within* and a *How Things Work* somewhere.'

'Seeds?'

'You would be able to grow most things – and think how they would proliferate, with so little competition. In a few hundred years' time, before your death almost certainly, what a peculiar ecology would develop upon the Earth! Millions of years of evolution would be by-passed. There is time-travel for you, if you like!'

'Time to create a race almost entirely lacking in primitive instincts – and without need of them!'

'Hopefully.'

She addressed Jherek, who was having difficulty coming to grips with the point of the conversation. 'It would be our trust. Remember what we discussed, Jherek, dear? A combination of my sense of duty and your sense of freedom?'

'Oh, yes!' He spoke brightly, breathlessly, as he did his best to assimilate it all.

'What splendid children they could be!'

'Oh, indeed!'

'It will be a trial for you, too,' said Jagged gently.

'Compared with the trials we have already experienced, Lord Jagged, the ones to come will be as nothing.'

The familiar smile touched his lips. 'You are optimistic.'

'Given a grain of hope,' she said. 'And you offer much more.' Her grey eyes fixed on him. 'Was this always part of your plan?'

'Plan? Call it my own small exercise in optimism.'

'Everything that has happened recently — it might have been designed to have led up to this.'

'Yes, I suppose that's true.' He looked at his son. 'I could be envious of you, my boy.'

'Of me? For what, Father?'

Jagged was contemplating Amelia again. His voice was distant, perhaps a touch sad. 'Oh, for many things . . .'

The Iron Orchid put down an unfinished walnut. 'They have no time-machine,' she said tartly. 'And they have not the training to travel without one.'

'I have Brannart's abandoned machine. It is an excellent one — the best he has ever produced. It is already stocked. You can set off as soon as you wish.'

'I am not sure that life in the Palaeozoic is entirely to my taste,' said Jherek. 'I would leave so many friends behind, you see.'

'And you would age, dear,' added the Orchid. 'You would grow infirm. I cannot imagine . . .'

'You said that we should have several hundred years, Lord Jagged?' Amelia began to rise.

'You would have a life-span about the same as Methusalah's, at a guess. Your genes are already affected, and then there would be the prevailing conditions. I think you would have time to grow old quite gracefully — and see several generations follow you.'

'That is worthwhile immortality, Jherek,' she said to him. 'To become immortal through one's children.'

'I suppose so . . .'

'And those children would become your friends,' added his father. 'As we are friends, Jherek.'

'You would not come with us?' He had so recently gained this father, he could not lose him so soon.

'There is another alternative. I intend to take that.'

'Could not we . . .?'

'It would be impossible. I am an inveterate time-traveller, my boy. I cannot give it up. There is still so much to learn.'

'You gave us the impression there was nothing left to explore,' said Amelia.

'But if one goes *beyond* the End of Time, one might experience the beginning of a whole *new* cycle in the existence of what Mrs Persson terms "the multiverse". Having learned to dispense with time-machines – and it is a trick impossible to teach – I intend to fling myself completely outside the present cycle. I intend to explore infinity.'

'I was not aware . . .' began the Orchid.

'I shall have to go alone,' he said.

'Ah, well. I was becoming bored with marriage. After today, anyway, it could scarcely be called a novelty!'

Amelia went to stand beside a rock, staring landwards.

Jherek said to Jagged: 'It would mean that we should be parted forever, then – you and I, Jagged.'

'As to that, it depends upon my fate and what I learn in my explorations. It is possible that we shall meet. But it is not probable, my boy.'

'It would make Amelia happy,' said Jherek.

'And I would be happy,' Lord Jagged told him softly. 'Knowing that, whatever befalls me, you and yours will go on.'

Amelia wheeled round at this. 'Your motives are clear at last, Lord Jagged.'

'If you say so, Amelia.' From a sleeve he produced pale yellow roses and offered them to her. 'You prefer to see me as a man moved entirely by self-interest. Then see me so!' He bowed as he presented the bouquet.

'It is how you justify your decisions, I think,' She accepted the flowers.

'Oh, you are probably right.'

'You will say nothing, even now, of your past?'

'I have no past.' His smile was self-mocking. 'Only a future. Even that is not certain.'

'I believe,' said Jherek suddenly, 'that I weary of ambiguity. At least, at the Beginning of Time, there is little of that.'

657

'Very little,' she said, coming to him. 'Our love could flourish, Jherek dear.'

'We would be truly husband and wife?'

'It would be our moral duty.' Her smile held unusual merriment. 'To perpetuate the race, my dear.'

'We could have a ceremony?'

'Perhaps, Lord Jagged —'

'I should be glad to officiate. I seem to remember that I have civil authority, as a Registrar . . .'

'It would *have* to be a civil ceremony,' she said.

'We shall be your Adam and Bede after all, Jagged!' Jherek put his arm around his Amelia's waist. 'And if we keep the machine, perhaps we could visit the future, just to see how it progressed, eh?'

Lord Jagged shook his head. 'If you go further forward, once you have stopped, you will immediately become subject to the Morphail Effect again. Therefore time travel will be impossible. You will be creating your future, but if you ever dare try to find out what the future will be like, then it will almost certainly cease to exist. You will have to reconcile yourself to making the most of one lifetime in one place. Amelia can teach you that.' He stroked his chin. 'There will be something in the genes, I suppose. And you already know much about the nature of Time. Ultimately a new race of time-travellers could exist, not subject to the Morphail Effect. It might mean the abolition of Time, as we have understood it up to now. And Space, too, would assume, therefore, an entirely different character. The experiment might mean —'

'I think that we shall try not to indulge in experiments of that sort, Lord Jagged.' She was firm.

'No, no, of course not.' But his manner remained speculative.

The Iron Orchid was laughing. She, too, had risen to her feet, her orchids whispering as she moved. 'At least, at the Beginning of Time, they'll be free from your further interference, Jagged.'

'Interference?'

'And this world, too, may go its own way, within its limitations.' She kissed her husband. 'You leave many gifts behind you, cunning Lord of Canaria!'

'One does what one can.' He put his hand into hers. 'I would take you with me, Orchid, if I could.'

'I think that temperamentally I am content with things as they are. Call me conservative, if you will, but there is a certain predictability about life at the End of Time which suits me.'

'Well, then, all our temperamental needs are satisfied. Jherek and Amelia go to work as colonists, founding a whole new culture, a new history, a new kind of race. It should prove very different, in some aspects, from the old one. I travel on, as my restless brain moves me. And you, dearest Orchid, stay. The resolution seems satisfactory.'

'There might be others here,' Amelia said, after an internal struggle with her conscience, 'who might also wish to become "colonists". Li Pao, for instance.'

'I had considered that, but it complicates matters. I am afraid that Li Pao is doomed to spend eternity in this particular paradise.'

'It seems a shame,' she said. 'Could you not —?'

He raised a hand. 'You accused me of manipulating Fate, Amelia. You are wrong – I merely offer a certain resistance to it. I win a few little battles, that is all. Li Pao's fate is now settled. He will dance with the others, at the End of Time.' He made references to her quotation and as he did so he lifted his hat as if he acknowledged some previous point she had made. Jherek sighed and was glad of his own decision for, if nothing else, it would, as he had said, mean no more of these mysteries.

'Then you condemn them all to this terrible mockery of existence.' Amelia frowned.

Jagged's laughter was frank. 'You remain, in spite of all your experiences, a woman of your time, Amelia! Our beautiful Iron Orchid finds this existence quite natural.'

'It has a simplicity, you see,' agreed the Orchid, 'which I did not find, for instance, in your age, my dear. I do not have the courage, I suppose, to confront such complications as I witnessed in 1896. Though,' she hastened to add, 'I enjoyed my short visit thoroughly. I suppose it is mortality which makes people rush about so. This world is more leisurely, probably because we are not constrained by the prospect of death. It is, I would be the first to admit, entirely a matter of taste. You choose your work, your duty, and your death. I choose pleasure and immortality. Yet, if I were in your position, I should probably make the decisions you have made.'

'You are the most understanding of mothers-in-law!' cried Amelia, hugging her. 'There will be some things I shall regret leaving here.'

The Iron Orchid touched Amelia's neck with a hand subtly coloured to match her costume; her tongue moistened her lower lip for an instant; her expression caused Amelia to blush. 'Oh, indeed,' breathed the Orchid, 'there is much we might have done together. And I shall miss Jherek, of course, as I am sure will Jagged.'

Amelia became her old, stern self. 'Well, there'll be little time to make all the arrangements necessary before we leave, if we go tomorrow.'

'Tomorrow?' said Jherek. 'I was hoping . . .'

'It would be best to go as soon as possible,' she told him. 'Of course, if you have changed your mind and wish to remain with – your parents, and your friends . . .'

'Never. I love you. I have followed you across a world and through Time. I will go with you wherever you choose, Amelia.'

Her manner softened. 'Oh, my dear.' She linked her arm in his.

Lord Jagged said. 'I suggest we stroll along the beach for a bit.' He offered an exquisite arm to Amelia and, after scarcely any hesitation at all, she took it. The Iron Orchid took Jherek's free arm, and thus joined, they began to walk along the pale yellow shore; as handsome and as happy a family group as any one might find in history.

The sun was starting to sink as Amelia stopped, dropped Jherek's arm and began to turn one of her power-rings, 'I could not resist a last indulgence,' she apologized.

The yellow beach became a white promenade, with green wrought-iron railings, stretching, it seemed, to infinity. The rocky interior became rolling green hills, a little golf-course. She created a red and white-striped bandstand, in which a small German band, not dissimilar to the larger one made by the Duke of Queens, began to play Strauss. She paused, then turned another ring, and there was a white and green rococo pier, with flags and bunting and variously coloured lamps decorating its ironwork, stretching out to sea. She made four deck-chairs, brilliantly striped, appear on the beach below the promenade. She created four large ice-cream cornets so that they had one each.

It was almost twilight now, as they continued to stroll, admiring the twinkling lights of the pier which were reflected in the calm, dark blue sea.

'It is beautiful,' said the Iron Orchid. 'May I keep it, when you have gone?'

'Let it be my monument,' she said.

They all began to hum the tune of the waltz; Lord Jagged even danced a few jaunty steps as he finished his ice-cream, tilting his topper over one eye, and everyone laughed. They stopped when they came close to the pier. They leaned on the railings, staring out across the glistening water. Jherek put his arm about her shoulders; Lord Jagged embraced his own wife, and the distant band played on.

'Perhaps,' said Jherek romantically, 'we shall be able to make something like this in the Palaeozoic – not immediately of course, but when we have a larger family to build it.'

She smiled. 'It would be pleasant to dream about, at least.'

The Iron Orchid sighed. 'Your imagination will be a great loss to us at the End of Time, Amelia. But your inspiration will remain with us, at least.'

661

'You flatter me too much.'

'I think she is right,' said Lord Jagged of Canaria, producing a pale yellow cigarette. 'Would you mind, Amelia?'

'Of course not.'

Lord Jagged began to smoke, looking upward at the infinite blackness of the sky, his features once again controlled and expressionless, the tip of his cigarette a tiny glowing ember in the gathering twilight. The sun, which he and the cities had created, burned deepest crimson on the horizon and then was gone, leaving only a smear of dusky orange behind it; then that, too, faded.

'So you'll leave tomorrow,' said Jagged.

'If it is possible.'

'Certainly. And you have no fears? You are content with your decision?'

'We are content.' Jherek spoke for them both, to re-assure her.

'I was truly divorced from Harold,' she said, 'when he refused to let me return with him. And, after you have married us, Lord Jagged, I do not think I shall feel even a hint of guilt about any of my decisions.'

'Good. And now ...' Lord Jagged drew his wife from the rail, escorting her along the promenade, leaving the lovers alone.

'It is growing a little chilly,' she said.

Jherek produced a cloak for her, of gold-trimmed ermine, and placed it around her shoulders. 'Will this do?'

'It is a trifle ostentatious.' She stroked the fur. 'But since this is our last night at the End of Time, I think I can allow myself the luxury.'

He bent to kiss her. Gently, she took his face in her hands. 'There will be so much, Jherek, that we shall have to learn together. Much that I will have to teach you. But do not ever, my dear, lose that joyous spirit. It will be a wonderful example to our children, and their children, too.'

'Oh, Amelia! How could I lose it, for it is you who

662

make me joyful! And I shall be a perfect pupil. You
must explain it all to me again and I am sure that I shall
learn it eventually.'

She was puzzled. 'What is it I must explain to you, my
dear?'

'Guilt,' he said.

They kissed.